SOUND THE TRUMPET

The Liberty Bell

♜ ♜ ♜

1. *Sound the Trumpet*

The House of Winslow Series

★ ★ ★ ★

SOUND THE TRUMPET

GILBERT MORRIS

BETHANY HOUSE PUBLISHERS
MINNEAPOLIS, MINNESOTA 55438

Cover illustration by Chris Ellison.

Copyright © 1995
Gilbert Morris

Published by Bethany House Publishers
A Ministry of Bethany Fellowship, Inc.
11300 Hampshire Avenue South
Minneapolis, Minnesota 55438

Printed in the United States of America.

Library of Congress Cataloging-in-Publication Data

CIP applied for

ISBN 1–55661–565–5   CIP

To Johnnie—From her husband

A bag of golden coins is mine.
Each one is made of precious days, my dear,
A glowing token of each lovely year
We've spent together. Ah, what a lovely time
Those tender days when first we knew such bliss—
When we were young and tasted love's desire!
Why, every second seemed a jewel of fire—
Each minute precious as a crown of amethyst!
Those youthful days—they are not gone from me.
When my spirit fails, from my treasure chest
I count my golden coins! Like flowers pressed
They breathe a fragrant memory of thee!
A miser soul, my six-and-forty coins I hold—
Each one, my love, with you a year of gold!

GILBERT MORRIS spent ten years as a pastor before becoming Professor of English at Ouachita Baptist University in Arkansas and earning a Ph.D. at the University of Arkansas. During the summers of 1984 and 1985 he did postgraduate work at the University of London. A prolific writer, he has had over 25 scholarly articles and 200 poems published in various periodicals, and over the past years has had more than 60 novels published. His family includes three grown children, and he and his wife live in Orange Beach, Alabama.

CONTENTS

PART FOUR
The Shot Heard Round the World
1770–1775

PART ONE

—

ENGLAND

1743–1749

1

A BLEAK CHRISTMAS

BY THREE O'CLOCK IN THE AFTERNOON, myriads of snowflakes had gathered in the dull skies over the royal palace and soon were drifting to earth, some of them as big as shillings. Within an hour the dark and dirty street leading up to the palace was covered with a light blanket of clean white snow. The palace itself no longer looked dark and foreboding with its turrets now robed in white. In the fading light of the late afternoon, it seemed transformed into something out of a fairy tale.

As the snow continued to fall, the crowd that had gathered in front of the palace gates began to shiver. The cold air whipped across the grounds and the open courtyards, turning noses red and ears blue. Most of the people who stood milling around the palace grounds on this twenty-fourth day of December in 1743 were poorly dressed. It had been a difficult year for England. The War of Austrian Succession had drained England of many of her resources and had stripped even the poorest commoner of any hope of securing warm, new clothing. In fact, it was a common sight to see people dressed only in thin woolens, or even less, as a guard against the cold, bitter wind that numbed their faces and hands and feet like frozen blocks of ice.

Yet today the crowd hoped to find a few moments of respite from the hard times surrounding them. The memory of how the royal court's generosity was sometimes displayed on Christmas Eve brought these poorly clad onlookers here in hopes of receiving some free morsel to celebrate Christmas. From time to time the royal family would have more food than was necessary—prepared for the royal banquet during these festive days. As a demonstration of His Majesty's benevolence, the leftovers would be dispersed to the poor who had gathered outside.

This particular year the crowd was larger than usual. A great many children stood shivering against the cold—children who should have been at home in front of their warm fireplaces on this freezing Christmas Eve had been drawn by the hope of food.

As the crowd shifted, a woman up near the front gate stumbled and fell into a tall, burly man who was standing in front of her.

"Wot's this?" The man turned his face, pinched with the cold, and shoved her back. "Watch wot you're doing, woman!" he growled, giving her arm a rough shake. "Bad enough to freeze my toes off waiting for them blighters in there to give us a crumb without having you fall all over me!" He gave her another shove, which caused her to stumble back and fall. Just as he was about to turn his back on her, he heard the challenge.

"You leave her alone!" A tall and gaunt boy about thirteen years of age shoved himself between the fallen woman and the large man. The lad was dressed in tatters, his worn shoes wrapped with rags to keep the soles from flopping. His bony arms protruded from an ancient black coat that had obviously belonged to a much larger person, and his fingers were blue from the biting cold. "You leave her alone!" he said again, louder this time, with anger in his voice.

The burly man did not complete his turn but whirled to face the boy. "What'll you do if I don't?" he growled. When he reached down to touch the woman again as she struggled to her feet, the young boy threw himself forward, fists flying, and pummeled the large man in the ribs. He caught the man off guard and drew a *woof* of shocked surprise from the lips of the bully.

"Daniel! Don't do that!" the woman cried, reaching out to stop the boy.

But she was too late. The huge man's face flushed with rage, and with a bearlike motion of his hand he caught the boy a blow on the side of the head, sending him sprawling in the snow. "Keep your 'ands to yourself!" he grated. Then he reached down, grabbed the boy by the frail coat lapels, and jerked him to his feet. Raising his fist to strike the boy again, he snarled, "I'll teach you to 'it a man, you young rogue!"

Suddenly a powerful hand reached out and clasped the man's wrist in a steely grip. Surprised at the strength he felt restraining him, the bully cried out, "Wot's this—?" He dropped the boy and turned to face the man who was holding him with one hand. "I'll bust your face!" the bully scowled. He tried to wrench his hand loose but to his surprise found it as fixed as if it had been bound in cold steel.

The man who held it stared at the attacker with a pair of menacing pale blue eyes and lips drawn thin with anger. He was not as large as the bully, but there was a solidness in his upper body and something in his face that gave warning to the large man to pause.

" 'Ere now, I wasn't going to 'urt the boy."

"Take yourself out of here, then," said the newcomer as he released the man's wrist. "Get off with you. If I see you again, you'll be the worst for it."

The bully weighed him carefully, then decided to leave, muttering, "Too cold to fight, otherwise, I'd show you something."

"Henry!" The woman came and stood beside her rescuer, a small smile on her face. "I'm so glad you came."

The boy got to his feet and glared after the departing form of their assailant. "If you hadn't come, I'd have given him something!"

"I suppose it's well that you didn't get into too serious a brawl with the likes of him," the man called Henry said. Then he turned to the woman and said, "Leah, you shouldn't be out in this weather."

"I know," Leah said quickly, "but I wondered perhaps if we couldn't be here when the food was given away."

Henry Partain had known Leah Bradford in better days. It grieved him now to see the thinness of her face and the paleness of her cheeks. He remembered suddenly how rounded and beautiful and rosy she had been when he had first seen her. Things had been much better back then, when she had a home and a husband. Now all that was gone, and Partain felt a flash of anger to think that such a fine young woman had suffered such loss and hardship. "Come along, now," he said. "It's too cold. They won't be giving any food away here, I can tell you that."

"But, Henry, sometimes they do."

"Sometimes they do and sometimes they don't—but you can't

stay out in this cold." Even as he spoke, Partain saw the woman sag and begin to cough. "Come along, now." He put his arm around Leah and began to edge through the crowd. "I'll see you home. Come along, children."

The boy, whose name was Daniel Bradford, set his teeth, and his jaw formed a firm line. He had wheat-colored hair that crept out from beneath the wool cap, and eyebrows of the same color. He looked at the man with a pair of penetrating hazel eyes, which were oddly colored with just a touch of green. "I'll come along after a while, Mr. Partain," he said. "You take Mum and Lyna home."

At once the girl who had not said a word began to protest, "I want to stay with you, Daniel."

"No, you go on with Mum," Daniel insisted. "I'll be home soon."

"You be careful!" Partain said. "Don't you get into any mischief." Then he turned and led the woman and the girl away.

As they left, Daniel called out, "And I'll bring you home something for Christmas dinner, too—see if I don't!"

He looked around angrily as a laugh went up from those around him. One ancient crone cackled, "You won't get nothing 'ere except some stale bread, maybe, and you'd 'ave to fight the rest of us to get that."

Casting an angry look at the woman, the boy shook his head, then pressed his way through the crowd. For some time he had been carefully studying the grounds and the garden. Trying not to draw attention, Daniel slowly moved along the street until he came to an iron gate that barred the entrance between two buildings. He glanced quickly around. *Nobody looking*, he thought. *I can get over that gate.* He reached up and caught the gate, the cold metal burning his bare hands. As agile as a squirrel, he scampered over the top, dropping to the other side. At once he got up, brushed the snow from his ragged knees, and darted into the gathering darkness between the two buildings.

Alert and wary, Daniel made his way out from the buildings and followed the curve of a long hedge that led to a lighted section of the palace. His nose told him that he was getting near the kitchen, and his mouth seemed almost to water as he smelled the rich aroma of food cooking. His stomach was knotted up and he muttered, "I'll get something for Mum to eat. See if I don't!"

16

Daniel Bradford was a bright lad. And thirteen years on the streets of London had sharpened his wits considerably. However, the last three years since his father had died had been a hard struggle for him, for he felt the heavy burden of caring for his sister and ailing mother. He darted silently as a cat into an open space in front of one of the buildings, determined somehow to find something for them to eat. When one of the servants came out, Daniel slipped in unnoticed through the door. He found himself in a large, open room flanked on one end by four large fireplaces burning brightly. He kept his head up and walked along as if he were one of the helpers in the kitchen. Past experience had taught him that people will trust someone who seems to know where they are going and what they are doing. So, with an air of determination, he moved along toward the outer door.

As Daniel looked around, he couldn't believe what his eyes saw. In all his days, the young lad had never seen so much food. The kitchen of the palace was filled with the smell of cooked meat, baked bread, and all sorts of delicious-looking food. Daniel took in the turkeys that were roasting on spits over open beds of hot coals, the steaks that were sizzling over hot fires, the huge loaves of bread that the cooks were removing from mammoth brick ovens. He moved directly onward, having no plan but knowing there was food enough here to feed an army—and he only needed a few handfuls of it.

" 'Ere now—where you going, boy?"

Alarmed, Daniel turned, ready to dash out the door, but saw one of the cooks staring at him impatiently. "Make yourself handy. Take this 'ere to the end of the banquet room and be quick about it."

"Right you are," Daniel said with alacrity. He picked up a pewter dish weighed down with a huge turkey just removed from the spit over the hot coals. The cook stared at him and said, "Can you 'andle that?" he asked suspiciously. "You don't look strong enough if you ask me."

"I can handle it," Daniel assured him, then marched away toward the large doors from which issued the sound of music. His shoulders and wrists ached from the weight of the heavy platter. The huge bird was right under his nose, and he longed more than anything else to lean down and take a bite out of the crusty breast that lay so close. Just then an attendant swung open the large door

17

and Daniel quickly passed through it, finding himself in a room the likes of which he had never even dreamed of, much less seen.

The royal banqueting room was *enormous*. The vaulted ceilings rose high, with windows to allow light in from the outside during the day. On this dark wintry evening, the huge hall was brightly lit with countless candles and warmed by blazing fires from the large hearths on each side of the room. As Daniel looked around, he saw that every square inch was packed, it seemed, with long tables. Having no idea which way to go, Daniel moved along between two lines of tables, noting that they were loaded with every sort of food imaginable. When he reached the end of the line, a tall man said, "There, boy, put that turkey down for His Lordship."

Quickly Daniel obeyed, putting the large platter down, half reluctantly. One of the richly dressed men at the table grinned at him and said, "You look like you'd like to bite that bird in half, boy."

Daniel blinked, not knowing what to say, and finally muttered, "It looks very good, sir."

"Why, here. Try a bit of it yourself." The man reached out, lifted a knife in his left hand and, grabbing one of the huge legs, severed it from the body. "There!" he said. "How does that suit you, lad?"

Daniel looked at him suspiciously, but seeing that he had a friendly look on his face said, "Thank you, sir." He took a bite of it, trying not to snatch at it like a hungry wolf, and nodded. "It's very good, thank you."

"Here, you can eat that on your own time." Daniel turned and saw a tall man sitting across the table frowning at him. "Clear these dishes off the table," he ordered. "Get busy, boy! Bring in some more food."

Holding the huge drumstick in one hand, Daniel moved quickly. Whirling around he headed back through the door and for the next half hour moved from the banqueting room to the kitchen, carrying empty trays and returning with new ones laden with succulent dishes. All the time he kept his eyes moving, making his plans for his own Christmas dinner. He had carefully stashed the turkey leg the nobleman had given him behind a pile of dishes, hoping it would be there when he returned.

King George II of England had caught sight of the young boy

18

as he left with the dishes in one hand and the turkey leg in the other. He had smiled and said in his thick German accent, "That boy got himself a turkey leg!" He laughed so uproariously that the queen, who was seated across from him, took notice and looked toward where Daniel had just disappeared through the door.

She smiled at her husband. "He deserves a drumstick, I suppose, dear."

The king was a small man, frail and rather ugly. His face was characteristic of the Hanoverian features: he had a long receding forehead, with bulging eyes and baggy eyelids. His nose was thick and long, drawn down to a pouting mouth above a flabby, swinging double chin. Unlike his father, George I, who had spoken no English at all when he had come to the throne as the first Hanover, George II had made the effort to learn to speak English—although his speech was amply carried along with a rather thick German accent. Like his father, George had never learned to like England. At one time he was heard to say emphatically, "No English cook can dress a dinner. No English player can act. No English coachman can drive, nor are any English horses fit to be ridden. And no English woman can dress herself." Left to his own desires, he might have gone back to his native land, but one does not easily give up the power and prestige of the throne of England.

"Your Majesty, you have outdone yourself," a thick-bodied man sitting next to the king remarked casually.

"Aye, Walpole." King George nodded with satisfaction. "We have a good feast, *ja*?" He looked over at his prime minister, Horace Walpole, and his eyes gleamed as he said, "You remember what we were doing earlier this year?"

Walpole, who was the first prime minister of England and the primary reason King George II had not destroyed himself politically by his own foolish actions, leaned back and said what he knew the king wanted to hear. "Why certainly I remember, Your Majesty. You were courageously leading your troops into battle at Dettingen." He smiled, adding, "England has never seen a king lead a charge with more ferocity than yourself."

The fulsome flattery pleased the king and served to bolster his confidence. He nodded with satisfaction. "*Ja*, and I will do the same to the filthy Scots. See if I don't!"

Queen Caroline, who had been endowed with a better sense

of judgment than her husband in these matters, said quickly, "Perhaps they will draw back. We do not need another war, my dear."

"I fear they will not draw back, Your Majesty," Walpole addressed the queen. He shook his head desperately and added, "Those Scots! You can kill them to the last man before they'll change their stubborn heads. It was a sad day for England when our two countries were united."

But George was not disturbed. "I will lead the charge that will trample them to the earth!" he cried out. He grasped a tankard of ale, lifted it high, and shouted, "Blast the Scots!"

All around the room a laugh went up and the cry echoed, "Blast the Scots!"

As the king and queen and Walpole carried on a lengthy conversation about how best to crush the Scottish rebellion sure to occur, Daniel had returned from the kitchen with another huge platter of food. As he distributed it among the nobility, he was amazed at the dress of the people attending the royal banquet.

Never in his life had he seen such a display of color and craftsmanship. The brilliance of the aristocratic male reminded him of the colorful plumage of a royal peacock. The men's coats sported every imaginable color and shade—blue and green, scarlet and yellow, violet and pink. Most were lined with ermine or white satin, laced with gold and silver thread, and had brocade sleeves.

Every piece of their outfits was an elaborate declaration of wealth and artistry, carefully designed and sewn with expertise by gifted tailors from throughout the city. Even their waistcoats were elegant, blooming with embroidered flowers or birds. And upon every button was a family crest in gold or silver or a miniature of the weaver's latest love. Their breeches, of contrasting silk or satin, were worn with silk hose of every color. Their shoes shone with buckles crafted from precious metal, and on their heads rested the powdered wigs of nobility.

The ladies were no less varied in the brilliance of their attire. Their billowing gowns and sacques, spread over lace petticoats, upheld by vast hooks of whalebone, conferred upon them a daintiness and feminine allure. Upon these flashing, rippling gowns were embroidered baskets of colorful flowers, fruit and grain, golden seashells, or silver branches. The light cast by the candles on the tables along with the blazing fires from the hearths made the jewelry donned by the ladies of the court a living sunburst. It seemed every head was crowned by a tiara, and all the bare white arms gleamed and glittered with bracelets studded with precious stones, while at the waist was laced "the stomacher," woven almost solid with diamonds and other precious gems in intricate patterns.

As fascinated as Daniel was with the sights and sounds and myriads of lords and royalty, he knew that he was in a dangerous position. Passing by the very platter that he had left on his first journey into the room, he saw that the turkey had lost its remaining leg but otherwise had not been touched. A thought came to him and his eyes narrowed. Quickly, he picked up the platter and started out of the room. His heart was beating faster, but he kept his head high and tried to appear as busy as the other servers. As he passed through the door, he spied a white apron hanging by a nail on the wall. Casting a furtive look around, and seeing that no one was watching, he placed the platter on the floor. He ripped the white apron from the nail and in one quick motion wrapped it around the turkey. To avoid drawing attention, he straightened up and looked around the room. Everyone was busy scurrying about, trying to keep the food served up, so he dodged quickly around the side of the room and passed out the same side door he had used to enter not more than an hour ago.

Instantly he was enveloped by the welcome darkness. For a moment Daniel stood there, his heart pounding in his chest for fear someone had seen him leave. Knowing that he could not go through the hungry crowds that waited outside, he made his way back to the iron gate. It took some agility to climb the gate, holding the heavy turkey, but he dropped on the other side, snatched up his precious burden, and began to run. The raucous noise of the banquet slowly faded behind him as he made his way down the dark streets, illuminated only by the yellow gleam of street lanterns that cast eerie shadows as he ran by.

☨   ☨   ☨

The snowfall that had started that Christmas Eve lasted only for a day or so. As fires were continually stoked in thousands of fireplaces, clouds of black smoke rose from the chimneys, creating an ebony cloud that hung over the white city. Instead of perfectly formed flakes of dainty creations, dirty particles of ash began to flutter to the ground. Soon the city was covered with a mantle of blackened snow. The day after Christmas the weather turned warm, and as passersby made their way through the streets, the snow was transformed into a leprous-colored mass that stained the boots and clothing of all who ventured out. The warming did not last long, as a cold, bitter wind moved in, causing the city to suffer under an intense cold snap. The streets remained dismal and the air itself seemed almost palpable with a choking flood of half-burned coal fumes that seemed so heavy it could not rise from the earth.

Late on a Thursday afternoon, a few days after Christmas, Daniel approached the door to a small building, carrying an armload of wood. He shivered as a fierce wind came sweeping down the street. It bit at his face and bare hands and seemed to suck his breath. When he loosened one hand to open the door, several pieces of wood fell, but the door swung open and he quickly entered.

"Daniel! You're back." Lyna came quickly to pick up the pieces of wood that had fallen and then shut the door.

Daniel moved across the dark room, dumped the wood beside the fireplace, and turned quickly to ask, "How is she?"

Lyna Lee Bradford, though only eleven, already gave promise of a grave beauty about to blossom. She had gray-green eyes set in an oval face. Her skin was smooth and fair, and her mouth was graced with clean, wide-edged lips and a firm chin. The bony structure of her face made definite, strong contours, making her seem older than her actual years.

She glanced at the door that broke the side of the single room and shook her head. "Not well. She's very sick." Feeling the fear rise again, she said, "Daniel, we've got to fetch a doctor!"

The thin lips of the boy tightened. They were blue from the cold, and he hugged himself, trying to soak up the faint heat that came from the fireplace. "How would we pay him?" he demanded as he angrily pulled his cap off and threw it across the room. "I don't know what to do, Lyna."

From behind the door a faint voice came, and the two young people looked at each other. "Has she eaten anything?" Daniel asked.

"No. She won't eat a bite."

"She's *got* to eat! Come on, I'll go talk to her."

When they entered the adjoining room of the small apartment,

22

Daniel moved at once to the wooden bed and bent over the frail form that lay under several worn blankets. He was chilled by the gauntness of his mother's face but tried not to let it show. "Well now, I've got some firewood, Mum, and I'm going to cook up some of that turkey. Turkey stew is what we'll have tonight!" he said.

Leah Bradford's body had shrunk to almost a skeleton. The sickness that had ravaged her had left her eyes sunken, and her lips were thin as she put them together, obviously in pain. Her breathing was shallow and she whispered, "Daniel—"

"It'll be all right, Mum. Mrs. Green is coming over. She said she's got some medicine that will do you some good."

"Daniel, you and Lyna come closer." She held out one hand to each of the children, and they came and sat beside her on the bed. "Listen to me," she said. "I've been praying, asking God what to do."

"He's going to make you well, Mum," Lyna said eagerly. "I know He will."

"But if He doesn't," the sick woman said, "I want you to go to my uncle who lives in Bedfordshire. His name is George Porter. Can you remember that? George Porter. If anything happens to me, you're to go to him."

"Nothing's going to happen to you, Mum," Lyna whispered in a frightened tone, but the pale gray of her Mum's face and the fragile feel of her hand brought fear to her eyes. "You're going to be all right."

"Write it down, Daniel," their mother insisted. "George Porter. He was good to me when I was a child. He's getting on in years now, but I've written him a letter. He was always a kind man. He'll be glad to take you in. I should have taken you there and made a place for you after your father died."

"We'll get you well first, Mum, and then we'll go," Daniel said. "Now then, I'm going to make up some of that stew and we'll have a nice supper."

The two young people went back into the other room, and Daniel asked, "How much of that turkey's left, Lyna?"

"Not very much. We've been living on it ever since Christmas. I'll get what there is." She stepped outside, went to a crevice in the house, and pulled up a loose board. The meat she had kept there was frozen, and when she brought it back inside she shook her head as she took it out of the paper it was wrapped in. "Not very much."

"I've got two potatoes," Daniel said. "We'll bake those. Then we can slice everything up and make a stew."

While Daniel threw more wood on the small fire, Lyna did the best she could to help with the meal. Shortly they had concocted a bland stew from the remains of the turkey.

"That's all there is," Daniel said, looking at the bones that were left. "We'll have to do something else tomorrow."

"Let's see if we can get Mum to eat some of this," Lyna said. She filled three bowls and carried them into the other room.

"Let me help you up, Mum," she said, putting one of the bowls down and helping her mother into a sitting position. "Now then, this is going to be real good. It'll make you feel better. It's hot and will help take some of the chill out."

The sick woman managed to get down two or three swallows, then gently pushed Lyna's hand away. "No, that's all I want right now. You eat the rest of it."

No amount of persuasion would change her mind, and finally, when the children had eaten, she said, "Daniel, read me some more from the Bible."

"All right, Mum." Daniel went to get the worn Bible, the only book in the house. When he returned he sat down with it on his lap and asked, "Where do you want me to read?"

"Read from the last chapter of the Book of Revelation. . . . It's the last book in the Bible." She waited until Daniel had found the place, then whispered with a thin, reedy voice, "Start with the third verse."

Leaning forward so that the light from the single candle illuminated the pages, Daniel put his finger on the lines and began to read: "And there shall be no more curse: but the throne of God and of the Lamb shall be in it; and his servants shall serve him: and they shall see his face; and his name shall be in their foreheads. And there shall be no night there; and they need no candle, neither light of the sun; for the Lord God giveth them light: and they shall reign for ever and ever. . . ."

Daniel read on throughout that old book, and the longer he read, the quieter and more peaceful the woman became. She lay back, her eyes closed, her frail body scarcely seeming to breathe. Finally, Daniel looked over at her and for a moment felt fear. He

24

leaned forward and asked in alarm, "Mum, are you all right?"

The pale eyelids fluttered open and the lips moved in a whisper, "Yes, I'm all right. Read some more."

As the candle slowly burned down, Daniel read on far into the night. When they were sure their mother was resting, Daniel and Lyna quietly slipped out and lay down in the next room on pallets.

With the first rays of dawn, both children were awakened by their mother's faint call. They jumped up, a look of fear in their eyes, and ran into her room. When they entered they saw their mother half fallen out of the bed.

"Mum!" Daniel cried. Gently he lifted her and put her back in bed, her arms draping to the sides. He put her arms under the cover and slid the pillow under her head. Tears rose in his eyes, for he did not know what to do. "Mum! I'll go get a doctor—"

"No." The woman's lips barely moved. Her eyelids opened and she said more strongly, "No! There's no time."

"Mum! Mum!" Lyna cried and threw herself across her mother's thin body.

Leah Bradford's hand slowly caressed the honey-colored hair. With her other hand she reached out to Daniel, who caught it with both hands and put his face on it. She felt his hot tears and whispered, "Don't cry! You must not cry."

"Mum!" Daniel whispered. "You can't die! You can't!"

"It's hard, but the Lord's told me that you will be all right. You will be in His kingdom. Promise me you will serve Jesus all your life. Promise me!"

Daniel lifted his head. He looked at his mother and saw that her eyes were not cloudy, but clear. He whispered, "I'll do the best I can, Mum."

Lyna lifted her tear-stained face. "Mum, what will we do?"

Their mother's voice grew weaker, and she whispered, "You'll have no father or mother—but God has promised to be the Father of the fatherless. He will take care of you. It may be hard at times, but never forget that Jesus is Lord of all. Will you promise to remember that?" she asked again, her voice falling away.

They both promised, nodding, unable to speak. Their voices were choked by the tears that rose. The dying woman looked at them and began to talk. She spoke of how God had come into her life and how she had always served Him. How their father, Matthew, who had died four years earlier, had been a fervent Christian. Finally, she said, "You see me now, sick and dying. I can't even walk. But, do you know what I'll be doing in just a little while?"

"What, Mum?" Daniel whispered.

A smile touched the thin lips of Leah Bradford. She squeezed his hand and raised her other hand to gently stroke Lyna's cheek. "I'll be dancing on streets of gold . . . !" she whispered.

The two children stared at her and Lyna said, "What? What did you say, Mum?"

"I always wanted to dance and I never could. Life has been hard, but as soon as I leave this place, I'll be with the King and I'll be dancing on streets of gold. I'll be with my Lord!"

She closed her eyes and grew still. At first the two young people looked at each other, overcome with grief. They thought they had just heard her last words, but then she stirred. For the next hour Leah Bradford whispered many encouragements to her children. Finally she lifted herself up in the bed.

"It's time for me to go. Be faithful," she whispered. "I love you more than anything on earth, but I must go to be with the Lord. Don't forget your promise." And then she settled back and took a deep breath. When she released it, her body lay completely still.

Daniel held the limp hand as he put his other hand on Lyna's shoulder, who was weeping. Tears were running down his own face. The children had seen death before, but now the one thing on this earth that they loved more than anything else had been taken from them, and the sorrow and grief bit bitterly in Daniel's throat. He looked over at the small form of his sister and put his arm around her. "Don't worry. We'll be all right, Lyna," he whispered.

For a while they stayed there, holding on to that limp form and staring at the peaceful expression on their mother's face. Then Daniel rose up and said, "I'll go get the neighbors."

♜   ♜   ♜

Death, for the rich, meant heavy oak caskets, carriages filled with mourning relatives and friends lining the streets, elaborate sermons by bishops in ornate cathedrals, and then interment in the magnificent inner-city cemeteries.

But for Leah Bradford, it meant a small gathering of a few poor neighbors, dressed in thin coats standing around an open grave, a curate who had come after much persuasion to say a final prayer, and then the throwing of the red clots of raw earth on the top of the simple pine box.

Daniel and Lyna Lee stood beside the casket as the overweight curate read from the Scriptures in a hurried fashion, drawing his scarf around him to keep the cold wind out. He finished by reading a few lines from the Book of Prayer, reached down, picked up a clot of dirt, and threw it in on the coffin. "Dust thou art to dust thou returnest," he said, then put his eyes on the two young people. "God be with you in His mercy."

Then it was over. But when Lyna and Daniel turned to go, they found themselves confronted by two gentlemen they had never seen, dressed in long, thick black coats, well protected against the biting cold by fur gloves and heavy boots. One of them, the taller of the two, said, "I am Mr. Peevy and this is my assistant, Mr. Havelock. We are the agents for the county."

The two young people looked at each other, and it was Daniel who spoke up. "Yes, sir? What is it?"

"I'm afraid," the taller of the two said, "we have distressing news for you young people. We have contacted your mother's uncle in Bedfordshire, and I'm afraid there is no possibility of your going to live with him. He is, as a matter of fact, very ill and requires others to take care of him."

Daniel swallowed hard, not knowing what to do, for he and Lyna had no other plans. "Well," he mumbled, "we'll have to do something else."

"I'm afraid," the shorter of the two men said, "you cannot go back to your house. The rent is due and the owner insists on your vacating it immediately."

Daniel shot back angrily, "We paid our rent every month! We never missed."

"Ah," Mr. Peevy said, "but that is over now and your mother, rest her soul, is gone. Now, you must make other plans."

"We'll get by." At the age of thirteen Daniel Bradford had learned to struggle for life. He lifted his chin and said, "We don't need that old room anyway!"

"But I'm afraid you must do something," Mr. Havelock said, "and all that remains is the workhouse."

"The workhouse?" Lyna Lee asked, her voice trembling. Somehow the word had an ominous character, and she clutched Daniel's hand. "What is that—the workhouse?"

"It's the place where people are cared for who can't care for themselves," Mr. Peevy explained. "Arrangements have been made for you to go. You, my boy, are almost old enough to make your own way, but your sister is not. I assume you will choose to go with her for a time?"

Daniel wanted to tell both of them to go to the devil. He felt overwhelmed by the black grief within him, but he would not allow these callous men to see the tears he had shed. "Yes," he replied, "we'll go there. Let us go get our things first."

"No need for that. We've already gathered them," Mr. Havelock said. "Come along, we'll take you to the workhouse."

☙ ☙ ☙

The workhouse was a bleak building located in one of the poorer sections of London. It was a dank, wooden structure that seemed shrouded with an aura of misery. As the carriage pulled up to the front of the building, Lyna Lee looked at it and whispered, "I'm afraid of this place, Daniel."

"It'll be all right," the boy said quickly with more assurance than he felt. "If we don't like it, we'll run away."

The two got down out of the carriage and were directed to the front door, which opened when Mr. Peevy knocked firmly. A tall man in a dark suit stared down at them. "Ah, Mr. Peevy, Mr. Havelock. I assume these are the two orphans? Please come in."

"Yes, sir, we leave them in your charge," Mr. Peevy said promptly. He looked at the two young people. "I trust you will be duly grateful for the mercies of God. This is Mr. Simon Bardolph. He and his good wife, Emma, run this respected establishment and will see that you are fed and clothed. We bid you good day. Thank you, Mr. Bardolph."

As soon as the two men left, Bardolph closed the door, then turned to look at the two newcomers. He was a tall, thin man with pale eyes and brown hair. His hands had long, skinny fingers that he clutched and rubbed together as he examined the pair standing before him. "Well," he said rather sharply, "I'll expect no trouble from you two. I do not permit trouble here at the workhouse. You understand me, young man?"

"Yes, sir," Daniel muttered.

"Speak up! No sullenness here, boy, no sullenness."

He turned and called, "Mrs. Bardolph!"

A short, fat woman soon appeared in the hallway. She had a red face, and when she spoke, her voice was louder than it should have been. "Are these the pair?"

"Yes, my dear. Now, we must give them instructions. I have already warned them that no trouble will be tolerated in the workhouse."

"I hope you made it plain," Emma Bardolph said loudly. "If they don't keep the rules, they know what to expect. You've told them that?"

"A touch of the stick! A touch of the stick!" Bardolph had the habit of repeating everything twice, and his own words seemed to amuse him. He stared at the two grimly and nodded. "Come along. I will show you your places."

Daniel and Lyna Lee Bradford never forgot that first day at the workhouse. Etched in their memories were the long, narrow rooms where they shared hard cots with the other unfortunate clients. The evening meal was composed of one bowl of rather watery soup, one hard roll of bread, and a quarter of one potato. They would never forget the same hopeless expression of desperation and defeat on the faces of every denizen of the workhouse. Whatever hope had once been there of youth and goodness and joy had been washed out. And now, both the old and young moved about as if they were slaves condemned to a galley, an empty hull of a ship that would take them nowhere.

The next morning after a breakfast consisting of another bowl of the same watery soup and another hard roll of bread, Lyna Lee looked at her brother. Her eyes were red from weeping long into the night. "We can't stay here," she whispered. "I'll die. I can't stand it, Daniel! Let's run away."

Daniel felt much the same way, but he knew what lay outside the walls—the dead of winter with hard times across all of England. There was no hope. "We can't," he said grimly. "We'll stay here until we're able to go." Then he reached over and took her hand in his and tried to smile. "I'll get us out of here, Lyna. I promise."

"Will you, Daniel, will you?" she whispered, holding on to his hand with both of hers.

Daniel looked around the sooty, grim surroundings and noted

29

the hopelessness in the face of an old man shuffling along, ready to die, ready for the grave. Then he looked back at Lyna. "Yes, I'll get us out of here, Lyna. We'll stay here as long as we have to. If it gets too bad, we'll run away, but we'll wait until spring."

At that moment, Simon Bardolph came by and saw the pair talking together. "None of that! None of that!" he barked. "Get to work."

Daniel squeezed his sister's hand and breathed his promise again. "I'll get us out of here, Lyna. You just wait and see!"

2

DANIEL MAKES AN ENEMY

WHATEVER HOPES DANIEL AND LYNA HAD of finding the workhouse to be more pleasant than its reputation were shattered during those first few days. They were not physically beaten, but the grim existence they endured proved at least that they were hardy. Day after day the food was mostly the same, with little variation. For breakfast they were usually served a thin gruel, a bowl of some sort of greasy soup for lunch, and a sparse serving of vegetables with a single slice of bread for dinner. The monotony of the diet did not, however, cause their appetites to diminish, for every night they went to bed hungry. They both lost weight, and by the time they had endured fifteen months of such scant rations, the coarse garments issued to cover them that first day they arrived now hung on them loosely.

The barracks where they slept were crowded with hard cots, and often they were kept awake by the coughing and wheezing of their fellow inmates. In winter they shivered from the numbing cold, and in summer they gasped for breath in the sweltering heat. Not infrequently a still form would be discovered in the morning, having given up the feeble struggle for survival during the night. The body would be carried out and wrapped in a blanket, then placed in a raw hole in the ground, whereupon Simon Bardolph would read the funeral services to the collected inhabitants of the workhouse.

It was on a raw morning in 1745 that an old woman was found

dead in the barracks. A shabby group had already gathered for the funeral outside, and they stood there shivering in the cold March wind. Lyna had been late for breakfast and her stomach ached as she moved closer to Daniel. He slipped her two pieces of hard bread, whispering, "I filched it for you. Eat it later. . . ." She squeezed his hand, but then before she could thank him, Mr. Bardolph came to stand at the head of the gaping grave.

A blanket-wrapped form lay beside the hole in the red earth, and the head of the institution frowned and shook his head with displeasure. *A shame to waste a blanket—she won't need it now*, he thought. He had once resorted to dispensing with the covering, but the dirt falling on the naked, helpless face of the dead man was more than even *he* could take. *Well, it's an old blanket—cheaper than a coffin, and will serve just as well.* Stepping forward Mr. Bardolph glanced sternly over the thin, pale faces—rather blue with cold—and began to read the now-familiar service they had heard several times during the winter. He was wearing a fine heavy wool topcoat bought with the funds reserved for clothing for the paupers. He had spared no expense in his selection, for a man in his position could hardly be seen in an inferior garment for such a solemn occasion!

He read the service quickly, skipping over the more lengthy sections, then slapped the book shut. "We will now pray for the departed soul of this sinner. . . ." Simon Bardolph had a nasal voice that always raked on Daniel's nerves, and when he was finished, he nodded at the two men who stood back with shovels in their hands. "Very well, do your duty," Bardolph said impatiently. Then he turned to the band of spectators who stood silently. "Be off with you now—get to your work! Get to your work!"

Daniel and Lyna turned with the others and made their way back to the shed where they both had been picking oakum for use in the Royal Navy. It was a dreary, monotonous work, and their fingers were soon rubbed raw from the tedious task. After a few more hours, the bell used to announce meals was rung. At once they moved along with the others to the dining hall where they ate their watery soup as slowly as possible to make it last longer. When they arose and started back to the oakum shed, Emma Bardolph appeared, snapping, "Go to the office, both of you."

"The office, ma'am?" Daniel asked, startled. He felt Lyna

clutch his sleeve. He could sense her fear, for a visit to the office of Mr. Simon Bardolph usually meant a caning for some minor offense. As they walked slowly toward the red brick house that served both as home and office for Mr. and Mrs. Bardolph, Daniel whispered, "Don't be afraid, Lyna—we haven't done anything wrong."

He knocked on the front door, swallowing hard, for in the last six months he himself had taken more than one beating from the hand of the cruel master. But as he waited for the door to open, a stubborn anger rose in him. *He can beat me—but he isn't going to touch Lyna!*

When the door opened, Mrs. Mason, the housekeeper, was standing there looking at them. "Come into the kitchen," she said abruptly, then motioned them over in front of the large fireplace. She poured a basin of hot water and commanded the two, "Wash your faces—and get into them clean clothes."

Astonished at her command, Daniel and Lyna obeyed when the tall, angular housekeeper spoke sharply to them. She grew impatient and finally took a cloth and began to scrub their faces until Daniel and Lyna both feared their skin would be removed. Next she brushed their hair with a harsh brush, then stripped off their dirty clothes from working in the oakum shed and had them put on the clean clothing laid across the chair. She tossed them shoes, which were not new but had soles and tops, and nodded. "Now into the study, both 'o you—and mind your feet!" Both the young people obeyed and followed Mrs. Mason down the long hall toward the study.

Lyna cast a questioning look at Daniel just as they reached the door, but he said nothing and shrugged his shoulders.

"Here they are, sir," Mrs. Mason announced, leading the pair inside.

Daniel glanced quickly at Mr. Bardolph, who was standing by the fireplace beside a very large, portly man with brown hair and brown eyes. Beside the well-dressed man sat a very short and overweight woman in a large chair. When the children entered, the woman turned to look at them. She had light hair, rather faded blue eyes, and was wearing expensive clothes. "Are these the children, Mr. Bardolph?" she asked, peering at them in a shortsighted fashion.

"Yes, indeed, Lady Edna," Mr. Bardolph answered. He gave a warning glance toward the pair, nodding shortly. But he smiled cheerfully, saying, "I thought of them the moment I received your request, Sir Edmund. I believe they are just the right young people to meet the needs you mentioned." He walked over and, standing between them, put his hand affectionately on the respective shoulders of Daniel and Lyna, giving them a fond look. "They're rather favorites of Mrs. Bardolph and myself. Since the tragic passing of their mother, we've been like a father and mother to 'em!"

"I trust they're not spoiled," the large man said, his eyes fixed on the pair. "We'll expect them to know how to work and to keep their station."

"Why, I should hope we've instilled those good qualities into them, Sir Edmund!" His hand closed cruelly on Daniel's thin shoulder, and he demanded, "I think you'll be able to give Sir Edmund and his good wife, Lady Edna, assurance that you're not afraid of hard, honest work, eh, Daniel?"

"No, sir," Daniel spoke up. He was mystified by the sudden change of behavior in Mr. Bardolph but quickly decided that the couple here in the study in search of some sort of workers was the best opportunity they had of escaping the dismal workhouse.

"What we are in need of," Sir Edmund went on, "are two young people to be servants. Particularly, we need a young man who can learn the skills of working with the horses and later drive the carriage. And we need a young woman who can do housework and later become a lady's maid." Staring at the two youths, he asked pointedly, "Do you think you might be able to do that?"

The offer was the open door Daniel had been praying for, and without a moment's hesitation he said with alacrity, "Yes, sir. My sister and I would very much like to do such work, wouldn't we, Lyna?"

"Yes, please," Lyna whispered. "We'd try very hard to please you both."

Lady Edna smiled at the girl but turned to her husband and said, "They're both very young, aren't they, Edmund?"

"Daniel is fifteen and the girl is thirteen," interjected Mr. Bardolph politely. Then he turned to address the two young people. "You will be taken into service as indentured servants. That means that for five years you will serve Sir Edmund Rochester and his good wife, Lady Edna. At the end of that time, you will be given the choice to serve longer if you wish. If you choose to go elsewhere, you will be provided with clothing and a small sum of money." Mr. Bardolph then turned back toward the woman and added smoothly, "I'm sure Your Ladyship is aware that in such matters as these, it's important to get the children at a youthful age. In that way they won't have picked up any vicious habits and can be trained to please you."

"I rather think that's true," Sir Edmund nodded. He was a bluff individual with a red face, and he had a tendency to bluster. He prided himself on his ability to make quick decisions, which were as often wrong as they were right. Pleased with their selection he now said, "Well, sir, I believe they will do fine. When shall they come to us?"

"Why, at once, I think," Mr. Bardolph said, smiling benevolently at Daniel and Lyna. "We'll miss them greatly, of course, but I couldn't think of depriving them of an opportunity to serve such as yourself, Sir Edmund—and you, Lady Edna!"

"Very well, send them by carriage—I'll pay their fare, of course." He turned to his wife, saying with satisfaction, "Now, my dear, I think we may consider the matter settled. Come, we'll be on our way."

As soon as the pair was gone, Mr. Bardolph dropped his feigned smile. "Now, I trust you will be properly grateful—but I doubt it." His cold eyes examined them critically, and he added, "If I ever hear of your speaking a disparaging word of your experience here, I'll convince Sir Edmund that you don't deserve positions with him. You'll be brought back—and I'll have you for it! You understand?"

Daniel nodded at once. "Yes, sir. We—we thank you for your kindness—don't we, Lyna?"

Lyna held tightly to Daniel's arm, and when the pair had satisfied their benefactor that they would never entertain any thought other than warm gratitude, he promptly dismissed them. His wife came in at once, demanding, "It went well?"

"Yes, my dear, very well." He picked up a bag of gold coins from his desk and smiled briefly. "I wish that we could get rid of the rest of the beggars on such profitable terms." He opened the bag and let the coins fall into his palm, making a most satisfactory musical tinkling, more enjoyed by the happy pair than any other form of music. "I'll make arrangements for a carriage to take them tomorrow. No sense paying for food when we'll not get any more work out of 'em!"

⚜   ⚜   ⚜

"Daniel—it's so *big*!" gasped Lyna.

Daniel stepped out of the coach and reached up to help his sister make the long step. Only then did he look at the imposing brick house that dominated the green lawn outlined by hedges and flower beds. The house consisted of three stories, with large mullioned windows on three sides. Enormous chimneys crested the structure, emitting curling tendrils of smoke, and to the rear was a carriage house larger than any dwelling either of them had ever seen.

A tall, thin man with salt-and-pepper hair came forward to meet the carriage and said, "Daniel and Lyna Bradford, I take it? I'm Silas Longstreet, manager of Milford Manor." He had a kindly look and nodded at their luggage—which consisted of two small bags. "Didn't come overloaded with this world's goods, eh? Well, come along and I'll show you around." He turned on his heels, adding, "You'll sleep in the carriage house, Daniel, and you'll have a place with the house servants in the attic, Lyna. Did you have a good trip. . . ?"

Daniel could feel Lyna holding his hand tightly and gave it a squeeze. "Yes, sir, a good trip." The two of them followed the manager to the carriage house, then to the second floor where a small room had been framed up at one end.

"This will be yours, my boy," Longstreet said. "Not fancy, but I daresay it will do."

Daniel glanced over the small room. It had one window which allowed the warm sunshine to fall over the simple furnishings: a cot, a table, two chairs, and one chest topped by a white basin and a pitcher.

"Well, you wait here," Longstreet ordered, "while I take your sister to the house."

"Yes, sir," Daniel said. He smiled at Lyna, saying, "We're in a good place, sister. Go along and be a good girl."

Lyna seemed a bit frightened by the newness of it all, but she

36

returned the smile. "I will—and you be a good boy!" she said, winking at her brother.

Longstreet chuckled, shaking his head. "I see she knows you, Daniel! Well, both of you do your work, and you'll have no trouble. Come along, lass."

Daniel opened his bag and put his few clothes on nails, arranged his other belongings in the small chest, then sat down on the bed. *This will be good!* he thought. *I like Mr. Longstreet—he seems like a kind man.* He lay down on the cot, found it comfortable, then rose and went downstairs to look at the horses he heard in the stalls below. He was stroking the nose of a black horse when an elderly man came in and gave him a searching glance. He was small and bent with either age or illness, and when he spoke it was in a querulous tone.

"Ye'll be the new boy. Wot's yer name?"

"Daniel Bradford."

"Humph. I'm Bates." He was carrying a small saddle in one arm and gave the boy a sour look. "Do ye know horses, boy?"

Daniel was tempted to say he did but knew he'd be found out soon enough if he lied. "No, Mr. Bates—but I'm a quick learner. Just show me what to do, and I'll try my best to do it!"

The boy's eagerness and good manners seemed to pacify Bates, and his tight lips relaxed. "We'll soon see about that," he grumbled. "Might as weel start now. I'll saddle Midnight there, and then we'll see if ye'll do."

Daniel had never saddled a horse in his life, so he watched carefully as the gnomelike little man went into the stall and saddled the horse. "All right," Bates said, stripping the saddle from the horse and stepping outside. "Let's see what ye can do."

At once Daniel stepped into the stall, and for one moment he felt a jolt of fear. The horse towered over him, a mass of nervous muscle and hard hooves and large teeth. But he pushed the fear away and spoke quietly to the animal. Giving a snort, Midnight turned to look at him curiously. Daniel picked up the small mat and placed it on the broad back, then put the saddle over it. He had some difficulty getting the straps buckled but did the best he could. Finally he stepped back and turned to face the old man. "Is that right, Mr. Bates?"

"Not bad," Bates admitted grudgingly. Stepping into the stall, he examined the saddle. "A bit tighter, mind you." Then he turned to look at the boy. "Ye've never saddled a horse, ye say?"

"No, sir," answered Daniel.

"Weel, maybe I'll make a good helper out of you." This was high praise, as Daniel was to learn later, and the Scotsman nodded, saying, "Now, the bridle—that is a harder thing. Watch how I do it, boy. . . ."

By the time Silas Longstreet returned, Daniel had managed to put the bridle in the horse's mouth. "Well, what about it, Bates?" Longstreet asked. "Can you make a horseman out of him?"

"I'll nae say so—but we'll see." A dour smile came to the thin lips of the old man, and he nodded slightly. "We'll know better after he gets nipped and his toes trod on a few times. He's nae afraid of a horse—but he don't know how dangerous the beasts can be."

Daniel asked hesitantly, "Do . . . do you think I might learn to ride, sir?"

"Ride!" Longstreet exclaimed. "Why, Daniel, that'll be a big part of your work. Midnight here needs a workout every day— and you'll see to it that he gets it—after you learn how. Bates will teach you. Oh, your sister, she'll be rooming with one of the maids, Martha Ives. She's a kindly sort of girl—so you don't need to worry about her."

"We're very glad to be here, Mr. Longstreet."

"Be easier than the workhouse, I'll vow!" Longstreet shook his head. "You had a pretty hard time there, I suppose?"

A temptation to speak of the hardships leaped into Daniel's mind, but remembering Mr. Bardolph's threats, he shook his head, saying, "It . . . wasn't too bad. But I'm very glad to be here, sir. I'm not too smart, and I don't know much about horses—but I'll work as hard as I can."

The two men exchanged glances, and Longstreet gave the boy a friendly slap on the shoulder. "I expect you're smart enough for the work here, Daniel—eh, Bates?"

Bates took out a clay pipe and slowly stuffed it with coarse black tobacco. He searched for a match, found one, then struck it on the post of the stall. When he had the pipe going, he took a long look at the eager, thin face of Daniel Bradford. Bates was growing old, coming to the end of his active life, and knew he was facing his replacement. For a long time he had dreaded the meeting, afraid that the new boy who'd come along would be cheeky and intolerable in the manner of some he'd met. Fortunately, Sir Edmund had heeded Bates' insight on some of the young hired help and had to dismiss a few of them along the way. The old man knew his horses and was not one to give his approval quickly.

"Weel, we'll have tae see," he said, the burr of the Highlands rough on his tongue. He sent a curl of purple smoke into the air, then nodded. "I think we can do something with the lad, Silas—if he don't get his neck broke first." Then as if he'd been too kind, he plucked the pipe out of his mouth and jabbed it at Daniel, saying harshly, "Don't be gettin' yerself killed, ye hear! It's too hard to break in a new boy!"

"I'll do my best, Mr. Bates," Daniel said. He was feeling a gust of relief, for he knew that these men might be hard, but they would be fair. "I'll do my best to please you both," he murmured.

♱   ♱   ♱

Lyna found her work easy—a pleasure really—after the endless harsh toil in the workhouse. She enjoyed polishing the heavy silver knives and forks, and helping to take care of Lady Edna's fine silk and linen dresses pleased her. She liked to let the smooth material run through her fingers—so different from the coarse linsey-woolsy most garments were made of.

She found Mrs. Hannah Standridge, the housekeeper, difficult—though not as harsh as Mrs. Bardolph or Mrs. Mason had been. Mrs. Standridge was a tall, angular woman with an imposing bust and manner to match. She demanded perfection from the staff, and the house servants despised her for it. Lyna quickly learned, however, that the housekeeper was not cruel, and the girl managed to do her work so well that she seldom incurred the sharp tongue of the woman. In fact, the older woman gave a rare nod of approval at Lyna's work from time to time.

The first two weeks of their service went well. Daniel and Lyna usually ate together and after supper often had a few moments to walk together around the grounds of Milford Manor. After the workhouse, they both were happy in their new situations, and when Daniel complained, it was Lyna who was able to end his bad mood by saying, "Think how it was at the workhouse." Her reminder always worked, and Daniel would smile and take her hand. "Right! God's been good to us, Lyna. I'm an ungrateful whelp!"

Daniel seemed to have a natural ability with horses, and so his work progressed very well. He exceeded Bates' expectations—which came as a shock to most of the other workers.

"Ain't nobody ever been able to please the old goat!" Rob Mickleson complained sourly. He was a heavyset man of twenty who worked on the farm under Longstreet. "I started out doin' yer job," he told Daniel once. "But there warnt no satisfying 'im! Don't see 'ow you done it, Dan'l."

Daniel had laughed, saying only, "I guess I like horses so much, it don't seem too hard."

This was, indeed, the "secret" of young Bradford's success with the animals. He loved the horses and even tackled the job of mucking out the stables with as much enthusiasm as any boy could. Bates watched him carefully as the days went by, noting the lad's gift with the horses. Pleased by what he saw, Bates poured his vast knowledge into Daniel, flattered at the devout attention the boy paid to his every word. When Sir Edmund asked him about the boy, he'd said, "Weel, sir—except for meself—I've never seen anybody who took to horses as the boy does. He'll make a fine jockey—except he'll be too big if he keeps growing. He's skinny now, but if he grows into his frame, he'll be a big 'un!"

Sir Edmund and Lady Edna were well pleased with their latest acquisitions. Although it had been his wife's idea, Sir Edmund took full credit for the addition to their house. He boasted of the pair to his neighbor, Mr. Henry Davon, saying firmly, "I told Edna it would be well to look to the workhouse for servants. They aren't guilty of spoiling them there!"

One fine afternoon, Lyna was helping to clean the master bedroom, when Mrs. Standridge entered. "Lyna, take these bedcovers out to the washhouse. Be sure and tell Maud not to use the strong soap on them."

"Yes, Mrs. Standridge," Lyna answered. She gathered the bedcovers into her arms and left by the back door. The washhouse was located close to the carriage house, and Lyna saw a plume of smoke rising from fires under the huge black pots where the clothes were being washed.

She passed through an opening in the hedge that led to the area, but the bedcovers were piled so high in her arms she failed to see the young man standing with his arms crossed in the middle of the path. She bumped into him, drawing a surprised grunt, and she staggered, dropping the load of bedcovers.

"Well, what have we here?" A tall boy with very light blue eyes and a carefully combed head of brown hair stood grinning at her.

He was not over sixteen, Lyna judged, but was very tall and strong. He was wearing a pair of tight doeskin trousers and a white linen shirt with full sleeves that was open at the throat. His bold eyes fastened on Lyna in a way that made her feel uncomfortable.

"Haven't seen you before—you must be the new maid."

Lyna scrambled to pick up the bedcovers, but he reached out and took her arm and held it with a strength that made her gasp. "You're a pretty little thing—what's your name?"

"Lyna—please let go, you're hurting my arm."

The young man slackened his grip but still held her fast. "Lyna? Why, that's a pretty name—to go with a pretty girl."

"I—have to get my work done," Lyna said. She had no idea who the young man was. She didn't think he could be one of the servants; his clothing was too fine for that. *Maybe he's one of the young men from the neighborhood,* she thought. "Please, let me go—"

"Yes, let her go!"

Lyna turned and saw Daniel standing in front of them. His face was pale, his lips drawn into a thin line. He reached out and struck the arm of Lyna's captor, then pulled her to his side. "Go back to the house, Lyna," he said. "I'll take—"

But he never finished what he intended to say, for a hard fist caught him on the cheek. He was driven to one side but caught his balance. Without a word he threw himself at the tense form of the young man, and in a moment the two of them were swapping blows. Daniel got the worst of it, for his opponent was taller and heavier than he. Three times Daniel went to the ground, and three times rose again. His mouth was bleeding and his left eye was closed, but he refused to give up.

"Here, now—!" Strong hands caught Daniel, and he recognized the voice of Silas Longstreet. "Daniel, stop this!"

"Who is this lout?" demanded the young man.

41

Longstreet held Daniel firmly. "His name is Daniel Bradford—and this is his sister." Silas kept his hold on Daniel's arm and his voice was firm. "I don't think I should mention this to Sir Edmund. He's still upset over your—attention—to Mary."

Anger washed over the bold features of the young man. "Oh, very well," he muttered. He glared at Daniel, adding, "You put your hands on me again, and I'll have you horsewhipped and driven out of Milford!"

As the young man strode away, Daniel wiped the blood from his mouth. "Who is he?"

"Someone you shouldn't have touched," said Longstreet, shaking his head. "That's Leo Rochester. He's the only son of Sir Edmund and Lady Edna."

"I don't care—he shouldn't have bullied Lyna!"

"He's done it to other young women," Longstreet said grimly. "But his father and mother won't hear any bad word about him. Just stay away from him, you hear?"

Longstreet turned away, and as soon as he had gone back to the carriage house, Lyna whispered, "Daniel—let's run away from here!"

But Daniel knew that leaving was not the answer. He shook his head slowly. "No, Lyna. We've got to stay. We've got no place to go—except back to the workhouse. We can't do that."

"I hate him! He's awful!"

"Just stay away from him."

"He'll try to get back at you, Daniel," Lyna warned. "Did you see how he looked at you?"

"I can't help that." Daniel knew he'd made an enemy, but he managed a smile. "Come on, now, don't be afraid. It'll be all right." Daniel bent down to pick up the bedcovers, saying, "You go on back to the house, now. I'll take these things to the washhouse for you."

Lyna gave Daniel a grateful smile and helped pile the bedcovers into his arms.

"Let's go down to the river tonight after supper," Daniel offered. "Maybe we'll see the kingfisher again. . . ."

His words had helped distract Lyna from what had just happened, but as she turned and walked back to the house, Daniel was thinking of the blazing anger he had seen in the eyes of Leo Rochester. *Lyna was right—he hates me. I'll have to watch my step all the time, or he'll find a way to get even with me.*

3

The End of a Season

"HAPPY BIRTHDAY, LYNA."

Startled, Lyna took the small package that Daniel extended toward her. Her face flushed with pleasure, and she exclaimed, "Oh, Daniel, you didn't have to get me anything!"

"Why, sure I did," Daniel exclaimed. "A girl's fourteenth birthday is important." He leaned against the wall of the milking shed, smiling at his sister. The year of good food, plenty of rest, and outdoor exercise had transformed him from a skinny, pale-faced stripling into a sturdy young man. He had shot up during this year to only an inch under six feet. He was lean, but his upper body, after long hours at the forge and in the saddle, was padded firmly with strong muscles. At the age of sixteen, he was stronger than many fully grown men. He brushed a shock of wheat-colored hair from his forehead and grinned. "And, besides, if I didn't get you something, you wouldn't get me a present on *my* next birthday."

Lyna laughed, then carefully untied the string. When it slipped off, she unfolded the paper and stared at the gift. She stared at it so long without speaking that Daniel shifted uncomfortably, asking finally, "Well, what's the matter? Don't you like it?"

"Oh, Daniel—it's *beautiful!*"

She picked up the locket, letting the paper flutter away, caught by the soft May breeze. When she lifted her eyes to face Daniel, she was blinking back tears and her lips were trembling. Holding

45

the small gold chain with the heart-shaped gold locket up to him, she whispered, "It must have cost all the money you had!"

Daniel had been saving money for a year—working in his free time for a neighboring farmer—in order to buy a fowling gun. He had used one belonging to Silas Longstreet's brother when they invited him to go hunting once. Since then he'd borrowed it often and longed for his own gun. But when a traveling peddler had passed through the village two weeks earlier, Daniel hadn't been able to resist using the money he'd saved to buy the locket for Lyna.

He was rewarded by the look of delight on Lyna's face and said quickly, "Oh, don't worry about that. Put it on."

"It's too fine for work—but I'll just try it on now."

As she reached back and fastened the catch, Daniel thought, *She's grown so much in this past year—won't be long until she's a woman.* He admired the long honey-colored hair that caught the sun and the graceful form which was not hidden by the plain brown cotton dress. *Some man's going to get a fine wife in a few years.* Aloud he said, "Now that looks fine, sister!"

Lyna reached up and kissed him on the cheek. "Thank you, Daniel. It's—it's the best present I've ever had." She hugged him, then stepped back and removed the locket. The paper had blown down the path, and she went to retrieve it. Carefully replacing the locket, she tied it up, then put it in her pocket.

"Maybe you can wear it when we go to London," Daniel suggested.

"Yes! I can do that. With my new green dress." The "new" green dress was one that had been given to Lyna by Eleanor Rochester, Sir Edmund's daughter. It was out of style and had scarcely been worn, since Eleanor never really liked it. "I'm so excited, Daniel," Lyna went on. "Do you think we can have some time to ourselves?"

"Hope so." Daniel straightened his back, adding, "Be plenty to eat from what Josh tells me. Well, I've got to get busy. There's work to get done."

Lyna watched him go, then turned and entered the milk shed. One of the farmhands saw her and said, "Come to get the milk, 'ave you?" He gave her a bucket of frothy milk and pinched her arm. "Wot about givin' me a kiss, lovely?"

Instantly Lyna pushed him away. She had grown defensive,

for her youthful beauty had the unpleasant side effect of drawing many of the men and boys to her like flies to honey. "Keep your hands for the cows, Simon!" she said stiffly. She ignored his rude reply and hoarse laugh and turned and made her way back to the house. She poured a glass of the frothy milk, then left the kitchen and went upstairs. She knocked on the door of the large bedroom and waited.

When Lyna heard Eleanor say, "Come in," she opened the door and entered.

"Here's your milk, Miss Eleanor—fresh as can be," she said brightly.

Eleanor Rochester took the milk and sipped it languidly. She was a tall girl with rather small brown eyes but a beautiful complexion. At sixteen, she was already being sought after by suitors—which had the effect of making her proud. She was both kind and cruel to Lyna, according to her mood. "Bring me my white dress—the one with the red lace," she commanded. She rose and Lyna started to help her dress, but Eleanor cried out and cuffed the girl. "You're so clumsy! Watch what you're doing."

"Sorry, Miss Eleanor. I'll be more careful."

"See to it, then. If you don't do better, I'll leave you here and take Mary to London instead."

"Oh, please, Miss Eleanor—don't do that!" Lyna's face grew distressed and she begged, "I'll be very careful, indeed I will!"

"See that you do, then!" Satisfied that her maid was properly cowed, Eleanor allowed the girl to brush her hair. She had no intention of taking the other maid, for Lyna was very quick and had learned what pleased her mistress very well. She closed her eyes and said, "I suppose your brother is going to London?"

"Yes, miss. He'll be driving the big carriage."

"Better keep him out of my brother's way." Eleanor had heard of Leo's encounter with Daniel and knew he had taken a dislike to the young man ever since. And time had only intensified the rancor the younger boy seemed to stir in Leo. "He dislikes Daniel—I suppose he still resents him from that fight they had when you two first came."

"I wish he still didn't hold that against Daniel, miss. But Mr. Leo—"

Eleanor caught the hesitation in the girl's voice and demanded, "What about Mr. Leo?" She drew her head back and stared at the girl, noticing her attractive figure and full lips. "Has he been after you?" When Lyna stared back at her, speechless and flushing, Eleanor laughed. "Well, he's been after everything in skirts ever since he was out of nappies! It's a compliment, in a way."

"I—wish he wouldn't, Miss Eleanor. Couldn't you—ask him not to bother me?"

"No. It's really none of my business. You'll have to take care of yourself." Actually Eleanor well knew that her brother was beyond any sort of rebuke she might give. Her mother had long since given up trying to exert any authority, and her father could only control Leo by threatening to cut off the money the young man spent so recklessly. Curiosity, however, got the better of Eleanor and she demanded, "What did he do to you, Lyna?"

"Oh, miss—I don't like to say!" But when Eleanor insisted, Lyna dropped her head and said in a low voice, "He . . . he's always touching me. And he grabs me and kisses me when none of the family is around. He says . . . that I have to give in to him because I'm only a servant." Lyna lifted her troubled eyes and begged, "Please, Miss Eleanor, don't you think you might talk to your father—ask him to speak to Mr. Leo?"

"Oh, don't be such a *puritan*, Lyna!" Eleanor exclaimed. "He's not going to force you. And a few stolen kisses won't kill you." She rose and put the matter from her mind. "Now, we'll take the rose dress and this one!"

🔔   🔔   🔔

The London that Lyna and Daniel found on their journey in June of 1746 bore little resemblance to the one they remembered. The Rochesters and the attendants who had accompanied them were guests at the palatial home of the wealthy family of Colonel White. The home contained numerous rooms and a ballroom ornately decorated for the special festivities to be held that very week. The room was so large that two hundred people could easily be accommodated.

Lyna was kept busy, for Eleanor was constantly changing clothes—or else out on a shopping spree buying new dresses to keep up with the latest fashions. Lyna accompanied her most of the time, and the effort of keeping the spoiled young woman washed, made up, dressed, and in good humor for the numerous social events was enough to exhaust the young maid. But Lyna was grateful for the privilege of accompanying Eleanor, and thoroughly enjoyed the music and color of the balls that were held almost every night, so she made no complaints.

Daniel was kept busy, too, driving the family through the streets and into the country. He had become an expert driver and soon learned the major routes of the great city. Bates was getting on in years and had been left at home, too stiff with aching bones to make the trip, so Sir Edmund charged Daniel with the task of transporting the family on their many trips around the city.

Colonel Adam White, the youngest son of the Earl of Wilton, took notice of the young man's efforts and was appreciative for all of Daniel's help with his own horses. Daniel had gone out of his way to shoe some of the colonel's favorite mounts. It did not go unnoticed, for Colonel White was a professional soldier, holding a commission in the Cavalry of King George, and had extensive knowledge of both men and horses.

"That young fellow is very able," the colonel remarked one afternoon to Sir Edmund. "See how firmly he handles that horse? We could use some like him in my troop." He watched with interest as Daniel hitched a pair of spirited matched bays, then added, "He's been with you for quite a while, I expect, Sir Edmund?"

"As a matter of fact, no." Sir Edmund glanced at Daniel, who sprang into the seat. "My wife and I took him and his sister from the workhouse a little over a year ago—more or less as an experiment. I thought it might be easier to train young people accustomed to discipline." He smiled with satisfaction. "It's turned out very well, sir—the young fellow has a positive gift with horses. Can do anything with them, it seems. And he's become quite a good blacksmith. Does a great deal of the shoeing for my stable."

"Very interesting," Colonel White commented. The two of them climbed into the carriage that Daniel pulled up in exactly the right spot. The colonel leaned forward and said, "Your master gives a good account of you, young fellow. What's your name?"

"Daniel Bradford, sir." He spoke to the team, which moved away smartly, then added, "I'd be a poor servant indeed if I couldn't serve Sir Edmund."

Sir Edmund's face flushed with pride and he said, "Tell Colonel White your new idea about forming and fastening the shoes, Daniel. I'm sure he'd find it most interesting."

As they rode on, Daniel explained how he had been experimenting with a new method of forming the shoes of the horses, one that seemed to be superior to the established method. When he ended, Colonel White nodded with appreciation. "Why, that sounds very practical, my boy. I'd be interested in learning how the experiment comes out." Leaning forward with a sly gleam in his gray eyes, he whispered, "Now I'm not a man to recruit from a good friend, but if you ever *did* decide to leave your present position, I think I could make you an interesting proposition."

"Here now, none of that, Colonel!" Sir Edmund protested.

Colonel White acquiesced, lifting his hand and laughing. "I surrender, sir! But I congratulate you on finding and training such an excellent young man for your service."

Daniel dropped the two men off at their destination, and as he waited for them to return, he smiled to himself. Colonel White's compliments had made his day, and he felt proud to be of such valuable service to Sir Edmund. When Sir Edmund and Colonel White returned, Sir Edmund slipped a crown into Daniel's hand and said, "Take your sister and see a little of London, my boy."

When Daniel completed his duties and finally found Lyna that afternoon, she told him Eleanor was exhausted from all the activities and had decided to spend a few hours in her room resting. Lyna had been ordered not to bother her mistress until it was time to dress for dinner.

With the crown in his pocket and a few hours of free time, the two set out walking along one of the busy streets of London. Daniel told Lyna of Colonel White's words, and she beamed at him. "How nice of him to say so—but it's only what you deserve."

They wandered around taking in the sights. After a few hours they headed back to the home of the Whites. As they walked through one of the poorer streets, Lyna shivered and said, "This reminds me of where we used to live—I don't like to think about it."

"Nor I. It was a bad time, Lyna." He saw that she had lost her gaiety and said gently, "We're better off now, aren't we? Mum would be happy for us."

At the mention of her mother, Lyna grew silent and pensive. Finally she said, "I still miss her, Daniel."

The woeful look on Lyna's face troubled Daniel. Putting his

arm around her, he said quickly, "Why, Lyna, don't you remember the last thing she said to us?"

Lyna looked up and asked, "What was it?"

"She said, 'I'll be out of this dark place—and I'll be dancing on the streets of gold!' Remember that?"

"Yes!" Lyna brightened and gazed up into the skies. "Think of that—Mum dancing and singing in heaven!" They walked on for a time, thinking of those early days. "We made her a promise, didn't we, Daniel? To serve God all our lives."

"Yes, we did."

The two walked on, and when they reached the front of the imposing mansion, they stopped for a moment. Daniel reached out and touched the gold locket, smiling at her. "It looks nice on you, Lyna. And so does the dress. You're very pretty."

With chores to be done, Daniel hurried to the carriage house to check on the horses. And Lyna rushed inside to finish some last-minute tasks before waking Eleanor. An hour later Lyna was walking down one of the broad hallways that opened up into a number of bedrooms, thinking of which dress Eleanor was to wear for that evening. Suddenly she heard a door open, and without warning, a pair of strong arms went around her, causing her to cry out with alarm.

"My, don't you look pretty!" Leo Rochester spun her around and grinned as she tried to pull away. "Where'd you get that gold locket? One of your lovers?"

"Please—let me go!" Lyna pleaded.

"All right—just one little kiss, and I will."

Lyna was helpless, for Leo Rochester was an extremely powerful young man. He pulled her closer, and when she tried to turn her head, he simply grabbed her hair and held her face toward his. His lips fell on hers and he kissed her despite her pleas. Then he released her hair and said, "Why don't you be nice to me, Lyna?" he demanded in a hoarse whisper, his penetrating eyes full of lust and craving. "A girl needs to be loved. Come on—" He pulled at her, dragging her toward his bedroom and laughing as she tried to wrench free of his grasp.

Lyna felt a choking kind of fear and did the only thing she could do. She was on the threshold of the bedroom when she turned and sank her teeth into his forearm, biting as hard as she could! At once Leo cried out and yanked his arm away. Instantly,

Lyna whirled and dashed down the hall with Leo's curses ringing in her ears. "I'll have you—you hear me?" he screamed after her.

Running into her small room she quickly closed and locked the door, then fell on her bed, trembling and crying at the same time. She was afraid of what could happen if she tried to mention anything. The one time she had brought something like this up to Eleanor, her mistress had simply laughed. So Lyna said nothing to anyone about Leo's actions. She understood that the family would not listen, and she was afraid of what Daniel might do.

She kept away from Leo that night, but when she met him while attending to Eleanor, she couldn't help but notice his pale blue eyes were as cold as ice when he looked at her.

He'll be after me all the time—I'll have to be very careful, she thought. The pleasure of the trip to London was over for her.

✠   ✠   ✠

Leo Rochester was born with a capacity for doing tremendous good—or enormous evil. Like most firstborn in titled English families, the cultural and economic system of that nation had endowed him with power and means denied others. Leo was gifted with more than an average share of intelligence, not to mention a strong body and fine appearance. This combination could have made him a champion of virtue, a potent enemy of vice.

However, like most who enter this world with such power conferred upon them at birth, the young lord quickly learned that his social position could be used to indulge his own avarice and self-serving motives. After a few less-than-chivalrous indiscretions, he soon discovered that the system rarely called those in his social standing to account for their actions.

By the time Leo had reached early manhood, those who watched him most carefully knew that nobility was not the major element in his character. Over the years his parents had turned a blind eye to his faults, so often excusing his behavior as youthful exuberance that they became powerless to deal with it. But the people beneath him quickly learned that the young lord had a personality bent on cruelty. His "idle pranks," as his mother called them, went well beyond the limits of childish play. If he had been a commoner, he would have been beaten—or worse—for his behavior. However, who could stand against the future lord of the manor, especially when his parents were so indulgent?

A few unfortunate ones painfully learned about Leo's vengeful nature. He never forgot a fancied wrong, and even his equals in society learned to their sorrow that to cross Leo Rochester was to court a bitter harvest. Timothy Defoe, one of Leo's best friends, learned this early in life. He beat Leo at a horse race three times in a meet and thought little of it. He remembered it six months later, however, when his favorite hound was found with its throat cut. No evidence was discovered to link Leo to the cruel act—but one look into Leo's cold, triumphant eyes and Timothy knew the truth.

Leo might appear to forget offenses, but deep down he nurtured hatred against those who crossed him—and he never forgot his first meeting with Daniel Bradford. True, he had not been injured by the few blows that the young man had been able to land. Leo had been the stronger of the two back then and had bloodied young Bradford considerably. The thing that Leo could not stand was being challenged, and Daniel had done that before his friends. Ever since that day, Leo had made life unpleasant for the young servant.

And Lyna's resistance of his advances burned in the heart of the young man. He was used to having his way with the servant girls, even if it meant coercion. His father had warned him sternly about this, and he had repented—on the face of the thing. But the people who served Sir Edmund well knew exactly how much Leo could be trusted. They kept their daughters carefully away from him—and those young women who had no such protection either left or suffered humiliation.

Leo sat in his room late one morning, his head aching from too much ale the night before. He was in a foul humor, and when he glanced into the mirror on his wall and saw the marks of Lyna's teeth on his upper arm, rage surged through him. "I'll teach her better than that!" he muttered. As he dressed, he thought of the pleasure he would derive from breaking the girl's spirit, but he thought of his father's warning: *"Stay away from the servant girls, Leo. Some of them have brothers and fathers who are capable of killing a man for such things. And I'll not stand for such crass behavior in my son. One more incident—and you'll discover what a world without money is like—I warn you!"*

Leo wasn't sure if his father would really carry out that threat, but the thought of losing his inheritance gave him sufficient reason to plan his moves carefully. "All right—so the brother is in the way. Get rid of him, and who's to stop me from having her? Without Daniel around, Father will most certainly never find out." Leo spoke this aloud, and a thin smile touched his lips. He had a quick mind, and by the time he'd gone down to breakfast, he'd already thought out the details of his plan.

The working out of his scheme was going to take some time, but the doing of it was pleasing to him. Horses played a large part in Leo's life; he was an expert rider and owned several fine racers. The one thing in young Bradford's favor, in Leo's mind, was that he was good with the horses. Daniel groomed them properly and had learned from old Bates how to keep them in top form. Leo had always been rough with his orders to the young groom, but from that day forward, he became vicious. Every day he found some reason to get at Daniel, cursing him for the least fault and inventing offenses where none existed.

Bates observed this, of course, and tried to intervene—but he was roundly cursed for his efforts. "He's got his knife out for you, boy," Bates warned Daniel. "Don't aggravate him."

As much as Daniel tried, he found no way to please young Rochester. Time after time Leo would strike and curse him, and somehow Daniel managed to control his growing anger. But finally the time came when Daniel couldn't stand it anymore.

Leo had invited a group of young people to Milford for a week-long visit. It was common enough, but it threw a great deal of extra work on Daniel. Bates was physically almost helpless by now, kept on at the manor only for his expert knowledge and experience with the horses. Consequently, Daniel was responsible for seeing that all of the guests had animals to ride. Inevitably there were delays, and Leo never failed to give him the rough side of his tongue when they occurred.

One day the group came for their day's riding, and Daniel worked feverishly. He had all the group mounted, except for a young woman named Emmy Price. "The mare for Miss Price is lame, sir," Daniel explained to Leo.

"What? Then saddle King for her."

Daniel shook his head. "Mr. Leo, King's too much horse—"

"Shut up and do as I say!"

Daniel nodded slowly, but as he saddled the big rangy bay he knew it was a dangerous thing to do. Reluctantly, he brought the horse forward, gave the young woman a hand up, then handed her the lines. But even as he stepped back he saw the whites of King's eyes roll—and knew he was going to buck. "Miss—look out!" he called out, but it was too late. The horse gave one tremendous thrust with its hind legs, throwing the surprised young lady out of the saddle. Daniel managed to catch her before she hit the ground, then quickly helped her away from the bucking animal. She was unhurt but visibly frightened by the ordeal. "It's all right, now—" Daniel soothed.

Suddenly a blow struck his neck like a streak of fire. "You imbecile!" Leo raged, his face red. "You frightened that horse—Miss Price might have been killed! You need a whipping—and I'll see you get it!"

Daniel covered his head with his arms, but the riding crop struck him with cruel force. It cut through his thin shirt and left red welts on his shoulders and back. He gritted his teeth and backed away, but Leo followed him, his powerful arm delivering whistling blows of the crop.

All of the young men knew better than to interfere, but Miss Price ran forward. She grasped Leo's arm, crying, "Do stop, Leo! It wasn't his fault!"

Leo was breathing hard but allowed her to hold his arm. "He might have killed you, Emmy!" he said angrily. Then he put his arm around her and said, "Go back to the house. Ted—see to her." He waited until the girl was escorted away, then turned and delivered a blistering speech to Daniel, shaking the crop in his face. He ended by saying, "This is just a taste of what you'll get from now on! Now get out of my sight!"

Daniel turned away, shaken and angry. His upper body burned like fire, and he gingerly touched the painful welts on his neck and left cheek. He went at once to the carriage house and packed his belongings in a sack, then walked to the house. He asked to see Lord Rochester and waited until Sir Edmund came down.

The color drained from Sir Edmund's face as he caught sight of Daniel standing at the foot of the stairway. "What's happened, Bradford? Who did this to you?"

"I'm asking to leave your service, Sir Edmund," Daniel said in a dead voice. "I thank you for your kindness—but I must go. I'll have to owe you the amount of my indenture."

"Why, we can talk about this, Daniel—"

"No, sir." Daniel was certain that Sir Edmund knew very well who had done this to him. He had an affection for the older man and knew that to speak of his son would have been both painful and useless. "I have to go, sir."

"I'm so sorry, Daniel. I'm sure this wasn't your fault. Perhaps we can work something out—we certainly don't want to lose you."

"No, sir. I've made up my mind. I believe it's in everyone's best interests for me to leave." He hesitated then said, "I will ask one favor of you, sir. Not money. Would you—look out for my sister? She'll be all alone when I'm gone. And the world's a hard place for a young girl with no family."

Sir Edmund looked into the eyes of this young man who showed so much maturity and promise—and felt deep shame over what his own son had become. He knew, of course, what lay behind Daniel's request. He had heard of Leo's attentions to Lyna and had spoken at length to him about it. But now he knew he was being asked to do more than that. A thread of anger ran through him that Leo's indiscretions had created this situation. His son was a constant embarrassment, and now his behavior would cost Milford Manor a good worker. He said forcefully, "My boy, I give you my word as a gentleman—no harm will come to your sister while she is under my roof." He added with determination, "I will make it plain to the staff—and to *anyone else*—that she is under my protection."

Daniel swallowed hard, a look of relief and gratitude on his face. "That's very good of you, sir—but you were always good to me and Lyna. Goodbye, sir—please tell your good wife how much I thank her for all her kindness to me."

Later that afternoon Leo found himself enduring the most painful half hour of his life. He had been called into his father's study, and as soon as he saw the wrath on his father's face, the young lord knew he had to be very careful. He stood at attention as his father thundered out loudly his many faults—knowing that his friends could hear most of it. Finally Sir Edmund said in a quieter tone, "I will be speaking with the boy's sister from time to time. And I will ask her if you have shown any insolence or offered her any affront. If she merely *nods*—I promise you, Leo, you will not be the next master of Milford. You will be thrown out of this place and on your own! I have tried to show kindness to you, but apparently force is all you understand. Do I make myself clear?"

"Yes, Father."

When Leo left his father's study, his hands were trembling and black fury raged in his heart. He was shrewd enough, however, to realize that he had gone too far. *The wench isn't worth it,* he thought, and from that day decided to leave Lyna strictly alone.

Lyna had no idea of what had transpired in the study, for she was busy helping Eleanor with a new dress that had just arrived from the seamstress. There was a light tap on the bedroom door, and a maid entered, saying, "Your brother wants to see you. I think he's in trouble."

Lyna excused herself with her mistress's permission and went down at once. When she saw the welt on Daniel's cheek and his bag at his feet, she began to cry.

Throwing her arms around him, Daniel held her, telling the story. Finally he said, "Sir Edmund won't let Leo bother you. I have his word on it, and he won't break it."

"But what will you do? I want to go with you, Daniel!"

"I'm going to join the army," Daniel said. "I've been thinking about this for some time now. Colonel White offered me a position—and it will be a place where I can learn a profession. . . ."

He spoke quickly, then finally drew back. "When I'm able, I'll send for you, Lyna. We'll be together again."

Lyna watched him as he walked away, watched until he disappeared down the road. Then she turned blindly and ran away into the garden, where she cried until her body ached. Finally she rose and walked dully toward the house, feeling more alone than she had ever felt in her entire life.

4

"GIVE THEM COLD STEEL?"

IN THE MID–1700s ENGLAND FOUND HERSELF surrounded by enemies—so much so that His Majesty's army made a thin red line protecting her borders. France had declared war on England and Austria, with Prussia forming an alliance with France. The repercussions were even felt across the sea in America, where part of this conflict became known as King George's War. This was only one in a series of bloody struggles for control over Canada, which eventually drew the Colonies into the fray.

As if foreign battles were not enough, England now faced a challenge on her own shores. Charles Edward Stuart, known as Bonnie Prince Charlie, landed in Scotland, gathered supporters, and started a Jacobite rebellion. He was victorious at Prestonpans but, for lack of support, dallied for weeks in Edinburgh. His failure to press forward after that initial victory gave the beleaguered English sufficient time to assemble an army to meet the challenge from the north.

Daniel Bradford was among the thousands of British troops who were sent to crush Bonnie Prince Charlie's insurrection. The entire force consisted of ten thousand men under the command of William, Duke of Cumberland.

Daniel knew little of politics and was rudely awakened one morning by his lieutenant, a blustering old soldier misnamed Jolly. "Get out of that sack, soldier!" shouted Lieutenant Jolly as he ripped off the bedcovers without apology. Daniel awoke instantly as the freezing air hit him. The officer grinned at the shivering young man, jeering, "Come on now, the troop's pullin' out."

Jerking his uniform on hurriedly, Daniel stared at the big man in confusion. "Pulling out for where?" he asked, yanking his boots on.

"For Scotland—now, no more questions. Get over to the mess tent and get a bit of breakfast, then see to the gear." Jolly turned to leave, then wheeled around, his red face serious. "You'll hear the cannon this time, Bradford. We're going to put a cap on the Young Pretender! About time we stomped on the cursed Jacobites!"

Daniel stared at the lieutenant blankly, but he had become enough of a soldier since he had enlisted to know that it was his job to obey, not to understand. That's why there were experienced officers in command. Throwing his coat on, he hurried to the mess tent, ate his portion of corn mush and salt meat, washed down with a large draught of ale, then went at once to tend to his work.

The time he'd spent serving in the 6th Royal Cavalry had been hard—but exciting. As soon as he had left Milford Manor, Daniel had gone to see Colonel White. The man had asked no questions but said instantly, "Here's your shilling, Daniel Bradford." He handed the boy a shilling, which sealed the enlistment, then added, "Obey orders and you'll make a fine soldier. After your training, I'll see what can be done about using you in my personal service."

The training had been rigorous those first months, but Daniel was accustomed to long hours and hard work. His keen ability with horses was recognized from the start, and he was assigned to work with the army's mounts. He was with the horses constantly, and Lieutenant Jolly was very pleased with what he observed. "He'll make a good 'un, sir," the big lieutenant nodded one day as he gave his report to Colonel White. "For a young man, he knows more about horses than most—and he's a good blacksmith."

"Will he make a good trooper?"

"Sir, he will! Rides like a centaur, he does!"

A few days later Daniel had been called to the tent of the commanding officer. "I need someone to take care of my own mounts, Private," Colonel White said. "Would you be interested?"

"Why yes, sir," said Daniel, shocked to hear of his new duties.

"I remember your theories about a new method of fastening the shoes on a horse. Did it work out?"

"Oh yes, Colonel White," Daniel nodded. "And I've figured out a way to put the weights on the shoes to make the gait easier, too."

"Very well, you'll serve me personally. I need a messenger fairly often, and when none of my officers are available, you can see to that." He smiled as he added, "I can't have a private serving me personally. I promote you to sergeant as of this moment."

"Thank you, Colonel. I'll try my hardest to do my best," said Daniel, pleased with the promotion.

"I have no doubts about that from what I've seen and the good reports Lieutenant Jolly's been giving me." With a smile, the colonel said, "You're dismissed, Sergeant. Go see to your new duties."

Daniel had proved a valuable asset to the colonel, who took great pride in seeing that his horses were well cared for. At first, Daniel had to endure severe taunts from some of the troops because of his rapid promotion, but he shrugged them off, determined to make the best of his time in the army so that he could make a place for Lyna. In fact, a day never went by that Daniel didn't think of his sister back at Milford.

That cold morning the camp was in a state of confusion as Daniel went about getting the gear ready. Finally, however, the 6th moved out in advance of the foot soldiers. They expected no contact with the enemy for several days, and soon the order of the march became clear. Daniel kept busy seeing to the mounts each day, picking up what information he could along the way about the battle to come.

Fires dotted the countryside on the third evening of the march, and Daniel worked late with the horses and gear. Several of the officers' mounts needed attention, and Daniel toiled with Simms, the blacksmith, at a portable forge. Daniel was cinching the last shoe on Colonel White's favorite horse, a mottled gray stallion named Ranger, when he heard steps behind him.

"Well, now, how does he seem, Sergeant?" Daniel looked around to see Colonel White, who had come to watch. The officer approached and bent over to peer at the shoe. "Looks fine to me."

"Yes, sir, it'll hold." Daniel dropped the hoof, patted the side of the horse, then took off his apron. "That's the last of them, sir. All in good shape."

"Fine—you and Simms come along. One of my officers found a suckling pig. There's a good bit of it left, and you two have earned it."

Ten minutes later Daniel was eating the roast pork with relish, listening as Simms spoke to the colonel about the condition of the troop. Since the troopers were only as good as their mounts, both Simms and Daniel played an important part in the scheme of things as the army advanced.

The brawny blacksmith gnawed thoughtfully on a bone, then said, "Colonel, I don't rightly understand this war we're going to fight." Simms was a Cornishman and spoke with such a thick accent that it had taken Daniel some time to understand him. "Who will we be a-fightin'? The frogs or the Spaniards?"

Colonel White was sitting in his camp chair, holding a pewter cup filled with ale. Shaking his head, he answered, "Neither of those, Simms."

"Who, then, sir?"

"Scotsmen, mostly, with some English."

"Another civil war, Colonel?" Daniel asked.

"Not really." White leaned forward, his hair giving off reddish tints from the leaping tongues of fire. "When James II was driven from the throne, many people thought he was the rightful king of England. Since then we've had several rulers, now a German prince named George, one of the Hanoverian line. But the supporters of James II have never given up their hope of seeing him and his descendants returned to power. They're called 'Jacobites,' which means 'James' in another language." He sipped his ale, nodded thoughtfully, then added, "The son of James is called the Old Pretender. And *he* now has a son whom many call the Young Pretender."

Simms shook his head, took a large bite of meat from the bone in his hand, and chewed thoroughly. "And it's him who's coming to take over."

"His friends call him Bonnie Prince Charlie," White explained. "I think he must have a powerful way to stir people. He's managed to draw considerable support—much of it from our own people. . . ." The colonel spoke on for some time, relating the course of Charles's victories. "It's not a civil war—not yet," he said grimly. "Call it a rebellion, for that's what it is. In any case, our standing army is very small here in England. We're stretched to the limit, what with the war against Spain and the one in North America."

"Will we win, sir?" Daniel asked.

Colonel White gave the boy a direct glance, then stood to his feet. "We have to," he nodded sharply. "If we don't, England will become Catholic again. And if that happens, we'll see days such as we saw under Bloody Mary. Get to bed when you finish—it'll be a hard day's march tomorrow." He drained the last of his ale, then said almost to himself, "When we meet Bonnie Prince Charlie—the fate of England will be on our lances. . . !"

🛡   🛡   🛡

When Charles Stuart led his army across the English border, he proved to be a wily foe for the soldiers of His Majesty's army. For weeks there were pitched battles in the Scottish Highlands. Daniel did indeed hear the cannons and endured the rigors of war. During much of the fighting he was not on the front line where the action was. He spent his days tending to his duties, making sure there were always fresh mounts, or carrying messages for Colonel White. At times he rode with the cavalry when it was sent on wide sweeping movements to seek out enemy positions. He rode for hours in the van of the troop, his eyes constantly on the mounts.

On two occasions, he was caught up in actual battle, when the troop made wild charges against the enemy. Once Colonel White's horse was shot from under him, and immediately Daniel was there to provide a fresh mount. "Good man!" White shouted, then turned and rode right into the mouths of the cannon. Daniel, having no orders, kept just to the colonel's rear, and he saw men go down, their breasts stained crimson. One of the lieutenants riding directly in front of Daniel uttered a shrill cry. Throwing his hands up, he went down, falling in a heap. Daniel pulled up his mount to protect the still body, and when the troop roared by, he slipped to the ground and bent over the wounded officer. "Are you hurt bad, sir?" he asked.

"Bad enough—but I'd be worse if you hadn't kept me from being trampled under the horses." Lieutenant Mullens struggled to his feet, and Daniel helped him onto his own horse, then swung up behind him. "We'll get you to the field surgeon, sir," Daniel said. Holding on to the sagging form of the lieutenant, he rode until he found the medical staff. When he pulled up in front of the tent, two attendants helped him carry the wounded man into the tent.

Later, after the battle was over, Daniel was working with a black mare with a gaping wound in her flank when Colonel White stopped by. "You probably saved Lieutenant Mullens' life, Sergeant," he said. "He told me how you pulled him off the field." He smiled and nodded. "It was a fortunate day for me—and for Lieutenant Mullens—when you took the king's shilling."

"I was glad to be of help to the lieutenant," Daniel flushed. He was weary and saw that the colonel was dirty and very tired as well. "Will we be moving on tomorrow, Colonel?"

"I think not—but very soon." White removed his hat and mopped his brow with a soiled handkerchief. "How many horses did we lose?"

"Too many, sir. We'll need replacements—and some like Lady here will need to rest up until they're healed."

For over a week, the troop remained in camp licking its wounds. One night after his duties were completed, Daniel wrote to Lyna. A few days later he was delighted to receive a long letter from her.

She assured him that there had been no more trouble from Leo—but she also informed him that Sir Edmund was very ill. "He had pneumonia earlier and can't seem to get over it," she wrote. "I pray that he recovers, for he has been very kind to me ever since you left."

Daniel had been saving every penny of his wages and had worked for some of the officers to make a little extra. As he read the letter, he thought, *If something happens to Sir Edmund, Lyna will have to leave. I've got to have enough money so I can find her a place. . . .*

The rebellion was slowly crushed by the English forces, though not without some cost. Daniel learned firsthand about the horrors of war. And what few romantic illusions he'd had about military exploits were gone by the time winter set in. Death on the battlefield was a terrible thing, and by the time the 6th Royal Cavalry came to grips with the last remnants of the rebels, Daniel heartily hoped he'd never again see a bloody corpse or endure the lingering stench of dead bodies strewn across a battlefield.

The end came at Culloden Moor. Daniel had risen early and taken extra care to prepare the horses for the colonel and several of his staff. At nine o'clock the Duke of Cumberland, the son of George II, came thundering up on a white horse, followed by his staff officers.

"Colonel White," he called out, his bulging blue eyes glittering with excitement, "we have them now—send your troop across that field! Swing around behind the enemy and we will crush them to chaff!"

"Yes, General, at once!"

"And there will be no quarter given, do you understand?" The duke's face was firmly set, his mouth drawn up into a grim line. "I want them finished! There are to be no more Jacobite rebels to disturb our kingdom!"

Colonel White shouted, "All right, my brave fellows—charge!"

The charge across the broken field was like nothing Daniel had ever experienced. The troop kept together fairly well at first, but soon gaps began to appear in the ranks as the desperate enemy found the range for their cannons. Nonetheless, they were cornered and knew that they could expect no mercy from the army of George II, so they fought like demented wolves.

The cannon's breath touched the face of Daniel Bradford, but it merely blew his hat off. He charged his horse into the midst of the enemy gunners, sending two of them sprawling. The third wheeled, pulled a sword from his belt, and hacked at Daniel with a vicious backhand blow. Daniel had drawn his own saber, with which he had never drawn blood, and managed to parry the blade. The force of it nearly tore the saber from his hand, but he wheeled his mount around and slashed at the tall soldier with desperate strength. The tip of the saber seemed to barely graze the man's throat, but Daniel had sharpened it to a razor's keenness.

The man nodded and blinked his eyes, then stared at Daniel with a look that haunted the young soldier for months. Blood cascaded from the soldier's throat, drenching his shirt with a rich crimson. Dropping his sword, the man grabbed his throat in a futile effort to staunch the flow, and his cries were pitiful—a series of gurgles that continued as he fell to the ground. He looked up at Daniel, his brown eyes pleading, held up one bloody hand as if for help, and then his heels dug into the earth as he kicked in protest against the end he could not flee.

Daniel, trembling uncontrollably, whirled and saw Colonel

White far ahead urging the riders forward. Ahead of the colonel loomed a wide ditch, too wide for a horse to jump, it seemed to Daniel. Nevertheless, White's red stallion lunged forward, sailed through the air, and hit the ground, staggering from the force of the impact. Daniel saw a group of the enemy move forward with gleaming bayonets, determined to capture the officer.

Right then Lieutenant Jolly came flashing by, shouting, "Come, boys! We've got to save the colonel!"

Daniel yelled something, a rage coming over him, and he spurred his mount forward. When he came to the edge of the gully, he saw several of the troop who had tried and failed to make the jump and were wallowing with their floundering steeds. He had a good horse, a fine jumper, and screamed as he reached the edge and threw his weight forward. "Up—Jupiter—up!" He felt the powerful legs of the animal as it lunged and left the earth and, for a frozen moment of time, felt gravity lose its power.

At first he thought the horse would fall short—but the powerful animal landed on the brink. Daniel kept his seat by some sort of miracle. With a wild look he turned around and saw that he and Lieutenant Jolly had succeeded in making the jump. Even as he mastered Jupiter, Jolly yelled, "Come, Bradford—give them cold steel!"

The two riders drove their horses into the midst of the enemy, driving four of them to the ground. But they could not get them all, and Daniel saw one of them riding furiously to where Colonel White struggled to get to his feet. The soldier had his blade lifted as he bore down on the colonel. Daniel wheeled his horse and drove into the fifth soldier, but saw that he was too late to help the colonel.

Just before the soldier reached Colonel White, Lieutenant Jolly, screaming and cursing, rode up from the side and struck the man in the head with his saber, killing him instantly. Daniel cried out, "Good, Jolly! Good—!"

But then an explosion rocked the earth, and Daniel suddenly found himself flying out of his saddle. The world seemed to whirl and finally came up and struck him a blow in the back that drove the breath from his body and his mind into a black, whirling pit.

T   T   T

"Come, my boy, wake up!"

Daniel woke to find himself looking up into a smoke-blackened face. He coughed and then realized that it was Colonel White who was holding him.

"There, now, that's better!" Colonel White's face showed relief, and as Daniel sat up and looked around, he saw that the battle was over—or almost so. The enemy was fleeing, but the remaining Jacobites were being cut down without mercy. The colonel pulled him to his feet, saying, "I was afraid they'd done you in, my boy. Are you all right?"

"Y-yes, sir," Daniel stammered. He looked to his left and gave a start—Lieutenant Jolly lay with his eyes open staring blindly at the sky. "Lieutenant—!" he cried out but knew at once that the man was dead.

"Poor fellow—he caught the blast of the cannon," Colonel White said, shaking his head. Then he took a deep breath and said quietly, "If it hadn't been for you two, I'd have been cut to pieces." He placed his hand on Daniel's shoulder and his eyes were sad. "I wish I could bring the lieutenant back. He was a fine soldier. I can't do that—but I'll never forget him. And I'll never forget you, Sergeant Bradford. A man would be a poor wretch indeed to forget the sight of you and Lieutenant Jolly sailing over that ditch!"

"I'm glad we were able to help, sir." Daniel looked over the field and was sickened by the senseless slaughter that was taking place. "Do they have to do that, Colonel? They're beaten badly enough."

But Colonel White knew there would be no mercy. "The king has ordered the Jacobites eradicated. There will be no future rebellions from that source!"

In the end the clan chiefs were stripped of their authority, and the wearing of tartans and kilts, and the playing of bagpipes and the owning of weapons were forbidden on point of death.

Daniel had survived the battle, but the aftermath left haunting memories he would never forget. He looked away as often as he could from the execution of the prisoners. Some of the captured were cruelly allowed to starve, while others were sold as slaves to American plantations. The prisoners were kept in the open, chained to trees and exposed to the inclement weather. Daniel noted one of them was a dark-skinned individual and stopped to ask, "You're not a Scot, are you?"

A pair of obsidian eyes met his, and for a moment the prisoner kept his silence. "I am Mohawk," he muttered.

"What's that?"

"Indian—from across the great sea."

Daniel was fascinated. He had read of the red savages of America but had never seen one. He noted that the man's lips were cracked with thirst. "I'll get you a drink and something to eat." He ran to get some provisions, but when he returned, the guard protested. Daniel boldly used Colonel White's name and had no more trouble from the guard. He squatted down and watched as the Mohawk eagerly drank the water, then devoured the food.

"Why do you help your enemy?"

Daniel could sense the man's suspicion and shrugged. "Why, I guess we've had our fight. I'd let you go if I had my way." He studied the coppery face, then asked, "What's your name? How'd you get all the way to this place?"

The Mohawk proved to be talkative. "My name is Orcas. I am the son of a great warrior chieftain." He related how he'd become friendly with some of the officers fighting against the British, and they'd offered to make him a great chief if he came to the Continent with them. "They lied—white men always lie," Orcas said bitterly.

"I'm sorry you got captured," Daniel said. "I'll do my best to bring you food until—"

"Until they kill me?" A grim smile touched the face of the Indian, and he seemed totally unafraid.

For the next three days, Daniel saw to it that Orcas had food and a blanket to stave off the cold. He talked often with the Mohawk, and Colonel White asked him once, "What do you find so fascinating about that savage?"

"Why, he's a long way from home, sir, and about to die." Daniel struggled to find the words to describe what he was feeling. "I guess I can't hate him much. If I was in his shape, I'd sure appreciate it if someone was kind to me."

"Very commendable," White said absently. "But he'll be shot tomorrow morning, I understand. Perhaps you'd like to take him a good meal tonight."

"Yes, sir. I'll do that."

Daniel never knew what possessed him, but after the camp had quieted down and the soldiers were asleep, he crept out of his blankets and quietly made his way to the tree where Orcas was tied. "Be very quiet—" he whispered as he cut the ropes that bound the Mohawk and handed him a small leather purse and a knife. "There's a little money there—if you can get to a port in Scotland, maybe you can make it home. It's all I can do, Orcas."

The dark eyes of the Indian never left Bradford's face. "Why do you do this?" he demanded.

Daniel shrugged. "I don't know. Now—get going."

Orcas suddenly reached out and grasped Daniel by the shoulder. "Give me your hand," he whispered. When Daniel only stared at him, Orcas lifted his own left arm and made a cut in his forearm. Then reaching out, he took the arm of the young man, made a similar cut, and held the two wounds together. "We are one blood now—blood brothers."

Daniel felt the pain of the cut and, staring into the Indian's eyes, could only say, "Go now, before they catch you—God be with you!"

Orcas nodded, his eyes gleaming. "Maybe not *all* white men are bad." Then he faded into the darkness without making a sound.

The next day the sentry who had been in charge of the prisoners was given ten lashes for permitting one of them to escape.

Colonel White said nothing for two days, then he murmured casually, "That Indian you liked so much—you did give him a good last meal, didn't you?"

Daniel looked into the eyes of the officer and said evenly, "Yes, sir. He was glad to get it." He waited for the colonel to speak, but the officer merely smiled strangely and turned to move away. For days Daniel was tense, waiting to hear that Orcas was recaptured. Finally he decided that the Mohawk had managed to get safely away or perhaps had even made it to a port and secured passage back to America.

🎺　　🎺　　🎺

Finally the battle at Culloden Moor was over, and when the troop returned to England, Colonel White didn't forget Daniel's faithful service, nor the fact that he had saved his life in battle. He kept Daniel close, praising him to one and all. A few days later, the colonel called Daniel to his headquarters. With a smile on his face, he said, "Draw a horse and go see your sister, Sergeant.

You've earned leave, so have a good time."

Daniel obeyed instantly, and two days later, he drew up in front of Milford. Wanting to surprise Lyna, he tied his horse in the rear of the main house, then made his way toward the cottage occupied by Silas Longstreet. Longstreet was very pleased to see Daniel and, after getting a report on the young man's travels, agreed to bring Lyna to his house. "Be quite a surprise for her," he smiled. "She's kept the whole household informed of your heroic deeds."

Daniel waited impatiently, then when he saw Lyna walking toward the cottage, he stood behind the door. When Lyna entered, he grabbed her and lifted her clear from the floor.

Lyna cried out in alarm, but when she twisted her head and saw who it was who held her, she squirmed free and threw her arms around him. "Daniel! You beast! Why didn't you tell me you were coming!"

"Because I didn't know," Daniel grinned. He held her at arm's length and shook his head at what he saw. "I leave a little girl, come back later—and find a woman!"

Lyna flushed, but her eyes were bright. "*Me* grown up! You've grown a foot!"

"Only an inch or so," Daniel protested. But he stood at attention for her while Lyna walked around him, admiring his soldiery stance. "If you don't look fine in that uniform!" she exclaimed. "How many girls have you had chasing you?"

"Not so many—and none as pretty as you." He caught her hand, saying, "Come on, let's go down to the river. I'll tell you how I won the battle at Culloden Moor singlehanded. . . ."

For the next three days, the pair had a wonderful time. Sir Edmund was still very ill, but Daniel was permitted to make a brief visit. He was shocked at how frail his former master was but did not allow it to show in his expression. "I'm very grateful for the kindness you've shown to my sister, sir," he said warmly.

"Nothing at all—nothing!" Sir Edmund was sitting up in bed, and his eyes were bright with fever. "I received a letter from Colonel White, Daniel. He told me what a heroic thing you did at the battle. Lady Edna and I are very proud of you, my boy!"

Daniel tried to make little of his deed, but he could see that the sick man took pride in his accomplishment. His visit was brief, for he didn't want to tire Sir Edmund. As he closed the door and turned to leave, he met Lady Edna in the hallway. "I'm very sorry to see Sir Edmund so weak."

Lady Edna's face was thin, and she shook her head. "I fear for him, Daniel. He's not making progress."

The days sped by, and Daniel said to Lyna one evening, "I have to rejoin my regiment day after tomorrow." He saw her face grow apprehensive, and he added quickly, "I've got some money saved. In another three months I'll have enough to send for you. Then we'll be together. Just be patient a while longer."

On the day before Daniel's departure, Leo Rochester returned. He had not heard of Daniel's visit and was more than a little drunk that day. As he rode in, he saw Lyna walking across the back pathway. He rode his horse across the yard and quickly dismounted. Coming to the ground, he blocked her way, saying, "Well, now, aren't you glad to see me?"

Lyna had not been troubled by Leo since Daniel left, but she saw at once that he was drunk. "Your father will be glad to see you, Mr. Leo," she nodded briefly.

She would have turned, but he caught her and, despite her struggles, kissed her roughly. He would have kissed her again, but he was suddenly seized and thrown back so forcibly that he staggered. Catching his balance, he glared at Daniel, who had stepped between him and Lyna. "You again!" he gasped. "You dare to put your hands on me!"

"Keep your hands off my sister and we'll have no trouble." Daniel turned and took Lyna's arm. The two walked away, not looking back. With a maniacal look in his eyes, Leo moved to his horse and opened the saddlebag. He pulled out a brace of pistols, checked the loads, then cried out, "Bradford—!"

Daniel turned to see the muzzle of the pistol in Rochester's hand level on his chest. Instantly he shoved Lyna to his left, falling with her. The explosion rang out, and he heard the hissing of the ball as it went by his ear. He leaped up and ran toward Rochester, who had dropped the one pistol and was coming up with the other loaded one. Daniel caught Leo's wrist, and the two struggled for possession. Daniel's months working with the forge had given him great strength, and he twisted the pistol away from himself.

Leo cursed and tried to resist—and then the air was shattered by a loud report. Daniel was shocked as Leo released his grip and fell to the ground, his side drenched with a sudden flow of blood. "You've killed me—!" he gasped.

The two shots drew an instant audience, one of them Silas Longstreet. His eyes widened as he saw Leo on the ground and the smoking pistol in Daniel's hand. "What have you done, boy?" he gasped.

"He tried to murder me!" Leo shouted. He propped himself up on one elbow, glared at Daniel, and cried out to the men who were running to the scene. "Take that pistol away—and hold him. He's a murderer!"

Lyna started to protest, but Longstreet knew there was no use. "There'll be a fair hearing for you, Daniel," Longstreet said sadly.

But Daniel was staring at the face of Leo Rochester. He had risen to his feet and apparently had suffered only a superficial wound. His eyes were burning as he glared at Daniel. "You'll hang for this, Bradford—I swear it!"

Daniel was taken at once to the local jail, and when Lyna was allowed to see him, he sat silently with her. "It was *his* fault!" she protested. "They can't hang you for that."

But Daniel had seen enough to know that his chances for gaining his freedom were slight. He held her hand and tried to pray, but when she left, he lay down on the filthy straw and wondered if there even was a God in heaven.

5

THE TRIAL

IF SIR EDMUND ROCHESTER HAD BEEN ABLE to attend the hearing, the trial of Daniel Bradford might have been more charitable. Judge Brookfield was an old friend of Sir Edmund's, and it is possible that he might have been prone to listen to the background surrounding the case.

However, Sir Edmund's health was in critical condition, so that even his wife was not able to be present at the hearing. At her husband's request, however, she did send the family barrister to defend the young man, but Emmett Sissons was more of a solicitor than a trial lawyer. He had plenty of experience in handling wills and torts, but he was out of his element when it came to a criminal case.

On his first visit with his client, he said, "Well, Mr. Bradford, what have you to say for yourself?"

"I'm not guilty, Mr. Sissons."

"Oh my! Dear me!" Mr. Sissons clucked his disapproval and insisted, "But, sir, you were found with the weapon in your hand and Mr. Leo Rochester on the ground with your bullet in him! Not guilty? Oh, dear me, no!"

When Daniel offered his sister as a witness to what had really happened, Sissons sighed and looked pained. "I will call her as a witness, but the prosecution will make short work of her, I warn you!"

On the day of the trial, Mr. Ronald Child, arguing for the prosecution, brought forth a series of witnesses who testified they had come on the scene to find Leo Rochester lying on the ground

73

wounded and Daniel Bradford standing over him with a smoking pistol. After skillfully questioning each of the witnesses, the shrewd lawyer capped his case by calling Leo Rochester to the witness stand—who proved to be a most effective witness.

"And do you insist, Mr. Rochester, that the defendant removed your pistols and shot you without provocation?"

"Well, I must admit, sir," Leo said calmly, "Daniel Bradford has never liked me ever since he came to Milford Manor. We have had trouble more than once, I daresay."

"What sort of trouble, may I inquire?" said Mr. Child, leading the witness on.

"Oh, he was careless with his work, and I had to rebuke him many times."

"Were these serious rebukes?"

"One of them was. . . ." Leo then proceeded to give a twisted account of how Daniel had nearly caused serious injury to one of Leo's guests. "I was so provoked that I struck him with my riding crop. I shouldn't have done that, of course."

"What did Bradford do at that time?"

"He left my father's service—and the last thing he said to me was, 'I'll kill you for this—see if I don't!' "

"I never said that!" Daniel burst out as he came to his feet. "He's lying!"

"Mr. Sissons! Keep your client silent, do you hear me?" ordered Judge Brookfield.

"I apologize, m'lord!" Sissons pulled at Daniel, whispering, "Sit down, you young fool! Keep your mouth shut!"

Mr. Child was very adept at making the most of Leo Rochester, who presented a very good appearance to the judge. He showed no sign of anger, and at one point during the questioning Leo even said, "I feel very sorry for Bradford. He has good stuff in him, but he's got a temper like fury, and I had the misfortune to anger him."

When the prosecution was done, Sissons was given time to cross-examine Leo, but his manner and style were so gentle that there was no danger that Leo's testimony would be damaged in the slightest.

"Why didn't you make him tell the court how he's persecuted my sister?" asked Daniel when Sissons sat down.

"He'd deny it—and nobody would believe her."

Finally Judge Brookfield asked Mr. Sissons to give the defense.

When Lyna was called to testify, she related the story of what had happened. But when Ronald Child began to cross-examine her, she was soon reduced to tears. "The defendant is your brother. Is that correct, Miss Bradford?"

"Yes, sir."

"Your *only* brother—in fact, your sole living relative?"

"Y-yes, sir, but—"

"You love your brother very much, don't you?"

Lyna twisted her fingers nervously and nodded. "Yes, I do."

Mr. Child put his eyes on the girl and asked in a kindly fashion, "You would do a great deal to help him, would you not?" When the girl nodded, he insisted, "You would, in fact, do *anything* to keep your brother from being hanged or from going to prison?"

By this time Lyna was in anguish. She stared at Mr. Child and again nodded.

"I put the question to you, Miss Bradford," the tall man said, his eyes fixed on hers. "Would you lie to save your brother's life if necessary?"

Lyna cried out, "Yes, but I'm not lying!"

Child lifted his eyebrow. He had expected the girl to be more difficult. "M'lord, you have heard the witness. She has declared that she would lie to protect her brother. I move that she be declared no proper witness and that her testimony be stricken."

"So moved and so declared," said Judge Brookfield. He turned to Sissons then and said harshly, "Do you wish to call any other witnesses, Mr. Sissons?"

"Yes, m'lord. I call Colonel Adam White as a witness for the defense."

A stir of surprise ran over the courtroom as the well-known officer moved to the front of the courtroom to stand at the bar. He took the oath, and then Sissons said, "Colonel White, please state your profession, and tell the court your opinion of the defendant, Daniel Bradford."

"I am in command of the 6th Royal Cavalry," White said, his voice clear and even. "I first met the defendant when he was an indentured servant of Sir Edmund Rochester. . . ."

Daniel kept his eyes on the colonel as he set forth his account— a very fine one. But Daniel was also watching the judge and could tell he was not impressed.

" . . . and I can say that Sergeant Bradford is a fine soldier, one who has defended his country with honor and courage. I find it impossible to believe that he is guilty of attempted murder."

Sissons, feeling quite pleased with his witness, said, "Thank you, Colonel White." Then turning to the prosecution with a satisfied look, Sissons said, "Your witness, Mr. Child."

Child approached the officer carefully. He was a crafty man and had no intention of trying to intimidate such a formidable man as the one who stood watching him. "Colonel, the prosecution is second to none in its admiration of our fine officers and men. We are all aware of the noble service you and the 6th performed at Culloden Moor. We would be degenerate indeed were we to do anything to degrade any man in His Majesty's service." He waited until a murmur of approval had died down, then said smoothly, "Colonel, I will put to you a single question. I know you have confidence in the defendant—but were you present when the shooting took place?"

Colonel White had no choice. "No, sir, I was not."

"Thank you, Colonel," Child nodded, then turned to the bench. "It was thoughtful of the colonel to come and give a testimonial concerning the defendant. However, his testimony has no bearing on the case, for as he himself admits, he did not witness the incident."

Child waited until Colonel White had been dismissed from the stand and then proceeded to summarize the case with great skill. "The case is quite simple, m'lord," he shrugged. "We have called *many* witnesses who all agree that they came upon the scene immediately after the shots were fired. They all agree that Mr. Rochester was on the ground, and that standing over him with a smoking pistol was the defendant. You have heard Mr. Rochester testify of the bad humor of Bradford, and there is no other possibility but willful attempted murder. The prosecution rests."

Sissons realized his client had no hope of being acquitted and made a feeble plea for mercy on the grounds of Daniel's youth and his good service for the king.

Daniel sat quietly, observing the final proceedings, knowing that he was lost.

Judge Brookfield said finally, "Let the defendant rise. Daniel Bradford, I find you guilty as charged of attempted murder." Ignoring the cry that came from Lyna, he proceeded, "I sentence you to ten years in prison, term to be served in Dartmoor prison. This court is adjourned."

Lyna fought her way past the guard and fell against Daniel, sobbing. She wept until she was led from the court by Silas Longstreet. When she looked back, she saw Daniel being shackled hand and foot. When he looked at her, his eyes were bleak and hopeless. He didn't move or return her cries but turned and shuffled away, his arm grasped by a heavy guard.

🛡   🛡   🛡

For two weeks after Daniel's trial, Lyna listlessly moved about doing her work, her face pale and her lips tightly drawn together. It was a difficult time in any case, for Sir Edmund was dying. The servants were kind, and Lady Edna said only, "I'm sorry about your brother, my dear."

Leo stayed at Milford, saying nothing at all to Lyna. He showed concern for his father and gave himself to comforting his mother and his sister. Only once did he speak to Lyna. They met by accident in the hall, and he halted, his eyes on her. She stared at him silently, and in an odd tone of voice he said, "After my father is gone, we'll make better arrangements for you."

The words echoed in Lyna's mind for a week. She knew very well what Leo's *arrangements* would be! She began to think of leaving, but she had no place to go. Sir Edmund had been her sole protection from Leo, and when he was gone, she would be helpless.

When the doctors showed up early one afternoon, whispers spread the word that the master was dying. Just before dinner the family was called, and Mrs. Standridge announced, "Sir Edmund, Lord of Milford Manor, is dead—God rest his soul!"

For the next few days the house was very busy making preparations for the funeral. It was an impressive occasion. The church was packed, and the bishop came from London to give the funeral sermon. Lyna attended, as did all the servants, but she heard very little of what the bishop said. She was thinking about how she could get away from there.

However, the apprehension that she entertained faded as the days passed. Leo was forced to spend a great deal of his time in London on legal business, and when he did come home, he did no more than give her a penetrating glance.

Maybe it's going to be all right, she thought. She was miserable and lonely, weeping over Daniel's fate and longing to see him. Dartmoor was far away, and she was not even certain that visitors were permitted—but she determined to go and see him somehow. Night after night she lay awake, and during the day she spoke little to anyone. She had never felt more alone. When her mother had died, she'd had Daniel, but now she had no one.

"I'll find a way!" she murmured one morning after a sleepless night. "I'll go to see him, no matter what it takes!"

6

THE RUNAWAY

THE DEATH OF SIR EDMUND ROCHESTER brought great changes to the estate of Milford. The family, of course, made the adjustments to the loss of the head of the family with some difficulty. Lady Edna Rochester took the loss the hardest. She had been totally dependent on her husband, and it was perhaps natural that she should now look to her son for every need. If she had been a more robust woman, she might have remarried, but she was overweight and given to nervousness, which did nothing to attract any suitors. Sir Edmund had left the estate to Leo, with provisions that he would care for his wife and daughter, and Leo saw to it that his mother's needs were met. Soon she settled into the dull routine of a wealthy widow.

Eleanor Rochester was an astute young woman, and though she missed her father greatly, she quickly adapted to a new way of life. She and Leo were much alike and came to an understanding almost at once. "Look around and find yourself a rich husband, sister," Leo advised her. "You're good-looking and have some property to offer as a dowry. Shouldn't be too hard to snare the son of an earl."

"And what about you, Leo?" Eleanor had countered.

"Oh, I'll marry, of course," he had shrugged. "But I intend to enjoy my liberty for a time. Father was all right, but he kept me on a pretty short chain. Now I'm my own man and can do as I please."

The servants of the house and the farm were all somewhat doubtful of their new master. Leo had never made any attempt

79

through the years to befriend any of them, and some of them had been abused by him. He was totally selfish, they well knew, and the young maids were careful to avoid him whenever possible. Now that Sir Edmund had died, there was no one to restrain him.

Lyna had been warned by Silas Longstreet shortly after the death of Sir Edmund. He drew her aside one afternoon, saying, "Lyna, I'm leaving Milford."

"Oh, Mr. Longstreet—!" Lyna exclaimed. "You've been here so long!"

"Aye, but it's time to go. We'll be moving next week." Longstreet had grown fond of the girl and now said, "It'll be hard on you here with Sir Edmund gone."

Lyna knew exactly what he meant. "I wish I could leave here— but my time of indenture won't be up for two more years," she sighed.

"That's what I want to talk to you about," Longstreet nodded. "I've spoken with my new employer about you. He says he can use a maid and is willing to buy the time remaining in your service from Sir Leo—if you want to come."

"Oh yes!" Lyna said instantly. "There's nothing for me here— now that Daniel's not here. Please, will you speak to Sir Leo?"

Later that day Longstreet was going over the books with Leo, and when they were finished, he said, "I think all's in order, sir. The new man should have no trouble."

"It seems very well, Longstreet."

"One more thing, sir. My new employer needs a lady's maid. I thought of Lyna and mentioned her. He's willing to buy the remainder of her indenture if you'd care to sell."

Leo shot an angry glance at Longstreet. "The girl will remain here!" he snapped.

Longstreet gave Leo a steady glance. "Sir, I have an affection for both Lyna and her brother. Not to be offensive, but the girl has no friends here. I feel responsible for her. As a matter of fact, I promised Daniel—"

"You heard me! The girl stays—now you're free to leave!"

Longstreet had seen Leo Rochester before in such angry moods. He said no more, for he knew to push it further was useless, and it would only make things worse. Sadly he went to his house and told his wife, "I spoke to Sir Leo about Lyna." His brow clouded, and he shook his head. "He won't let her go." He ran his hand through his gray hair, adding, "He'll have the girl now. I hate to think of it!"

When Longstreet told Lyna of Leo's refusal to release her, the poor girl began to cry. She had dared hope that she would be able to go with the Longstreets, but at the thought of having to stay, a heaviness settled over the young girl.

For two weeks after the funeral, Lyna went about her work, seeing little of Leo. He was spending most of his time with the new manager, so he was seldom seen in the house. Lady Edna became more demanding, and Eleanor increasingly more so. The house servants seemed to settle into the new way of life, but Lyna feared that sooner or later Leo would notice her.

Two days after the Longstreets left Milford, Lyna was approached by Betty, one of the housemaids. "Sir Leo, he wants to see you, Lyna—in his study."

Lyna at once grew wary. "What does he want, Betty?"

"You'll have to ask him that," Betty shrugged. "He don't tell me his business." She gave Lyna a sly grin and said, "Better watch out for him, though. He's a one with the girls, he is!"

Lyna moved down the hall and knocked on the door of the study reluctantly, her heart beating faster. When a voice said, "Come in," she opened the massive oak door and entered. Leo was sitting at the walnut desk, which was littered with papers and ledgers. Looking up, he smiled, "Well, come in, Lyna."

"Yes, sir." Lyna moved closer. "You sent for me, sir?"

"Yes, I did." Leo replaced the goose quill into a gold holder. Then he rose and moved to stand beside the high window that admitted bars of yellow sunbeams. He was a handsome man— and well aware of it. He had a tall body, kept strong through an active life of riding and hunting, and always wore the finest of clothing. He was wearing a pair of ash gray breeches cut to fit very tightly.

Leo's shirt was pure white, his cuffs cut back in the newest fashion, his collar high in the latest style, and a pure silk ruffle blossomed at his throat. He wore a maroon waistcoat and a pair of shining black boots that covered his calves. On his right hand he wore a large red ruby set in a massive ring, which glowed as he lifted his hand and ran it through his thick brown hair.

"Well, now," he said, his blue eyes fixed on her, "I haven't seen much of you lately, have I, Lyna?"

"No, sir," said Lyna nervously.

"You're looking well. Let's see, how old are you now?"

"S-seventeen, sir."

"Ah, yes, seventeen." Leo moved across the room, coming to stand beside her. His eyes roamed over her, and the corners of his lips turned up in a smile. "I remember when you first came to Milford," he said. "You were skinny as a stick and pale as paste." He reached out and let his hand fall on her shoulder. "You've blossomed since then—my word, you have!"

Lyna felt uncomfortable and desperately wanted to pull away from his hand. She looked up quickly, saying, "You wanted to see me, Sir Leo?"

Leo gave her shoulder a squeeze. "I can make things a lot easier for you, Lyna. No need for you to work so hard."

Quickly Lyna said, "I don't mind work, sir." She moved away from his touch and lifted her chin in a defiant manner. "If that's all, sir. . . ?"

The girl's quick movement away from his touch amused Leo. He was accustomed to easy successes with women, especially with young servant girls. Somehow Lyna Bradford's resistance pleased him. He saw it as a challenge, and now that his father's heavy hand was not present, Leo knew it would be only a matter of time before he bent the girl to his will. "That's all—for now," he said and watched as she left the room. "You've got pride—but so did your brother," he murmured, then smiled at the thought of Daniel Bradford buried alive in a dark and foul prison cell at Dartmoor.

☙   ☙   ☙

A sound broke through her fitful sleep, coming to Lyna only faintly. She rolled over, moving restlessly under the heavy weight of blankets, vaguely aware of the absence of Betty, her customary bed partner. A faint clicking sound caused her to start. She struggled out of sleep, lifted her head, and asked, "Betty—is that you?"

When no answer came, alarm flooded her at once. Betty, she remembered, had gone to spend the weekend with her parents. It had been a luxury, having the tiny garret room to herself. The room was located in the extreme east corner, over the ballroom. It had become a citadel for Lyna, a haven where she retired as soon as her duties were over. She had a few books and a candle, and reading had been her only entertainment.

One window broke the west wall of the small room, and as Lyna sat up with alarm, the full moon sent silver beams through it—outlining a large form that loomed beside her bed!

Lyna cried out, but at once Leo Rochester's voice broke the silence, "Now, don't take on, Lyna—" When he pulled the covers back, Lyna made a frantic lunge to escape. A powerful hand caught her, closing on her arm with a viselike grip. Lyna caught the smell of liquor and knew that he was drunk. His voice was hoarse, and he pulled her back, holding her fast.

"Let me go!" she panted, pushing at him with all the strength of her arms. Fear ran along her nerves, and she knew if she didn't think of something soon, all would be lost!

Leo captured her wrists and held them tightly in his big hand. "That's all right, sweetheart," Leo gloated, his voice slurred with too much wine. "Fight! I like it—but you'll give in soon enough!"

Lyna screamed, "Help me—someone!"

"Nobody to hear you. You can't hear anything in this room in the main house. Scream all you want—"

Lyna could see his face in the cold moonlight, and her mind reeled with terror. No one would come to her aid. Unexpectedly, an idea broke through her panic. To Leo's surprise, she suddenly went limp. When she stopped struggling, Leo lifted his head and laughed.

"You give up pretty easy, girl." He released her hands and started to pull her close—but the moment she felt her hands free, Lyna lunged away from him. His hand slapped at her, but she managed to come off the bed as he cried angrily, "Come here—you can't get away!"

Lyna knew he would put himself between her and the door. Her mind was racing now. She had only one hope. A heavy pewter candlestick sat on the table beside the bed—the only thing that could be used for a weapon. Desperately she seized it, then turned to face him.

The moonlight fell on Leo's face, which was twisted with drunken anger. "Come here, Lyna! You can't get away!"

Lyna held the heavy base of the candlestick tightly in both hands. When he came toward her with his hands reaching for her, she thrust it at his face with all her strength! It caught Leo in the mouth with a sickening sound of breaking teeth, and a wild cry burst from his lips. He lifted both hands to his mouth, and when he did, Lyna took the candlestick by the top of the stem and with all her force swung it again. It caught Leo in the left temple, and he crumbled to the floor instantly. He lay there so loosely that Lyna thought she had killed him. But when she leaned over, she saw that he was still breathing.

"Got to get away!" she gasped. Instantly she wheeled and went to the small closet. Frantically she threw on a dress and her one heavy wool coat, then stuffed her meager possessions into a rough cloth bag. Leo was beginning to groan as she stepped past him. She took one look at his face, which was covered with blood, shuddered, then ran from the room.

Lyna quickly went to the kitchen. Opening a cloth sack, she put a few potatoes, two loaves of bread, and some dried meat inside. Quietly she stepped outside into the numbing cold wind and went at once to the barn. Daniel's old room was vacant except for his old trunk containing his personal belongings he'd had to leave behind when he was arrested. Digging through the trunk, she took some of his things, including two books and one of his old outfits—not knowing why, but wanting something of his. As she left the barn, she heard the sound of the horses stirring but nothing else.

The moon cast a silver glaze on the fields as she made her way south. She had no destination, but Lyna knew instinctively that Leo would search for her. *He'll never forget what I did*, she thought grimly. *I'll have to hide during the day and walk nights. Maybe I can reach the coast and get on a ship. . . .*

She made a pathetic figure as she fled from Milford. Several times she passed cottages where warm fires burned. And each time she thought of how nice it would be to have a little house— to be safe inside. But she knew no house in the country would be safe for her, and as the moon gazed down on her, she walked doggedly along the road, not looking back a single time.

🔔   🔔   🔔

Drifting snow streaked across the fields in a ghostly haze and swirled in little eddies at her feet as Lyna made her way down the frozen road. Dawn was beginning to redden the low-lying hills to her left as she stumbled over the rutted way. She was cold and tired, and her shoes, never made for heavy outside wear, had not stood the journey. Both soles had come loose sometime during the night, and her attempts to bind them up with strips of an old blouse had not been very successful.

She stopped, dropping the heavy bag, then pulled off her thin gloves and blew on her fingers. *Got to find a place to stay!* she thought numbly. It was her third night on the road, and twice she had been forced to sleep in haystacks. She had burrowed into the musty hay to shiver through the cold, lying there all day until night came. The other time she had been fortunate to find an abandoned barn and had managed to make a small fire. She had roasted two of the potatoes she had brought and ravenously ate them along with some of the bread.

The wind was picking up now, and the blowing snow was forcing its way into every opening in her scant clothing. She knew she would freeze if she didn't find shelter. Slowly she turned and saw, against the glowing red of the early morning sky, the outline of a large house. Picking up her sack she moved toward it. A dog's bark broke the frigid silence and stopped her dead still. A small mongrel appeared from around the corner of the house, its head down and a menacing growl in its throat.

"Good dog!" Lyna whispered and held her hand down. The dog halted, seemed to consider her—then began to wag his stubby tail. He came closer, and Lyna pulled a piece of bread from her sack and offered it to the animal, who took it eagerly. "Good dog," she said, patting his ragged fur. "Come on, now."

She skirted the house, having seen the outline of a barn in the meadow behind it. She was frightened, knowing that if seen she could be shot for a prowler. But in the icy wind the swirling snow soon screened the house. When she reached the back she saw two barns—one new and the other ancient. The older one was leaning at an impossible angle, ready to fall, it seemed. The sound of animals in the new barn gave her an idea. She slipped inside and, by the dim light of the rising sun, saw three cows in stalls, chewing slowly.

At once Lyna found a bucket, then speaking soothingly to one of the cows, sat down on a three-legged stool. Soon the rhythmic sound of streams of milk hitting the bottom of the pail came, and when she had drawn about a pint, she lifted the pail and drank thirstily. The rich taste of the frothy, warm liquid was the best thing she'd ever tasted! She quickly milked the other two cows, not taking much from either, and drank until she could hold no more. Then she made her way to the older, deserted barn—a better hiding place, she surmised.

Climbing into the rickety loft, she found enough old straw to cover herself. Outside, the wind moaned, muting all other noises. Exhausted from walking all night, and comfortably full from the warm milk, Lyna fell asleep as if drugged. Once she woke up to the sound of a voice from the next barn. But soon that ended, and she knew that the farmer had milked the cows and fed them, so she dropped off to sleep again.

When she awoke, the sun was declining in the west. She rose stiffly, blew on her hands, and wished for a fire. The dog met her as she came down the ladder, and she spoke softly to him. "Nice dog," she murmured, noting that her lips were stiff with the cold. She peered out the door and could see a man chopping wood in the backyard. Smoke was rolling out of the chimney of the big house, and she longed for the warmth of a fire.

A fresh snow had fallen while she slept, for the land was covered with a pristine white blanket that reflected the golden rays of the dying sun. She drew her coat around her, and then slipped unseen into the new barn. After making her supper of all the fresh milk she could hold, Lyna began a careful search of the barn. Toward the back wall, she found a small barrel of apples, which she sampled at once and found good. She took half a dozen of them and also a small sack of the corn used for horse feed. It could be soaked and cooked, she knew.

As the last rays of the sun slowly faded, Lyna got ready to start another night's walk. Though the food and rest had helped, she knew that she was in great danger. She had come some twenty miles from Milford, but a long journey still lay ahead of her. *If I could just travel during the day,* she thought, *I'd be all right—but I'll freeze trying to walk at night.* She looked outside and saw that it was finally dark—but also that fine grains of snow were being swirled by a rising wind. It would be harder going now in the deeper layer of snow. Discouraged, she went back inside the barn and sat down. The small dog whined and came and put his head in her lap.

"I wish I had fur like you," she whispered. She rubbed his head, trying to think. "If I were a boy, it would be easy," she added, pulling at his ragged ears.

If I were a boy—

The thought echoed in her mind, and she stood up so suddenly that the dog gave a startled yelp and backed away. Lyna had a quick mind, and once the idea had come, she rapidly worked it out.

"I've got some of Daniel's old clothes," she muttered, "and nobody would be looking for a *boy* runaway." She thought for no more than two minutes, then nodded, her eyes gleaming with determination. "I can't make it to safety as a girl—so I'll become a boy!"

At once she pulled Daniel's old clothes from the bag, stripped off her dress and petticoat, and put on the trousers and shirt. They were too large for her, but the very shapelessness of the garments helped hide her figure. She picked up the soft cap—then paused. Her hand went to her long hair and she whispered, "Got to get rid of this—but I don't have scissors—or even a sharp knife."

She made another search of the barn and was delighted to discover a pair of sheep shears. She tested their edge, then with her left hand took a heavy lock of her blond hair. Placing the shears in position, she took a deep breath, then snipped the hair. It fell to the floor, and soon was followed by other locks. Cutting her own hair was awkward, but Lyna worked carefully, leaving it long enough to fall over the edge of her collar.

"There—now you're a boy," she said to herself. She ran her hand over her head, whispering, "It feels so *odd!*" Then she carefully scooped up the loose hair, wrapping it in her cast-off petticoat. She stuffed everything into the bag and determined to rest until nearly dawn the next day.

"I've got plenty of food here, and I'll leave before dawn. Maybe I can get a ride on a wagon," she murmured. She started to walk across the floor of the barn and laughed. "It feels so—*funny!*" Lyna had been wearing skirts all her life, and now the feel of the rough trousers on her legs was shocking. She walked around and thought, *Boys walk different than girls—they take bigger steps—and they swagger sometimes.* She practiced a few times, and after several strides was finally satisfied. Finding a blanket in one of the horse stalls, Lyna decided to risk staying in the snug new barn. She milked one of the cows, drank all she could hold, then patted the side of the animal, saying wistfully, "Wish I could take you with me, cow."

She wrapped up in the blanket and slept well. An hour before dawn she woke, had her last liquid breakfast, then picked up her bag and left the barn.

The dog came to nose her, and she bent over to pat his shaggy head. "Goodbye," she whispered. Then she shouldered her bag and made her way around the house to the road. By the time the sun cast its first rays across the land, Lyna was already two miles away, walking down the snow-packed road.

She heard the sound of horses' hooves and looked back to see a wagon with runners replacing the wheels. The man who drove it was wrapped up in a huge coat and his cap nearly covered his eyes. However, as he pulled alongside her, he called out cheerfully, "Hello, young fellow. Goin' to town?"

"Yes, I am."

"Hop in. It's too cold to be a-walkin'." When Lyna climbed into the seat beside him, the farmer asked, "Whereabouts you headed, lad?"

"Going to Dover."

"Well, I ain't goin' so far as that—but I can put you down in Faxton. What's your name, boy?"

Lyna had not yet thought of that, but the answer came naturally. "Name is Lee." Daniel had called her by her middle name when she was small, and now she smiled at the thought. "Just call me Lee," she said. She sat there beside the driver, suddenly filled with hope for the first time since leaving Milford. For some reason, she thought of her mother and the last prayer she'd prayed for her and Daniel.

As the sled moved smoothly along the glistening ribbon of snow, Lyna Lee Bradford prayed a childlike prayer: *Lord, help me find my way!*

7

An Unexpected Visitor

DARTMOOR PRISON WAS DESIGNED for the confinement of prisoners—not for their comfort.

The guards were callous men who often vented their anger and frustrations on the inmates. Warden Pennington G. Sipes was dedicated to wringing the last pence from his budget. The last thing either he or anyone else cared about was the misery and dismal suffering of criminals. He was fond of stating his philosophy of penology to the inspectors who made rare visits to see that funds were not wasted on excessive food or fine clothing for the prisoners.

"It is my task to demonstrate to the prisoners that those who break the law must suffer for their crimes. We are not running a resort here at Dartmoor, but a prison. Those who have pride will be broken—and if some perish, what complaint can they have? Had they been respectable citizens, they would not be here."

After almost a year of fighting to survive the rotten food, the sweltering heat in the summer, and the numbing cold in winter, Daniel Bradford had lost almost every normal reaction that he'd brought into the prison. The days were endless drudgery, and the nights a horror. The thought of spending ten years in a hell such as Dartmoor brought a mindless terror so consuming to Daniel that he wanted to scream and beat his fists against the stone walls.

From the very beginning, however, he learned to obey orders instantly—*any* orders—for any minor infraction in the eyes of the cruel guards was ruthlessly punished. His spirit was crushed almost at once, and he soon found out what the inmates meant when they spoke of "going to the shower." Something in their voices and the fear in their eyes frightened Daniel. If these hardened men were filled with terror over whatever the punishment was, how could he bear up to it?

The grim reality came one day when he failed to put away his tin plate used for all meals. A hulking guard named Jesperson caught him by the arm, his small eyes gleaming. "All right, Bradford, you didn't last long, did you now? Come along—you can use a shower."

Fear threaded Daniel's nerves, but he kept his face stolid as the guard dragged him away. He saw the grins on the faces of the other guards—and some of the inmates joined them.

Jesperson led him to a section of the prison walled off from the rest. When they entered a room set off to the back, Daniel looked around apprehensively.

"Got a new man, Pinkman, name of Bradford." Jesperson grinned. "Needs a taste of a shower."

"Well, I reckon we can accommodate him." The guard was small and had a sharp face like a ferret. He measured Daniel with his slate-colored eyes in a way that frightened the young man. His smile was a mere twitch of thin lips, and he nodded toward a device against the wall. "Just 'ave a seat, and we'll take care of you right enough."

Jesperson shoved Daniel into a heavy wooden chair fastened to the back wall. Over the chair was a pipe with a circular head pierced with many small holes. Daniel had time only to glance at it, when Jesperson fastened his wrists with leather straps to the arms of the chair. Then the other guard swung something that was attached to the wall in front of his face. It was a large cuplike device that pressed against his throat and came up to the level of his eyes, clamping his forehead tightly with a steel band.

"Not too tight, is it?" Pinkman asked anxiously. "Let me know if it binds. We aim to please. Are you ready now?"

"He's ready," Jesperson grinned. "Let 'im have it, Pinkman."

The small guard reached out and turned a handle, and at once cold water sprayed over Daniel's head. The shock of it made him gasp, and he struggled to move, but his head was clamped fast by the steel band. He opened his eyes and saw the two men grinning as they watched. When he looked down he saw the water collecting in the cup, and suddenly terror ran through him.

They're going to drown me!

He felt the water touch his chin, then slowly rise until it lapped against his mouth. He shut his lips, but as the water crept up over his upper lip and touched the base of his nose, he fought against his bonds with all his strength.

The water soon rose over his nose, and he held his breath as long as he could. Finally the pain in his chest forced the air out—and when he inhaled, water choked him instantly. It was agony, and he coughed and gagged as the water hit his lungs. His arms and legs strained mightily, but the horrid torment went on until finally he passed out.

He came to, coughing and gagging and heaving as he recovered. He shivered and opened his eyes to see Pinkman and Jesperson watching him with interest. "All right now?" Pinkman asked, his voice strangely gentle but his eyes filled with an unholy joy.

Daniel nodded weakly, and Pinkman winked at his companion. "A tough one, ain't he, now? Well, let's have another shower, eh?"

Daniel almost screamed as the guard turned on the water again. A mindless terror clawed at him, and as the torment was repeated, he fought until he went under again.

How many times the ordeal went on, Daniel could never remember afterward. The world became a fiendish nightmare as the two guards again and again waited for him to regain consciousness, then watched as he strangled and gagged helplessly.

Finally Pinkman looked down at the pale face of the young man and nodded regretfully, "Guess that'll have to do—for this time. He's a tough one, eh?"

"He ain't no crier, that's for sure," Jesperson said, a reluctant admiration in his pale eyes. "Not a word out of 'im!"

"Well, well, next time we'll do better," the small guard nodded as he unfastened the straps and allowed the limp head of the prisoner to fall to one side. Pinkman's ferret eyes gleamed and he urged, "Be sure you bring this one back, Jesperson—he's an interesting case. Kind of a challenge, you might say. . . ."

Three times during the past ten months Daniel had been taken to the "shower," despite every attempt to avoid it. He had nightmares now of those times, and a deep-seated hatred for Jesperson and Pinkman burned in his belly. He would have killed them instantly if the chance had ever come, but it never did, of course.

Dartmoor had few individual cells, only large tomblike rooms in which fifty prisoners were crowded together. These oversized "cells" were little kingdoms, where Daniel had discovered those first days after arriving that the strong ruled and the weak served. He had been challenged almost at once by a hulking inmate named Perry, who demanded that Daniel give him his blanket. When Daniel refused, the big prisoner struck out at him. Though the man was muscular, he was slow and ponderous. Daniel slipped under the impact and instinctively drove a tremendous right-hand blow into the convict's mouth, knocking him down. Daniel was strong and healthy and had had his share of fights in the army. When the convict got up, cursing and raving, Daniel proceeded to coolly knock him down again and again.

Finally Perry crawled to his feet, his face a bloody mask. He stared at the young man, who was not even breathing hard, spat out a tooth and muttered, "Who needs yer blasted blanket?"

"Good on you, lad," one of the prisoners murmured. "He'll leave you alone now."

"That's what I want—to be left alone," Daniel muttered. He turned to face the prisoner who had spoken to him, an undersized man of some thirty years. He was emaciated and bore the marks of suffering on his gaunt face, but he seemed to be of a better sort than most of the others. "My name's Bradford," Daniel offered, sitting down next to the thin man and leaning back against the dank, foul-smelling wall. "You can call me Daniel."

"James Boswell—call me Jamie." He extended a bony hand, then asked, "How long is your sentence?"

"Ten years."

"And the charge?"

"Attempted murder."

"Ah? Well, Daniel, ten years is better than goin' to the gallows."

Daniel looked around the abysmal surroundings and shook his head. "I don't know about that," he said bitterly. Then he stared at Boswell closely, asking, "What about you?"

A slight smile appeared on Jamie Boswell's thin lips. "Well, the charge was treason. I was arrested for being a supporter of Bonnie Prince Charlie—for being a Jacobite."

"And were you?"

"Oh no, not really. But the hunt was up and I'd made political enemies. The Crown needed a scapegoat and my enemies needed to get rid of me, so—there it was."

Daniel had been filled with bitterness since his arrest and was puzzled at how calmly the small man seemed to take his fate. "I guess you'd like to pay those back that put you here?"

"Oh no, that's not for me, Daniel. The Scripture says, 'Vengeance is mine, I will repay.'"

Incredulous, Daniel stared at the man, and Boswell quickly added, "But I can't take any credit for not harboring hatred. In the natural I suppose I'd be filled with hatred by now, what with the way I've been treated. But since the Lord Jesus came into my heart, why, I find it's possible even to pray for those who locked me up here."

"I'll never pray for the man who put me in this place!" spat Daniel.

Boswell didn't answer for a time but gently laid his hand on the young man's shoulder. "Well, I'm sorry you're in this place, my young friend, but we'll make the best of it. Perhaps I can be of help from time to time. I've learned how to get by, and you shall too."

Daniel relaxed in the presence of this calm and gentle man. "It's a terrible place. How long are you in for, Jamie?"

"Six more years to go. Now, first of all, come and make your bed next to mine—if you'd care to, that is."

Daniel liked the open honesty of the small man and agreed at once. Those next few days Boswell had guided him through the worst of it all. And when Daniel saw how badly some of the newcomers had fared, he was very thankful for the advice.

He was able to repay Boswell almost at once. On the second day of Daniel's imprisonment, Perry came to stand over the pair. He ignored Daniel, but putting his eyes on Boswell, he demanded, "You got yer money today—hand over me share."

At once Daniel realized that the hulking bully had been forcing Boswell to pay extortion. Standing to his feet, he said, "Perry, get away from here or I'll smash your face to jelly."

The words were not loud, but Perry immediately took a step back. He glared at Daniel, but his lips were still crushed from the young man's hard fist, and he whirled and walked away, cursing under his breath. Daniel took his seat, saying nothing. But Boswell clapped his thin hand on Daniel's shoulder. "Thanks, Daniel. He's been robbing me for months."

From that time on the two kept together, and Daniel profited from the relationship. He discovered that his new friend was a scholar of sorts and had been a writer and a printer before he'd been imprisoned. "Had to learn how to print to get my things published," Jamie informed him. "My pen gets out of hand at times."

Visitors were rare at Dartmoor. The prison had been built in a location very difficult to reach, so that it involved considerable expense and trouble to make a visit. Getting letters out was hard, for the guards demanded a bribe, and Daniel had almost no money. He did send one letter to Lyna but received a reply from an unexpected source—Sir Leo Rochester.

When the letter came, Daniel stared at it in disbelief. The envelope was sealed in wax with the family crest of the Rochesters. The letter itself was written on fine paper with the same crest at the top of the page.

"Your sister is no longer at Milford," the letter read. "She left shortly after my father's funeral. However, I have gone to great lengths to find her. I know you will be pleased to know that when I do, I shall see to it that she is properly cared for. My father having passed away, I am now master of Milford. I trust you are enjoying your present environment."

Daniel felt a wave of hatred rush through him, and he tore the letter to shreds. He was so troubled about Lyna's plight that he shared his history with Jamie, who showed quick sympathy.

"Well, from what you tell me, she's better off away from Leo Rochester. Thank the Lord she's out of his power."

"But—where *is* she?" Daniel groaned. "She could be hungry or sick—"

"Let's think better things," Jamie answered at once. "She's an orphan, and God has a special love for those people. He calls himself the Father of the fatherless." Boswell had a pair of mild light blue eyes, and he spoke quietly as a rule. "When I came here I raged at God—cursed Him and dared Him to strike me dead."

Somehow this side of the man didn't fit the image that Daniel had formed of Boswell. "Can't see you doing that," he said finally, "but it's what I'd *like* to do. What changed you?"

"God did—but not until I'd almost destroyed myself." Jamie hesitated, then said, "Mind if I tell you about it, Daniel?"

"Go ahead—but it won't do me any good."

Boswell ignored Daniel's skepticism. He settled down with his back against the stone wall and began to speak. He went far back, relating how his own family had been devout Christians. Then he spoke of how he'd gotten away from their faith when he went to the university.

"Which one was that?" Daniel asked.

"Christ's College, Oxford," said Boswell.

A bit surprised, Daniel paid more careful attention to the quiet voice, for he'd formed a high opinion of educated men.

"I became an atheist," Jamie acknowledged. "I made fun of my parents' simple religion and used to laugh at ministers." He paused and asked, "I don't suppose you're an atheist, are you, Daniel?"

"No. Only a fool would deny there's a God!"

"Well," Jamie shrugged, "I was a fool for several years. Made myself a reputation in the printing world, plenty of money—everything I needed." He paused and ran his hand over his sandy hair. "You know, there are times now as a Christian when heaven and all that seems terribly improbable—but there were many times when I was an atheist when hell and judgment seemed terribly probable. . . ."

The two sat there, and for almost an hour Boswell described how he nearly lost his mind buried alive in Dartmoor. Then he told how a minister had come once and held a funeral service—and had preached the love of Jesus for all sinners. "It hit me like a physical blow, Daniel," he confessed. "I began to tremble, and when the minister finished, he came to me. He said, 'Man, call on the Lord for forgiveness! Jesus died for you—don't miss out on heaven!' "

"What happened?" Daniel asked. He could not doubt the sincerity of the small inmate, for there was a quiet light of joy in those blue eyes.

"I did what the man said. I called on God, and the moment I asked for forgiveness in the name of Jesus Christ—everything changed!" He shook his head, saying, "Oh, I still grew weary and sick—the food was still awful, and I still endured some misery from Perry and the guards—but there was a peace inside me that I can't explain, Daniel! Before I was converted, Jesus was just a man who lived two thousand years ago, but by some tremendous miracle I can't explain—why, He's inside me now!"

Daniel listened but made no comment. Later, as the weeks passed, from time to time Jamie would share something from the Bible with him. He quoted scripture liberally, and once after quoting the entire eleventh chapter of Hebrews, Daniel asked, "How much of the Bible do you know by heart, Jamie?"

"Why, all the New Testament—but not that much of the Old."

Daniel stared at his friend in disbelief. "*All* the New Testament? You must be a genius!"

"Oh no, not really," Jamie denied. "I've always had a good memory, and since I've been in here, I've had little else to do. I memorized most of Plato when I was an atheist. But it's nice to have the Bible with you all the time."

The months passed slowly, and Daniel grew more and more sullen and withdrawn. He never heard from Lyna and dully assumed that she had left the country—or perhaps had died. He moved through the days like an animal, sitting for hours staring at the walls, his mind a blank. He deteriorated physically, of course—as did all those in Dartmoor. The deplorable conditions, the rotten food, the lack of exercise, and the horrors of "the shower" reduced even the strongest of men to empty shells of hopelessness. Some had even committed suicide to escape the baneful existence.

If it had not been for Jamie, Daniel would have found a way to kill himself. Weapons could be obtained—for a price. He could have hanged himself by making a rope of his clothing, which one poor soul had done a few days earlier. But though he came close to killing himself, just when things grew worse, Jamie Boswell would be there, encouraging him. Jamie was a ray of light in that dark place, and Daniel vowed if the time ever came, he would find a way to repay the man for his kindness.

Finally winter came again, and the bitter cold gripped every man in an iron fist. Each inmate put on every thread of clothing he owned and spent the days and nights wrapped in the thin ragged blankets that served as bed and cover alike.

One bleak December morning, Daniel was sitting beside Boswell, half asleep. He shivered involuntarily from time to time, but this had become so habitual that he paid no mind. He was dreaming of the time when he and Lyna had walked beside the small stream that flowed through the woods close to Milford. A vivid image of her dear face, fresh and eager, came to mind. It almost seemed as though he could hear her clear laughter.

And then he felt a boot nudge him, dispelling the pleasant reverie. He looked up and saw Adams, one of the better guards, standing over him. "You've got a visitor, Bradford. Come along, now."

Daniel blinked with astonishment, then came to his feet at once. "It's got to be Lyna," he whispered to Jamie. Then he turned and followed Adams, stumbling on numbed feet. He walked behind the guard out of the cell, then down a long hall that led to the main section of the prison. Door after door opened, then closed behind him with a clanging that echoed down the cold corridors. Adams came to a door, opened it, then nodded. "Wait here, Bradford."

The room was not heated, but it was warmer than his cell. A table and three chairs sat alone in the otherwise bare room. Daniel stood staring at the door, trembling with excitement. He had given up hope long ago, but now it came back with a strength that flooded him.

He waited for five minutes, then the door opened. Daniel stepped forward, expecting to see Lyna—but a shock of bitter disappointment ran through him when Leo Rochester stepped inside!

Rochester stopped and stared at Daniel, a look of smug satisfaction creeping over his face. "Well, I suppose you were expecting your sister, Bradford." He removed his heavy black wool coat and hung it on the back of a chair. Daniel's ragged condition stood in marked contrast to Leo's elegant attire—finely woven gray woolen trousers, a green brocade waistcoat, and a white silk shirt. Leo carefully set his beaver hat on the table, dusted off the chair with his kid leather gloves, and sat down. "Well, now, let's have a talk," he said brusquely. "How've you been? Not too badly, I hope?"

Daniel would have allowed himself to be pulled to pieces with hot pincers before giving Rochester the satisfaction of hearing him beg or complain. "As well as can be expected," he said. "What do you want?"

Rochester slapped his thigh and laughed. "Well, sink me! If you aren't as incorrigible as ever. I thought Dartmoor would take the starch out of you—but I'm glad to see it hasn't."

"Glad to see you're still interested in my welfare," Daniel said bitterly. He was struggling with the rage and hatred that rose in him at the sight of the man—but kept his face immobile. "You have nothing better to do than come torment me?"

"Torment you?" Rochester lifted his eyes in mock horror. "Now *there* you do me an injustice."

"Just pure Christian charity, is that what brought you here?"

Rochester seemed pleased with his caustic responses. "Daniel, you're as tough as a boot! I always said you were, you know. We've had our differences—but I confess, you've got the one quality I admire in a man—and that's toughness."

"I'd like to go back to my cell, Mr. Rochester. The company's better there."

Leo shook his head, saying, "Why, you haven't heard what I've come for." He sat forward and leaned on the table, studying Daniel carefully. "You'll be pleased to hear that I've managed to lose a great deal of money since I came into my property."

Daniel smiled for the first time. "I'm pleased to hear it."

Rochester blinked, then laughed. "I knew you would be. Well, let's talk business. I have an offer to make you." He waited for Daniel to ask what it was, but silence filled the room. "Oh, you're not going to ask? Well, I shall tell you anyway. I want something from you, and I'm willing to make it worth your while if you give it to me."

"What could you possibly want from me?" Daniel spoke abruptly. "Your lies put me in this place! Isn't that enough revenge even for you?"

"All right, I did lie. You infuriated me—always have. But that's over, past history as it were." He leaned back and studied Daniel carefully. "I actually *do* have a proposition for you. I'll make it, and if you choose to say no, I'll walk out of here and you'll never hear from me again. Here it is—I've sold everything I own in England and bought a large tract of land in Virginia—a plantation, you'd call it." Rochester uttered a nervous laugh. He bit his lips, then shrugged his shoulders. "I haven't the least idea of how to manage such a place, but it's a chance for me to recover my fortune. Land's very cheap there, and with luck and time, it can be done."

"And what do you want from me?"

"I need all the workers I can get—and I want your life for the next seven years."

Daniel was stunned, unable even to utter a response. Rochester smiled at the young man's obvious shock. "That surprises you, I see. Well, there it is, Daniel. You go with me to America as my indentured servant. Serve me for seven years, during which time you'll be well provided for. At the end of the time, you'll be a free man. I realize you have good cause to hate me—but anything would be better than this place, I'd think."

Daniel stood stock still, wild thoughts racing through his mind. He thought of spending the next nine years like a blind worm in the hole of Dartmoor. He knew if he remained here he would come out a broken man. On the other hand, he had heard many speak of land that could be had for pennies in America. A man at least had a fair chance there!

Rochester watched Bradford's face but said nothing for a time. Finally he said, "I'm leaving next week. I'll have to have somebody—if not you, I'll hire another man. Make up your mind."

Daniel asked, "How do I get out of here?"

"I've already taken care of that. It's done all the time—prisoners released to go serve as indentured servants." He rose and picked up his coat and hat. "Well, what shall it be?"

Daniel knew that he was putting himself into the hands of a man who hated him, who would humiliate and grind him down as much as possible. But he would be out of the dank dungeon of Dartmoor. And he'd never have to suffer "the shower" again.

"I'll go," he said abruptly. "But only on one condition."

"And that is?"

"There's a prisoner here, his name is Jamie Boswell. You see to it he gets out, and I'll do what you want. . . ."

Leo listened carefully, then nodded. "Very well. I'll get him a place here with one of my friends. Agreed?"

"Yes."

Rochester said instantly, "Done! I'll see to it that you go as my servant." Reaching into his coat, he drew a legal-looking paper from his inner pocket, saying, "I had the papers drawn up for you. Sign it, and I'll have someone come for you." He gave Daniel a long, searching look, then said in an odd voice, "Seven years— you'll do as I say. You know I'm not an easy man. There'll be no turning back, you understand."

"Have you found Lyna?"

The question took Rochester off guard. He put his hat on, pulled it down over his brow, then looked directly at Daniel.

"I thought you knew," he said finally.

"Knew what?"

"I wrote you about her—you never got the letter?"

A chill gripped Daniel. "What—did the letter say?"

Rochester dropped his eyes as he pulled on his gloves. "This will be hard for you," he said. Looking up he said, "I traced her to Liverpool, but by the time I got there—" He shook his head and his voice fell. "By the time I got there, she had died. There was an outbreak of cholera, and she was one of the first to go."

Daniel felt as if his heart had been ripped from his body. He stood staring at Rochester, a burning hate raging through him. *If you hadn't driven her away from Milford, she wouldn't have died*, he thought.

Rochester said only, "Sorry—I thought you knew." He turned and banged on the door, and when the guard opened it, he left without a backward glance.

Daniel stood in the room, not moving. When the door slammed shut, he said out loud, "I'll be serving the devil in human form—no mistake about that. Leo Rochester will make life miserable for me!"

Finally Adams returned and led him back to the cell. Jamie took one look at his face and asked, "What's wrong, Dan?"

"My sister—she's dead."

"Ah, lad, I'm sorry to hear that—!"

100

The two sat for a long time, and finally Daniel said, "Jamie, we're leaving this place . . ." He explained what he had done, then said, "Leo will see you get out—if you don't, write to me and I'll see it's done."

That night Daniel couldn't sleep. All he could think of was Lyna's dear face and how they'd loved each other. He finally whispered, "Lyna, I'll never forget you—and I'll try to live a life for both of us!"

PART TWO

—

THE
MASQUERADE

1750–1752

8

AT THE RED HORSE TAVERN

VERY FEW THINGS DISTURBED SIR LIONEL GORDON so much as the behavior of his younger son. Gordon had served with distinction under the Duke of Marlboro, who had commended him to his staff, commenting, "Gordon is a *steady* man. He never allows the enemy to rattle him. A man like that is invaluable!"

But if the great duke could have seen the object of his admiration on the morning of June 4, 1750, he might have been forced to revise his high opinion of the man.

Mild summer weather had ushered out the last traces of the terrible winter. A warm, gentle breeze stirred outside, carrying the sound of birds through the window of the smaller dining room where Sir Lionel sat with his wife and older son. The grass spread out from Longbriar Manor like an emerald green carpet, but the owner of the great estate was taking no pleasure in the fair weather or the beauty of his estate.

"Well, so he's managed to get himself thrown out of Oxford!" he exploded.

Sir Lionel's fist struck the heavy mahogany table, causing the china dishes and crystal goblets to tremble as if in alarm at the loud voice. He was a large, well-built man of fifty, with steady blue eyes and a thatch of reddish hair. "I'd have thought that was impossible—even for Leslie. Some of the greatest chuckleheads who ever drew breath have managed to stay in that place!"

"I told you it would come to this, Father." Oliver Gordon was a small man of twenty-eight years, made in the mold of his mother rather than his father. His eyes were brown like hers, and there was a cold, almost impersonal air in his sharp features. Oliver held his hands out and studied them thoughtfully. His fingers were long and tapered, and he was an expert musician—almost his only passion. Picking up the knife from the snowy-white tablecloth, he pared a slice of beef from the portion on his plate, then took it into his mouth. Chewing slowly, he nodded toward the woman who sat across from him. "Mother and I warned you that he would never settle down there. He's not the type to become a man of letters."

Lady Alice Gordon was not yet fifty years of age. She was plain, though all that could be done to improve a woman's looks was evident. Her brown hair was carefully arranged in the latest fashion, and cosmetics made her smallish eyes appear larger. She wore a maroon silk dress trimmed with Dutch lace at the collar and sleeves. When she lifted her wineglass to sip the clear wine, the light from the chandelier reflected from the large diamond ring on her finger. "You really *must* do something with him, dear," she insisted.

"Do *what*?" Sir Lionel demanded. "He's twenty-four years old, Alice—a little late to take a stick to. And too strong, I might add." He allowed some of his pride in his younger son's physical strength to creep into his voice, but at once shook his head. "I wish he'd marry some rich woman and waste *her* money instead of mine!"

"I think you should send him to one of the Colonies, Father," said Oliver, looking up suddenly to meet the older man's stern eyes. "We need a man to oversee the property in Virginia that Uncle Robert left. Send Leslie."

"Why, he can't even take care of his *clothes*! He could never manage a property in a place like that—" But the idea caught at Sir Lionel. He stroked his neat beard thoughtfully, then said, "On the other hand, it just might do, Oliver. It's a rough sort of place, filled up mostly with criminals and Indians. The experience might do him some good."

"Leslie needs some sort of challenge like that, Father," Oliver said. He had little use for his younger brother, and the idea of sending him to America had come to him sometime earlier. He was aware that despite his father's anger at Leslie's wild ways, he concealed a streak of fondness for his younger son. Oliver would one day be master of Longbriar, and at the age of twenty-eight he was already as competent in the running of the vast estate as his father. He was his mother's favorite and now turned to her for support. "Don't you think it might do Leslie good to be on his own, Mother?"

"You've often said that it was the making of you, Lionel—leaving home and serving with the regiment." Lady Alice knew how to handle this husband of hers. She had brought him a large sum of money as her dowry and knew quite as much about managing their affairs as he. "Think about it, at least, my dear. You're so good at things like this."

Sir Lionel Gordon was better at managing his horses than at managing his family. He stared at the table, thinking hard, then sighed. "I'll have it out with him, then. He can't go on like a schoolboy for the rest of his life. . . !"

Oliver and his mother exchanged satisfied glances, and later in the afternoon, Sir Lionel faced his younger son in the library. The two men were much alike, having the same tall, robust frames and the same half-handsome features. They had been close when Leslie was at home, as they shared a love of hunting and fishing. But the later years had not been happy, for Leslie Gordon had not found his way. He had no desire to enter a profession—especially law or medicine, which he hated equally. He knew the estate well but had become a profligate as he passed through his later teens, spending his time with a small group of rather wild young men.

Now Leslie braced himself for the lecture he was certain lay before him. Oliver had smiled when Leslie had arrived, saying, "Father wants to see you, Leslie." Something about the smile of his older brother gave Leslie caution.

Standing before his father in the study, he said tentatively, "It's good to be home, Father. I've missed our times of hunting."

Sir Lionel did not smile but said sternly, "You may get a different kind of hunting, Leslie. I'm sending you to America to manage the plantation there."

The statement struck Leslie like a bucket of cold water thrown into his face. For a moment he stood stock still. "But—sir," he finally managed to say, "I don't know anything about that kind of thing."

"You don't know about anything, Leslie—except fast horses and tavern wenches. But you're going to learn. There's no point arguing. My mind's made up!"

But Leslie *did* argue, giving his father several very good reasons why he should not go to America. Finally he said, "Father, I'd be a waste over there. But there's one thing I could do well, I think."

"I'd be pleased to hear it," Sir Lionel said bitterly, more disappointed in the young man than he showed. *He's so much like I was at his age,* he thought, studying the broad shoulders and electric blue eyes. *Full of life—and of the devil! What a waste!*

Leslie loved his father and was heartily ashamed of his own life. At Oxford he had tried to throw himself into the life of a scholar. But almost from his arrival Leslie had discovered that the dusty world of books was not meant for him. He loved activity and physical action, but as much as he tried, he could never apply his mind to his studies as Oliver had done.

He had, however, come home with a plan, which he now presented. "Father, I know I've been a great disappointment to you— but no more than to myself." He began to pace the floor, speaking for some time about how he had learned that the life of a scholar was not for him. "I have no talent for it—nor inclination," he said, pausing to stand before his father, who was slumped in a chair behind a massive rosewood desk. "But there is one profession I think I might be suited for. It's what I hurried home to speak with you about."

"What profession might that be?"

"One you love very much, sir," Leslie said instantly. "You've always spoken of your time in the army. I've often thought it was the part of your life you liked best."

Sir Lionel stared at Leslie somewhat surprised, and his features relaxed. "You know, I think that's true—but don't say so to your mother. She hates the army." He stroked his beard thoughtfully, his eyes half-lidded. "I remember those days. It was a fine time for me. Hard, mind you, but a man needs hardness, Leslie. I still think of those times with old comrades. Many of them are dead now, but I think of them as they were—bronzed, strong, and filled with life. By Harry, we had *life* in those days!" He blinked, then demanded, "Are you saying you want to go into the army?"

"Yes, sir, I am."

"I offered to buy you a commission when you were twenty. You laughed at the idea."

"Yes, but that was before I knew what other professions were like."

"It's a hard life, Leslie. Oh, I loved it—but there's danger, boredom, and injustice in that world. And quite frankly, you haven't shown any inclination to accept discipline. I'm not so sure you would succeed. A soldier has to accept rebuke—something you've never been able to do."

To Sir Lionel's surprise, Leslie admitted, "You are right, sir, I never have. But I've thought of this for almost six months. And I've been talking with General Drake, your old friend."

"Morton Drake?" Sir Lionel's eyes opened wide. "Why, he must be as old as the hills!"

"No, sir, he's hale and healthy. I've gone to see him, and he talked a great deal about your military service together. He still thinks the world of you, sir."

"Morton Drake—I haven't seen him in years!"

"He's retired, of course. But he introduced me to Colonel Adam White, who's in command of the Royal Fusiliers, stationed at Sandhurst. . . ." Leslie saw that this information interested his father, so he spoke rapidly of his visits to the general. Finally he said, "I asked him for his advice—about going into the army, and he said the same as you, sir. But he took me with him to meet Colonel White."

"Did he now? I'd like to see him again."

"Why don't you, sir? He's very fond of you. He'd be glad to see you again after all these years."

"Well—perhaps I will."

"I'd like to make the army my career, sir. I believe I'd make a good soldier." Leslie said no more but stood before his father, waiting, his face serious.

"I'll think on it," was Sir Lionel's only response. But for the next two days he thought of little else. He was aware that his wife and older son were waiting for him to announce that Leslie was to be sent to America, but somehow he could not bring himself to do it.

Finally at dinner on Tuesday, he said abruptly, "Alice—and Oliver—" He put his fork down and looked toward Leslie. "Leslie has made an interesting proposal. He wants to make the army his career." Sir Lionel sat there listening quietly as the two protested, but finally he shook his head. "I feel he would not do well in America, but he has the qualities to become a good solider—if he can learn discipline."

"He never has," Oliver said shortly. But it was obvious that his father had made up his mind, so he shrugged and added, "It's as good as any for him, I suppose."

Lady Alice hated the army and said so, but Sir Lionel stuck to his guns. "It's a chance for him to make something of himself. I'd like to see him learn how to be a man—and the army is the place for that," he said with finality.

For the next two weeks Leslie and his father spent most of their time hunting and riding while they waited for the legal processes of purchasing his commission to settle. It was the finest time they had enjoyed for years, and when it was time for Leslie to leave, he took his father's hand, saying, "I'll do my best, sir." He'd made his farewells to his mother and brother, but parting with his father was different.

Sir Lionel felt the strength of his son's grasp and said huskily, "I'd like nothing better in this world than to see you become a good soldier! I . . . I sometimes wish I'd stayed with my regiment, but that's past praying for." He suddenly stepped forward and embraced Leslie—something he'd not done for many years. Then he stepped back, saying brusquely, "Well, be off with you—and take care of those horses, you hear me?"

Leslie was moved by his father's embrace, so much so that he could not speak for a moment. He covered his confusion by turning and stroking the nose of Caesar, one of the two fine horses his father had given him to take along. Grabbing the reins, he mounted and took the lines of the other horse, a mare named Cleo, then smiled, "I'll write you often, sir—but come and visit when you can."

Sir Lionel watched the departure of his son with a feeling of hope. He stood there until the distance swallowed up the young man, then turned and slowly walked back into the house.

"He's got the makings of a fine soldier—if he can just put his mind to it!" he said to himself.

🕮   🕮   🕮

Lyna paused wearily and looked up at the sign that swung

gently in the slight breeze. A bright red horse with flaring nostrils and long legs was outlined against an ebony background.

Red Horse Tavern, she thought wearily. The hot sun had sapped her of strength. Weak and thirsty, she moved to the wooden trough where two horses peered down at her. Grasping the pump handle, she had to struggle to get a trickle of water flowing, then drank thirstily. She caught some of the cool water in her cupped hands and splashed it on her hot face, then dried it with a ragged cloth she used for a handkerchief.

Got to have something to eat, Lyna thought as she turned to face the door of the tavern. It was late afternoon, and she had plodded along the road all day since early morning. She had left the farm two days ago where she'd spent most of the winter and spring. When she'd been allowed to stay and work for her keep at the place, she'd been grateful. The winter had been unusually bitter that year. Henry Tate, the owner of the small farm, had said roughly, "Can't pay you nothin', but you can sleep in the shed and you won't starve. Expect you to work hard, though."

She hadn't starved, but she had worked long hours, and the food had been sparse and ill-cooked. Tate's wife, Harriet, was a sour-faced woman who measured out each morsel of food as if it were fine gold, and she demanded hard labor from everyone.

Though it had been difficult, she'd had a place to sleep and something to eat. But Tate's nephew had arrived the previous day, and the farmer had said, "Can't keep you no more, Smith. You'll have to find yourself another place."

Lyna had left at dawn without a word of farewell. Hoping to find work on another farm, she stopped at several. Soon, however, she discovered that no one needed help. *"Get to London—you'll find something there, boy,"* had been the last advice she'd gotten.

But after two days of hard walking in the heat of summer, she was exhausted. A kind lady from a small farm had given her a bowl of fish soup for breakfast, but that had been hours ago. Now with her stomach knotted from hunger, she approached the Red Horse and entered without much hope.

The interior was dim, lit by two small windows and several candles. A big man was standing beside a table, pouring some sort of liquid into the cup of a customer. The smell of hot food caused another contraction of Lyna's stomach. It was a small place, with only three customers, and Lyna knew it was unlikely that they'd need more help.

She waited until the innkeeper went back to the bar along one wall, then moved toward him. He turned and took in her ragged clothes and pale face with a practiced glance. "No begging here, now—on your way!"

"Please, could I work for something to eat?"

"Don't need nothin' done."

Lyna was desperate. "Please, I'm starving. Let me work for scraps—anything."

"I told you, there ain't nothin' here for you!"

Lyna would have been intimidated by the man's roughness, but she stood before him, saying, "I'll do anything!"

The innkeeper came from behind the bar. He was a short, burly man with a bald head and a fish-hook mouth. Grabbing her arm, he began to drag her toward the door, saying, "You deaf? I said for you to get out!"

"Just a minute, Tapley. . . ."

The innkeeper swiveled his bullet head to glance at the man he'd just served. "I don't mean to be hard, sir, but these beggars come around like stray cats! Why, you feed them once, and they ain't no way to get rid of them!"

"I think I can spare half my meal. Let the boy sit down."

Tapley hesitated, but then shrugged and released his grip. "None of my business," he muttered. "You 'eard the gentleman— now mind yer manners!"

Lyna was feeling very faint, when the man at the table said, "Here, lad, have a seat." He kicked one of the heavy chairs out from the table. "Bring another plate and cup, Tapley." When the innkeeper left, he added, "Well, sit down. You look like you could stand a good meal."

Lyna walked unsteadily to the chair and sat down. "I . . . can eat in the kitchen, sir," she whispered.

"No need for that. What's your name?"

"Lee Smith."

"My name is Leslie Gordon." When Tapley came with the extra utensils, Gordon cut a generous slice from the large slab of roast pork and put it on the pewter plate. "Bring us a pitcher of ale," he ordered. Then he cut a large slice from the bread that was on his left and transferred it to the plate of his guest. "Get yourself on the outside of that, Lee," said Gordon, then he began to eat his own meal.

Gordon didn't stare at the youth, but he noted that despite being at least half-starved, the young fellow ate in a mannerly fashion. *If I were that hungry, I'd stuff my mouth like a dog,* he thought. Without appearing to pay attention to Smith, he made some quick observations—*Pretty frail—and not much good for heavy work. Looks like he's had a hard time of it—ragged as a scarecrow. Not a bad-looking chap, though—if he were cleaned up, he'd look fine.*

"Been on the road, have you, Lee?"

"I've been working at a farm—but I got put out for another fellow."

"Oh? Well, that's too bad, but you'll find something. Here, wash that down with some of this ale. It'll put some color in your cheeks." He watched as Smith drank the ale, then asked, "Do you have any family?"

"No, sir."

The brief answer took Leslie Gordon by surprise. The idea of having no family and no place to go was something he'd never had to think of. He stole another glance at the small form, taking in the fineness of the face and the hollow cheeks. Now as he studied the young man, pity rose in him. *I'll have to give him a little money,* he thought, *and maybe buy him something to wear. Those rags are past help!*

Lyna ate until she was full and then said, "Sir, can I groom your horse for the meal?"

"Do you know horses?"

"My brother taught me a little."

"All right, come along." Leslie rose and led her to the rail. "I think I'll stay the night. Come along to the stable. Here, you can lead Cleo."

Lyna was glad for the times she'd spent helping Daniel with the horses at Milford. Some of the good advice Daniel had learned from Bates and passed on to her helped her now. She spoke gently to the mare, who eyed her, then followed docilely.

Gordon made the arrangements with the hostler, then said, "Lee, I'll be leaving soon. Give them both a good grooming and I'll pay you well."

"Yes, sir." Lyna didn't waste any time in setting about her task.

She liked horses, and by the time Leslie Gordon returned, both the animals were gleaming.

"Why, they look fine!" Leslie said with pleasure. "Never saw a better job of grooming!"

"Thank you, sir," Lyna said. Then she swallowed hard and asked the question she'd been planning. "Would there be a place for me at your home? I'll work for food."

The question caught Leslie. He looked into the gray-green eyes that were fixed on his and stammered, "Why, I . . . I'm sorry . . ." Seeing the sudden disappointment sweep over the boy, he said quickly, "You see, I'm leaving my home. I'm going into the army— as a lieutenant."

Lyna pleaded, "But won't you need a young man to take care of your horses? Don't officers have servants?"

"Why, yes, I believe they do."

"Then take me, sir!" Lyna began to speak quickly. "I can cook for you, Mr. Gordon—and I worked for a tailor for a time, so I can keep your clothes and boots for you—and I'll see that your horses are in good shape—please, sir!"

Leslie knew that it was customary for officers to have servants, but he had not thought of hiring one. Still, the idea of having someone to take care of his uniforms was appealing—and the boy *could* groom a horse.

Lyna stood before him anxiously waiting. She felt as if her fate were hanging in the balance. Her eyes were enormous as she kept them on the young man's face. And she prayed as hard as she ever had in her life.

"Well, I don't know—" Leslie said slowly, then he slapped his side and grinned. "Why not, though? It'll have to be all right with my commanding officer, you understand?"

Lyna blinked in surprise at his answer and quickly said, "Why, thank you, Mr. Gordon. I'll be a good worker, you'll see."

"I'm sure you will, Lee. But—you can't be my servant in those clothes."

"I . . . don't have any more, Mr. Gordon!"

The notion took a swift hold on Leslie. He fished into his pocket, pulled out some coins and said, "There's a shop beside the Red Horse. Go buy yourself something to wear. Better get two outfits, I think."

Lyna was stunned with the suddenness of it. She took the

coins, then looked up into the face of the man. "How do you know I won't steal this?"

"Never thought of it," Leslie said. "You won't, will you?"

"No, sir!" She turned and left the stable at a run.

Leslie laughed and slapped Caesar's side. "Well, you'll get all the attention you want now, I think." He turned to the hostler saying, "Saddle them both."

"Yes, sir, that I will!"

Lyna found the shop, and when a tall man came to give her a disparaging look, she opened her hand to show the coins Gordon had given her. "Mr. Gordon wants me to dress well enough to be his servant," she said.

At the sight of the coins, the shopkeeper beamed. "Well, I think we can take care of that!" He soon discovered that his advice was little needed, for the young man knew *exactly* what he wanted. Lyna went through the stock, made her selection, then went into a back room to change. Quickly she took off her brother's old clothes. She tore the shirt into strips and bound them around her bosom, then put on the loose-fitting tan shirt and brown breeches. Over the shirt she donned a dark green vest that helped disguise her figure. She sat down and slipped on a pair of white stockings and the new shoes. Stepping outside, she stopped to look at her image in the mirror and was startled. For a final touch, she chose a tricorn felt hat. After paying the shopkeeper, she left the shop and went at once to the Red Horse.

Leslie looked up from his seat at a table in the back of the room when she entered and exclaimed, "Well, now—clothes do make the man, after all! Let me have a look."

Lyna felt her cheeks burn as he studied her and she held her breath.

"You look very well, Lee. Now, let's see if we can make a few miles before dark."

"Yes, sir."

When they left the tavern, and Lyna realized Gordon intended her to ride his other large horse, she had a moment of panic. She'd ridden a few times, but never such a spirited horse. She put her foot into the stirrup and awkwardly got into the saddle.

Cleo began to buck, and Lyna would have fallen if Leslie had not come to grab the lines. "Calm down, Cleo!" he ordered. When the animal had quieted down, he looked at her. "You've not ridden much, I take it? Well, no matter. You'll have to learn if we're to get on. Now take the lines. . . ."

Five minutes later the two were on the road to London. Gordon gave instructions from time to time, and Lyna soon was able to handle the mare.

Leslie was pleased with himself, glad that he'd been able to help the lad, and that he now had a servant. "How old are you, Lee, fifteen?"

"At least." Lyna turned to smile at him, then said, "I thank you for taking me with you. I . . . I was in poor shape, sir."

"Well, we'll both have new careers, Lee," Leslie smiled. "I'll learn to be a soldier, and you'll learn to take care of me."

"Yes, sir!" Lyna stole a glance at the strong figure and the masculine profile. "I'll take care of you the best I can!"

9

"He's As Good As a Wife, This Lad?"

AS SOON AS GORDON ARRIVED in London, Colonel White greeted the new officer with a cheerful air.

"First, you'll have to find a house, Lieutenant," he advised. "The regiment will be stationed here for at least a month, probably longer. The king wants his subjects to see His Majesty's military strength, so we'll be having regular parades and exhibitions to provide that. It'll be a good time for you to learn the ropes."

"I thought we'd all be living in tents, Colonel."

"We'll see plenty of that, Gordon—but for now, either rent a room in an inn or find a small house. Perhaps you could share one with one of the other officers. I'll ask around."

That very day Leslie met Captain George Mullens, a tall, rather plain man with a shock of straw-colored hair. When he mentioned that he had been advised to find a house, Mullens said at once, "I've got a small place—two bedrooms. If you'd care to come and share it, I'd be happy to accommodate you."

Leslie protested that he didn't want to be a bother, but Mullens shook his head and insisted. "Be company for me. I'm not too much of a social person, Leslie. And I could use some help with the rent. Come along, but it might not be fine enough for the son of an earl!"

Leslie found Lee, who was waiting outside headquarters, and said, "I think we may have a place to stay. Come along and we'll take a look."

As the two swung into the saddle, Captain Mullens joined them, mounted on a fine brown mare. "This is my servant, Lee Smith—Captain Mullens, Lee."

"Ah, yes. Been with you long, Gordon?"

Leslie winked at Lyna and said, "Long enough, I suppose."

Lyna felt nervous as the tall soldier examined her, but she met his eyes evenly. "Glad to know you, sir," she said, nodding at him.

"Can you cook, Smith?" Mullens asked.

"Why—yes, sir—a little."

"By George, you've got to come with me on the house, Gordon! I'm sick of my own cooking—if you could call it that! Come along, now."

Lyna took in the sights as the three of them passed through the busy streets of London. The streets were packed with people so determined to get to their destinations that they jostled one another furiously. One vendor driving a wheelbarrow of nuts yelled in a stentorian tone, "Make way there!" but he was drowned out by a tinker who stood at the door of his shop, bellowing, "Have you a brass pot, iron pot, kettle, skillet, or frying pan to mend?"

As they made their way down the twisting streets, sooty chimney sweeps with grave and black faces shoved past some fat, greasy porters. Some of the porters were laden with trunks and hatboxes, while others struggled along bearing aloft a wealthy woman in a chair. The noise was deafening and the rank odor of the garbage and ordure that had been thrown into the gutters burned Lyna's nose as they rode along.

They passed scores of inns bearing colorful images of their various names: Blue Boar, Black Swan, Red Lion, not to mention Flying Pig and Hog in Armor. The streets were lined with all kinds of vendors who hawked their wares. Lyna could have purchased a glass eye, ivory teeth, spectacles, and even cures for corns. She saw chemists' shops, where drops, elixirs, cordials, and balsams were advertised as cures for all ailments.

When they were out of the main section of London and riding through a neighborhood of houses, Mullens pointed with his riding crop. "There's the place. Not bad looking, eh?"

The small house was made of red brick with white windows and a slate roof. It sat right on the street, as did the others that joined it. Mullens led them through a gate into a spacious backyard that included a small stable, where they dismounted and tied the horses.

"Nice little garden," Leslie said, noting the profusion of colorful flowers that had been arranged in beds.

"Yes, I like to fool with them," Mullens shrugged. "So many things in this world are ugly and smell bad. It makes a difference to have a rose now and then. Come along."

He led the way through a door into a hall, then directed them to a drawing room lined with bookshelves filled with books. "They came with the house," he informed them. "The former owner must have been quite a reader." Next he led them into a small dining room. The room had a kitchen that occupied a small shed off the side of the house, which had been added to keep the heat out. Mullens waved at the shelves, which contained a random supply of food. "If you decide to stay, Gordon, perhaps your servant can try his hand at making us a decent meal."

Lyna was tense, waiting for the matter of sleeping arrangements to come up. She was relieved when Mullens led them to a large bedroom, which he said Gordon might like. "And there's a small room in the attic, used for a servant, I expect. It'll do well for you, Smith. Go take a look—right up those stairs."

"Yes, sir!" Lyna climbed the stairs and was delighted to find a tiny bedroom, complete with small bed, table, chest, and a washstand. Though the room was small, it was clean and had a large window that allowed in plenty of light and fresh air. *Oh, I hope he takes it!* she thought. When she descended the stairs, the two men were smiling.

"We'll be staying here, Lee. You like the room?"

"Oh yes, sir—it's lovely!" As soon as she said the word "lovely," she caught herself and made a quick mental note to be more careful about her speech. She knew certain words weren't right for a young *man*. Quickly she said, "Do right well, sir." Then she asked, "Could I fix a meal for you, Captain Mullens?"

"Yes, by Harry!" Mullens' long face brightened and he said, "You'll need to go to the green grocers and the butcher, I expect— right down the street."

Leslie drew out some coins and passed them to Lyna. "Get what you need—let's have a feast to celebrate our new home and our new friend. Captain Mullens wants to show me around, but we'll be back for supper."

Lyna left the house at once. As she walked along, she was very grateful that she'd been trained to do some of the cooking at Milford. She had a natural talent for it and enjoyed fixing meals. Determined to make the meal a success, she bought the ingredients necessary for her most successful dishes. It took almost all of the money Gordon had given her, but she wanted to make a good first impression.

When Lyna returned she set about getting a fire going. Then she cut the best meat from the leg of mutton and put it on to parboil. Afterward, she added three pounds of shredded mutton suet and seasoned it with pepper, salt, cloves, and mace. She also put in currants, raisins, prunes, and a few sliced dates. Mixing all this well, she put it all into a pan and placed it in the oven to bake.

While the mince pie was baking, Lyna decided to try her hand at baking a cake. She had made only two—and those were while she was at Milford—but both had turned out quite successful. So she began mixing flour, currants, butter, and sugar in a bowl she found. As she worked, Lyna thought of how things had favorably turned around for her in just one day. She smiled, remembering some of her mother's last words of encouragement, of how God promised to be the Father of the fatherless and take care of them. "I'd have been sleeping under a hedge if Mr. Gordon hadn't come along," she mused out loud.

Next she added cinnamon and nutmeg. When the spices had been mixed in well, she put in the yolks of four eggs, a pint of cream, and a full pound of butter. As she beat the mixture, the sun flooded into the kitchen, and the heat of the stove made her face glow. She worked quickly, finally pouring the mixture into another pan. Setting it aside, Lyna let it lie for an hour until it began to rise. Then she put the pan into the oven along with the mince pie.

Glancing at the position of the sun, Lyna decided that she had time to do more. So she put on a chicken to boil while she made two loaves of fresh oat bread. While the loaves were baking, she went into the dining room and found the settings for the table. Spreading a white cloth over the oak table, she set out silver plates, knives, forks, and goblets. She found a silver candlestick that held six candles and the tapers to go with it and inserted them firmly into their bases.

By then the sun was almost down as she lit the candles. *They ought to be back soon,* she thought. As she walked back into the kitchen, she smelled the pleasant aroma of the bread. Checking it and finding it done, she quickly removed the loaves and set them on the sideboard. As she lifted the lid on the mince pie, she heard the door open and the sound of voices. Quickly she stepped out of the kitchen and met the two men, saying, "Supper is ready, sir."

"Is it?" Leslie exclaimed. He sniffed the fragrance of fresh-baked bread and grinned at his friend. "Think you could eat a bite, George?"

"I could eat whatever that is that smells so good!"

"If you'll sit down, it's all ready." Lyna returned to the kitchen, picked up the mince pie, and took it into the dining room. When she lifted the lid and placed generous servings on the plates of the men, she was glad to see them both pleased.

"That's not mince pie?" Leslie exclaimed. "My favorite dish!"

"I hope you enjoy it, sir." Lyna made several trips to the kitchen to bring all the food she had prepared. While they helped themselves to the other dishes, Lyna brought a bottle of ale—part of Mullens' store—and poured their glasses to the brim. She hovered over the two men, pleased with their praise for the food.

Finally she brought in the cake and Mullens stared at it. "By Harry—I can't believe it!" he exclaimed. He took an enormous bite, and with his mouth full, nodded toward Lyna. "Smith—if you can't cook anything else—I can live on what I've had tonight!"

"Where'd you learn to cook like this, Lee?" Leslie inquired.

"Oh, I worked in a large house once as a cook's helper," Lyna answered quickly.

"Well, you certainly were a good pupil!"

"Thank you, sir. I'll bring your tea to the library if you like."

The two men moved to the library, where they smoked and drank tea for some time. Mullens spoke of the regiment, giving Leslie a quick analysis of the officers and the state of the troops. He was an astute man, knowing the army well, and was glad to help his new friend begin his military career.

"I'm glad we've met like this, George," Leslie said. He lay back in the Queen Anne chair, smoking a pipe and feeling pleased with his new surroundings. "I've been dreading it a bit. A fellow can put his foot wrong, and it's the devil's own trouble trying to get it right."

"You won't go wrong, old fellow," George replied. "Soldiering's a hard life—but a good one. If you're cut out for it."

"You've never married, George?"

"No. Not much of a ladies' man. I suspect you are, though." He laughed at the expression on Leslie's face. "No, dear fellow, I don't know your history. But it would be strange if you hadn't been subjected to the wiles of the fairer sex. Son of an earl, handsome and rich. I suspect you've had your share of love's delights."

"Oh, I suppose I've been a fool a few times."

Mullens smiled and looked over toward Lyna, who'd come in with a fresh pot of tea. "When your master's not present, Lee, you must give me the juicy details of his love life."

Lyna shot a startled glance at Leslie, then flushed. "I couldn't do that, Captain Mullens!"

"Don't tell him a thing, Lee," Leslie spoke up. "It's none of his business."

"No, sir, I won't."

Lyna kept the tea flowing, and while the men talked, she had her own meal in the kitchen. She enjoyed the sound of the two men speaking quietly at times, but sometimes they laughed rather loudly. While they were in the library, she went to Gordon's room, made the bed, and unpacked his uniforms. She had time to go downstairs and iron his shirts and trousers, taking pride in her ability to handle the iron.

She was hanging the garments neatly in the wardrobe when Leslie entered. He gave a startled look at the freshly made bed, then at the uniforms. "Why, Lee, you've done it all," he exclaimed. He grinned at her, his heavy eyebrows rising. "You're going to spoil me."

"I hope so, Mr. Gordon," Lyna smiled back. "It's the duty of a manservant to spoil his master."

"Well, if you ever want to leave me, you'd have a place. Captain Mullens is very pleased to have you."

"I . . . I won't be leaving you, sir."

Something in the tone of the youthful voice caught Leslie's attention. He studied the clear features, noting that the drawn cheeks made the gray-green eyes appear very large. There was, he noted, a vulnerability in the face, the expression of one not accustomed to kindness. He suspected that the lad had been mistreated by someone and determined to provide something better. "Well, I'm glad to hear that."

He stripped off his coat and began to remove his shirt. At once Lyna moved toward the door and said hastily, "I'll have your hot water when you're ready to shave in the morning, sir."

"Fine. And, Lee—"

"Yes, sir?"

Leslie smiled at the youthful face. He put his hand on the thin shoulder and said, "I'm glad to have you with me. I can see that life is going to be a lot easier with you around."

Lyna felt her eyes sting and blinked rapidly. Clearing her throat, she was very much aware of the pressure of his hand. "I'm very grateful for the chance to serve you, Lieutenant. Good-night, sir."

"Good-night, Lee."

Lyna went to her room and wanted to drop into bed at once. She undressed and washed in warm water, then put on the night shirt she'd purchased. She glanced at her reflection in the small mirror, noting that her hair needed cutting. It had a tendency to curl, and she knew that she had to make herself look as masculine as possible. Tired from her busy day, she slipped between the sheets and lay there exhausted. She was so tired she could not go to sleep at once.

She thought of Daniel for a time, then forced those thoughts away. Sleep began to come, and she smiled as the events of the past few hours came to her.

He's so kind—to take in a ragged beggar!

She had doubtful thoughts, knowing that to keep up the masquerade would take great skill—and some luck. She breathed a prayer of gratitude, then as she slipped into the warm darkness, a single image of the face of Leslie Gordon came to her—and she smiled faintly. . . .

🎺　　🎺　　🎺

Learning to transform herself from a young woman into a young man proved to be more difficult than Lyna had expected! Fortunately she had a rather low-pitched voice for a woman, which was a great help. The fact that she was taller than most young women was also a factor in her favor. Aside from those two elements, Lyna had to remain constantly alert, lest the many pitfalls cause her to slip up and reveal her identity.

As the weeks passed, however, she perfected her art. It was

like being on stage, and after the initial fright was over, she took a strange delight in the masquerade. The obvious danger was that someone would somehow take notice of something and recognize that she was not a young man but a young woman. At first she had feared that being in the presence of soldiers might be a dangerous thing—but it didn't prove so. As the days slipped by she went about her duties serving her master, and the times she was around the other officers, she was treated no differently than the other servants.

The regiment's assignment in London made her introduction to the world of the army much simpler than if it had been out in a field camp. Primarily she remained at the house, but at times she accompanied Leslie Gordon to the reviews and to meetings of the staff, along with other servants. The two officers found it very convenient to have their horses taken care of by the youthful servant—and even more enjoyable was the luxury of well-cooked meals and uniforms always clean and pressed.

"By Harry, Leslie," Mullens exclaimed one day when the two were eating a fine supper, "he's as good as a wife, this lad!"

Leslie glanced up at Lyna, who was bringing in a pudding. Her face reddened at the compliment, but he was accustomed to that. "Better than a wife, George," he said fondly. "From what I hear, that breed demands all a man has and makes life miserable for him if he doesn't provide it."

"That's the best definition of marriage I've ever heard," Mullens grinned. As Lyna passed by he gave her a slap on the backside. "Lee, don't ever leave us two old bachelors!"

Lyna flinched and quickly moved away from the captain's reach. "No, sir," she said shortly, turning and heading back to the kitchen.

Leslie laughed. "Don't embarrass the lad, George. We'd have a devil of a time without him."

"Well, he's so blasted *sensitive*, Leslie!"

"I know, but when we take the field we'll need a good servant. And I don't expect we could find a better one."

That night after finishing all her work, Lyna took an extra candle to her room when she retired. She had begun keeping a secret diary. She had no one to talk to during the day, since the men were gone attending to their army duties. So at night she would sit up and read until she was certain that the two men were asleep. Then she'd pull out a notebook from under her mattress, and by the light of the candle she would put her thoughts on paper.

The entry for the night of August 15, 1750, was typical:

> Captain Mullens is a kind man—but I could have crowned him when he slapped me on the backside! I know I blushed like a—well, like a *girl*—and Mr. Gordon saw it. He must think I am the most tender young man in the world. He was watching last week when Lieutenant Givins told that awful story at dinner. It was worse than anything I've heard yet, and I know my face lit up like a candle! Later he said, "Lee, the men are rough but don't mind them." I tried to laugh it off, but I'm sure he noticed it.
>
> Five weeks we've been here, and it's been wonderful! A place of my own to sleep, plenty to eat, all the books to read, and Leslie gives me a crown every week for spending money. If it weren't for thinking about Daniel in prison, I wouldn't have a worry—except for keeping my secret, that is. But I've managed so far, and God willing, I'll be able to keep it up!

Two days later, however, Lyna was almost unmasked.

It began when Leslie said at breakfast, "We'll have guests tonight, Lee. How much money will you need to fix a meal for six?"

Lyna thought for a moment, then named a sum. Leslie pulled out a pouch from inside his vest pocket and handed her a number of coins. "And here's an extra shilling to get something special," he said as he and Mullens left for their duties.

As soon as the men had gone, Lyna cleaned up from breakfast. Then she hurried to the market to buy the fixings for the meal that night. She spent the better part of two hours walking amongst the vendors trying to find all she needed. Besides, she wanted to make sure she didn't pay any more than she had to. Finally satisfied with her purchases, she started home. As she rounded the corner of the street where the small brick house was, a vendor stuck a bunch of flowers in her face.

"Flowers, sir, for yer sweetheart?" said the old lady.

Lyna almost laughed at the thought and, on impulse, handed the woman the last shilling she had and hurried on her way.

The first thing she did when she entered the kitchen was stir up the fire and add some wood. She quickly set about making meal preparations for the guests who were to come. In the last few weeks Lyna had experimented on some new dishes, which had turned out quite nicely. She planned to prepare some of them for the meal that night.

The rest of the day seemed to fly by, but everything went smoothly. Just as she finished setting the table and placing the flowers in the middle, she heard voices in the hall. On the way to the library, Gordon entered the dining room and said the guests should arrive in an hour or so. When Lyna heard a knock on the door half an hour later, she was surprised when she opened it. Standing there were not three officers, but Lieutenant Givins— and three women!

"Ah, Smith," Givins smiled. "We're a little early. Are your masters home?"

"Yes, sir. Won't you all come in?"

Gordon and Mullens came out of the library at that moment, and the air was filled with laughter as Givins introduced the three women. "This is Henrietta, this is Alice, and this is my own treasure, Mary."

As soon as they were seated at the table, Lyna was kept busy with the serving. But she was not deceived by the women. They were all of the same stamp, heavily made up and wearing cheap and rather revealing gowns. When some of the stories that Lieutenant Givins told grew ribald, they protested lightly but joined in with shrill laughter.

After the meal was over, the guests moved into the library. As Lyna was busy washing the dishes, Leslie came and said, "Bring some ale in, will you, Lee?"

"Yes, sir, right away." She wiped her hands, cut pieces of the cake she had baked that afternoon, then took them in on a platter. The three couples were playing a game, but Lyna paid little heed. However, the game involved some sort of penalty, it seemed, and Henrietta shrieked as she lost.

"And the penalty is a kiss for the handsomest man in the room," Givins laughed. "And I think we all agree on exactly who *that* gentleman is!"

But as Givins moved to collect the kiss, Henrietta winked at Gordon, saying, "No, I think not, Lieutenant." She turned and, without warning, embraced Lyna and planted a kiss on her cheek.

"Now *that'll* do you, Givins!" Captain Mullens laughed loudly. "Let that be a lesson to you!"

Givins flushed and gave Lyna an angry look. "I wasn't including babies, Henrietta," he said shortly. "Only *men!*"

Henrietta was thoroughly enjoying her joke. "Why, he's very handsome, Robert," she jibed. Lifting her hand she ran it through Lyna's shortly cropped blond hair. "He's young and innocent— just what I like!"

Leslie had been laughing at Henrietta's antics. But now he noticed Lee's embarrassment and said at once, "Well, let's get on with the game. My turn, I think."

Lyna fled to the kitchen and stayed there as long as she could. She went outside once. When she returned she found Leslie kissing Henrietta. "Oh—excuse me!" she gasped and hurried from the room.

Later that night after the guests were gone, Lyna moved about cleaning the house. Mullens had gone to bed, and when she went to the library to pick up the empty mugs, she found Leslie staring out the window. He turned and said, "It was a fine meal, Lee." He smiled and added, "Don't be embarrassed by Lieutenant Givins. It's just his way."

"No, sir."

"I think Henrietta took a shine to you." He grinned, but when she looked troubled, Leslie said, "She takes a shine to anything in pants, so never mind it." He crossed his arms and said seriously, "I've got news. The regiment is going into the field."

"Really, sir?"

"Yes, we'll be leaving London shortly." He shook his head thoughtfully. "There's trouble in India, I'm afraid. Colonel White has informed us that we'll be leaving in two weeks."

"India—that's a long way, sir!"

"Yes, and it will be very dangerous. You may not want to go along."

Lyna gave him a sudden look, which he could not fathom, but said, "Yes, sir, I'll go with you if I may."

"Of course both Mullens and I would like to have you." A smile crossed his lips. "In fact, he said he *wouldn't* go if you didn't. He's grown quite attached to your cooking. You've really spoiled us both, Lee."

Lyna felt strangely warmed by his words. "You've been very

kind to me, Lieutenant Gordon—you and Captain Mullens. I . . . wouldn't know what to do if I couldn't serve you."

Gordon came and stood before her. His eyes were gentle and his voice was low. "Why, Lee, you're a part of me—and a part of Mullens, of course." He put his hand on her shoulder and squeezed it gently. "We'll go together, then."

"I'm glad, sir!"

Gordon nodded, then dropped his hand and started for the door. He stopped and turned. "It'll be harder in India than in this little house." He looked around the room fondly, then back to Lyna. "I'll never forget this place."

He turned and left, and Lyna, still feeling the pressure of his hand on her shoulder, whispered, "Neither will I, Leslie Gordon!"

10

LYNA MAKES A DISCOVERY

THE SHIP THAT FERRIED THE ROYAL FUSILIERS from Liverpool to India was so crowded the men had to take turns sleeping in the narrow hammocks. Adding to the discomfort was the heavy weather the low-lying ship encountered almost as soon as the shores of England faded from sight.

For Lyna the misery of the voyage proved to be a mixed blessing. She felt queasy the first night out, but by dawn of the second day she had gained her sea legs. But Lieutenant Leslie Gordon did not fare as well. He was a poor sailor, worse than most. He turned pale even as the ship hit the first rolling swells of the open sea, and throughout the long voyage he never completely recovered.

Lyna had been nervously wondering how she could keep her secret on the crowded ship, but Leslie's seasickness made it possible. He had been assigned a small cabin with two bunks. Under normal conditions, any man would have discovered his roommate was a woman—but Leslie was so sick he would not have noticed if his partner had been the Queen of Sheba!

The two had made their way on board and found their tiny cabin. Excited about the voyage and what lay ahead, Leslie commented cheerfully as they stepped inside, "It's not a palatial suite, is it, now?" The room was only large enough for the narrow two-tiered bunk, a tiny table, a diminutive chest, and one chair. He smiled at Lyna. "You'd better take the top, Lee. If we hit rough weather, I'd crush you if I fell out of that top bunk."

"Yes, sir, that will be fine."

Leslie sat down on the lower bunk, speaking with excitement about the possibility of facing action in India. Lyna began to unpack his personal things, storing them carefully in the tiny chest. She found a place for his razor and shaving soap, wedged his pistols and loading equipment under his folded clothing, then began trying to do something with his wrinkled uniforms.

"Oh, we won't be able to do much about those," Leslie said as Lyna searched for a suitable spot to hang them. "Just stuff them anywhere. We won't be on a dress parade, Lee." He groaned and lifted his right boot, tugging at it. "These blasted boots! I *knew* they were too small! Give me a hand, will you, Lee?"

Lyna grabbed the heel of his boot. It was skin tight, and only when she gave a tremendous wrench did it budge. She fell backward, striking her head with a resounding *thud* against the oak bulkhead. Pain caused her to cry out involuntarily, and bright lights danced in front of her eyes.

"Lee! Are you all right?"

Strong hands touched Lyna, and she felt herself being lifted up. Leslie put his arm around her and sat her down beside him on the lower bunk. "That was a nasty bump! Let me see. . . ." He used his free hand to explore her head, moving it gently under the heavy blond hair. "That's going to be a pretty bad knot—but I don't think the skin is broken. Just be still for a moment."

Lyna was desperately aware that Leslie was holding her in a tight embrace. Afraid that he would notice he was not holding a tough young man but a softly rounded young woman, she pulled away from his grasp.

"I—I'm all right, sir!" she said, standing up. She made a joke out of the thing, saying, "Good thing I landed on my head, or I might have been hurt. My pa used to say it was the toughest thing about me!"

"Look, you just lie down, Lee," said Leslie, his voice still anxious. "I'll take a turn around the ship. Can't have you getting down, can we? Who'd take care of me?"

After he had pulled his boots back on and left the cabin, Lyna collapsed onto the bunk, trembling slightly. *If I'd been knocked unconscious,* she thought, *he'd have undone my clothes—and it would all have been up with me!* She lay there for a time, worrying about how she would share such a tiny place without being discovered. Finally she rose and made the cabin as neat as possible. "Maybe I can . . . can go out when he undresses for bed," she muttered. "But how will *I* ever undress with him in this little box of a room?"

But one factor came to her rescue—the weather. Just before the ship set sail, Leslie had eaten a large meal for supper at the captain's table. But as they pulled out into open waters less than an hour later, he felt the ship suddenly nose downward. Up until that time the deck had been as steady as his own floor at Longbriar— but as the ship slowly rose, his stomach turned over. Almost instantly he became deathly nauseous. He was walking with Mullens at the time, who gave him a sharp glance. "Are you all right, Leslie?" Then Mullens saw his friend make a lunge for the rail, and he shook his head. "No, I see you're not. Well, perhaps it'll be brief. It sometimes is, you know."

But two hours later Mullens found Gordon still hanging to the rail. "Look here, old fellow, you need to go below." He took Gordon's arm and steered him to the small cabin. When the two stepped inside, Mullens said, "I say, Smith—your master is a little under the weather. Put him to bed and see to him, won't you? That's a good fellow!"

Lyna had seen several officers suffering from the same malady as she had gone up top to get some fresh air herself. "I'll see to him, Captain," she said quickly. Mullens left, and she turned to Gordon and said, "Let's get that hot uniform off, sir."

Leslie's mouth was drawn up into a tight, puckered line, and his face was ashen. "Never knew—a man could be so *sick*—!" he gasped. He allowed her to pull his coat and shirt off, then she slipped a cotton nightshirt over his head.

"Lie down, Lieutenant—that's right—now, let's have these boots." She tugged the boots off, then the socks, and finally pulled his tight trousers free. "Now, cover up and let me bathe your face with cool water. . . ."

All night long Lyna stayed beside her employer. He lay still as though afraid to move—and when the ship began to roll more violently from side to side, he kept his eyes tightly closed. Whenever he quieted down, Lyna would go topside to empty the bucket over the rail. She could do little except bathe his face with tepid water and hold his head when he threw up. After a time he had nothing left in him, but the ugly retchings continued.

Sometime during the early hours of the morning, Leslie said

weakly, "Lee—go to bed! There's nothing more you can do for me."

"Yes, I will, sir—in a little while. Try to take a little water, Lieutenant Gordon." Lifting a cup to his lips, she gave him tiny sips of water, some of which he kept down. The only sleep she got consisted of short naps in the chair by the lower bunk. At dawn Lyna heard the door to the tiny cabin open. She looked up and saw Captain Mullens, who had come by for a report.

"He's so sick, Captain!" Lyna whispered. "He looks like death!"

"He may be sick all the way to India, Smith," Mullens said doubtfully. "Can you handle that?"

"Yes, sir."

Mullens gave Lyna an encouraging nod. "Good man! If it's a chronic case, you'll have to feed him like a baby. He'll spit it up, mind you, but he's got to have nourishment. I'll leave word with the cook to make some clear broth—and you just make him take it, no matter how much he curses!"

As soon as Mullens left, Lyna tried to sleep more. But an hour later she awoke when Leslie stirred. After fetching fresh water from the barrel in the galley, Lyna poured some into a basin and bathed his face. The day wore on and Lyna endured his bad temper as she alternately forced him to sip water and some broth the cook had prepared. Sometimes he was able to keep some of it down, but whenever the ship rolled, the poor man was overcome with nausea and the cruel retching plagued him once again.

For the rest of the voyage, Lyna had her hands full with caring for Leslie Gordon. He grew to hate the feeding sessions and did indeed curse on more than one occasion when she persisted in spooning food down his throat.

"What's the use of eating when it just comes right up again?" he cried once. "Leave me alone, can't you?"

"Some of it stays down, sir, and you *must* have some nourishment!"

Later Leslie looked up at her. His eyes were sunken and his skin had a gray pallor. "Didn't know you'd have a blasted puking baby to take care of, did you, Lee? Wish you'd stayed at home?"

Lyna took a cloth, dipped it in water, and then bathed his face. "No, sir, I don't wish that." She felt a strong maternal instinct, and for one moment Lyna had the impulse to put her arms around him and hold him—but she quickly put that thought aside! "You'll be fine when we get ashore, sir," she said softly.

"I might die before then," he muttered bitterly.

"No, you won't do that," Lyna said, trying to comfort him.

"Sure of that, are you? I wish *I* were!"

Most of her days and nights were spent sitting beside him for long hours. When she could, she took short naps in the bunk above. The other times were spent bathing his face or trying to feed him broth. She managed to change her clothes when he drifted off into fitful short sleeps, and once thought wryly, *He's not likely to be noticing he's got a woman for a roommate—and even if he did, he's so sick I don't think he'd care much. . . !*

One afternoon she left the cabin and stood beside the rail. Captain Mullens came to stand beside her. "How is he?"

"A little better." She looked out over the long line of waves that rolled endlessly, then asked, "When will we get there, sir? It's been a long trip."

"Not long now—maybe two days." Mullens leaned on the rail and gazed at the blue sky above. He seemed a lonely man, with no family except one sister in Yorkshire. More than once Lyna had wondered why he'd never married. Although he was not handsome, he had a kind spirit and flashes of humor that she found most appealing. Now he put his sharp blue eyes on Lyna and smiled. "Well, Leslie sure made the right choice for a manservant. You make a fine nurse, Lee—as well as being a great cook and valet."

Two days later, the ship dropped anchor in India. The months at sea had taken their toll on Gordon. He had lost a considerable amount of weight and was so weak he could hardly button his shirt. As Lyna helped Gordon dress, he complained, "I'm weak as a kitten! Don't know if I can walk down the gangplank, Lee." He slipped into his coat, then turned to face her. His face was gaunt and his eyes sunken, but he managed a smile. "Lee—thanks for everything."

Lyna dropped her eyes and stepped back. "Oh, I'm glad I was here to help you, sir. Once you get some land under your feet, you'll feel better."

"I sure hope so—I'd hate to think I was going to feel this bad the rest of my life." A trace of humor flickered in his eyes, and he nodded. "Now, sometime *you'll* have to get sick. Then I can take care of you—sort of even things up, eh? You've worn yourself out feeding me and giving me baths. Maybe I'll be able to do the same for you someday, right?"

Lyna smiled broadly at her employer and shook her head. "I hope not, sir—no, indeed!"

☖   ☖   ☖

Lyna never understood properly the political issues that ignited the battle which brought Englishmen so far away from the shores of their homeland. For several weeks after the regiment marched down the gangplank, she had all she could do taking care of her employer. Gordon recovered quickly from the seasickness and now spent long hours day after day drilling his men—and learning the art of war from Captain Mullens and Colonel White. Finally, the troop marched to the outskirts of a small city called Trichinopoly, where they made their camp.

The heat of India was oppressive, and the sanitary conditions of the camp bred all kinds of sickness. Sometimes as many as a fourth of the men were down with some sort of illness. Lyna worried that sooner or later either she or Leslie would be added to the list.

Rumors began to fly through the ranks that they would soon be going into battle. Lyna's fears mounted as that day approached and the tension in the camp grew. Then one night Colonel White stopped by to caution the officers that the next day would bring on the battle. He was accompanied by a twenty-five-year-old officer named Robert Clive. As the officers sat around the fire drinking tea mixed with whiskey, Lyna hovered close, listening to the discussion.

Gordon said little at first as he sipped at his tea. He listened for a while, then finally said, "I hate to admit it, sir, but the issues of this thing still elude me. Exactly *what* are we fighting for out here?"

Colonel White smiled at the question. "Better men than you have asked that, Lieutenant. As a matter of fact, I suspect that few members of Parliament really know. Clive, why don't you enlighten our young friends?"

Clive was a man of no more than medium height, but he seemed taller because of his erect posture. He had a pair of steady gray eyes, and his voice was clear and confident.

"It all has to do with the East India Company," he said, looking around at the officers, who paid him close heed. "The nationals here have been fighting among themselves, so France sent a man named Joseph Dupleix to take over for France. And he succeeded—oh, my yes!" Anger swept over the face of the young officer. "I was at Madras when it fell to him. Only a few of us escaped to tell the tale. With that victory, France became master of southern India."

A wild dog not far from the camp lifted its voice in a long howl, and Clive waited, listening to the mournful sound. Then he waved his hand toward the east. "The French intend to drive us out—and we're here to make sure they don't succeed! They've besieged Trichinopoly, and in the morning we'll go out and hit them hard."

"It'll be a bit of a chore," Colonel White said evenly. "We'll be outnumbered considerably."

"But we are *Englishmen*!" Clive insisted. "We are soldiers of His Majesty—and we will overcome!"

The next morning Lyna was helping Leslie pack his gear for the battle when he said, "We'll be back to the base when we've whipped the Frenchies." His face was glowing with excitement, and he reached out and slapped Lyna on the shoulder. "We'll have a victory celebration, won't we?"

Lyna bit her lip, trying not to show the fear she felt. "Be careful, sir," she said, lifting her eyes to meet his. "I . . . don't like to think of . . . of anything happening to you."

"Bosh, nothing's going to happen!" A bugle blared and the roll of drums caught his ear, and he turned and left at a run.

As Lyna watched him go, Colonel White's servant, a burly man named Boswell, came to stand beside her. "Well, there they go, flags a-flyin' and drums a-poundin'! I've seen 'em go like that many a time—and some of 'em won't be a-comin' back."

Lyna shot him a startled look. "You think it'll be bad, Boswell?"

Boswell spat on the ground and shook his bullet head. "A battle's always bad, Smith," he grunted. "Ain't nothin' fine or noble about it, no sir! Oh, my eye! When they come a-draggin' the wounded back with their guts all hangin' out, you'll see!"

Lyna went about her duties nervously—and just before noon

135

she heard the distant boom of cannon. Running outside, she encountered Boswell.

"Startin' up, it is. I 'opes our lads give it to 'em!"

Lyna walked around the camp for hours worrying about Gordon. Late in the afternoon the wagons used for ambulances started arriving. She moved in close to watch as the wounded men were unloaded, praying she would not see Gordon. And she learned at once that Boswell had been right—there was no romance in war!

The wounded were moaning with pain, some of them covered with blood. As each wagon arrived, the downed soldiers were unloaded and placed on the hard floors to wait their turn with the field surgeons. Screams of agony rent the air, and more than once Lyna covered her ears to shut out the hideous sound.

Finally, moved by compassion for the suffering Lyna saw, she went over and offered to help. A doctor exclaimed fervently, "Lord, yes—we can use all the help we can get! See that those poor fellows waiting over there get water, will you—except those with belly wounds."

Lyna worked arduously all afternoon and even after darkness fell. She saw more than one man die, and her hands and clothes were stained with blood from helping raise men up for a drink of water.

When she finally fell onto her cot, she was relieved that Leslie had not been one of the wounded soldiers. But the thought that he might be dead gripped Lyna with a terrible fear. She slept in fits until dawn, then arose and began her vigil again as she helped tend the wounded. The distant sound of gunfire began and continued intermittently throughout the day. The wagons started arriving with the wounded, and once again she was relieved when Gordon was not among them.

Late in the afternoon, while Lyna was feeding a soldier who had lost his arm, Boswell came by. "They're a-comin' in—the regiment!" he said hurriedly.

Lyna carefully fed the soldier the few remaining bites and smiled at him. "Now, you try to sleep, Corporal." Then she moved with a hurried step outside the hospital. She saw at once the long line of men and horses coming back from the front line. Nervously, she searched for a glimpse of Gordon's company.

She heard a familiar voice behind her and turned to see Captain Mullens dismounting. When he faced her, she knew immediately the news was bad.

"I . . . I'm sorry, Smith," said Mullens.

"Is . . . is it bad, Captain?"

"I'm afraid it is." A bloody bandage was tied around the captain's left arm and he moved carefully, his face lined and hard. "He took a bullet in the stomach about noon."

A cold wave of fear ran through Lyna, for she knew how few who suffered that sort of wound lived. Most of them died of infection. "Where is he?"

"Come along. We'll see the surgeon gives it his best."

For Lyna the rest of the night was blurred. She could remember only bits and pieces of helping lift Leslie out of the wagon and into the hospital. He was barely conscious and didn't even recognize her. She was scarcely aware of Mullens beside her while they waited for the surgeon to do his work. Fear had a paralyzing effect on her, slowing down her thoughts. It was as if somehow she'd been numbed by the impact of the bullet Gordon had taken.

Finally the regimental surgeon came out, his apron stained with blood. "He's not going to make it, I fear," he said to Mullens, his face stiff and cold. "We got the bullet out, but it was a bad one. I think it may have done a great deal of damage to the organs."

"What can we do, Doctor?" Mullens asked. "He's a good man. I'd hate to lose him."

"Nothing much, I'm afraid." The surgeon looked at the young man beside the captain and asked, "You've been helping us—are you his servant?"

"Yes, sir," said Lyna, struggling not to show the emotion that was choking her.

"Well, he'll have fever. They always do. Try to keep it down. Keep him from moving too much. And pray. I wish I could be more hopeful."

"Can we go to him now?" Lyna asked.

"Yes. We'll have him put in one corner of the ward. You can stay with him all the time."

"A bad break," Mullens said soberly as they followed the doctor. "I'm very fond of him—as you are."

"Yes, sir, I am," said Lyna, her lip trembling.

When they stood looking down at the pale face of the wounded man, Mullens said, "I'll be on duty, but I'll come by when I can. Let me know what I can do, Smith." He started to leave but hesitated, saying, "Don't get your hopes up, my boy. I've seen this sort of thing often. He's in very poor shape. There . . . really isn't much hope, I'm afraid."

"He won't die!"

Mullens blinked in surprise at Lyna's adamant response. He said no more but left at once.

Lyna sat down and picked up Gordon's limp hand, holding it with both of hers. All around her the cries of men in pain rose, but she was scarcely conscious of them. Her eyes were fixed on the still face of the man who lay on the cot. Sometime later the doctor came by, looked down at her, then shook his head and left.

Lyna fought down the fear that lodged in her throat and held her head up straight. Reaching forward, she smoothed the reddish hair from Gordon's forehead, her touch gentle.

"He won't die! I won't let him die!" she whispered.

Finally she leaned back and took a deep breath. The clock ceased to have meaning for her, for she had thrown her spirit into the task of saving this man. And as she sat there long after the ward had grown quiet, except for an occasional groan, a startling thought came to her. *Why am I hurting for him so much?*

She leaned forward and studied the pain-wracked face and whispered, "I think . . . I love you, Lieutenant Gordon. . . !"

Her voice was low and there was no one to hear or see her. Picking up the still hand, she kissed it, then held it to her cheek. . . .

11

DISCOVERED?

It was like drifting in a sea of murky darkness . . . with muffled sounds that held no meaning.

Occasionally a voice broke through—unembodied, thin, far away. After a while, one of the voices became familiar, for it was different from the others—gentle and quiet. It somehow brought release from the fear that enveloped him as thoroughly as the darkness.

And searing pain—always pain that stabbed like the sudden thrust of a fiery sword, sending him back into the stygian blackness.

He could feel the difference between the hands that touched him. One touch was brisk and rough, probing, sending great waves of pain through his body. He would struggle faintly, attempting to get away, but there was no escape from the relentless torture.

But other hands were gentle, bringing relief from the scorching sense of burning. They would linger on his face and body, bringing coolness that washed away the heat of the fever. And he would relax at their sensitive touch.

Time had no meaning as he drifted in this realm of semiconsciousness. For all he knew, the Pyramids might have been built while he lay on the hard, narrow bed. Or it might have been a wild nightmare lasting only a few seconds. Darkness, heat, pain, coolness, the touch of hands—these were the boundaries of his shadowy world.

At times he dreamed of home—of Longbriar. Scenes from his

childhood drifted by, events he hadn't thought of for years—had long since forgotten. A trip to Portsmouth with his father, the delight of seeing the tall masts of the ships, and his father's hand holding his. A fragment of memory touched him briefly, of the first girl he'd kissed—her face turned up to his in the moonlight along the shore in Brighton. He twisted as he dreamed of the fight he'd had with Carleton Bennett when he was fifteen, almost feeling the hard knuckles on his face.

Gradually the dreams and the darkness faded, and he became aware of *real* voices.

One day he opened his eyes when he felt gentle hands touching him. A face swam into focus, and he whispered, "Lee—!"

The hands that were bathing his face stopped, and a familiar voice said, "Leslie, you're awake!" The tired-looking eyes brightened. "Well, it's about time you woke up! How do you feel?"

Leslie stared at his servant as if he were seeing a spirit. "I got shot," he murmured. He looked around the ward, noting the line of cots—most of them empty. "I'm in the hospital?"

"Yes, sir. You've been here since you were wounded—almost two weeks ago." Lyna felt the patient's forehead, then nodded. "You don't have a fever anymore. Let me take a look at your wound."

Leslie lay still while his servant carefully removed the bandages on his stomach. He lifted his head to look at the ugly, puckered scar, trying to pull his thoughts together. "You've been here all the time?"

"Yes, sir. But the infection's all gone. Doctor Simms will be by soon. Can you drink some water?"

Leslie's mouth felt as dry as the Sahara. He nodded and drank noisily from the cup of water held to his lips.

"Don't strangle yourself," Lee scolded. "You can have all you want after the doctor says so."

"What's happened?" Leslie asked. "Did we win?"

"Yes, you won," Lyna said, then described in detail how Clive had directed the troops and won a great victory.

Doctor Simms strode down the aisle between the rows of cots and stopped, his expression incredulous. "Well, Gordon, I see you're awake."

Simms examined the wound, giving Leslie a quizzical glance. "You're a very fortunate man, Lieutenant. Most men don't survive wounds like this." Turning toward Lyna, he said, "I'd say this young servant of yours made the difference. He hasn't slept a full night since you were brought in."

Leslie saw that his servant was indeed thinner. "I knew you'd do me good, Lee. . . ."

He dropped off to sleep in that alarming manner of badly wounded men, as if he'd been drugged. Simms was satisfied, however. "He's on the mend, Smith. Just needs lots of rest and good food. It's going to take some time for him to get his strength back." The doctor studied the tired face, then said gently, "I wish there were more nurses like you—but I'm prescribing more rest for you."

"Yes, sir. Have you heard when we'll be going home?"

"Yes, Colonel White said the wounded will be leaving at the end of the month. I think by then this young man will make the trip fine. See that he eats all he can."

"Yes, Doctor Simms, I'll do that." Lyna looked down at the drawn face of Leslie Gordon and murmured, "I'll take real good care of him."

🛡   🛡   🛡

The voyage home was delayed for a few weeks, which was fortunate, according to Doctor Simms. It gave Leslie more time to regain his strength, so that when the *Dorchester* was ready to weigh anchor and set sail for England, he was able to walk on board. He needed a cane and Lyna's support, but he was out of danger and improving daily.

Every day at sea Leslie grew stronger; his color improved and he gained some weight.

"I can't believe it, Lee! I thought I'd be sick to death as soon as I got back on another ship!"

Leslie turned his gaze from the endless expanse of ocean stretching over the horizon to look at Lyna. The bow of the *Dorchester* dipped and rose, sending white foam over the deck. "Not like our trip over, is it? Thank God for that!"

Lyna held the rail to steady herself and gave Leslie a warm smile. "No, I was dreading it for you. But it's actually done you good, this voyage."

He took a deep breath of the salt air. "I don't know why I haven't been seasick. A miracle, I think." He studied Lyna carefully, then shook his head. "You've taken care of me, but now it's time for you to look after yourself. You've lost weight, Lee."

Lyna's brown trousers hung loosely; the short jacket and cotton shirt appeared too large. Although thinner, her face glowed from the invigorating sea air, tanned slightly by the southern sun. "You have some freckles—right across your nose," Leslie observed. "I had them when I was a boy, millions of them."

Lyna looked out at the rolling sea, thinking of the weeks that had gone by since the battle. She had been with Leslie Gordon almost constantly, nursing him day and night after he'd been wounded. As he got better, her role had changed to one of companionship. They had plenty of time together, so he'd taught her to play chess. To his chagrin, Lyna proved to be the better player.

They spent long hours playing chess, letting the days slip by. There was a strange peace about the time for Lyna. She could not remember when she'd been so free from pressures. She didn't think of England or their return, but let the days roll over her. They talked endlessly as Leslie grew stronger. And for hours she would read to him—usually a novel. She had always been a reader, though her selections had been limited. They disagreed on the worth of some of them and argued rather noisily defending their favorites.

One day as they stood at the rail, enjoying the serenity of the sea and sky, Leslie suddenly said, "You know, Lee, it's a strange thing, but I've gotten closer to you than I ever got to anyone."

"I suppose it's because you had no one else."

"No, I've been alone before. I think perhaps it's because I was so dependent on you." He stared out across the gray expanse, then turned and gazed at her, a smile on his broad lips. "First I was your patient on the voyage over—and after I was wounded, I was your patient again. You were always there." He placed his hand on Lyna's shoulder. "I suppose I've been the worst trouble you ever had—having to take care of me, I mean."

Lyna looked up at him and smiled. "No, sir. I'd not say that. We've had good times—since you got better." A mischievous light touched her gray-green eyes. "And I'd never have been able to teach you good taste in novels if I hadn't had you at my mercy—nor beat you at chess."

Leslie laughed at her impudence. "I just *let* you beat me at chess," he said airily. "And your taste in writers is *terrible*. . . !"

The two of them walked around the deck for a time, arguing about the merits of Henry Fielding and Samuel Richardson. When Leslie grew tired, they returned to their small cabin. Lyna went to get his meal from the galley and, as had become their custom, ate her own meal with him.

When they were finished, she cleaned up, then set up the chessboard. This time Leslie won. With a hint of triumph in his voice, he said, "See, I told you so."

"I'm still ahead of you three games," she retorted. "Shall I read to you?"

"Yes—but not that interminable *Clarissa* by Samuel Richardson! I don't see how you can stand that sentimental book. All that silly woman Clarissa does is run away from the rascal who's after her—and squall! Lord, she runs on water power!"

"What do you mean sentimental? She's a respectable woman! It makes me so *angry* the way he treats her!" Lyna's eyes glinted and her back grew straight. "That man Lovelace—he should be hanged! He has no sense of decency or honor."

"Oh, come now, Lee!" They had had this argument before, and Leslie was mystified as to why his servant grew so incensed at the plot of a mere book. In the novel, a nobleman named Lovelace was determined to seduce an innocent young servant girl named Clarissa. "Lovelace isn't so bad. Most of our nobility have drunk from the chalice of love in their green years."

"I suppose *you* did?"

Leslie was taken aback by the anger in Lee's eyes. It was the only time he'd ever seen his young servant angry. "Why, I suppose I did. But she was willing enough," he added quickly. "I never forced myself on a woman."

"But many men do exactly that. They take advantage—it's wrong!"

Leslie studied Lee's face for a moment. Perplexed, he finally shook his head. "You ought to know this world's not a very fair place. You've had some hard knocks. Why does it shock you to see it set out in a mere novel that some men are evil?" A thought came to him, and he asked, "Has some woman given you a hard time, is that it?" He leaned back and said, "You've never shown any interest in the girls, Lee. You're too young to have had many serious problems along that line—or am I wrong? You're a handsome young fellow. Did some beauty do you in?"

"No!" Lyna shook her head, then realized she was getting into deep water. "It's not that, sir. It's just that—oh, I don't know, Lieutenant, things just aren't fair!"

"Well, go on and read the blasted book. Maybe someone will shoot the villain dead before he has his way with the innocent Clarissa." He sat on his bunk and rested his head against the wall. "Maybe by the time we get to Longbriar you'll finish the thing. . . ."

🪶 🪶 🪶

"Well, I must say, my boy, I'm proud of you!"

Leslie looked up startled, for his father had not made a remark like that for years. The two of them were riding across the meadows two days after Leslie had returned home. "Why, that's good of you, sir—but really, I didn't do much." He patted the mottled gray mare and shrugged. "I was just getting ready to start fighting, and the beggars cut me down like a cornstalk."

Sir Lionel shook his head, his voice firm. "Colonel White wrote me about you. I want you to read the letter. He speaks most highly of your gallantry under heavy fire. He's proud to have you in his command. Sees a great future ahead for you, Leslie."

The two men rode slowly, making allowances for Leslie's wound. Sir Lionel had welcomed his son home with delight, making much of him to his wife and Oliver. In fact, the two had been together almost constantly, so much so his wife had protested one day when they returned from hunting. "After all, Lionel, you can't neglect the rest of the world for Leslie!"

Oliver had been friendly enough, but he had little in common with his younger brother. His mind was occupied with business and music, and he spent little time with Leslie. "He'll be gone soon enough, Mother," he said when she had objected. "Father's always been fond of military things. Let them have their little visit."

Lyna had been nervous about coming to Longbriar. She knew a little about Leslie's family, for he had spoken of them at times on the voyage from India. When she arrived, Leslie had praised her to the skies. "This young fellow has been my good angel," he'd said warmly to his family in her presence. He told them of Lyna's faithful attention, and Sir Lionel had at once said, "Why, we're in your debt, young man! I thank you for your faithful service to my son!"

The living arrangement during the visit proved to be safe. Leslie had taken her upstairs and showed her where she was to sleep. "Look, this is my room, and it's joined to a smaller one—right through this door. You'll have a little privacy for a change—but it'll be convenient for you to serve me."

"It's very nice, sir," Lyna said, looking around the small room—which was much larger than any she'd ever had. It was a welcome relief from the cramped quarters on the ship, where it had been difficult on the return voyage to hide her identity. With Leslie feeling so much better she had had to come up with clever ways of concealing her secret. Somehow she had managed, but Leslie had teased her often, saying he had never before seen such modesty in a young man.

"Well, we'll be here until I'm fit enough to rejoin the regiment," Leslie went on. "I think you'll like it here at Longbriar."

Lyna did enjoy her stay. Her duties were light, and she had a great deal of time to herself. She took her meals with the rest of the servants, but made no friends among them. After three weeks she wrote in her diary:

June 12, 1752

I went for a long walk deep into the woods today. It's so lovely in the spring. Flowers blooming everywhere. I slept beside a bubbling brook, collected a bouquet of wild flowers. Leslie said he didn't know young *men* collected flowers—I must be more careful!

One of the maids has been flirting with me outrageously—her name is Rosaline, Lady Alice's personal maid. She thinks I'm a handsome young fellow, and yesterday she made an excuse to press herself against me—the hussy! She gives me all sorts of rather obvious invitations—and is quite peeved when I don't respond. It amuses me, but I keep away from such things. It could be dangerous.

I like Sir Lionel very much. He's kind to me and very grateful for what I did for Leslie. I wish all English lords were so considerate.

We will be leaving here soon. Leslie is almost completely recovered, thank God!

I will find a way to get to Dartmoor after we get back

with the regiment. I must see Daniel—I must!

🔔　　🔔　　🔔

A few days later, Lyna stayed up very late reading, enjoying the luxury of an evening off while Leslie had ridden to the home of an old friend to spend the night. It was a hot night, and being alone she decided to risk a complete sponge bath. Usually she bathed during the day when Leslie was out with his father.

She undressed and poured fresh water into the basin on the washstand. Taking fragrant soap and a clean cloth she washed her face, then began to sponge carefully. The water felt good, and she refilled the basin twice, savoring the coolness of it.

She was almost finished when she heard a slight sound behind her. She spun around and was horrified to see Rosaline standing in the doorway staring at her, her mouth open in amazement!

Lyna desperately made a grab for her robe, but it was too late. The girl whirled and disappeared, the sound of her footsteps fading as she ran down the hallway. Lyna stood motionless, then began to tremble. *She'll tell—I know she will!*

And she was correct in her assumption, for the maid went straight to her mistress the next morning. Lady Alice listened with disbelief, scoffing, "You've lost your mind, Rosaline! Or else you've had a dream."

But Rosaline said indignantly, "Do you think I don't know a man from a woman, ma'am?"

"What were you doing in that room anyway?" Lady Alice demanded—then nodded grimly. Rosaline was a pretty girl who could think of nothing but men. She'd had numerous affairs with the men on the estate and, no doubt, had had intentions that night of seducing Lee Smith while Leslie was away. "Oh, it's like that, is it!" Lady Alice raged. "No, don't bother to deny it. Don't say a word, you understand—or I'll have you whipped!"

Lady Alice was waiting when Sir Lionel and Leslie returned. As soon as they entered the house, she was there to meet them. "Come into the library, Lionel—and you too, Leslie." Her face was grim as she added, "This concerns you."

When the door was shut, she turned to lash out, "I thought I knew you, Leslie, but this deception exceeds even *your* misdeeds!"

Leslie blinked with surprise. "Deception? I don't understand—"

"Oh, don't bother to deny it!"

"What do you mean, Alice?" Lionel broke in. "What's wrong?"

"What's wrong? Leslie has brought his doxie into this house, that's what's wrong!" When she saw the perplexity on her husband's face, she snapped, "That servant of his—Lee Smith—is *not* a young man! She's a hussy dressed up as one!"

"Mother, don't be ridiculous!" Leslie broke out.

"Don't deny it!" Lady Alice cried. "I know you've been with women—but to bring that creature into your own home!"

Sir Lionel turned to stare at his son. "Is this true, Leslie?"

Leslie was stunned. "I . . . I don't know what to say. I had no idea!"

"You *must* have known!"

Leslie stared at his mother, then shook his head slowly. "I met him on the road—" He was thinking more quickly now, remembering how Lee had always been very private in personal things. He said suddenly, "Let me see about this."

He left the room and went at once to the second floor, entering his own room, then crossing to the adjoining door. For one moment he hesitated, then knocked. "Come in," a voice said quietly. He opened the door and saw Lee standing beside the window. One look and he knew it was all true!

Lyna said, "I almost left last night, but I wanted to see you one more time—to explain."

Somehow she had changed—or he himself had changed. She was still dressed in men's garb, but now that he knew the truth, Leslie saw as for the first time that the eyes were too large for a man, and the sweep of the jaw was smooth and feminine.

"Sit down, Lee," he said quietly. "Tell me everything."

"My name is Lyna Bradford. . . ."

Leslie listened patiently as Lyna related her story. She told him of her mother's death and the time at the workhouse with Daniel. Of how they had worked as indentured servants for a family. And of her brother who had been falsely accused and sent to prison. Twenty minutes later, Lyna ended her story. For a while, they both sat in silence. Finally, with a sad look in her eyes, Lyna said, "I'm sorry, sir, for bringing shame to you. I . . . I don't regret anything but that."

Leslie had not one doubt about the truth of her story. Everything suddenly made sense: comments she had made, her sensitivity Mullens always joked about, her modesty, her cooking, the flowers—so many things. He stood up and walked to the window, thinking of the unselfish care she'd lavished on him all this time. Turning back to her and seeing the anguish in her eyes, he said gently, "Lyna, you have nothing to be ashamed of. You did what you had to do to survive. And as long as I live—I'll never forget that you saved my life."

"Oh, I hardly did that!"

"Doctor Simms said so."

Lyna's heart was too full to speak. She knew he was not angry with her—and that was what she had feared most. But he was looking at her in a strange fashion, and she could only say, "I'll be going now, Lieutenant Gordon."

"Going? Going where?"

"Why, I can't stay here!"

"No, I don't think you can," Leslie said. His mind was working swiftly. He knew that his mother was angry to the bone. His father—well, he would be able to make him understand. But the situation would be intolerable for both Lyna and himself. Quickly he made a decision. "We'll be leaving together, Lee—I mean, Lyna."

Lyna stared at him, not understanding. "Sir, you can't leave your family—and I won't be able to serve you—"

"One problem at a time," Leslie interrupted. He sat back down beside her, looking into her tragic eyes. "Don't feel bad about this, Lyna," he said gently. "We'll manage—both of us. Now, you take your things and go saddle the horses. I've got some explaining to do."

Lyna quickly obeyed, and thirty minutes later Leslie entered the stables, carrying a small traveling bag. He looked tense but said only, "Let's be on our way."

The two of them mounted, and she noted that he didn't look back as they left the grounds. When they reached the top of the ridge, he did draw up and turn to look down on the estate. He was silent for a few moments, and finally Lyna could not bear what she suspected. "Sir, you can't leave your family on my account!"

Leslie faced her. "I've been estranged from my family for some time, Lyna. My mother and my brother are very angry with me— but my father believes me." He saw the tears of frustration in her eyes and said quickly, "Come now, things aren't so bad as that."

"I feel terrible!"

"No need." He marveled that he could have ever been so blind to the feminine qualities of the girl. Despite some doubts of his own, he said cheerfully, "Come along now, we'll be all right!"

The two rode away from Longbriar, and Leslie wondered when he would ever look on it again.

12

SIR LEO ROCHESTER'S VISIT

THE CANDLE GUTTERED IN THE HOLDER, and Lyna glanced up, then snuffed the wick so that it burned more brightly. Her small room was still, as was the entire house. Outside her window the apple tree stirred in the rising breeze. It seemed to be clawing at the clapboards with bony fingers, but she was accustomed to this. Dipping the tip of her quill in the ink bottle, she poised it over the sheet of paper, a thoughtful expression on her face, then began to write:

> For two weeks we've been back in this house, and I still feel very—strange. I had expected Leslie would rent me a room and help find work, but he wouldn't hear of it. The night we arrived, he said, "George kept up the house, and he told me to stay in it until he gets back with the regiment— and you're staying here, too."
>
> I remember how I argued, but he would not listen. He is a most *stubborn* man! When I said it wouldn't be right for a single man and a grown woman to live together under the same roof, he said we'd been living together under the same roof for months! I hinted that people would talk, and he just shook his head, saying, "Let them wag their tongues. We'll do nothing wrong, so it's none of their blasted business!"
>
> So, we did as he said. I kept to my same little room, and he moved back into his downstairs. I keep the house, and he is busy getting ready for the return of the regiment.

She heard a faint sound and looked up to see the mouse that came to take the crust of bread she always put out for him. He sat up and nibbled the bread, his silver eyes watching her. "Hello, Your Highness," Lyna whispered. He was a bold fellow, and she felt a companionship with him. He came regularly, and she enjoyed his antics. "Now, what have you been up to, sir?" she demanded.

He stopped eating, cocked his head, and studied her calmly. His nose twitched, then he began to nibble in an incredibly rapid fashion. When he was finished with his meal, he proceeded to calmly give himself a thorough bath. Lyna smiled as he suddenly scampered away; then she began writing again.

We were like two strangers for those first days—indeed we were. I'll never forget the look on Leslie's face when he came home and got his first glimpse of me in a dress. I'd gone to a shop and bought it, for we had agreed that would be best. It wasn't a fancy dress, just a simple blue gown, but with nice lace trim around the bodice and sleeves. I hadn't worn one in so long that it felt peculiar, to be sure! Anyway, when he came into the house I was dusting. He took one look at me—and I never saw a man look so shocked! His eyes flew open and his jaw actually dropped! I would have laughed—but I was too nervous! He swallowed and nodded, mumbling, "I see you got a new dress. You look—very nice."

I'd hoped for more of a compliment, but he seemed to be stunned. Two days later, however, he did say, "When I saw you for the first time in that dress, Lyna, I actually realized you were a woman." I did laugh at him then, for we'd gotten a little more relaxed about the whole thing. I said, "It takes a great deal to convince you, sir." After that I would notice him stealing glances at me—as though he had to constantly assure himself that I was a young woman and not Lee Smith.

The regiment will arrive soon, and I asked Leslie how he would explain me to his fellow officers. He looked doubtful and said only that he was sure they would understand. I wish I were sure of that!

Since he will never see this diary—nor will anyone else— I'll write here what I shall never be able to say aloud: I love Leslie Gordon! It's a hopeless love, for he is high above me— but I will never find a man as kind! He tells me he's been wild—but to me he has been nothing but gentle.

Lyna slowly read over the last lines, then wiped the quill and put it down. Lifting her mattress, she hid the diary, then went to bed, thinking of the strange fate that she'd fallen into.

"I'll talk to Leslie about Daniel tomorrow," she murmured. "I want to write him. Leslie will know if it's safe. . . ."

🔔　　🔔　　🔔

"Good to be back in England, isn't it, sir?"

Colonel White looked out at the ship that was disembarking the troops, then nodded. "Very good, Mullens! And I suppose you're ready for a little time off?"

"If it's convenient, sir."

"Of course! You've done a fine job! I'm mentioning your fine service in my report. I think it could be helpful to you."

"That's good of you, sir!"

The two men parted, and Captain Mullens caught a cab. As he moved through the city, he was thinking, *Glad I kept the lease on the house. It'll be good to have a place to rest in—and it's been good for Leslie.* He had told Leslie when he left India to be sure to use the house when he and Smith got back to England. Leslie had assured him he would keep the house fit until the rest of the regiment returned.

"Here we are, Captain," said the driver as he pulled his horses to a stop.

Mullens stepped out of the cab, paid the fare, then walked up to the front door. He had not known how much he missed the place until this moment. It was merely a rented house, but he'd been in and out of it for three years—the longest stay he'd had in any one spot. "By Harry—it's *good* to be back!" he exclaimed. He opened the door and stepped inside, calling out, "Leslie—are you here?"

Receiving no answer, he took two steps down the hall, then halted abruptly as a young woman stepped out of the door that led to the kitchen. Mullens yanked off his tricorn hat, somewhat confused. "Oh, I hope I didn't—ah, frighten you, ma'am."

"Not at all. Won't you come in, Captain?"

George Mullens' first thought was that his friend Gordon had married—or had taken a mistress. He stood there—his mind working rapidly—studying the young woman. She was very young, he saw, not over seventeen or perhaps a year older. She wore a simple blue dress that set off her trim figure well. Her hair was blond and she had a fine pair of gray-green eyes. Yet there was something about her that baffled him.

"We've met, have we not?"

"Yes, sir, many times."

The reply provoked Mullens, for he prided himself on his good memory. He cocked his head, thinking hard, but could not remember the woman. "I'm afraid you have me at a disadvantage, ma'am," he said. "My memory is failing me at the moment."

"Come in, Captain. Let me take your things."

As the young woman took his hat and coat, Mullens took a long look at her. Then when she turned, he said, "Why, you must be Smith's sister!"

Lyna's face became pale, but she faced him squarely. "I wish Lieutenant Gordon were here, Captain Mullens. It would be better if he could explain."

Suddenly a wild thought flashed into Mullens' mind—brought on by the sound of her voice. He exclaimed with astonishment, "Why—why, you're *Lee Smith*!"

Lyna nodded and stood quietly before the soldier. "Yes—I was. My real name is Lyna Bradford." She shook her head at the shocked expression on Mullens' face. "Come and sit down, sir. It's a long story. . . ."

Mullens accompanied the young woman into the library, where he sat and listened to her for the next quarter hour. When Lyna had finished, she said, "I feel you must despise me, Captain."

"Why, not at all!" Mullens was amazed, but he had no great social conscience. The girl's behavior might shock some, but he was a soldier—and had only admiration for the courage and ingenuity she had shown. "Why, Miss Lyna, you are a daring young lady!" He sat forward, staring at her, and shook his head in wonder. "You certainly fooled me—and Leslie as well!" He laughed with delight, exclaiming, "I'll have him for this! Imagine, living all this time with a lovely young girl—and not even *knowing* it!"

"Oh, please, Captain—don't tease him about it!" Lyna's eyes were filled with apprehension as she pleaded, "He's done so much for me! For my sake, don't torment him!"

Mullens sat staring at the lovely face of the young woman, wondering how he could have been deceived. But for her sake he agreed at once. "Well, it will be a sacrifice—but I promise. Now tell me more. How do you two get on? Are you staying here?"

The two talked for half an hour more, and as she explained, all of Lyna's fears vanished. She had always liked Mullens, and now knew that he was no threat to her. She heard the door close and rose at once, joined by Mullens. "Thank you for being so understanding, Captain," she whispered, then turned to face Gordon as he stepped inside.

"George!" he cried out, and the two men greeted each other warmly. Leslie glanced at Lyna, who nodded and gave him a warm smile. "Ah, Lyna has told you of our adventures? Well, now that the secret's out, will you throw us out?"

"Throw out the best cook in England? Not likely! You're welcome to stay as long as you like. Now sit down and let me fill you in on the regiment. I expect you'll be getting a medal, but I say you should hold out for a promotion. . . ."

While Lyna went to finish the meal she had been making, the two men sat and talked all about the regiment. Later, when they were alone after dinner, Mullens made his only comment about Lyna. "You did a noble thing for Lyna, Leslie. Most men would not have been so charitable."

After George had gone to bed, Leslie and Lyna sat down in the library to have a cup of tea. "I'm glad he's back," Leslie said. "He's a fine fellow."

"Yes." Lyna hesitated, then said, "I . . . wasn't sure he'd want me to stay. It's not a regular thing, is it?"

"You're a housekeeper for a pair of lonely bachelors. That's all there is to it."

They spoke quietly, and when she rose, Leslie stood and suddenly reached out and took her hand. Lyna was startled, for he had never done such a thing. He held it quietly, his fine eyes looking down on her. Finally he lifted her hand and kissed it gently.

Lyna's hand seemed to burn from the kiss, and when he released it, she whispered, "Why did you do that, sir?"

"I don't know. Perhaps because I admire you so much."

"Me, Lieutenant?"

"For heaven's sake, Lyna, *must* you call me that? After what we've been through, you might at least call me Leslie."

155

"It . . . wouldn't be right, sir!"

He put his hands on her shoulders and swayed her toward him. "I think all the time of how you cared for me—on the ship—and in India." Leslie could smell the faint fragrance of violets. He saw her eyes fixed on his. "You're a lovely young woman, Lyna." He hesitated, then said, "I know you've been misused. But do you trust me?"

"Yes! Yes, sir, I do!"

"Then . . . may I kiss you?"

If Leslie had tried to kiss her without asking, Lyna would have been frightened. But he was not demanding. She knew that if she said no, he would not be angry. She thought of all he'd done for her—when he'd thought she was a young man—and a sense of warmth and trust enveloped her.

She lifted her face, and when his lips fell on hers, she felt a gentleness she'd not known could come from a man. At the same time, there was a strength in his arm and a tender force in his lips that stirred her. She was aware of the muscles of his chest as he drew her close, and without thought, she lifted her hands and put them on his neck. Her lips had a pressure of their own, and a strange fluttering rose in her heart—reminding her that she was a woman. His hands were warm and firm, and he held her as if she were a very fragile and precious thing.

She felt herself pressing closer to him. Then to her surprise, he released her, but kept her in the circle of his arms. He looked into her eyes and whispered, "Lyna Bradford, you're woman enough for any man!"

Lyna was moved by his kiss, and she knew that most men would not have stopped as Leslie had just done. "I . . . I must go."

"Yes—but not until you call me by my proper name!"

Lyna reached up and laid her hand on his cheek. It was something she had longed to do but had not dared. She whispered, "Good-night . . . Leslie!" And then she was gone, slipping out of the room and leaving young Leslie Gordon to his thoughts.

🛡   🛡   🛡

A fresh layer of snow lay on the rooftops and streets of London, and though Christmas was still two weeks away, Lyna was looking forward to it. She had been working for weeks on two new shirts for Leslie, taking them out of hiding when he was gone with Captain Mullens to drill the men. Sometimes she would sit in bed sewing the fine seams, thinking of how happy she'd been in the past weeks.

Leslie had not kissed her again, but he was not unaware of her as a woman—she was certain of that. Often as they sat before the fire, reading or simply talking in the easy way that people who enjoy each other do, she would look up to find his eyes fixed on her. His expression she could not define, not completely. *Does he love me?* she would ask herself—then force the question from her mind.

She had written, on his advice, to the warden at Dartmoor prison, asking what procedures must be followed to visit a prisoner. Leslie had promised to take her as soon as they knew what the regulations were—and as soon as he was able to get a short leave.

The sun was glistening on the fresh snow as she made her way down the street to the market. Every post had become a rounded beacon, flashing with diamondlike gleams, and all the houses that had dirty, sooty roofs were now castles of smoothly rounded peaks. There were no sharp edges or angles—all the city had been smoothed and rounded as if by a magic hand.

Lyna bought her supplies, then walked home, delighting in the beauty of the city—white, sparkling, and fresh. A group of small boys emerged from behind a fence, waging war with snowballs, their shrill, yelping cries muted by the thick blanket of soft snow. One of the older boys called out, "Hey, now—watch out!" and sent a snowball winging toward Lyna.

She twisted quickly, causing it to miss, then put her package down and made a hard-packed snowball. "Watch out, yourself—" she cried, and hit the boy in the stomach with the missile. The rest of the pack began jeering at the wounded member, and one of them waved at her, hollering cheerfully, "Good on you, miss!"

Lyna retrieved her package and smiled. The incident brought back memories of how she and Daniel had learned to survive on the streets against rougher boys than those she'd just seen.

After arriving home, Lyna worked all morning cleaning. Later she began cooking for the evening meal. She prepared a thick roast in the large black pot, then stewed several vegetables. She also decided to make a plum pudding—a favorite dish of both men. She had learned from her mother how to make savory puddings by stuffing meat or blood, spices, and other ingredients into skins of an animal's intestine. Sometimes they'd smoked them, adding pepper, which improved the flavor and hid any foul taste if they started to spoil.

"I'm glad some smart person invented pudding *cloth*," she murmured. "I always hated those old intestines!" For the sweeter plum pudding, she carefully stuffed the cloth with fruit—mostly raisins and currants—and sugar, then added some rich cuts of beef. Forming the mass into a ball, she tied the top, then dropped it into a cooking pot.

At four o'clock she heard the front door open and close, followed by the boisterous sound of voices in the hallway. The kitchen door burst open and the two officers entered, their faces ruddy. Captain Mullens went at once and pulled the lid from a pot, then exclaimed, "Pot roast! Gordon, we're likely to end up with bellies as big as the general's if she keeps feeding us like this!"

Leslie winked at Lyna. "You ought to keep your trim appearance, George—as an example to the rest of us. Tell you what, I'll eat my share and most of yours. Can't say fairer than that, can you?"

"You two go wash your dirty hands," Lyna said. "You look like you've been playing in the mud." She shooed them out of the kitchen and began to set the table. By the time they returned with faces and hands clean, the food was on the table. They sat down and she served them; then she sat down and said, "It's your turn to say grace, Captain."

Mullens blinked. "Begging your pardon, Lyna, but what good does it do for a heathen like me to say a blessing? I mean to say—well, dash it all—God knows what a bounder I am!"

Lyna had insisted on one of them asking a blessing at every meal—a custom both of them found strange. But Lyna said, "You're not a bounder, Captain. And you *are* thankful for the food, aren't you?"

Mullens grimaced but nodded. "Can't deny *that*—since I intend to demolish a large portion of it. But I'm not a believer in God."

Lyna turned to him and said gently, "That may be, George—but He believes in *you*. That's why He sent His Son to die for you—and why He sent this food to you. Now—don't argue."

Mullens bowed his head and stumbled through a rather un-orthodox blessing, exploding with a loud, "*Amen!* Now, let's do our duty, Lieutenant."

The men ate with gusto, and when Lyna brought in the plum pudding, Leslie groaned. "Why didn't you *tell* me you had a plum pudding? I would have saved room!"

"Well *I* saved lots of room," Mullens asserted. "Just give me his share, Lyna—" Interrupted by the sound of knocking, he glanced toward the door. "Who could that be, I wonder?"

"I'll get it," Leslie said. "Don't let him have all that pudding, though." He made his way to the door and opened it. A tall, well-dressed man stood looking at him. He wore a heavy black over-coat, a tall silk hat, and carried a heavy cane with a gold head.

"I'm looking for a young woman named Lyna Bradford."

At first Gordon thought the man must be one of the officials of Dartmoor, come to give news of Lyna's brother. But there was something of the peerage about him; one could never mistake the air that such men had. "Yes, sir, Miss Bradford is here. Won't you come in?" Leslie said, stepping aside.

"Thank you."

As the man passed by, Leslie noted a rather wicked-looking scar on his left cheek. "If you'd like to wait in the library, I'll fetch her."

"Very well."

"And your name, sir?"

A smile touched the thin lips of the man. "Just say that an old friend has come to call. I'd like to surprise her."

Leslie was not entirely satisfied with that, but he nodded and returned to the dining room. "Lyna, there's a gentleman to see you."

"Oh, it must be about Daniel—about the letter I wrote."

"I don't think so," Leslie said slowly. "He said to tell you he's an old friend."

Lyna was surprised. "Oh, it must be Mr. Longstreet, then—the gentleman I told you about from Milford. He was very kind to Daniel and me." She rose and left the room. Leslie shot Mullens a troubled glance, then followed her. He was behind her when she stepped into the library and a startled cry burst from her lips. He moved into the room to find her standing before the tall man, her face twisted with fear.

"Ah, my dear Lyna, we meet again. It's been a long search, but I can tell you, it's worth all the trouble I've had."

Lyna was trembling, her face pale. Instantly Leslie stepped beside her, his eyes fixed on the face of the man, who was watching him carefully. "Who is this man, Lyna?"

"I am Sir Leo Rochester—and your name?"

"Lieutenant Leslie Gordon." Turning to Lyna he said, "Don't be afraid, Lyna."

"No indeed, I say the same as this officer." Rochester smiled with his lips, but it did not reach his eyes. "I don't suppose you've told this gentleman much of me? No, I thought not. Well, sir, I will inform you that this young lady is a runaway. She is indentured to me, with a year left to serve."

Leslie saw that Lyna was petrified. She was trembling violently, and he put his arm around her, as much to comfort her as to quell the red rage building in him. He had always known that someone had abused Lyna, and now he was positive that this arrogant man standing here was the man.

"Sir, the amount of the indenture will be paid. If you will name the sum—"

"Ah, but I do not choose to part with the girl. As a matter of fact, I intend to take her back with me this very night."

"Then I must inform you, sir, that you are bound to be disappointed."

Sir Leo Rochester stared at Gordon, anger twisting his face. "The girl is a thief, Lieutenant. She left my house with a large sum of money. She is liable to the law, and if you persist—"

"He's lying!" Lyna cried. "I ran away because he wouldn't leave me alone. I never stole anything!"

Leslie said, "Sir Leo, you have my permission to leave."

Rochester's face grew dusky with rage. "You realize that you are harboring a fugitive? And you must know that I will return tomorrow with representatives of the law to take the girl?"

"Get out!" Leslie snapped.

"I won't!"

Leslie Gordon stepped forward, his eyes blazing. "Do you need help to get out of this house, Rochester? I can provide it if necessary."

For a moment Rochester seemed ready to fight—but he forced himself to say, "I will not dirty my hands on you." He walked stiffly out the door, pausing to turn. "Tomorrow, we shall see who will give way!"

As the door slammed, Lyna turned blindly and fell trembling into Leslie's arms. She began to weep, and he held her tightly. She finally looked up, her face stained with tears. "I—I *can't* go back—not to him!"

"You're not going back!"

Lyna stared at his face. "I'll have to run away again."

Leslie shook his head. "No, you won't run away. But you won't be going back with him." When she started to protest, he suddenly bent his head and kissed her. Then he lifted his lips to whisper, "Will you trust me, Lyna?"

Lyna Bradford had known little kindness from men—but she knew that Leslie Gordon was different. She thought fleetingly of his kindnesses, then nodded. "Yes, Leslie—I'll always trust you!"

T   T   T

"This is the house. Are your men ready for trouble?"

Sir Leo Rochester had led the three large men to the door of the house early the next evening. He had informed them that there would be resistance, and he had paid them well, instructing them to batter anyone who defied them.

"Don't trouble yourself about *that*, Sir Leo," one of the men answered. He was slightly smaller than his two companions, but there was an air of authority about him. "We have the warrant, and it shall be served."

"Very well." Rochester knocked on the door, and it opened at once. A small man stood there, dressed in a rather dapper fashion.

"Yes, what is it?"

Leo nodded, and the sheriff said, "We have come to arrest a young woman named Lyna Bradford. We understand she's in this house."

"There is no woman by that name here, sir."

"He's lying!" Rochester said. "Make a search!"

The small man smiled. "Why, of course. Come in, all of you."

Leo walked in and moved down the hall, followed by the three officers. He turned into one door, saw the room was empty, then entered another. He stopped instantly. "There she is, Sheriff! Make your arrest!" He pointed at Lyna, but his eyes were on Leslie Gor-

161

don—who stood with his arm around Lyna—and on another officer next to the couple.

The sheriff stepped forward, but the small man who had opened the front door interrupted him. "My name is Jaspers, Sheriff. I think you know me?"

"Indeed, I do, sir." The sheriff had instantly recognized the foremost lawyer in London but had kept silent. He knew that the little man was feared by every opponent he'd faced, for he had a knack of winning cases that were supposed to be lost. The sheriff said carefully, "I have a warrant for Miss Lyna Bradford, sir."

"And there she is!" said Rochester.

Mr. Jaspers put his cool eyes on Rochester but then turned to the sheriff. "This is Mrs. Lyna Gordon, Sheriff. Here is a copy of her wedding license. And as you see, *I* am one of the witnesses, so there is no doubt of the legality of the marriage."

Rochester stared at the lawyer, then turned to face the man and woman who stood together. "You can't get by with that! I'll have you both arrested!" He saw the peaceful expression on Lyna's face—and how the tall soldier held her carefully, a smile in his eyes—and it infuriated him. "Sheriff—do your duty! Arrest her!"

But the sheriff was no fool. "Sir, the warrant is for a single bound girl. This lady has a husband."

"She broke her indenture by running away!"

"For which you may bring action for the refund of any money owed to you. I can recommend several good solicitors who will be glad to handle the matter—but Mr. Gordon has indicated that he will be happy to pay the sum. If you will submit it, it will be paid."

A silence fell over the room. Leo Rochester's face was pale as chalk, so that the scar stood out like a flag. He would have killed both Lyna and her husband if he could have done it without hanging. But he knew he was defeated. With a wild curse, he shouldered his way past the policemen and left the house. The sheriff and his burly assistants followed, after apologizing to Mr. Jaspers.

"Mr. Jaspers," Lyna said, coming to put her hands out to the diminutive lawyer, "how can I ever thank you?"

He took the hands of the young bride, leaned forward, and kissed her cheek. "I wish all my cases ended so happily. My congratulations to both of you!" He turned to Mullens, saying, "Now, sir, you come with me. This is the wedding night for these two."

Mullens was subjected to rather overwrought thanks—including kisses from Lyna and a massive bear hug from the groom. He grinned as he left, winking, and said rather loudly, "Our regiment has a reputation to maintain, Lieutenant. See you do your duty tonight!"

Then they were gone, and the house was quiet. The two stood in the middle of the library, stunned and subdued. Lyna came to him, burying her face against his chest. "I . . . I can't believe we're married!"

"You can't?"

"No . . . it all seems like a dream." She lifted her face to his. "I really can't believe it!"

"Well, then, Mrs. Leslie Gordon—I shall have to prove it to you."

A flush touched Lyna's cheeks, but she held his gaze. As he took her into his arms, she whispered, "Oh, Leslie—I love you with all my heart!"

She was soft and warm and sweet, and there was an innocence in her lips. He held her tightly, saying, "This isn't a dream, sweetheart. I'll love you until the day I die!"

PART THREE

—

THE VIRGINIA INCIDENT

1753–1760

13

A New Acquaintance

LEO ROCHESTER STEPPED OUTSIDE INTO the bright sunshine that sometimes comes in September in Virginia. He lifted his eyes to the rolling hills, feeling a sense of satisfaction with the fine yearlings that frolicked inside the white fences. He missed England, but he was quite pleased with the success of his plantation, which he had named Fairhope. Though it had been a risk leaving Milford Manor and starting over in the Colonies, it had proved to be a wise decision. Leo smiled at how profitable the venture had turned out to be.

The house was not equal to the ancestral home in England, of course, but, for the Colonies, it was splendid. He glanced at the two-storied structure with satisfaction. It was a square house, painted white with blue shutters. Smoke curled out of the six chimneys, scoring the blue sky, and a long white portico spanned the entire front of the house, whose roof was supported by white columns. Large and spacious stables lay to the back of the main house, and to the left of them were the slave quarters.

As Leo approached the stables, he found Daniel Bradford showing a chestnut stallion. He was intent on the job, and Rochester halted and studied his servant. Leo noted that the years at the forge had given Bradford a deep chest and broad shoulders. He had seen him once take a steel horseshoe and twist it as if it were made of putty. *Strong as a bear,* Rochester thought. *He'd be hard to put down in a fight.*

He knew the prosperity of Fairhope was to a great degree the result of Bradford's keen ability with horses. The young man seemed to have been born with an uncanny knowledge of which foals would be champions, and the planters in the area had flocked to Fairhope to buy the horses Daniel bred. He trained them as well, which had put a great deal of money into Leo Rochester's pocket.

He's done better than I expected, Leo thought grudgingly. *A good thing I brought him along.* Then he touched the scar on the left side of his cheek, and a flash of anger ran through him. The memory of how Lyna Bradford had escaped him had not faded. Even now he took a vicious pleasure in the memory of how he'd gotten at least a taste of revenge on the girl. He'd bribed the warden to alter the records concerning his agreement with Daniel, so they read that Daniel Bradford had died in prison. Then he'd made it a point to write a scathing letter to Lyna, telling her he was glad her worthless brother had died in Dartmoor—and wishing her the worst of fortunes.

It was a cruel sort of revenge, and looking at the swelling muscles in the back and arms of Bradford, Rochester had an uneasy thought of what might happen if Daniel ever found out his master had lied to both brother and sister. *He's capable of crushing a man's throat; and he'd do it, too!* However, Leo knew that Lyna's husband was in the regulars and that his military duties would take him and his wife to the distant assignments of the Royal Fusiliers. *I hope the wench gets fever and dies in one of those Godforsaken places,* Rochester thought.

Stepping forward, he said briskly, "Hurry it up. I've got a job for you."

Daniel didn't even look up but carefully continued to pare the hoof he was working on with a file. He was seldom hurried and over the years had learned to keep his dislike for his employer under control. His time at Fairhope had not been unhappy. After the horrors of Dartmoor, his freedom and responsibilities here were a paradise. From the very beginning, Daniel had thrown himself into the work with an intensity that surprised Rochester. As a result, he was now recognized as one of the best men with horses in the state. His time of indenture would be up in two years, and he didn't think beyond that.

He carefully set the hoof down, slapped the horse on the

shoulder, then turned to face Rochester. "What sort of job?" Daniel asked calmly. He pulled a clay pipe out of his pocket and filled it methodically as he spoke. "Whatever it is, you'd better get Ralph to do it. I'm busy training the new foals."

"Do what I tell you and keep your insolent remarks to yourself!" snapped Leo. He hated to admit that it was Bradford's efforts that drew the income to the estate, and he took every opportunity to display his spite.

"Suit yourself," said Daniel, knowing that nothing angered his employer so much as having to admit that he needed the help of his servant. "What is it?"

Leo had hoped to anger Daniel, but he seldom could. He suddenly grinned. "You won't like it," he said. "It's a matter of trading one female for another." He laughed at the surprise that came to Bradford's face. "We're selling Lady and getting a new maid."

"I don't mind a new maid, but it's not wise to sell Lady. She'll make you a lot of money if you hang on to her. She's the finest mare on the place."

"I know that—but I've got to have some ready money."

"If you'd learn that you can't play cards with the sharpers you run with, you'd not have to sell your finest stock."

Leo flushed and cursed Daniel. "Mind your own affairs! Do what I tell you or I'll have you flogged!" Leo looked into Daniel's steady eyes and knew it was a foolish threat. "I've sold the mare to young Washington."

"I thought Lawrence Washington bought the stock."

"He died last year. His younger brother George is handling the estate now. Do you know how to get there?"

"Mount Vernon? Yes, I know it."

"He'll give you cash. Give him a receipt."

"What's this about a maid?"

Rochester shrugged. "My mother thinks she needs a new maid to help with the house. She ran Ella off."

"That was foolish. Ella's a good girl."

"Bradford, you're insolent! What my mother does about a maid is none of your business! Now, the new girl will be at Pine Bluff—that's close to Mount Vernon. She's a raw girl, never worked out, but comes recommended by Squire Thomson. Her name's Holly Blanchard. Stop at his place and he'll give you the directions how to find her."

"All right. I'll leave right away."

Rochester said as he turned to leave, "If the girl's ugly, don't bring her."

Daniel stared at the retreating back of Rochester and thought, *If she's pretty, I'd like to leave her where she is.* Daniel shook his head as he thought about it. He knew well enough that though Rochester had come to a new country, he had brought along all his old ways where women were concerned. Daniel knew that several of the maids had left because of Leo's advances, and rumor had it that he was known to frequent the brothels along with his profligate friends. *I'll warn the girl—that's about all I can do.*

🔔　　🔔　　🔔

"Well, Daniel, I've never seen a finer mare!"

Daniel flushed with pleasure, for the praise from the tall young man, he suspected, wasn't given often. "Lady's the finest horse I've ever trained," he said proudly. "She can carry your weight I think, Mr. Washington."

It would take a strong steed to bear the weight of the master of Mount Vernon. At the age of twenty-one, Washington stood six feet three with broad shoulders, wide hips, and heavy legs. He gave the impression of great strength, and as Daniel had watched him ride the mare, he knew that Washington was the finest horseman he'd ever seen. Washington had bold features, including a broad nose and a determined chin. His eyes were deep-set, a gray-blue that seemed to look right into the heart of a man.

"I've heard fine things about your horses, Bradford," Washington nodded. He had met Daniel earlier on a trip to Fairhope, and the two had gone over the fine points of Lady then. "Your reputation has spread, Daniel. Mr. Rochester is fortunate to have a man of your skills. How did you learn so much about horses?"

Daniel warmed to the man, saying, "I had a good mentor back in England, sir. And I served a time in the cavalry."

"Did you indeed?" Washington's eyes lit up with interest. "I'd like to hear about that. Come along. We'll have something to eat." He led Daniel to the kitchen of the large house, where the two sat down and ate the meal set out by a female slave. Daniel was not a great talker, but Washington's genuine interest in his service with the cavalry was so intense he found himself speaking more than usual.

He halted once, laughing ruefully. "I'm talking like a magpie, Mr. Washington!"

"Why, I'm fascinated, Bradford!" He took a long pull at the mug of cider, then asked, "What did you think of the English as a fighting force?"

"The cavalry? There's none finer, sir!"

"So I'm told. What about the infantry?"

Daniel thought of the battles he'd seen and shook his head. "Well, Mr. Washington, to tell the truth, I wouldn't care to be a foot soldier in the king's service."

"Why not?"

"Well, the men are poorly paid, and they have to furnish some of their own equipment. It's a hard life, sir. But what I couldn't understand was how they could march into the face of enemy fire."

Washington pulled his chair closer. "I've never seen a battle fought that way," he admitted. "But someday I may. What's it like?"

"Well, the troops are trained to advance in close ranks. If a man in the front rank goes down, the man behind him in the second rank steps forward and takes his place."

"That must be fairly disconcerting to the enemy," Washington observed. "To see the lines keep filling up with new men."

"I suppose so—but it's chilling, at least it was to me." Daniel lifted his mug, sipped the cider thoughtfully, then set it down. "It's the way all armies fight in Europe, sir. The French do the same. What that kind of fighting means is that the army with the most men wins the battle. They just keep feeding troops forward until they overcome the enemy."

"Well, that's the object, isn't it?"

"Of course, sir, but in England and France there is more open farmland on which to fight." He glanced out over the fields toward the woods that lay in the distance. "That sort of tactic wouldn't work in this country. Here, there are too many forests and hills—no place to form large groups of soldiers."

Washington's eyes narrowed. "I've wondered about that myself. And I've heard that some of the king's troops haven't fared so well using those tactics in Canada against the French." His craggy face broke into a rueful smile. "I've heard that the French used the Indians to attack massed troops. *They* don't line up in nice neat formations, not the Indians! They hide behind trees and shoot from ambush."

Daniel grinned suddenly. "I expect the officers in His Majesty's army look on that with disfavor?"

"Indeed! They call them cowardly—but they don't seem to have found any new tactics to meet them." He frowned and shook his head. "We've fought two wars over territorial claims to the Ohio Valley and are about to wage a third, I fear."

"Against the French again?"

"Yes." Washington hesitated, then said, "As a matter of fact, that's the reason I bought the mare from Mr. Rochester. I'm leaving right away on a long, difficult trip. Governor Dinwiddie has commissioned me to take a warning to the French commander at Fort Le Boeuf against further encroachment on territory claimed by the king."

Daniel asked instantly, "Will they heed the warning, sir?"

"No, I think not," Washington answered. "It's gone too far for that. England's got her armies spread all over the world. The French are determined to keep their share of this new world. They'll never give it up without a fight."

"My indenture is up in two years, Mr. Washington," Daniel said. "I'd thought to settle in the Ohio Valley. With the way things stand, would you advise against it?"

Washington shook his head. "I'm afraid it would be unsafe. The French already are inciting the Indians to attack English settlers in that area." He paused for a moment, then smiled and added, "Come to Mount Vernon, Bradford. I can use a man who handles horses as well as you do."

Daniel was flattered by the offer and promised to think about it. Finally he rose, saying, "Good luck on your mission, sir. I wish I could go with you."

"When your indenture is up, come and see me. Governor Dinwiddie has made me an adjutant over a military district in this state. I could use a good man like you in the militia."

Daniel left Mount Vernon, highly impressed with Washington. The man possessed a steadiness that pleased him. Daniel would have liked the adventure of accompanying the big man on his trip to warn the French, but he knew that Rochester would not hear of it. His time of indenture stipulated seven years of service, and Leo would demand he fulfill the terms to the very day.

Two more years—and I'll be free to do as I please, he thought as he headed the team down the winding road.

He arrived at Pine Bluff at dusk and put up at an inn for the night. After a good meal, he retired early and slept soundly the whole night. Daniel woke up at the sound of the animals stirring in the stable. He went out to wash at the pump, combed his hair with his fingers, then entered the small dining room for breakfast. "I need to find a gentleman named Thomson," he said to the man who came and set a plate in front of him.

The innkeeper, whose name was Shockly, was a burly man with black curly hair. "That'll be Squire Thomson. He lives six miles down the road—but he ain't there. He's gone to Boston."

Daniel said, "I'm supposed to find a young woman named Holly Blanchard. She's going to work for my employer, Mr. Rochester. Do you know the girl?"

"Why, it happens I do." Shockly shrugged his heavy shoulders. "I heard her ma died. Didn't know she was leavin' the homeplace."

"How do I get there?"

Shockly gave careful directions as he filled Daniel's cup, adding, "The Blanchards are backwoods people. Don't come to town more'n three—four times a year. I knowed her pa and her brother. The old man died a few years ago, and I heard that young Blanchard married and moved on down to Georgia." He shrugged, adding, "That's all the family the gal had—guess she's got to work out."

Daniel finished his breakfast, thanked the man, then started out to find the Blanchard place. He had difficulty finding the old homestead, for it was far back in the woods. He finally drove up a narrow, twisting road and stopped in front of a dilapidated cabin. A man stepped out, and Daniel said, "I'm looking for a young woman named Holly Blanchard."

A voice came from inside the cabin, and a young woman stepped outside, carrying a small bundle. She was no more than sixteen or seventeen, he judged. "I'm Holly Blanchard," she said, stepping off the porch.

"My name's Daniel Bradford. Mr. Rochester sent me to fetch you to Fairhope."

The girl nodded, rather nervously, Daniel thought, then

climbed into the buggy as the man on the porch went back inside without saying a word.

"I'm ready," she said evenly.

Not much of a goodbye, he thought. Aloud he said, "Just put your things in the back."

"Yes, sir."

"You don't have to call me sir, Holly. I'm a servant for Mr. Rochester, just like you."

The girl nodded but said nothing. Daniel spoke to the team and guided them as they wound around the narrow road. "You lived here long, Holly?" he asked idly.

"All my life."

"Guess you'll feel bad leaving it." When she didn't reply, he said quietly, "I heard you lost your ma. I'm sorry about that."

The girl nodded slightly, and when Daniel glanced at her, he saw a tear running down her cheek. It disturbed him, and he remembered his vow to warn the girl about Leo Rochester. But she was filled with her private tragedy, and he refrained from adding to her burden. She would need some time to adjust to a new place and to settle in to a different way of life. He would keep an eye on her and talk to her at another time.

As they rode along, Daniel thought about his time at Fairhope. He had not formed close friends since he arrived in Virginia. He was fatalistic in his own way, preferring to keep those who would have been friendly at arm's length. It was not so much hardness, but rather caution that made Daniel build a wall around himself. Those difficult years after his mother died, along with the hard times in prison, had proven to him that life was fickle, so he had chosen not to make new friends. Better not to have them than to have them and lose them.

Daniel kept silent as they rode along, and the girl sat staring straight ahead at the road, saying nothing. At noon he stopped and brought out the lunch he'd had the innkeeper pack. "Well, let's eat," he said.

"I'm not hungry."

Daniel ignored her, saying, "I'm getting stiff. Here, we'll take a rest under those pines." He helped Holly down and handed her the satchel with the food in it. "You fix the lunch, and I'll take the team down to that creek for a drink." Without waiting for an answer, he unhitched the team and led them away. He took his time, giving the girl a few moments to herself. After the team had had a long drink from the winding creek, he led them back.

"That looks good," he commented, coming to where she'd spread the sandwiches and onions on a flat rock. He brought a jug out of the wagon and smiled at her. "No cups, but we can take turns with this ale." He sat down and began to eat. "Go on, Holly," he urged gently. "We've got a long ride ahead of us before we reach Fairhope. You need to eat something."

Slowly the girl reached out and took one of the sandwiches. As she ate, Daniel studied her covertly. She was not tall, and even though she was wearing a plain gray dress, Daniel saw that she was fairly pretty. She had thick brown hair and a beautiful complexion. Finally she looked at him with dark brown eyes and a heart-shaped face. "What's it like—where we're going?" she asked.

"Why, it's a nice plantation, Holly," Daniel replied. He told her a little about Fairhope, then asked, "You had no place else to go?"

"No. I got no kin—except my brother. He's gone to Georgia, with his wife's people."

Daniel bit into one of the onions, enjoying the strong flavor. "You didn't think to go with them?"

The girl hesitated. "We . . . didn't get on."

Daniel glanced at her and saw the troubled light in her eyes. *Well, she's got no other choice. She'll have to go to Fairhope, I reckon. And Leo will just have to keep his distance from her.*

The air was chilly, and when they got back into the buggy, he said, "Getting cold. You got a coat, Holly?"

"No, just a sweater." She rummaged through her sack, pulled out a worn brown sweater, and put it on. She had kept her right hand out of sight, but his eyes fell on it. She was missing the small finger and the one next to it.

Holly saw him looking at her hand and instantly thrust it under her sweater. Her fair cheeks flushed as if she'd done something shameful.

"How'd you hurt your hand, Holly?" Daniel asked, making his voice easy and natural.

"I . . . was holding a stick of wood . . . and my brother, he missed with his ax and cut my fingers off."

"That's too bad—but I'll bet you've learned to make do."

Holly turned and stared at him, her eyes betraying her fear at having to leave home. "I can do most anything," she said eagerly. "Even sew and spin and milk a cow. It don't hurt my work none a'tall, Daniel!"

She was so pathetically eager to convince him that Daniel was touched. "Why, I'm sure of it, Holly. You'll make out real fine."

The buggy moved along, and Holly whispered, "I ain't never worked out, Daniel. I'm scared I won't please them."

"Sure you will," Daniel assured her. "You'll be working for a housekeeper named Mrs. Bryant. She's real nice. I'll put in a word for you with her—you know, tell her you're new at this sort of thing and ask her to be patient."

Holly turned to him, her eyes warm. "Would you really?"

"You have my word on it." Daniel didn't tell her about Leo—or about how fussy Lady Edna was. He knew she'd just have to learn to put up with them as everybody else did.

By the time they reached Fairhope, the sun was almost down. "Come along and I'll take you to Mrs. Bryant," Daniel said. He leaped to the ground and came around to her side of the buggy. She picked up her bundle, holding it in her good hand—and looked to see Daniel extending his hand to help her. She had kept her maimed hand hidden. Now, however, she slowly withdrew it—and placed it in his hand.

Daniel was certain this was the first time she'd ever done such a thing. He saw the trust in her dark brown eyes as he gently closed his fingers on the injured hand and helped her to the ground.

"I . . . I thank you," Holly whispered.

I'll have to be a friend to her, he thought as he led her to the back door. *She's a pitiful little thing. . . .*

🔔   🔔   🔔

For the first two weeks of Holly's service, Daniel made it a point to stop at the house and visit with her whenever he could. He had spoken to Mrs. Bryant, who was a kindly woman, asking her to help the girl. The housekeeper had agreed, and just one week after Holly's being there, she reported, "Why, Daniel, she's as hard a worker as I've ever seen. Real awkward, but that's because she's never been in a fine house like this. But tell her once, and she never has to be told again. She's a fast learner."

One morning Holly came out to the barn to milk the cows.

Daniel had been busy working on one of the carriages when he saw her cross the yard. Leaving his work, he walked over to the barn and entered. Holly was sitting on a three-legged stool, busily filling the pail. Seeing him come in, a smile brightened her face. "Oh, hello, Daniel."

"I hear good reports about your work from Mrs. Bryant," he said as he leaned against the wall.

"That's nice—I like Mrs. Bryant." She suddenly bit her lip, started to say something, then fell silent.

Daniel asked quietly, "What's wrong, Holly?" When she only shook her head, he asked, "Is it Mr. Rochester?"

Instantly her cheeks flushed, and she looked up at him, surprised at his question. "I'm . . . I'm afraid of him, Daniel!"

"I'll speak to him, Holly. Don't you fret anymore about it, you hear?"

"Thank you, Daniel," she said, a troubled look still in her eyes.

"Well, I need to get back to my chores," said Daniel. He went back to fixing the carriage and waited for a chance to talk with his master. Later that morning, Leo came to the stable to get a horse.

"Saddle Highboy for me," he said, his mind on his errand.

"Mr. Rochester, I want you to leave Holly Blanchard alone."

Rochester blinked with the shock of the blunt statement. His handsome face reddened, and he slapped his riding whip against his thigh. "Keep your mouth shut! I'll do as I please!" he blurted out.

Daniel came to stand before him. He was wearing a thin shirt and his chest swelled against it, the corded muscles clearly outlined. His hazel eyes were half-shut and his voice was controlled as he said coldly, "If you bother her again, Leo, I'll break your back."

Rochester lifted the whip, preparing to strike Bradford's face. However, something he saw in the eyes of the young man caused him to withhold the blow.

"Second thoughts are usually best," Daniel said.

Rochester flared out, "If you ever lay a hand on me, Bradford, I'll see that you rot in prison."

"Then who would make money for you to throw away at cards?" Daniel taunted. He had hoped Leo would strike him, for he was ready to retaliate.

Rochester hated to admit the truth. "You must be enjoying her favors, Daniel." He saw this as a way to extricate himself with some sort of dignity. "I want none of your leavings—go on and have the wench!"

Daniel said no more. He turned and went to saddle Highboy while Rochester glared at him. When he returned with the mount, Leo quickly mounted, struck the horse hard with his crop, and took off at a fast gait. Daniel stared after him as he disappeared down the lane. Later in the week Daniel questioned Holly. "Has Mr. Rochester been behaving himself?"

"Oh yes—thank you, Daniel!" She reached out and touched his arm with her left hand. Her eyes were bright and she whispered, "I don't know what I'd have done—without you!"

Daniel laughed and without thinking reached out and gave her a hug. "Really, it was nothing, Holly," he said, then walked back to the stables.

At the end of the day, Daniel stopped by the house. When he entered the kitchen, Mrs. Bryant looked up from her work. She walked over and slyly nudged him. "You've got a way with the girls, Daniel!"

"What's that?" said Daniel.

"I saw how Holly was staring after you today."

A little embarrassed, Daniel said, "What do you mean, I just gave her a little hug. That's all."

"You never looked at any of the girls—but you could have had some of them." Mrs. Bryant was a born matchmaker, and she leaned close and whispered, "She's a pretty little thing—and downright foolish about you! Why, she never takes her eyes off you!"

Daniel laughed. "She's from the backside of the woods, Mrs. Bryant. I don't think she's been around many men. You just wait and see. She'll take up with Henry or Jake!"

But as the weeks passed, Mrs. Bryant watched Holly and could tell that the girl was hopelessly enamored with Daniel. *She's moonstruck over him—that's what she is!* she said to herself. *And a good girl she is, too—not like some I could name!*

14

Daniel and the Lady

"I've never been to a dance—I wouldn't know how to act,"
Holly said as she leaned on the fence rail and stroked the nose of
the frisky new foal Daniel was training.

Daniel shrugged his shoulders and smiled at her. "Why, I'm
not much of a dancer myself—but I could teach you enough to
get by."

A few days earlier, George Washington had invited Daniel to
a dance to be given by the local militia the following week. Daniel
had mentioned it to Holly in an offhanded fashion, not knowing
if she'd even consider his invitation. Now as she watched him
work with the young chestnut stallion, he hoped she would say
yes.

The colt lifted his head, snorted, then wheeled and galloped
out across the pasture. Holly laughed. "He's a rowdy one, he is!"
She had fit into her role as maid for Mrs. Bryant very well and,
after almost a year's service, had become the lady's strong right
arm. Holly had gained weight, and as Daniel glanced at her, he
thought she looked very pretty in her blue dress covered with a
white apron. Her glossy brown hair escaped from the white
starched cap, and he noted that she still used her left hand to tuck
it in. "I expect Micah will be jealous if you go with me," Daniel
teased her. "He's moon-eyed over you!"

Holly made a face at him. "I'd as soon go with a *moose* as with

179

Micah." She looked up at him and asked abruptly, "When will your time be up, Daniel?"

"First of 1756." He walked over beside her and leaned on the rail. "It'll be a glad day for me," he said, staring out over the fields.

Holly's gentle eyes grew troubled. "I'll . . . I'll not know what to do without you here, Daniel. If you hadn't taken care of me . . . speaking to Mrs. Bryant . . . and to Mr. Leo . . ." She hesitated, then shook her head. "Maybe you'll settle close, do you think?"

Daniel shrugged his shoulders, saying, "Haven't decided." He reached over and picked up the bridle he'd stripped from the chestnut, then stopped and said thoughtfully, "I've thought of going into the army. Washington has asked me to join him. I could be an officer, in time."

The previous year, George Washington had been commissioned by Governor Dinwiddie to raise a force and proceed to the Forks of the Ohio and take command. He had asked Daniel to accompany him, but Daniel had to fulfill his time of indenture. Daniel was deeply disappointed at not being able to join the colonel's troops when they moved out. Washington's force met the French in battle but were completely outnumbered. Forced to retreat, he led his men to Fort Necessity, a small log stockade he'd constructed for just such an emergency. The French followed and Washington's small army was forced to surrender the fort. The French allowed Washington and his men to retreat to Virginia.

After Washington returned to Virginia, he spoke of the battle to his brother Jack. "I fortunately escaped without any wound, for the right wing, where I stood, was exposed and received all the enemy's fire. I heard the bullets whistle, and believe me, there is something charming in the sound."

Later Daniel had a meeting with Washington, who laughed at himself as he recounted his own words. "I spoke like a callow youth—which Horace Walpole insists that I am. He says that if I knew more of bullets, I would not find them 'charming.'"

But the excitement of the battle had bolstered Washington's confidence, Daniel could see, and he said, "Sir, if you take the field again, I hope to ride with you. My indenture is up in January of '56, so please keep me in mind."

"Of course I will! When we were having trouble with the horses, I told my second in command that if Daniel Bradford were here, we'd not be having such a hard time."

All this ran through Daniel's mind as he moved with Holly toward the barn. He was startled to hear Leo Rochester's voice to his left, calling out, "Bradford!"

At once he went to stand in front of the owner, noting that Holly quickly walked back toward the house. "Yes, sir?" he asked.

Rochester stared after the girl, then turned and glared at Daniel. It was obvious the proud man was still galled by being warned away from Holly. Despite Leo's threats, Daniel knew he'd never have any more trouble over it. He did, after all, bring in much income for the estate.

Leo struck his leg with his riding crop, then said, "We're having a visitor soon—a young lady. Her name's Marian Frazier."

"Yes, sir?"

"Well, she's crazy for horses, Bradford. I want you to see that she has a nice mare to ride while she's here—or whatever will please her." Daniel eyed him strangely, and Rochester laughed. "She has a very rich father in Boston. I may marry her someday, so I want her to see the best side of Fairhope."

"Is she a good rider?"

"Have no idea—but you see to it that she doesn't get hurt, hear me?" said Leo, an edge to his voice.

"I'll take care of it personally, Sir Leo."

The request was not unusual, for Daniel was normally asked to see to proper mounts for all the visitors that came to Fairhope. A week later, as the two of them rode to the small village where the dance was to be held, Daniel related Rochester's orders. "He's never mentioned marrying, that I know of. Her father must be pretty rich."

"Why would a rich man want to marry for money?" Holly asked in a puzzled tone. "He's got everything he wants."

"He that loveth silver shall not be satisfied with silver," Daniel responded. "That's in the Bible somewhere—can't remember where." He slowed the horses down to a walk and gestured at the cluster of houses that lay ahead. "There's Duttonville—the dance will be in the town hall, I hear." He sat loosely in the seat, his tall, strong form relaxed. He wore his best suit—a pair of brown knee breeches, white stockings exposing his muscular calves, and a maroon coat over his white shirt. Over his wheat-colored hair he wore a brown tricorn, which he now pulled down over his brow. "I'll bet she's homely—Miss Marian Frazier."

"But you've never seen her, have you?"

181

"No . . . but somehow I got it in my mind that she's a skinny old maid with a pointy nose and a shape like a rake handle!"

Holly laughed outright. "You're just silly! Why should she be plain?"

"Dunno. Just think she is." They were entering the village, and he admired the bright colors of the houses. They were mostly clapboard, with a few sober red brick homes. "Look like rows of dollhouses, don't they?" Daniel commented.

"I think they're pretty. Look, that one with the gingerbread trim—it's so nice!" A touch of longing came into Holly's voice, and she added, "I'd love to live in a little house like that. It wouldn't have to be big, though."

"You might have ten children," Daniel remarked, then laughed at her sudden surprised expression. "Why not? The girls would all be pretty—like you." He saw her flush as she always did when he paid her a compliment, then added innocently, ". . . and the boys would all be big and ugly—like Micah."

Holly sputtered and struck him hard on the arm with her fist. "You—you *blacksmith*!" she cried.

"*Blacksmith?* What kind of cussing is that? Maybe I'd better teach you something a bit stronger," Daniel said. He smiled at the reaction he saw in her face. He knew that Holly was a devoted Christian. From the day she'd arrived, she had faithfully attended the little Congregational church. "I tease you too much, don't I, Holly?"

Holly smiled slightly and blushed, then quickly changed the subject. "I don't think I want to try to dance. I'm too awkward."

But Daniel merely shook his head. "You don't go to a dance *not* to dance," he replied. "Besides, nobody will be looking at us."

He drove the wagon to the line of buggies and tied up the team. Reaching up, he helped Holly down—thinking of how she'd been ashamed to give him her maimed hand the first time he'd helped her down. *She's gotten over being uneasy about her hand—at least with me,* he thought. He liked the girl very much and took pride in the way she'd taken hold with her work. Even Lady Edna had made mention to the housekeeper how pleased she was with Holly's work. She reminded him of Lyna—whose memory was never far from his thoughts. Holly looked nothing like his lost sister, but she was kind, and Daniel felt like a brother to her.

When they were inside, Holly's eyes opened wide when she

saw all the decorations and the lights that glittered from a myriad of candles. "Oh, it's beautiful, Daniel!" she exclaimed.

He helped her off with her coat and, when he saw the dress she was wearing, shook his head in admiration. "Why, Holly . . . ! You look very nice indeed."

Holly had been anxious for him to admire her dress. It was actually a dress that Edna Rochester had worn a few times, then tired of. Lady Edna had given it to Mrs. Bryant, telling her she could do with it as she pleased. And as soon as the housekeeper had heard that Daniel had invited Holly to the dance, she promptly offered it to Holly. It wasn't really stylish, but she'd worked on it, and now was happy at the admiration reflected in Daniel's hazel eyes. The dress itself was made of pink satin, and the Empire style with the bodice gathered lightly above and below her bosom looked very good on her. The skirt was full and clinging, with a row of satin swags near the hem line. The only jewelry she wore was a pair of small pearl earrings—borrowed from Helen, one of the other maids.

"Come along, Holly," Daniel said. "We'll see what sort of dancers we make." Taking her hand, he led her to the floor, noting that her heart-shaped face was tense with fear. *She's petrified*, he thought, and so he determined to make this an evening she'd never forget. "Now, isn't the music fine?" Daniel asked. To calm her he kept encouraging her as he led her through the sets. His tactic was successful—Holly moved over the floor with more ease than he'd hoped for.

The room was crowded with many Virginians who belonged to the militia. The uniforms were wildly different, for each unit chose its own, and yet there were many men, such as Daniel, who had no uniforms at all. The dresses of the women added touches of scarlet, green, pink, blue, and even such exotic colors as orchid and turquoise to the whirling kaleidoscope made by the dancing pairs.

It was a democratic sort of dance, for some of the wealthy planters such as the Lees and the Washingtons had come—mostly to encourage the men who served under them. Holly felt very much out of place among all the people, and when a tall man wearing a buff uniform came to speak to Daniel, she instinctively moved her right hand behind her back.

"Good evening, Daniel," Washington smiled, shaking hands

with Bradford. "Glad you could attend the Militia Ball. And this young lady is. . . ?"

"Miss Holly Blanchard, sir. And this is Colonel Washington, Miss Blanchard."

Holly curtsied and managed to return the greeting the tall man gave her. She had heard so much about Washington from Daniel and others that she was very glad to have a close view of him. He was not handsome, she saw, but there was a strength in his rugged features, mixed with a courteous demeanor. After the colonel left, she said, "He looks very kind, Daniel."

"He has a temper," Daniel replied. "But somehow he has a way with people. He can make men follow him."

The evening went by all too quickly for Holly, and when Daniel helped her down from the buggy back at Fairhope, he asked, "Did you have a good time, Holly?"

"Oh yes! I never thought I'd get to go to such a party."

It was late and a huge silver moon poured waves of light over the yard. "I'm glad," Daniel said, smiling at her. The light from the moon reflected in her eyes, and he said, "You looked nicer than anyone, Holly. I was proud to be with you."

She didn't speak for a moment, then she whispered, "Daniel . . . I want to tell you—"

She halted and Daniel saw that she was choked up. He leaned forward, put his hands on her shoulders, and gave her a kiss on the cheek—much as he might have done with Lyna. But then she leaned against him and looked up—and he kissed her lips. It was, he thought, a brotherly caress, but when her body brushed against his, he tightened his grip for a moment. Her lips were sweet and innocent, and he savored the youthful touch of them. Then he was aware that the kiss was not as brotherly as he had thought—so he drew back.

Holly had been roughly kissed twice and had disliked it each time. But there was a strength and comfort in Daniel's embrace that touched her. She was breathless as she looked at him, whispering, "Good-night, Daniel." She went to her room at once, which she shared with Sally, another maid, and went to bed. As she lay there, she knew she would never forget the evening, and she touched her lips with her fingers, thinking of his kiss—wondering if he would ever kiss her again.

✝   ✝   ✝

"Are you Daniel Bradford? Mr. Rochester informs me you're to see that I get a suitable mount."

Daniel was examining the hoof of a tall jumper named Dunmore. When he dropped the hoof and turned to the young woman who'd entered the stable, he was speechless for a moment. He'd heard that Miss Marian Frazier had arrived—but he hadn't heard that she was a beautiful woman. He remembered telling Holly that she was probably very homely—but there was *nothing* homely about the attractive young woman who stood waiting for him to speak.

"Why, yes, miss," he said finally. "I'm Daniel. Welcome to Fairhope."

Marian Frazier was very tall, and her height was accented by the long green skirt she wore. She had a wealth of dark auburn hair, light green eyes, and a glowing complexion. In a day when many people had blackened or missing teeth, she had very even, white teeth.

"I've got a nice gentle mare that you'll like, Miss Frazier," Daniel said. He led her to the stalls and nodded. "Very good-tempered, Molly is."

"I'd prefer a more spirited horse. That stallion over there, I think might suit."

Daniel at once shook his head. "Oh, that's King, Miss Frazier—and he's a handful. Wouldn't be at all suitable."

"Put a sidesaddle on him, Bradford," the young woman commanded. When Daniel hesitated, she laughed at him, a musical sound. "Don't worry, I won't fall off."

Daniel protested, "I'm to give you whatever you require, Miss Frazier, but King has thrown some very good men."

"Well, he won't throw me!"

Daniel objected again, but in vain. He could tell from the determined look in her eyes that Marian Frazier was a strong-willed young woman, accustomed to having her own way. Finally she hinted that she would have to resort to speaking to Mr. Rochester. She was nice enough but totally determined to ride King, and in the end Daniel reluctantly gave in to her request.

He saddled the big horse and then his favorite in the stable, a black gelding named Midnight. When the horses were saddled, he came to hand her up. She mounted so gracefully he hardly felt the weight of her hand on his. He was holding the lines and handed them to her with a warning, "He'll try to get the bit in his teeth—so be careful!"

Even as he turned and mounted Midnight, he saw that King was up to his old tricks. The big stallion lunged forward in a move that would have unseated most riders—but the young woman merely swayed and laughed. She struck King lightly on the flank with the crop and turned to say, "Come along—see if you can catch me, Bradford!"

Daniel was a fine rider and had ridden and won many of Rochester's races. He leaned low over the gelding, whispering into his ear. Midnight was a fine horse, but not the speedster that King was. Still, the skill of the rider meant something, so he fully expected to catch the big horse soon enough.

The dust rose, swirling from the hooves of the two horses, as they galloped off. The young woman was riding perfectly, Daniel saw. He was a little shocked, for he was not accustomed to seeing such skill in a woman. And when Miss Frazier abruptly turned King's head and left the road for the rolling pasture, he was alarmed.

"Miss Frazier—there are holes in this field!" he called out. But she merely looked back and laughed at him. Gritting his teeth, he drove Midnight at top speed, intending to catch the fool woman and stop her!

But he had no chance at all, for King was running at top speed. Daniel looked ahead and called, "Don't try that fence—he's not a good jumper!" But there was no sign of obedience, and he held his breath as King took the fence, knocking down the top rail with his rear hoof.

Crazy woman—she'll kill herself!

Daniel guided Midnight over the fence, angry yet at the same time impressed with Marian Frazier's skill. Finally she pulled the stallion up short, and when Daniel caught up, he drew his own mount up alongside. He wanted to shout at her, but he knew that would never do—not after what Leo had told him.

The light green eyes of the young woman were gleaming, and her wide mouth turned upward in a delighted smile. Her cheeks were bright with color, and there was an air of freedom about her as she said, "Now—let's not argue about which horse I can ride, all right?"

Daniel felt his anger fade and was forced to smile at her. "Your father would probably take a stick to you, Miss Frazier," he said. "But my guess is that he didn't do too much of that when you were small."

"Not nearly enough!" Marian leaned forward and patted King's neck. "There have been plenty of people to tell me so. Now, show me the best trails."

Daniel spent the rest of the morning showing Miss Frazier around the plantation. She was intensely interested in every-thing—the crops, the advantages of slaves over free laborers, the problems of running a large business—and by the time they re-turned to the stable, he laughed, "You must be one planning to write a book!"

"Meaning I'm a nosy young woman? Well, I'm never bored, Daniel. Life is too short for that."

Daniel dismounted, and as she slid out of the saddle, King bucked unexpectedly. Daniel yanked his bridle down with a tre-mendous pull, at the same time catching the young woman with his free arm. He felt the pressure of her body for a moment, then set her on her feet.

Marian was embarrassed. "After all my boasting—to get thrown like a beginner."

"King's very clever. I think he stays awake nights thinking of ways to humiliate people." He held the big horse effortlessly with his iron grasp.

At first, Marian had not thought Daniel a very large man, but now she noticed with admiration the heavy muscles of his shoul-ders and arms and the swelling chest molded by the thin shirt. "You're very strong, Bradford," she remarked.

"A blacksmith has to be," he shrugged. "Can't shoe a horse with your brain."

Marian smiled. "Thank you for the tour. I expect we'll be see-ing a great deal of each other. I love to ride—but your employer doesn't care much for it, does he?"

"Well, Sir Leo thinks of a horse as a means of getting from one place to another."

"And you don't?"

"No, I like the process." Daniel stood holding the lines of the big horse, the sun glinting on his light-colored hair. He was tanned and his hazel eyes grew warm as he added, "A horse is— well, more than just transportation. When you're on a fine horse and feel his muscles working as he flies over the ground, why, that's about the most exciting thing I know."

Marian stared at him, her eyes wide. "Why, that's the way *I* feel!" she exclaimed. "I get too emotionally involved with my horses—I cry when they hurt, and when my mare Lily died, I thought I'd like to die, too!"

The two stood there, sensing the excitement that comes when two people discover they have an interest in common. It actually matters little what it is, for it is the unity of the thing that joins them. When these people meet and discover that the other shares the same burning interest, the one wants to exclaim, "What! You *too*?"

Marian came to herself, conscious that she was showing too much of her inner heart to a servant she'd just met. Brusquely she nodded, "Well, we'll be seeing each other," and turned and walked back to the house.

And they did see each other—every day. Sir Leo had guests over, and riding around the grounds on the trails was a regular part of the activities. At night there were elaborate suppers and even a concert of chamber music one evening. But during the days, Marian spent a great deal of time in the saddle. Leo was tolerant, telling Daniel, "See she doesn't break her neck. She's worth too much money for that!"

Marian tried to keep a wall between herself and Daniel Bradford, but it proved impossible. She was a very rare creature—a wealthy woman with a genuinely democratic spirit. Most young women of beauty and wealth were snobs, but not so Marian. Her independent nature had no trace of arrogance, but rather an insatiable thirst to learn and experience everything she could. She enjoyed Daniel for his quick wit—and for his mastery of everything about horses. She would watch as he shoed a horse, asking question after question, and finally would sigh. "I wish *I* could do all the things you do—but I'm not strong enough."

"I don't think you'd like to have a blacksmith's muscles, Miss Frazier," Daniel grinned. "You'd look a bit odd."

A week flew by, and Leo sent for Daniel. When the young man entered his office, he saw Marian Frazier sitting in the window seat. He greeted her, then turned to Leo, who said, "Bradford, I've got a letter here from Colonel Washington. He wants to hire you for a time."

"Hire me for what, sir?"

Rochester frowned and snapped his fingers with some irritation. "You've heard about General Braddock's arrival from England?"

"Yes, sir. He's supposed to whip the Frenchies in the Ohio Valley."

"Yes. Well, Washington is going along as his aide. He wants you to accompany him. He's willing to pay for your time, so I'm sending you to join him." He scowled and flung himself into a chair. "I suppose you like the idea of playing soldier?"

"I'm sure he just wants me to help with the horses, sir—but I'll be glad to go."

"All right, be off with you—but don't dally after General Braddock whips the French, you hear me?"

"I'll come straight back to Fairhope, Sir Leo."

Marian looked up to smile at Daniel. "Good luck. Don't get yourself shot. You still haven't shown me how to train a horse to take a fence."

"I'll do that, Miss Frazier—and you watch out for King."

After he left, Leo stared at the young woman. "You like Bradford, don't you?"

"He knows more about horses than any man I've ever known. And he's handsome," she added slyly. "Does that make you jealous?"

Leo went to her, pulled her to her feet, and tried to kiss her. She avoided it, then laughed and left the room. "Come on, I'll let *you* ride King today!"

Daniel went and gathered his gear together, then headed for the barn. As he saddled Midnight, he was surprised that Sir Leo had granted his request to take the fine horse. When he turned to lead his mount out, he saw Holly standing at the entrance of the barn.

"Daniel, you're going to the army!"

"Just to shoe the horses for Colonel Washington, Holly. I won't be doing any fighting." There had been a reserve between them since he'd kissed her after the dance, and now he smiled and put

189

out his hand. "Come now, say goodbye. I'll be back soon. We'll go to another dance."

She took his hand, felt its pressure, then he mounted and was away at a gallop. Turning slowly, she made her way back into the house, feeling lonely and a little afraid.

15

BLOOD AT
MONONGAHELA

"We must wipe out the shame of Fort Necessity!"

This one statement by King George set in motion the wheels of war. Determined to prove English soldiers were the finest in the world, he sent General Edward Braddock to America with two regiments of five hundred men each to fight the French. The general arrived in Virginia in February of 1755 with his troops. The Virginia Burgesses added their support by voting £40,000 to pay and equip four hundred fifty Virginians in nine companies to accompany the newly arrived general.

Braddock had had an exemplary army career for forty-five of his sixty years. However, his military expertise was about to be challenged. He was soon to learn that the wilderness of America was not suited for the tactics used on the expansive battlefields of Europe. As he organized his troops along with the colonial militia, he made one good decision. He had learned of George Washington and his military prowess and persuaded the tall man to accompany him as his aide.

Daniel Bradford joined Washington at Mount Vernon. Washington was accompanied by a deep-chested young man whom he introduced as Adam Winslow. "You two will be a great help to me," he smiled. "Adam is the best gunsmith in Virginia, Daniel, and you are the best with horses." The three men left at once, leading a string of fine horses for Washington's service. As they traveled, Washington explained his position to the two young men. "I will not be a part of the army itself—but an advisor on General Braddock's staff."

Later when the two young men were alone, sitting in front of a fire, Daniel said, "I don't think it's right, Winslow. Colonel Washington knows more about the enemy than the whole of Braddock's staff."

"I expect that's right, Daniel," Winslow nodded. He spoke slowly and thoughtfully. Adam was a husky man, with a ponderous strength in his movements. "It'll be more of a fight than these English officers think."

By the time Daniel and Adam arrived at Fort Cumberland, the two young men had become fast friends. The fort was bustling with activity as an army of 2,400 men was assembling. Daniel's first assignment from Washington was terse. "I'll meet with the general, and I want you to examine the horses. I want a thorough report on their condition. They will be vital to this campaign."

"Yes, sir," said Daniel.

Daniel moved among the troops, observing the various groups that had gathered. Some of the units included volunteers from Pennsylvania, Maryland, and the Carolinas. At one point Daniel stopped to talk with a steady-eyed man dressed in buckskin breeches named Daniel Boone and discovered that quite a number of the men were not soldiers at all. Many of them were simple backwoodsmen who had come along to help.

"Some of us are axmen," Boone informed him. "Our job is to clear a road to Fort Duquesne for the troops and all the equipment."

Daniel spent the rest of the day studying the horses carefully and was disappointed, to say the least. Many of them were spavined, broken hocked, and wind galled. He was staring at a sorry-looking specimen when a burly woodsman noticed him.

"Ain't much, are they?" grunted the large man. He studied Daniel carefully, asking, "Which unit you with?"

"I'm not with any unit. My name's Daniel Bradford. I came with Colonel Washington. . . ."

The man listened carefully while Daniel spoke, then spat an amber stream of tobacco juice at his feet. "Well, I was hired to drive this here wagon, but the shape these horses are in, I might have to pull it myself. I'm Daniel Morgan. You had anything to eat?" asked the man.

"No, and I have a friend who could use some grub, too."

"Well, go and fetch 'im whilst I fix somethin', and come have a bite."

Daniel went and found Adam Winslow and returned to Morgan's wagon a few minutes later. As the two sat down in front of the fire, Morgan poured cups of steaming coffee and handed them to the hungry men. Then he filled some plates with the stew he had made.

While Bradford and Winslow ate with the husky wagoner, Washington was speaking with General Braddock. The two men liked each other, and after introducing his new aide to his staff, Braddock outlined the tactics he was planning. The man was so thorough he had mapped out the expedition down to the last pound of bacon in the supply wagons.

Standing next to Washington, Braddock was a foot shorter, with more fat than muscle in his bulk. He wore a powdered wig under his winged hat, and his uniform blazed with bright decorations. "Tell us, George, what kind of fighting conditions can we expect?" asked the general.

"Well, it's not going to be like some of the fighting you're used to. The terrain around our objective," Washington said, noting the officers' reactions, "is one of thick forests and broken gullies. It will be difficult to maneuver troops, General," he explained. "And you will discover that the enemy will not meet you with a massed force. Indians know nothing about that sort of warfare."

"Ah, yes, they fight from behind trees, I am told." Braddock's bulldog face had a stubborn cast. "We will see them flee when they meet trained troops of England. They will be no match for us."

🎺   🎺   🎺

Later, when Washington received Daniel's report on the condition of the horses, the colonel looked doubtful. "The train will break down, I fear," Washington said. "The general is taking two dozen six-pound cannons—not to mention four big howitzers and fourteen small mortars."

"Sir, the man has no idea of what he is getting into."

"I believe you're right, Daniel. I got the same impression when he asked me to explain to his staff about wilderness fighting. Some of those cannons he plans to take weigh over a ton." The tall man bit his lower lip, adding, "And then there's all the food for two thousand men and all the equipment."

"I met some of the men who'll be clearing the road," Daniel nodded. "But what bothers me is the lack of food for the horses. The general seems to have planned for his men but not for the animals. There's not enough in the train, and no horse can keep going on leaves!"

"Daniel, I want you to go buy a wagon and carry enough grain for our own animals," Washington decided.

Daniel waited until the man finished with some other instructions; then he went and found Winslow. They spent the next two days gathering sufficient supplies to take along. Daniel knew from his army days in England the rigors and demands that fighting put on the horses. He had learned in the battle at Culloden Moor against the Jacobites that if the animals weren't properly cared for, the army would suffer. It proved to be a wise decision, for later in the campaign, it was this food that kept their horses strong and active while others were starving.

The trek itself turned into a nightmare. The army moved out with all its equipment and slowly began its march north. Braddock sent a guard of highly trained British riflemen ahead of them with six blue-clad Virginians selected for their knowledge of the woods. On the flanks he kept outriders, and behind all these the three hundred axmen labored long and hard to clear the road. Every day was marked with endless hours of arduous toil. And the long train of men, horses, and supply wagons could only advance as fast as the axmen cleared the road ahead of them. The terrain proved to be an obstacle, as Washington had tried to inform the general. And the cannons Braddock had insisted on bringing were so large and cumbersome they slowed the advancing army down even more.

Washington wrote to his brother Jack about the difficulties they were having. He had tried to give advice to Braddock many times, but the general's arrogant responses had finally silenced him. As the days wore on, Washington learned to never give advice to Braddock unless asked for it.

In late June, the troops were plagued with dysentery, the old enemy of the soldier. Washington was among those who were afflicted. He became so weak he was forced to ride in the wagon, which Daniel drove. Unfortunately, the sickness came at a time when Braddock sorely needed the man's wise advice.

As time passed, Braddock grew more frustrated with the situation. He refused to listen to Washington's advice on fighting the enemy. And it was this inability to adapt to a new way of fighting and his harsh treatment of the troops that resulted in many bad choices along the way.

Braddock had been trained differently. For decades he prided himself as the general of highly trained soldiers who followed orders concerning military protocol down to the very details of a soldier's attire. The battles he had fought in Europe were often staged on large fields, where each day flanks of fresh troops in crisp red uniforms would advance across the battlefield like a colorful parade with guidons, drums, and trumpets. Here, each day was a lesson in survival as they cut through the thick forests. Some days the progress was slowed down by gullies, inclement weather, or broken wheels on the wagons. And as the troops trudged along through the wilderness, the stark contrast between the ideal soldier and the rag-tag appearance and behavior of the Americans grew daily in Braddock's mind.

The general made a grievous error one afternoon when a group of men from Pennsylvania came slouching in, offering to serve as scouts without pay. Their rugged appearance was so abhorrent to Braddock that he refused to use them. He was short with the Indians who accompanied the army, commanding them to wash off the grease on their faces—which they applied to repel mosquitoes. By alienating these men who knew the wilderness better than anybody, Braddock, in effect, lost the "eyes" of his army.

The British officers demanded the same sort of respect from the Americans as received from their own troops—which was impossible. One afternoon Daniel and Adam Winslow witnessed a scene neither of them would ever forget. Daniel was in line behind his friend Daniel Morgan, who was rebuked by an officer for moving along slowly. Morgan answered the man with a rough retort. At once the officer drew his sword and rushed toward the driver. Morgan snapped the sword from the hand of the officer and easily gave him a sound thrashing.

The cries of the officer drew instant help, and when Morgan was grasped by soldiers, the officer shouted, "Tie him to that wagon—give him twenty-five lashes!"

Morgan's shirt was stripped off, and a burly soldier stepped forward with a whip. Drawing it back, he brought it down across Morgan's naked back, raising a red welt. The beating went on forever, so it seemed to Bradford. Washington had heard the commotion and had lifted himself from his bed in the wagon to mutter, "Bad business!" When the last stroke was given, he said, "Take care of him, Daniel!"

Daniel and Adam joined Daniel Boone in cutting the unconscious man down. They bathed Morgan's back, applied ointment, then offered to drive his wagon.

"No! I'll drive it myself!" Morgan said, cursing the officer under his breath as he painfully climbed into the wagon. From that hour he nourished a bitter hatred for everything English.

🛡   🛡   🛡

Braddock's army arrived at the banks of the Monongahela River on July 9. The enemy lay directly ahead, and Washington had Daniel bring one of his horses with a pillow placed in the saddle. He had no fever, but he was extremely weak from suffering twenty days of the illness.

Getting into the saddle, he said, "Look—that's a beautiful sight, isn't it, Daniel?"

Bradford looked to see the red-coated regulars parade with unfurled guidons and drums beating and trumpets blaring. "I suppose the general's doing it to frighten the enemy," he said.

Adam Winslow said in his slow voice, "Somehow I don't think the enemy's going to run when they see a parade."

"Let's hope they do," Washington said, tight-lipped. "I don't like this ground. There's not much space to maneuver the troops and equipment. We need to get out of this thick wood."

The French commander, Captain Daniel Lienard de Baujeu, was well aware of the terrain and used it to his advantage. He was leading a heterogeneous army of Indians, and his scouts had kept him well informed on the progress of the advancing army. Now as Braddock crossed the Monongahela, Baujeu detected a weakness he could exploit. The British had moved into a *cul de sac*, with thickets on all three sides, and were flanked by deep gullies. At once he cried out, "Fire—kill the English!"

Lieutenant Colonel Thomas Gage was in the group that received the first fire from the enemy. He ordered his men into the battlefront and commanded them to return fire. The soldiers could see nothing, but they pointed their muskets at the bush and fired. The volley tore off leaves and twigs, leaving heavy smoke lingering around the trees.

Gage ordered his men to reload, then ordered again, "Fire!" Baujeu fell with a bullet in his forehead, and cannon came up to reinforce the foot soldiers.

The French fell back, and Captain Jean Dumas took command. "Do not fear them, my children!" he rallied. "See, when their officers order them to fire, there will be a time when they must reload. Take cover, then, after the volley, we will move in and have them!"

At this point, Braddock could have moved back to clear ground, but to retreat in the face of the enemy was a sign of weakness. His inflexibility in changing his style of fighting prevented him from ordering his men to take cover behind the trees. Instead, he rode to the forefront of the battle to urge the troops on. He was shocked to see the Virginians and the Pennsylvania axmen taking cover behind the trees. With the flat of his sword he beat his own men out of the cover and sent his aides to order the Virginians to fight in the open.

Boone was fighting beside Daniel Bradford and Adam Winslow. "It's like sending a cow to catch a rabbit!" he exclaimed. "Them Indians will cut them redcoats to ribbons—look at 'em, Dan! Going into them woods like they was on parade!"

Daniel Bradford was appalled at what he witnessed. To him it was plain suicide.

Adam shook his head, muttering, "They'll get slaughtered!"

Washington was also horrified at the sight. He rode up to Braddock to tell him to pull back.

Braddock saw him draw up at his side mounted on a powerful steed and said, "Now, sir, you will see how the English soldier handles an enemy!" He lifted his voice, shouting, "Charge!" and the troops slowly moved forward.

"Sir—this is the enemy's main body. We're outnumbered!" Washington protested.

"Nonsense! It's just a few skirmishers!" Braddock scoffed. But suddenly the general's horse was struck with a ball, and as he fell, Braddock screamed, "Charge the enemy!"

The massive force moved forward, marching in ranks, officers

197

on horseback, drums beating the cadence. A wall of red filled the entire road as the men walked shoulder to shoulder.

Suddenly the woods erupted with a blaze of musket shots. Bullets hailed from the unsecured heights, and every bullet seemed to find a target! Within minutes the column was decimated. Yet the officers continued to order volleys into the woods at an enemy they could not see. Washington pleaded with Braddock to allow the Virginians to seek shelter, but Braddock insisted, "Let the French play the coward, but not we English!"

And so the senseless slaughter continued. The only remarkable thing about this battle was that the English lasted as long as they did. The first volley was fired early afternoon, and they remained on the field for more than three hours.

As the British officers fell, confusion and panic began to grip the remaining soldiers. Washington knew what would happen if they lost all sense of leadership. Seeing that most of Braddock's staff was killed, he took command and rode tall in the saddle, amid the screaming bullets, carrying out Braddock's orders. The soldiers sensed the man's courage and threw themselves back into the battle. Four bullets left burns where they cut through his coat. Two horses were shot from under him, but he never faltered. He secured a new mount and plunged back into the fray giving orders.

When a Mingo chief saw that no shot took the big man, he ordered his warriors, "Aim at somebody you can kill. The Big Man is under the protection of the Great Spirit!"

The fighting was so fierce that men were falling like flies all around. Daniel Morgan, his back a mass of scabs and scars, was struck in the back of the neck by a bullet that lodged in his mouth. He spat it out and kept firing!

Shortly after five-thirty, Braddock finally gave up hope. In two hours he had had four horses shot dead under him. Finally a bullet found its mark, passing through an arm and penetrating his lung. The fall of their leader sent the English army retreating in wild disorder. It was Washington who was the marvel of the day. He saved them by quickly organizing the Virginians and the Pennsylvania axmen into a rear guard, which held off the enemy.

Daniel Bradford was in the thick of the battle the whole time, fighting alongside Adam Winslow and Daniel Boone. The battle had been bad, but the retreat was even worse. All night they rode under the failing light of a dim moon. The casualties had been heavy, and at times their horses stepped on wounded men. Daniel was numbed by the agonizing cries of the dying. Some of the screams in the distance, he knew, came as Indians stopped to collect scalps. He shuddered at the thought and plodded on.

Fortunately the French were not able to follow up their victory. The fourth night after the battle Braddock died of his wound. Just before he died, he muttered faintly, "Who would have thought it? His Majesty's troops defeated by the French and Indians. We will know better how to deal with them another time."

The next morning Washington chose a burial place in the middle of the road and directed a brief funeral service. After the shrouded body was lowered into the grave, he ordered every wagon, every horse, and every soldier to march over it. The mound was flattened and no epitaph was written, so that the fallen general's body would not be dug up for a victory scalp and a resplendent uniform.

And so the battle was over—and the vaunted general and his trained troops were defeated.

As Washington and his two young aides made their way back home, they spoke little of the humiliating defeat they had just suffered. Only once did Washington give any indication of the tremendous grief he felt. The three were sitting before a campfire one evening, eating beef roasted on sticks. "All those brave men," he said suddenly, shaking his massive head. "And all for nothing!" Neither Adam nor Daniel replied, and finally George Washington added thoughtfully, "Perhaps one thing came of it—we know that the English method of war will not work in this country. Though it was a costly lesson that could have been avoided."

Washington and Adam Winslow left Daniel when they came to the crossroad that led to Mount Vernon. Daniel made his way back to Fairhope, depressed. His time of indenture was almost up, however, and he consoled himself with the thought that he would soon be a free man. Boone had invited him to join a group going over the mountains to settle in Kentucky, and Washington had offered him a job at Mount Vernon.

Finally he said aloud, "I'll be my own man—and that's more than I've been lately!" He thought of Lyna with sadness, wishing she were still alive so that the two of them might find a life together in this new world. Then he spurred his horse toward Fair-hope, anxious to see Holly—and thinking about Marian Frazier.

"I wonder if Marian has missed me." But then he shook his head, knowing that even if she had, such things were not to be.

16

TWO WOMEN

AFTER THE EXCITEMENT OF MILITARY LIFE, Daniel discovered that getting back into the flow of life at Fairhope was difficult. He had hated the blood and the suffering he'd seen at the Monongahela. But after years of indentured servitude, the freedom the adventure had offered was very appealing. It had opened up new vistas to Daniel and made him anxious for his time to come to an end at Fairhope.

Leo Rochester noted Daniel's restlessness as soon as he returned. One day Leo came to the stables and said sarcastically, "I suppose farming is too tame for a military hero?" Daniel said nothing but continued to fix the strap on the saddle he was working on. Rochester impatiently slapped his hands against his sides. "I'll not get much work out of you before you leave, I suppose."

"You've gotten your money's worth out of me," Daniel shrugged. His time of indenture would be up on the first day of 1756, and he was aware that the scent of freedom from Rochester was another factor that added to his restlessness.

Rochester hesitated, then nodded. "I can't deny that. Your knowledge of horses has helped line my pockets quite well. As a matter of fact, I'd like you to stay on." He laughed at Daniel's look of astonishment, adding, "I know—we've not been friends, but I need you around here. I'm no farmer—never will be. You've got the experience it takes to run this place properly." Leo had been mulling it over for weeks. Things had not run as smoothly during Daniel's absence. "You'll be manager of the whole estate. I'll give you a percentage of all the profits. Contract for five more years,

201

and at the end of that time, you'll have enough money to buy your own farm if that's what you'd like."

"A generous offer, Mr. Rochester—but I'll be moving on."

Rochester felt a tinge of regret, but he was not surprised by Bradford's response. He had expected no other. "Very well, I'll have to get what I can out of you before you leave. I have an important errand for you. I want you to take six horses to Boston and deliver them to John Frazier."

"Miss Marian's father?" said Daniel in surprise.

"Of course." Leo noted the interest in Daniel's eyes and laughed. "You two were pretty thick when she visited here— spent almost every minute together riding. Well, one of the horses is a gift for her. I think it'll make her give in—stubborn wench!" His courtship of Marian had not prospered, but Rochester was a patient man when he wanted something—and he wanted the fortune that would come along with the only child of John Frazier, who owned a profitable foundry.

"When do you want them delivered?"

"Leave in the morning," said Leo.

Surprised at the suddenness of it, Daniel listened as Leo discussed the details. He had misgivings about Leo's interest in Marian, but said nothing as Leo went on.

Finally Leo cocked his head and smiled sardonically. "I don't suppose I can expect you to put in a good word for me, Daniel— just don't pour any of your hatred for me into my intended's shell-like ear." He laughed, then turned and walked back to the house.

Daniel was glad for the chance to get away from Fairhope. He even found himself anxious to see Marian Frazier again. He had never met a woman who intrigued him so, and he felt rather foolish for thinking of her. *She's in another world, Dan Bradford! Besides, Leo Rochester has his eyes on her,* he scolded himself.

He spent the rest of the afternoon preparing Lonnie Bates, his helper, on what to do during his absence, then went to say good-bye to Holly. Since his return he had spent little time with her. As he walked toward the kitchen, he wondered again what was troubling her. When he'd left, she'd been happy, but on his return he'd found her pale and subdued. She kept to herself and didn't talk as much to him as she used to. He was worried about her, for he could tell that something was wrong, yet he could not find a way to help.

"Well, Holly, I'm off again," he said when he entered the kitchen. She was sitting at the table shelling peas, and at his words, she looked up at him with an expression he couldn't define. Her eyes, which were usually bright, were dull, and her lips were drawn into a thin line. He hesitated, then sat down across from her. The kitchen was deserted for the moment, and he hated to leave her in such a despondent condition. "What's the matter, Holly? Are you sick?"

"No. I'm all right," she said as she worked.

Daniel noted that her voice, which was usually cheerful, had no joy in it. She looked—*different*, somehow, though he couldn't put his finger on what made her appear so.

She asked diffidently, "Where are you going, Daniel?" She listened as he explained his errand, then said quietly, "I hope you have a good time."

Daniel sat beside her for twenty minutes, but she was withdrawn, responding to his questions in a lackluster manner. Finally he said in a perplexed voice, "Something's wrong with you, Holly. I wish you'd tell me what it is. Maybe I can help."

For a moment, he thought she meant to speak out about whatever troubled her. She lifted her eyes to him, and for one brief instant he saw a ray of hope, and her lips opened slightly—then she closed them and shook her head. "There's nothing, really," she said, but he thought he saw tears beginning to form.

"I've got to leave, but as soon as I get back, we'll have a long talk," Daniel said. He rose and put his hand under her chin, entreating her to look up at him. Seeing the pure misery in her eyes, he said gently, "I don't like to see you like this, Holly. Whatever's bothering you, when I get home, I want you to tell me about it."

He gave her a quick farewell, then spent a troubled night worrying about her. Awake before dawn, he saddled up Midnight, and, with Mr. Frazier's horses in tow, started out on his journey to Boston. All along the way he thought about the troubled look in Holly's face. *She was so happy when I left to go with Washington— and now she's downright miserable. Guess I know a little of what that's like.* He realized how fond of her he'd grown, so he determined to get to the bottom of it as soon as he returned from delivering the horses.

T   T   T

The city of Boston was a busy place, and Daniel had some trouble guiding his small herd of horses through the crowded streets. He threaded his way through multitudes of horse-drawn wagons filled with heavy loads of produce. As he led his animals past Back Bay and through the town gates, geese and chickens exploded in noisy flocks in front of him. He had some difficulty finding the Frazier residence, but finally, after getting two sets of wrong directions, he pulled up in front of a very large white house set thirty yards back off the street. Most of the houses opened up right on the sidewalks, but this one, he saw, was built more like a country house, with large pillars holding up a portico and mullioned windows on the front and the sides.

He led the horses down the circular drive, stopping to ask the black man who was carefully clipping the green grass, "Is this Mr. Frazier's house?"

"Yes, indeed, sir." The man was tall and thin, with chocolate-colored skin and large intelligent eyes. "These must be the horses Mr. Rochester is selling. I'm Cato. Come with me, sir, and I'll help you stable them." He led the small procession around to the back of the house, where a brick stable offered ten stalls. As Cato helped Daniel put the horses into individual stalls, he said, "I'll feed them, Mr. Bradford. You'd best go see Miss Frazier." His white teeth gleamed as he smiled. "She ain't talked 'bout nothin' but these here horses for a week. Just go to the side door, and Emmy will fetch Miss Marian."

Daniel followed his instructions, and shortly Marian Frazier came running into the foyer, her green eyes alive with pleasure. She came to him, offering her hand, exclaiming, "I thought you'd *never* get here, Daniel! Did you bring the horses?"

Very conscious of her smooth hand in his, Daniel nodded. "I don't think I'd be very welcome if I'd come without them, would I?" He released her hand, intensely aware of her vibrant beauty. She was wearing a rose-colored dress that clung to her body, and her full lips were smiling with the same excitement he remembered.

"We'll go riding right away—but first I want to see them." She practically towed him out of the house and into the stables. Going from one horse to another, she demanded to know the names, the virtues, and the shortcomings of each one. When she came to the fine chestnut mare, the prize of the lot, she whispered, "What a beauty!"

"This one's for you, Miss Frazier—a present from Mr. Rochester."

Instantly Marian turned to face him, a strange expression on her face. "A present? What sort of present?"

Daniel couldn't repeat what Rochester had said, so he merely shook his head. "Just a present, I guess. She's the finest mare I've seen since I've been at Fairhope. Her name is Queenie."

Somehow the gift disturbed Marian. She stood there, absently stroking the nose of the mare, her eyes thoughtful. Finally she turned and asked, "Did he give you a message to go with the present?"

Daniel felt very awkward and wished she hadn't asked about Leo Rochester. He felt that she would be making a terrible mistake to marry the man—but how could he tell her that? Looking at the clean lines of her face, he hated the idea of her being the wife of a man who had no scruples or sense of decency. But he could only say, "No, Miss Frazier—no message."

The first wave of excitement that had brightened her eyes now faded away. Her voice was more restrained as she said, "Come along. I'll take you to my father and you two can get acquainted. Later, perhaps you'll come for a ride with me."

"Like we used to do at Fairhope?" Daniel suggested. "I've thought of our rides many times."

Marian looked at him and her good humor returned. "Have you? So have I." Mischief caused her eyes to gleam, and she suddenly laughed. "I can still beat you in a race—you'll see!"

Daniel spent a pleasant half hour with John Frazier and took an instant liking to the man. Frazier was a rather short man with piercing blue eyes and a set of fine whiskers, which he stroked fondly. He was an astute businessman, having worked his way up from a hired hand to becoming the owner of one of the largest foundries in the Colonies.

"My daughter tells me you're a fine blacksmith, Bradford," he said after they had settled the details of the sale. "Perhaps you'd like to see my foundry before you leave Boston. Be glad to show you around."

"I'd like that very much, sir," Daniel said eagerly.

"Well, *if* you can get away from Marian in the morning, you can go with me. She thinks you know more about horses than any man alive, and I think she has plans to keep you pretty busy."

The gentleman's words proved true, for Daniel spent the rest of the afternoon with Marian, trying out the new mare. They rode outside the city, and he discovered that she knew every inch where a horse could be ridden. When they were on a level green bordered by fences, she gave him an arch look. "Are you prepared to let me beat you in another race?"

Daniel was mounted on a tall, rawboned gelding named Fred and knew he had little chance to beat the speedy mare. "No bets—but we'll see."

Marian spurred her horse and took off across the field. Daniel followed her in pursuit, but as he had expected, Queenie beat the big horse easily, but he didn't care. He pulled up beside Marian, whose light green eyes were gleaming with pleasure. "You like to win, don't you?" he asked.

"Of course! Don't you?" she breathed, her face aglow from the ride.

"Haven't had much experience along those lines." Not wanting to sound pitiful, Daniel quickly added, "Next time I'll ride Big Red—he'll show you his heels."

"Tomorrow morning," Marian nodded. "We'll come early."

"Your father offered to show me around the foundry in the morning."

"Oh, Daniel, it's just a sooty, black, noisy old place!"

"It makes the money that buys you fine horses and pretty outfits like that one." She flushed slightly at his compliment, which surprised him greatly. *I'd think she'd be up to her pretty neck in pretty speeches.*

They moved along through the countryside, and he enjoyed the ride more than anything he could remember. When they returned and pulled up in front of the stables at the back of the house, Daniel helped her down.

"So you'd rather go with Father to the foundry than go riding with me?" she pouted. "I think I resent that, Daniel." But she was smiling and added, "All right—but tomorrow afternoon is *mine!*"

Daniel agreed, and the next morning he went with Mr. Frazier to see the foundry. He enjoyed his visit and watched everything carefully. Once he offered a suggestion that brought an approving glance from Mr. Frazier. Afterward, when he was leaving, pleading his promise to ride with Marian, Mr. Frazier said, "I'm always looking for good men, Bradford. Would you ever think of leaving your present position? I think I could find a place for you."

Daniel thanked him, and later when he was riding beside Marian down a shady lane, he told her of her father's offer.

"But would you like to leave Fairhope?" she asked at once. "Leo told me he planned to offer you a good position there when your indenture is up."

Daniel hesitated, then shook his head. "I'll be leaving the first of the year."

A few minutes later they came to a stream and dismounted. Daniel held the lines and let the horses drink, then tied them to a sapling. Coming to stand beside her, he looked around, "Pretty here—like Virginia."

The clear water murmured in a sibilant fashion over the smooth stones, reflecting the sunbeams with tiny flakes of light. The trees formed a natural canopy, giving the spot the air of a cathedral, and the green turf was soft under their feet.

"Daniel . . ." Marian said hesitantly, her eyes coming to rest on him. "What sort of man is Leo?"

"Why, you know him, Miss Frazier!"

"No, I don't. He's handsome and witty—and rich, of course." She bit her lower lip, which was a most attractive gesture to Daniel. She seemed uncertain for the first time since he'd met her. "I . . . I suppose all young women about to be married get nervous. It's . . . such a big thing, isn't it? I'll have to live with the man I marry until one of us dies. What if I make the wrong choice?" She suddenly took his arm, her grip tight, and there was something close to fear in her eyes. "You've been with him for a long time—and nobody knows a person as well as a servant does. You've seen him when he's off guard. So tell me, Daniel, what's he really like?"

Daniel had never been at such a loss for speech. All the years he had known Leo Rochester only confirmed the first opinion he'd formed that day so long ago in England. Leo was a self-serving man spoiled by his aristocratic upbringing, a man of unbridled desires who did not care what happened to others who got in his way. Marriage to such a man would be disastrous for this young woman. He knew that Leo Rochester was selfish to the bone, that he would never be faithful to any one woman. *How can I say that to her? But she needs to know what he is like,* he thought as they stood by the stream.

Turning to her, he said quietly, "I can't tell you what to do. But I can say, be very careful, Marian. He's a strange man."

Marian listened to his words, and for one moment she seemed completely vulnerable. She was an impulsive young woman, filled with the joy of living, but as she looked up into his eyes, she seemed to be begging for assurance.

She closed her eyes and whispered, "Oh, Daniel—I just don't know anymore!"

Daniel felt a great desire to protect her, knowing what lay ahead for her if she married Leo. He didn't deserve a woman who could give herself so totally to life. Moved by his thoughts and the moment, Daniel put his arms around her. She looked up, a startled expression in her eyes. He expected her to draw back, to protest, but she did not. Instead she leaned against him and whispered, "Daniel!"

Somehow a dream formed that he knew he'd had for years—yet he could not bring it out of the misty background, nor cause it to take shape. When she looked up at him with those light green eyes, he bent down and kissed her. He felt her wishes come up to him and suddenly knew that she was thinking of him as a woman thought of a man.

Marian welcomed his kiss. She had never given herself to a man's tender touch, but now as she felt the power of his arms, she made that surrender that she'd never been able to make. She had been struggling with her decision, but as she leaned against Daniel's chest, all that seemed far away.

Somehow a barrier had fallen, and she knew it would never be completely restored. In one brief moment, they had crossed the line between friends who care for each other to a man and a woman who feel the powerful surge of a new love. The effect of this kiss, she knew, would be with her for a long time. They were on the edge of the mystery which made love so desperate and so desirable a thing—and she wished she could always have this feeling of security—and of being loved.

"Marian . . ." he whispered as he looked at her. In that brief instant, he had hoped that what he felt could last forever. But he knew there could be no future for them. "I . . . didn't mean to do that."

Marian straightened at once and saw the desire in his face—and the hopelessness. She suddenly understood what he was thinking—*We're separated by everything. No one would understand—and life would be impossible.*

Marian felt a sharp stab of regret but knew what she had to do. "We're entitled to one mistake, Daniel," she said in a weary tone. She turned to the horses, and he helped to hand her up. They rode in silence for a few moments, then finally began to speak of unimportant things.

The next day Daniel left Boston at dawn. He had bid farewell to Mr. Frazier the night before, but he had not seen Marian. Daniel knew he would not see her again.

All the way back to Virginia, he was morose and withdrawn. Somehow he knew he'd lost something precious—*But it was never mine—never could be mine!* he told himself.

When he finally pulled up in front of Fairhope, he stared at it and said aloud, "I can't have her—but I'll not stay here and watch her be married to him!"

🎺   🎺   🎺

If Daniel had not been so depressed by what happened on his trip to Boston, he might have noted that Holly was even more withdrawn than ever. But he was kept busy by new orders from Rochester, and on his free time, he kept mostly to himself.

About a week after he'd been back, Mrs. Bryant approached him while he was working with a new horse. She came right up to him, put her hands on her hips, and said, "Daniel, can't you talk to Holly?"

Later that day Daniel came to the house to get some scraps of linens, and her words caught at him. "Holly? What's wrong with her?"

Mrs. Bryant clucked her tongue and shook her head. "Men! You're all as blind as bats! I could drown the lot of you!" Her face was red with anger, and she faced him squarely. She was an angular woman, as tall as Daniel, and there was something formidable about her. She studied the face of the young man, then lowered her voice. "She's in trouble—bad trouble!"

Daniel stared at her blankly. "What kind of trouble?" he asked.

"What kind of trouble would a pretty young girl be in?" Mrs. Bryant was a plain woman and had been exposed to a bad marriage. She had a low opinion of most men, and now she shook her head almost fiercely. "Poor thing! She's green as grass, and some man's gone and taken advantage of her, Daniel."

Shock rolled along Daniel's nerves. "She told you this?"

"No, she didn't tell me—but I have eyes, don't I?" The angry eyes of the woman fastened on Daniel. "I thought it might be you—she's been in love with you ever since she came."

"Why—that's foolish!" Then Daniel added abruptly, "No, I've done nothing to her. And you may be wrong."

"She's leaving, did you know that? Why would she leave here if she didn't have to—and where's the poor thing going to go?"

Daniel felt a heaviness settle on him. Then anger rose at the thought of some man deceiving the innocent girl, but he fought it down, "I'll talk to her, Mrs. Bryant."

The woman studied him, then nodded, pain etched in her eyes. "Be kind to her, Daniel. She's the sort who knows all too well what rough treatment is." She turned, saying, "I'll send her out to you—go down to the grape arbor. It's quiet there."

Daniel left the house and walked down toward the arbor, his mind struggling with the tragedy. He felt a mixture of sympathy and concern; but at the same time, a burning anger at whoever had done it gripped him. He knew that Holly was a devoted Christian—and if this was true, it would make it even worse for her. He knew she had no place on earth to go, and the weight of that lay heavily on him.

Ten minutes later, she came down the path slowly. Daniel rose at once. "Holly, sit down," he said. Her face was pale and drawn, and her eyes were pools of despair. She sat down dumbly, and Daniel said, "Mrs. Bryant's told me about . . . about your trouble." He waited for her to speak, but she seemed to be paralyzed. Finally he asked quietly, "Are you going to have a baby, Holly?"

She dropped her head and tears rolled down her cheeks. Daniel put his arm around her, murmuring, "I'm so sorry, Holly. Is there anything I can do to help you?"

Holly turned to face him, her soft lips forming the words, "Oh, Daniel—I wish I were dead!"

"Don't talk like that!" Daniel was deeply moved by the terrible grief and shame he saw in the girl's eyes. His heart went out to her, and for a long time he sat beside her, gently assuring her that things would work out. Finally he said, "You can't leave here, Holly—"

Instantly she said, "Oh, but I must! I can't stay here!"

Abruptly Daniel thought of why she was so determined. "Who's the father of the child, Holly? He may want to marry you."

"No!" Holly cried. Leaping to her feet, she ran back up the path, leaving Daniel to stare after her. A mockingbird hopped up on the limb of the cherry tree to his left and began to chirp. Daniel stared at the bird, then whirled and ran after the girl, calling her name. . . .

17

A Free Man

AS THE LAST DAYS OF HIS INDENTURED time passed, Daniel became strangely moody, going about his work in a half-hearted fashion. His fellow servants couldn't understand his lack of excitement.

"Lord, if I was about to get myself out of this place and be my own man," Micah Roundtree exclaimed, "I wouldn't be mopin' around like you've been, Daniel! What's wrong with you?"

But Daniel had merely shrugged and gone about his duties. When the last week of his time rolled around, Leo called him to his office in the house. It was not as large as the one at Milford Manor, but Leo had furnished it quite well with the profits from selling the fine horses Daniel raised. When Daniel walked in, Leo was standing behind a large oak desk, a glass of brandy in his hand. Coming around the side, he shoved a small sheaf of bills at Daniel, saying, "There's the cash your papers called for." He hesitated, then said, "Now that you're a free man, what will you be doing?"

Daniel had kept his plans secret until now, but he saw no reason not to tell Rochester. "I'll be opening a blacksmith shop in Dentonville," he said evenly. It was a small town far enough away from Fairhope to escape his memories but close enough to Mount Vernon to serve as Washington's blacksmith. He did not add that it was George Washington himself who had suggested the matter and had, in fact, underwritten Daniel's initial expenses.

Leo Rochester stared at Daniel and said only, "You've earned your freedom, Bradford. We're not the same sort, are we? The first

213

time we met, it was a fight. We're just not the same cut of cloth. But good luck to you."

Daniel took the bills, then turned and walked out of the office, hoping he never would have dealings with Leo Rochester again. He strongly disliked the man's vile character, and that would never change. He had suffered at the hands of the man more than once during his indenture. Many times the anger almost consumed him, causing him to strike out. But over the years Daniel had learned to control it, knowing that Rochester would have no qualms at throwing him back into prison.

He spent the rest of the day in the forge, his mind on the future—but when dusk came, he laid his tools down for the last time at Fairhope and went to gather up his belongings. As he tidied up the cabin he'd built and put on clean clothes, he thought of Holly—as he had done almost unceasingly since he'd found out she was in trouble. Every day he'd sought her out, trying to cheer her, but nothing seemed to lift her spirits. She had insisted that she was leaving, and when he tried to discover her plans, she seemed to have none—except to escape from Fairhope as soon as possible.

The wind was sharp when he stepped outside, and he sniffed the cold air. Tiny flakes of snow burned on his face, and he knew that by morning the ground would be covered. He went to the back door of the house, entered and found Mrs. Bryant cooking supper. "Where's Holly?" he asked at once.

Mrs. Bryant gave him a sharp look. "She's not been down this afternoon. I think she's getting ready to leave, Daniel. There's no talking to her."

"Go and get her, will you, Mrs. Bryant?"

Wiping her hands on her apron, she left the kitchen to get Holly. Daniel waited, and shortly Mrs. Bryant came hurrying back, her eyes wide with disbelief. "She's gone, Daniel—look, she left a note."

Daniel took the note and read it quickly. He could tell it had been written in a hurry. It simply said, "I can't stay here any longer. Thank you for your many kindnesses, Mrs. Bryant. Tell Daniel I couldn't bear to say goodbye to him."

Daniel scanned the note again quickly, then his mind began working. "You didn't see her leave?"

"I haven't seen her since two o'clock. She was in her room

then. Oh, what will the poor child do in her condition?" Mrs. Bryant said, her voice breaking.

"She's headed for town," Daniel said instantly. "It's the only place she could get a coach to leave here. I'll find her, don't worry." He left the house, hitched a horse to the buggy, and drove out at a fast gait. Doxbury was the closest stage stop, and it was fully ten miles away. He turned west and kept the horse at a trot as the snow began to leave a soft white blanket on the ground.

As he drove he thought of Holly's plight, and the image of her tragic face came to him. His affection for her had grown over the months, and now he realized he was going to have to do something. *She can't take care of herself,* he thought, his eyes probing the road ahead. *She's as helpless as a kitten!*

He had not gone three miles when he saw her—a pathetic figure trudging along the whitened roadway struggling with a bundle. He felt a gust of relief and hurried the horses on. When he drew close, he pulled the buggy to the side of the road.

"Holly!" he called, leaping down and running to her. She turned to him and met his eyes with a hopeless expression. He took her arm and held it tightly. "Come on, get in the buggy."

"I can't go back, Daniel."

Seeing that she was adamant, Daniel nodded. "All right, we won't go back. Give me that!" He took her small bundle and led her to the buggy. When he'd helped her in, he put the bundle in the back and wrapped a blanket around her. "We'll go to Doxbury," he said. "I'll get you a room in the inn."

She didn't answer. All the way to town, Daniel tried to get her to speak, but she could only answer in monosyllables. Finally they reached the small town, and he pulled up in front of the White Hart Inn. "Come along," he said. When they entered, they were greeted by the innkeeper, a rotund, elderly woman named Mrs. Bixby. "I need a room for this lady, ma'am," he said quickly.

"For how long?"

"Well, overnight at least."

Mrs. Bixby gave a curious glance at the pair, then nodded. "Come along, I'll show it to you." She led them to a room upstairs. It was small, but at least it was clean. Besides the bed, it had a stand with a washbasin, a single chair, and a fireplace. "That'll be two dollars—in advance," she said. Taking the coins from Daniel, she asked, "Will the young lady be wanting supper?"

"Could you bring something to the room—for both of us?" Daniel asked.

Mrs. Bixby's eyes narrowed, but she nodded at Daniel. "Certainly, sir."

When she left, Daniel said, "I'll get a fire started, Holly. It's going to be cold tonight."

Soon a cheerful fire was blazing in the fireplace and Mrs. Bixby brought them some roast beef, bread, and a pitcher of ale.

"Here, this looks good," Daniel said, offering one of the wooden trenchers to Holly.

"I'm not hungry."

Daniel hesitated, then said, "You've not got only yourself to think of. There's the baby to consider now."

Holly started and gave Daniel a shocked look. It was as if she had not been aware that the child she bore was a person who had to be considered. She had been so overwhelmed by the shame of her tragedy that she had forgotten the baby growing within her. In her mind this little one was not yet a living, breathing human who would be a part of her life. Now she was brought face-to-face with the hard fact that she could never again think only of herself—the baby would be part of her in everything.

She took the wooden plate, ate a bite, then took a swallow of the ale. "It's . . . it's good, Daniel," she said, trying to smile.

"Did you eat anything this morning?" asked Daniel, a tender look in his eyes.

"No. I was too sick."

"Well, you'll have to have good food. Even *I* know that much about having babies."

He was encouraged as Holly ate a little more, and as the fire crackled, he began to speak gently of unimportant things. Finally she finished her meal, and he stirred up the fire. The flames flared up, sending myriads of sparks swirling up the chimney. "Fire's nice—nothing like a good warm fire when snow's falling."

"I've always loved the snow." Holly curled up in the chair, drawing her feet under her. The food had made her sleepy, and she sat quietly as Daniel spoke of his boyhood, and of the heavy snows he'd seen back in England.

Seeing that Holly was exhausted, Daniel said, "You need to rest. I'll be leaving you now." When fear leaped into her eyes he added reassuringly, "I'll be back tomorrow. You sleep late, and we'll have dinner together. Maybe take a walk in the snow—might even build a snowman." He saw her relax and smiled at her. "Good-night, Holly. You get some rest, now."

Daniel left the White Hart and started back to Fairhope, but he was troubled with Holly's situation. All the way back his mind was filled with disturbing thoughts. She was so young and vulnerable. He shuddered at the thought of what could have become of her if she had run away. As soon as he arrived back at Fairhope, he unhitched the horse and rubbed it down, then went to the kitchen and told Mrs. Bryant where Holly was staying. "She's all right, but something's got to be done," he said, shaking his head.

"She's too young, Daniel, to be facing this alone. She only has her brother, but she don't get along with that wife of his. What's she going to do?" she said, wringing her hands.

"I don't right know, Mrs. Bryant, but we have to figure out something." Excusing himself, Daniel went to his cabin and sat at his handmade desk, racking his brain. An hour later he heard a knock at the door and got up to open it.

"Hello, Mistuh Daniel." Horace, the slave in charge of the grounds, smiled at him. "I come to ask you how Miss Holly is."

"Come in, Horace." Daniel stepped back, and when the small man stepped inside, he said, "She's all right for now. I got her a room in Doxbury."

"Poor little chile!" Horace was the pastor of the small black congregation that gathered every Sunday. He and his wife, Molly, had become very fond of Holly since the first day she had shown up for the Sunday service. She had come to his services faithfully, and now Horace asked, "Whut she gonna do, Mistuh Daniel? I is worried about her."

"So am I, Horace. . . ." Daniel bade the man sit down, and for some time the two of them talked over the problem. Finally Daniel said, "I can't think of a thing, Horace. Don't know *what* to do! She's got to go somewhere to have the baby."

Horace shook his head. "If we could, me and my Molly would take her in—but Mistuh Rochester ain't gonna allow dat." His kindly face was twisted as he sat there thinking. Finally he looked at Daniel and said, "Is you a praying man, Mistuh Daniel?"

"I . . . I don't think I am," said Daniel, a bit surprised by the man's gentle question.

"Well, mebby you ain't been up to now—but it 'pears to me

217

dat you is gonna *have* to start lookin' to de Lawd." Horace spoke for some time, giving Daniel several scriptures, including one that Daniel had never heard. "De Book, it say, 'And thine ears shall hear a word behind thee, sayin', This is the way, walk ye in it, when ye turn to the right hand, and when ye turn to the left.' Now *dat* is the promise of God, Mistuh Daniel!"

"Where is that, Horace?" Daniel demanded. "I never heard it."

"Right smack dab in Isaiah thirty, the twenty-first verse."

Daniel was not a great reader of the Scriptures, and his religion had been of a perfunctory nature. He had never forgotten his promise to his dying mother, however, and now he said doubtfully, "I don't think I'm in much favor with God, Horace. I haven't served Him like I should have."

"Why, dere's no better time to start than now. De good Lawd, He ain't particular 'bout dat! If He *wuz*, why, ain't none of us sinners could get nothin' from Him! But He say He loves you—and when you find a promise, why, jest hang on to it!"

Daniel suddenly nodded. "Well, I sure *need* to hear from God, Horace. You better pray that He gives me an answer—and pretty fast."

After the slave left, Daniel went to his trunk, pulled out his Bible, and found the verse Horace had just quoted to him. He read it several times, then found pen and ink and marked it carefully. He sat for a long time, doing what he'd never done—seeking God. . . .

🔔   🔔   🔔

On the fourth day of the year 1756, Holly was in her room waiting for Daniel. He'd promised her that he'd come early, and she had risen and was already dressed when his knock came.

"Come in," she said, opening the door. The days she had spent at the inn had restored some of her good nature, and she smiled as he entered. "Well, you're a free man now, aren't you, Daniel Bradford?"

"Yes, I am, Holly." Daniel was somber, she saw, and looked tired. But there was a peace in his eyes that was different. He suddenly took her hands, saying, "I'm not a servant of Leo Rochester, anyway." He hesitated, then said, "Holly, something's happened to me. . . ."

Holly listened as he told her of Horace's visit, and how he'd spent the last three days seeking God. She was very much aware that he was still holding her hands.

" . . . and I've been praying for God to tell me what to do—and He has, Holly!" Daniel's eyes suddenly grew misty—something that was rare indeed—and he was struggling for words. Finally he said, "Last night . . . God spoke to me!"

"Daniel. . . !"

"Oh, not in a literal voice, Holly, but it was God, I know it!"

"What did He tell you?" said Holly, looking at him intently now.

"He told me what to do with my life—and it was about you, Holly." Daniel dropped her hands and gripped her shoulders. With a tenderness in his hazel eyes, Daniel rushed on, "Holly, I know this is sudden, but I truly believe God has shown me that He wants me to be your husband and a father to your child. Holly, you and I will be together! You'll never be alone again!"

Holly was so shocked she couldn't speak. Daniel's words fell on her ears, but she couldn't believe she'd heard him rightly. And then he took her in his arms and kissed her. She surrendered to his strength, clinging to him fiercely. Leaning against him, she whispered with her face pressed against his chest, "Daniel . . . are you *sure* it's of God?"

Daniel Bradford held her possessively, whispering, "Yes, I'm sure, Holly. We'll have our troubles to face, like anybody else . . . but whatever happens, I'll always know that God is with us . . . because He's the one who's telling me to take you for my wife!"

🜚   🜚   🜚

April sunshine splashed on the big man as he galloped into Dentonville. He pulled his gray stallion up with a flourish under the sign that read, DANIEL BRADFORD, BLACKSMITH. He came off his mount with the smooth motion of a natural-born horseman and greeted the man who came out to him. "Good morning, Daniel—what a day, eh?"

Daniel wiped his hands on his apron, then took the hand offered him. "Yes, it is, Colonel Washington. Reminds me of the time we were on our way to the Monongahela."

Washington smiled briefly, saying, "That seems long ago now, but it was just last year. I'll never forget it." Since that time, Washington had thrown his energy into restoring Mount Vernon. In the last year, he had already erected new buildings, refurnished the house, and even experimented with some new crops.

"How is the farm, sir?"

"Oh, business is excellent. And your good wife? Anything new? I'm ready to fulfill my duties as godfather anytime."

"Any hour, the doctor says, Colonel." He glanced toward the house where Holly was in bed on Doctor Fox's orders. "I'm more nervous than I was in that battle with the French."

Washington laughed. "Natural enough for a first-time father. Now, two things—first, you'll have to come to Mount Vernon sometime next week. That will be easier than bringing all the horses here. Second, I've got to press you to join the militia. I know it's taken all your time getting established in a new business—and it's commendable that you'd want to be with Mrs. Bradford for the birth of your firstborn. However, as soon as possible after the child is born, I would very much like for you to join. I need good men like you in places of leadership, Daniel. You'd be a tremendous asset."

Washington was a man to whom Daniel could refuse nothing. "Yes, of course, sir. I'll do my best for you."

Washington smiled with pleasure, then swung into the saddle and left at a fast gallop. Daniel thought of how fortunate he'd been to have had Washington's support. His business had been highly successful, for the patronage of the colonel had been enough to bring him more work than he could handle. He had been forced to hire an assistant, and now he was working on plans to build a larger shop and hire on another man to keep up with all the work.

He returned to his work, but half an hour later, Mrs. Stevens, who had been sitting with Holly, came hurrying into the smithy. "Mr. Bradford—it's time!"

Daniel dropped his tongs and ripped off his apron. "Take over, Tim!" he called over his shoulder as he ran toward the house. When he reached the bedroom, he took one look at Holly, then said, "I'll go and get Doctor Fox!"

He made a wild ride to the doctor's office, practically carried the physician to his buggy, and harried him all the way back to his wife's bed. Fox, irritated by the jostling, said shortly, "Go back to your shop, Bradford. I'll tend to this. You'll just get in the way!"

Daniel, however, remained in the house, pestering the doctor and Mrs. Stevens with nervous questions. It was a hard birth, but finally at midnight, Doctor Fox came out of the bedroom. He was tired as he wiped his brow, but he had a smile on his face. "You have a fine son, Daniel—go give him greetings."

Daniel rushed into the room, fell down beside Holly, and took her hands. "Are you . . . all right?" he whispered.

Holly was pale and worn, but she turned a tender smile at him. "Yes, I'm fine."

"And here's this fine boy!" said Daniel proudly.

Daniel rose to take the bundle Mrs. Stevens handed to him. He stared down at the little red face, unaware that Holly was watching him intently. Although Daniel had assured her repeatedly that he would love the child regardless of who his father was, she was still apprehensive. She had never spoken of the father, and Daniel respected her silence about the matter.

Looking down at the child, Daniel said nothing for so long that Holly grew fearful. But then he turned to her, a smile on his broad lips. He reached down and took her hand.

"I have a fine son," he said quietly. "What would you think of Matthew for a name?"

"Yes!" Holly's eyes filled with tears, but she squeezed his hand and whispered, "His name is Matthew—and may God make him the finest son a man ever had!"

18

Marian's Mistake

THE GREATEST ARGUMENT AGAINST MONARCHY as a form of government might well be the century-long reign of the Hanoverian kings over England. Foreign bloodlines, political incompetence, and even insanity began to weaken the monarchy in the eyes of nobles and paupers alike.

George I ruled for thirteen years and never learned to speak English. His ineptitude was known throughout the empire. Rumors flew out of the palace and all through the kingdom that George I loved pleasure and would gladly add to his mistresses any woman who was very willing and very fat. The German-born ruler had little interest in the internal affairs of the country. As a result, he left politics in the hands of his incapable ministers, ushering in the role of Prime Minister—and letting the real power of the empire slip from the hands of the monarchy. The stage was set for others to wield tremendous power over the people of England.

Unfortunately, the royal bloodlines produced no competent successor to the throne, for George II was no improvement. Short and stout with the puffy, gargoylelike features of a true Hanoverian, he possessed all the petty vices, including raw avarice. He had an undying hatred for his son, Frederick, the Prince of Wales, whom he banished from the court. Once he stated flatly, "My dear firstborn is the greatest beast in the whole world, and I most heartily wish he were out of it." The true power behind the throne came by subtle influence from a very capable source, his wife, Queen Caroline, along with Horace Walpole, the Prime Minister.

But on June 4, 1738, a son was born to the Prince of Wales, a boy named George who was destined to rule England after the death of his father. He was so frail at birth that his parents had him baptized at midnight, fearing that he would not live through the night. He survived, however, and was so carefully sheltered in his nursery that by the time he was eleven he was still unable to read English. His education was flawed, lacking in the preparation required of one who was to ascend to the throne. When his father was killed in 1751 in the most undignified manner—struck in the head by a tennis ball—his mother turned his upbringing over to Bubb Dodington, whose evil influences greatly effected the ruining of the mind and character of young George. His mother then took a lover, Lord Bute, who completed the task.

At the age of seventeen, the young prince read a book that changed his life. Unfortunately it was not the Bible, but a political tract titled *Idea of a Patriot King* by Viscount Bolingbroke. It set forth the notion that monarchs should be above all influences, including party or profit. His only concern should be the welfare of the people. Corruption should be stamped out wherever it existed.

The American patriotism that cried for independence was just such corruption. Young George took the motto of this book as his creed and determined to crush any resistance to the monarchy. When George III was crowned King on October 15, 1760, the angels in charge of England wept!

🕮   🕮   🕮

The crowning of a new monarch may have been all important to some, but Daniel Bradford took no notice of the event. He had more pressing matters to consider. His wife, Holly, was pregnant with her fifth child and was not doing well.

He was trying to keep the children entertained while Doctor Fox examined Holly. Rachel was the only one who was quiet, but at the age of one she had not yet developed the lungs her three brothers had. She sat propped up against the wall, her thumb in her mouth, large green eyes watching owlishly, her bright red hair glinting in the amber beam of the whale-oil lamp that glowed on the table.

Dake and Micah, identical as two beans, swarmed over Daniel, who was sitting on the floor. At two the twins were large for their age, and their wheat-colored hair and hazel eyes made them miniatures of their father. They had his high cheekbones and broad forehead, and the same cleft in their rather pugnacious chins. The resemblance to their father was almost comical, but Daniel delighted in it. "Now you'll never have to ask what I looked like when I was a boy," he was fond of telling Holly.

The twins loved to wrestle, and when Daniel allowed himself to be pinned to the floor, Dake yelled, "See, Pa! We win!"

"You sure did, Dake." He had named the boy Drake—after the great English seaman—but Matthew could not quite manage that, so he had become "Dake" to all of them.

"Come on, Pa," Matt pleaded. "You promised to take us for a ride." At the age of four, Matt was not as large as the twins, though he was quicker in mind and body. He had light brown hair and blue eyes, and gave promise of becoming a handsome man someday. His features were more sharply chiseled than those of the twins, and he was far more restrained. Dake and Micah were loud, boisterous, and outgoing, while Matt was given to quiet periods and was somewhat withdrawn when it came to meeting new people.

"A little later, Matt. You can ride to Mr. Lassiter's with me." Looking at the boy, he thought of the years that had passed since he'd first held him. Daniel was proud of Matt, and he had been careful to play no favorites between him and the twins. It had not been difficult, for somehow he had never been troubled by the fact that Matt was not his real son. He'd asked God to give him a love for the boy—and his prayer had been more than answered. Time had softened the memories of the circumstances surrounding the birth of his firstborn, and he was tremendously grateful for Holly and for the wonderful children God had given them.

When Doctor Fox walked out of the room, Daniel rose quickly. "You fellows wait here. Take care of Rachel, Matt." He led the physician into the parlor and asked at once, "How is she, Doctor Fox?"

Fox had aged somewhat since Matt's birth. His hair and beard had turned silver, and his face was more lined. He stroked his beard slowly, hesitating as he formed an answer. "She's having a hard time, Daniel." He shrugged, adding, "I'm sorry she's having this child, to be truthful. She nearly died when Rachel was born."

Daniel remembered the doctor's warning that Holly should not have other children, but she had longed for another baby. Now he felt a stab of regret that he had allowed her to override his own wishes. He talked to Doctor Fox quietly, attempting to elicit an optimistic outlook, but the physician was gloomy. "Don't let her out of bed and send for me as soon as the labor starts. Will Mrs. Taylor be with her?"

"Yes, and her daughter will help take care of the children." Mrs. Taylor was a widow who lived close-by, and Fox had great confidence in her. After giving a few instructions, the doctor picked up his black bag and left the house, shaking his head.

As soon as Doctor Fox left, Daniel went at once into the bedroom. Going to the bed, he leaned over and forced a hearty note into his voice as he kissed Holly. "Well, now, Doctor Fox says it won't be long."

Holly looked very ill. The pregnancy had been worse than her others, and her skin had a pale color. Her cheeks were drawn in, and her eyes sunken. "He's not happy with me," she said quietly. Reaching up, she took his hand and held it, her grip weak.

"Oh, you know Fox." Daniel forced a grin. "He's never satisfied with any of his patients. You're going to do just fine, Holly." He sat down and held her hand for some time, speaking of the arrangements he'd made with Mrs. Taylor and her daughter, then of the children.

Holly lay very still, her eyes on his face as he spoke. She had been different during this pregnancy, Daniel had noticed—quieter and somehow lacking in the joy that had been with her before. Once Daniel had found her weeping—something that had very rarely happened in their marriage. She had shrugged it off, saying that she was just weepy and that there was nothing to worry about.

Now as she lay quietly, Daniel saw some sort of expression in her face that he could not read. He finally asked tentatively, "Holly, what's the matter? Are you frightened?"

"No, Daniel . . ." Holly hesitated, then a struggle seemed to take place in her. Her drawn face moved, and her lips seemed to draw into a tight line. She stirred restlessly, then finally whispered, "Daniel, I've been thinking so much of Matthew these last few days."

"Matthew? Why, he's fine, Holly!"

But she shook her head, and her grip on his hand tightened. "I don't mean that he's sick or anything like that." The sunlight streaming through the window fell across her face, a pale yellow

light that accented the lines in her face, making her look older. "It's
. . . about his father."

Daniel blinked with surprise, for they had not spoken of this
since their marriage. He had told her that the past was dead, and
that Matthew was his son. Holly had been happy with that, and
now he was somewhat shocked at her words. But he saw she was
troubled—more than he'd seen her in years. "What is it, sweetheart?" he asked gently.

"If anything happened to me, no one on this earth would ever
know who Matthew's father is." She reached up with her maimed
hand and stroked his face in a tender fashion. "Oh, Daniel, you've
been a *real* father to Matthew—and I've loved you for it! No man
ever loved his son more than you love him!" Allowing her hand
to drop, she fell silent. Daniel waited, troubled by this, and wondered why she was so burdened.

"Does it matter, Holly?" he finally asked.

"I hope not . . . but somehow I keep feeling that I should tell
you. I've been praying about it, and I think I must." She looked
up at him, her eyes filled with pain. "I think you should know,
Daniel . . . though I don't know why I feel this way. Somehow I
think God is putting this on my heart."

Daniel could see the hesitation in her eyes, yet he could tell it
was very important to her. "All right, Holly, if you feel that way,
maybe you should tell me." He was suddenly aware that she had
carried this burden alone for all these years. The important thing,
he realized, was not that he knew Matthew's father, but that Holly
must not carry the weight of it alone any longer.

"It . . . was Leo," she whispered, her lips twisted. "He forced
me, Daniel. He caught me alone and had his way with me. I
fought him . . . but he was too strong." Tears overflowed and ran
down her pale cheeks. "When I found out I was with child, I was
afraid I'd hate the baby—because of that. But then you came and
I loved you so much! And you've been so good to Matthew!"

Daniel was not too shocked at her words. He hadn't allowed
himself to think much about whom the father had been, but he
remembered now that back at the time, he'd been suspicious of
Leo Rochester. It had been wise of Holly not to tell him the father's
name. *I'd probably have killed him,* he thought—but the passage of
time had dulled the rage that would have come when the wound
was fresh. Now he felt a dull anger and bitterness. But he knew

as well that he would never say a word to Leo Rochester about Matthew.

He leaned over and stroked Holly's hair, then kissed her cheek. "Now I know," he said softly, "and you've done what God asked you to do. I don't want you to have one more troubled thought about this. It means nothing, Holly—nothing! Matthew Bradford is my firstborn son—and nothing under God's heaven is going to change that!"

"Oh, Daniel—" Holly cried, a light touching her eyes. "I love you so much!"

Daniel sat beside her, speaking of other things. He could tell she was relieved, and soon she grew sleepy. He kissed her, saying, "You sleep now. I'm going to make a quick trip to Mount Vernon. Mrs. Taylor is here if you need anything."

When he emerged from the room, Matthew and the twins swarmed him, reminding him that he'd promised to take them for a ride. "All right, but just a short one," he agreed. While they were scrambling to get ready, he went to Mrs. Taylor in the kitchen. "I'm going to take the boys for a ride," he said. "I won't be long, but I'll have to make a quick trip to Mount Vernon. You'll see to Mrs. Bradford?"

Mrs. Taylor was a motherly woman of fifty. "Of course, sir. You go right on." After he left the kitchen, she resumed mixing dough, but her thoughts were on Holly Bradford. Mrs. Taylor was knowledgeable in all matters relating to childbirth, and her brow wrinkled as she thought, *I don't like the way she looks—she's going to have a bad time, I fear. . . .*

🔔   🔔   🔔

Martha Washington smiled as she said, "Mr. Bradford, have you met Mrs. Rochester?"

Daniel kept his expression free of the quick stab of emotion that ran along his nerves. He bowed to Marian, saying, "Oh yes, Mrs. Washington. Mrs. Rochester and I met several years ago."

Marian had seen Daniel coming across the room talking to Colonel Washington, so she had been able to compose herself. She had seen Daniel Bradford only once since he had left Fairhope, and that had been a brief encounter at which they had murmured but a few words. Daniel had never returned to Fairhope, and their paths had not crossed anywhere else. As the wife of Leo Rochester she normally moved in higher social circles and was taken aback to see him now.

"Yes, Mr. Bradford is responsible for the fine stock we have at Fairhope." She managed a smile, adding, "Queenie is still my favorite, Mr. Bradford."

Daniel had gained control of himself enough to make a comment about the horses, and then Colonel Washington and his wife were called by a servant. When they had moved away, Marian said, "Colonel Washington has told me how you've prospered. I'm glad to hear of your success." She took in the plain dark broadcloth he wore, noting that he still looked roughly handsome.

Daniel asked, "Mr. Rochester isn't with you?"

"No. He's in London on business," she replied, her answer very clipped. Afraid that Daniel might suspect how unhappy she was in her marriage, she at once asked, "You have a family, I understand?"

"Yes, three boys and one daughter. Mrs. Bradford and I have been greatly blessed." He hesitated, then added, "We're expecting our fifth very soon. As a matter of fact, I must hurry back home right away."

Marian nodded. "I have no children," she said, the statement stark and unadorned. "I hope to see you again—but give my best wishes to your good wife."

"I will, and thank you," Daniel said politely, yet noticed how distant she seemed.

She turned to go, but then suddenly said, "I still remember our rides, Daniel. They were very good."

"Yes, I think of them often. You were very kind to me."

Her lips parted and her eyes brightened—and then she abruptly said, "I must go now. Goodbye."

The brief encounter unsettled Daniel somehow. All the way home he thought of how troubled she seemed. *More beautiful than ever—but her eyes have so little joy! She was always so full of life, and now it's as if she's been drained dry.* He thought of the kiss they'd shared, and how he'd never forgotten it. For years he'd felt guilty and disloyal, had tried to bury the memory, but it would lie dormant for months—only to rise again.

His marriage to Holly had been good. She had been a loving wife, and he loved her dearly. But it had not been a grand passion—in all their married life he had never felt for Holly what he had felt for Marian Frazier that one day by the creek. As he approached his home, he thought, *What sort of a man are you, Daniel Bradford? You've got a wife who's been faithful and true in every way—and you think of a boyish love!* He shook his head angrily, determined to put out of his mind forever that feeling he'd had for Marian Frazier—no, for Marian *Rochester.*

Dismounting in front of his house, he was met at the door by Mrs. Taylor. One look at her face and his heart seemed to contract. "What is it?" he demanded. "Is her time come?"

"No—not yet. But she's having other problems." Mrs. Taylor's plain, round face was drawn with worry. "I think Doctor Fox had better come and look at her, Mr. Bradford." She shook her head, adding, "She's not strong—and I'm concerned."

Daniel left at once and went to find Doctor Fox. Fortunately, he was not out making rounds. He was sitting behind his desk in his office when Daniel burst through the door.

"Doc, you've gotta come. Mrs. Taylor thinks something's wrong with Holly," said Daniel, his face drawn with worry.

Fox grabbed his coat and bag and quickly followed Daniel outside to where his horse was hitched in front. He told Daniel to ride on ahead and he'd be there shortly. Daniel took off at a fast gallop as the doctor followed behind at a fast gait. When Fox arrived and entered the kitchen, he saw Mrs. Taylor coming out of the bedroom, concern etched on her face. Daniel was in the kitchen trying to keep the children quiet, but Fox could tell from the drawn lines on his face, he was scared.

Doctor Fox examined Holly, then came out into the kitchen. "Stay with her as much as you can. I don't know exactly what the problem is—but she's having difficulties, Daniel."

For the next three days Daniel scarcely left the house. He tried to help out with the children the best he could, but he spent most of the time just sitting beside Holly. A gnawing sense of dread was growing inside him, and he was frightened. The other births had not been easy, but this one was—different. Holly was suffering terribly, and when she did sleep, it was a fitful rest, waking up in pain and drenched in sweat. Daniel tried to comfort her, soothing her brow with a cool cloth. Often, she would lift her hand to his cheek and tell him how grateful she was for his presence.

Finally she went into labor, and Alice Taylor came and took the children away. Daniel walked the floor, enduring the strain badly. He slept in short naps and ate only when Mrs. Taylor forced him to.

After hours of hard labor, a baby boy was born. Doctor Fox came out, wiping his brow, and said in a hard tone, "Get the children here!" He chewed his lip, then shook his head. "She's going, Daniel—there's nothing I can do. I'm sorry."

Daniel's mind went numb. Mrs. Taylor left instantly at the doctor's word and returned a few minutes later. When they came through the door, they all looked at once toward their father. Daniel took Rachel in his arms, saying, "Boys—your mother—she wants to see you."

Matthew gave him a look that Daniel never forgot. His eyes were filled with fear and he whispered, "Is she dying?"

Daniel could not answer the boy nor bear to look into his face. He said hoarsely, "Hurry, son—!"

They all gathered around the dying woman, and when she held up her arms and called them by name, Matthew, then Dake and Micah were embraced. "Let me have her—" Holly said and took Rachel in her arms. She kissed the silken hair, whispered endearments, and then asked for the baby. Cradling the small form in her arms, she tenderly looked into the tiny face. She said softly, "Tell him his mother loved him dearly—and call him Samuel." Then she held up her hand to Daniel, whispering, "Husband—" When Daniel bent and held her, she whispered faintly in his ear, "All my love—to you, my dear husband—as it's ever been!"

Daniel's eyes were burning with scalding tears, and he held her with trembling arms. He felt the strength going out of her, and wanted to call her, to keep her from slipping away.

But he heard her whisper, "I love you—but—I must go—to Him who loves me—!" She said clearly in a stronger voice, "Lord Jesus—!" and then she was gone.

Daniel held her for a long moment, then straightened up. He kissed her cheek, and the boys came, all of them weeping. Daniel picked up the baby, held him tightly and, looking down at his face, thought, *I'll do the best I can with the children, Holly, I promise!*

🛡   🛡   🛡

The funeral was difficult, and afterward the children were a problem—especially Matthew. The sudden loss of his mother affected him terribly. He would sit for hours staring at nothing. He became irritable easily, and at times would cry inconsolably. The twins were not affected as deeply, but it took all the patience that Daniel had to keep his promise to Holly.

He let his assistants run his business, and for two weeks he threw himself into caring for the children. The women of the neighborhood came and helped, often bringing some sort of dish or baked goods to help out. But Daniel was growing weary and cast down by the tremendous grief and responsibility that he bore. Finally Mrs. Taylor took him in hand one day and said, "Go hunting—go to town, Mr. Bradford!" she exclaimed. "You can't stay with the children all the time. Now go!"

Daniel stared at her, but realized that she was right. He left the house and walked all day in the woods. He was spiritually and emotionally exhausted, and for three days he roamed the hills. Slowly the silence of the forest seeped into him. At night he built a small fire and cooked a rabbit he'd shot earlier. Finishing his meal, Daniel lay on his blanket looking up into the starry heavens. The gentle breezes rustling through the leaves soothed his jangled nerves, and finally he began to pray. On the third day, God gave him a great peace that settled down into the depths of his troubled heart.

When he returned home, he entered the house, calling out, "Matt, where are you? Micah—Dake?"

The three boys came running to greet him. He picked them up, hugged them, and was relieved to see that they were well.

And then he turned to see a woman holding Rachel. At first he thought it was Mrs. Taylor—but it was not. He swallowed hard, then exclaimed, "Marian—!"

Marian was holding Rachel tightly in her arms, and her eyes were fixed on Daniel. "I—came to offer my respects." She seemed embarrassed, and said quickly, "Mrs. Taylor's daughter is ill, so I volunteered to help with the children until she recovered."

Micah cried out, "She can make the *best* taffy, Pa!" And at once Dake and Matthew joined in with Micah and began singing the praises of their new keeper.

Daniel went at once and held out his arms to Rachel, who was squirming in Marian's arms. "How are you, sweetheart?" he asked, kissing her silken cheek. She patted his cheeks and began pulling at his hair.

Finally Daniel and Marian were able to get the children settled.

She had made taffy and put Matthew in charge of letting them throw it at a nail on a board. While they were noisily engaged in pulling the sticky confection, Marian found herself alone in a corner of the big kitchen with Daniel. She was flushed, but her eyes were bright as she related how she'd kept the children entertained. When Daniel tried to thank her, she shook her head. "It's been such a joy, just being around them," she said softly. "I love children, and they're so sweet!"

The two of them spent some time with the children, and then Marian said, "I must go, now that you're here to take over."

Daniel asked before he thought, "Will you come back, Marian?"

Marian gave him an odd look, then shook her head. "I don't think that would be wise."

At once Daniel knew what was in her reply, what Leo Rochester might do if he knew his wife was seeing a former servant. He said quietly, "I understand."

Marian left at once, and on her way back to Fairhope, she thought in bleak despair, *I've made the worst mistake a woman can make. I never loved Leo—not as I love Daniel Bradford!* It was the first time she'd allowed that thought to surface in her mind. And now as she rode along under a gray cloudy sky, she knew that the future would be as bleak as the sky above.

As for Daniel Bradford—he went about pulling his life together, refusing to entertain thoughts of anything except his promise to Holly. *I'll do the best I can for the children.* He knew that he had missed something that could not be replaced, but doggedly he set his heart to give his children—including young Samuel who would never know his mother's caress—the best he could.

PART FOUR

THE SHOT
HEARD ROUND
THE WORLD

1770–1775

19

MASSACRE IN BOSTON

THE BRAZEN CLANGING OF HAMMERS on iron filled the enormous high-ceilinged room. Men blackened by smoke from the furnaces pounded white-hot steel into curves, angles, and concentric shapes, sending showers of sparks swirling upward, flickering brightly, then fading like diminished miniature stars. The air was thick with scorching leather, sweat, and acrid smoke that burned Daniel's eyes as he passed along between the two lines of workers. His quick glance took in the apprentices who pumped the leather bellows, and he stopped long enough to ask one of them, "How's your mother, Timmy?"

The young man, no more than sixteen, nodded quickly. "Oh, she's better, Mr. Bradford—and she says to thank you for lettin' me off to help until she got better." A rash grin flashed from the boy's sooty face as he added, "And she said to tell you she's prayin' for you every day!"

Daniel slapped the young man's shoulder, saying as he moved on, "Well, I need all the prayers I can get, Timmy. Tell your mother I'm glad she's better."

Moving on, Daniel was not aware of the glances of approval his simple act of pausing to speak to the boy drew from the other workers. When he had bought a half interest in John Frazier's foundry, the workers had been aloof, but soon they'd discovered that not only was Daniel Bradford as good at the forge as they, but he was a good boss as well.

When John Frazier had written and offered him a partnership, Daniel had almost refused. *It will put me too close to Marian,* he had thought instantly. However, after thinking it over and deciding that his feelings for Marian were not a factor, he accepted Frazier's fine offer. As soon as he'd found a buyer for the smithy, he had packed up his family and moved to Boston in 1765. Now five years later he was in charge of the day-to-day operations of the foundry—and not a man was unhappy with Bradford.

Leaving the shop by a side door, Daniel walked up a flight of stairs, moved down a narrow hall, then stepped through a door into an outer office. He nodded at Blevins, the bookkeeper, asking, "Is Mr. Frazier still here, Albert?"

"Yes, sir, he is. Said he wanted to see you before he went home." Blevins was a tall, cadaverous individual with sharp features and a thin-lipped mouth. He had been with John Frazier from the beginning, and the astute man knew every aspect of the company better than either partner. He had been stiff with Daniel at first but had warmed to him when he'd discovered that Bradford was willing to learn. Despite his craggy, rather sour look, Blevins was a kindhearted man who was thoroughly devoted to John Frazier. "I don't like the way Mr. Frazier's looking," he said. "He's never gotten over his bout with pneumonia he had last year. Why don't you try to get him to go south for a time?"

"I'll do that." He winked conspiratorially at the bookkeeper, adding, "You're the real boss around here, but don't let anybody find out about it." He moved through the door to the inner office and found his partner sitting at the desk, staring at some designs. "Hello, John," he said, taking off his apron and hanging it on the wall. He peered down at the drawings and nodded, "What do you think? Can we do it?"

John Frazier had sold half interest in his business to Daniel five years earlier because he was beginning to have health problems. He needed a young, energetic partner, and he had found him in Daniel Bradford. It had proved to be a wise decision, for his health had not gotten better. Frazier was only fifty-nine, but he had the frail look of an invalid. His color was pale and ashen, and he had lost considerable weight since Daniel had come.

Looking up, he nodded, "Yes, these are good, Daniel. But can we make money on casting cannon?"

"Don't know," Daniel shrugged. "Not much market in the Colonies, and we can't sell them in England. But we ought to find a market, John. Men are going to fight, and they need cannon."

Frazier's mouth drew into a straight line. "If those fools in Parliament keep digging at us, we might need cannon to teach them a lesson." Seeing the surprise on Daniel's face, he laughed shortly. "I sound like one of Sam Adams' Sons of Liberty, don't I? Well, I don't go that far—but it's getting worse, Daniel."

"Yes, it is. I had hoped that the Stamp Act fiasco would have brought the Crown to its senses."

As the two men talked about the growing tensions between the Colonies and the Crown, Daniel expressed his incredulity at the king's stubbornness in the face of American resistance. England's attempt to tax all legal papers in the Colonies had exploded when Sam Adams and his Sons of Liberty had gone into action. These patriotic rowdies had rampaged through the Colonies, spreading their zeal for liberty from Maine to South Carolina, encouraging people to refuse to buy the stamps, and stirring up a storm of violence. King George was stunned by it all and quickly backed down.

But no sooner had the king repealed the Stamp Act than he suffered the first of his terrible fits of madness. He hid from the public behind his palace walls, existing on potatoes and water, and avoiding any direct contact with the people. He blundered into handing over control of the empire to Charles Townshend— the new Chancellor of the Exchequer—who used his power to cripple the Colonies further by slapping heavy duties on all imports from England, which only fueled the colonists' growing hatred.

The death of Townshend in 1767 did nothing to alleviate the situation, for the mad King George replaced Townshend with the *one* man in England who could stir the anger and bitterness of the colonists even more than Charles Townshend—Lord North. North pursued a headstrong course of forcing the colonists to obey his predecessor's tax laws.

Daniel recalled that tense day in May of 1768 when two British warships had sailed into Boston Harbor and began "impressing" men into service—a British euphemism for kidnapping unsuspecting colonists and enslaving them into service in the Royal Navy, with no chance to alert their families of their whereabouts. Incensed, the Sons of Liberty mobbed the Crown's Inspector of

Customs, and England retaliated in typical fashion by sending troops into Boston.

"If only Britain hadn't sent those troops here," Daniel said. "It was like pouring gunpowder on a fire! No good can possibly come of it."

John nodded solemnly. "No, I expect not, Daniel. I'm afraid we are facing difficult times indeed." Rising painfully to his feet, Frazier took his coat and allowed Daniel to help him into it. He settled his tricorn hat on his head, then said, "A letter came from Marian this morning."

At the mention of Marian, Daniel felt a peculiar jolt. He had felt odd about becoming a partner of John Frazier's—for he had known for years that his love for Frazier's daughter was hopeless. He had kept his relationship with her under careful control. He had seen her and Leo only a few times, but neither he nor Marian ever referred to their brief moments of intimacy they'd shared during her first visit to Fairhope years earlier.

"How is she?"

"Very well. She doesn't like it in England. Says she's coming home soon." Frazier hesitated, then said briefly, "Leo won't be coming—he's not finished with his business, Marian says."

Daniel knew that Frazier was very much aware of what kind of "business" his daughter was referring to. Through the years he had sadly discovered that Leo Rochester centered his life around wenching, gambling, and heavy drinking. Leo's reputation was bad, and it was the grief of Frazier's life that his daughter had not gotten a different husband. However, Daniel carefully avoided any mention of Leo's name, saying only, "You've missed her, John. It'll be good for you two to have some time together."

"Yes, it will. Well, good afternoon, Daniel. Let me know what we're going to do about casting these cannon," said Frazier as he turned and left the office.

Daniel moved to the window and watched the frail figure climb painfully into his carriage. He thought for one instant of Marian but quickly put away the small but insistent feeling that rose at the thought of seeing her again. *Can't be thinking like that!* he rebuked himself, then turned and sat down to work on the drawings of the cannon.

After working for an hour, he rose and put on his coat. He left the office, bidding Blevins a good day. He saddled his gelding at the stable and rode out, his mind filled with cannon designs. It was a project he'd been interested in for years, and now he was determined to be one of the few men in the Colonies who could produce such powerful guns.

As he passed along the streets of Boston, Daniel saw several red-coated soldiers and thought of how tense the situation was getting. Confrontations between soldiers and citizens were growing uglier each week. The animosity had grown so deep that there had been a few incidents of rocks being thrown at the soldiers, and the soldiers had retaliated by leveling their bayonets and threatening to draw blood. They had not made good on those threats—not yet.

He pulled his coat closer about him and shivered in the early March chill. The gray skies and raw wind seemed a portent of troubled times ahead. Daniel jumped as a man on the street shouted, "Filthy lobsterbacks!" He swung around in the saddle to see two British soldiers riding by, their faces stoic, staring straight ahead, ignoring the taunts and jeers of a small group of men who had joined their comrade.

Daniel had never had a hatred for the Redcoats. He knew too well that they were a miserable lot themselves—so poorly paid that most of them were forced to seek part-time work to furnish the bare necessities. And for this the working class in Boston resented them highly, since jobs were hard to come by.

Lobsterbacks! He really couldn't blame the colonists for using the epithet, a reference to the bloody floggings with which the British army enforced its brutal discipline. He remembered such a flogging years before on his trip to the Monongahela. *Daniel Morgan—he's become quite a leader in resisting the Redcoats. Little did that British officer know what he was doing when he laid a whip to Morgan's back,* thought Daniel as he rode along. He continued on toward home, anxious now to get out of the cold and rest by a warm fire.

As Daniel drew close to his house, he saw a small crowd gathered in the street, surrounding a tall British soldier. It was easy to identify the man by his red woolen overcoat and the pointed hat of an infantryman.

A poorly dressed workman was standing in front of the soldier, and Daniel heard the man cry out, "Lobsterback—go back where you come from. We're tired of the looks of you here!"

241

"Out of my way, Yankee Doodle!" replied the soldier. He lifted his Brown Bess rifle and the bayonet gleamed faintly. "Let me pass—I have work at the docks."

The colonist shouted, "Work at the docks?! You already have a job!"

"I need the money—now back up!" he threatened, nervous at the gathering crowd.

Daniel caught a flicker of movement, and even as he dismounted, he saw a stone flying through the air. It struck the soldier's hat and a cry went up from the crowd. Daniel caught a glimpse of the boy who'd thrown the stone and saw others reaching down for more.

"Stop that!" he cried loudly and, stepping forward, put himself between the soldier and the crowd. He made a formidable shape in the fading light, his broad shoulders and solid neck tense. "Be off with you now!" He watched the crowd reluctantly move away, then said to the soldier, "Sorry about this."

"Thank you." The soldier nodded, turned on his heel, and marched stiffly down the street.

Daniel went back to his horse and led him to the small stable behind his house. After he unsaddled and fed the animal, he descended the narrow stone steps leading to the back door of his house. When he stuck his head into the kitchen, Mrs. White said, "Dinner's ready, Mr. Bradford."

"All right. I'll wash up and be right there." Mrs. Letty White was his housekeeper, a strong woman of sixty who served as cook—and kept the children under her strong hand. Daniel asked, "Children give you any trouble today?"

"No, sir—none that I couldn't handle," she said as she stirred a thick soup in the cast-iron pot suspended over the open fire.

Daniel went to his bedroom, washed, changed clothes, then came back to take his seat at the head of the table. After greeting each of his children, he bowed his head and said grace, then helped himself to a generous serving of the rich soup. "How was school today?" he asked. He listened as the five of them related the events of their day, examining each one—thinking of how different they all were.

Matt, only thirteen—so different from the others! So quiet that I wonder what's going on in that head of his—and sometimes something seems to break out in him and I see a temper that could be frightening. He studied the straight back, the light brown hair and blue eyes, wondering if he had done his best for the boy. *Holly could have drawn him out, but I haven't been able to touch whatever's in him. Maybe it's the artistic streak in him—not at all like me in that way.*

He shifted his eyes to the twins, who were two years younger than Matt, but broader and stronger. He took in their straw-colored hair and hazel eyes—so much like his own—and noted the small scar on Dake's left eyebrow, almost hidden by his hair. He remembered how Sam had administered that scar. Dake had been teasing his younger brother and Sam had hit him in the head with a stick. Ever since then, it had been an identifying mark—the only way most people outside of the family could tell the two apart, but the twins' personalities and behavior were distinctive to their own father.

Dake will always be that, not Drake which I named him. Matt couldn't say it—so Dake it is. Always involved in some kind of mischief—too quick to speak and just as quick to jump into things. A temper like a firecracker— but never holding a grudge. I wish he had more of Holly and less of me in the matter of temper.

He looked over at Micah, who was sitting across from him, noting how precisely he used his knife. Whereas Dake shoveled his food into his mouth, Micah cut his meat into small, neat portions and ate almost as daintily as a woman. *That's Holly, that gentleness,* he thought almost sadly. *Never loses his temper and always has a smile for everyone. Loves books just like she did, but the best worker of the three—steady as a rock!*

Now Daniel had to smile as he looked on his youngest son, age nine. *Sam—you're a different breed!* He admired the strong, short figure, the rich auburn hair and abundant crop of freckles and the electric blue eyes. *You'd take the house—or anything else— apart if I didn't watch you! Got the most mechanical touch I ever saw in a boy—and not afraid to tackle anything.*

Finally, there was Rachel—with her red hair and green eyes. Daniel hardly ever looked at her without thinking of Holly, for she had her mother's heart-shaped face and widow's peak. *More beautiful than your mother—but not as sweet, perhaps.* At the tender age of ten, she was the tyrant of the household—able to get her own way, in most cases, from her brothers or her father. She looked at him now and smiled—and a poignant memory touched Daniel, for he'd seen her mother look just so a thousand times.

243

Finally the meal was over, but they stayed at the table talking, a custom Daniel both enjoyed and insisted on. It was a time he used to instruct the children in something, and now he said, "There was a soldier in front of the house as I came in. Someone hit him with a rock." He saw Sam cast an involuntary look at Dake but ignored it. "I'm asking you not to join in harassing the soldiers. Those men you see had no choice about coming here. They're only following orders, and most of them hate it."

Dake stuck his chin out pugnaciously. "But, Pa—it ain't *right*! They make hardworking colonists quarter them!"

Daniel saw in Dake's set features a reflection of himself at that age and said easily, "I know, son, but we can't do anything about that. What we can do is act like gentlemen."

"The Sons of Liberty say we ought to fight them," Dake argued.

"That's treason, Dake," Matthew spoke up, his lips drawn tight. "They're the servants of the king—and we are, too."

"Aw, who cares about Old Mad George?" Sam quipped. His hair was standing up wildly, and he waved his square hand in a wild gesture.

Daniel allowed the argument to go on for some time. He believed his children had the right to think and speak their minds. He often joined in heartily, taking sides with one of the boys. This time it was Dake and Sam against Matt and himself. Rachel merely sat and listened. The argument came to an end when Sam lifted his head and said, "Listen—it's the bells, Pa! There must be a fire!"

Daniel heard them, too, and said, "You all stay here!"

"Pa, let me go with you," Dake begged, and the others joined in. But Daniel rapped out his order to stay in the house, then rose and grabbed his coat.

Outside he found men running toward the center of town. "Is it a fire?" he asked Thomas Sealy, his neighbor.

"No, it's the Redcoats—they're shooting some of our people!"

The words cut along Daniel's nerves, and he ran with the rest toward the commotion. When he reached the Customs House, he saw Henry Knox and went up to him at once. Knox was a fat young man who owned a prosperous bookstore, but who was highly interested in military matters. He and Daniel had gotten to know each other well, and they had spent much time talking about guns and cannons.

"Ed Garrick's been hurt by that lobsterback," Knox said, his fat face glowing with anger. He looked around and muttered, "This is an ugly crowd, Daniel—and it could get worse."

As more people gathered in the street, the scene started to get out of hand. Soon they began throwing snowballs and chunks of ice at the soldier. Dodging the missiles, he tried frantically to get inside the Customs House, but the door was locked. In the dim flickering light of the moon, Daniel could read the hatred on the faces of the mob. "Henry, these are toughs from the waterfront," Daniel said. "We've got to do something."

Knox nodded and the two men shoved their way to the front, trying to speak, but loud voices kept screaming, "Kill him! Knock him down!" The situation was getting worse by the minute. Then Daniel saw a British officer and a few soldiers at the edge of the crowd. He knew the officer, Captain Thomas Preston, and respected him. Daniel pushed his way through the mob and said, "Captain, take care of your men!"

Knox was alongside him, his face pale. "If they fire on these people, they're dead men!"

"I'm aware of that," Preston replied. He looked over the crowd, which seemed to contain much of the male population of the town. "Fall in, Private White," Preston ordered the beleaguered soldier.

At the officer's command, a roar went up from the crowd, and when they charged forward, Preston ordered his men to form an arc. By then snowballs and ice and curses began to fly from all directions toward the soldiers, and the mob began chanting, "Fire! Why don't you fire!"

The situation had turned into a powder keg ready to explode. Just as Preston was moving his men slowly away, a club came flying out of the crowd, striking one of the soldiers and knocking him down. The soldier struggled to his feet, fury spreading over his face. He fired but the shot flew high, hitting no one. The crowd yelled and surged forward, and a private lifted his musket, aimed, and squeezed the trigger. A man fell dead with a hole in his head, and another musket roared, downing a huge black man named Crispus Attuck.

Daniel knew Crispus well, and he dived into the crowd to try to reach the dying man. His attempts were futile, though, as he was carried helplessly along by the surge of the angry mob. Pandemonium broke out and other shots were fired, wounding more men. One man broke free from the crowd and ran, only to be struck in the back and killed instantly.

At the sight of dead and wounded men lying in the street, the crowd suddenly grew silent. In the dim light of the pale moon Daniel saw the shock on wild faces. Rumor had it that the muskets of the Redcoats were loaded with only powder, but now in the face of death, a pall fell over the mob.

Henry Knox said in a strained voice, "Daniel, this means war! American blood has been shed—and our people will never forget!"

Sickened by the sight, Daniel turned and stumbled down the street—the crowd dispersing now in all directions. He knew that what had taken place this day would never be forgotten. Blood would bring forth blood, and he felt the crushing weight of it as he slowly made his way home.

20

A Spot of Tea

DAKE SMELLED THE RICH AROMA OF COOKING even before he entered the house. He'd been outside chopping wood, and when he entered and dropped a huge armload of split oak into the box, he turned at once toward the fireplace. "Donkers!" he exclaimed and moved to where Rachel was cooking.

"Stay away from here, Dake!" Rachel said sharply. At the age of fourteen she was on the verge of young womanhood. "You can wait to eat with the rest of us."

Dake suddenly swooped down and picked Rachel up, swinging her lightly as a feather around the kitchen. At fifteen he was as tall and strong as most men, and he delighted in tossing Rachel around as though she were a child. "Aw, sis, you wouldn't deprive a starving man of food, would you?"

"Put me down, you—bear!" she squealed.

Dake set her down but managed to sample the donkers. This was his favorite food, made out of leftover meat from the past week's meals. Rachel had chopped it all up along with bread and apples and raisins and some savory spices. Fried and served up with boiled pudding, it made a delicious dish. "Nobody makes donkers like you, Rachel," he said and gave her a hard hug. "No girl in Boston's as pretty, either!"

Rachel sniffed, but she allowed Dake to sample the donkers. She knew very well that he was getting around her, but she was very fond of Dake. The two of them were close—much closer than Dake and his twin, Micah. Rachel had said once, "I think God got mixed up and put the wrong twin with you. Twins are supposed

247

to be alike—but you and Micah are as different as night and day. You and me are the same inside."

"Go call everyone to breakfast," Rachel ordered.

Dake smiled and simply stuck his head outside the kitchen door and yelled in a stentorian voice: "Breakfast! Come and get it!"

"Well, *I* could have done that!" Rachel said tartly.

"It isn't polite for young ladies to yell."

"And it is for young men?" she asked in a teasing tone.

"Sure. That's because men are crude and rough, and you ladies are sweet and nice." Dake grinned at her, then helped her set the table in the dining room. As he did, Sam came stumbling in, his eyes puffy with sleep. Dake rubbed the head of the thirteen-year-old, saying, "Don't you *ever* get enough sleep? Wake up!"

"Let me alone or I'll bust you, Dake!" Sam was a good-tempered lad—after he'd had breakfast. Until then he was as sullen as a young boy could be.

Micah entered, and he and Dake sat down beside each other. Except for the clothing, few could have told the two apart. Looking at her identical brothers, Rachel smiled to herself and thought, *If it weren't for that tiny scar on Dake's face, our friends would never know who is who.*

Daniel came in, dressed in a dark green suit, and Rachel smiled at him. "You look nice, Papa." She came over and straightened out his cravat, then patted his cheek. "Try not to get so dirty, will you?" She took her seat, adding, "You're the *owner* of the foundry, not one of the hired workers. You can just tell people what to do."

Daniel grinned at Rachel, for they'd had this argument often enough. Even though he was a partner in the foundry, he often worked side by side with the workers, showing them what to do. "It's just not in me to sit in an office and shuffle papers all day," Daniel joked. "A man's got to get his hands dirty or he doesn't feel like he's done a day's work!"

Sam said rebelliously, "Well, when *I* get to be boss, you won't see *me* working myself to death!"

Dake laughed outright. "I don't remember seeing you ever hurt yourself working. That wood I split this morning was supposed to be your job. Now you get out there and split the rest of it after breakfast."

"You're not my boss, Dake!" snapped Sam.

"Well, I'm your father, Sam," Daniel spoke up. "And Dake's right. You get all that wood split today." He eyed Sam, waiting for an argument, but Sam saw something in his father's eye that caused him to keep silent. Daniel bowed his head and asked the blessing, and as he said "Amen," he saw Sam's hand close on a piece of bread.

Micah noted Sam's grabbing hand and asked with amusement, "How do you time it so well, Sam? You always have your hands on the food just as Father says the amen."

Sam stuffed a mouthful of donkers between his lips, mumbling, "Because he always says the same thing. I know when he's almost finished."

Despite himself, Daniel laughed aloud. "I'll have to cross you up, Sam. Next time I'll ask a blessing that lasts for ten minutes."

The family enjoyed their mealtimes together. They had managed to keep house with the aid of Mrs. White. And now that Rachel was older, she had taken over much of the responsibility for the meals. Looking around the table, Daniel had a quick thought: *Holly would be very proud of them!*

"When's Matthew coming home, Papa?" Rachel asked.

"Not for a while, Rachel. He's enjoying his time in England studying painting." Daniel had reluctantly given his permission when Matthew had asked him to go. Yet Daniel knew the lad was intent on following his art, so in the end he had given in to Matthew's wishes. He had only been gone a few months, but Daniel already missed him considerably.

Rachel sipped from her cup, then made a face, exclaiming, "This is *awful!*"

"Might as well drink dishwater," Dake agreed. "But it's better than nothing."

The tea was raspberry tea, or "liberty tea," as it was sometimes called. Most Americans—except for Tories—had substituted this for tea shipped from England. None of the Bradfords liked it, and Sam shoved his cup away. "Don't see why we have to drink this slop!" he grunted.

"I've explained that to you fifty times, Sam," Dake snapped. "The English are trying to make us pay for the French and Indian War. And that's not right!"

"I can't see how drinking this swill is going to make things any better!" Sam shot back.

Dake stared at his stubborn younger brother and began to speak loudly. "Look, Sam, the East India Tea Company lent the Crown money to fight the war. Now to pay them back, King George has slapped a stiff tax on tea."

"And that's like taxing the Company's customers to pay off the Company," Rachel nodded. "It's stupid!"

Daniel said mildly, "The East India Company has seventeen million pounds of tea in London warehouses. If they don't sell it, the Company could go bankrupt."

"That's *their* problem, Father," Dake said heatedly. "They don't have the *right* to tax us for their stupid wars!"

"If the English hadn't stood against the French," Daniel remarked, "we might be living under the French flag—and then you'd be going to mass instead of to a Protestant church."

The discussion became heated, with Dake and Rachel hotly disputing the right of England to tax the tea without the consent of the colonists—while Daniel and Micah took a more moderate view. Sam didn't care about anything but his own tastes and said, "I don't see why we don't drink what we want!"

Daniel rose and slipped his coat on. "You just split the wood, Sam," he said. Then he turned to the twins, saying, "I'll be getting a report from your tutor later in the week. It had better be good."

After their father left, Dake said, "Don't see what good it does to study Latin. Everybody's dead who spoke it."

Micah grinned at Dake. "It's an exercise for your mind, Dake."

"If that old man hollers at me one more time over some stupid verb, I'll throw him in the bay!" The "old man" was Dr. Silas Jennings, a retired minister and scholar who had taken the twins as students in his school.

"If you do, Father will do worse to you," Micah replied calmly. "Come on, we're going to be late. . . ."

🔔   🔔   🔔

"Dake—you can't get mixed up in this crazy business!"

Paul Revere stared at the two young men, his dark eyes gleaming with excitement. "You must be Micah," he nodded, then turned to say, "Dake, Mr. Adams has sent us word that we must do something about this tea tax." He hesitated, glancing at Micah.

He had grown rather close to Dake Bradford, but he was uncertain about his twin brother. Dake had simply pushed himself into the Sons of Liberty, coming with an older friend. Revere had found the young man just the sort of recruit he needed and overlooked his youth. He had talked with Dake about his family and discovered that neither his father nor his twin was sympathetic with the Sons of Liberty.

Dake saw Revere hesitate. "You can speak in front of Micah, sir. He won't say anything."

Micah said at once, "I'm going to Dr. Jennings' house, Dake—I wish you'd come with me." He stood there feeling uncertain, disturbed as he always was over Dake's rabid enthusiasm for the revolutionary activities of the Sons of Liberty. He was a calm young man, not given to bursts of excitement as was his twin.

"You go on, Micah," Dake said. "I've got to do this."

Micah started to say something, then shook his head sadly, turned, and walked away. Revere waited until Micah had gone, then said, "It's not just another meeting, Dake." His eyes glowed with excitement as he added, "This time we're actually going to *do* something!"

"What's going on, sir?" asked Dake, curious at the man's obvious excitement.

"We're going to raid three of the Crown's ships," Revere said, speaking quickly. "It could be dangerous, Dake. You may not want to go on the actual raid, but I want you to help me get word to all the Sons of Liberty. Will you do that?"

"Of course! But I'm going on the raid, too!" Dake was twitching with anticipation and soon was off at a dead run. In his pocket he carried a list of men to be alerted. As he ran, Dake thought of his father, knowing he wouldn't approve of what he was doing. *I hate to go against him,* he thought grimly, *but I have to do this!*

🝔　　🝔　　🝔

Thomas Hutchinson, the Governor of Massachusetts, was a flexible man—but his fine home had been wrecked earlier by a "patriot" mob. He responded to the crisis with a bitter spirit and set in action the events that had long-reaching effects. Patriots at New York and Philadelphia had prevented ships carrying tea to their ports from docking and unloading their cargo. The resistance was so strong that the ships' captains had been forced to return to London. In Charlestown, shiploads of tea had been landed, but it had been locked up in a warehouse near the docks. With the unrest growing throughout the Colonies, people were asking, "What will Boston do?"

Hutchinson made a fatal decision. He allowed three ships— the *Eleanor*, the *Beaver*, and the *Dartmouth*—to enter Boston Harbor, all loaded with tea. He then ordered Admiral Montagu to close the harbor mouth so that no ship could return to England.

Sam Adams seized the opportunity and called for a quick assembly of the Sons of Liberty at the Old South Church. Adams had sent a warning to Hutchinson, but he knew what the governor's answer would be. Standing in front of the gathered men, Adams could sense the excitement coursing through them. He looked out over the group and asked, "Who knows how tea will mingle with salt water?" At once a great shout of laughter erupted around the room.

Dake was one of the crowd that milled around the church, and at six o'clock when Governor Hutchinson's refusal to heed the warning came, he was waiting outside with the rest for Adams to respond.

Sam Adams read the paper and looked out over the faces that looked at him eagerly. "This meeting can do nothing more to save our country," he cried in a shrill voice. Instantly yells rose from the throats of the men.

"Are you sure you want to do this, Dake?" Paul Revere demanded.

"Yes, I'm sure!"

"Well—so be it! Here's the paint—and get into this outfit!"

Dake scrambled into the Indian garb Revere handed him and then smeared his face with paint. When he was ready he joined the others and went screaming like a true Mohawk toward the harbor where the ships were anchored. Adams had planned for fifty men in each of three parties to attack the three ships. Dake fought for a place in one of the small boats and soon was standing on the deck of the *Dartmouth*. Captain Hewes, who was in charge of the raiders, demanded of the ship's captain, "Give me the keys to the hatches!"

The captain put up no struggle, and soon Dake and the others were wrestling the heavy chests to the deck. Dake took great delight in splitting them open with his tomahawk, laughing with the other men as the tea fluttered down to coat the surface of the water.

Everything was done in an orderly fashion, with no interference from the captain or crew. Finally the "Mohawks" returned to their bobbing boats and rowed back to shore.

Dake made his way home, his heart stirred with the event. He knew his father would have stern words for him—but he could bear that.

"At last—we've actually *done* something!" he cried aloud, throwing his tomahawk high into the air. He'd kept it for a reminder of the tea party, and as it spun in the air, he shouted, unable to keep back what rose to his throat, "Now, George the Third—how did you like *that* little tea party?"

21

OUT OF THE PAST

BOSTON HARBOR LOOKED LIKE A FOREST of masts, but Daniel only had eyes for one of the ships. He stood straining his eyes, and when he saw Matthew making his way along the rail of the *Bristol Queen*, he shouted, "There he is, Dake!"

The two waited until the passengers came ashore; then they made their way through the bustling crowd to the trim young man. "Matt—by George—it's good to see you!"

Matthew dropped his luggage and rushed forward to take the hug his father gave him. He was slender but only an inch shorter now than his father's six feet. At the age of nineteen he had grown into a handsome man with thick brown hair and fine blue eyes. "Pa, it's good to be back," he said, then took his brother's hand, saying, "Dake—how are you? You look strong enough to pick up the ship!"

Dake nodded, his blond hair ruffled by the sea breeze. "Good to have you back, Matt. Let me take that suitcase. . . ."

Dake made it his business to get Matt's trunk, then the three men made their way to the carriage. "I'll drive, Pa," Dake announced. He was six feet tall and weighed one hundred eighty-five pounds, all solid muscle. When the three were on their way, Dake asked, "Well, are you ready to start painting portraits? I'll be your first model!" He grinned at his brother, adding, "You don't find good-looking fellows like me to pose very often, I bet!"

Matt gave Dake a smile, saying, "My rates are pretty high, but I'll put you on my list." His interest in art had taken him to England and France to study painting. He turned now and looked at

255

his father, asking, "Have you ever forgiven me for becoming a painter instead of a blacksmith, Pa?"

"Why, Matt, I never put up that much of a struggle," Daniel protested. At first he had been apprehensive over Matthew's choice, but he had been supportive, which included paying his son's expenses for the past two years. "I'm proud that a Bradford has that kind of talent."

Matthew touched his father's arm, saying at once, "I was just joking, Pa. You'll never know how much I appreciate your help." He looked at the crowded streets, noting the many red-coated soldiers. "Looks like half the British army's here," he remarked.

Dake gave the lines a sharp jerk, which caused the horses to quicken their pace. "I wish they were all back where they came from," he growled. "They've got no business here in Boston!"

Matthew gave his brother a sharp glance. "You don't think so, Dake?"

" 'Course I don't! And if I had my way we'd send them packing."

"Be a little difficult to do that, I'd think," replied Matthew.

Matthew spoke more crisply, Daniel noted, and he looked different—the effect of the English style of clothing. He was wearing a maroon velvet jacket and a pair of ash gray wool trousers tucked into a fine pair of leather Hessian boots. He also wore a square-cut vest of colorful striped satin, and a watch fob of striped red and green silk. His hat was made of beaver, high crowned and narrow brimmed.

"After all, Dake, this is an English colony."

"We're not slaves, Matt!" Dake shot back. "I guess you've been listening to the wrong people over there. I hope you've not come home a Tory."

"I'm a subject of His Majesty King George the Third, Dake—and so are you. There's such a thing as loyalty to one's country."

Dake was framing a hot reply, but Daniel said quickly, "Now, let's not get into political arguments. I want to hear about your painting, Matt. What are your plans? I don't have the vaguest idea of how an artist goes about getting started."

The tense moment passed as Matt began to speak of the future, but Daniel knew that the peace was only momentary. In the year of 1775, Boston was a powder keg, waiting for only one spark to set off a war. Dake had become such an enthusiastic member of the Sons of Liberty that he was one of Sam Adams' favorite fire-brands. As much as he had tried, Dake had failed to entice Micah into the group. And Samuel, at the age of fifteen, had to be forcibly restrained by Daniel from getting involved.

Finally they arrived at the house, and Rachel ran out to greet Matthew. "Why—I can't believe it, Rachel," he exclaimed, stunned by the change in his sister. "You were a scrawny pest when I left—and look at you now!"

Rachel was now sixteen and had blossomed into a beautiful young woman. She had her mother's heart-shaped face, but little else from her. Her hair was flaming red and her eyes were green as eyes can be. This along with a flawless complexion combined to make her very attractive. She kissed Matt, saying, "Now, when will you paint my picture?"

But Sam had come to stand before his older brother, claiming his attention. "Tell me about the machines in England," he demanded. He was not tall, but strong and filled with an endless supply of energy. He was fascinated by any sort of machinery, and Daniel boasted that he would become another Benjamin Franklin someday.

Micah stood back, letting the others greet Matthew, which was typical of him. He was a carbon copy of Dake, tall and strongly built, with yellow hair and blue eyes, but he was very quiet, almost withdrawn. He loved books, Dake often said, more than people, and there was some truth to this charge.

When they all had settled down, Rachel said, "Now, we're going to the Fraziers' for dinner, Matt, and I want to show you off. You wear your best clothes and we'll show them what a real artist looks like!"

Matthew Bradford looked around at his family. "I've missed you all," he said. "It's good to be home."

Daniel was warmed by his words. "We've been looking forward to your return for months. The family's not the same without you, Matt." He was happy and thought, *I wish Holly could see him—she'd be so proud!*

🎺   🎺   🎺

Marian looked over the dining room, pleased with the arrangement. The room was illuminated by a suspended gleaming ceiling lamp which threw amber gleams that reflected on the large sideboard and long table. She noted the Wilton carpet that was protected by a baize floor cloth. The portraits on the wall caught the light from two small patent lamps set on tripods resting on the mantel. It was a rich, lovely room, which held many special memories for Marian.

Hattie came in, saying, "Everything's ready, Miss Marian. Is Mr. Frazier going to come down?"

"Yes, Hattie. He's feeling better this evening—" A knock on the door sounded, and she said, "I'll let the guests in, Hattie." She moved down the hall to open the door. Her eyes went at once to the central figure. "Good evening, Daniel," she said softly. She smiled to cover the stirrings of old memories, then said, "Come in—all of you, please."

Daniel had not seen Marian but a few times in all these years, yet he felt awkward as he stood there in the doorway facing her. Old memories stirred unbidden in his mind, and he felt drawn by her beauty, which had not changed since their first meeting. Finally he said, "I think you've met all my family, Marian, but they've all grown up, so let me introduce them."

Marian warmly greeted each of them. To Rachel she gave a compliment on her lovely dress; to the twins she avoided making the usual trite remark about telling them apart, which pleased them greatly. "Sam, you weighed only about ten pounds the last time I saw you," she smiled. When Daniel informed her about Matthew's recent study in Europe, she extended her hand. Matthew took it and kissed it with a grace that startled Daniel and made him rather envious. "Did you meet Mr. Joshua Reynolds in London?" asked Marian.

Matthew's eyes widened. "Why, he was one of my teachers, Mrs. Rochester."

"He's my favorite painter," Marian smiled. "We dined with him several times the last time I was in England. You had a fine teacher, Matthew."

Matthew at once attached himself to Marian, monopolizing her. This attention continued all through the dinner, and finally Dake leaned over and whispered to Micah, "You'd think he'd never seen a woman before! He's a pretty slick talker, isn't he?"

Micah smiled and nodded. "She's a beautiful woman. Pa never told us that. He's known her forever, hasn't he? You'd think he might have mentioned it."

Dake shrugged his broad shoulders. "You know Pa, Micah. He's not looked at another woman since Mother died."

Rachel, who was seated beside Dake, had been listening to their conversation. "Sometimes I wish he would marry. He gets lonely," she added. She looked across the table where her father was sitting between Major John Pitcairn of the Royal Marines and John Frazier. He was wearing a new dark brown suit that she'd bullied him into buying and looked very handsome. At the age of forty-five, Daniel Bradford looked ten years younger. Rachel had been surprised by the beauty of Marian Rochester and noted that her father hardly ever looked directly at her. *He acts as though he's afraid of her—I wonder why?* she thought as she observed them.

Daniel was not aware of Rachel's eyes. He was listening as Matthew and Major Pitcairn were speaking. Pitcairn was a fine-looking man of forty who had gotten acquainted with John Frazier when he'd first arrived in America. Frazier had been drawn to the officer, and he'd become a frequent guest. The major had traveled all over the world and was a fascinating spinner of tales.

Matthew asked, "What sort of a commander is General Gage, Major?"

"A little cautious for my taste, but a sound man."

Dake started to speak, but his father caught his eye and he clamped his lips shut and listened to the men discuss the political matters of the day. He knew that Adams felt that General Thomas Gage had been sent by George the Third to clamp a lid on the rebellious activities of the Colonies. Since it was Gage's troops that had precipitated the Boston Massacre in 1770, Adams had warned the Sons of Liberty that Gage had come back to destroy their liberties. The Tories joyfully welcomed him, rejoicing that the king had finally sent them a man to make the Yankee Doodles dance.

"The man has pressed the colonists so hard with his strict regulations that Massachusetts, I hear, has called for the First Continental Congress," said John Frazier casually.

Pitcairn only smiled and shrugged. "Nothing to worry about. They will blow off steam and do no harm, John."

After dinner Pitcairn excused himself, pleading another engagement. Before he left, he turned to Daniel and said, "I mentioned to General White that we'd be dining together, Mr. Bradford. He sends you his invitation to attend a reception for the new officers who've arrived. It's tomorrow at six."

"My compliments to the general—and tell him I'll be there."

Pitcairn gave Daniel a curious glance. "He tells me you served under him once. Says you had the makings of a fine soldier."

Daniel was embarrassed, saying, "I think he makes too much of that."

"A man's likely to make much of a thing like that." Pitcairn studied the large man in front of him, then asked abruptly, "What would you do if these Sons of Liberty led Boston into a treasonous rebellion?"

Daniel shook his head. "I pray it won't come to that, Major Pitcairn. It would be tragic!"

After the major left, Daniel went to sit with John Frazier. He was worried about the older man, thinking, *He looks worse every time I see him.* The two of them listened as Rachel played the harpsichord and sang. When she was finished with the piece, they all joined in the applause. Afterward, Marian came to sit beside Daniel. "She's got a marvelous talent, Daniel," she said warmly. "You must be very proud of her."

"I am—and of all of them," he said.

They sat there talking about the rest of his family, and Daniel enjoyed her company. When it grew late, he said, "Marian, this has been most pleasant."

"We must do it again," she said quietly. She was very much aware that Leo's name had not been mentioned except by her father, who'd explained his absence. When she arose, he rose with her, and she turned to him suddenly, saying, "I'm surprised you never married again, Daniel."

Daniel hesitated, then said slowly, "I never found a woman I could share life with. I've often thought that was a selfish view. For the children's sake I should have married. They were so young when their mother died."

He stood there, the past rising unbidden like a faint echo from a far distance. Daniel was thinking of the time so many years ago when he'd kissed her—and she'd responded so passionately. He felt stirred by the memory, then wondered, when he saw her smooth cheeks color slightly, if she too remembered. She was, to him, more beautiful at thirty-two than she had been when she was eighteen. He wanted to put his arms around her, to take her from this place where they could be alone—but he knew it was a foolish thought. Carefully he said, "Marian, you've been in my thoughts for years. I'll never forget—" And then he broke off, bitterly knowing he was making a fool of himself. He said abruptly, "It's late. We must be going home."

The moment passed, and when the guests were all gone, John Frazier said, "A fine family, eh, daughter? I wonder why Daniel never remarried after the death of his wife. He'd be a fine catch for a woman—still would be. He's a young man."

"I don't know, Father," Marian said quietly, her face paler than usual. "I suppose he didn't fall in love with anyone." Even as Marian spoke, she knew it was false, for in her heart she was saying, *He loved me when he was young—and he still loves me! He couldn't even look at me tonight.* And then she suddenly admitted to herself what she had long denied: *If he asked me—I'd leave Leo and go with him!* Her lips trembled, and she blinked back the tears as she said good-night to her father and quickly went to her room.

♜   ♜   ♜

When Daniel arrived at the reception the next night, he was warmly greeted at once by Major General Adam White. White was over sixty and was retiring from the army. When he'd come to Boston, Daniel had looked him up and the two had shared some good memories. The general was beaming and shook his hand firmly. "Now then, this *is* fine! Come in and let me introduce you to the staff, Bradford."

Daniel allowed himself to be pulled into the large room and introduced to General Gage himself. Gage had come to welcome his new officers, and he impressed Daniel as a man of sense. White spoke highly of Daniel, insisting, "If you want a man to see to your horses, General, here he stands. I've always said he was the best in the army!"

Gage smiled at White but then added, "I may need some help with the horses, Mr. Bradford. Would you be able to serve in that capacity?"

Daniel was somewhat taken aback by the suddenness of the question and said only, "I have a business that takes most of my time, General Gage. About all I can offer is advice—which is cheap enough, I believe."

General White took Daniel to meet the other officers and finally said, "Well, that's the lot, except for a colonel I'd like you to meet. Where *is* the colonel, Simms?"

"Oh, he said he'd be a little late, Major." The man who spoke was a small lieutenant with a bristling mustache and a pair of sharp gray eyes. "I think his wife lost a shoe or something."

"It's a chronic disease with wives," White grinned. "Never knew one of the fairer sex to be on time for anything!" He led Daniel to the reception table loaded with food and drink, saying, "You'll like this man, Daniel. He's a fine officer!"

Daniel and General White moved to a small room where they could talk more easily. They sat at the single table drinking some of the cider and reminiscing about old times. Daniel had a thought and spoke it to White. "You know, General White, if things had gone differently, I might have been one of you. I always liked the army."

White grinned, saying, "No, Daniel, you're a rich colonist—no ducking lead for you—" He broke off abruptly on seeing a couple pass by the door. "I say—Colonel!—come in, will you? There's someone here I want you to meet."

Daniel set his tankard down on the table and rose to meet the tall officer and the woman who heeded General White's invitation. "This is Colonel Leslie Gordon—and this is Mr. Daniel Bradford, Leslie. Present your wife to him."

Gordon stepped forward and took Daniel's hand. "Happy to make your acquaintance, Mr. Bradford."

Daniel was impressed with the officer, and then he turned to meet the woman who was standing slightly behind her husband. "This is my wife, Mrs. Gordon."

Daniel turned to the woman with a smile—and then he saw her face and halted. He felt as though he'd been struck in the pit of the stomach, for he could neither speak nor move, so great was the shock that paralyzed him.

Lyna Lee Gordon's face turned chalky white, and her husband at once came to take her arm, exclaiming, "Lyna—what's wrong? Are you ill?"

Lyna's eyes were staring with wild disbelief at the man in front of her. She was trembling and was aware that her husband and General White were staring at her, asking her what was wrong.

Then she took a deep breath and moved forward.

Colonel Leslie Gordon could not have been more shocked if the sun had fallen—for his wife walked right into the arms of the tall man and clung to him fiercely! Gordon saw Bradford's arms go around his wife—saw him hold her tightly. He felt as if the world had gone suddenly insane and whispered hoarsely, "Lyna—who *is* this man?"

Lyna was clinging to Daniel with all her strength, but at the sound of Leslie's voice, she drew back and stared up into a face she'd never expected to see again until she reached heaven.

She turned and held to the arm of her brother, tears unashamedly streaming down her face.

"Leslie—this is—my brother, Daniel!" She swayed and suddenly the room seemed to spin around her. She was aware that she was losing consciousness—and the last words she heard were, "Lyna—I thought you were dead. . . !" She felt his hands reach out to support her and then she fainted.

22

A MOMENT OF PASSION

"DANIEL—COME IN!"

Lyna took Daniel's arm and practically hauled him into her small house. She turned, saying proudly, "This is your uncle Daniel!"

Lyna had come out of her faint at the reception the night before to discover that she was not dreaming—that Daniel was *alive*! She had clung to him, and he to her. They had seemed unwilling to lose physical contact and sat holding hands, taking turns relating what they had each been through over the years. General White and Leslie Gordon had sat back, shocked by the revelation—not understanding how the two could have been separated, each thinking the other dead.

Lyna and Daniel understood instantly, however. They didn't mention Leo Rochester's name—but it was clear that he had lied to both of them. Daniel felt a streak of fury roar through his brain as he thought of the deceit the vile man had used for revenge. *What kind of a devil would take pleasure in separating us?* thought Daniel, but he forced the tormenting thought away.

Finally Lyna had said, "Come visit us tomorrow, Daniel. I want you to meet our children."

"Of course—and then you and Colonel Gordon must visit us."

Daniel had left the reception in a daze. Finding his sister alive after all these years was a miracle to him. He had said nothing to any of his family when he arrived at the house but kept it to him-

265

self. That night he had lain awake thinking of Lyna. The next morning he'd gone at once to the house where Lyna and her family were living.

Now as he stepped forward and saw the face of Grace Gordon, he smiled, saying, "Well, I've never had a niece to spoil—but I intend to begin at once."

Grace was a small girl of seventeen with dark honey-colored hair and gray eyes. She had an oval face and was clearly flustered by the appearance of an uncle she'd never dreamed of having. "Mother's told us all about you, Uncle Daniel," she said at once. "She's never forgotten a thing the two of you did together, I don't think. She still laughs when she remembers how you carried that turkey off right out from under the noses of all those nobles."

"And this is Clive, our older son," continued Lyna. "He's twenty-two and wants to be a rich businessman, don't you, Clive?"

"Oh, don't be foolish, Mother!" Clive Gordon was very tall, at least six feet three, and roughly handsome. He had reddish hair, cornflower blue eyes, and a strong tapered face. He took his uncle's outstretched hand with a firm grip and said, "Happy to meet you, sir. But I warn you, Grace is right. Mother's made you out to be quite a fellow! No man could live up to her tales of that older brother of hers!"

"I'll not try, Clive." Daniel turned to shake the hand of David, who was fifteen and too forward, or so Lyna informed him. David was a lean boy, with dark brown crisply curly hair and merry brown eyes.

"It's customary for uncles to give their nephews a shilling or two from time to time," he announced brashly. "If you'd care to catch up for lost opportunities, Uncle Daniel, please feel free to do so."

"Why, you young rascal!" Lyna exclaimed. "You're incorrigible."

Daniel laughed and winked at David. "See me when we're alone, David. I think some sort of arrangement for back payment might be made."

"Don't spoil him, Daniel! He's the world's worst at getting exactly what he wants!" warned Lyna, enjoying the moment.

She was, Daniel saw, very fond of her children, and as they sat down to tea, he demanded to know more about them. He sat there looking from face to face, and finally when Lyna shooed the children away, said, "Lyna, what a wonderful family! God's been good to you!"

"Yes, He has," Lyna nodded. She was wearing a simple dress, but somehow she lent grace to it. She was as attractive as a young girl, and her hair was crisp and still glowed like honey in the sunlight streaming through the window. Sitting down beside Daniel, she took his hand and squeezed it. "I can't believe it's true, Daniel—that you're alive and we're together!"

Daniel put his hand on her cheek, whispering, "I thank God for bringing you back to me, Lyna. Part of me died when Leo told me you had died in that cholera epidemic. Now I feel alive again."

They sat in front of the fire, and Daniel listened as Lyna related how she'd nearly died—and how she had the best husband in the whole world! Her eyes glowed as she proudly spoke of how kind Leslie Gordon had been to her from the first time she had met him at the Red Horse Tavern when she had run away from Milford Manor. He listened quietly as she told him how Leslie was all that a woman could desire in a man. "His brother Oliver is Lord of Longbriar now—rich and secure. But I wouldn't give the love I've found with Leslie for all of it!"

When she was done, Lyna insisted that Daniel tell her his story, leaving out none of the details. It took a long time, for she wanted to hear everything. And he was unaware of how much of himself he gave away as he spoke, for he didn't know that this sister of his had a quick mind and was very observant. When he finally ended his story, Lyna asked one question, "What about Marian Rochester, Daniel?"

Daniel stared at her, confused. "What about her, Lyna?"

"It sounds as if you were in love with her when you were younger," Lyna said. "Are you still in love with her?"

"Lyna—she's Leo Rochester's wife!" said Daniel, shocked at the bluntness of her question.

Lyna leaned forward, her eyes fixed on him. "Of course—but you're not answering my question. Do you love her?"

Daniel felt awkward, for he had tried to keep his love for Marian Rochester buried deep down in his most secret thoughts. Now he could only stammer, "Why . . . do you ask such a thing?"

Lyna's face was filled with compassion. "Why, Daniel, you can't even say her name without showing how you feel! And you're not the first man to love another man's wife."

"Don't . . . don't say such things!" Daniel looked down to see that his hands were trembling. He clenched them but saw that Lyna had noticed his weakness. "I've got a family and she has a husband—and that's all there is to it." He looked at Lyna but could not hide the misery in his eyes. "Please, Lyna—let's not mention this again!"

Lyna nodded slowly. "Very well, Daniel. I'll not speak of it— but if you ever need to talk, I'll be here for you." She began to speak of other things, and soon afterward Leslie arrived. Kissing Leslie as he entered, she left the two of them to talk while she began to fix the noon meal.

🔔   🔔   🔔

Daniel had been badly shaken by Lyna's intuitive assertions, and as he made his way back through the city, he thought about his behavior, wondering how many other observant people had seen his feelings for Marian that he'd tried so desperately to mask. The gusty March wind pulled at his hat and snatched his coat open, but he paid no heed. *Got to learn to keep my feelings for Marian hidden—no, I've got to forget—God knows I've tried to do just that!*

He made his way to the foundry and spent the rest of the day burying himself in the work. When he finally arrived at home, he was exhausted not only physically but emotionally. As soon as he came through the door, Sam clamored for his help on a clock he was attempting to make. The two of them worked on it until Mrs. White came to announce that dinner was ready. "Come along and let's wash up, Sam," he said, and the two of them made a quick job of it.

When everyone was seated, and after Daniel said a brief prayer, he smiled, saying, "It's good to have you here, Matt. Tell me what you've been doing today."

Matt was wearing a fine wool coat and an elegant white silk shirt from Paris. "Oh, I walked along the harbor and studied the light."

Dake had lifted a knife loaded with peas to his mouth. He dexterously ladled them in, chewed hastily, then demanded, "Studied *what*, Matt?"

"The light—the sun and the way it changes the color of the sea." Matt's eyes grew distant and he seemed to be *seeing* the ocean through the wall of the house. "Sometimes in the morning when the sun is red, the sea is sort of a pale green—about the color of Rachel's eyes—but an hour later it turns to a whispering blue."

"*Whispering* blue?" Dake said with a puzzled look on his face. "What in thunder is *that*?"

Micah rarely interrupted his twin, but now he leaned forward and said, "I know what you mean, Matt—it's sort of pale, like the first violet, just *tinged* with blue. And it sort of—well, *quivers* when you try to stare at it."

Matt stared at his younger brother with interest. "You may be a painter yourself, Micah. That's as good a description of that color of the sea as I've ever heard."

Micah, not accustomed to compliments, flushed, and Rachel reached over and ruffled his hair. "You could do it if you wanted to, Micah." She was partial to Micah, for the two of them had been close all their lives. *"You should have been Micah's twin, Rachel,"* Daniel had told her once. *"You're closer to him than Dake is."*

Dake scoffed loudly. "Well, just plain old *blue* is good enough for me. I reckon it's all right for you, Matt, but I like to have things black or white."

"Most things aren't that simple, Dake."

Dake stared at Matt and shook his head. "Don't see why not. If a thing's right, it's right."

"The Bible says, 'Thou shalt not kill,'" Matt responded, "but good Christians kill all the same. In a war soldiers have to obey their orders, even Christian soldiers. So 'Thou shalt not kill' becomes a little more complicated, doesn't it?"

Dake was an argumentative young fellow and at once plunged into the fray. "Why, that makes no sense, Matt! The Bible means not to kill anyone—like to *murder* somebody. But it's different in a war. . . ."

Daniel listened as the two young men went on, noting that Sam agreed with whatever Dake said, but that Micah seemed to be less willing to go along with his twin's opinions. And as he knew would happen, Dake grew angry when he discovered that he could not answer Matt logically.

He said angrily, "Look, we've got a king over in England, but he's not an American. He sends soldiers over here to enforce all his taxes. And *you* may have forgotten that they butchered some of our people right here in Boston a few years ago, but some of us haven't!" Dake was a handsome young man, and now his hazel eyes were glowing with feeling. "And I don't think God will hold it against me if I shoot a lobsterback who's killing my people with his bayonet!"

"I don't think it's that simple, Dake," Matt said evenly. He had determined not to argue with Dake, and he could see that his father was distressed. He picked up his knife and began slicing his meat into bite-sized portions. "But I'm not going to argue with you about it."

The evening went fairly well after that, but later Daniel took Dake aside and said, "Don't pester Matt with politics, Dake."

"But, Pa—"

"No, don't argue with me. I know you think he's wrong—but he's your brother. I won't have this political mess causing rifts in my family."

"But he doesn't—"

"I'm not going to argue about this, son," Daniel said firmly. "I don't usually demand something from you, and I don't like to order you to stop your wrangling. I'm *asking* you to do it. Will you heed my wishes?"

Dake was a good-hearted young man and at once nodded. "Well, I'll *try*, Pa—that's the best I can say."

Daniel slapped Dake's shoulder, smiling with relief. "I've never known you to try something you couldn't do, son. And I appreciate it."

The next day at the foundry Daniel worked hard on getting the final designs ready for the cannon he hoped to cast. He spent the whole day working with Isaac Cartwright, the most experienced man in the shop. Finally, at four o'clock, Daniel smiled at him, saying, "This thing will probably blow up and kill both of us, Isaac."

"No, sir!" Cartwright denied vehemently. He was a short barrel of a man who knew iron and other metals like most men know their own bodies. "It'll be a *fine* piece, Mr. Bradford! Good enough to blow a few of King George's red puppets to bits!" Cartwright was a fiery patriot and had already been jailed twice for insulting Gage's officers.

Knowing that talking to Cartwright was like talking to a lamppost, Daniel shrugged and went back to his office. As he entered, Albert Blevins met him. "A note from Mr. Frazier. He wants you to stop by on the way home with all the information on the Miller project. I have it all ready."

"I'd better leave now, Albert." Daniel took off his working apron, donned his coat, and left the office. It was growing dark, but he reached the Frazier house shortly. The black woman Hattie opened the door, saying, "Mistuh Frazier, he say for you to come right to his room, suh. Lemme have your hat and coat, Mistuh Bradford."

"Thank you, Hattie."

Daniel found Frazier feeling poorly, so he stayed only a few minutes, going over the papers on the project he'd been working on. "I'll stop by tomorrow, John, and we'll go over these more thoroughly."

"Thank you, Daniel. I appreciate how hard you've been working on this," said Frazier.

Daniel bid the man good-night and left the room. When he reached the foot of the stairs, ready to leave, he was startled to see Marian.

"Do you have a moment, Daniel?"

"Of course," he said as she motioned for him to follow her into the parlor.

"I'm worried about Father. He's not doing well at all."

"What does the doctor say?"

"Oh, just that he's never recovered from the fever he had last month. But he had a strange spell of some sort yesterday. It frightened me, Daniel."

Daniel saw that her eyes were cloudy with doubt and said, "What kind of a spell?"

"He . . . couldn't describe it very well. Just said he felt peculiar and had trouble breathing. And he said the fingers on his left hand were numb . . . as if they were asleep."

Daniel listened as she spoke of her father. He noted that she was no less attractive when she was dressed in a plain dress than when she wore a rich gown and glittering jewels. He knew he should leave, but he hated to leave her when she was so distraught. Just then Hattie entered the parlor and said, "You want me to take Mr. Frazier's dinner up to him, Miss Marian?"

"Yes, please." Marian looked at Daniel and asked, "Would you stay for dinner?"

Daniel could tell that she was lonely and worried about her

father and made a quick decision, "Well, I haven't had anything since noon—"

"Come along—I hate to eat alone."

Daniel followed her into the small dining room, and soon the two were eating a simple meal of lamb and vegetables. Hattie returned and served them from time to time, then said, "I got to tend to Enoch, Miss Marian—you just leave them dishes when you gits through. I'll tend to them when I gits back."

"All right, Hattie. Be sure and tell Enoch I said for him to get well."

When Hattie left, Marian said, "Enoch is her youngest boy. He's got some sort of ague." She sipped the wine from a crystal goblet, then added, "She's a wonderful cook—and a fine nurse. I don't know what we'd do without her."

"She's a fine woman from what John's told me. He said he's setting her free," said Daniel.

"I'm glad!" Marian nodded and her light green eyes glowed. "It must be awful to be *owned*—like you were an animal!"

Daniel listened as she spoke for some time about her hatred for slavery. He was pleased to discover she felt exactly the same as he did. They talked for a time, then Daniel said reluctantly, "I've got to go, Marian."

"Oh, just one cup of tea before you leave! I've got a new service and a fresh shipment in the library."

Daniel was starting to feel awkward but agreed. He waited while she went and fixed a kettle of boiling water. When she came back they moved to the library where she brewed a pot of tea.

"I feel guilty drinking tea," she said, pouring the boiling water into a cup. "Most of my friends have fasted from drinking it. They've made it a symbol of independence ever since the Boston Tea Party. In fact, some of them have sworn not to drink the brew until England stops taxing the Colonies."

"I don't see how my refusing to drink tea helps the situation much," Daniel said dryly. He spoke for a time of the volatile politics of the country, then somehow found himself telling Marian of his sister, Lyna—how he'd found her after believing she was dead all these years.

Marian was fascinated by the tale and kept asking questions about the matter. She was half aware that she was drawing Daniel out to prevent him from leaving. Somehow she felt no shame over this and wondered at herself.

As for Daniel, a sense of comfort had come to him. He had not had anyone to share his inner thoughts with for years. Since Holly had died, he had kept to himself. All of his time was spent working hard at the foundry and giving himself to the task of being a good father as he'd promised. There had been little time for any social life. He'd been attracted to two women, but not seriously. Now as he sat in the light of the fire drinking the delicious tea—and speaking with a woman who listened so carefully—he longed to stay.

Finally he got up and she rose with him. "This has been very pleasant, Marian," he said. "I can't think of an evening I've enjoyed more."

Marian came to stand in front of him. The amber light of the fire gave her face a coral glow, and her dark auburn hair had been loosed so that it cascaded down her back. Her green eyes glowed and she seemed infinitely desirable as she said softly, "It's been good for me, Daniel—very good!"

He could smell her scent, a faint sweetness that came to him with a strange potency. She looked exquisite in the simple dress she was wearing, and there was an innocence in her face that reached out to Daniel. "You . . . you're very lovely, Marian," he said unsteadily.

Marian felt powerful feelings stir at his words, and yet she knew she should not listen. She was a lonely woman, married to a brute who had never given her tenderness. For years she had hoped that this kind of love would come between her and Leo, but he grew more thoughtless and even cruel. She had learned in a short time that she had made a tragic mistake in marrying Leo, but there was no retreat in her world. She had thought often of Daniel Bradford, with a bittersweet memory of things that she had allowed to slip past her.

And now as she faced him, tracing the strength in the solid planes of his jaw and the steadiness of his hazel eyes, she longed for him. And being a woman, she knew that he longed for her in the same way. She leaned forward, spoke his name in a broken whisper, and he came to her—as she knew he would.

His kiss was firm and inviting, and she responded equally so. She clung to him, knowing only that he loved her and that there was something good in him. His arms were enfolding her closer, determined and strong, and there was a protectiveness in his embrace that made her weak.

For how long they stood there, holding each other, swayed with passion that threatened to break out in a flood, she never knew—nor did Daniel. They were both like two enraptured people, their minds blinded by their love, on the edge of a deep chasm, teetering on the brink—

And then a voice broke through the moment—loud and jeering.

"Well, my dear wife—I see that you're entertaining your lover! Quite a welcome home from England!"

Marian and Daniel broke apart, and Marian uttered a cry of distress. "Leo—I didn't know—!"

"Obviously you didn't," Leo said. He had been drinking, and his mouth was tight with anger. He was wearing an overcoat and carrying a gold-headed cane, which he gripped until his knuckles were white. He stared at Daniel, finally saying, "I think I will kill you, Bradford!"

Daniel had never felt so helpless. Guilt raced through him, and he knew that nothing he could say would have the slightest influence on Rochester. He said evenly, "I wouldn't blame you too much, Leo. And I make no defense. But it's all my doing. Marian has never—"

But Rochester laughed harshly and glared at Daniel with red-rimmed eyes. "Oh, *spare* me that, Bradford! Don't play me for a fool. Do you think I don't know a guilty woman when I see one? Just look at her—she's guilty as Jezebel!"

Daniel glanced at Marian. She looked so vulnerable and pale standing there, her lips trembling. "Leo, I've never lied to you," Daniel said. "You know that, don't you? Never!" When Rochester hesitated, he said, "I swear to you that this one moment of indiscretion is the first—and you must blame me, not Marian."

Rochester seemed for a moment to sway, as though he were half convinced of Daniel's impassioned plea. Drunk as he was, he did know that Daniel Bradford was a man of honor. Perhaps it was, for some complex reason, the cause of his hatred for the man. But it lasted for only a moment, then he sneered, saying, "A man will lie for a woman when he'll lie for nothing else. Get out of my house, Bradford."

Daniel moved stiffly past Rochester and picked up his hat and coat. When he reached the door, Rochester cried out, "This isn't over, Bradford! You'll regret touching something of mine!"

Daniel did not respond but left the house. He moved woodenly and was so shaken by the scene he had difficulty mounting his horse. He never remembered riding home, for the ugly scene played itself again and again in his mind.

What a fool I was—and it's Marian who'll have to pay for it!

As soon as Bradford left the house, Rochester crossed the room where Marian stood and struck her with his fist. She fell to the floor, blood salty in her mouth, but as he cursed her, punctuating his curses with more blows, she did not utter a word. Her silence infuriated Rochester worse than anything else she might have done. After he finally stopped hitting her, he snarled with a terrible intensity, "We'll see how much you love him after he's a corpse—which is what I intend to make of Mr. Daniel Bradford!"

23

LEO SEES HIMSELF

THE EVENTS LEADING TO THE SHOTS heard round the world at Lexington and Concord were only a preamble of what was to come. Much later those in Massachusetts would look back upon them as a series of dress rehearsals for the inevitable war that broke out between the American Colonies and Britain.

General Gage had been steadily accumulating troops, but when he called for workmen to build barracks, none came forward to help. He sent to New York and Halifax for workmen, but the Sons of Liberty began a campaign of sabotage. Brick barges were sunk, straw for soldiers' beds was burned, and supply wagons were overturned.

Enraged by this show of resistance, Gage sent soldiers to Charlestown and Cambridge to seize colonial powder and cannon. When the Continental Congress heard the report of Gage's action, it exploded in outrage. Many of the patriots viewed it as a violation of the very fundamental liberties that had been set down in the original charters. Almost overnight four thousand armed and angry men thundered into Cambridge, while all over New England others organized units and were on the march. This unbelievably swift response would have alerted most that the colonists were on a trigger edge, teetering on the brink of a revolution. But Gage was a general and did not read the signs of the times. Instead, he kept his head well hidden in the sand of military protocol. The fact that the men of America could gather almost instantly into a host seemed not to trouble him.

Another incident occurred when Gage sent a military expedition to Salem on February 16, 1775. The British met the colonial militia under Colonel Timothy Pickering's command at an open bridge. The staunch Pickering faced the British troops down! As they turned to march sullenly back to Boston, a nurse named Sarah Tarrant taunted them from an open window, "Go home and tell your master he has sent you on a fool's errand and broken the peace of our Sabbath. What, do you think we were born in the woods to be frightened by owls?"

Angered by the woman's jeering, one of the soldiers lifted his musket and aimed it at her. Sarah Tarrant scoffed at him, "Fire if you have the courage—but I doubt it!"

And so the British empire was challenged by Americans willing to sacrifice all to defend their rights. All through the Colonies fiery voices demanding freedom from the English Crown began to blaze. The fire was fanned in Virginia by Patrick Henry, who was well known as a revolutionary and great orator. He rose before the newly formed Virginia Provincial Convention and declared:

"There is no retreat but in submission and slavery! Our chains are forged. Their clanking may be heard on the plains of Boston! The war is inevitable—and let it come! I repeat it, sir, let it come!

"It is in vain, sir, to extenuate the matter. Gentlemen may cry, 'Peace! Peace!'—but there is no peace. The war is actually begun. The next gale that sweeps down from the north will bring to our ears the clash of resounding arms! Our brethren are already in the field! Why stand we here idle? What is it that the gentlemen wish? What would they have? Is life so dear, or peace so sweet, as to be purchased at the price of chains and slavery? Forbid it, Almighty God! I know not what course others may take, but as for me, give me liberty or give me death!"

The thundering rhetoric of Patrick Henry was soon carried well beyond the walls of the Virginia Convention. It was carried on the lips of all true patriots throughout the Colonies. Unrest was mounting and troubles were stirring again in Boston.

General Gage was facing a dilemma that threatened to weaken his military strength. It was not with American militia, but with his own troops. Sick of the poor pay, rotten food, and the unforgiving lash, the disparaged soldiers were deserting by the hundreds. The offer of a new start in a new land appealed to many of them, causing them to flee from Boston. Gage, with the typical mentality of many British officers, gave orders to severely punish anyone who was caught trying to escape. Ordinarily under military law they would have been hanged, but with the growing resistance among the colonists Gage could not spare them, so the sentence was "milder"—a mere 1,000 lashes to be administered at the rate of 250 per week! The only effect this inhumane discipline had was to encourage more men to flee!

The tension between the militia and Gage's soldiers continued to build as April approached. The British soldiers tried to ignore the dismal conditions by staying comfortably drunk, for liquor was cheap in Boston. Their officers found feminine companionship of the lower sort and even went so far as to put on amateur theatricals at which the more effeminate of the officers sometimes quarreled over who should play the feminine parts, complete with dresses.

Colonial Leslie Gordon was appalled by the deteriorating morale of the men. As an officer in His Majesty's service, he was repulsed at how the troops were behaving. "We're looking like buffoons, Lyna," he said one morning at breakfast. "I can't imagine what General Gage must be thinking!"

Lyna poured him a fresh cup of tea, concerned about the situation. "But it won't come to a war, will it, Leslie?"

"It might if Lord North doesn't stop issuing those idiotic regulations. His taxations have already pushed people to the edge."

Later in the day, Gordon was walking through the camp on an inspection with Major John Pitcairn. They paused to watch a squad of soldiers taking target practice—and were disgusted when every single soldier missed the mark.

An elderly farmer had come along with his son to bring a load of lumber to the camp. He stopped unloading long enough to watch the shooting, then laughed aloud. The sergeant in charge of the squad cursed him, asking what was so funny.

"They ain't much for shootin', are they?" the farmer grinned. He was one of the few who had agreed to sell supplies to the British, so he was not afraid of the sergeant's scowl.

"I suppose you could do better?" the officer scoffed.

"Why, I got six boys—and this here"—he waved at the dark-haired fifteen-year-old boy who stood watching—"he's the worst shot of 'em all, but I reckon he can do better than them soldiers."

"Let's see if he can!" challenged the Redcoat.

Leslie said at once, "That's a mistake, John! We'd better stop it."

"Oh, let him try," Pitcairn said carelessly.

The sergeant set five loaded muskets in front of the lad, and the boy proceeded to hit the target five times in a row, two of them bull's-eyes.

Leslie Gordon turned away in disgust, stating flatly, "Just what we needed! Our men beaten at their own game by a farmer boy! And the old man is probably telling the truth, John. These Americans have grown up with a musket in their hands, and a man is a lot easier to hit than a squirrel!"

"Aye, but squirrels don't shoot back, sir," Pitcairn shrugged. "They're a rabble in arms, this militia of theirs. They'll never stand against the trained troops of the Crown."

☙ ☙ ☙

Dake Bradford stood before the three men, his heart beating fast. Sam Adams, Paul Revere, and Dr. Joseph Warren had asked for him to remain after the meeting was over! He had seen them at many of the secret meetings the Sons of Liberty had convened, where he'd listened to them speak many times. But now face-to-face with his heroes, Dake could barely keep still.

Sam Adams had pretty much failed at everything he'd tried. He was a man fueled by a passion for freedom and soon turned his zeal into writing. He was born for this moment in time. He had become a gadfly, able to powerfully stir up the people of America against the British rule with his polemical writings. Every time he gave an impassioned speech, his eyes burned with the light of a true believer. His clothes were shabby, and he was an average man in height, weight, and appearance. He had a great head, which he held at an angle, always in motion.

"Mister Bradford, I have had good reports of you," Adams said abruptly.

"Why, I want to do my best, sir!" said Dake, drinking in the man's praise.

"You're a fine horseman, I understand? And you have a fast mare?"

"Fastest in Massachusetts!"

Dr. Warren laughed at the quick response. "I like a man who believes in himself—and his horse, Mr. Bradford." Warren was the most popular physician in Boston, a hero to many for his work in the smallpox epidemic of 1763. His chief interest, however, was not medicine, but liberty. He had opposed the Stamp Act with all his power and had risen steadily in the hierarchy of the patriots' cause, serving as the chairman of the Committee of Safety and president of the provincial Congress. And this tall, handsome man would be the first to be clapped into prison—and perhaps hanged—if a real war broke out. "Would you be willing to use this fabulous mare of yours for the cause?"

"Yes, sir!" said Dake eagerly.

All three men smiled at the instant and enthusiastic reply. Adams nodded, saying, "Fine! Fine! Mr. Revere will give you your instructions." He hesitated, then asked, "Your father—is he a patriot?"

Dake hesitated, then answered carefully, "Well, Mr. Adams, he doesn't really understand what we're trying to do. But when the fighting starts, I assure you, he'll be with us!"

"He's a good man by all reports," Revere said. He was a short stocky man, dark complected and square faced. "He's working on a new project—learning to cast cannon. That would make him an invaluable man for our cause."

Dake blinked with surprise. He knew nothing of his father's work in casting cannon and realized that the Sons of Liberty had spies in practically every house in Boston. "I wish you'd talk to him, Mr. Adams," he said. "You could make him see how important this is."

"I will try to see that we have a talk, your father and I."

As soon as Adams and Warren left, Revere waved Dake to a table, his dark eyes glowing as he said, "Now, when the revolution begins, we must have men who can get the word out to our people all over New England. I will be one of those, and you will do the same, Dake."

"Will it be soon, Mr. Revere?" Dake asked as the short man rose finally.

"Sooner than you think, young man!"

🔔　　🔔　　🔔

Resentment had burned with a vitriolic rage in Leo Rochester ever since he'd seen his wife in the arms of Daniel Bradford. He had not been completely sober since that night, and abusing

Marian had not been enough. He had not struck her again after that first outbreak of anger, but verbally he lashed her with cruel words that cut deeper than any whip.

If it had been any other man, he thought as he sat in the Eagle Tavern three days after his return, *I wouldn't have been greatly disturbed. She's never been the kind of woman I've wanted! I've had to find warmer women than her!* He was just drunk enough for his thinking processes to be slowed down considerably, and he defiantly drained the glass of whiskey and shouted, "Innkeeper—blast you! Bring me a bottle!"

He snatched the bottle from the resentful innkeeper, poured a glass, and drained it off. As the liquor hit his belly and sent a fine mist of fiery fumes into his head, he thought of Marian. Their marriage had been a disaster from the start, and he had a brief moment of regret, knowing that he had been a poor husband. He thought of their wedding night—how she'd looked so beautiful in her white gown—and how fear had overwhelmed her that night. He'd been drunk and had thought of nothing but himself. He was rough, without a thought to tenderness. He remembered he'd felt bad the next day, but the damage was done. When he approached her, she shrank back, her eyes filled with fear and disgust.

The memory angered him, and he took another swig. "Let her have her men," he muttered. "But not *him*—not Bradford!" For years he had bred resentment for Daniel Bradford, knowing that he'd wronged him. Now he reveled in the savage pleasure of knowing that Bradford was not the perfect man some thought him to be.

"Hypocrite—blasted hypocrite! No better than me! Puts on a front, but he's as rotten to the core as the rest of us!"

Rochester drank steadily, and finally a purpose grew in him. *Got to show him—he can't treat Leo Rochester this way!*

Rising to his feet, he had the innkeeper fill the silver flask he always carried with brandy. Tossing several coins to the host, he staggered out of the tavern. "You—over here!" he shouted. When a carriage pulled up, he had to grasp the side of the vehicle to keep from falling. "You know where Daniel Bradford lives?"

"No, sir, don't know the gentleman."

"Well, do you know the Frazier foundry?"

"Oh yes, indeed, sir!"

"Go there, find out where Bradford lives—then take me there—but first go by Anderson's shop over by Faneuil Hall."

Half an hour later, Rochester walked out of Anderson's Gun Shoppe with a pistol, primed and loaded, under his coat. He climbed into the carriage and ordered the driver, "Take me to Bradford's house!" He then drew the flask and drank half the contents, swallowing convulsively. As the carriage rattled along, he muttered, "Nobody will blame me—injured husband! Got a right to—defend my honor!" He soon grew dizzy and lay down on the seat, falling at once into a drunken stupor. He was aware once that the carriage stopped, but he could not rouse himself. He felt sick and fought down the nausea that came as the vehicle started up again. He fell asleep and did not move until he heard a voice that seemed to come from far away.

"Sir? This is where Mr. Daniel Bradford lives."

Rochester muttered, "Go—away—" but the voice became more insistent. He struggled to a sitting position and blinked uncomprehendingly for a moment at the round face of the coachman.

"Shall I get help, sir? You ain't feeling too well, are you?" the coachman asked diplomatically, noting the drunken stare on Rochester's face.

"No, blast you!" Rochester heaved himself out of the carriage, cursing when he staggered, but shoving the stocky driver aside when he tried to help him. "Keep your hands off me—!" Fumbling in his pocket, he tossed a crown at the cabman, but then realized he had no way to get back to his home. He shook his shoulders together, blinked his eyes and said, "Wait here—there'll be another fare and an extra crown for you."

"Yes, sir—I'll wait right here!"

The street was nearly empty and darkness was falling over Boston. Leo felt sick and his legs trembled as he walked toward the white clapboard house set back from the street, but the bitterness that had burned in his belly seemed to ignite again. He reached the door, touched the pistol in his belt, then lifted his hand and knocked resoundingly on the door. As he waited, he thought of what he was about to do, and fear ran through him. He had never killed a man, nor even been involved in a brawl. But he was too drunk to realize much, and when the door swung open to reveal a tall woman with white hair, he muttered, "Mr.

Bradford—have to see Mr. Bradford!"

Mrs. White gave him a cautious examination, then nodded. "Come in, sir. I'll tell Mr. Bradford you're here." She stepped back, and as Rochester stepped into the entryway, she smelled the raw liquor and saw that he was very drunk. "The family is at dinner, sir. If you'll wait in the library, I'll tell Mr. Bradford you're here."

"All right." He followed the woman into a small room lined with books and illuminated by a whale-oil lamp. The woman turned and left, and he stood there, sobering considerably as the significance of what he planned to do began to sink into his mind. He was not at all concerned with the wrong of killing a man, nor was he at all troubled by what might follow. Men who took the wives of others were fair game, and no jury or judge would convict him for killing a man who had violated his home and his wife. He was thinking only of the possibility that his hand might not be steady enough, that he might miss with his one shot. He knew the prodigious strength of the man. If Bradford didn't fall dead, he might well get his hands on his assailant. Rochester had seen Bradford twist a heavy horseshoe with his bare hands, and he shuddered at the thought of what those hands would be like on his neck.

He positioned himself with his back to the bookshelves, directly opposite the door, and waited. A large clock on the mantel over the fireplace filled his ears with an ominous, steady cadence. As it ticked off the seconds, the thought leaped into Leo's mind: *In a few minutes—if I miss—I may be dead, and that clock would go on with its infernal ticking!* He had given little thought to death, for despite his indulgences, the man had never been ill. Now, however, as the *ticktock, ticktock* of the clock repeated in a remorseless rhythm, he felt fear crawling along his nerves. *To be dead—to die at the hands of Bradford!*

And then the door opened and Daniel Bradford entered. Instantly Rochester's hatred revived, and he watched as the big man closed the door carefully, then turned to face him squarely. "Well, Leo," he said evenly, "what brings you here?"

Bradford's coolness served to anger Rochester, for it made his own weakness seem suddenly contemptible. He wished he were sober, for he hated the thought that his drunken condition must seem a flaw to Bradford. But the sight of Bradford's face gave him a sudden determination to finish what he'd come to do.

"You're a hypocrite, Bradford!" he cried. "I've known it for years. You've deceived some, but all that religious talk of yours—that pious churchgoing you've shown to the world—it's all an act!"

"I've given you cause to think so, Leo," Daniel said quietly. He had known as soon as Mrs. White had come to whisper in his ear that a gentleman somewhat under the influence was in the library asking to see him that his visitor was Leo. He had been expecting such a thing but had rather thought that the encounter might occur elsewhere. Now as he looked at Rochester, he saw the hatred that burned in the man's bloodshot eyes. "Sit down, and I'll try to tell you how—"

"I know how it was! You're a liar and a cheat, Bradford!"

"As I say, I've wronged you, but not as you think."

"Go on, Daniel," Leo taunted. "Tell me how it was all just an innocent little embrace. You felt *sorry* for the neglected wife, I suppose? And I know she's told you what a beast of a husband I've been!"

"Marian's never said one word against you, Leo."

"Oh, that's likely, isn't it, Bradford?" Leo's anger rose higher, for he had convinced himself that Marian had indeed revealed the truth about her failed marriage. The thought enraged him and he shouted, "Don't bother to lie—I know what you've done! You're both alike, you and her! Why, she hasn't even given me a son! She's barren as a brick—!"

Rochester broke off, for he had not intended to say this. It was a shame—the only one—that lay in him. He had wanted a son for years, had expected one from his marriage. But none had come, and he was angered and hated Marian for failing to provide him one. Deep down he was not at all certain that the lack of a child was her fault—as he often told her it was. For all his affairs, he had never heard that he had fathered a child. This would have been something to boast of, but it had not happened—and deep inside, a scalding sense of inadequacy had burned in his heart. He had hated Daniel for his sons as much as for anything else, and now staring at him, he realized he'd blurted out something about himself that he never wanted anyone to know.

Daniel had not missed the desperation in Rochester's voice. He thought at once of Matthew. Knowing that the son for which Leo Rochester so obviously longed was no more than a few feet away troubled him. However, he masked his alarm, saying, "You're not able to talk about this in your condition, Leo. Go home and sober up. Tomorrow we'll—"

But he had no opportunity to complete what he planned to say, for Leo had drawn the pistol from beneath his coat. Had Leo been sober, Daniel would have died, for he was only five feet away. But Leo fumbled as he drew back the hammer of the pistol. In that one small instant, Daniel leaped forward and knocked the weapon aside.

The pistol exploded. The powder burned Daniel's coat, but the ball passed through the fabric, tearing the shirt underneath, and plowing into the heavy oak door instead of into his heart.

Daniel easily wrenched the pistol away from Leo, and one look at the man's face revealed fear. "I'm sorry you did that, Leo," said Daniel. The echoes of the shot reverberated in the small room, and the sound of running feet came down the hall outside. Then the door burst open and Dake ran in first, followed by the family and Mrs. White.

"Pa—are you all right?" Dake cried, rushing to his father's side, his eyes fixed on Rochester. He noted the pistol in his father's hand and the powder burns on the coat. "Are you shot?" he demanded.

"No, I'm all right." Daniel swept the faces of his family, wishing heartily that the incident had not happened. He did not think of the fact that except for the short interval of time Leo took to draw the pistol's hammer, he would be on the floor with a bullet in his heart. He saw all of them staring at Rochester and said quickly, "We've had a little accident—nothing to worry about. This is Mr. Leo Rochester. You met him once, but you were all very young."

Rachel came and looked at the bullet hole, her face pale. "Let me see, Pa," she said. "You're hurt!"

But Daniel took her hands, saying quickly, "No, there's no harm done." He shot a quick glance at Rochester and saw that the man's complexion had turned pasty white. "Why don't all of you go back? I'll have a few more words with Mr. Rochester—"

At that moment Matthew came into the room. He had left the table early, going to his room, and now he came rushing in, demanding, "What's the matter? I thought I heard a shot!"

Instantly Daniel shot a glance at Rochester and saw that the man's gaze riveted on Matthew. Quickly, he stepped in front of Matthew, saying, "Just an accident—all of you, please leave us alone."

They all reluctantly moved to the door, but Dake turned to put his eyes on Rochester. "I'll be right outside, Pa, if you need me."

"Thank you, Dake," Daniel nodded, then shut the door and turned to face the ashen-faced man opposite him. "That was a fool thing to do, Leo," he said tightly. "You'd have swung from the gallows if you'd killed me."

But Leo Rochester was staring at the door, his lips drawn in a thin pale line. His voice, when he spoke, was a hollow whisper. "Who was that?"

Daniel knew it was hopeless to try to turn Rochester's mind from what he had seen. Both he and Holly had seen from the time Matt was an infant that he bore an astonishing resemblance to Rochester. To both of them it was a tragedy, and especially for Holly. Every time she looked at him, she saw the features of the man who had so brutally taken advantage of her. She had never mentioned the resemblance, nor did Daniel while she was alive—but they had both watched silently, dreading the day when somehow the two might meet. However, there had been little chance of that—at least so it seemed.

And now it had happened—in his own home—but Daniel resolved to give no ground to Matt's real father. "It's time for you to go," he said, ignoring Leo's words.

But Rochester turned to face him, his eyes wild. "Who is that?" he repeated. He forgot himself enough to come closer and grasp Daniel's arm. "Tell me—who is he?"

"He's my oldest son, Matthew Bradford."

Rochester blinked and stared at Daniel. "No—he's not!" A shiver seemed to run through him, his body shaken by the young man he'd seen. "He's as like me as a mirror image! He's me—when I was his age!" He grabbed wildly at Daniel, catching the lapels of his coat, whispering hoarsely, "He's my son, isn't he, Bradford?"

Daniel removed Leo's hands with his iron grasp. "Don't be a fool! He's my son—"

"He's Holly's son—but not yours!" Leo was thinking quickly and gave a startled look at the door. He was suddenly aware of a tremendous surge of joy. He was not childless—he had a son! "She was with child by me when she left Fairhope," he said slowly, tracing the history in his mind. "You married her and gave the child a name, didn't you?"

A grim despair seized Daniel Bradford. *All for nothing—all the years we kept the secret—gone in one second.* He had often wondered about the right of keeping Holly's secret from the boy, but never once had he seen any profit for the boy in telling him the sordid story. Now he knew that all that was changed. He knew instinctively that Leo wanted a son desperately, and he knew as well that there would be a fight to save the boy.

"Forget what you've seen, Leo," he said finally. "The boy is my son. He was born to me and Holly, and any court in the world will certify that I'm his father. Holly is gone, and she's the only one who knew the truth. Go away and leave the boy alone. You can bring him nothing but misery."

"I can give him the truth—and I can give him his heritage!" The sight of his son had sobered Rochester completely. He stared at Daniel for a long time, then nodded. "He'll know the truth, Bradford. He has a right to that—and I have a right to my son!"

At that moment Daniel Bradford felt overpowered by a blinding rage. "You have a *right*? You who disgraced an innocent girl and never gave it a thought? If justice were served, you'd die for that!" Daniel stepped forward and lifted his powerful hands, unconscious that he was doing so. Fighting off the rage, he slowly lowered his hands and said, "Get out, Leo. And don't ever come near me—or my family!"

Rochester stared at Daniel. "I'll go, Bradford—but this isn't over." He walked stiffly to the door, then turned abruptly, his face changed. A light came to his eyes, and he said, "There may be a way out of this."

"There's nothing for you, Leo. Get out!"

"You love my wife, I take it? And I want a son. Does that suggest anything to you?"

The hideous offer, veiled as it was, revolted Daniel Bradford's sense of honor. He stepped forward, uttering through clenched teeth, "Rochester, you're a *monster!*"

Rochester didn't flinch. "You want Marian—and I want Matthew. Sooner or later, you'll come to your senses and see that it would be best for all of us. I assume she loves you, and she detests me. We have no marriage—never have! As for Matthew, I can give him the world! And I will!" He turned and purposefully strode out of the house, his footsteps firm and determined.

Daniel stood in the center of the room, not believing what he had heard. "He'd trade Marian to get what he wants!" he gasped—and then with incredible power, the whisper came to him—something deep inside, from a place he'd kept locked and bolted.

Why not? Matthew would be rich—and you and Marian would be happy!

Daniel was paralyzed by the enormity of the evil thought. Whirling he picked up the pistol that lay on the desk and threw it at the wall with all his strength. It clattered to the floor, and he stared at it, then cried, "Oh, God forgive me!" Then, gaining control of his emotions, he picked up the pistol, placed it on the desk—and walked out of the room. He forced himself to smile, but when he entered the dining room and saw Matt looking at him, a sword seemed to pierce his side. He looked like Holly—something in his eyes—but his face was an unspoiled version of Leo Rochester's visage.

"Come now, let's finish our dinner," he said calmly.

Matt looked at him carefully. "Is . . . everything all right, Pa?"

"Yes, Matt. Everything is all right."

24

A Town Called Lexington

GENERAL THOMAS GAGE HAD LITTLE USE personally for spies or traitors. "If they will betray their own," he once remarked to General John Burgoyne, "what's to prevent their betraying us?"

Now as he listened to his visitor, an urbane, handsome gentleman by the name of Dr. Benjamin Church, he felt stirrings of disgust. He kept an impassive look on his face, however, for he knew that Church was a longtime member of the Committee of Safety—the heart and core of the resistance against the king. Gage was also aware that Church had fallen in love with a wealthy woman and was in need of funds to carry on his courtship.

Church looked over his shoulder nervously, as if afraid of being seen. He had come late under cover of darkness, and even so, he spoke in a whisper. "Ah, General, I trust things go well with you?"

"They do not, sir." Gage's voice was almost harsh, and he had to force himself to modify it. *The fool may have something for us—have to smile and charm him.* "Sorry to be so short, Dr. Church, but I've just received orders from London. The Crown is unhappy with me. They demand that action be taken at once." He rose and went to stare out the window into the inky darkness. He was caught in a trap and well knew it. Gage knew the Americans better than Lord North, better than the king—better than any man thousands of miles away insulated from this boiling spirit of revolution. But he was a soldier and bound by duty to obey orders.

Turning to Church he said, "I need your help, sir. I must make a showing of some sort. I intend to arrest some of the leaders—Sam Adams and John Hancock to begin with. Where are they, can you tell me?"

"In Concord," Church rapped out. "You must move quickly, however, for they won't stay there long." He coughed and said, "I find myself a little strapped for funds, General, but I might give you a very good bit of information if—"

Gage knew the rules of the game and pulled out a bag of coins from a small desk. "There—" he said, counting out a quantity of them into Church's hand. "What do you have for me?"

"When you send a force to arrest Adams and Hancock, you can seize the arsenal of the Committee. It's in Concord, well hidden, but I can give you the location."

General Gage's eyes widened at the news. He did not expect such valuable information from Church. This was more than he had hoped for. "Give me their guns and powder, and I'll have them! Give me the details. . . !"

𝕴   𝕴   𝕴

"What is it, dear?" asked Leslie Gordon as he hurriedly donned his uniform. Drawing on his boots he turned to Lyna, who had entered the bedroom.

"Who was that at the door?"

"Orders, Lyna. I've got to be gone for a time."

"Can you tell me what it is?" Lyna knew Leslie didn't like her to pry for information, but she was worried about the growing tension between the colonists and the soldiers.

"General Gage has decided to arrest some of the rebel leaders and to seize their store of muskets and powder."

"Will there be trouble?"

"Gage doesn't think the rebels will fight—but he's wrong." He stood and pulled on his coat, then turned to her. "Don't worry about me—but that's foolish for me to say. You always do when I may be in action, don't you?"

Lyna went into his arms and lifted her face. She took his kiss, returned it, then drew back with a frown on her face. "Yes, I do worry about you. And now I worry about my nephew. Dake is caught right in the middle of this trouble. Daniel's worried sick about him."

Leslie hesitated, weighing something in his mind. Finally he said carefully, "Lyna, I can't give away military information, but if you could tell your brother to keep his son at home for a few days, it might be wise. This thing will blow over, hopefully, but I like that young man—hate to see him get hurt."

As soon as Leslie had ridden away, Lyna dressed quickly and left the house. She drove to the foundry and was shown into Daniel's office by Blevins.

Daniel smiled as he rose from his desk and greeted her, but he saw that she was troubled. "What is it?" he asked. He listened as she spoke, then the two of them talked for a long time. Finally he said heavily, "This is hard. I wish you and Leslie were stationed anywhere but here."

Lyna nodded but said, "God will have to take care of Leslie and Dake. There's no way to stop this thing, is there?"

"No, I'm afraid not. It's certain to break out—just a matter of time." He shook his head doubtfully, adding, "Dake's seventeen years old. He's a young man now, not a boy. If I tell him not to fight, he'll leave the house, and I don't want that to happen."

"What will you do, Daniel?"

"I don't rightly know. But we're all in God's hands. My family comes first, of course."

"Will you fight if it comes to a war?" Lyna knew that her question was a painful one and said quickly, "I shouldn't have asked that." She rose, and when he thanked her for the warning, she said, "I'll be praying for you, Daniel, and you must pray for Leslie and my own boys."

"I already have, Lyna, and I will continue," said Daniel.

🛡   🛡   🛡

Paul Revere spoke hurriedly, his dark eyes glowing with excitement. He and Dake were standing under the shelter of a large elm tree, watching the British officers as they harried their men into formations. Revere had sent for Dake and now pointed toward the soldiers. "Those are the grenadier and light infantry companies—the best troops Gage has," he murmured.

"I've been watching the harbor, sir," Dake spoke up. "They've been pulling the whaleboats up for repairs."

"Have they now? Good work, Bradford!" Revere thought rapidly, then said, "I think these troops will be sent from here to Cambridge—then they can take the road to Concord—that's about twenty miles." He gave the younger man a steady look. "I must see Dr. Warren—I suspect we'll have some riding to do!"

The next morning Warren sent Revere to Lexington to warn Sam Adams and Hancock to be ready to make their escape. He returned that night, having agreed that if the British went by water he would have two lanterns placed in the North Church steeple, and only one if Gage sent them by the overland route.

On April 18, Gage sent patrols along the Concord road on the alert for rebel couriers. That night eight hundred of his elite troops were awakened, startled out of a sound sleep. They fumbled into their uniforms, then formed ranks under the eyes of their commander—a fat, slow-thinking man—Lieutenant Colonel Francis Smith. Smith had under his command Major John Pitcairn. Also accompanying the troops was Lieutenant Colonel Leslie Gordon. At half past ten the British ranks began to move out. As soon as word reached Dr. Warren, he sent William Dawes and Paul Revere flying from Boston to warn the countryside.

Revere rowed over to Charlestown, sprang onto a waiting horse, and rode off at top speed. Behind him two lanterns began to glow in the steeple of Old North Church. When Revere reached the home of Parson Jonas Clark, he shouted the names of Adams and Hancock. When they emerged Revere excitedly relayed the news to them. Sam Adams turned to Hancock and exclaimed, "What a glorious morning this is for America, Hancock!"

On his way back to Boston Revere was captured by the British. The senior officer put a pistol to Revere's head and threatened to blow his brains out if he didn't cooperate. Revere admitted that the whole countryside was aware of the march of the British on Concord and would be ready for it. Later Revere was released and returned to the Clark house. With fresh mounts, the three patriots began their journey to Philadelphia where the Continental Congress was in session.

And on the clear, cold morning of April 19, 1775, the pale sunlight fell on the long British columns that were marching into Lexington.

🜨   🜨   🜨

"The men are in poor shape, John." Leslie Gordon rode alongside Major Pitcairn, and both men were dismayed as they watched the troops move out. The Sons of Liberty were constantly making it difficult to secure adequate supplies. And the continuing desertions had greatly affected the morale of the remaining soldiers. The march itself lacked the professional manner Pitcairn expected of his men.

Pitcairn was a strange choice for second-in-command, for there were no Royal Marines in the column. Nevertheless he was a fine officer and agreed with Gordon's statement. "Poor business!" he nodded. "We'd be better off to pull back and try on another day."

The soldiers were angry, wet from the waist down because of the moist white paste that was used to keep their breeches white. Now the breeches were stained with mud, and their slow-thinking commander had kept them waiting two hours for rations before forcing them to wade up to their chests in cold water to get into the whaleboats. They had been on their feet now for five hours. Each man was dragged down by sixty pounds of equipment in a pack and a ten-pound musket, the unreliable Brown Bess, which was carried at their side.

At the sound of bells and a musket being fired, a private lifted his head and said, "Well, they knows we're 'ere, Simon," he announced disgustedly to the man beside him. "We ain't about to sneak up on 'em, is wot I says. Wisht I was back at the tavern with Molly!"

Even as he spoke the brightly polished barrels and glittering bayonets of His Majesty's troops were visible to a handful of patriots drawn up on Lexington Green.

🎺   🎺   🎺

"Pa—? Wake up!"

Daniel came out of a fitful sleep with a start at the whisper that penetrated his bedroom door. Throwing back the thin sheet he used for a cover, he came to his feet and stumbled through the darkness to open the door. He was blinded at first by the yellow light of the lamp that flared in the darkness of the hallway, then made out Micah's face. "What's wrong?" he demanded quickly.

"I have to talk to you," Micah said. The amber light threw his face into sharp planes, making dark shadows of his eyes. When his father stepped back, Micah entered and stood waiting until Daniel took the taper and lit the lamp. Micah could see the troubled expression on his father's face.

"What is it?" Daniel asked. Of his four sons Micah was the most steady, the least likely to be alarmed—and yet Daniel could tell he was disturbed.

"Pa, I hate a sneak," Micah said, looking down at the floor for a moment. "But I got to tell you—Dake's gone to fight with the militia."

Daniel felt a coldness seize him, but he said only, "I knew it would come to this. You're right to tell me, Micah—don't worry about it."

"But that's not all, Pa—he took Sam with him!" he blurted out.

"Sam!" Daniel knew Dake felt he had to be a part of this, but he was disappointed that Dake had influenced Sam.

"Yes, Pa. I tried to stop him, but Sam said he'd bellow and wake you up, and Dake didn't want that. He said he'd look out for Sam—but I don't like it."

"Nor do I, Micah." Daniel stood there, thinking quickly, then asked, "Did Dake say where he was headed?"

"He said Mr. Parker was calling the Lexington militia out. The whole countryside's up in arms, Pa. The British are going that way—a lot of them," Dake said.

"I'll have to go bring Sam back," Daniel said at once. "Dake's old enough to do as he wants, but I'll not have Sam mixed up in this thing."

"What's wrong?" asked Matthew, who had stepped into the room. "It's something about the Sons of Liberty, isn't it?"

"The British are on their way to Concord to arrest Sam Adams," Micah explained. "Dake took Sam with him to join the militia."

"Why, that's foolish! The militia can't stand against regulars!"

"I don't know about that, but I'm going to get Sam," said Daniel.

"I'm going with you, Pa," Micah insisted. "I'll saddle the horses." He glanced at his older brother. "Want me to saddle your mare, Matt?"

"No. I won't get involved. And if you're wise, Pa, you'll grab Sam and get out of it. Everyone who's in this thing could be arrested and even hanged."

"That might be—but I'll have my son or know the reason why! Go get dressed, Micah. We'll take the road to Roxbury, then cut north to Cambridge. The British will be taking the northern road directly into Lexington, but we can beat them if we ride hard!"

Fifteen minutes later the two men were riding at a full run, muskets tied to their horses. They kept up a steady pace, and Daniel was thankful for the fine horses they had. They passed through Roxbury and found the town up in arms. Men were scurrying around, gathered into a line of march by their officers. Later when they passed through Cambridge, they found the same activity. They rested the horses and got what news they could from the excited officers of the militia.

They rode at a steady pace through the night, and as dawn began to turn the east into a reddish glow, they saw the town outlined ahead of them. Drawing the tired horses to a walk, Daniel nodded. "I think we're in time, Micah. Don't hear any kind of firing."

As they rode into the town, a sentry stepped forward and challenged them. But when he identified them, he said, "Captain Parker's got the men out on the Green—go join 'em!"

The two men moved forward toward the masses of men ahead and dismounted and tied their horses. "Come on," Daniel said tersely. "We'll find Sam and pull out of this."

"Yes, sir."

They walked over to two young men who were standing tensely observing the Green. Daniel asked the older one, "What's going on?" When the tall young man hesitated, Daniel said, "I'm Daniel Bradford."

Instantly the young man turned to stare at him. "I think you might know my father—Adam Winslow."

"Why, I certainly do! We served with Colonel Washington together back in fifty-five."

"I'm Nathan Winslow, and this is my younger brother, Caleb." He indicated a very young man standing beside him, "This is Laddie Smith." His face was grim and he said, "My father always speaks highly of you, sir."

"I'm glad to hear it. He's a fine man," Daniel said. "I'm trying to find my two sons. I want to get them out of this affair."

Nathan Winslow grimaced. "And I, sir, am trying to get my brother out of it. This is going to get bad!"

Daniel stared at Nathan, then at the stubborn face of his brother. Shaking his head, he said, "Both of you should leave. As

297

soon as I find my sons, we're all getting away."

Daniel turned away, feeling a sense of hopelessness. Finding Sam was less difficult than he feared. They had not gone more then twenty paces before Micah said, "Pa—there's Dake and Sam!"

Daniel at once spotted the two and walked up to where they stood waiting. He led Micah toward the pair, noting that they had seen them. Dake's face was stubborn, and Sam's no less so. "Dake, I'm disappointed in you," Daniel said, stopping to face him.

"It wasn't his fault, Pa!" Sam protested. "I threatened to wake you up—"

"Be quiet, Sam," Daniel said firmly. "Dake, you're old enough to decide for yourself about this—but why did you bring your brother along? I thought you had more sense."

Dake was unable to meet his father's eyes. He had known from the moment he'd agreed to take Sam that it was the wrong thing to do. Several times along the way he told Sam to go home, but Sam had stubbornly refused. Now he lifted his head to meet his father's eyes. "You're right, Pa. I'm sorry."

"Well, that's something. I want to—"

"Here they come!"

Daniel was interrupted by a shrill, yelping cry. He whirled, hearing at the same instant the clipped cadence of drums. He saw the flash of bayonets and red uniforms approaching. Captain Parker called out an order, and the seventy or so men of the militia fell into line inside a triangle formed by the three roads. The road to Concord was at its base. Parker's men stood about a hundred yards above it, and Daniel and his sons could see the approach of the advance guard.

"There ain't many of us, Captain," one of the militia called out. "And they's a heap of them lobsterbacks!"

"The first man to run will be shot down," Parker responded.

Across the way, John Pitcairn ordered his men into a line of battle. At once the trained troops formed a line three men deep. They made an awesome sight to the untrained Americans—a solid mass of soldiers, all carrying glittering bayonets.

"Stand your ground," Parker ordered. "Don't fire unless fired upon. But if they want to have a war, let it begin here!"

Daniel watched helplessly, knowing that one false move would ignite the battle fury. He watched as Pitcairn rode forward, shouting, "Lay down your arms! Disperse!"

The militia seemed to hesitate, and it seemed that the crisis would pass. Parker realized that the situation was impossible and commanded his men to disband, taking their weapons with them. But a shot rang out.

Afterward, the arguments raged about who fired it—both sides claiming that the other had done so. Pitcairn and Gordon both moved out, ordering the men to hold their fire, but the regulars were angry. A volley rang out from some militia behind a wall. One British soldier was wounded and two balls grazed Pitcairn's coat.

One of the officers yelled out, "Fire!" and the regulars fired a volley. One of the shots must have been high, for an older man standing not ten feet from Daniel fell back, clawing at his side. Daniel saw that the militia had no chance to stand and said, "Come on, we've got to get out of here!" The four of them turned, and as they moved back from the Green, Dake turned to see Jonas Parker standing alone. He was reloading his musket, and Dake cried out as four British soldiers reached him, thrusting their gleaming bayonets into his body.

Dake lost his reason and turned to run toward the oncoming soldiers. Daniel raced after him, followed by Sam and Micah. He caught Dake, swung him around, saying, "Don't be a fool, Dake!"

At that moment Sam cried out, and Daniel and the other two whirled to see the boy falling. He grabbed his upper leg, and Daniel saw that he'd taken a ball. Without a word, he leaped at Sam and picked him up. The balls were whistling around the four of them, and he yelled, "Come on, boys!"

He glanced over and saw that Caleb Winslow had been shot and that his brother Nathan had picked him up and was running with him. He felt a stab of grief, thinking how terrible it would be for Adam Winslow if he lost a son in this useless slaughter.

The militia were all scattering in the confusion. And if Daniel ever was grateful to God for his prodigious strength, it was during those minutes when he raced along bearing the sturdy form of his son. He kept up with Dake and Micah, and finally they drew up in the shelter of a clump of large trees.

"Let's have a look at that leg," Daniel said. He pulled Sam's trousers down and with glad relief said, "Missed the bone!" Pulling off his scarf he made a quick bandage and bound up the wound. Sam pulled his pants up, his face pale. "It don't hurt much, Pa," he said grimly. Then he looked around and said, "Look, there's some of the men forming over there."

Daniel looked in the direction and saw that Sam was right. One of the men, evidently an officer, had managed to stop the rout. They could hear him saying, "All right, men, they got the best of us—but we'll have our revenge. They're bound for Concord—but they've got to come right down that road to get back to Boston!" He was a tall, thin individual with a hatchet face. "By the time they get back, we'll have reinforcements. We'll lay for 'em, and by the Great Jehovah and the Continental Congress we'll show 'em they can't kill our people! Are you with me?"

A cry went up, and Dake said abruptly, "Pa, I'm staying. You and Micah take Sam back home."

"No, I'm not going!" Sam Bradford got to his feet, his face pale. "They murdered Captain Parker and the others. If they can do it to them—they'll do it to anybody who stands against them!"

Daniel saw the determination of his son. Despite his objection, Daniel felt a thrill of pride at the spirit of this youngest son of his.

"Pa, I'm only fifteen, but I'm old enough to fire a musket— don't make me go home, Pa!"

At that moment a strange thing happened to Daniel Bradford. He was an Englishman—had never had a desire to be anything else. He'd stayed clear of the rabid politics of the day, hoping to walk a middle road. But now he thought of the dead who lay on the Green at Lexington, and he looked down at the bloody bandage on Sam's right leg. *It could have been him—or Dake or Micah— lying dead*, he thought. Suddenly he knew that the shots that had been fired had changed the world for him. Sam had put the matter into its simplest form. *If they can do it to them—they can do it to anybody who stands against them!*

Dake and Micah were watching their father closely—as was Sam. He was the best man they knew. Now they saw that his face was tremendously sober, his eyes half closed. Dake held his breath, and then he heard his father say, "I guess you've been right about this thing all along, Dake. No man's going to be able to straddle a fence anymore." There was a deep sorrow in Daniel Bradford's voice, but he straightened himself, and anger glowed in his eyes as he added, "We'll do whatever honest men can do."

Micah knew what this cost his father to say, and he remained silent for a moment. Then he said, "Pa, I don't think I can do this."

Daniel said instantly, "Go home, Micah. Stay out of it if you can."

"No, I'll stay, but I won't fire on British soldiers—not yet."

Dake looked at his twin, not understanding. But he said only, "You'll have to come to it someday, Micah." Then he said to his father, "Sir, I honor you!" Then he turned and walked away toward the officer and began speaking to him.

"Sam, can you make it on that leg?"

Sam's broad face was pale, but he smiled. "Yes, sir—if you'll give me a hand from time to time."

"We'll have to do that from now on, son!"

🅣   🅣   🅣

"We're being cut to pieces, sir!" John Pitcairn was hot and thirsty as he came to protest to Colonel Smith. The column had proceeded to Concord, found a few stores, had a brief engagement with some local militia, then turned and headed for Boston.

But four thousand men had gathered around that sixteen-mile gauntlet running back to Charlestown. They had not formed into ranks but had fired from behind stone walls or trees. Redcoats slumped to the dust, dozens of them, and there seemed to be no defense. The wagons were piled high with wounded, and still the carnage went on.

Gordon had come with Pitcairn to reason with the commander. "Sir, we've got to get in their flanks!" he exclaimed. "If we can double back on them, we can drive them from those fences."

"All right, Colonel Gordon, take some men and do so!"

Gordon quickly formed a force, and for a time his tactics worked—but the militia faded into the woods, only to re-form farther down the road. They would allow the column to get even with them, then rise up and fire a solid sheet of volleys, mowing down the exhausted soldiers like ripe wheat.

The strain of the long march and the heat of the battle caused the discipline of the British to fade. They had been on their feet for more than twenty hours, carrying heavy packs of equipment. As the men continued to fall, some of them tried to escape in a stumbling run, only to be shot down by the sharpshooters positioned along the road.

Finally at three o'clock a relief column led by Lord Percy appeared, and Gordon whispered, "That's good, John. They'd have killed us to a man if Percy hadn't come."

The fight continued all the way to Charlestown, and the casualties continued to mount. The British had 73 men killed, 27 missing—probably dead—and 174 wounded. The Americans had 49 killed, 5 missing, and 41 wounded.

Sam had fought for a time, but Micah had taken him home when he grew faint. Dake and Daniel had followed the fight, moving along the road all the way. When they were less than a mile from Charlestown, Dake finally ran out of ammunition and ran back to get more. Daniel was behind a fallen tree as the column passed. The soldiers were firing at his group, and he heard the whistle of musket balls like tiny bees around his head.

He lifted his musket and carefully trained it on the tall officer who was helping a wounded soldier into the creaking wagon. His finger started to pull on the trigger. Suddenly the man's face came into focus, and Daniel saw that he was aiming at Colonel Leslie Gordon, his sister's husband.

Time stood still for Daniel in that instant. He had killed men that day, hating every moment of the battle. He had taken a stand from which he could not retreat. Now he was committed, and the man in the red coat was his enemy.

In that frozen fraction of a second, a picture of Lyna's sweet face rose in Daniel's mind. He thought of their terrible times as children, and he thought of how much she loved this man—and he her.

Slowly he loosed the trigger and let the muzzle drop. He watched as Gordon straightened up, his face twisted with pain. *He hates this as much as I do,* Daniel thought.

As the column moved out Daniel stood up, his shoulders slumped with fatigue from riding all night and then fighting. He turned and walked wearily along the road looking for Dake. Deep inside he had the premonition that the last few hours had brought the Colonies to a pivotal place in history. The yearning for freedom had now broken out into a fight for the pursuit of inalienable rights that every patriot longed for. And he knew that the world that had existed for him the day before when he set out to come after Dake and Sam was gone forever. Whatever lay ahead, it would not be the peaceful life he so valued. He studied the faces of the tired men around him and realized that his own face had the same determination as theirs. Sides had been taken, and there would be no turning back!

It'll be a long time before I can find what I had before this day—maybe never. . . . The sun slowly dipped down behind the hills, casting a purple haze over the world, and a nightingale murmured a few notes in a plaintive voice.

25

FAITHFUL TO GOD

"LESLIE!" LYNA RAN ACROSS THE ROOM and threw herself into her husband's arms. His face was smeared with black powder stains and his uniform was filthy. Lyna clung to him fiercely, feeling a tremendous gust of relief that he had come home safely from the battle. She kissed him and placed her hand on his cheek. "Sit down—I've got tea."

Leslie slumped into a chair beside the trestle table and began to pull off his boots. He had not slept since the battle and was trembling with fatigue. His feet were aching, and he groaned with relief when the high-topped boots were off. "Lord, that feels good!" He picked up the mug of black, sweetened tea and drained it.

Lyna refilled the cup, saying, "Are you hungry, dear?"

"No, but I'm so tired I could sleep on the floor."

"You'll have to eat a little—then you need a bath." As she moved quickly around the room throwing a hot meal together, she asked, "Was it very bad, Leslie?"

"Bad? It was terrible, from beginning to end, it was awful!" Gordon sipped the tea, then as he ate the hot stew, he told Lyna of the carnage that had taken place on the road back from Concord. "As ill-planned and awkwardly executed as ever a battle I've seen!"

"Did we lose many officers?" Lyna listened closely as he gave her the details of the British losses, then, when he finished, asked,

"Were . . . were many of the Americans killed?"

Instantly Leslie understood what was troubling her. "I'm afraid so, Lyna. Not as many as we lost, but some of the men went wild—started killing civilians who'd done nothing."

Lyna felt a cold fear grip her heart but said no more. After Leslie had eaten and she'd seen to it that he had a hot bath, she bullied him into bed. She kissed him, whispering, "Thank God you came back unhurt!" Then she moved to get her cloak, saying, "I'm going to find out about Daniel. I'll be back as soon as I can. Sleep well, my dearest!" When she reached the bedroom door she turned and looked back. Leslie was already asleep. Slipping out the front door, she hurried her step, trying to control the cold fear that rose inside her.

🔔   🔔   🔔

Leo stepped into the bedroom to find Marian sitting in front of her dressing table. Coming to stand behind her, he studied her face in the mirror for a moment before speaking. He had never ceased to admire her beauty, even though their relationship had deteriorated years earlier. The afternoon sun slanted through the window, bringing out the rich auburn tints in her hair. Over the years she had kept her trim figure. Many of his friends had wives who had turned fat, and a faint regret threaded its way through him for what he had lost. However, Leo Rochester was a realist, with a strong cynical strain in his makeup, so he put away the thoughts of what might have been.

"Have you heard about the battle?" Leo noted with interest that his question caught her attention instantly. "I expect your lover is right in the middle of it," he said, then took out a cigar and lit it, waiting for her to answer. When she said nothing, he grunted, "Don't play games with me, Marian!"

"I've told you the truth, Leo," she said quietly as she continued to pin her hair.

Irritated at her simple answer, Leo snapped, "I come home to find you in the arms of another man, and you tell me it's all innocent? I'm not a simpleton, Marian!"

Marian had fastened the last pin and stood to face him. She was wearing a pearl gray dress with green trim at the bodice and sleeves. Except for her wedding ring, her only jewelry consisted of two small pearl earrings. The strain of the whole thing had left its traces on her face, small lines at the outside corners of her eyes and a tenseness in her mouth. But she answered evenly, "I'm sorry for what happened. I was wrong. I can only say again that what you saw was all there was."

Somehow Leo knew she was telling the truth—and that was somehow painful. He had been with dozens of women, and when he'd found Marian in Bradford's arms, he'd been incensed—but somehow almost pleased. He wished to see her brought down to his level—both her and Bradford—but deep inside he knew that Marian was telling the simple truth.

He asked suddenly, "Are you in love with him?"

"I'm your wife, Leo."

"That's not what I asked—but I think we both know the answer to my question." A faint, humorless smile crossed his lips, and he said, "I know you pretty well, I think. You're cold to me—but you'd never let another man kiss you unless you loved him." He gave her a sudden angry gesture of his hand, his voice hard. "I didn't come here to talk about you and Bradford—or maybe I did." He puffed on the cigar, studying her thoughtfully. "He loves you—I think he has for a long time."

"Leo—!"

"Did you know that he's not the father of that oldest boy?"

Marian stared at him blankly. "What do you mean?"

Leo's eyes grew suddenly bright and he straightened his back. "He married Holly Blanchard when she was carrying a child—and the child was mine!"

"I don't believe it!"

"Don't you? All you have to do is *look* at him."

An image of Matthew leaped into Marian's mind. She had been vaguely aware that he looked nothing at all like Daniel physically. And she had noted that he was very different from his three brothers. She had assumed that he resembled his mother, but at Leo's words she now was forcibly reminded that every feature of the young man was like that of her husband.

"Comes as a shock to you, doesn't it?" Leo walked to the window and looked out, not seeing the tall trees that spread their large branches over the house. He had thought of little else but the fact that he had a son since he had seen Matthew Bradford. He had not admitted to a single soul how the failure of his marriage to produce children had been a sign of personal failure in his own mind. If Holly Blanchard's child had been a girl, he would not have been so affected, but he was very English in the deep-seated desire to see his name carried on through a son.

Turning to face her, he said, "I want Matthew to become my son. He's the only hope of the Rochester line. I don't want my name to die with me."

"It's too late, Leo. He's not a child anymore—and even if he were, Daniel would never give him up."

"It's not up to Daniel," Leo snapped. "As you say, Matthew's not a child. He's nineteen years old and able to make up his own mind."

Marian stared at him, the shock of the thing etched on her features. "You can't do this thing, Leo," she said, a pleading light in her eyes. "It would shake his whole world. Daniel Bradford's the only father he's ever known. Think what it would mean to him!"

"Mean to him? It would mean that he'd be the son of nobility instead of a blasted tinker! The boy's not a fool, I can tell you that, Marian. Why, I only saw him for a moment, but I could read his face like a book! He's sensitive and there's nothing of Bradford in him. When I offer him everything—including Fairhope and a proud name—he won't hesitate!"

Marian could see that Leo was set on the thing and, for a moment, felt a twinge of pity for the man. She had been humiliated by him for her failure to produce children. And in truth she did feel the sting of that failure more keenly than she ever allowed him to know. But somehow she knew that the desire of Leo to have a son would not be met in Matthew Bradford. But she had never had the slightest influence on Leo and saw that it was hopeless to try to dissuade him now.

Leo gave her an odd look, his lips twisting into a travesty of a smile. "I've already made Bradford an offer. He wants you, and I want a son. Not a bad trade, I'd say."

"Leo!" gasped Marian.

"Why looked so shocked, my dear? It happens all the time. You must know that." Leo shrugged lightly. "Men get rid of their wives as they get rid of horses or houses. Most of the time they do it to get a younger woman. I think my motive is a little more noble than that."

"You—can't be serious!"

"I am serious—deadly serious." He suddenly fixed his eyes on her in an intense stare. "You're so conventional, Marian—you and Bradford. He was as shocked as you are. The two of you are alike, and I think you've found that out. But after all, I'm not trying to trade you off for another woman. You love the man, and he's so in love with you I can read it in his eyes. And for what it's worth to you," he added, "I believe you're telling the truth about your *affair.* Both of you are so self-righteous you wouldn't consider doing anything sinful. But if you were free, you'd go to him in a heartbeat."

Marian tried to protest—but she knew instantly that this much of Leo's speech was true.

He saw her hesitate and nodded. "I see you agree with me. Well, let's be honest with each other. Divorce is an ugly business and pretty difficult to come by—but there are ways. Money will buy anything."

"That's not so!"

"Isn't it? But think what it could be like, Marian—you could have Bradford—which is obviously what you want. He could have you, which is what *he* wants. I could have a son, which is what *I* want. And despite what you or Bradford think, it would be a good thing for Matthew. So all four of us get what we want. Can't you forget your little moral quirk and see that I'm right?"

"Leo, marriage isn't like other agreements," Marian protested. "It's forever in God's eyes."

"I know that's the way the storybooks speak of it. 'And they got married and lived happily ever afterward.' But life isn't a fairy tale, my dear. I sometimes wish it were." Strangely enough the cynical side of Leo Rochester gave way to what seemed to be a wistful air, and for that brief moment, he appeared more vulnerable than Marian had ever seen him. He dropped his eyes and seemed to study the pattern of the carpet for a long moment, and when he lifted them, he had none of the hard edge that a life of self-indulgence and dissipation had brought him. He said almost gently, "I know I'm not a good man—never have been. But in this one thing at least, I think I'm not asking for myself—at least not *only* for myself."

"Leo, you can't just step into a thing like this. You can buy a house or a carriage, and it's yours as soon as you pay for it. But you must see that being a father isn't like that—not at all!"

"It's too late for me to go back and change nappies and walk the floor with the boy," Leo said sharply. "I know that—and I'm not fool enough to think I'd have been any good with an infant. But I can be good with Matthew as a man. He's just ready to begin his life, and I can give him everything a young man needs—money, a fine name, an estate. . . ."

Leo spoke for a few moments of the advantages Matthew would enjoy and finally said, "I see you don't agree. Well, I don't care whether you do or not, Marian. It would be easier if you and Bradford would see this thing in the proper prospective. You'll do all you can to turn him against me—but in the end, he'll come to me!"

Leo spun around and left the room. Marian stood staring after him, her mind seeking some sort of answer—but none came. She well knew the stubbornness of her husband, and a heaviness settled over her as she moved out of the bedroom and made her way to see to her ailing father.

She found him sitting in his chair, fretful and nervous. "I'm worried about this battle, Marian," he said at once. "I want to know what's going on." She tried to soothe him, but he shook his head. "I'm stuck in this house like a mouse in a trap. I don't get any news about anything. Go see what you can find out, won't you, daughter?"

"All right. I'll be back as soon as I can. Try not to be upset."

"Why shouldn't a man be upset with the world falling down around him?" John Frazier halted abruptly, then smiled and reached out his hand. "I'm sorry, Marian. Don't pay any mind to my ways."

"It's all right, Father," Marian said quickly. Leaning down, she kissed him, saying, "I want to know as badly as you do. I won't be too long."

"Go by and see Blevins at the shop. He seems to know everything."

Marian left the house and went at once to the foundry. As she expected, Daniel was not there, and she learned that Blevins had gone to the town hall, where there was a meeting of the leadership.

"He'll be back soon, Mrs. Rochester," Edward Jenns, the foreman, assured her. "Why don't you just wait in 'is office?"

"Thank you, Edward, I think I will." She went to Blevins' office and tried to be patient but found she was more nervous than she'd been in years. Finally the door opened, and she turned from the window expecting to see Blevins. Instead Jenns said, "Lady 'ere to see Mr. Bradford—but I expect she can wait in 'ere."

"Quite right, Edward." As Jenns left the room, Marian nodded to the woman who entered. "I'm Mrs. Rochester," she said. Marian was curious, wondering who this tall, attractive woman could be. There was a genteel air about her, and she looked familiar somehow.

"I'm Lyna Lee Gordon, Mrs. Rochester—Daniel's sister."

"Oh—yes!" At once Marian saw the strong resemblance between sister and brother—the same light hair and features. In the sister, these were smoothly refined, of course, but she had the same steady eyes and strong chin. "I've heard about your marvelous reunion with your brother. You must be very happy."

Lyna answered, "Yes, it's been like nothing else in my life. . . ." She was very conscious of the woman who stood before her and was favorably impressed with Marian's bearing. *This is the woman Daniel loves*, she thought and determined to probe deeper than a casual conversation. "I'm very concerned about Daniel," she said, seeing a flicker of fear flash in the large green eyes of Marian Rochester. "He's gone to fight with the Americans, you know."

"I . . . didn't know for certain." Marian felt that Lyna Gordon was one of the most perceptive women she'd ever met. There was a steadiness in her gaze that revealed a more than casual interest. *I wonder how much Daniel has told her about . . . how we feel?* Aloud she said, "It must be very difficult for you, Mrs. Gordon—with your husband in the king's forces."

Lyna could sense that Marian was a woman of compassion. She moved closer and nodded. "It is difficult—and will become worse, I fear. My husband is a soldier and is very loyal to the Crown. I know Daniel will be drawn to the patriot cause. Two of his sons are already involved. . . ."

For half an hour the two women talked, and each discovered the other to be kind and gentle. Finally Lyna decided that honesty was what Marian needed. "I'm very fond of Daniel," she said quietly, then added, "And I believe you are, too, Mrs. Rochester." When Marian started and turned pale, Lyna came to put her hand on the arm of the other woman. "Oh, he's not said how he feels about you—not directly, that is. But he's such a dear, honest man! He can't speak your name without revealing how he feels."

Marian was trembling and said, "I . . . I can't speak of him, Mrs. Gordon!" She hesitated, but the kindness in Lyna's face gave her the courage to say, "Once—a long time ago—we were very close. But that's all over!"

"Is it?" Lyna murmured, then started to say more when the door burst open. The two women turned to see the tall form of Albert Blevins. Seeing them he halted and exclaimed, "Mrs. Rochester—Mrs. Gordon—!"

"Albert—what is it?" Marian asked.

Blevins was flushed and for once his stolid features were contorted with worry. "It's Mister Bradford!" he exclaimed. "I was on my way back from the city hall when some of the militia got back from the battle—some of 'em wounded. I knew the sergeant, and he'd heard that Mr. Bradford was hurt bad!"

"Where is he, Blevins?" Marian demanded.

"The sergeant didn't know for sure—but it's likely they took him to Doctor Rush's house—that's where they're setting up a hospital for the wounded."

"Where is it, sir?" Lyna cried out. "I must go to him!"

"Yes, Mrs. Gordon," Blevins nodded. "I'll take you myself."

But Marian spoke up, "My carriage is downstairs, Albert. You wait here. Someone may bring word. I'll take Mrs. Gordon to her brother." Turning to Lyna she said, "Come with me. We'll find him, Mrs. Gordon . . . !"

☥   ☥   ☥

"Why, it's nothing but a scratch!" Sam protested vehemently. "I could have stayed at the fight if—"

Doctor Claude Bates was a short, rotund man with a shock of gray hair and a pair of sharp black eyes. "You hush, Sam Bradford!" he said loudly. He had the loudest voice in Boston, though he was not aware of it. His great booming baritone voice numbed the ears of all his patients, and he seemed incapable of whispering. "Your father ought to give you a caning!" He looked down at the bandaged leg and turned to the men who stood around Sam's bed. "Keep him off that leg," he thundered as though they were half a mile away.

"What's that you say, Doctor?" Dake asked, cupping his hand behind his ear. "I didn't quite get that."

"Stop your foolishness, Dake!" Micah had taken over Sam's

312

care, ignoring his protests. He'd rousted Doctor Bates out and now asked, "Any chance of infection, Doctor?"

"Certainly! Always a good chance of that." The doctor collected his gear and said irritably, "Well, I'll go see to some of the other fools who didn't have sense enough to stay out of a fight!"

"The doctor's not a patriot," Daniel said as the door slammed. He looked down at Sam's leg with concern. "But he's a good doctor. You'll mind what he says, Sam."

"But I want to be in on the fighting!"

Dake shook his head. "Won't be any fighting for a spell, Sam. The lobsterbacks have holed up here. They can't get out, either," he added grimly. "Our men have thrown a ring around Boston. We've got 'em!"

"There's a little more to it than that, Dake." Matthew had been sickened by the whole thing. Now he looked at the pale face of his brother Sam and shook his head. "King George will send twenty thousand trained soldiers here if he has to. He's vowed to stamp out patriot rebellion!"

"So—we'll train ourselves," Dake countered. "We did all right in the battle, Matt. Whipped them completely!"

"And what would have happened if the battle had been fought in the open?" Matthew shook his head. "Sooner or later the British will catch you in a battle where you can't hide—and that'll be the end of it. But I won't be here to see it."

Daniel lifted his head sharply. "What does that mean, son?"

Matthew turned to face Daniel. "I'm going back to England—maybe to France. All I want to do is become a painter—the best artist I can be. And you know that until this revolution is over, there's no place for that in this country." He saw the disappointment on his father's face and said, "We'll talk later."

Dake stared at the disappearing form of his brother and shook his head. "I don't understand him, Pa. I guess I'm just too dumb to see why a man won't fight for his family and his country."

Micah saw that Sam was looking sleepy. "Come on, Dake," he said at once. "Let's go see if we can find out what's going on."

"That be all right, Pa?" Dake asked, obviously anxious to go.

"Yes, both of you go on. I'll stay with Sam."

The twins left and Daniel sat down and talked with Sam for the next fifteen minutes. He saw that the boy's face was tense and said quickly, "That leg's hurting. Let's see if some of this medicine Doctor Bates left will help."

Pouring a large spoonful of the dark liquid down Sam's throat, he said, "That smells bad enough to be good medicine."

"Yahh—!" Sam grimaced. "Tastes awful!" He squirmed in the bed, then asked, "Pa, what's going to happen? Is Matthew right?"

Daniel pulled his chair closer to the bed and began to talk with Sam. Soon he saw the boy's eyelids droop, and finally his breathing became slow and measured. Rising to his feet, he tiptoed out of the room and went to the library. He sat down and began to think of all that had happened and wondered about the future.

Sometime later, he was startled by a knock at the door. Quickly he came to his feet, and when he reached the door and opened it, Daniel was surprised to see Lyna.

"Thank God, you're all right, Daniel," said Lyna, throwing her arms around him and embracing him. "I was so worried!"

"Lyna, what's wrong? Is it Leslie?"

"No—I'd heard that you were wounded. . . ." She explained what she had heard from Blevins, then asked, "Are the boys—?"

"Sam got a ball in his leg—but he's all right."

After Lyna had listened to the details of the battle, she said quickly, "I'll sit with Sam. There's someone in the carriage who's very worried about you." When he stared at her, Lyna said, "It's Marian Rochester. She was at the foundry when we got word that you'd been hurt, so she offered to bring me in her carriage to help find you." Lyna hesitated, then put her hand on his arm. "Go to her, Daniel. She's very concerned."

Daniel blinked with surprise, then gave his sister a straight look. "All right—I will." He stepped outside and walked to the carriage. Marian gasped when she saw him approach. "I'm all right, Marian," he said quickly. She was staring at him, her face pale. "Come into the house," he offered. "It was Sam who was wounded, not me. But he's going to be all right."

Marian shook her head, saying, "No, Daniel, I can't come in. Please get in and tell me about Sam."

Daniel stepped into the carriage and sat down beside her. When he turned to face her, explaining Sam's wound, he saw that she was shaken. Finally he said, "Marian—!" and reached over and took her hands. They were cold and he held them tightly. "I . . . I don't want to make things worse for you."

"I know, Daniel!" Marian was struggling to hold back the tears that formed in her eyes—but in vain. She had been terrified that he was dying, and now that he sat beside her, she knew that never would she love any man as she loved this one. His hands held hers tightly, and she longed to know the strength of his arms around her, holding her close.

Daniel saw the tears gather in her eyes and run down her face. "Marian...!" he whispered. "I hate to see you like this!" His voice was husky, and he wanted to kiss the tears away—but knew that would be wrong, and such a thing would only make matters worse. He sat there, aware that they were trapped in a hopeless situation. He wanted her more than he'd ever wanted anything in his life, but deep down he knew that he must let her go.

"Marian," he said softly, "I'm not a wise man—but one thing I know—" He paused, thinking how to frame words to express what he felt, then said more strongly, "I want you more than I want anything except heaven. But I've watched people all my life take things that they wanted—and leave God out. And every single time, I've seen the thing they wanted most turn to bitter ashes in their mouths."

Marian nodded, very conscious of the warmth of his hazel eyes. She noted the scar on the bridge of his nose, the high cheekbones, and the strong forehead. She wanted to reach up and touch the cleft in his chin, to smooth his thick hair back—but knew that she must not. "Yes, you're right," she nodded. "I've seen the same thing."

They sat there quietly, and finally Daniel said, "If you and I took each other, Marian, we might have some joy for a time—but it would be wrong. Sooner or later we'd lose what we have now— respect and trust—and love." He hesitated, and then spoke again, saying, "But I feel something inside me—something I can't really understand. It's like God is saying, 'Be faithful to me—and I will give you the desires of your heart.' My desire is to wholeheartedly follow God. I love you, but I *must* honor your commitment to Leo."

"Oh, Daniel—I feel that, too!" Marian exclaimed. She stared at him, her eyes filled with tears, but now there was joy in them instead of misery. She had been unhappy and alone for so long, and the future looked even more bleak—but somehow his words had touched a spring deep inside her heart. The weight seemed to lift, and she whispered, "If I remain faithful to God—He won't fail me, Daniel. And He won't fail you, either."

He lifted her hands and kissed them, then reached out and put his hand on her cheek. A quietness filled his spirit and he said softly, but with a strength that gathered in him like a rising wind, "No matter what the future holds, God will uphold you, my dear!"

Marian felt his strength in the touch of his hand, heard it in the firmness of his voice—and somehow she knew that what he said was true.

"Yes, Daniel," she nodded. "God will not leave me!"

He got out of the coach and entered the house, not looking back. Marian sat quietly in the carriage, her heart beating strongly, then picked up the lines and spoke to the horses. As she drove along the streets, she was aware that the city was humming with the excitement of the beginning of the war. Ahead the future looked bleak and terrifying. The sound of the trumpet had roused the specter of war, and soon there would be men dying on bloody fields. The wheels of destiny were turning, and the world would never be what it was since the first shots fired at Lexington. A great beast was slinking over the land and would demand the blood that war always seeks.

But despite all this, Marian was more conscious of the feel of Daniel's touch on her cheek, and of his words that seemed to linger in her heart.

Looking up into the sky where dark clouds marched along in ranks, she whispered, "Thank you, Lord God—for a man with strength to love You more than he loves his own way!"

TREAD
UPON
THE
LION

BOOKS BY GILBERT MORRIS

THE HOUSE OF WINSLOW SERIES

1. *The Honorable Imposter*
2. *The Captive Bride*
3. *The Indentured Heart*
4. *The Gentle Rebel*
5. *The Saintly Buccaneer*
6. *The Holy Warrior*
7. *The Reluctant Bridegroom*
8. *The Last Confederate*
9. *The Dixie Widow*
10. *The Wounded Yankee*
11. *The Union Belle*
12. *The Final Adversary*
13. *The Crossed Sabres*
14. *The Valiant Gunman*
15. *The Gallant Outlaw*
16. *The Jeweled Spur*
17. *The Yukon Queen*
18. *The Rough Rider*
19. *The Iron Lady*
20. *The Silver Star*

THE LIBERTY BELL

1. *Sound the Trumpet*
2. *Song in a Strange Land*
3. *Tread Upon the Lion*

CHENEY DUVALL, M.D.
(with Lynn Morris)

1. *The Stars for a Light*
2. *Shadow of the Mountains*
3. *A City Not Forsaken*
4. *Toward the Sunrising*
5. *Secret Place of Thunder*

SPIRIT OF APPALACHIA
(with Aaron McCarver)

Over the Misty Mountains

TIME NAVIGATORS
(For Young Teens)

1. *Dangerous Voyage*
2. *Vanishing Clues*

TREAD UPON THE LION

GILBERT MORRIS

BETHANY HOUSE PUBLISHERS
MINNEAPOLIS, MINNESOTA 55438

Published by Bethany House Publishers
A Ministry of Bethany Fellowship, Inc.
11300 Hampshire Avenue South
Minneapolis, Minnesota 55438

Printed in the United States of America.

Library of Congress Cataloging-in-Publication Data

Morris, Gilbert.
    Tread upon the lion / Gilbert Morris.
        p.   cm. — (The liberty bell ; Book 3)
    I. Title. II. Series: Morris, Gilbert. Liberty Bell ; bk. 3.
ISBN 1–55661–567–1
813'.54—dc20   96–25296
                                                                      CIP

To Mickey and Sondra Williams—

There's an old song entitled "Precious Memories." That describes very well how I think of you two. Time erases many things, but I keep the memories of our days together locked up safely. Often I take them out and am reminded of how much I treasure both of you!

GILBERT MORRIS spent ten years as a pastor before becoming Professor of English at Ouachita Baptist University in Arkansas and earning a Ph.D. at the University of Arkansas. During the summers of 1984 and 1985, he did postgraduate work at the University of London. A prolific writer, he has had over 25 scholarly articles and 200 poems published in various periodicals, and over the past years has had more than 70 novels published. His family includes three grown children, and he and his wife live in Colorado.

CONTENTS

PART FOUR
The Fall of Fort Washington
October—November 1776

THE LIBERTY BELL

🕭 🕭 🕭

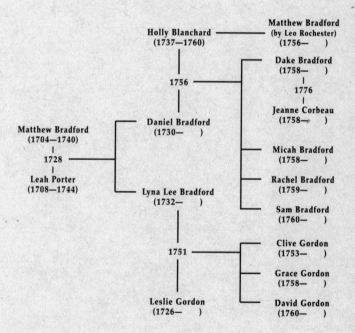

Holly Blanchard
(1737—1760)

Matthew Bradford
(by Leo Rochester)
(1756—   )

1756

Dake Bradford
(1758—   )

1776

Jeanne Corbeau
(1758—   )

Daniel Bradford
(1730—   )

Matthew Bradford
(1704—1740)

1728

Leah Porter
(1708—1744)

Micah Bradford
(1758—   )

Rachel Bradford
(1759—   )

Lyna Lee Bradford
(1732—   )

Sam Bradford
(1760—   )

1751

Clive Gordon
(1753—   )

Grace Gordon
(1758—   )

Leslie Gordon
(1726—   )

David Gordon
(1760—   )

PART ONE

EXODUS FROM BOSTON

March—May 1776

1

Wedding Day in Boston

KATHERINE YANCY HAD HATED the ugly brown sofa from the day her parents had picked it out—and now as Malcolm sat down on it and gave a startled grunt, she wished for the old Windsor chairs the sofa had replaced.

I don't see why they couldn't have bought that pretty little sofa I liked so much, she thought ruefully. She had picked out one with a pleasant green color that was well padded and gracefully shaped. It would have fit perfectly in the corner across from the fireplace, but her choice had been disregarded, and her father had chosen the monstrosity that now dominated the best parlor.

Sitting down carefully, Katherine felt an intense disliking for the sofa—a miserable, nasty, narrow thing with wood jutting out at every corner on which to break your elbows. To Katherine it was, as she had told her father, "unimpressionable as flint," and she hated the unyielding, slippery seats and the bolsters that were as hard as hickory logs! Aside from the discomfort of sitting on it, the piece was covered with a horsehair fabric of a leprous brown color and cast a pall over the entire room.

"I say, this sofa is a bit hard, isn't it now?"

Malcolm Smythe lifted his eyebrow in mock anguish and thumbed the bolster with his knuckles for emphasis. He smiled then and moved closer to Katherine, adding, "But at least it's better than standing up." Smythe was a rather handsome young man of twenty-three. He had pale blond hair, light blue eyes, and a pleasant set of features. In one sense he liked sitting down better, for he was long waisted with rather abbreviated legs. This meant that he was slightly taller than the young

13

woman sitting down. They were both, he knew, exactly five feet ten inches in height, but he liked to be taller than the woman he was courting.

Smythe was quite a dandy in dress, and for his call that early afternoon he wore a brightly colored green waistcoat, a pair of charcoal knee britches, and his neck was adorned with a pure white neckcloth and a ruffle that spun out below his chin. Even in the heat he wore a frock coat with buttons down to the edge just below his knees, and the cuffs, which were dotted with silver buttons, were turned back almost to his elbow. He appeared to have dressed for this occasion with a special care. This was not the case, however, for Smythe loved fine clothes and had a room full of the latest fashions at his home.

Katherine Yancy allowed him to take her hand as a smile creased her lips. She had a wide mouth, far too wide for beauty, but which somehow held a sensual cast. A tiny dimple appeared on the right side of her cheek, and her light gray-green eyes seemed to reflect the humor that lay just beneath the surface of a rather sober exterior. She had a wealth of rich brown hair with just a few tints of red or gold that caught the sun as it shone in through the mullioned windows. Her face was square, her eyes were wide spaced and very large, and, as always, they crinkled when she grinned or laughed, so that they became almost invisible. She was an attractive young woman—not beautiful, for she had features too bold for that. It was an age that valued petite prettiness rather than strong features—and Katherine Yancy was strong if nothing else!

Looking down at Malcolm's hands, she laughed suddenly. She had a deep voice for a woman, and when she sang it filled the rooms of the largest buildings with a rich contralto. "This is a *miserable* sofa!" she announced firmly. "Even the dog won't sleep on it, will you, Pluto?"

The large, shaggy dog with a massive head blinked and thumped the carpet with his tail but did not lift his head.

"It shows he's got better sense than we do. Come on, I can't *stand* this sofa!"

Rising quickly to her feet, Katherine drew the young man after her. Since she knew he was sensitive about his height, she had learned to wear low slippers and had been amused to discover that Malcolm always wore the highest heels he could find when he came to call on her. This gave him an advantage of two inches, and now she said, "That's a new suit, isn't it?"

"Yes, I picked it up in Philadelphia. Do you like it?" Malcolm asked as he straightened out his frock coat.

"Very colorful, and it fits you so well."

"Well, a man must have a good tailor, or what's he good for?"

Katherine almost replied, *A man is more than his clothes, isn't he?* But she had learned that Malcolm did not take teasing easily, so she said, "Come along, let's taste these tea cakes that I made this morning." She led him to a drop-side Hepplewhite table against the wall, between the two windows, and poured two cups of steaming tea from a silver teapot into beautifully executed china cups. She watched as Malcolm tasted the tiny cakes and nodded his approval. She sipped her tea then, and the two moved before the window.

Spring had come early in March of 1776, and the warm rays of the sun had coaxed the sharp blades of emerald grass up through the dull clods of earth, making the tiny yard in front of the Yancy house look as though it were sprouting fine green hair. "The flowers will be up soon," Katherine murmured. "We'll have a lot of them this year, I think."

The two stood by the window talking for some time, speaking of unimportant things, then finally Smythe set his teacup down and turned to face Katherine. "Katherine, I've got to talk to you," he said, his brow wrinkled with effort of serious thought.

Katherine inwardly grew tense, for she sensed what was coming. "What is it, Malcolm?"

"It's about this awful rebellion. We've talked about it before and we don't agree." Smythe took her hand and put his arm around her, drawing her close. He pressed her closely against him, and his hands moved across her back in a caressing gesture. "You know how I feel about you, Katherine," he whispered, and then he moved forward to kiss her.

Katherine knew that she was going to be kissed, and for one moment she almost drew back. She sensed that Malcolm, for all his ardent declarations of love, was not doing this out of passion. Nevertheless, she remained still as his lips fell on hers. He held her tightly, and she neither resisted nor encouraged him. Finally he drew back, an annoyed expression on his face. "You've got as much passion in you as a . . . as a dead woman!" he exclaimed.

"I don't think you're interested in kissing right now," Katherine said. She stood before him very straight, and the bright yellow sunlight that streamed through the window highlighted her, bringing out the color of her dress. It was a simple dress made of patterned fabric, light blue on darker blue. She wore a small lace apron, and the bosom of her dress was adorned with light yellow taffeta bows. A tiny white cap perched on her abundant auburn curls that fell freely down her back rather than being put up in the popular styles. She made an attractive picture as she stood there, but she was not aware of it. She felt that she was too tall for true beauty, and her features were not dainty enough.

Her eyes were fixed on Malcolm and she said, "I can't change my mind. How could I, Malcolm? This is my country."

Smythe shook his head violently. "No!" he exclaimed. "*England* is your country. I'm an Englishman and you're an Englishwoman. This rabble in arms—why, it's doomed. They haven't got a chance!"

Anger quickly flashed in Katherine's eyes, and her lips drew firm in a tight line. She held herself tautly upright and said, "And what about my father and my uncle? Were they fools for fighting for their freedom—and for your freedom?"

"We *have* freedom, and your uncle and your father were simply caught up in a riot. It came to little more than that."

Malcolm felt uncomfortable speaking of Katherine's father, Amos Yancy, and his brother Noah. The two of them had fought with the patriot forces at Breed's Hill during the first full-scale battle of the rebellion but had been captured during the retreat. They had both been held in the hulks, as they were called—old rotting ships where prisoners of war were kept. Smythe was aware that squalid conditions were every bit as bad on those vessels as rumor had it, and he could not meet Katherine's eyes.

"If you'd listen to reason, Katherine, I have an idea that might do something to get your father and your uncle released. My family does have some influence with the Crown, you know."

The Smythes were an old New York family, well-off and loyal Tories to the very bone. The thought of challenging the Crown and the British empire was a horror to them. Malcolm's courtship of Katherine had begun a year before the revolution broke out at Lexington and Concord. He was genuinely fond of Katherine, but the course of true love had not run smoothly between them.

Katherine turned away from Malcolm, anger coloring her cheeks. Most of the time she possessed a placid and calm temper, but at times anger would come almost in a blinding flash. She had learned to control it for the most part by simply waiting until it passed. Now she looked outside and forced herself to watch a robin that had snared one end of an enormous angleworm. The robin had braced his claws against the earth and was pulling with all of his might. Katherine fancied she could almost hear the bird grunt as it tugged at its next meal. Finally, he succeeded in yanking the worm out, mounted to the air with a flutter of wings, and flew directly to an apple tree, where he completed his meal with relish.

Turning back to Malcolm, Katherine said quietly, "I'm sorry, Malcolm, but I can't agree. The Colonies have tried everything to get justice from England. Neither the Crown nor Parliament understands what we are all about over here. We are not just a little branch of the British empire. The Colonies are the beginning of a great nation, a whole new continent. It can't be run from a Parliament thousands of miles across the sea."

Malcolm began to speak rapidly, but he soon saw that it was useless to argue with her. "I'm sorry," he said stiffly, "I hope that you'll think this over, Katherine." He started to say something else, then shook his head slightly as if denying the thought. "I must be going now. I have an appointment with my tailor."

Katherine walked with him to the door and handed him his tricorn hat. She watched as he pulled it firmly over his head, and for one moment she thought that he would try to kiss her again.

Opening the door, he stopped and turned toward her. "I'll see you soon, I hope," he said.

"I'm going to a wedding this afternoon. Dake Bradford is getting married."

"Yes, well, perhaps I'll call tomorrow then."

"Goodbye, Malcolm." Katherine watched as he turned and walked down the brick pathway to where his horse was tied to an iron hitching post fashioned in the shape of a horse head. He took the reins, swung into the saddle rather awkwardly, touched his hat, then rode off down the street. Katherine listened as the horse's hooves rang on the cobblestones, then she slowly turned and went back inside.

She was still disturbed over their disagreement twenty minutes later when her mother came in, carrying a basket under her arm. Katherine spoke to her shortly, and her mother demanded at once, "What's the matter, Katherine?"

Susan Yancy, at forty-five, still had the dark-haired beauty that she had possessed as a girl. She had beautiful mild brown eyes and attractive features, but she was thin, and her face had the worn lines of a chronic invalid. Setting the basket down on a table in the hall, she moved over to Katherine and looked into the girl's face. "Malcolm didn't stay?"

"No, he didn't."

From the very brevity of Katherine's tone, Susan Yancy knew something was troubling her daughter. "You two quarreled, didn't you?"

"Yes, over the war, of course. Malcolm just can't understand how I feel about it."

"Well," Susan said as cheerfully as she could, "you'll make it up. Come now, you must put on your best dress for the wedding."

"All right, Mother." Katherine turned and moved away to her room, but even as she entered and began to prepare for the wedding, her thoughts were on Malcolm and the impassable gulf that seemed to be widening between them. She stared at herself in the mirror for a moment, and the thought came to her, *I don't see how we can ever marry—not until this question about England is settled once and for all. . . .*

T   T   T

Daniel Bradford stood at the front of the large auditorium, observing the crowd that had come to celebrate his son's wedding. Every seat and every pew was filled, and a number of latecomers stood lined along the back of the wall. Moving his head slightly, he glanced to his right where his son Dake stood, his eyes fixed on the front doors of the church. *He's only eighteen. Too young to be married, especially with a war facing us,* Daniel thought. He took in the strong form of this son of his, fully six feet tall and one hundred eighty pounds. Dake's straw-colored hair was drawn back, tied with a black ribbon. His hazel eyes were clear, and a happy expression drew his lips upward into a slight smile as he waited for his bride to appear. He was wearing a simple suit of brown with white stockings and black shoes with silver buckles. *A fine-looking bridegroom—but too young.*

Dake and Jeanne had planned to wait until the war with England was over before marrying, but then they had decided to take advantage of any time they could have together, as no one knew what the future held.

Just then a brief whisper swept the crowded room, and both Daniel Bradford and his son looked to see the bride entering.

As Jeanne Corbeau came down the aisle, Daniel thought of the strange fashion in which this beautiful young woman had come into the Bradford family. She was a lovely girl of eighteen. Her black hair was too curly for many of the popular hairstyles of the day, so she arranged it loosely around her face. She had blue-violet eyes, the most unusual Daniel had ever seen, high cheekbones, and beautifully formed lips. *She's beautiful, all right, but it's a wonder she didn't wear buckskins,* Daniel thought wryly as she reached the front of the church.

Dake's bride was from the woods of the North. She had encountered Clive Gordon, Daniel's nephew, on his return trip from Fort Ticonderoga to Boston. Stranded in the forest, sick with fever, Jeanne had saved Clive's life. With her father gone, Clive could not leave her alone in the wilderness, so he had brought her to Boston and courted her—but it had been Dake who won her heart.

Poor Clive, he lost a beauty, and it hit him hard, Daniel thought. He thought of his sister, Lyna Lee Bradford Gordon, Clive's mother. He, himself, had come to America as an indentured servant. Lyna Lee had

18

married Leslie Gordon, an officer in the king's army. They had been reunited only recently, and sorrow came to Daniel Bradford as he thought of the Gordons, who served King George III, and the Bradfords, who were patriots and determined to follow General Washington and fight for their freedom. *It must be hard on Lyna Lee,* Daniel thought soberly. *Truth is, it's hard on all of us.*

The bride came to stand facing the minister, who wore his black robe and held a large worn Bible in his hands. Dake took his position beside her, and the ceremony began. As the minister led them through their vows, Daniel found himself unable to concentrate on the words. Looking out over the congregation, he noted his own family in the front pew on the right. This included Matthew, his oldest son, and Micah, at eighteen, the identical twin to Dake. Next to them sat Rachel, his only daughter at seventeen, who looked to him more beautiful with her red hair and green eyes than even the bride. She had a heart-shaped face like her mother, and Daniel loved her very much. Finally, beside Rachel, sat his youngest son, Samuel, already quite a handful at sixteen.

Shifting his eyes he looked on the other side, halfway back where Leo Rochester sat with his wife, Marian. A sharp anger touched Daniel as Leo stared back. He was actually *Sir* Leo Rochester, and had been Daniel's master in England. Because of Leo's lies, Daniel had ended up in a cold prison accused of attempted murder. In the end, Leo had offered him his freedom if Daniel would agree to come to the Colonies as a bound servant. As Leo Rochester smiled, Daniel felt a sense of satisfaction in noticing one tooth that did not match. His sister, Lyna, had knocked that tooth out years ago when Leo had attacked her one night in a drunken stupor. Leo, he noted, was overweight, and his face was lined with dissipation.

Beside him sat Marian Frazier Rochester—at forty-one still the most beautiful woman that Daniel Bradford had ever known. She had dark auburn hair, green eyes, and a heart-shaped face. She looked at him suddenly, her eyes catching his, and Daniel quickly turned away. He had fallen in love with her, and she with him years ago on her first visit to Fairhope, Leo's estate in Virginia, but Daniel had been an indentured servant and Marian was a wealthy young lady. Daniel had finally married Holly Blanchard, who was carrying Sir Leo Rochester's child. By the time his wife, Holly, had died, Marian had married Sir Leo Rochester. Though Daniel had moved his family to Boston to work in John Frazier's foundry, he still could not forget his love for Marian—and knew that he must never speak of it to anyone.

He shook himself as the silence was broken by the clear voice of the minister, rising up to the high arches of the ceiling. The gray stones that formed the sides seemed to capture and soak the words into themselves as they had many other ceremonies of this nature. Through the stained-glass windows the light filtered in and bathed everything in beautiful reds, yellows, greens, and amethyst. As the minister's voice spoke clearly, a holy silence settled in the room.

Finally, the minister said, ". . . and I now pronounce you man and wife."

Daniel grinned as Dake reached forward, without reservation, kissed his bride thoroughly, and noted that Jeanne Corbeau Bradford held to him with all her strength. He moved forward and said, "Have you got a kiss for an old man, Jeanne?"

Jeanne turned from Dake and threw her arms around Daniel and kissed him soundly on the cheek. "Now, you have another daughter," she smiled, "and I promise to be much more trouble than Rachel."

"I don't doubt it," Daniel grinned. He liked this girl and suddenly was glad that she and Dake had found each other. It always had seemed like a miracle to him when a man and woman found each other out of the millions on earth—and were happy. This brought a touch of sadness to Daniel Bradford, for he knew that he'd had such a chance with Marian—but had lost it years ago. Now he was happy that his son had found the one God meant for him.

Stepping back, he made his way to the side of the church while the newlyweds were swarmed by those who came forward to congratulate them and wish them well. His eyes were drawn irresistibly across the room where, once again, he encountered the gaze of Marian Rochester. He tried to turn away, but was almost powerless to do so. It was, indeed, a power that Marian held over him—one which he would not deny, although he never spoke of it to a living soul.

🔔　　　🔔　　　🔔

The reception was held in the pastor's home—a large parsonage with an enormous parlor designed, no doubt, for exactly such festive occasions.

Leo Rochester stood beside the table, sipping from the goblet in his hand. He looked down at Marian and muttered, "You'd think they'd serve some real whiskey at an event like this, wouldn't you?"

Marian looked up without comment. She had been surprised when Leo had informed her that he was attending Dake Bradford's wedding. When she had allowed the surprise to show in her eyes, he had grinned and said, "That takes you off guard, doesn't it, my dear? Well, at least I'll have a chance to see one of Bradford's whelps out of the way. Besides," he had added, and a grim look had settled in his face, "I want to talk to Matthew."

Now Marian studied his expression and found something that had troubled her before. "Don't you feel well, Leo?" she asked quietly.

Leo blinked his eyes, and his lips twisted into a scowl. "Why this sudden wifely interest in my health?" he snapped. "You haven't cared for me in years."

This was not exactly true, but close enough. Leo Rochester had been disappointed in his marriage. He had wanted a son to carry on the family name, and Marian had produced no children. This failure, as he saw it, drove him from her. He had proved to be a womanizer, and their marriage, for all practical purposes, had ended years before. Now he studied her face and said, "You'd like that, wouldn't you? If I got ill and died you'd end up with Fairhope and all my money—then nothing could stop you from marrying your lover, Daniel Bradford."

"That's not true, Leo," Marian protested.

"Of course it's true. Do you think I don't know? Didn't I catch you two in each other's arms in my own home?"

"It was . . . just a mistake, Leo. Nothing had happened before. I'm not his lover."

Leo grinned sarcastically. "So you tell me, but every time he looks at you he's like an infatuated schoolboy." It was his custom to taunt her with this, but Rochester privately was convinced that nothing scandalous had ever taken place between his wife and Daniel Bradford. Nevertheless, he hated the man, and had ever since he was a boy back at Milford Manor in England. He had used Daniel—with his fine sense with horses—to build up his plantation, Fairhope in Virginia, and now Leo's obsession to have an heir gave him even a greater reason to use the man he despised.

"I'll have Matthew one way or another!" he spoke abruptly.

"You can't have him, Leo, can't you understand that?"

"He's my son!" Leo kept his voice low, but there was a fierce determination that glittered in his light blue eyes. He ground his teeth together, then said fiercely, "He's my son, Marian! Can't you understand that—what it *means* to me?"

"You forfeited all right to Matthew. You abandoned his mother, and Daniel married her just to give her son a name. There's no proof that he's your son anyway, and no court of law would ever admit it. Daniel was married to Matthew's mother when he was born."

"There's proof all right," Leo said. "Look at him! He's the mirror image of what I looked like when I was his age."

Marian looked over toward Matthew Bradford and could not help but agree, although she said nothing. This son was not like the other Bradfords, who were all strong, husky men. Matthew was slender with none of the rugged features of the Bradfords. He had brown hair and blue eyes. He looked, in fact, exactly like the picture of Leo Rochester that hung in her own parlor, one that had been painted when Leo was twenty.

Still, she was aware of how fiercely Leo hungered for a son—a man to carry on the Rochester name. She was also aware that he had gone to Matthew and told him the truth—that he was his father. He had offered him his name and all that wealth could bring. So far Matthew had resisted, but Marian wondered how long the young man would hold out. She knew he wanted to return to England to continue his study of art, and that Leo had offered to introduce him to many of the famous artists he knew.

To change the subject she said, "Look, I must go speak to Abigail."

"The Howland girl?" Leo's interest was caught. "I'll go with you," he said. "She's a toothsome wench. Alluring eyes if I ever saw them."

"Hush, Leo, she'll hear you!"

Leo grinned but said no more. They came to stand before Abigail Howland and Douglas Martin, who had once been one of her suitors. Seeing the two approach, Douglas said, "I'll see you later, Abigail. I'll come to call."

"That would be nice, Douglas."

Abigail Howland, at the age of nineteen, was as beautiful a woman as Massachusetts could boast. She had an oval face, hazel eyes, and brown hair. She was very full-figured with an exquisitely tiny waist, and always wore exactly the right thing. She wore an amber dress with deep pleats and, unlike most of the women, a wide pannier. It emphasized the smallness of her waist, and her figure swelled against the bodice, which was made of pleated taffeta. She was one of those women who would look good in anything. There was an air of sensuality about her, even as Leo had stated, but she looked somehow troubled as she said, "How are you, Sir Leo—Lady Rochester?"

"Very well," Leo said, "and how is it with you and your mother?"

For one moment Abigail Howland hesitated. She was usually a rather outspoken young woman, but there seemed to be a reticence in her that neither Leo nor Marian had ever noticed before. "Not as well as I might like."

Instantly Leo said, "Since Washington drove the British out, it's been a little hard on us Tories."

"Not on you, Sir Leo, but on my family." Her father had been a staunch Tory before his death, and now only her mother was left, and she was not well. The two of them had been driven out of their fine home by the patriots and were staying in a small cottage, which belonged to an old friend of Saul Howland's.

As they stood there speaking, Matthew approached. He nodded toward Leo, calling his name, spoke to Marian, then turned and said, "Abigail, it's good to see you again."

Abigail's face lit up at once. The presence of a young man seemed to bring new life into her. Leo did not miss the sudden change. He watched intensely as the two spoke, his eyes going from the face of this son who would not claim him to the young woman he so eagerly spoke with.

Why, I think the pup is in love with her! At least he wants her—which is about the same thing, Rochester thought. *I don't blame him. She could bring a statue to life—but she's in poor shape—as all the Tories are here in Boston.*

Marian said, "I'll be coming over to see you and your mother. I'm sorry I haven't called earlier."

"Mother's not too well," Abigail said. She turned her eyes toward Matthew and said, "I've missed you."

"I've been busy painting. I want to show you some of the things I've done."

"I'd like to see them. I don't know much about painting, though, as you well know, but I love the portrait you did of me."

"Well, I'll do better ones later." Matthew smiled and had apparently forgotten Rochester. He was not a typical colonist, having spent the last few years in England and on the Continent studying painting. He was not in sympathy with the revolution, and having been confronted with the secret of his birth, he felt out of place with the Bradford family. Now he suddenly turned and looked at Leo, saying, "I received the paints and the brushes you sent me, sir. Thanks very much."

"An artist must have the best," Leo nodded. He started to say more, but a sudden, odd feeling had come to him. It had happened like this a month before. He stood there unable to speak a word, for it was suddenly as if his heart and everything within him were composed of very fine, fragile glass. He felt that if he moved or spoke all would be shattered! He had never experienced anything like it before—until three weeks earlier. Then he had been so stricken he had gone straightway to bed. It had passed away—or so he thought—but now the same disturbing sensations were coming on again. He stood there listening as the others talked, aware that Marian was watching him strangely, but he did not dare to move. His breath came shallowly, and he stood absolutely still.

Finally, the moment passed. He took out his handkerchief, mopped his forehead, and turned away without a word. As he left the house, he was aware that Marian had followed him.

"Are you ill, Leo?"

Again the question angered him. He'd never had a sick day in his life, and the thought of sickness was something he had never considered. He had been, as a matter of fact, rather contemptuous of those who were ill, and now he looked at her with anger in his eyes. "Stop pestering me! I'm all right!"

Marian knew Leo very well, and she had never seen him look like this. His face had turned almost gray. She knew that he was not well despite his protestations. "Perhaps we'd better go home," she said quietly.

"I'll go home by myself. Go on in. You and Daniel can get together—maybe plan what to do with all of my money after you've buried me. How long would you wait if I died?" he said, turning toward her. "A week? A month? Maybe even a year to make things look respectable."

Marian shook her head but said nothing. Finally she said, "I'd rather come home with you."

"No, I want to be alone. Go on back inside." Rochester turned and moved toward the carriage. He got into it, moving carefully, saying, "Take me home, Rogers."

"Yes, sir." The cabbie spoke to the horses, and they moved out smartly. He threaded the carriage down the streets until the church was out of sight. A short ugly dog with clipped ears came out to bark at the horses' heels. Rogers leaned over and struck at him with his whip. With satisfaction, he caught the animal across the rump and laughed when the hound yelled and tucked his tail between his legs.

"That'll teach you to snap at my horses' heels," he said, then chuckled in his chest. "Come on, boys, home now. . . !"

2

A Man's Word

THE STREETS OF BOSTON were almost deserted as Leo Rochester made his way down the main thoroughfare. Before the British army had departed, driven off by General Washington and the guns of Henry Knox, the British soldiers had done their best to destroy and deface as much of the city as they could. Some of the shops that Rochester passed were boarded over, having had their windows broken and the interiors raided by the furious troops of King George III.

Rochester passed by a small shop, then halted as a thought came to him. Turning, he entered, ducking his head as he passed through the doorway. He was greeted by a small, wizened shopkeeper who bowed mechanically three times as if he were wound up. His name was Phineas Johnson, and his tiny, dark eyes glowed as he fairly bubbled over to greet his customer. "Ah," he said, exposing a mouth full of obviously artificial teeth carved out of hippo ivory, "Sir Leo, a pleasure, sir, to see you, sir!" He came across the shop wringing his hands, stood before Leo, and bowed three times again quickly, then said at once, "How can I serve you this afternoon, Sir Leo?"

"This filthy wig—it doesn't fit properly. It won't stay on," Leo growled. Removing his tricorn hat, he jerked the powdered wig from his head and practically threw it at the shopkeeper.

"Oh, to be sure! Let me take care of that." Quickly Johnson moved over to a table where several wig stands had their station, fastened the wig to one, and began working with it at once. As he snipped and poked at the artificial hairpiece, Leo stood impatiently waiting. *This wig business, it's idiotic! If I had any sense, I'd stuff it down this miserable shopkeeper's throat and never put one on again!*

He knew he would never do so, however, for the wig craze, which had begun in England years before, had become *de rigeur*. No self-respecting aristocrat would be seen without one! *This craze has,* Roch-

25

ester thought, *become more bizarre*. Some women wore towering mounds of false hair, filled with puffs, feathers, and any number of fancy ornaments. Young girls cut off their own hair or shaved their heads sometimes so they could be fitted for a wig. Poor girls who needed money sold their hair to wigmakers. Rochester had heard that one Virginia father, William Freeman, paid nine pounds for a wig for his seven-year-old son. With the average worker making twenty-five to thirty pounds a year, it's obvious that the wig craze was in full sway.

Phineas Johnson worked like a squirrel, chirping and turning his hippo teeth in a broad smile from time to time as he moved around the wig stand making adjustments to the hairpiece. Finally, he pulled the wig off and came forward, bowed three times, and said, "Now, Sir Leo, let's try this. . . ." Leo bent his head, and the wigmaker put the wig on, settled it, and stepped back. Smirking with satisfaction, he rubbed his hands together, bowed three times, and in his mechanical ritual said, "There, sir."

"Very well," Leo said. "Oh, my servant has lost his wig pick."

"Oh yes. Here. This is a very fine one made of silver."

Rochester took the instrument, gave it a caustic glance, then stuck it in his overcoat pocket. Wigs were so hot and heavy they made the head sweat—and sweat attracted lice. The pick was for removing those tiny visitors. Since wigs were washed very seldom, the invaders made themselves happy homes and had to be picked out by the servants with wig picks.

"Well, sir, the army is gone—a sad day for loyal subjects of King George," Phineas Johnson said, pocketing the coin that Rochester handed him. He looked around furtively, then whispered, "The patriots have threatened to raid my store. There's no one to hold them back now that the blasted rebels are in charge."

"Well, we had our good days, now we'll have to take the bad," Leo said callously. He left the shop, well aware that the wigmaker's plight was not uncommon. The Tories had ridden high as long as the British army held the city, but now many of them had been tarred and feathered. Some had been thrown out of their homes, and their property seized by the Continental government. Leo, himself, had not been affected, for his own plantation in Virginia seemed safe and secure, and he owned no property in Boston.

Bright April sunlight illuminated the streets as he moved along, dodging refuse that piled up on the sidewalk. There was little attempt at street cleaning, especially in the middle of a war. Some shopkeepers simply threw their trash out, and passersby had to walk around it or wade through it.

Arriving at a two-story red-brick structure, of which the first floor was occupied by a shipping agent, Leo turned to the stairs that led up one side and slowly ascended them. He passed under a sign that read *Henry Settling—Surgeon.*

Opening the door, he stepped inside and shut it behind him. For a moment he stood there, taking in the long narrow room that served as a reception area. It contained only seven cane-bottomed chairs, a desk, and a cabinet at one end. At the other end, a small window looked out on the street below.

"Settling!" Rochester called out. He waited for only a moment, and the single door leading to the interior opened.

Dr. Henry Settling stepped into the reception area and peered over his glasses. "Oh, Sir Leo. I didn't hear you come in." Settling was a gaunt man of fifty with a set of light blue eyes and a Vandyke beard. He wore a powdered wig, knee britches, and a white shirt, over which he had on an apron that was stained with a few splatters of brown, dried blood. "Will you step inside, Sir Leo?"

Leo stepped into the inner office, which was rather crowded with a large rosewood desk, a skeleton on a rack in the corner, and a collection of various instruments and paraphernalia in glass-fronted cases flanking the walls. An acrid smell of chemicals filled the room—distinctly unpleasant—and Leo wrinkled his nose with distaste. "It stinks in here, Settling."

"The penalty of my profession, I'm afraid." Settling's steady gaze rested on Leo and he asked, "Is this a social call or a professional one?"

Leo hesitated for one moment. He took off his hat, tossed it onto a chair beside the wall, then turned to face the physician squarely. "Something's wrong with me, Settling. I don't know what it is, but I've got to find out."

"What are your symptoms, Sir Leo? Will you sit down while we talk?"

Reluctantly and nervously Rochester sat down. "I've been healthy all my life. Never had a surgeon put his blasted knife on me. Stayed as far away from you fellows as I could."

"I'm glad to hear it." Settling smiled slightly. "But all of us have our physical problems. How old a man are you, Sir Leo?"

"Forty-seven." Rochester shifted uncomfortably on the chair, then looked up at the doctor. There was a trace of fear or deep anxiety in his eyes. He ran his hands over his wig, straightened it, then shook his head sadly. "It's in here," he said, tapping his chest. "And here . . ." He held up his left hand.

Doctor Settling listened as Rochester described the pain in his chest and the numbness in his left hand. When Leo finished he said, "Remove your coat and shirt, and we'll have a look." He waited until Leo pulled off his shirt, and he noted that the man was not in good physical condition. He was overweight and his face was marked with the signs of heavy drinking. He said nothing, however, but kept up a cheerful line of patter as he leaned his head over and listened to Leo's heart, took his pulse, and thumped him front and back. Next he looked down his throat, pulled the pouches of his eyes down and stared in his eyes, then smelled his breath. Finally, he leaned back and gave his patient a thoughtful glance. "You do seem to have some problem."

"Well, I know *that*, blast it!" Leo growled. "What's the matter with me?" He took a deep breath and felt again the light fluttering, the sense of intense fragility, and expelled it carefully. "What is it—this ache in my chest?"

"Impossible to say for sure. Have you ever had a sharp pain, somewhat recently, here in your chest?"

Leo thought for a moment. "Yes," he nodded finally. "About three weeks ago. I woke up in the night and felt almost stifled. It was like my chest was full, and I could hardly get a breath." He thought hard then nodded. "This arm"—he held up his left hand—"was tingling. I remember that too. I had trouble flexing the fingers the next day." He fell silent then, studying the face of the surgeon, trying to read his fate there. Sir Leo was not a man given to fears, but this physical weakness had hit him hard. He asked almost timidly, "What is it, Settling? You've got to know *something*."

"You do have a bit of a problem. That's obvious. As to the exact nature of it, that's difficult to say."

"Is it a stroke?" Leo asked abruptly. This had been what he had come to ask the doctor, and now he waited as a felon waits at the bar of justice for the judge's sentence.

Settling saw the fear in Rochester's eyes. He was a good doctor, and one of his policies was to always speak the truth to his patients. "I think you may well have had either a stroke or perhaps a heart attack." He held up his hand quickly as the fear filled Leo's eyes and said, "Both are apparently quite minor at this point."

"What can you do for me? Is there medicine for a thing like this?"

"The best medicine is a reasonable diet, no alcohol, and regular exercise."

Rochester scowled. "You mean turn from my sins and lead a clean life?"

"I'm afraid that's it, Sir Leo. There's no substitute for the things I've mentioned."

Leo sat there. He was pasty-faced from indoor living, and his long hours spent in the taverns of the city consuming large amounts of alcohol had blunted his features. He flexed the fingers of his left hand, then said, "What if I don't follow your advice?"

"I think you already know the answer to that," Settling said flatly.

Settling knew well the disreputable reputation of Leo Rochester. He had treated Leo's wife, Marian, and was impressed with the woman's quiet demeanor and modest behavior—as well as with her beauty. Settling was an inveterate collector of gossip, but he kept to himself what he had learned about his patients' personal lives. He knew that Sir Leo Rochester had shown no moral restraint and spent many nights away from home rather than with his wife. Settling could not understand this, but then he had given up trying to understand human nature some years earlier.

Now he spoke, convinced that he was wasting his breath. "I'll make out a diet, things that you should eat and those you should avoid. Of course, your drinking will have to be moderated. Maybe a glass of whiskey at night. One, perhaps, in the midday—but if you continue to drink as heavily as you have, I guarantee you'll be signing your own death warrant before long. You're not getting any younger," he said quickly, seeing the stubbornness start to gather on Rochester's features. "You should have several years ahead of you if you'll listen to sound advice and take care of yourself."

Rochester stared angrily at the physician as if it were somehow his fault. Leo was a spoiled man, having been given everything the world values at much too early an age. For years he had sought his pleasures in every form without a thought to the consequences that might catch up to him someday. Now a cloud of ominous thoughts seemed to gather over him, and he shook his head. "Not much to live for. I might as well become a Quaker."

"Something to be said for their clean living," Settling shrugged. "Now—while you get dressed I'll make out a diet and also a tonic. Maybe something to help you sleep at night."

Leo dressed, took the paper the doctor gave him, paid the fee, then left in a somber mood. As he made his way down the steps, he was filled with a sudden apprehension about his future. He shook it off as he got into a carriage and rode out to the edge of town where Marian's father, John Frazier, had built a fine home many years ago.

When he arrived, he stepped out of the carriage, gave the driver a coin, and entered the house. He was met at the door by Cato, the butler, a black man of some forty-five years, who took his coat and hat at once, murmuring, "Good day, Sir Leo."

"Is your mistress at home, Cato?"

"Yes, sir! She's in the small parlor."

Leo walked down the hall, which was floored with cypress, and turned into the small parlor that occupied part of the lower floor of the large house. The room into which he stepped was bright and colorful, though no larger than twelve by sixteen. On one wall hung a painting made of French wallpaper, a rather graphic scenario that had been designed by Joseph Dufore. It portrayed an exotic scene, a blue-green river flowing in a serpentine path through a dense forest. On the fore bank, two Indians, copper-skinned natives, were in the process of killing a spotted leopard that had climbed up in a tree. One stood over the leopard's head, chopping at him with an ax. The other on the ground had pulled a hunting bow to full draw and was about to send an arrow into the beast. To the right of the picture a series of craggy rocks was capped by two Indians wearing turbans and puffy white britches. One of them was sounding an alarm on a curling ram's horn. Far off to the left rose a strange-looking tower—some sort of Maya Indian structure—and at the base of it a turbaned man clothed in a white robe and red sash sat astride a powerful steed that was rearing up in the air.

Leo had chosen this picture, although he knew that Marian had never liked it. Now he turned his eyes and swept the room that he had furnished and had become his favorite room in the house. Several side chairs flanked the wall, backed against the chair rail. Two padded Windsor chairs were at one end of the room, but there was a comfortable sofa with Griffin feet and a gaily colored covering of wine and yellow. Two large windows in the room let in the yellow sunlight, and in the center of the room a large walnut table rested under an ornate glass chandelier. The surface of the table was covered with a silver tea service and some fine china imported from Holland.

"Have you eaten, Leo?"

Rochester looked to where Marian had risen from her chair, laying her sewing to one side. She stood to face him, and he studied her as if he had not seen her for some time. He was struck with her beauty and her choice of dress. Rochester knew a little something of women's fashions, having spent some time with those who were interested. His wife wore a modified empire gown with a low neckline edged with a narrow, sheer collar. The sleeves were puffed and flared, and the skirt of the dress, though full, was made of a soft fabric that fell straight to her feet. It was a simple dress, white with vertical pale blue stripes, and it set off her figure admirably. *She always was beautiful*, Leo thought, and regret came to him as he considered the years he had spent chasing other women. However, he said only, "Yes." Going over to one of the horsehair-covered stuffed chairs, he slumped into it and looked up at her, waiting for her to speak.

"Father's better today. I think he can come down. Will you be at home for dinner?"

"I suppose so."

Marian was puzzled by his behavior. He had been acting strangely, as a matter of fact, for several weeks now, and she could not fathom it. For one thing, he was staying home more. It was not uncommon for him to leave for weeks at a time, and even when he stayed in Boston, he spent every night in the taverns and with other women. She had long since resigned herself to the failure of her marriage and to the fact that Leo's actions were something over which she had no control. Long ago, she had determined to keep her own manner as gracious as possible. That was all she could do.

"Leo, do you think we'll go back to Virginia soon?"

"Do you want to?"

"I miss the horses," Marian said simply, "and the quiet there. It's been a trying time here in the middle of this war."

"Yes it has." Leo looked up at her suddenly. "Would you leave your father?"

"I thought I might persuade him to go with us."

"I doubt it," Leo said morosely. He sat there for some time, and the two spoke of the possibility of returning to Fairhope in Virginia. After his meeting with Settling, he now had no desire, really, to go there, and finally he said, "No, I'll stay here."

He rose abruptly and went to his study, leaving her alone. When he closed the door, he went at once to his desk and began going through his papers and books. There was an intensity in his manner that was unusual, for he did not like bookwork. Later that afternoon he left the study and headed for the front door.

"I'll be back for dinner," he said and left the house abruptly.

Marian watched him go, puzzled by his behavior. His face was puffy and his color was bad. She had a way of noticing things, and had caught the fact that his left hand was giving him problems. Once she had even seen him reach over with his right hand and pull the limp arm into position. "Something is wrong with him, but he'll never tell me," she said. Then she turned and went upstairs to see to her father, wondering what all this would mean for their lives.

🦁 🦁 🦁

"Katherine, this letter came!" Susan Yancy had met her daughter as she came back from the market. Her face was troubled, and she thrust the one-page letter at Katherine, saying, "I'm afraid it's not good news."

Placing her market basket on a table, Katherine quickly scanned the few lines written on the piece of rough paper. The writing was almost illegible, but clearly it was her father's. She did not like the wavering looks of the handwriting and squinted at it as she read aloud:

> My dear wife and precious daughter—
>
> I take this occasion to send word that Noah and I have endured our imprisonment as well as could be hoped. The conditions here are not good. The food is poor, and the prison itself is uncomfortable. I regret to say that Noah has contracted some sort of disease, for such things are rampant here. I myself, at this point, praise God, am not affected. I know that you must be concerned about us, and I encourage you to pray to our Heavenly Father that we will be strengthened and kept in this place. I pray for you daily, and, indeed, there is little else to do. The Scripture says, "Whom the Lord loveth, he chasteneth," and we must look upon this as part of the discipline of a loving father. Try not to worry any more than you can help about us.
>
> With all my love and affection,
> Amos Yancy

Despair overwhelmed Katherine, filling her like a black cloud as she thought of her father and uncle locked in the cold and squalid skull of a ship. "This is awful!" she exclaimed. She read the letter again, then she and her mother talked about the poor quality of the handwriting.

"Father always was such a careful penman," Katherine said.

"Yes, look how the lines waver. I'll be bound he has fever himself and didn't want us to know it."

Biting her lip, Katherine shook her head. "And poor Uncle Noah! He wasn't a well man when he was taken prisoner." Noah Yancy was fifty-five and had already endured some severe health problems before he had been captured and taken away as a prisoner.

"From what I hear of those awful hulks, even if a person was well he'd be sick soon enough down *there*," Katherine said, clamping her lips together.

"Where did the British take their prisoners?" Susan asked.

"Halifax. That's in Nova Scotia," Katherine said sullenly.

"It seems so far away," Susan sighed as she folded the letter and stuck it in the pocket of her apron. She moved over to the window and stared out. Hot tears spilled from her eyes, and there was a catch in her throat as she said, "My . . . poor husband! Would God he had never gone into the army!"

"He felt he had to do it, Mother," Katherine said. "He was doing what he thought was right." The two women comforted each other as well as they could, but both felt the despair of being so far away and helpless to ease their suffering in any way.

For the next two days Susan grew more and more morbid. She was not well herself, and it was all Katherine could do to keep her mother's spirits up. Finally, on Wednesday afternoon when her mother had lain down to take a nap, Katherine was surprised to hear a knock at the door. She went at once to open it and blinked with surprise. "Why, Malcolm," she said, "I didn't expect you."

Malcolm Smythe stood there awkwardly and pulled his hat off. He was dressed rather formally, but this was common enough for him. "I have to talk with you, Katherine," he said quickly.

Alarmed by his manner, Katherine said, "Of course—come inside." She led him into the parlor and turned to him at once. "What is it? Is something wrong?"

"Nothing new," Malcolm said carefully. He bit his lip, chewing on it nervously, a mannerism of his when he was disturbed. Clearing his throat he said, "I've been . . . thinking of our situation, Katherine."

"Our situation?"

"Yes, I mean, we've been seeing each other for two years now, and I'm very fond of you."

Katherine suddenly knew what was coming next. The very choice of words, "Very fond of you . . ." was not the language of love. Malcolm had said much more passionate things in the past when he was pressing his suit with her. Now Katherine stared at him and said quietly, "What have you come to say, Malcolm?"

"I . . . I don't know how to put this," Smythe said carefully. He cleared his throat nervously, stared out the window, and fumbled with the tricorn hat that he held in both hands. He turned it around several times, as if trying to find the best way to hold it, a ploy to give him time while he sought for the proper words. "I consider myself a man of honor," Malcolm said finally, and managed to meet her eyes. "And I intend to be. But I think we need to . . . reconsider our relationship."

Like a signal given in the night that suddenly mounts up and explodes, Katherine understood immediately his meaning. She was a perceptive young woman, far more than most her age. Now looking at the young man in front of her, she knew exactly what he was stumbling to say. "Are you trying to tell me that you want to break our engagement, Malcolm?" she asked flatly.

Malcolm turned the hat over several times rapidly and crushed it in his hands. "Well," he said, "I wouldn't want to put it that way. . . ."

"What other way could it be said?" Katherine demanded. "I want to look at this thing straight on, Malcolm. Tell me what you're thinking."

"Well, I'm concerned about our future. We're so . . . well, *different*, Katherine. For some time now, I've been afraid that our political differences might be too . . . well, too great for us to bridge."

At that moment Katherine knew that she would never marry this man. Standing there, she watched him continue to twist his hat around nervously. A sudden flash of anger came to her as it sometimes did. She forced herself, however, to remain still and wait until the worst of it passed, then finally said calmly, "I think you're right. We would never be able to overcome this part of our lives." She saw relief leap into Malcolm Smythe's eyes and knew that she had been correct. It was a hopeless match between them.

"Perhaps after things settle down, we can begin to see each other again?"

"Goodbye, Malcolm," she said. "You don't want to see me again. Go find a nice Tory girl with lots of money. Marry her and have lots of Tory children."

Smythe flinched at the bluntness of her words. He saw the anger and resentment in her face and swallowed hard. "I . . . I'm sorry it's come to this, Katherine." He sought to say something to ease the tense moment, but was intelligent enough to realize that there was nothing more to say. "I think it might be best if you announce that you've broken our engagement."

"Yes, that would be best."

The words were stark and bare and even. This was a side of Katherine Yancy that Malcolm had seen before. Truthfully, he was somewhat overwhelmed by the almost fierce independence of this young woman. His parents had been apprehensive as well, not only of her political convictions, but that she was not appreciative enough of their family position and status. Relief came again, and Malcolm Smythe gave her a compassionate look—at least for him it was compassionate.

"You're a strong-willed girl, Katherine. I wish you well, but we would never have been happy together."

"No, we would not. Goodbye, Malcolm."

Katherine led him to the door, opened it, and felt a sudden impulse to give him a shove as he passed through it. Restraining herself, she shut the door and leaned heavily against it. Despite herself she began to tremble as tears filled her eyes. She had fancied herself in love with this man. It was true enough that she had wondered at times if their love was strong enough to build a marriage on, but a woman must marry, and Malcolm had been witty, amusing, had come from a good family—and if he had not been as romantic and challenging to her intellectually as she might have liked, still he had been a stabilizing factor in her life for the last two years.

Abruptly she dashed the tears from her eyes. "Now, what'll I do, trying to explain to everyone what's happened?" she muttered. She knew all too well the wagging tongues of Boston and was aware that the next few days would be a tiresome, difficult time explaining such a, thing—even to her own mother. Slowly she moved away from the door, knowing that her mother would not understand. With her father and uncle gone, her mother would have considered a marriage to Malcolm some welcome stability to their plight.

♯   ♯   ♯

Katherine had been exactly right. Explaining the broken engagement had proved difficult—very difficult. She had spoken about it to her mother first, of course, and Susan had stared at her with an air of incomprehension in her mild brown eyes. She had protested, "But, Katherine, it's all settled. He's so well connected, and you two get on so well. I don't understand it."

Katherine had wearily explained the situation to her mother, but it had been hard. It had been almost as hopeless when she had announced the broken engagement to her friends and to her pastor. All of them were mildly shocked, and they all equally disapproved of what they considered an ill-advised and hasty course of action. However, she had weathered the worst of the storm and for almost a week had endured.

During this time she had spent a great deal of the days alone, either in her room or walking the streets of Boston. There was a park not far from her house that she often retired to in the heat of the day and watched the children who played there. She enjoyed watching the squirrels as they eagerly scampered around her feet for the scraps of food that she tossed to them. She fed them absentmindedly, laughing at their playful antics at times—but it was a sobering time for Katherine Yancy.

She was a young woman who needed activity, and now there was little enough to do. With Malcolm no longer calling on her, she mostly took care of her mother, who was unable to do the housework. Katherine saw to the meals and cleaned the house, but all of this occupied little of her time. She was concerned, deeply concerned, about her father and uncle, and spoke once to her pastor. All he could do was recommend prayer, which she, of course, was already engaged in daily.

The thought that finally came to her was startling at first, and she put it aside. It came back, however, very strongly, and one night she stayed awake practically the entire night, thinking of how the idea that had forced itself on her might come to pass. It seemed difficult and impossible, but slowly she thought and worked out the details.

The next morning she met her mother at the breakfast table, and after she had asked a simple blessing said, "Mother, I'm going to Halifax."

"To Halifax!" Susan stared at her daughter wide-eyed, sure that her broken engagement with Malcolm had sorely affected her senses.

"Yes, I must go," she said. "Father is not well and Uncle Noah needs care."

"But it's so far away!"

"I could get a ship. It'll not be a long voyage. I'll take food and warm clothing and blankets for Father and Uncle Noah."

"But will the officers let you see them?"

A stubborn look swept across the face of Katherine Yancy. "They'll be so sick of me, I think they will," she said, nodding firmly. She thought ahead then of the trip, the voyage, the trouble she would have with the officers in charge of the prison, but her courage rose and she said, "I'll stay until Father and Uncle Noah are well. I must do this, Mother!"

3

THE HULKS

BANKS OF LOW CLOUDS hung heavily over the harbor at Halifax. They seemed to be drenched with their own weight and had the texture of heavy dough, though they were much darker. Katherine moved down the gangplank of the merchant ship *Dominion*, glad to be finally free from the foul smells and unruly pitchings of the ancient vessel. For all her fine name, the *Dominion* was afloat only by the herculean efforts of a doughty captain who drove his men like galley slaves. They had left the port of Boston six days earlier and had hit rough weather almost at once. The ship had bobbed like a cork and leaked at the seams so severely that Katherine became frightened, fearing that they would never make port.

Now reaching the land, she took a deep breath, savoring the freshness of the air and the firmness of earth. A drizzle was beginning to fall, but the inclement weather did not bother her. *At last I'm off of that awful ship*, she thought. *I didn't know anything could stink so bad!* The small cabin she had been assigned to she had shared with three other women. As soon as the ship began to pitch on the white-capped waves, two of them got sick immediately. They remained sick all the way, throwing up continuously. The only escape from the clammy foul air was to go topside, where one ran the risk of being washed overboard by the heavy swells that came crashing down across the deck. Katherine had tried to take walks a few times to escape the confines of the cabin, but the deck was filled with gear, and more than once, leering sailors had grabbed at her when the officers were not looking. *Not that the officers cared a great deal*, Katherine thought with distaste as she made her way across the wharf toward a series of low, weather-beaten wooden buildings that leaned against each other for support.

Finally she reached a narrow cobblestone street and stopped an elderly man who was pulling a small cart with large wheels. "Can you tell me the way to the British camp?" she asked.

The old man stopped and straightened up and peered at her out of a face that was as wrinkled as a prune. Deep lines marked his face and eyes, and he had no teeth, so that his nose and stubbled chin attempted to meet. He suddenly looked like an ancient nutcracker to Katherine, and when he spoke she could barely understand his mumbled words. "That way—down toward the church on your left. Aye, that's where the soldiers be."

"Thank you." Katherine smiled, then turned and made her way down the street. It was a poor enough city, not at all as nice as the wharves and docks at Boston. Moving along at a rapid pace, she began to see the red coats of soldiers and wanted to ask one of them for directions. She waited until she saw a tall, erect officer in a spotless crimson jacket with crossbelts across his chest and a saber at his side. He wore the tricorn hat of the British officer, and his shirt was white enough to have put the clouds to shame. "Pardon me, sir. Can you tell me where your headquarters is located?"

"Why, I'm headed that way now, miss. If you would permit me to accompany you. . . ?" He gave her a careful examination out of a pair of watchful gray eyes and said, "I'm Lieutenant Steerbraugh."

"Thank you, Lieutenant. That would be most kind."

Lieutenant Steerbraugh positioned himself to Katherine's right and shortened his long steps to accommodate her pace. "Did you just come in on the *Dominion*?"

"Yes." She hesitated, then added, "My name is Katherine Yancy, Lieutenant. I would like to see the officer in charge of the prisoners."

"Indeed?" Steerbraugh was interested and tried not to appear too curious. "I'm not sure exactly who that would be. There aren't very many of them, though, Miss Yancy."

"Who would you suggest I see? My father was taken prisoner in Boston, and I think all the prisoners were brought here, were they not?"

"Yes, I believe so." Steerbraugh took several more strides, thinking deeply. He had a long face with a prominent mustache that covered his upper lip. "I think, perhaps, you may as well see General Howe."

"Oh, that would be wonderful!" Katherine exclaimed. "Do you think he will see me?"

"Not to be familiar," Steerbraugh grinned behind his dark mustache, "but I don't think General Howe ever refused a chance to meet an attractive woman. No offense, Miss Yancy."

"None taken."

Steerbraugh led her through a labyrinthine path, passing through ranks of soldiers that were roaming the mean streets of Halifax to a camp just outside the town itself. Tents had been set up in neat, orderly rows, and a squad was presently drilling, directed by the raspy voice of a sergeant. A troop of cavalry passed by, their hooves kicking up spongy turf from the wet earth. Finally they arrived at a house centered in the middle of the camp, and Steerbraugh said, "This is General Howe's headquarters. Let me accompany you, Miss Yancy."

"That would be very kind, Lieutenant Steerbraugh," Katherine said, grateful for his help. She had not missed the stares from the soldiers as they had made their way through the streets.

Steerbraugh led her up the steps to the house, which was old and covered with peeling white paint. Stepping inside, she saw that the foyer had been made into an outer office. A sergeant sat behind a small desk, but he rose at once and saluted the lieutenant.

"Is General Howe in, Sergeant?"

"Yes, sir, he is. Shall I see if he's busy?"

"Yes, tell him that I have a young lady here who would like to speak with him."

The sergeant gave Katherine a thorough examination, but nodded and turned to disappear through the door at his back.

Steerbraugh turned to face Katherine and made polite conversation, asking how her voyage had been. The sergeant came back, however, almost at once. A grin tugged at the corners of his lips, for the general had asked, "What sort of a looking wench is she?" Upon being told that she was a peach—in the sergeant's words—Howe had straightened his wig and said, "Have her come in then, Sergeant."

Steerbraugh moved forward and opened the door for Katherine. She entered and found herself in a room filled with worn furniture, including a couch, chairs, and a large rosewood desk, beside which General Howe was standing.

"Sir, I have a guest who's just come off the *Dominion*. May I present Miss Katherine Yancy from Boston. Miss Yancy, General William Howe."

"Good morning, Miss Yancy," Howe said, stepping forward. He was a fine-looking man, very tall, yet rumpled in his dress. His dark hair curled in unruly knots and escaped the ribbon that fastened it behind his neck. His eyes were large and fun loving, and his full-lipped mouth made him look generous.

Lieutenant Steerbraugh said, "Miss Yancy has come to visit her father and uncle."

"Oh," Howe said with some surprise, "and how is that, Miss Yancy?"

"My father's name is Amos Yancy, General. He and his brother,

Noah, were taken as prisoners at the Battle of Breed's Hill."

At the mention of Breed's Hill, Howe's features clouded. Neither he, nor Gage, nor any who took part in that battle remembered with pleasure the sight of so many slain Redcoats that had covered the green hill. It had been a senseless slaughter. Howe's generous mouth tightened somewhat, and he said, "I see, and what is your purpose in coming, Miss Yancy, may I ask?"

"I'm afraid he's not well, General. I would like to visit him and provide him with warm clothes, blankets, food, and medicine that I brought, if possible."

"I'm afraid that is not possible," General Howe said. "It wouldn't do—a young lady like you out on the hulks."

Katherine was not wearing ornate clothing. She was, however, looking very pretty in her simple gray dress. The bonnet framed her squarish face, and her cheeks were rosy from the walk from the harbor. "Please, sir," she pleaded. "I know it's an unusual request, but it's very important to me that I see my father and my uncle. In the last letter we got, my father said my uncle was very ill. I would so much appreciate it if you would let me visit them."

"I'd be happy to accompany Miss Yancy to the *St. George* to see that she's safe," Lieutenant Steerbraugh said quickly.

Howe's features grew less stern, and he almost winked at the lieutenant. "I'm sure you would, Lieutenant, but we have no precedent for this kind of request."

"Not to put too great a point on it, General," Steerbraugh said, "but I can't see what harm it would do—just one visitor. We're not likely to have many all the way from Boston out here in Halifax." He nodded at the young woman who was waiting, almost holding her breath. "I know she's shown great courage in coming this far alone."

Howe was of the same opinion. If he had not had Mrs. Loring with him—the wife of a civilian supplier of goods to the army—he might have pressed his own case. But for the time being, Mrs. Loring's charms were sufficient. Waving his well cared for hand, he said airily, "Well, I suppose it can do no real harm."

"Oh, thank you, General." A flush tinged Katherine's cheeks, and she looked very attractive as she stood before him. Impulsively she put out her hand, and he squeezed it at once. "I'm so grateful to you. Will I need a pass for my visits?" She took the chance of making a way for a series of visits instead of one.

Howe recognized the ploy immediately. He smiled, however, and winked at the tall lieutenant. "Have my sergeant make out a pass and I'll sign it."

"Yes, sir," Steerbraugh said with alacrity. He stepped outside the office, and Howe inquired more closely into the situation of the Yancys. Soon, however, Steerbraugh returned with the slip of paper. "Here you are, sir." The two waited as Howe moved to his desk, pulled a quill from a holder, dipped it in a bottle of ink, and scribbled something on it. He poured fine sand over it to serve as a blotter, cleared it with a puff of his breath, then folded it and handed it to Katherine. "There you are, Miss Yancy. Let me know if I can be of further assistance. I know this is a difficult time for you."

"You've made it much easier, General. Thank you very much."

Steerbraugh led Katherine out of the building and said, "Do you have a place to stay, Miss Yancy?"

"Why, no, I don't."

"I think that might be somewhat of a problem. With all the troops that we brought in, and many of those faithful to the Crown who have accompanied us, it's very hard to find accommodations."

"I'll find something," Katherine said.

"Let me recommend the Dolphin Inn. I have friends who are staying there, civilians from New York. I'm sure you could work out some arrangement with the innkeeper. I know you're tired, so perhaps we ought to see to that first."

"Thank you, Lieutenant. That's very thoughtful of you." Katherine was very tired, and she surrendered to Lieutenant Steerbraugh's kindness. It did not take long to walk to the Dolphin Inn, and she stood waiting as Steerbraugh practically forced the innkeeper to make room for her. She finally was placed in a tiny room in the attic, barely eight feet square. The room had a single bed, a small chest that served as a washstand, a small window of diamond-shaped glass that let in a few feeble rays of sun, and a worn green carpet.

"This isn't much," Steerbraugh said cautiously.

He then accompanied her to the *Dominion* and commandeered an army wagon to carry her small chest full of supplies that she had brought with her. When they returned to the inn, he carried the chest to her room. Now he shook his head doubtfully, "Not much in the way of luxuries, I'm afraid."

"This is fine, Lieutenant. I'm very grateful to you for your help. I don't know what I would have done without you."

Steerbraugh flushed at the compliment. He found himself attracted to this pretty, young American, and said, "Perhaps you'd like to freshen up. Later on this afternoon I'll take you to the prison ship."

"Oh, really, Lieutenant. I'd rather go now. I'm so anxious about my father—and I can rest later."

"Very well. What would you like to take to your father?"

At once Katherine began pulling items out of the chest and placed them in a small canvas bag. She had randomly thrown in some food and warm clothing before she had hastily left Boston.

When she had gathered it all together she said, "I think this will do for a start."

Steerbraugh insisted on carrying the bag, and Katherine carried the blanket folded beneath her arm. They left the Dolphin Inn, and he led her back to the wharf. When they arrived at the docks, a misty haze had fallen over the harbor so that it was almost impossible to see. The sun filtered through it, making iridescent reflections on the water. He pointed and said, "There's the hulk out there. There's only one now, an old ship called the *St. George*."

"How do you get out there?"

"I'll hire a small boat. There are always men around the docks wanting to pick up a few coins."

"You're very efficient, Lieutenant," Katherine complimented him. She followed him down to the shoreline where the water lapped at the pilings of the dock. Soon he found a small dory and a fisherman who offered to row them out to the *St. George* for half a crown.

Steerbraugh helped Katherine into the boat, then stepped in, placing the bag on the floorboards of the dory. They sat in the bow, facing the stern of the boat, and watched as the fisherman jumped in, shoved off from the dock, and began rowing with strong sweeps of his oars. The tiny craft bobbed up and down, but this was nothing to Katherine, who had endured much worse during the voyage. Overhead, gulls wheeled and swept down making raucous cries. "They're not very pretty birds, are they? And they sound awful," Steerbraugh said with a grimace. "I don't know what they're good for."

"I suppose all of God's creatures are good for something."

Her words caught at Steerbraugh. He turned toward her and studied her more carefully. The wind tugged at her bonnet, and strands of her dark brown hair had escaped. When she turned to smile at him, he noted that her eyes were the most unusual color. *Green like the sea sometimes*, he thought. *But gray too. Most unusual. A deucedly pretty girl.* He chatted with her on the way, and when they pulled up beside the *St. George*, the oarsman shipped his oars and held on to the cleats of the ladder that was nailed to the side. "Ahoy," Steerbraugh called out, "Lieutenant James Steerbraugh. Visitor by order of General Howe."

"Come aboard, Lieutenant," a voice hailed at once.

"Perhaps you'd better go first, Miss Yancy. If you fall, I'll be there to catch you."

She was a strong, athletic girl, and climbing the ladder was no problem. However, it was a little awkward for Katherine. She was aware that the oarsman and Steerbraugh himself were staring at her as she climbed up the wooden ladder. When she reached the top she saw a tall man in a blue coat with a strange-looking hat staring at her. He stepped forward at once and thrust out his hand. When she took it, it had the texture of hard tree bark. His eyes were half-lidded after many years of sun on the sea, and he said, "Watch your step, miss." Then he turned to Steerbraugh and said, "Do you have authority from General Howe?"

"I have it," Katherine said. She reached into the small reticule that she carried by a string around her wrist and fished out the pass.

The officer read it and looked at her. "Somewhat unusual," he muttered. He pulled at his muttonchop whiskers, then turned his light blue eyes on the Lieutenant. "You vouch for this young lady?"

"Yes I do, Captain."

"And this is General Howe's signature?"

"It is, sir."

"Well, I suppose it will be all right." Still he hesitated. "You can't go down in the hulks. It wouldn't do for a woman to be down there."

"Perhaps you have a room somewhere where Miss Yancy could meet her father."

"He's a prisoner, is he?"

"Yes," Katherine said at once. "His name is Amos Yancy. His brother, Noah Yancy, is also a prisoner aboard this ship."

The captain clawed at his muttonchop whiskers for a moment, then shrugged. "If you'll step this way, I have a room that might serve for a visit."

The two followed the captain, whose name was Simms, down the deck. The *St. George* was an old vessel that had seen its share of use. It smelled of tar and rotten wood. She had once been a fighting ship, but that had been years ago. Now she was barely afloat, and the trip from Boston to Halifax proved likely to be her last. Another foul and unclean smell filled the air. It rose, Katherine realized, from the prisoners' quarters below deck.

The captain opened a door and stepped inside what appeared to be a general meeting room. A man was sitting at one of the two tables eating something out of a dish. He rose at once and Captain Simms said, "May I introduce Miss Yancy. Miss Yancy, Major Saul Banks. He is one of the surgeons of our army. He is in charge of all the prisoners confined to this ship."

"Happy to meet you, Miss Yancy." Major Banks was short, fat, and red faced. He had blue eyes and strangely colored cinnamon hair that he kept slicked back with some sort of grease or oil. He had a froggish expression almost, with bulging eyes and an extremely wide mouth. When he spoke, it was as if his tongue was too large for his mouth and he mumbled his words. "Pleasure to meet you, ma'am."

"Miss Yancy has traveled all the way from Boston to visit her father, Amos Yancy. Do you know him?"

"No, not by name, Captain. Too many for that, you understand."

"Well, I'll have one of my lieutenants fetch him." Turning then to Katherine, he said, "You can meet with your father in this room."

The captain turned and left the room, and Major Banks stared at the two. "Most unusual. You have permission for this, Miss Yancy?"

"General Howe has given her a pass to see her father," Steerbraugh said.

"Most unusual."

There was an awkward silence in the room. Katherine was aware that the surgeon was looking at her slyly. An attractive woman, she had learned to interpret this sort of expression, and in Banks' case it was not difficult. He licked his lips intermittently and turned his head to one side, studying her with his pale blue eyes. He asked several questions, which she answered as briefly as possible.

Finally, the door opened and a heavyset marine sailor stood there, saying, "I'll have to remain on guard outside. Let me know when your visit is up."

As soon as the door closed, Katherine turned to the prisoner standing there. "Father!" she cried out. She moved forward at once, grief in her tone and in the agonized expression on her face.

Amos Yancy looked like a thin scarecrow, not the strong, tall man she remembered. His hair, which he had always taken such pride in keeping clean, was now lank and hung in filthy strands. His clothes were nothing more than tattered rags, and his frail body showed through rips in the pitiful excuse for a shirt that he wore. He smelled as foul as any human Katherine had ever encountered. Nevertheless, she moved toward him and put her arms around him and buried her face against his chest, murmuring, "Father, I'm so glad to see you."

"Katherine!" Amos Yancy's face was gaunt, but a gleam of hope had sprung into his brown eyes, and he reached awkwardly to stroke her back as she clung to him. "I never expected to see you here, daughter."

"I've come to take care of you, Father. Now, how are you? Tell me about yourself and about Uncle Noah—" She turned suddenly and found Major Banks watching her and said, "Would you excuse me, Major, and you too, Lieutenant? I'd like to have some time alone with my father."

"Certainly," Steerbraugh said at once. "Naturally you'll want to see your father alone." He stared at the surgeon and said, "Major Banks, perhaps you'll show me the ship."

Banks' face reddened. He did not approve of leaving them alone. He put the best face on it, however, and said, "All right, Lieutenant." But he stopped at the door and said, "You'll be needing to talk to me about your father's physical condition. After you finish your visit, I'll be happy to do so."

"Thank you, Major," Katherine said shortly. She waited until the door slammed, then turned and hugged her father again. "I'm so glad to see you," she said, then she moved back and looked at him, shaking her head. "You're ill."

"I'm fine," Amos Yancy said. He still could not believe what he was seeing. He passed his hand before his eyes in an unbelieving gesture and whispered, "I can't believe that you're actually here, Katherine. How did you manage it?"

"Oh, we'll have time to talk about that, but let's get some good clothes on you. Here." She opened the canvas bag and fished out a pair of trousers, a clean shirt, and some socks that she had knitted herself. "I'll turn my back, and you change into these. Throw those rags away."

"Well, I don't know—"

"Father—now do as I say." Anger was running deep in Katherine Yancy. Ever since she and her mother had received the letter from her father, she knew the conditions had been bad. Even before she had made her decision to come to Halifax to help them, the stories of what Tory prisoner ships were like were the concern of many families whose menfolk had been captured. She had prepared herself as best she could, but the gaunt expression of illness that lined her father's face frightened her. At the same time, knowing the suffering he and Uncle Noah had endured made her furious. "Get into those clothes. If anyone gives us a problem, I'll go straight back to General Howe."

"All right, daughter," Amos said, taking the clothes she handed to him. When she had turned around, he slowly removed the rags that covered his frail body. Silently he thanked God, for the mere sight of his daughter standing there overwhelmed him with emotion. When he was finished, his voiced choked as he said, "It's . . . it's so good to see you, daughter."

Katherine came to him at once, saying, "What you need is a hot bath."

"There's not much of that on this ship. I haven't had a bath since I was captured."

Amos had been a prisoner aboard the *St. George* for many months. It seemed, indeed, like a lifetime. Belowdecks in the dreaded prison was a population of prisoners condemned to a dismal existence—all sick and starving. They were crammed in a space too low to stand up in, and too small to stretch out without ramming their feet into another prisoner. As the weeks passed, their number continued to dwindle as death claimed another life.

The prisoners' quarters were secured by an iron hatchway, and the only ventilation came through the tiny round portholes in the sides of the ship. As the days of captivity moved into an awful rhythm, every morning the prisoners heard the cry, "Throw out your dead." Amos had been one who had climbed the rope ladder with the wretched corpse of one who had died that very morning. It mattered not whether by starvation, disease, or their own hands. The names of the dead were taken whenever possible, and the bodies were slipped over the gunnels to a watery grave. Those who clung to life were thrown their pitiful rations for the day. They took turns boiling the poor scraps of meat and the peas in a huge brass cauldron of salt water that was set into a bricked-up furnace at the ship's bow. Some were so starved they ate their food raw, and those who were not quick enough to grab what they could were condemned to fast for another twenty-four hours.

Amos stared at this lovely, clean daughter of his and thought of the loathsome food. The bread was moldy and unfit to eat, the bits of meat alive with worms. There was an occasional gill of rum and hardly ever any fresh water. The only possible variance in the routine was when a prisoner disobeyed an order and was whipped—sometimes to death. Other times men were hung upside down from the bowsprit to strangle on their own blood. Each punishment served as a solemn warning against agitation or disobedience of any sort. He said nothing about this, but he thought of those turncoats who had enlisted in the British service. Always there were a few who did that. There were always those who buckled and traded loyalties to end their suffering. Now he stood there, his face haggard, his unkempt hair hanging down over the new shirt, his beard matted and foul, and whispered, "I'm glad you've come. Tell me about everything."

"First you will eat, or you can eat while I talk."

Katherine began to pull food from the bag. She pulled out a dried fish, cut a slice of hard bread, and said, "Eat this, and tomorrow I'll get some fresh vegetables and bring them to you." She watched as her father tried to keep from gobbling the food up. She opened one of the bottles of rum that she had brought and saw how his eyes lightened at once.

Finally he shook his head and said, "I'd better not eat too much."

He thought for a moment, then said, "I wish I could give some of this to every prisoner down below, but they wouldn't let me take it with me."

Katherine held her father's hand. "We'll get you out of here some-day. You'll be free."

"It's not myself. It's Noah I'm worried about." Amos shook his head. "He's very sick."

"Take some of the food to him," Katherine urged.

"Right, I'll do that. I know that'll help."

"I brought enough clothes for him, too. Can you take those to him?"

"Yes, it'd be good for him."

The two talked for some time, and then a knock sounded on the door. It opened at once and the surgeon stepped inside. "I'm afraid that's all the time permissible, Miss Yancy. Bosun, take the prisoner back down below."

Banks watched as the girl kissed her father. He eyed the new clothes and saw the pockets bulging with food. When the door shut behind them, he moved closer, saying, "Now, my dear, let's talk about your father's case."

"His case, Major, is that he's starving and he's sick. It doesn't take a physician to see that."

Banks blinked with surprise at the fearlessness in the girl's face. It only made him grin, however, and he said, "I like to see a woman with spirit. Now then"—he moved close enough to put his hand on her arm—"I think something, perhaps, might be done. We might make a— shall we say a *special* case for your father."

Something in the tone of his words alerted Katherine, and she pulled her arm away instantly. "I will appreciate anything you can do for my father. He needs care, and my uncle is even worse."

"As I say," Banks said, "I would be happy to see to it that they get a little something extra. In the meanwhile I would be delighted if I could show you Halifax—not much to see, but we do have a little society here of respectable people."

"Thank you, Major, but I didn't come for a social outing. I'll be most grateful for anything you can do for my father."

Banks saw her resistance. "Well," he said, "we will see about that. Will you be coming tomorrow?"

"I intend to come every day, Major. That's the way the pass reads."

"Is it, now? Well, we shall see about that." There was a threat in his words, and his pale eyes glittered. He had fat, pudgy hands, and as she passed by toward the door he put his hand on her back in a familiar pat.

She stepped away instantly and pulled the door open. Steerbraugh was there, and she said with some relief, "Lieutenant, I'm ready to go now."

Steerbraugh glanced at her, seeing the agitation in the girl's face. "Of course, Miss Yancy." He gave the surgeon a cold look but said nothing. "If you come this way I'll see you back to your inn."

The two left and Major Saul Banks stood in the center of the room, his face flushed with anger. Muttering, he said, "Thinks she's too good for me, does she? Well, we'll see about that. . . !"

🛡   🛡   🛡

For three days Katherine made the trip to the *St. George*. She purchased some green vegetables from a farmer and was glad to see her father's face take on fresh color.

"Noah's enjoying the food and the drink, and the warm clothes, too," he had said to her. "If we could just get him to some fresh air, I think he would be much better off."

"I'll ask the captain."

"No, it's the surgeon you'll have to ask—Major Banks." Amos did not notice the troubled look that crossed his daughter's face. "He's a hard man. Banks does practically nothing for the men. He's drunk half the time. When he does come, he doesn't do anything, but he's really in control of the prisoners, not the captain."

Her father's words sent a chill over Katherine. Nevertheless, the next time she saw Banks she said, "Would it be possible to get my father and uncle transferred to some sort of jail in town out of the hulks?"

Banks moved forward. "Anything is possible with the proper *friends*." He moved closer again and managed to put his hand on her arm. He was always touching her, and Katherine was furious but could not afford to show it. He put his arm around her and pulled her toward him. Katherine could not move for a moment. She managed to turn her head aside so that his lips planted a kiss on her cheek. She struggled, but he had strength in his stubby arms. "Now, don't be like that, my dear Katherine! After all, you want something, and I want something. What could be more natural than that we help each other. Eh?"

"Let me go!" Katherine struggled furiously. She ripped herself from his embrace and glared at him. "You're no gentleman, sir!"

Banks had risen out of the gutters of Glasgow, gotten the rudiments of medical training, and enlisted through the help of a friend as an officer, a surgeon in the British army. He had little skill as a surgeon and was shunned by most of the officers who were of the upper class. All his life Banks had longed to be a gentleman, and now Katherine Yancy had thrown it in his face that he was not. He stared at her, his froglike features twisted with anger. "Not a gentleman? Well, we shall see about that! The one thing I am is surgeon in charge—and I am declaring as of this day that your visits will cease until further notice."

"You can't do that! I have a pass signed by General Howe."

"General Howe is a busy man, and even if he questions me I will see to it that you do not set foot on this ship to see your father. You can depend on that."

His words were prophetic. Katherine, on the following day, was not permitted to visit her father. She had gone, at once, to General Howe's headquarters and found the General amiable but strict. "I cannot go against the advice of the surgeon. He tells me it's dangerous for you to be there. There's sickness on board."

Katherine begged and pleaded, but the general, in this case, would not be moved. She left the headquarters sick at heart and walked the streets searching for a way out. To give in to Banks was unthinkable— yet still she knew Banks was capable of making life more miserable for her father and her uncle. Finally she returned, dejected, to the Dolphin Inn, and as dark fell over Halifax it seemed to close around her own heart like a fist.

4

A Desperate Case

ON APRIL 13, 1776, George Washington arrived at Manhattan Island. He had sent Benedict Arnold off on a futile mission to Canada in December, and General Charles Lee, the most experienced officer in the Continental Army, had left the main force to take command of the segment of the Continental Army in the South.

When Washington arrived in New York, he found the city swelling with a population of nearly twenty-five thousand, much different from siege-worn Boston. Everywhere there was a bustle and elegance on the streets, which were wider and more regular than those of Boston. Broadway, its main thoroughfare, which ran northward a mile from the ancient stone fort at the Battery, was shaded by rows of trees and lined with fine residences, churches, and public buildings. Beyond the limits of the city, country roads meandered through the wooded hills, marshes, and farmlands that stretched some twelve miles to the little wooden Kings Bridge that crossed to the mainland. All of this began to change at once when Washington arrived with his troops. Without delay he put his men to work completing the fortifications that Lee had started to build in Manhattan. All kinds of ambitious barricades and obstructions had been thrown across streets, and some were sunk into the riverbed to defend what was truly indefensible—a long, thin island surrounded by waterways easily navigable by enemy warships.

One immediate effect of the arrival of Washington's army was the plight of the loyalists of New York. Fearing reprisal, many of them fled the city in terror. The streets were full of shouting men and women, stunned or sobbing children, as they scurried back and forth from their homes to the docks, trundling carts, trucks, wheelbarrows, and handcarts all loaded to overflowing with all sorts of baggage and personal belongings.

Those who did not flee were subjected to indignities on the part of the triumphant patriots—some of whom got completely out of hand. Dake Bradford, who had left his bride after a brief honeymoon to return to his unit, witnessed one nightmarish scene. He was walking down Broadway on his way to the camp when suddenly a man emerged from an alley dressed up like a grotesque, nightmarish bird. Out of this strange-looking creature, whose mouth was red and gap-toothed, came horrible screams of pain.

Dake realized at once that the poor man was probably a loyalist and had been tarred and feathered. A rowdy mob followed him, yelling and laughing at their victim. They finally seized him after poking him with pointed sticks and put him on a rail, holding him high enough so that he could not reach the ground with his feet. The more the man writhed and twitched, the more feathers flew into the air, and the louder his tormentors shrieked and laughed.

Dake was disgusted by the sight and shook his head. "We don't need that kind on our side," he muttered grimly. But the crazed mob was completely out of control and he could do nothing. When he arrived at the barracks that had been assigned to his unit, he took a great deal of ribbing from his friends about his new status as a married man. He managed to field the many jokes with a smile, knowing that the more he protested the more ribald they would become. Finally he spoke to his sergeant, a tall, lanky Virginian who had been at Bunker Hill with him. His name was Silas Tooms. He was thirty-five but looked older, worn down from a lifetime of hard work on a farm. He was, however, a good soldier and a fine sergeant, and Dake had taken a liking to him. "What do you think, Silas?" Dake asked when they had a moment alone. They had procured some cider and were sipping it gratefully, for it was an unusually warm spring day.

Tooms took several swallows, his Adam's apple bobbing up and down, before he answered. Finally he wiped his mouth with the back of his sleeve and shook his head dolefully. "Mighty poor place to try to make a stand," he rasped. His voice was high-pitched and filled with gloom.

"What do you mean?" Dake asked instantly. "General Lee's thrown up a lot of fortifications."

"Maybe he has, but we can't defend this whole island. Look over there." He pointed toward the East River, which ran by on their right, then swung around. "You can't see it, but the Hudson's over there. If the British come back with their navy, which they're bound to do, what'll we do then?"

"Well, they've got to get at us," Dake said.

"You gonna fight off a ship of the line with that musket of yours?"

Tooms demanded. "We'll be caught like rats in a trap if we're not careful."

"General Washington knows all that, Silas. We'll be all right. You wait and see."

Silas looked around at the troops who were drilling and considered the thing. "What we got here is mostly militia," he said. "They're not trained to stand and fight."

"They fought at Bunker Hill."

"Yes, they did, but then we were up on top of a hill, and the British had to come up. We could hide behind the walls and shoot them as they advanced. Here, they can anchor their warships all around us and pick us off with their guns. I wish we'd leave here."

"Leave? What about the city?"

"Let the lobsterbacks have it! It ain't nothing but a pest hole of Tories anyway," Tooms growled. "I say burn it to the ground!"

Although Tooms did not know it, several of Washington's officers felt the same way. They met in a council of war, and several of them almost came to blows over the question of whether to defend New York or not.

Washington, however, had put the matter at rest. He had stood before them, a tall man with a long face and deep-set gray eyes. "The Congress has expressed their desire for our army to hold New York. It would be giving too much away to the British for us to let them have it without a fight."

Lee had scoffed. "Burn it to the ground!" he had shouted. Others had disagreed.

"We will hold New York for as long as we can," Washington had said in the end.

Not all went smoothly for the general, for one plot emerged that almost took his life. The general's cook was a faithful black man who had traveled from Mount Vernon with Martha Washington. One Thursday afternoon he brought in a special dish of green peas, and one of Washington's aides, for some reason, became suspicious.

"Where did you get them?" he asked the cook.

"Why, someone's serving maid brought them to the kitchen."

Washington was about to begin the meal when the aide said, "General, there are those who would like to see you dead. Do not eat those peas."

Washington looked surprised but shrugged. "Very well, if you say so, Lieutenant." He pushed the dish aside, and later, when the cook cast the peas to the chickens he kept outside the kitchen door, the entire flock died.

The story of the dish of poisoned peas spread rapidly. A conspiracy was uncovered, and rumor had it that the Tory conspirators had planned to poison both Washington and General Putman, then stab them when they were unconscious. Other reports circulated widely, arrests were made, and many Tories took to the woods, although about twenty of them were caught before they could escape. The most active participants were captured, and some of them saved their necks from the gallows by telling all they knew.

One of them, Sergeant Thomas Hickey, refused to talk and was charged with treason, having been implicated by some of the other conspirators.

A general court-martial was convened by a warrant from General Washington. Samuel Parsons presided over the trial in which Hickey was accused of mutiny and treason. Washington, himself, made little of the matter, but the trial went on.

Hickey pleaded not guilty but was found guilty by the court-martial. He was sentenced to be hanged. A gallows was erected in a field near Bowery Lane, and the last day of Thomas Hickey's life was a fine one. The sun shown brightly and the breeze was cool. Eighty men with loaded muskets, twenty from each brigade, were ordered to guard Hickey. He was marched onto the field to the beat of drums, and the fifes struck up a tune called "Poor Old Tory."

Hickey was brought to the place of execution. All the buttons had been cut off his uniform coat, and the red insignia of a sergeant had been ripped from his shoulder. He looked scornfully at the crowd that had gathered by the hundreds and held his head up high. When he reached the foot of the gallows, he was met by a chaplain. For just a moment, Hickey's reserve broke down and he gave in to tears, but then quickly wiped them away with his hand. The blindfold was adjusted over his face, he mounted the steps of the platform, and the rope was placed around his neck. As the snare drums rolled dramatically, the platform was yanked away. Hickey's body swung, writhing for a moment, then finally went limp.

A yell went up from the crowd, but Dake, who was not far from the gallows, shook his head. "The death of one Tory won't help us much when the British get here," he murmured to Sergeant Tooms. He looked out over the water as if he expected to see the British battle fleet arrive, but there was nothing except the blank expanse of empty horizon shadowed by white clouds that wandered around the blue heavens like fleecy white sheep.

🦁   🦁   🦁

After the departure of the British, followed by the exodus of Washington's forces, Boston seemed much like a ghost town. Things went badly for those who had been loyal to the Crown. Abigail Howland and her mother had reached the end of their meager resources, and now they faced utter destitution.

Abigail had taken the last of their money and had gone searching for food. There was little enough to be had, for the siege had driven the prices of everything up. Many of the shops were boarded up, and the whole city seemed wrapped in gloom. Finally she managed to procure two loaves of bread, a small basket full of wilted carrots and onions, and a portion of lamb that had a rather rank smell about it. Carrying her provisions, Abigail passed through the streets of the city, a cloud over her spirit. When she arrived at the small house where she and her mother had taken refuge after being put out of the family home, she was met by her mother.

"Abigail," Mrs. Howland said, coming to greet her, "we have a letter from my sister-in-law, Esther."

At once Abigail put the basket down and came to take the single sheet of paper that her mother held out to her. She scanned it quickly, and a glimmer of hope came to her. The letter was a brief invitation stating simply:

> I cannot say how things will be in New York now that it seems to have been chosen for the next site for battle, but if you and Abigail would like to come and share my home, Carrie, I would be most happy to have you. At the present time there seems to be plenty of provisions, and I know things are difficult for you there in Boston.

Abigail instantly said, "Let's go, Mother!"

"Well . . . we don't know how it will be there. The loyalists have been treated rather badly, I understand."

"It can't be any worse than here," Abigail said firmly. She looked at her mother, noting the feebleness that had become much worse lately, and knew that she, herself, would have to make the decision. Firmly she said, "We have enough money to get to Aunt Esther's house. You can rest there, and there are fine doctors in New York. I'm worried about you, Mother."

Carrie Howland was too tired and sick to argue.

"Very well," she said. "It can't be any worse for us there than here."

Abigail nodded. "I'll pack our things, and we'll leave tomorrow by coach. It'll be a hard trip, but when we get there Aunt Esther will take care of us."

5

"Are You in Love With My Pa?"

"SAM..."

Rachel Bradford paused and placed her hands on her hips before calling out again. "Sam Bradford, you come out of that workshop this instant!" She turned her head to one side, and the breeze caught her red hair, making golden gleams in the heavy tresses. There was an alertness in her green eyes, and she called out again in a stentorian voice, "Sam Bradford, I'll have Pa take a strap to you if you don't come here this instant!"

The backyard of the Bradford house contained a small vegetable garden. Flowers occupied small plots, and on the property line in the back stood a neat rectangular shed with a low-pitched roof. Just then the door opened and Sam Bradford stepped outside. At the age of sixteen he was already five ten and strongly built like his father, Daniel. His uncombed hair caught the sun and glinted with the same trace of red his sister's had. He trudged toward the house, carrying some sort of object in his hands, and when he got to the porch he said, "Aw, you didn't have to bust my eardrums. I heard you the first time." He was a cheerful young man and had a great affection for his only sister. Now, however, he was put out, and when he came up to her he bumped her with his hip, sending her backward. "You want all the neighbors to hear you screaming like a wounded panther?" he complained.

Catching her balance, Rachel flew back at him. Reaching out, she grabbed a huge handful of his hair and yanked his head back and forth. "Don't you push me around," she cried, then tugged him into the kitchen after ignoring his cries of protest. When they were inside, she turned to him and pointed to a huge bowl of potatoes sitting on the

55

table. "I told you to peel those potatoes two hours ago," she snapped, "and you haven't done one of them. You sit right down there and peel them right now or I'll take a strap to you myself!"

Sam set the machine in his hands down on the table, reached for her, and pinioned her arms. She was one year older but was no match for his powerful grip. "I think I'll just squeeze you in two, sister," he said. "Then I wouldn't have to put up with your nagging anymore." He picked her up and swung her around, laughing at her futile protests. Finally he put her down and said, "Now, you mind how you speak to a gentleman from now on."

Rachel beat on his shoulder with her fist, but laughter danced in her eyes. She was very fond of this youngest brother of hers. Her twin brothers, Micah and Dake, were only eighteen, but it was she and Samuel who had grown up together fishing, exploring the woods that surrounded Boston, and now she could not but feel a surge of admiration for him. "You sit down there and peel those potatoes right now! The men will be in soon, and I want to have supper ready."

"No problem." Sam gestured in a grandiose fashion to the object on the table. "There you have Professor Samuel Bradford's patented, dyed-in-the-wool, world's champion potato peeler." He laughed at the disbelieving expression on Rachel's face and added, "It'll peel apples, too. Let me show you."

"I've seen enough of your crazy inventions, Sam. They never seem to get anything done," Rachel said. However, she was fascinated and moved closer. The contraption that Sam had placed on the table was simple enough. It had a metal arm that rose out of a base made of walnut, with another arm extended at right angles over which Sam jabbed a potato. Then he moved another upright arm forward, which had a blade of some sort attached. Grasping a small wheel attached to the second arm, he winked at her and said with excitement, "Now, you just watch this! It'll peel that potato in three seconds. No more sittin' there with a knife picking the eyes out and all that stuff," he crowed. "Watch this, Rachel!"

Sam advanced the second upright arm until the blade was touching the potato. As he began to turn the wheel, the blade performed a circle around the potato, which was held tightly. "Look at that!" he said proudly and pulled the peeled potato off its mount.

Rachel took it and shook her head in disgust. "Why, this won't work!" she exclaimed. Reaching down, she picked up the peeling. "Look at this. You've got peelings over half an inch thick." She held the potato in one hand, and the peeling in the other and shook her head. "We'd have to cook the peelings! All you have left here is half a potato."

Sam was disgruntled, for he had put great stock in this invention. "Well, that's just a technical problem," he mumbled. "I'll just have to set the blade a little bit farther back." He had already begun making adjustments to the invention in his head, for he loved to make things, but Rachel gave him no help.

"Get that thing out of the way," she said. Reaching over to the table she picked up a short knife and said, "Here, you peel those potatoes right now. I've got to tend to the rest of the supper."

"All right, but one of these days when I'm rich and famous from my potato peeler, see if I give *you* any of the money," Sam called out as she turned and busied herself at the stove.

🛱 🛱 🛱

Daniel Bradford entered the dining room after washing his hands and paused to look at the supper that Rachel had prepared. "Why, this looks good enough for a king!" Turning, he reached out and put his arm around Rachel and squeezed her, careful of his strength. He was forty-six years old and in perfect physical condition. One inch over six feet, he weighed one hundred eighty-five pounds, and there was not a spare ounce of fat on his body. His upper body was heavy and strong from the years he had spent at the forge, and there was an air of power about all that he did. He released her and said, "If that's as good as it looks—and smells—I'm probably going to commit gluttony."

He moved to the head of the oak table, took his seat, then waited until Micah, Rachel, and Sam had seated themselves. He bowed his head and said a simple prayer, then looked up and smiled at them. "I hate to say it, but I wouldn't regret it too much if Mrs. White stayed sick another few days. Your cooking is better than hers, Rachel." Mrs. White was the housekeeper and cook in the Bradford household since he'd come to Boston from Virginia with his family, and Daniel Bradford did not really mean what he said. He always liked to praise Rachel whenever he could, for he was fiercely proud of her, as he was of his other children.

"You eat so fast you never taste anything, Pa," Rachel said, but flushed with his compliment.

"Hurry and cut that meat up, Pa," Micah Bradford said. At eighteen he was within an inch of his father's height and weighed almost exactly the same. He also had the same straw-colored hair and hazel eyes of Daniel Bradford, and when he smiled his eyes crinkled the same way his father's did. His twin brother, Dake, had the same hair and eye color, of course, as did Samuel. There was a strong family resemblance between these three, and more than once Daniel had said to Rachel, "I'm glad you took after your mother and not after me, daughter."

The four ate heartily of the meal that Rachel had prepared. She had roasted a leg of lamb and baked some fish caught early that morning in the sea. They were expertly cooked, and the meat was tender, almost falling apart. She also had prepared potatoes, beans cooked with her own special recipe, and carrots. Sam ate so fast he hardly spoke for a while. "This is sure good bread," he said, breaking off a piece of the fresh baked loaf and stuffing it into his mouth. "Did you tell Pa about my new invention?"

"What invention's that?" Micah inquired. "A perpetual motion machine?"

"No, nothing like that yet," Sam said, swallowing a huge bite and shuddering as it went down. He cut a piece of lamb off, approximately half the size of his fist, lifted it on his knife, and bit off half of it. Chewing with great enjoyment he said, "It's a potato peeler, and it peels apples too."

"The only thing is, the peeling was so thick there was no potato left," Rachel laughed, her eyes gleaming in the lamplight. They all teased Sam for a time about his invention, and finally Rachel said, "How did it go at the foundry today, Pa?"

"It's going to be more trouble than I thought, Rachel," Daniel said.

He had fair skin by nature, but stayed outdoors as much as he could, which gave him a ruddy complexion. He had a rather thin face with high cheekbones, a broad forehead, and a cleft chin. A scar ran across the bridge of his nose, and with his wheat-colored hair and eyebrows he looked, Rachel thought, like the old Vikings might have looked on their sea-going ships. "What's the matter?" she asked.

"Just that we've never tried to make muskets before," Bradford said, "but General Washington wants me to try it."

"We'll get it, Pa," Micah said. He was a soft-spoken young man who talked with slow speech, unlike his brother Dake, who rattled off like a preacher. Micah chewed thoughtfully on a bit of the lamb and then nodded. "It'll just take a little longer than we thought."

Sam listened as they talked about the problems of turning the foundry into a musket factory. Finally he broke in impatiently. "Pa, I want to join the army."

"I believe you've mentioned that before," Daniel said dryly, "about a thousand times at the last count."

"Well, Dake's there, and he's only two years older than I am."

"Sam, we're not going to discuss this anymore—not at the table."

"But, Pa, James Seely signed up yesterday, and I'm two months older than he is."

"That is between him and his parents. This is between you and me."

"The war might be over before I get a chance at it."

A cloud crossed Daniel Bradford's face, and he said, "I doubt that, son. I very much doubt that." He put his fork down, leaned back in his chair, and stared at this younger son of his. His thoughts went back to the time in England when he had served in the cavalry of King George. He remembered the blood and agony and death . . . and he knew that this young son of his had no idea of what being a soldier really meant. He also understood the yearnings of youth for excitement and color and now said, "I know life's dull for you, Sam, but your first job is to get an education."

"You can't fight the lobsterbacks with a Latin book, Pa," Sam protested.

Micah listened quietly as Sam argued sturdily, knowing that his father would never give in. Micah, himself, had been under pressure to join the army. Many young men of his age had already signed up, and a few had already taunted him for being a coward. Yet something in him refused to join in the clamor to shake off the shackles of England. Dake, his identical twin, was like a brand fully ablaze. Already he was serving with Washington in the Continental Army, but Micah was a young man who thought slowly and somewhat more profoundly than his brother Dake. He finally said, "There's lots to do around here, Sam. You can help the army more by making muskets. Anybody can carry one, but the Colonies have to buy guns made in Europe."

"You don't care about the war, Micah," Sam said almost angrily.

"That's enough, Sam!" Daniel Bradford's voice clamped a silence on the room. When he spoke in that tone, everyone knew that it was not wise to push the thing any further. Daniel stared at Sam, daring him to speak, then when Sam tactfully kept the silence, he said, "We'll speak no more about this. You understand?"

"Yes, Pa." Rebellion ran through every line of Sam's body, but he understood his father well enough to keep his peace—at least for now.

"Oh, I forgot to tell you," Rachel said. "A note came from Marian Rochester today." As soon as she spoke she saw her father's head suddenly lift and knew that the others had not missed the attention that the name had for their father. "I'll get it." She got up, left the room, and came back with a small slip of paper. They all watched as he unfolded it, and all three of them had their own ideas about their father's relationship with Marian Rochester, though he had never spoken a word to them about it.

None of them actually knew how Mrs. Rochester and their father felt about each other. Outwardly they were polite, but there were rumors around and they had heard them. Rachel thought suddenly of her father's early life back in England. She knew the story well. He and his sister, Lyna Lee, were orphaned at an early age and had become indentured servants of the Rochester family. Leo Rochester, the oldest son, had developed a lust for Lyna Lee Bradford and a hatred for Daniel, who had stood against him, even as a servant. Rachel also had heard fragments of the story from her father—and some from her aunt, Lyna Lee Gordon. The two had been deceived, and Daniel had been driven away from the Rochester household and cast into prison. Lyna had been forced to run away to avoid Leo's attentions. Daniel and Lyna had been separated for years, and through the cruel lies of Leo Rochester each had believed the other dead. To escape dying in prison Daniel had accepted Rochester's offer and followed Leo to Virginia as an indentured servant for seven years. Only recently had the two had a spectacular reunion. Lyna Lee Bradford was now Lyna Lee Gordon, the wife of Colonel Leslie Gordon of King George's troops that had come to force the Colonies into submission.

But more than this Rachel thought of how Leo had become determined to marry the daughter of a wealthy Bostonian, John Frazier. Her name was Marian, and when she had come to visit Leo's plantation, Daniel had fallen in love with her—or so Rachel guessed. Her father never spoke of such a thing, but there was something in his manner toward Marian Rochester that had caught the quick-eyed girl's attention. Now, whenever the two met, Rachel always studied them closely. Her mother had died at the birth of Sam, and her father had never remarried. Rachel had decided it was because he was in love with Marian Rochester and, loving her, he could never marry another woman.

Unaware of his daughter's scrutiny, Daniel looked up from the note and put his eyes on Sam. "Marian says the plumbing you fixed for her won't work. You'll have to go tomorrow to fix it."

"All right, Pa." Sam was always ready to get out of school and said, "I thought of a few new ways to improve it. It may take all day."

A sudden smile turned the corners of Daniel Bradford's lips upward. "I was sure you'd find some way to get out of that Latin lesson," he said.

After the meal was over, Sam helped Rachel clean up while Micah and Daniel retired to the study to work on drawings and to talk about the problems of manufacturing the muskets. Sam complained loudly about the injustice of life, primarily because he was not allowed to join the army as he wanted to.

"I hope you never have to go in the army," Rachel said. Sadness came to her eyes then and she said, "I feel so sorry for Jeanne. Here she and Dake get married, and the first thing he does is run off to fight."

"Why, a man's got to stand for what he believes," Sam protested.

The two argued for some time, and finally Sam said, "Rachel—?" He hesitated for a moment, then reached up and clawed at his hair, leaving it to fall over his face. Brushing it back he said, "Do you notice how Pa always looks kind of—well, funny, every time anybody mentions Marian Rochester?"

Quickly Rachel shot a glance at her younger brother. He seemed totally caught up with hunting, fishing, and inventing things, but now she saw a worried expression on his smooth countenance. "Why, he's just interested in people, I guess."

"It's more than that, isn't it?" Sam turned a dish around in his hand, dried it thoroughly, then put it on the shelf. Turning to her he said, "I had a fight last week. Tim Denton said something about them."

"About Pa and Marian?"

"Yes, and I busted him for it. He won't say that again, at least when I'm around." He turned to her and chewed on his lower lip nervously. "It makes me feel kind of funny."

"Well, you don't have to worry about Pa or Marian. They're both fine Christians. And besides, she's married. But people have wagging tongues. That Mrs. Denton's got a tongue long enough to sit in the living room and lick the skillet in the kitchen!" she exclaimed vehemently. "I'd like to pull it out!" Anger flashed in her green eyes, then she turned to Sam and calmed herself. "Don't worry about it, Sam."

"Well, *I'll* never get into a mess like that!"

"You don't know what you'll get into," Rachel remarked, and suddenly her shoulders seemed to slump.

"Well, I won't!"

"Let him that thinketh he standeth take heed lest he fall," Rachel quoted. "That's what the Bible says." Then she reached out and mussed his hair again fondly. "How about another piece of pie?" She took his mind off the problem, but she, herself, was troubled by what Sam had said, and as the two sat there eating the remnants of the apple pie she wondered what would come of it.

🦁   🦁   🦁

The morning sun filtered through the tall window composed of small triangles of glass. The triangles broke up the yellow light into fragments as it fell on the silver and gold vessels that adorned the white tablecloth of the table where two men and a woman sat. A black servant moved around them, attending to their needs, his dark eyes watchful to anticipate their needs before they asked.

Marian Rochester ate sparingly of the eggs and fruit on the china plate before her and noticed that her husband, Leo, ate even less. *He doesn't look well*, she thought, noting his features were somehow gaunt yet puffy at the same time. Leo was a big man who until recently had been overweight. He was still somewhat fatter than usual, but the white shirt he wore was not as tight around his neck, and she knew that he had lost weight. She had asked him several times if he was ill, but he had always snapped at her, and now she dare not say more.

Matthew Bradford sat at the table too. He was the oldest son of Daniel Bradford, and at the age of twenty bore little resemblance to either his father or his twin brothers or Sam, for that matter. He was slender with brown hair and blue eyes, and he had none of the heavy muscular strength of the Bradfords. Looking across at Leo he said, "This might not be a good day for a visit, sir. Are you sure you feel up to it? You don't look well."

Rochester blinked and cast a warning glance at his wife, but he managed a smile and shook his head. "Just a little under the weather. I've been looking forward to it, Matthew. I've got some new prints in my study I'll show you after breakfast. I think you'll be interested in them. They came earlier this week on the *Argosy*."

Marian sipped her tea, listening quietly as the two men talked of art, and thought of the strangeness of the situation. She had married Leo Rochester in a romantic moment and had lived to regret it. She had learned quickly that he was a brutal man, for he treated her little better, if as well, as his fine horses. She knew also that she should have married Daniel Bradford, even though he was only an indentured servant at the time. This thought she could not bear, and even as it arose she thrust it away and tried to concentrate on the talk of drawing and painting and famous artists.

Studying the two, she saw the resemblance between the two men. She thought again of the painting of her husband when he was Matthew Bradford's age, and at that age he had looked exactly as did the young man sitting across from her. The tragic irony, of course, was that Leo was the father of Matthew Bradford. She had learned the story from Leo himself, told from his point of view, and then Daniel had told her the rest. After Leo had come to America, he had been attracted to a young woman, a servant in the house named Holly Blanchard. He had forced his attentions on her, and then when Holly became pregnant he cast her off without a thought. Daniel had married Holly out of pity and had given her child his name. He had never told Matthew, and it had been only recently that Leo had discovered that he actually had a son.

Marian sat there looking at the two as they spoke about art, and finally when she arose they stood with her. "Shall I bring coffee to the drawing room, Leo?"

"Not now," Leo said brusquely. "We have a lot of talking to do. Maybe later." He turned and left the dining room.

Matthew, however, paused long enough to smile and say, "Thank you for the fine breakfast, Mrs. Rochester."

Something about his smile touched Marian, for there was a gentleness in this young man that Leo lacked. "Since I didn't cook it, I can hardly take credit, but thank you, Matthew."

The two men went to Leo's study, a rectangular-shaped room sheathed in glowing walnut, furnished with a rosewood desk, Windsor chairs, and several fine pictures on the wall.

"Here we are. You sit here, and we'll put them on this easel," Leo said. He pulled a print from the large leather case on his desk, set it on the easel, and said, "Now, look at the lines of that. That's what I call real drawing! What do you think?"

The two men talked for a long time about the drawings that Leo produced slowly. Leo wanted to make the moment last, for he was a cunning man. He knew he had to convince Matthew that taking the name of Rochester was his one chance at a life filled with fame, success, and money.

As Matthew looked at the prints, he thought of the strangeness of his situation. How few young men had the chance to become rich without lifting a hand! After his brief visit to Fairhope, he now understood well how his mother had been forsaken. When he had confronted Leo, he had not denied it. Leo had pleaded that he did not know there was a child to come and was relieved to see that Matthew did not seem to harbor ill will.

Ever since his youth, Leo Rochester had been a man to seize things for himself. Through his trickery and skills of manipulation, he had honed his selfishness almost into a fine art. He had taken what he wanted without thought and, being wealthy, had indulged his every whim. But now the one thing he wanted the most he could not have. Marian had produced no children, no heir to carry on his name, and now this young man sitting there, so much like himself at an earlier age and even now, Leo desperately wanted to claim.

Finally, he hesitated, then said, "I've been feeling a little ill these days. You probably have noticed?"

"Why, yes I have, Leo. Have you seen a doctor?"

"Oh yes, but what do they know? I know what I need." Leo put his full attention on Matthew and said intently, "Sunny Italy—that's what I need. Have you ever been there?"

"No, but I've heard about it all my life, though."

"That's where all the great masters painted. With so many museums there, you could go for years and not see them all." Leo went on describing the glories of art that abounded in Italy, then finally took a deep breath. "Come with me, Matthew," he said quietly but with a steady force. When he saw the surprise wash across the young man's face he pressed him, "I need you. We could leave next week. There's a ship leaving Boston for the Continent."

"Why, I can't do that, Leo."

"Why not? What's holding you here?"

For one moment Matthew could not answer. The truth of the matter was that he longed to leave Boston. He was tired of the place, and the thought of going back to the Continent was enticing. Still, there was something that rebelled against the thought of giving up his name, and he knew this was on Leo's mind. He hesitated for one moment, then shook his head. "Well, I need a little time, Leo. Actually," he said tentatively, "I'm going to New York."

"New York? Whatever for!" Leo exclaimed. "That'll be the scene of the next battle, don't you know that?"

"Yes . . . I expect you're right about that." Matthew knew, as did everyone, that General Washington had turned New York into an armed camp. He also knew that the British who had fled to Halifax would return soon with a powerful force. New York would be fought over as two dogs fight over a bone.

"I have a friend, a man I met in England. He's a Dutchman," Matthew said slowly. "His name is Jan Vandermeer. We became great friends in England, although he's older than I, about fifty. He's a great painter, Leo, although he's never been recognized, and he's living in New York now with some relatives." Matthew's face lit up and he said, "I received a letter from him recently, and he asked me to come and visit with him. He said he'd like to teach me a few things. It's a great opportunity."

Disappointment rose in Leo, but he kept his voice even. "Well, of course, that would be fine, but there are so many fine artists in Italy that could teach you even more." Then he saw Matthew's face grow stubborn and said at once, "But, of course, I understand young men must have their way. Tell me more about this fellow Vandermeer. . . ."

🔔　　　🔔　　　🔔

Hearing the sound of banging outside her window, Marian drew back the curtains. Seeing Sam outside doing something to the plumbing, she opened the window and called out, "When you get through,

Sam, come inside. If you're hungry I've got something you might like."

"Won't be long, Mrs. Rochester," he said cheerfully, then turned again to bang on the hot water tank that he had invented and installed. It was a simple enough device—a steel tank with a wood fire box underneath where servants could build a fire. The water was heated in the tank, then ran through pipes that Sam had brought into the house. He was proud of this invention—a duplicate of the one that he had installed in his own house. Finally satisfied that he had solved the problem, he went to the back door and knocked. When Marian answered he said, "My hands are all greasy."

"Come on in—you can wash at the sink."

Sam marched over to the sink and pumped water out. Using the soap Marian furnished, he said, "You know, you ought to have hot water in the kitchen, too."

"Do you think that could be possible?" Marian asked. "It would be lovely."

"I don't see why not. If I can put it in a bathtub, I can put it in the kitchen sink. I'll work on it."

He dried his hands and said, "Are those donkers I smell?"

"Yes, they are. I made them just for you, Sam. I know how much you love donkers." Marian had saved meat leftovers during the last week. Earlier that morning she had chopped them together with bread and apples and raisins and savory spices, then fried them. As Sam sat down, she served it up with boiled pudding, and he ate as if he had not had a bite for days.

"Don't eat so fast, you'll choke yourself," Marian admonished him. She sat there looking at the boy fondly, then said, "I miss my hot bath, Sam. That's the greatest invention in the world, I think. Every house in Boston ought to have one."

"Well, that'll never happen," Sam shrugged. "It costs too much. Only rich people can have their own bathtubs, especially with hot water piped in from the outside."

"I'm glad I'm rich then—at least rich enough to have one of your nice bathtubs." She leaned forward and watched him eat, smiling at his eagerness. "Tell me about things at home. How's Rachel?"

Sam waved his spoon around, gesturing dramatically, as he described his new invention and how Rachel was going to love the potato peeler when he got it perfected. When he finished, she gave him a mug of hot coffee, which he loved, and as he drank it she sat back and listened to his youthful exuberance. When he told her about how his father had refused to let him join the army, she shook her head sympathetically, but inside was thinking, *Good, I hope the awful war's over before Sam joins up.*

For a long time Sam sat there talking with Marian, and finally without warning, in the way of youth, he asked bluntly, "Mrs. Rochester, are you in love with my pa?"

Taken completely aback, Marian's face suddenly grew scarlet. "Why—Sam, what a thing to ask!"

"Well, are you?"

"Why do you bring this up, Sam?" Marian tried to gain control of herself. She could not give him the simple truth, for if she said, "Yes, I am in love with your father," she knew what he would make of that. To gain time she replied, "It's rather impertinent of you to ask such a thing."

Sam stared at her and admired her as he always did. She looked much younger than her forty-one years, with her rich auburn hair, green eyes, and heart-shaped face. He was aware she loved horses, could play the piano, and do all sorts of things. He knew also that she was very unhappy in her marriage, for Leo's reputation was common knowledge to anyone who knew the Rochesters. Now he said lamely, "Well, I just wondered, that's all."

"Have you heard talk?" Marian asked, trying to hide the caution that threatened to make her voice waver.

Sam hesitated, then shook his head. Finally he said, "I've heard some. And you two act funny around each other. I mean, every time you come into a room Pa just kind of—well, he kind of lights up. Why does he do that, do you think, if he's not in love with you?"

Marian knew she had to say something. She breathed a quick prayer for wisdom, then leaned forward and put her hand over Sam's hand, noticing how strong and thick they were—like his father's. "Sam, I'm a married woman, and if you'll think about it, knowing your father's values, you'll understand that your father is the last man on the face of the earth to pursue any interest with a married woman—or anyone else. Isn't that true?"

Sam blinked with surprise, then swallowed hard. "Why, sure it is," he said. He stared down at her hands, so well kept and soft, yet strong on his, and it gave him a feeling of pleasure that she would touch him like this. "I guess I'm just an old blabbermouth like I sure don't want to be." Though he felt embarrassed, he looked up then and said, "You do like him, don't you?"

"Your father and I have admired each other for many years. It all began with my love for horses. He taught me how to ride—or thinks he did." She smiled and then began to tell stories of the time when she had

first come to visit the Rochester household in Virginia and Daniel Bradford had been the one who had helped her with her riding. Finally she
said quietly, "You were very worried about this, weren't you, Sam?"

"Well, kind of."

"I understand that. Your father is a very attractive man, and he's
never married again. He must've loved your mother very much."

Sam glowed with pleasure and said, "I'm glad I asked you. I feel a
whole lot better now."

"Well, why don't you talk to me like this more, Sam." Marian
squeezed his hand, then folded her own together and said, "You know,
I've never had any children. I've always wanted to have a family, of
course, as every woman does. Do you suppose I could be a sort of
mother to you? Kind of a combination friend and mother? I don't have
any practice with sons, especially big ones like you, but I'd like to have
you to practice on."

"I . . . I guess that'd be all right," Sam mumbled. The thought pleased
him immensely and he said, "I think that would be just fine."

Seeing the pleasure in his face, Marian suddenly rose, leaned over,
and kissed him. "There! Now, come along. I'll show you my new filly.
She can beat anything in Boston, I think. . . !"

🦁   🦁   🦁

Leo Rochester went about depressed for several days after the day
he spent with Matthew. He did not feel well, and the depression over
Matthew's refusal to go to Italy made him feel worse. He began to drink,
in spite of the doctor's strict orders, and knew that he was making a
fool of himself again in the taverns.

"There's got to be a way," he muttered one evening, going down to
dinner. He had put the bottle away and felt somewhat better as he entered the dining room. It gave him a sense of security, and he thought,
Maybe this sickness, whatever it is, is leaving. I could live a long time yet.

Marian was surprised at Leo's attitude. Her father, John Frazier, was
so ill he could not leave his bedroom. He was an invalid now, practically
confined to his bed, and Leo asked about him, which surprised her.
"Why, he's not much better I'm afraid, Leo."

"Too bad." Leo had never given much thought to Frazier's illness,
but now it was very real to him. "You think it would help to see another
doctor?"

"Why, I doubt it," Marian said. "Dr. Bates knows his case better than
any." She longed to ask about Leo's illness, but knew that he would not
like it. Encouraged by his manner, she began to speak of small things,

and finally she said quite by chance, "Have you heard about the How-lands?"

"Howlands? You mean Abigail Howland and her mother?"

"Yes, I feel so sorry for them. They've lost everything, I think."

"Too bad . . . the Tories haven't fared too well since the patriots took over." He made a grimace and said, "They'd have probably tarred and feathered me if I weren't here in this house. What about the How-lands?"

"Why, they're going to New York."

"Whatever for?" He thought instantly of Matthew and said, "Matthew wants to go there too, he tells me. What's the big advantage in going to New York? The whole place could be blown off by Wash-ington's cannons, or when the British come back they'll probably take it away again."

"Mrs. Howland has a sister-in-law there. She's invited them—a Mrs. Esther Denham."

Leo listened as Marian described the situation, and finally said, "Well, the girl's a beauty—a little bit shop worn. Everyone knows she had an affair with Paul Winslow and maybe with his cousin Nathan, but she's pretty enough. Men will be willing to forget that."

He left the table and moved to the study for a time, finally coming back to ask Marian, who was in the sewing room, "Did you hear when they were leaving, the Howlands, I mean?"

"Right away, I think. Why?"

"Oh, just curious. Matthew was quite taken with her at one time. I thought they might see something of each other when they're both there." He turned and left the room, and a thought that had come to him began to grow. He nourished it for a while, letting it take shape, then finally he said under his breath, "It might work—it just might work. . . !"

6

A Tempting Offer

A SONG SPARROW PERCHED on a branch of a blossoming apple tree just outside of Abigail Howland's bedroom window. She was sitting there stroking her long brown hair listlessly with a brush, and the song caught her attention. Turning her eyes outside she saw among the white, puffy blossoms a bird with his head tilted up throwing his song onto the morning air of May. Something about the joyful song of the bird caught at her, and she thought, *There was a time when I felt like you do and could sing a song. I wonder where it all went?*

Restlessly she turned from the window, tossed her brush down, and rose to head for the door. She stepped outside into the hall of the small house, intending to go to the kitchen, when a knock sounded on the front door. Abigail was in a bad mood, having had a difficult night. She had lain awake tossing restlessly, reaching out with her mind, trying to think of some other way to go with her life. She had come up with no answers, and finally tears of frustration had risen in her eyes and she had buried her face in her pillow, trying to blot out the bleakness of her future.

Moving toward the door when her mother did not appear, she opened it and stood stock still. "Paul!" she gasped with surprise. She was instantly aware that her face was puffy, and that she was wearing a drab brown dress that did nothing for her. At the same time a streak of anger touched her nerves. She held on to the door with one hand, preparing to shut it. "What do you want, Paul?" she demanded in a hard-edged voice.

Paul Winslow stood before her, dressed as if he were on his way to an evening ball. He wore a gray frock coat with a sloping shoulder line, a green double-breasted waistcoat, a pair of fitted dark brown britches, and striped stockings with figures in the form of embroidered clocks. He swept his hat off his head, a felt narrow-brimmed affair, and smiled

69

at her with one eyebrow cocked in a quizzical expression. "Why, Abigail," he said. "Is that any way to talk to your friend and former lover?"

Abigail stared at him almost with hatred and slammed the door—or tried to. Paul Winslow reached out and caught it easily and stood there looking at her. Even as she watched him she was impressed with him. He was one of those men who had a neatness about him, both in feature and in figure. He was of no more than average height, but there was a natural grace in his body—a depth to his chest that hinted at strength. He had a handsome face, and his dark hair lay smoothly in place like a cap. His large brown eyes studied her carefully, well set in the plains of a face smoothly joined to form a pleasing picture. Smiling easily he said, "I thought we might have tea together. We haven't seen each other in a while."

Abigail wanted to strike out at him, but there was something in the man that drew her. They had been lovers for over a year, and yet during that time she had not come to know him at all despite her efforts. She finally stepped back and said, "Well, you can't stand there in the doorway; all the neighbors will be talking."

Paul stepped inside the door, spun his hat in his hand, and tilted his head to one side. "I think they probably said all that could be said about us. We're no longer an item for the gossips, Abby. Now, how about that tea, and if you have any breakfast I'd be glad to share it with you."

Abigail shrugged her shoulders and said, "I'll see what there is. Come along."

Paul Winslow followed Abigail to the kitchen, and the swaying of her body, which he traced with his quick brown eyes, brought back memories of their torrid affair. It had ended when she had forsaken him for Nathan Winslow. This had occurred as a result of Abigail's strongly developed sense of self-preservation. When she had seen that the patriot forces were going to retake Boston from the British, she had immediately switched her allegiance to Nathan, whose family were prominent patriots. Paul had revealed the truth to Nathan, who had been shocked by Abigail's perfidy. Since that time, Abigail had not spoken to Paul, and now as he followed her to the kitchen he regretted it.

"I'll fix tea and some eggs if you like. We have a few left, not many."

Paul nodded agreeably. "Food has been scarce in the city. I thought it was scarce while the rebels were surrounding us, but it seems like all the food supplies have dried up. Boston's not the same as it once was."

Abigail shrugged. "No, it's not." She busied herself gathering the things together for a breakfast of sorts. As she prepared the meal, she listened closely to Paul, who related several humorous incidents of how he had managed to scrape by, even though he was regarded as a Tory.

He had always had the gift of charming her, and she found his conversation amusing after the dreary days she had endured.

Finally the two sat down and ate, and Paul smiled across the table at her. "It's good to see you again, Abigail. I've missed you."

"Have you?"

Ignoring her cold tone, Paul nodded. "Why, of course I have. After all, I've always been very fond of you." Paul took a bite of the scrambled egg, chewed it thoroughly, then swallowed it.

"You have an odd way of showing it."

"Because I revealed your little scheme to Nathan? You would never have been happy with Nathan. He's a holy man, you know, and you're not—"

Abigail's cheeks were suddenly flushed with red, and she said, "That's none of your business anymore, and I'm as holy as you are!"

"Exactly right!" Paul nodded. "Neither of us are good people, Abigail. Perhaps we ought to marry just to spare two other innocent victims from a life of tragedy if they marry us." Paul Winslow was a realist and knew himself to be worldly to the bone. He also knew Abby was no different. "What about it?" he said.

Abigail sat sipping her tea. She put it down, and then stared at him, asking him frigidly, "What about *what*?"

"Why, about us." Reaching across the table, he captured her hand. She tried to withdraw it, but he held it tightly. "Don't fight against me, Abby," he murmured. "As I say, I'm very fond of you. You're one of the loveliest women I know. There's still a great deal of fun to be had in Boston. Or, if you like, we could go to Philadelphia."

"And live on what?" Abigail asked. She jerked her hand back, picked up a piece of bread, and nibbled at it thoughtfully. Her lips curved upward in a bitter smile and she said, "We can't live on love, if that's what it was we had."

"Oh, there are ways. I might have a good day betting. And my family's always good for a touch."

"No thank you, Paul."

Paul leaned back in his chair and studied the girl carefully. Even dressed in a dowdy dress with her hair not fixed, there was a beauty in her that shone forth. Her skin was almost translucent, and there was an attractiveness in the set of her lips and in the shape of her eyes. She had the longest eyelashes he had ever seen, and she knew well how to use them. "What do you intend to do, then?" he demanded finally. "You and your mother aren't doing too well, I take it? I thought I might be able to help a little bit with the finances."

Abigail blinked with surprise. "Well . . . that's kind of you, Paul," she said, "but we're leaving Boston."

"Leaving? Where are you going?"

"New York."

"New York? You'll be caught right in the middle of another battle."

"I know. That's what everyone says, but that's where we're going."

"Why would you want to go to New York?"

"My aunt lives there. My father's sister. She's quite well-off—Mrs. Esther Denham. She's invited us to come and stay with her at her house."

"Quite well-off?" Paul sipped his tea and chewed on that information. "Perhaps elderly and quite infirm—not long for this world? Perhaps a little inheritance might be coming down the way to you and your mother?"

Abigail stared at him with distaste. "You always think of things like that, don't you?"

"Oh, you're just going because you love the dear old lady."

Abigail suddenly grew angry. Her eyes flashed and her lips drew tight. "You haven't a decent bone in your body, Paul Winslow. Not one!"

Winslow suddenly felt ashamed of himself—a rare occurrence for him. "You're right," he said, "the scum of the earth, and you're looking at him. Well, I wish you well, Abigail, you and your mother. Do you need help, money to make the trip to New York?"

Abigail hesitated. "Well . . . I . . . I really do, Paul. We're almost destitute."

"I have a little here. Had a good night at the tables last night." Paul Winslow reached into his inner pocket and pulled out a few coins. He divided them in half and gave some to her. "Partners in this at least." He stood up and said, "Thanks for the breakfast." And when she stood he took her hand and kissed it. "I do wish you well, Abigail. I'm a rotter and always will be, but you know I always thought there was something in you that I'd like to see come out."

Abigail stared at him in bewilderment. "What do you mean by that, Paul?"

"I mean, outwardly you're a diamond—beautiful and all that, and I see you have a hard streak in you—but beneath that I've always thought there was another Abigail." He thought for a moment, his brown eyes considering her carefully. He shrugged finally and smiled. "I guess I'm trying to say there's a sweetness in you somewhere that you've been hiding all these years. You've always been the hard, bright, beautiful Abigail Howland, and that's been enough for me, but anyway, I'd like to see some of that other Abigail."

Abigail followed him to the door and opened it. He took his hat from the peg, settled it firmly on his head, and smiled. "As my cousin Nathan would say, God bless you, Abigail."

He turned and walked briskly away, leaving Abigail to stare after him. She looked at the coins in her hand and wondered for a moment if she was making a mistake. Turning back inside, she shut the door and moved slowly back toward the kitchen, where she sat down and poured herself another cup of tea. For a long time she sat there staring at the wall, then took a deep breath.

"I've got to go, but I'd give anything if I had something more to look forward to than just being a long-term guest at Aunt Esther's house." She had a streak of pride in her, and it galled her to have to accept charity. Finally she rose and began to fix breakfast for her mother.

T   T   T

Abigail's second guest's visit came as even more of a shock than that of Paul Winslow. She had gone to the market and had come back with a few parcels of food. Her mother was sitting in the parlor embroidering when she came in, and called out to Abigail as she passed by. "Abigail, come here a moment, daughter, after you put the groceries down."

Abigail was somewhat surprised but did as she was bidden. When she returned to the small parlor she stopped abruptly, for she found her mother was not alone.

"Why, Mr. Rochester," she said, turning to meet the man who had risen as she entered. "I didn't know you were here."

Leo Rochester was wearing a fancy suit as usual. It was well tailored, but he had lost weight, so it seemed to hang on him, making him look gaunt. When he smiled she saw the hollows in his cheeks and that his eyes were not as bright as she remembered them.

"I took the liberty of coming to call on you, Miss Howland. Your mother and I have been having a very nice talk."

Abigail Howland knew that Leo Rochester was not the kind of man who made calls on uninfluential widows who were having financial problems. Quickly she understood that Leo had come to see her, but she made no mention of it. Instead she sat down, and for some time the three of them sat there as Leo spoke of various things.

Finally Mrs. Howland rose and said, "I'm sorry to be such a poor hostess, but I'm not too well, Sir Leo. If you don't mind, I think I shall leave my daughter to entertain you while I lie down for a time."

Leo rose at once, and a look of compassion came into his gaunt features. "I'm sorry to hear it, Mrs. Howland." He hesitated, then shrugged self-consciously. "I have not been too well myself lately, so I can have some sympathy. Odd how when we have health we don't appreciate it, and when we get sick, immediately we see what a blessing it was."

"That's very true, Sir Leo. Well, you will entertain our guest, daughter?"

"Of course, Mother. Try to get some rest. We'll be leaving tomorrow at ten. It'll be a difficult trip."

After Mrs. Howland left, Leo said, "You're going to New York, I understand."

"Yes, to stay for a time with my aunt."

"So I understand. As a matter of fact, that's why I've come to see you." They were still standing and he turned to say, "Could you sit on this sofa? I have something rather strange to say to you, Abigail—if I may call you by your first name."

"Of course." Abigail took her seat beside Leo on the sofa and turned to face him. She was struck again by the unhealthy pallor of his cheeks and wondered about the nature of his illness. She only knew him slightly, so she asked, "How is your wife, Mr. Rochester?"

"Marian? She's very well; she always is."

The very brevity of his reply strengthened Abigail's understanding of what she already had heard—the two had no marriage at all. Leo Rochester was a well-known rake, and everyone who gave ear to the wagging tongues about the city knew he not only visited the brothels in Boston but throughout the Colonies. She could not understand it, for Marian Rochester was a beautiful woman—however, Abigail had long since given up trying to understand such things. "And how is Matthew Bradford?" she asked.

"Ah, it's about Matthew I've come." Leo leaned forward, an intent look in his eyes. "I don't know how much you know, but you must understand that Matthew is more than an acquaintance." He quickly told her how he had discovered that Matthew was the son of his own blood—the son of a servant in his house. He spoke straightforwardly with some regret in his voice, to be sure, but the regret was that he was unable to convince Matthew to take his name and become his son legally. Finally, Rochester put his hands apart in an eloquent gesture of helplessness. "I've done all that I can to convince the boy to see that he can have a wonderful life if he'll do as I ask."

"But he refuses to leave his family, I take it?"

"Exactly!" Leo grasped his hands together, squeezed them, then shook his head. "It's a fine thing—loyalty to one's family—but he's not like the other Bradfords."

"Not like them in what way?"

"Well, he doesn't *look* like them for one thing, but that's not important. The fact is, the Bradfords are skilled tradesmen. They are blacksmiths and know how to run a foundry. Good people, I dare say. I've had my difficult times with Daniel, of course, but that's neither here nor there." He leaned forward and his eyes became more intent as he spoke almost passionately. "I could do so much for Matthew! He has real talent as an artist. If he would come with me to England and to Italy he could have the best teachers. Why, he could have his works hanging in the National Art Gallery in London."

"Portraits by Matthew Rochester—is that what you're thinking?" Abigail suddenly demanded.

"Exactly! I'll never have another son. He's the only hope I have and . . . and I want my name to go on. He'd be Sir Matthew Rochester, Lord of the estates in England, or he could live in Virginia at Fairhope, my plantation there."

Abigail listened as Rochester spoke on, and she was quite puzzled. Finally she asked, "Why are you telling me all this?"

"Because I think you might help me, and I certainly would be grateful for your help—not just emotionally, but in a financial way."

Immediately Abigail's attention grew sharper. "What could I possibly do for you?"

"I think Matthew's half in love with you, Abigail."

"I'm not so sure about that."

"Well . . . I've watched him pretty closely. That time he was painting your portrait, you were all he could talk about. Not just as a subject, but the times you spent together." Leo tapped his chin thoughtfully with a forefinger and nodded slowly. "I think I know men and women pretty well, and I think I recognize infatuation, at least, when I see it. I'm convinced you've caught his attention."

Abigail thought about those times she had spent with Matthew. She had liked him a great deal, but as far as she was concerned he was not the sort of man she would be permanently interested in. There was not enough money in the Bradford family—but with Sir Leo that was different. She knew he was immensely wealthy, and suddenly a door seemed to open and she said, "What would you want me to do?"

"Make him fall in love with you," Leo said at once. "He's already halfway there. You're a woman who knows how to use men."

Abigail stared at him. "What do you mean by that?"

Leo shook his head. "Well, let's not get upset, shall we? I think most of Boston knows you had an affair with Paul Winslow, and perhaps with his cousin Nathan. You're not a Puritan. I don't mean to be insulting by that, for I'm not the one to point the finger at anyone, but it's true enough, isn't it?"

Abigail flushed and said, "Yes, it's true enough."

"Well, I'm glad to see you are able to listen to reason. Now, here's what I want you to do. You're going to New York and so is Matthew. It would be natural enough for you to see him there. Draw him on, Abigail. You shouldn't have any trouble fanning that spark of interest he has for you. Make him fall in love with you; then you could be of some help to me."

"If you think I can make him do what you can't, that's impossible."

"I don't think so. A man in love doesn't think straight. Why, he may even want to marry you."

"And what would you think about having me for a daughter-in-law?"

"I wouldn't mind in the least," Leo said, smiling cheerfully. "As long as I have a son, I think it would be wonderful for him to have a wife. I'd want grandchildren. You look like a good bearer to me. You and Matthew would have a beautiful son. Think of that. You would be Lady Abigail Rochester one day."

Abigail sat there, her fists clenched tightly together, listening as he painted an enticing future. Finally she looked at him directly in the eye. There was no need to think further about this. She thought briefly about what Paul had said about her having a gentle side to her nature very far down, but she knew that it was very deep indeed.

"What about it, Abigail?"

She knew what her answer would be, but she said, "I'll have to think about it." Her mind was already made up, but she was seeking for better terms.

"Of course." Leo rose and said, "It's a big step. I'll pay your expenses to New York, and if you convince him to do what I ask, you'll never have to want for money again. And, of course, if you marry him you'll be getting a good man."

"When will you have to have an answer?"

"You're leaving for New York tomorrow. I could help with your expenses if I knew by then."

Suddenly Abigail said, her voice tight, "I can't put on an act with you. You know I'm going to do it, don't you?"

A sudden streak of regret filled Leo Rochester's eyes. He stepped closer to her and put his hand on her hand gently. "I don't want to force you to do this. I've done enough to be sorry for in my life. I think you might do me some good, and I think you'd be doing Matthew a great favor—and of course, I think you would be helped too. You've had to fight and struggle for money and position. If you had that, perhaps you might have time to find out what's really inside of you."

Instantly Abigail was shocked, since this was almost the same thing that Paul Winslow had said. Trying not to show her feelings, she said, "It's just a business proposition, Mr. Rochester."

Leo Rochester was not a man of sentiment. He looked down at this girl with the beauty that most women would have given most anything for and saw that she had steeled herself. "Very well," he said quietly. He reached into his pocket and brought out an envelope. "I came prepared to offer you this. There'll be more if you need it. Write me when you get to New York and let me know how things are going."

After Rochester had left, Abigail Howland stood in the hall holding the envelope. It was thick with bills, and she opened it and counted the money. Slowly she put it back, then walked down the hall. She thought about Matthew, his innocence, and a thought came to her. *He'll be easy. He is in love with me, or almost so.* Somehow the thought disturbed her, and she tried to shake it off, but it came again and again. She knew there was no other way out, and finally she shook her head and said angrily, "God, forgive me, what else can I do? We've got to live, Mother and I, and after all, it is the best thing for Matthew. He'd be a fool to choose a life of poverty and obscurity when he could have a title and the money and power that goes with it."

Such thinking did not assure her, however, and there was discomfort and almost pain in her eyes as she slowly made her way to her room and sat down to stare out the window. The bird with its joyful song was gone—only empty branches now—and she sat there staring at them for a long time.

PART TWO

—

SUMMER OF
INDEPENDENCE

June—July 1776

7

DAMSEL IN DISTRESS

THE SEA HAD ALWAYS FASCINATED Katherine, but on the morning of June 8, she paid no heed to the beauty that lay before her as she approached the harbor. A flight of screaming gulls wheeled around overhead, descending and opening their mouths wide as they clustered around her, hoping for a morsel of food. Several times she had brought bread crusts and scraps with her, for it had delighted her to watch the aerial acrobats swoop down to snatch fragments from her hand. One small boy had shown her a trick that had fascinated her. He had put a piece of bread on his head, and the gulls had simply scooped it off neatly. Grinning at her with a gap-toothed smile, he had said, "You want to try it, lady?"

Now as Katherine walked slowly toward the piers, she glanced out over the harbor, noting the stately naval vessels anchored there. A magnificent ship of the line had drawn in closely, the cannons run out and gleaming dully in the late afternoon sunlight. The water lapping at the shoreline as she approached was as clear as wine. Twenty feet out it turned into a pale green, and out farther still, into a dark blue. The horizon lay before her, sharp and level as the blade of a knife, and the light blue sky was dotted with high-flying, fluffy clouds that covered the sun from time to time, then let the bright rays pierce the earth as it rolled beneath them. Katherine breathed deeply, inhaling the salt tang of the sea unconsciously, for her thoughts were on her father and her uncle.

For over a week she had come every day to the *St. George*, but each time she had been turned away by the officers. Nevertheless, she had stubbornly made her way to the headquarters to see General Howe, but with the same result. A steady diet of failure to convince him to change Banks' orders had dampened her spirits. She knew now only a dull, glowing anger at the system that would allow helpless men to perish for lack of simple care that was readily available.

"Good morning, miss." A thin fisherman with a black stocking cap on his head and a striped jersey greeted her cheerfully. "Be you going back to the *St. George* again?"

"Yes, please."

The fisherman nodded his head, reached out, and helped the young woman into the bobbing dory. When she was seated, he sat down and grasped the oars. Shoving off with one of them, he aimed the small craft at the hulk anchored a hundred yards offshore. As he rowed with the skill of a lifetime of practice, he studied the young woman surreptitiously. Through half-hooded eyes he took in the simple blue dress, the bonnet that half shaded her eyes, and the white lace at her throat. *A good-looking wench, I'll say that for her*, he thought, taking regular strokes with the oars. *Too bad about her pa and her uncle—but that's the way it is in a war. Don't see that it'd do the British any harm to let her take a little food in to her folks* . . . . Aloud he said, "I hope your pa and your uncle be doing better today. Too bad they had to get caught."

Katherine gave him a slight smile. "Why . . . thank you. I don't suppose I'll be able to see them, but I've got to try." She sat there trying to think of new ways to convince the authorities to allow her to see her father, but nothing came to her. This was not a new thought, for day after day and night after night she had struggled with her hatred for Banks. She had seen him three times since he had closed the door to her visits, and each time she had to struggle to keep the white hot anger that rose within her concealed as much as possible. Even now as the dory skimmed across the sprightly white caps, she thought of his grinning red face, and her fist clenched tightly on the handle of the basket she carried. Almost with a physical effort she forced the thought of the surgeon out of her mind and tried her best to think more positively.

The dory arrived at the side of the ship near the wooden ladder, and, as usual, a lieutenant was waiting at the top to help her in. The fisherman said, "I'll just wait here, miss."

"Very well," Katherine said. She allowed the lieutenant to hand her aboard. His name was Smith, and glancing at his face she saw regret there and knew what he was going to say. He was a tall, thin officer with black hair and dark brown eyes. He was homely enough, but he had always been polite to her each time she had come aboard.

"I'm sorry, Miss Yancy, but you made your trip for nothing again, I'm afraid."

"Couldn't I see the captain?" Katherine pleaded.

"Miss, I'll have to tell you. The captain asked me not to bring you to him. There's really nothing he can do, Miss Yancy," Smith said regretfully. "In the service the surgeon has total control over the sick prisoners, and Major Banks has given strict orders that your father and his brother are not to be allowed any visitors. I'm sorry, but that's the way it is."

A huge bird flew over suddenly, and Katherine glanced up startled. "What's that bird?" she inquired.

Looking up, Smith took it in with a casual eye. "That? Why, that's an albatross, miss."

"Albatross? I never saw one of those."

"Supposed to be bad luck for sailors sometimes," Smith remarked. "Sailors are a superstitious lot, you know." He moved his feet uncertainly and said, "I could offer you a cup of tea, Miss Yancy, but there's no hope of seeing your father."

"Will you at least see that he gets this food?"

Katherine looked up and there was such anxiety in her gray-green eyes that Smith could not find it in his heart to say no. Banks had left strict orders that no food was to be given to the prisoners, but Smith was an independent sort for a lowly lieutenant. Leaning forward he took the basket and whispered, "I'm not supposed to do it, Miss Yancy—but I'll do the best I can. It'll be the worst for me if I get caught, but I'm sorry for your trouble."

Katherine's eyes glistened with sudden tears at the man's unexpected kindness. "Thank you, Lieutenant Smith," she whispered and dashed the tears away quickly. She gave him a tremulous smile and said, "May the Lord bless you for your kindness to my poor father and my uncle."

"Well . . . it's little enough to do," Smith mumbled. He was stricken with the girl's beauty, but having a wife and two children at home, he quickly put any romantic thoughts out of his mind. Glancing around he saw that several of the deckhands were watching and wondered how he would explain the basket of food to them.

Katherine said quickly, "I'll be going back then, but I'll be here tomorrow to try again."

Smith helped her down the ladder and watched as the oarsman pulled the dory away and made for the land. Turning around with the basket in his hand he caught one husky sailor staring at him with a broad grin on his face. With a voice that roared he said, "You don't have enough to do, Jenkins? I'll see if I can find a few more extra jobs for you." He watched with some regret as Jenkins hurried away, thinking, *He's a good man, and I shouldn't be ragging him like that.* He carried the basket at once to his quarters and concealed it, his mind humming with schemes on how he might get the food belowdecks to the Yancys.

As the dory reached shore, Katherine stepped out and handed the fisherman a few coins and thanked him. He touched his forelock quickly and said, "I suppose I'll be seeing you tomorrow, miss?"

"Probably so," Katherine nodded. She turned and made her way from the harbor, walking quickly through the town. The thought that her father and her uncle might get some of the food cheered her, and she thought, *Well, there are some good men among the British, at least. They're not all like Major Banks.*

When she reached headquarters she marched into the commander's office. The lieutenant who greeted her said at once, "Now, Miss Yancy, do we have to go through this again?"

"I would like to see General Howe."

Lieutenant Redman shook his head. "I've explained that eight days in a row, I think. The general cannot see you, miss. He's a very busy man, and even if he did see you he would give you the same answer. He cannot countermand the standing orders of the surgeon."

Katherine stood there helplessly, knowing that Lieutenant Redman was right. She turned and walked out of the room frustrated and angry as usual.

After she left, Redman heard the voice of the general calling him, and he entered the office immediately. Before the general could speak he said, "That young woman was here again, General—Miss Yancy."

Howe looked up and ran his hand through his thick brown hair. He was not wearing his wig, and he looked much younger. "She doesn't give up easily, does she, Redman?"

"No, sir." Redman hesitated then said, "I really can't see what harm it would do to let her see her father."

"I know. I feel the same, but we have a chain of command. Once I start making exceptions, there'd be no order left in the ranks." But Howe's tone was regretful, and for one moment he was tempted to break his rule. He was, however, basically a military man tied into a rigid system, and he would not break that system except with great provocation. The picture of the young woman's face swam before his eyes, but he said with resolve, "I just can't. We must keep order, Lieutenant."

Outside the headquarters building Katherine walked slowly. There was nothing now to do except go back to her room at the inn or spend the rest of the day walking aimlessly through the town. She had no friends, and loneliness bore upon her constantly. Halifax was no more than a small fishing village, but now had been stuffed to capacity by the influx of sailors, soldiers, and civilians who had fled from Boston.

For half an hour she walked along the main street, looking without interest into the shop windows. She was accosted more than once by soldiers attracted by her fresh beauty, but she ignored them as if they were invisible. Finally she straightened her shoulders, and a steely light came into her eyes. Her lips grew tight and she said, "I won't be treated this way!"

With resolution, she turned and headed back toward the headquarters. She found the building used for a hospital easily enough by simply asking a passing private, then marched up the steps to the plain, square brick building that had once been a barn of some kind. When she stepped inside, she found herself in a gloomy room whose darkness was broken only by some light coming from a few narrow dirty windows high up. The floor was made of stone, however, and echoed hollowly as she walked across it toward a desk where a youthful corporal sat watching her.

"Yes, miss, can I help you?"

"I need to see Major Banks."

"Why, yes, ma'am. If you'll come this way. His office is right over here."

Katherine followed the corporal to a room that had evidently been added. It was made of rough lumber, and when the corporal knocked on the door she heard Banks call, "What is it?"

"A visitor, sir. A young lady."

Katherine stood there, and when the door opened she saw satisfaction fill the pale blue eyes of Banks. "Ah, Miss Yancy. Please step inside my office. That'll be all, Corporal."

Apprehension filled Katherine at once, but without a word she stepped into the office. It contained a desk, a cot, a rough bookcase containing several worn volumes, and a washstand. Somehow the major had obtained a bright green rug that added a touch of color, and a window had been made—apparently as an afterthought—to let in the red beams of afternoon sunlight.

"Major, I've come to plead with you again," Katherine said.

"Well, now, sit down. Here, take this chair, and I'll sit on the bed. But first we'll have a little refreshment."

"Oh no, I couldn't really!"

"Nonsense!" Banks said jovially. "I just had some flip made. I think you'll like it." He took a glass decanter from the table, found two stoneware cups, and poured a liberal amount into each. "There," he said, handing her one of them. "Now, you'll find that the best flip this side of England!"

"Really, I couldn't!" Katherine said and saw his eyes grow tight with anger. "I'm not used to such things." She set the glass down and said, "Major, I've come to plead with you about my father. I haven't seen him in over a week. Please let me see him."

Banks drank the contents of his cup, belched slightly, and gasped as the fiery liquor bit at his throat. He blinked his eyes and came up off the bed. Moving over, he picked up her cup and said, "Well, if you're not going to drink this we can't have it go to waste. Aye?" He drank it down, then said, "All the sweeter for the touch of your fingers on it, Miss Yancy. Or may I call you Katherine?"

Katherine was aware that Banks was already drunk. He had the veins of a drinker in his face, and his movements were uncertain. He pronounced his words carefully, as drunks do, thinking that they are disguising their condition. Knowing that he might deny her request again, she determined to keep trying. "If you won't let me see him, would you at least allow my father and my uncle to receive the things I've brought?"

"Well, we will have to talk about that, won't we?" Banks was standing beside her, and he put the glass down, then turned to face her fully. His uniform was dirty and stained with food, and there was a carelessness about him not seen in most British officers. "Well now, my dear." Suddenly Banks reached down, took her hand, and pulled her to her feet. He held her hand as she struggled to free herself. Then without warning he threw his arms around her and kissed her.

Katherine twisted her head furiously. His lips, however, pressed against her own, and she was thoroughly disgusted. As he started to run his hands over her body she shoved him away with a desperate burst of strength. Banks staggered backward, but his drunken eyes were filled with lust, and he came back at her again. At once she stepped to the door and opened it. Banks stopped abruptly, for she said calmly, "I'll scream if you come any closer, Major Banks!" He stopped where he was and looked at her, befuddled. "I'll come back tomorrow when you're feeling better. I must warn you I intend to take this as far as to General Howe."

"That won't do you any good. You've already tried it," Banks muttered. "Now, why don't you be reasonable, my dear. You want something and I want something. We can make a bargain, you and me."

Disgust filled Katherine, and she turned at once without a word and left the hospital.

Banks stared after her, noting that the corporal was watching as well. "Keep your mind on your business, Corporal!" he snarled and moved back inside, slamming the door. He poured himself another drink, gulped it down, then nodded as he muttered, "She'll come around. Yes, she will, or I'll see that her father and uncle rot!"

T   T   T

Clive Gordon had no official standing in the British army, but since he had performed in a semiofficial way at Fort Ticonderoga under his father's orders, he had been accepted as a welcome civilian volunteer in the regiment. He entered the officers' mess and noted that the general was not there. Taking his seat beside Lieutenant James Steerbraugh, he asked, "Where's General Howe today?"

"High strategy, Clive, my boy." Steerbraugh nodded wisely and winked at him. "I expect he's having a meeting with Mrs. Loring to plan how to take New York away from the rebels."

Clive glanced around and saw grins on the faces of several of the other young officers. It was amazing to him how a man of General Howe's stature could lower himself to an affair with the wife of a subordinate. Everyone knew about Mrs. Loring. The patriots even wrote crude songs about them.

The two young men sat there speaking about the strategy that had brought them this far, and Steerbraugh said finally, "I just don't see how we've been beaten. We've got a well-trained army, and Washington's got nothing but a rabble in arms, mostly untrained militia. How did they beat us out of Boston? Why didn't General Gates lead us out?"

"You may have forgotten how far it is to England, James," Clive said. "It takes a great deal of money to get one British soldier here to the Colonies. If we lose him, another one has to be sent. That's double the money. Furthermore, he's got to be fed, clothed, and given ammunition. All that is straining the empire pretty thin to keep this stupid revolution fought back. If Gates had marched us out and we had lost our army, what would have happened then? Why, England would have lost her share in the New World."

Steerbraugh argued vehemently that the ragged troops of Washington should not beat the trained soldiers of England.

"They did pretty well at Breed's Hill and on the way back from Concord, in Lexington."

"Nothing to the purpose," Steerbraugh argued, waving his hand with disdain. "The cowards shot at our men from behind fences at Concord and Lexington. And we had to fight our way up that hill to get them when they were entrenched behind embattlements at Breed's Hill."

"Then we never should have gone after them," Clive said. That was his firm judgment, as it was many of the officers. He knew that General Gates, who had led the attack had been badly shaken at the terrible losses. "I think it will be a long time before any British officer leads troops against the Americans behind embattled positions."

The two were interrupted by two officers who came in and took their places. Steerbraugh said, "I see that the surgeon is drunk again."

"That's pretty well a chronic condition, isn't it, James?"

The surgeon sat down, and it was obvious to every officer at the table that he had been tipping the bottle again heavily. He was always an obnoxious sort of man, and when he was in his cups his temperament got even worse. Soon he began talking about a young lady who he was trying to force his attentions on.

"Who's he talking about, James?" Clive asked.

"A young woman named Katherine Yancy. She's come all the way from Boston to help her father and her uncle, I believe. They're prisoners on the *St. George*." He glanced with disgust at the surgeon and said scathingly, "Banks can't keep his eyes off the young woman, and word has it that he won't let her see her people until she gives him what he wants."

"That's pretty foul!" Clive said sharply. "Why does the general put up with the man's debauchery?"

"You know Howe—he's a stickler for organization. He won't go over his surgeon's head." Clive sat there and toyed with his food, listening to the surgeon as he boasted about his coming conquest. The man's ribald manner ignited an anger in Clive, and he left so as to avoid listening to the rest of the surgeon's crass boastings.

Leaving the headquarters, Clive walked along the streets that were now growing dark, making his way to the small house that his father, Colonel Leslie Gordon, had managed to rent for his family while they waited for the British troops to move into New York as was previously planned. When he stepped inside he was greeted by his mother, Lyna Lee, who came to him at once and kissed him.

"Why, you should've come back earlier, Clive. We waited supper for you." Lyna Lee Gordon, at forty-four, was a beautiful woman. She had hair the color of dark honey and large gray-green eyes set in her oval face. She had clean, wide-edged lips, a firm chin, and a fair, smooth skin. She was wearing a pale plum-colored dress that set off her figure admirably and laughed as she said, "You didn't miss much at dinner, though. You probably had better food at the officers' mess."

"I doubt that, Mother," Clive smiled. He was, at six three, much taller than she was and looked down at her with fondness.

She studied him as they moved into the kitchen where the family was sitting at a round wooden table. He was lean with long arms and legs, and he had reddish hair and cornflower blue eyes in his tapered face. Lyna noted as she sat down that there was still a sadness or a regret that his open features revealed. *He's still sad over Jeanne Corbeau*, Lyna thought and felt a touch of regret that her son had lost what he considered the love of his life to her nephew Dake Bradford.

"Sit down and tell us how we're going to win this war, Clive," said David Gordon, the sixteen-year-old son of Leslie and Lyna. He had dark brown hair that was crisply curled, and brown eyes, alert and set in a square face. He was not tall, not over five ten, and was very lean and quick in all that he did. Now he threw questions at Clive constantly.

"Leave your brother alone!" Colonel Gordon said. He smiled at his younger son, shook his head, then added, "You talk like a magpie." At fifty, Leslie Gordon looked no more than thirty-five. He was tall, well-formed, with reddish hair and blue eyes. He glanced over now at Clive and winked. "This one's been pestering me to let him join the army."

"Let him do it, Father," Clive said. "I'd like to have him under my thumb for a while."

"Are you going to join the army, too, Clive?" Grace asked. The only daughter of the family, at the age of eighteen, had the same dark honey blond hair and attractive eyes as her mother. She spoke of Clive's plan—whether to make the army his career, even though he had studied to become a doctor. "I wish you wouldn't," she said. "You can be a fancy society doctor in London."

"Then I could have lots of money to buy you pretty dresses, Grace," Clive grinned. He sat down, and the family talked for some time about affairs.

Finally, David demanded, "When is General Howe going to take New York?"

"It might not be quite that easy, son," Leslie Gordon said mildly.

"Why, everybody knows we're going to have enough soldiers to wipe the rebels off the face of the earth," David said impulsively. His eyes shone with excitement as he said, "I wish I could be in the army. Why don't you let me sign up, Father?"

Leslie Gordon ignored his question as Clive shook his head, saying, "I'm just not sure yet about what to do." He sat there for a while, enjoying the pleasure of being with his family, then his thoughts ran back to the surgeon and he frowned unconsciously.

"What's the matter, Clive?" Lyna Lee had caught the expression on Clive's face, and being sensitive to his moods she asked, "Is something wrong?"

He glanced over toward Grace and David, who were arguing loudly over some insignificant matter, and lowered his voice as he spoke to his parents. "Something happened that angered me—a matter about surgeon Banks." He saw his father frown and said, "He's not much of an officer, is he?"

"Well, surgeons are a little bit different. They don't have to keep the rules quite as rigidly as the rest of us—but he's really not much of a surgeon."

"Apparently not." Clive had worked with the army some, although he had little contact with Banks himself. Banks was a newcomer to the regiment, having arrived just before the troops were evacuated from Boston. Since they had been at Halifax, Clive had offered to help with the sick men several times, but Banks, jealous of his position, had simply shuffled him off.

"What's he done, Clive?" Lyna asked.

"There's a young woman come from Boston. Her father and her uncle are prisoners on the *St. George*," Clive replied. He drummed his fingers on the table, studying them for a moment, then looked up, a heated anger in his eyes. "She's an attractive young woman from what I hear, and Banks won't let her see her people—unless she—"

Seeing her son's embarrassment Lyna said bluntly, "Unless she gives in to his desires?"

"That's exactly it! A rotten thing—but then he's a rotten man, I think," Clive said. He sat there for some time and the three spoke of the situation. Then Clive rose and said, "I'm going to study for a while. Good night." He leaned over, kissed his mother, nodded with a smile to his father, then left the room.

As soon as he was gone, Lyna helped the other children clean up the kitchen, then she and Leslie retired to their small bedroom. She undressed for bed, put on a cotton nightgown, got into the featherbed, and waited as he hung up his uniform carefully, then got into bed beside her. They lay there for a while speaking quietly, then he picked up her hand and stroked it, kissed it fondly, and she moved closer to him. "I'm worried about Clive," she whispered. The walls were thin in the house, and she could still hear David and Grace talking about something." I don't think he's ever gotten over his love for Jeanne Corbeau."

"He ought to go back to England and get away from here. Maybe he could forget her." Leslie turned to her then and pulled her close. "You ought to go back with him. You and David and Grace."

Lyna put her arms around him, pulled his head closer, and kissed him. "No, I won't leave you," she said. "If I do, one of these attractive American girls will grab you. Leave a good-looking thing like you loose over here in the wilds of America? Not likely!"

Leslie laughed quietly, ran his hand down the smoothness of her back, savored the touch of his lovely wife, then he said, "You really ought to do it. We'll win New York well enough."

"Will we?" she asked anxiously.

"Yes, England's sending the biggest expeditionary force in history over to win this revolution. I'm afraid Daniel and his friends are a lost cause." He held her for a moment tightly, then said, "I'm sorry about that. I think a lot of Daniel."

Lyna was grieved, but there was nothing she could do about that. She whispered, "God will take care of them." And then she drew his head forward and kissed him, moving against him.

8

"Love Won't Be Put Into a Little Box?"

AFTER A RESTLESS NIGHT, Clive Gordon rose and found himself still thinking of the young woman that Major Banks had boasted of. Ordinarily he might have ignored such a thing, disgusted as he was, but in truth he still suffering over the disappointing loss of Jeanne Corbeau. At the age of twenty-three Clive Gordon had never suffered a casualty to his emotional life, and as he set out his toilette to shave, he let his mind run over those days not very long in the past. Working up a rich lather he applied it to his cheeks. Then he picked up a razor and, yanking a hair out of his head, tested the sharpness of the blade. Grunting with satisfaction, he carefully drew the blade down his cheek, wiped the lather on a towel, then gave his left cheek the same treatment. As he worked carefully around his throat, he muttered, "He's a bully boy, Banks is. A disgrace to the uniform he wears!" He continued thinking moodily of the situation, and by the time he had finished shaving and brushing his rather long reddish hair back with a pair of military brushes, Clive found himself growing more and more dissatisfied with the girl's plight.

"What was her name?—Katherine something, I think. I'll have a word with Banks." The decision made him feel better, and he donned his suit carefully. Since he had not formally joined the army he had no uniform. Instead, he put on a seal gray pair of tight-fitting trousers, a frilly white linen shirt, and topped it off with a simple waistcoat. Then after donning his black leather shoes, he shrugged into a fawn-colored frock coat. Plucking his tricorn hat off of a peg, he settled it firmly on his head and studied himself in the mirror. "All right," he spoke aloud to his reflection, "let's go see what kind of stuff Major Saul Banks is made of!"

Clive left the attic room that he occupied at his parents' rented house, went downstairs, and said to Grace, who was cooking breakfast, "I'll get something at the officers' mess, Grace."

He left the house and with long strides made his way across town. It was a fine morning, with the red sky in the east still glowing freshly. A slight breeze stirred against his face, and he inhaled deeply, enjoying the smell of the sea. It was a smell that he delighted in, and he thought, *I should have been a sailor—but that's a hard life. I'm not sure I'd want to do it for a lifetime.*

He passed by many uniformed soldiers, some of them in his father's regiment. Reaching headquarters, he went at once into the officers' mess, where he sat again with Steerbraugh, and the two enjoyed a hearty meal of eggs, bacon, and fresh bread.

"What are you up to, Clive?" Steerbraugh asked idly. "I wish I had some of your leisure time. King George's lieutenants don't have much of that."

"I'm going to have a word with Banks about that young woman."

Steerbraugh looked at him astonished. "Well ... by George!" he stammered. "Are you, now?"

"I think it's a disgrace the way the man's treating her."

Steerbraugh grinned broadly, his white teeth gleaming. "Good for you, Clive! You can get by with it. If I did it, I'd probably get court-martialed for assaulting a superior officer. I'll wish you the best with the scoundrel."

While the two ate Clive kept looking for the surgeon, but Banks did not appear. "Well," he said finally, "I can see him later. I'm going to meet the young woman. What's her name?"

"Katherine Yancy," Steerbraugh answered promptly. His eyes brightened and he said, "She's a pippin, Clive. I think I was the first one to greet her. By George, you'll be a knight in shining armor!"

"I don't know about that, but I'm going to do whatever I can to help her. I've asked around, and it seems Banks doesn't want any interference with his patients—but they're not patients. They're just poor devils trapped in that stinking hulk—most of them sick, and some of them are dying. I don't see why we have to treat prisoners like that!"

"They're probably treating our men just as badly," Steerbraugh shrugged philosophically. He had the typical soldier's callousness toward prisoners taken in a war and never stopped to think how it might be if he himself were suffering as a prisoner. "If you'd care to see the young lady, she's staying at the Dolphin Inn, not far from the harbor.

Small town like this, anyone can point you to it."

"Thanks, James."

As Clive Gordon rose and prepared to leave, Steerbraugh grinned again broadly. "Give the young lady my best," he said. "I'd step in myself, but I'd lose my commission if I punched the monster in the nose as I'd like to."

Clive nodded his assent and left the mess hall. He made his way down the street, and after a few inquiries found the Dolphin Inn without difficulty. It was a small inn with an overhanging second story, squeezed in between two larger buildings. When he entered, the barkeep, noting his well-cut suit, came at once from behind the bar.

"Yes, sir! May I be of assistance?"

"I'm looking for a young woman named Katherine Yancy. Is she staying here?"

"Why, yes, sir, she is. I'm not sure if she's up yet. First room at the top of the stairs if you'd care to go knock."

"Thank you."

Clive climbed the narrow stairs, and when he got to the second floor he peered down the murky hallway, illuminated only by small diamond-shaped windows at each end. He went to the first door, where Katherine had moved to from the attic, and knocked uncertainly. For a brief moment he thought no one was there, and had just raised his fist to knock again when the door suddenly opened. He stood there rather foolishly, fist in the air, staring at the young woman.

"Yes, what is it?" she asked rather abruptly.

"Miss Yancy?"

Katherine stared up at the tall young man standing before her, which she did not have to do with most men. She noticed that he seemed to be well-dressed and rather personable. Still she was wary, being a stranger with no family in town. "I'm Katherine Yancy," she answered curtly. "What do you want with me?"

"My name is Clive Gordon, Miss Yancy. I'm a physician. I'd like to speak with you if I could."

"You can't come in my room. If you'll go downstairs I'll meet you. What is it you want?"

"Well, I've heard your story from a friend of mine, Lieutenant Steerbraugh. I believe you have met him."

"Oh yes! He was very kind to me when I first arrived." Katherine peered more closely at the young man and said, "I haven't sent for a doctor. I'm not sick."

"No, but I understand your father is. I have access to the prison ship, the *St. George*. I believe I could arrange for you to visit your father again.

I understand you've had some difficulty along those lines."

Katherine's eyes lighted up, and her lips parted as she exclaimed, "You can? How wonderful—just let me get my cloak! And I have some food I'd like to take." She turned back into the room and came out almost at once, fastening a bonnet over her curls, and walked with him to the stairs. He stepped aside and let her go down first, then followed.

As they passed down the stairway and out of the inn, Clive noticed the innkeeper watching them closely. He saw Katherine look up and Clive thought, *She must feel uncomfortable. Still, this is too good an opportunity to miss.*

"Could you really get me in to see my father?" Katherine asked as they walked along.

"My father is Colonel Leslie Gordon. His regiment was stationed in Boston, but he's here now with the rest of His Majesty's forces. I'm not officially in the army, but I have been of some help to the doctors at Boston."

"Are you acquainted with Major Banks?"

There was a curtness in the girl's voice. She lifted her head high and turned to look at him. She had unusual eyes, he thought. At first he thought they were gray, but then he saw they had a greenish tinge to them. They were very large eyes with dark, heavy eyelashes that set them off well. She had a beautifully textured complexion, smooth as ivory, but a few freckles almost invisibly splattered across her nose. He thought of how Steerbraugh had described her as a pippin and found himself agreeing with the man's estimate. "Yes, I'm acquainted with him. I understand he's forbidden you to see your father."

"Yes, he has! I've been to General Howe several times, but he insists he can do nothing."

"Well, I hope I can be of some help—although I can't promise anything," Clive said. He had very long legs and slowed his pace to allow her to keep up. "You came all the way from Boston to see your father?"

"Yes, and my uncle. They were both taken prisoner earlier in the war—at Breed's Hill. I'm very concerned about them—especially my uncle. I haven't seen him, but my father says he's very ill."

"The hulks are a terrible place! I'm opposed to using them as prisons, but, of course, I have no say in such things."

His remark brought an approving look from Katherine. "That's very kind of you, Mr. Gordon." They walked several paces and she said, "I've been so discouraged lately. I've brought food and medicine to my father, but since the major forbids me to see him, I'm not ever sure if he gets them or not."

"Suppose we stop off at one of the shops and pick up some fresh fruit? I'm sure we could find something, and I'll stop by the apothecaries and replenish my supply. I didn't bring my bag, but I know pretty well what men in that condition might need."

"Oh, that would be so kind!" Katherine said, her cheeks glowing with pleasure. The two of them visited the two shops, and when they came out Katherine said, "These will help Father and Uncle Noah, I'm sure!"

"Well, come along and we'll see what we can do."

When they reached the docks, the same fisherman was waiting in his dory. He gave Clive a sharp look, then spoke to the young woman cheerfully. "Well . . . I see you have company this morning, miss. Same price for two." He watched as the tall young man helped the girl down, then sat beside her in the stern. Facing them, he shoved off and rowed expertly over the waves. He was a talkative fellow and did his best to discover the relationship between the two. The young woman merely answered noncommittally, so when he reached the *St. George* and let them up the side of the ship's ladder, he knew little more than he did before. "Shall I wait, miss?"

Clive tossed a coin down to the fellow and said, "Yes, wait. We shouldn't be too long. I'll make it worth your while."

"Thankee, sir!"

The lieutenant who had greeted Katherine each morning stepped forward. "Miss Yancy," he said, "I'm sorry but—"

"My name is Clive Gordon," Clive said crisply. "My father is Colonel Leslie Gordon, Colonel of the Seventeenth Regiment. I'm here in his name to give this young woman's father and uncle a visit."

Lieutenant Smith looked at him confused. "Well, sir. I'm . . . I'm afraid I can't permit that."

"You're going to violate Colonel Gordon's orders? I don't think that would be too wise, Lieutenant."

Smith flushed, then said hastily, "Well, I'll have to see the captain."

"We'll wait," Clive said firmly, "but not long! Hurry up, lieutenant!"

As Lieutenant Smith scurried off, Katherine giggled. "I'm so glad you did that. He's been nice enough, but I'm tired of his constant refusals. Do you think the captain will listen?"

"I have no idea. If he doesn't, we'll have to try something else."

Gordon's assurance pleased the young woman and she said, "I'm so thankful that you took the time to come. Why did you do it?"

"Well—" Clive Gordon was rather embarrassed—"I heard about your difficulties, and it bothered me. I'm not sure I can help, but I thought I'd have a try."

"That was very nice of you!" Katherine said. "At least some of you British are gentlemen."

Clive suddenly laughed aloud. "I thank you for your compliment and hope to be deserving of it. Tell me about yourself while we're waiting."

"Oh, there's little enough to tell. I have a mother back in Boston who's not too well. It's been rather hard with father being in prison like this."

She went on to tell how her father and uncle had been captured, and how she had been so concerned that she had made the trip with no assurance of success. As she spoke, Gordon admired her smooth features, her well-shaped lips, and the erect manner in which she carried herself. She had a trim figure, a very tiny waist, he noticed, and her hair caught glints from the sun as they stood on the deck of the *St. George*.

Lieutenant Smith came hurrying back, a smile on his face. "The captain says the navy can't be getting into the differences between officers. Since your father's a colonel, and the surgeon is only a major, he says to allow you to see anyone you want to, Mr. Gordon. If you'll come this way you can wait in here."

He led them to the usual room where Katherine had waited before and then left at once. The two stood there speaking quietly, and five minutes later the door opened and Katherine moved forward quickly. "Father!" she said. "It's so good to see you again."

Amos Yancy was blinking in the bright sunlight that streamed in through the single small window. The hold of the ship was dark and murky, and he held her hands for a minute until his eyes adjusted. His voice was husky as he said, "It's good to see you, daughter!"

He coughed, and the rasping sound of it caught Clive's attention. *That's not good*, he thought. *It could go into pneumonia.*

"Father, this is Mr. Gordon. He's been kind enough to help me to see you. He's a doctor, too. I want him to examine you and then Uncle Noah."

"Noah's not able to get up the stairs, I'm afraid." Amos Yancy coughed again, and he put his hand out to the younger man. "I thank you for your kindness to my daughter, sir."

"I'm only sorry to find you in such poor condition, Mr. Yancy. Sit down here, please, and let me listen to your chest. You know how we doctors are."

As Clive began to examine Yancy, Katherine asked, "Have you been getting the food that I've been sending?"

"The lieutenant brought something just yesterday. That's the first we've gotten. I suppose you've left more, but none of it ever got to us."

"That was Banks' doing!" Katherine said, then bit her lip. She did not want to complain during the time she had with her father. She stood to one side watching how the young man carefully examined the prisoner.

Finally after thumping and listening and asking several questions Clive said, "You shouldn't be in this damp place!"

"I suppose not, but it looks like I will be for a time."

Clive thought carefully and then said, "There is a smaller prison in town. At least it's dry, and there's some sunlight. I don't know if I can do it, but I'll see if I can get you and your brother transferred."

The father and daughter stared at the tall young man, and Katherine whispered, "Oh, that would be wonderful! Could you really do it?"

"I have no idea," Clive said honestly, "but I'll do my best. Now, suppose you visit with your daughter while I go below and see how your brother is doing. His name is Noah, you say?"

"Yes, the guard will take you down."

As soon as the tall young man left the room, Katherine said, "Isn't it wonderful, Father! He just appeared at the door this morning and said he wanted to help. I'd given up on finding any Englishmen with any manners or courtesy—but I was wrong."

"Yes you were, lass," Amos said. He managed a smile and coughed again. "It would be good to get to a dry place. I don't mean to be complaining, but it's Noah I'm worried about."

"Maybe Mr. Gordon can do it," Katherine said.

The two sat there talking. She gave him some of the food that she had bought and watched him eat, but he had little appetite. He had a fever too, she could tell, and when Gordon came back she saw at once there was a serious look on his face.

"I'm afraid your brother is in poor condition."

"Yes, he's not the only one," Amos Yancy said.

"Could you do anything for him?" Katherine asked.

"I think if we move him to a dry place he'll be much better off. Let me see what I can do. The only influence I have is through my father, and he would have to convince General Howe to make an exception, but General Howe's very fond of my father. In any case," Clive said, "I'll do what I can."

Suddenly the door swung open with a bang. The three turned at once to face Major Saul Banks. Banks had come on one of his periodical visits, and when Lieutenant Smith had informed him of the colonel's son who had insisted on Miss Yancy seeing her father, Banks had exploded with rage. His face now was glowing and his smallish eyes burned as he half shouted at Katherine, "What are you doing here? I gave strict orders that no one was to see my patients!"

Clive stepped forward at once. He towered over the short officer, which made Banks even more angry. "I'm responsible, Major Banks! I met Miss Yancy, and she told me of her father's illness—"

"I don't care what she told you! You have no authority on this ship! Now, get off! Don't let me see you back here again, Gordon!"

"I'm afraid I can't take that, sir!"

"This is a military ship. As a civilian, you have no authority here!"

"I hate to use my father's name, but I believe Colonel Leslie Gordon has some authority," Clive said coolly. He had no idea whether his father would back him up, but he rather suspected he would. In any case, it was the only defense he had. Now he said, "And furthermore, I'm not sure but what I should bring this matter to General Howe's attention!"

"Say what you please. The general will back me up," Banks said. "Now, get off this ship!"

Clive suddenly knew a moment of fury. He was ordinarily an even-tempered young man, but the injustice of it all suddenly infuriated him. "You, sir, are not worthy of the uniform you wear! You're no gentleman, and you should be ashamed of the treatment you've given a helpless woman! And, furthermore, I warn you, I'll do everything within my power to help Miss Yancy see her father and uncle off this hulk!"

Banks began to curse and rave, and in the same breath called Clive a vile name.

Angrily Clive said, "That's a term no gentleman would endure. I'll have my friend call on you, Major Banks."

Instantly Banks' mouth dropped open, for he had not expected Gordon to challenge him to a duel. He knew instantly that Clive Gordon would do exactly what he said, and he rather suspected the tall young man was a better shot and had a steadier hand than he did. He began to bluster, saying, "I would not dirty my hands on you, Gordon!"

Clive pressed his point. "If I hear one more word from you about this matter, I'll slap your face in the officers' mess! You'll have to accept my challenge then, and I promise you I'll shoot you right in the heart the next morning at dawn! It would give me great pleasure to do so, Banks!"

Banks stuttered and tried to find a way out, but the hard light in the young man's eyes convinced him he was in over his head. He gasped a few unintelligible words, then turned and stalked out.

As the door slammed, Katherine suddenly reached out and took Clive's arm. "Good for you! I wish you would shoot him in the heart! He deserves it!"

"Now, Katherine," Amos Yancy protested. "That's no way for a young girl to talk!"

"I know it. I'm sorry, Father—but he's been so mean, and he's done everything he could to keep you from getting well! You don't know what he's done!"

"I think this may make things much easier," Clive said quickly. "Let's go ashore, Miss Yancy. I'll go see my father at once. I hardly think the major is going to push this thing. He's a coward as well as a brute to women."

Katherine was so excited she could hardly speak. She kissed her father, saying, "It's going to be all right, Father. I know it is. Mr. Gordon's going to see to it."

The two left the ship, and when they were set ashore Clive said, "I'll take you back to your inn, Miss Yancy." The two walked briskly along, Katherine speaking brightly, her face suffused with excitement. When he left her at the inn he took his hat off, and she looked up at him with a grateful expression on her features.

"I . . . I can't tell you what this means to me, Mr. Gordon."

"I'm glad I could be of some help. May I come back as soon as I make the arrangements? I'm sure you'll want to hear."

"Please do," she said softly, and when he bowed and walked away, she stood watching his tall figure as he moved down the street. She had given up hope, and now Clive Gordon had brought it back into her life. She turned slowly and moved toward her room, thinking, *It's going to be all right! Thank you, God, for sending someone to help. . . !*

☩   ☩   ☩

"Why, you look beautiful, Katherine!"

Grace Gordon had been helping her guest into a dress that had once belonged to her, but had been carefully tailored to fit Katherine.

Katherine looked in the mirror and smiled, saying, "It is beautiful—the dress, I mean, not me!" She was very pleased with the way the dress had turned out. For the past week she had spent considerable time with the Gordon family and had learned to admire them greatly. Grace, at the age of eighteen, was only two years younger, and she and the young woman had quickly become fast friends. Katherine admired the dress, which was a close-fitting Basque jacket with a striped blue-and-yellow pattern. The sleeves were frilled just below the shoulders, and the full skirt was a patterned satin, a peach color that gracefully reached the floor. "I shouldn't let you do this, Grace!" Katherine protested, all the while admiring herself.

"Nonsense! It's been fun, and you needed a new dress to wear to our celebration tonight!"

Looking in the mirror, Katherine liked the cut of the dress. She reached up and touched her hair. "I like the way you've done my hair," she said. Turning to the young girl she reached out her hands, and when Grace took them she said warmly, "You've been so kind to me—as kind as anyone could ever be. Things look so different now than they did a week ago."

Katherine found it hard to believe that only one week ago Clive Gordon had appeared at her door. Then, like a whirlwind, he had brought so many wonderful changes to her life. She remembered suddenly how he had made all the arrangements to have her father and uncle transferred to the prison, and how he had made it possible for her to visit them every day. He had also brought her to meet his family, and they had accepted her without question. Now she said, "If the English were as nice to Americans as you and your family have been to me, I don't think there would have been any revolution."

Grace smiled quickly. "I hope we get all of our misunderstandings ironed out soon. It's a shame for our men to have to go to war when it could be settled if they'd let the women take care of it!" She laughed at her own remark and said, "Now, tell me some more about that young Quaker who's been courting you."

"Oh, that's nothing! He just wants someone to keep house for him, I think. I couldn't be a Quaker anyway."

"Why not?" Grace asked curiously.

"They're too quiet and silent—and I like colorful dresses—like this one," Katherine said, smoothing her skirt. "Nothing will come of him."

The two girls talked for a while, and just before they left to go to dinner Katherine said, "I wonder why Clive hasn't married."

The innocent question, or so it seemed, brought a smile to Grace's lips. "Well, he almost did. Just recently in fact," she said. "He fell in love with a young French girl named Jeanne Corbeau."

"Jeanne Corbeau? Didn't she just recently marry Dake Bradford?"

"Yes. Dake is my cousin. He and his family are from Boston—do you know them? His father's name is Daniel Bradford."

"Why, yes, I know of them, of course. I attended Dake and Jeanne's wedding. They're a fine family. Dake must have been quite aggressive to beat out a handsome fellow like your brother."

"Well, Jeanne was raised all her life in the woods, and Dake is a woodsman to the bone. I don't think Jeanne and Clive would ever have been happy together. He'll be a physician, I suppose, in London someday."

"You don't think he'll join the army?"

"Sometimes he talks about it," Grace shrugged, "but I just don't know. I don't think he knows himself." She hesitated, then shook her head. "He's been very downhearted lately. Can you tell that?"

"Well, the few times I've been with him he seemed cheerful enough, but I suppose he wouldn't go around complaining."

"No, he's not much of a one to wear his heart on his sleeve, but it hurt him dreadfully, I'm afraid. He's never been interested in a young woman before, not seriously."

Katherine said only, "I'm sure he'll find happiness with someone."

"I'm sure he will. He's such a fine fellow. Now, let's go eat that supper mother's worked so hard to prepare!"

The two young women left the bedroom and found the entire family gathering together in the cramped dining room. With their guest, there was barely enough room for the family around the table, and Katherine flushed with pleasure at the attention that Mr. and Mrs. Gordon paid to her. After the meal they sat in the parlor and enjoyed a fine time of singing a variety of hymns. Katherine discovered that they were a very devoted Christian family, and she also found that she knew most of the hymns.

"Why, you've got a beautiful voice!" Clive said with approval. "Do you play the harpsichord?"

"Yes, I do, and my father plays the violin very well! We used to play duets sometimes." A sudden sadness flooded her and she said no more. Thoughts of her broken home came to her with a rush, and for a time she withdrew herself, only speaking when someone asked her a question, and not a great deal.

Finally, the evening ended, and Lyna Lee Gordon came over and kissed the young woman on the cheek. "You must come back as often as you can. We get lonely here, don't we, Leslie?"

"Yes we do. Good to have young people around." Colonel Gordon smiled. He took Katherine's hand, bowed low, and kissed it. "Bring her back, Clive, every chance you get."

The two left, and Clive escorted Katherine back to the Dolphin Inn. They walked along the streets that were now darkened except for the occasional lanterns that cast golden beams into the night. It was a fine evening in June. The stars overhead glittered brightly against a velvet sky, and the full moon poured its silvery streams upon them. They moved slowly, and finally Clive said, "Let's go have a look at the sea. I always like to see the ocean at night, especially on a night like this."

"All right."

They made their way down to the docks and stood together admiring the white caps illuminated by the silvery beams of the moon. "You see that track, the reflection of the moon?" Clive said suddenly, pointing to the V-shaped, bright reflection on the water. "The old Norsemen used to call that the whales' way. I don't know if there are any whales there, but it certainly is beautiful."

Katherine was feeling especially happy at how things had changed. Her father had seemed much improved that day when she visited him. Thinking of her good fortune, she now looked up at the stars and murmured, "I wish I knew all their names. Do you know the stars, Clive?"

"Just a few." He looked up, named several of them for her, and said, "I think that's Venus over there."

"Where?"

"Right there." He moved behind her and held his arm up, holding her left arm loosely and indicating the bright star. "I think that's Venus."

Katherine was very aware of his closeness. "I'd like to see a sunset on Venus."

He laughed suddenly and turned her around, holding her shoulders. "You wouldn't see much of one," he said. "Venus rotates so slowly it only has two sunsets in an entire year."

"Is that all—only two?"

"It's what I've heard. I don't know if it's true or not. That wouldn't be many sunsets to enjoy, would it?" He suddenly was very conscious of her loveliness. The warm summer breeze was fragrant with the smells of the sea, tangy and sharp. The waves were licking the dock at their feet in a sibilant manner, but more than this Clive was conscious of the sweet fragrance that she had on and of the contours of her lips. Her face was touched with the soft light of the moon, giving her features an argent cast. He thought he had never seen anything more lovely. For that one moment he forgot Jeanne Corbeau—or perhaps he remembered her. He never knew which it was, for the spell of the girl's beauty drew him. Strong emotions stirred in him, and almost recklessly, with a touch of desperation as the loss in him seemed to rise, he drew her close and bent his head.

Katherine knew he was going to kiss her and knew she should turn away—but she did not. Her heart was filled with gratitude to this tall young man who had showed such kindness to her. When his lips met hers she meant it as a sign of gratitude—no more than that. Katherine had been kissed before a few times, but something about this kiss was different. Gordon's strong arms wrapped about her, and he was so tall and powerful that she felt almost like a child in his grasp. His lips were firm, and to her surprise she found herself returning the caress. For one moment she stood there feeling more like a woman than she had ever felt in her life. Something in her urged her forward so that she held her own lips firmly against his—and then she drew away.

"I'm . . . I'm sorry," Clive said quickly. "I shouldn't have done that!"

Katherine struggled for a moment to regain her composure. She then smiled up at him and said, "I suppose one kiss isn't so terrible, is it?"

Clive had been shaken by the embrace. Somehow he felt confused. *How can I kiss this young woman, as pretty as she is, when I fancy myself in love with Jeanne?* He was disturbed and pulled his hat off, running his hand through his crisp hair. "I don't go around kissing women as a habit," he mumbled.

"I'm sure you don't." Not wanting to prolong the moment, Katherine said, "We'd better go back now. Will I see you tomorrow?"

"We'll go back to our house."

"That would be too soon for a visit."

"Oh, what does it matter if it's too soon or not soon enough!" Clive said. He was anxious to see whether she had been offended by the kiss, and by the time they reached the inn, he was sure that she was not. "Good night," he said, taking off his hat again.

"It was a lovely evening! Good night, Clive."

All that night and during the days that followed Katherine was reminded often of that single caress under the starry sky. She found herself spending more and more time with Clive, telling herself that it was because her father and her uncle tied them together. However, one evening when she was spending the night with Grace, the younger girl said, "You look like a woman who's falling in love."

Katherine gave her a startled glance, then shook her head. "You mean with Clive?"

"You're not seeing any other men, are you?"

Katherine shook her head. "No, that can't be! We're on different sides of a war. You're wrong, Grace!"

Grace Gordon was a thoughtful young woman, and one who had deep insight into people. She considered the face of her friend and said, "Be careful. I know you think it's impossible—but love won't be put into a little box, Katherine!"

9

An Old Love

CLIVE HAD NO SOONER ENTERED the door than his mother stepped outside the small parlor and called him down the short hallway. "Clive, come here, please!"

Sweeping off his hat and hanging it on a peg, Clive moved at once to meet her. One look at her troubled face and he demanded, "What's wrong, Mother!"

Lyna Lee held a single sheet of paper out to him. "It's a letter from Daniel," she said. "You'd better read it!"

Taking the sheet of paper, Clive quickly scanned the few lines:

Dear Lyna,

I trust that you and yours are well, but I am afraid that I do not have good news here. Some sort of epidemic has gripped Boston by the throat. In almost every household there's someone down, usually more than one. As usual, the doctors refuse to say exactly what it is, but I don't mind admitting I am terribly concerned about my family. Micah and I have not been touched by it, but Sam, Rachel, and Jeanne are all in poor condition. The doctors here are running themselves distracted, and every day there are scores of funerals. I hate to ask, but do you suppose Clive could come and help take care of my family? If this is impossible, do not worry about it. We are trusting God to bring us through this. I trust again my prayers are for you and all of my nephews and my niece.

Your loving brother,
Daniel.

Looking up, Clive frowned and shook his head. "It sounds very serious, doesn't it?"

"I'm afraid it is. Daniel is not one to ask for help unless there's no

105

other way." For a moment Lyna looked up into his face, then asked, "Do you think you might be able to go, Clive?"

With an expression of surprise Clive said, "Why, of course! It's a good thing I'm not in the army. I couldn't go then, but I'll leave at once and try to find out about transportation."

"Your father's already taken care of that," Lyna said quickly. "I'm afraid there's no time to waste. He has booked passage for you on the *Lone Star*, which is sailing in less than an hour."

"Well, that doesn't give me much time, does it?"

Lyna patted his arm. "I'll help you get your things packed."

Clive smiled at her. "You were pretty sure I'd go, weren't you, Mother?"

"Yes, I knew you would!" Fondness was in her tone, but a touch of worry clouded her fine eyes for a moment. "Just be sure you don't get sick yourself. I couldn't bear that! I'd have to come down there to nurse you and all of Daniel's brood, too!"

"Well, it's a risk we doctors have to take. I'm not sure about medical supplies there in Boston. They were getting pretty scanty when we left. I think I'll go to headquarters and see if I can scrounge up a few things there to take with me."

"And I suppose you'll stop to say goodbye to Katherine?"

"Well—of course I feel I must do that! I'll stop in and have one last look at her father and uncle."

"How are they doing, Clive?"

"Her father is much better—her uncle . . . well, I'm not sure. He can't seem to shake off this sickness in his throat and chest. He wasn't a healthy man, Amos tells me, when they were captured. They had no business being at that battle in the first place, but those Yancys are evidently a pretty stubborn lot."

"Tell Katherine to come by and see us while you're gone. You don't have to be here for that."

"I'll tell her, Mother." Clive quickly packed his clothes into a small trunk, and then kissed his mother goodbye at the door. "I'll write you as soon as I get to Boston. I'm sure Uncle Daniel will be writing to you all the time."

"Take care, son," Lyna said, holding to him for a moment. "God be with you!"

Clive left, carrying the small case down the street until he found a carriage. Tossing the chest inside, he got in and said, "Drive me to army headquarters."

"Yes, sir!" the driver responded and slapped the horses with the lines. "Get up there, Bess—Charlie!" The horses responded by breaking into a smart pace, and within ten minutes Clive was getting out at headquarters.

"Wait here for me. I have another ride to make. I'll make it worth your while."

"Yes, sir, I'll be right here!"

Clive moved quickly into the hospital, where he found the quartermaster spinning a tall yarn with a corporal. He explained his predicament about his relatives in Boston. "I'll be glad to pay you for the supplies. I don't think there's any place else I could buy them."

The quartermaster, a short, stubby man with a pair of lead-colored eyes, gave him a caustic look. "I can't release supplies, especially for treating rebels," he said. "You'll have to get General Howe's permission."

Clive argued his case but the quartermaster refused to give him any medical supplies. He went at once to find General Howe, only to find the general was in a staff meeting with his officers. Glancing at the clock on the wall of the outer office, Clive saw he had no time to wait and turned and left the office. He knew of a small apothecary shop that sold a few drugs, so he rode there in the carriage, bought what supplies were available, then returned to say, "Take me to the Dolphin Inn." As the carriage moved through the narrow streets, he went over the things in his mind that he might do, but could think of nothing else.

When the driver finally pulled up at the inn, Clive said again, "Wait for me! As soon as I finish here I need to go to the dock right away! I have to catch a ship ready to sail within the hour." He went inside and ran up the narrow flight of stairs. Knocking on the door of Katherine's room he waited eagerly, but there was no answer. He knocked again, but was certain that Katherine was not there. Running back down the stairs he said to the innkeeper, "I'm looking for Miss Yancy."

"She went out some time ago, sir," the man said. "Probably be back soon."

"Well, I can't wait. Please tell her Mr. Gordon called." Clive thought for a moment, and asked, "Do you have pen and paper? I'd better leave her a note."

"Yes, sir! Right here."

Clive quickly took the scrap of paper and the pen and, dipping it in the bottle of ink the innkeeper provided, wrote a brief note:

Katherine,
    I'm called to Boston on business. My uncle Daniel's family needs medical care. I hope to be back soon. I will also pray for your father and your uncle.

He hesitated over the closing and finally wrote, "Your devoted friend, Clive Gordon."

Waving the paper in the air until the ink was dry, he then folded it and said, "Please see that Miss Yancy gets this." He handed a coin to the innkeeper, then hurried outside. Jumping into the carriage he said, "Make it fast. My ship leaves in fifteen minutes."

"Probably won't," the driver said matter-of-factly. "Them ships never leave when they're supposed to—and they never arrive in port when they're supposed to, but I'll get you there, sir. Hang on!"

Clive reached the ship in plenty of time, got aboard, and discovered that his father had already paid for his passage.

"You got here just in time," the captain said. "We're just weighing anchor. Ten minutes later and you'd have missed us."

Clive thanked him and, after stowing his gear in the small cabin that was assigned to him, went topside. Moving to the stern to keep out of the way of the sailors who were rapidly setting the sail, he listened to the clanking of the anchor chain. The *Lone Star* swung at once, catching the tide, and as the sails billowed out, surged forward. As she cleared the harbor Clive stood in the stern looking back at Halifax, which grew smaller and smaller. His mind was on Katherine Yancy, and he was surprised at the keen disappointment that touched him at the thought of not seeing her for a time. When the land became a thin, knife-edge along the horizon, he turned and walked slowly along the deck. His thoughts tempered by the whistling wind that shook the billowing sails with a clapping sound from time to time, Clive finally moved to the bow and looked forward, wondering what awaited him in Boston.

ᛏ   ᛏ   ᛏ

Matthew Bradford found New York a whirlwind of activity after the dormant quality of life in Boston. As he walked down the street with a large flat case of his paintings, looking for Jan Vandermeer's house, he was almost stunned by the furious activity all around him. Everywhere he looked men were busy digging, throwing up defenses against the British army that everyone knew would arrive soon. There was a colorful group that he saw on the streets—men in brown coats with green or yellow or red facings, with brown, black, or gray hunting shirts. He saw some of John Haslet's Delaware Continentals, and William Smallwood's Marylanders. These recruits interested him, for he knew all of them came from wealthy families from Annapolis and Baltimore. As he walked along he also caught a glimpse of John Glover's Marbleheaders.

Up and down Manhattan, picks and shovels made the dirt fly all the way down to the Battery, as men sweated and cursed as they dug like moles. Matthew took it all in. He even saw General Israel Putnam flying about bellowing commands everywhere. Not far behind Putnam was Henry Knox, now promoted to a full colonel of artillery. Knox and his men came by with guns and wagons clattering along the streets. Matthew stopped from time to time to listen to the talk of the soldiers and was impressed at how confident they were. He picked up the fact that they had an army of twenty thousand men and that they held a strong position. He was glad to learn they had powder in ample quantities, which he knew the Continental Army had lacked before during the siege of Boston.

Finally, Matthew sought directions, and a kind elderly shopkeeper pointed the way out for him. After walking another half hour through the busy streets, he arrived at the corner of Greenwich and Dey Streets, which contained several fashionable houses. One stately home had solid shutters on the ground floor, and venetian shutters above. All of the houses had shutters and blinds, apparently to keep out the worst of the sunlight. He finally came to a three-story house built of bricks, sitting almost on the street. The windows were all closed with green venetian shutters, and when Matthew knocked on the door he was admitted into a foyer, which surprisingly was cool and semidark despite the blistering sunlight that baked the streets outside. "I'm looking for Mr. Jan Vandermeer," he said, pulling off his hat as he faced the tall angular woman who wore a white apron and a white cap over her dark hair.

"He's up in the attic room. Take those stairs."

"Thank you, ma'am."

Matthew climbed to the third floor, then took the final steps, a twisting, winding, narrow way that led to a small landing. When he knocked on the single door, he heard a voice shouting something loudly from the inside. The door opened then, and Matthew was blinded by the bright light that flooded through the gable windows across the end of the large room. He was grabbed around the waist at once, and a thick guttural voice with a Dutch accent said, "Yah, here is my friend, Matthew! Come in, come in!"

Matthew was practically dragged into the room. He saw that it had a high ceiling and was terribly cluttered. He paid no attention for the moment, for he was grinning broadly at the short man who was pumping his hand and beating his shoulder at the same time.

"Gut! You haf come! Come, we have a drink together to celebrate your arrival!"

"How are you, Jan?" Matthew asked as Vandermeer towed him to a table that contained a tall wine cooler, various sorts of glasses and cups, and what seemed to be the remains of several meals.

109

"I am fine! Here, we drink!" Vandermeer poured a dark reddish liquid into two pewter tankards, shoved one into Matthew's hand, and said, "To the second-best artist alive today, my friend, Matthew Bradford!"

Matthew took a healthy pull at his tankard, then gasped for breath. It bit like fire and he wheezed, "What is this stuff?"

"You are spoiled, just a baby!" Vandermeer exclaimed. He stood there grinning, a short, round man with blond hair. Round he was, in form, with large round eyes set in a round head. His eyes, almost piercing blue, were excitable, and whenever he spoke he pumped and waved his hands in a wild fashion. Matthew grinned, for he remembered that Jan Vandermeer only spoke in the manner of an exclamation—even if it was just a simple sentence such as, "It's a nice day." Whenever Vandermeer said anything, it was half shouted, and so filled with emotion that if it were written it would have to be followed by an exclamation point.

"I've invited myself to stay with you at your invitation, Jan," Matthew said. He was still holding his suitcase and looking around the room. "If you have room for me, that is."

"Room? Of course, but what does an artist need mit room?" Vandermeer boomed. His voice seemed to fill the room, and he slapped Matthew on the back heartily. "Come, I show you!" Striding across the cluttered floor Jan kicked a stool out of the way, sending it flying until it hit the wall with a crash. "Here, this is all you need! A bed, a vashstand—" Grabbing Matthew's suitcase he threw it inside on the bed and slammed the door. "Come now, I vill show you what I haf been doing!"

Matthew could not help smiling at his friend, as he often did. During his time in England the two artists had become very close, but he had forgotten the wild excitement with which the Dutchman attacked everything. He had also forgotten the tremendous ego of the man. It had never occurred to Vandermeer to give Matthew a chance to get settled. Instead he was walking excitedly around the room, grabbing up canvases, some half finished, some barely started, others completed. Yelling and jabbing a round forefinger at them, he demanded an opinion from Matthew.

Finally Vandermeer put down a painting of a landscape that seemed to jump off the canvas with its bright, brilliant colors and demanded, "There, what do you think of this?"

Matthew stepped backward, for Vandermeer held the canvas approximately twelve inches from his nose. When he had gotten a good perspective he cleared his throat uncertainly, then said, "Well, Jan, to tell the truth it's a little—well, a little overdone, isn't it? I mean—the colors are all primary."

Vandermeer roared with laughter and whipped the canvas away. "Just an experiment, my friend, nothing more! An artist must try all forms! Now, let me see what you haf brought!"

Matthew hesitated, for Jan Vandermeer was prone to be excessive in his criticisms as he was in everything else. However, Matthew had come to New York for the express purpose of learning, and he knew that underneath the rather ridiculous facade of the small Dutchman lay a keen, analytical brain and a genius that allowed Vandermeer to grasp at once the failings and the virtues of any painting.

"Well, I only brought a few," Matthew said tentatively. Moving across the room he picked up the flat case, found a place on a table by moving several objects, then opened it up. Picking up one of the canvases, he held it up, saying, "This is a still life I did just last month." He eagerly watched the round eyes of his friend take in the painting. Suddenly he realized how much he wanted Vandermeer's approval. He, himself, was not certain whether he had genius, or talent, or nothing. Yet somehow Matthew felt that it lay in him to be a great painter, but he had not yet reached the stage that he had seen in others of absolute certainty of his gift.

"Let me see! Ve haf here a plate mit a loaf of bread, a fish, and a glass of wine!" Vandermeer cocked his round head to one side, closed one eye, and stuck his chubby hands behind his back.

As Jan stared at the painting, seeming to pull it into his own head, Matthew could almost hear the wheels grinding. Matthew watched his friend, but he got no hint at all of what Vandermeer was thinking.

Finally Jan said explosively, "It is a perfect painting!"

"Do you really think so, Jan?" Matthew asked eagerly.

"Yah, and that makes it a *bad* painting!" Vandermeer laughed loudly at Matthew's astonished expression. "You do not want a perfect painting, one that captures every detail exactly!

Matthew was dumbfounded. He had worked for weeks on this painting, doing exactly what Jan had suggested. He had tried to capture every detail and to make the still life as much as possible like it really was. It had been his best effort, he thought, and now he said rather stiffly, "I am sure I don't know what you're talking about. A painter is supposed to paint what he sees."

"No!" Jan practically jumped up and down and moved over to shake Matthew almost fiercely. "He must paint vot he *feels*! You do not understand? Have you ever heard of Andrea del Sarto?"

"I . . . I don't think so."

111

"His real name was Andrea d'Agnolo di Francesco! He was a painter who lived in the fifteenth century! He was called 'del Sarto' because he was the son of a tailor, which is sarto, and he painted perfect pictures! As a matter of fact," Jan said, pacing the floor and waving his stubby arms around, "the perfection of his frescoes in the Church of the Annunziata in Florence won him the title of 'The Thoughtless Painter,' and he was *nothing*!"

"What do you mean nothing? How can a faultless painter be nothing?" Matthew exclaimed with exasperation running through his tone. "I have spent years trying to paint what I see as well as I can—as much like the original as possible—but now you're telling me that's not what I need to do?"

"That's exactly vat I'm telling you to do! Look, my friend! Come and look out the window!" Jan grabbed Matthew's arm, dragged him to the window, and gestured down at the busy street below. "If you were to paint a picture of that street, what would you paint? You see there the soldiers, some old ladies, and a young woman who's carrying what seems to be a baby. There are horses. Could you paint every one of them exactly? No!" he yelled and jumped up and down in excitement. "You would paint the *impression* of that street—the colors, the movement, the *sense* of the street, not as if you were drawing a scientific illustration for a class of physicians! You must decide vat it is about that street which is important, and then you must render it in your own fashion!" He pounded Matthew on the chest, driving the young man backward. "You must take what is in your heart and mix it with your paints—then you vill have part of yourself on the canvas! What you haf here," he shook the painting of the still life before Matthew's eyes, "is paint on canvas. But it is *not* Matthew Bradford!"

Matthew stared at the painting that he had labored on so assiduously and shook his head in despair. "It sounds to me, Jan, like you're telling me I haven't begun to be an artist yet."

"That is right! That is right!" Jan practically shouted. "You haf learned certain tricks of the craft of painting, but now that you haf mastered that, what must come out of you is this!" Reaching forward, Vandermeer grabbed Matthew's shirt in the vicinity of his heart. He twisted and pulled and beat at Matthew, crying, "We must haf your heart on the canvas, not just smears of paint, and ve will do it!" He suddenly stopped and saw the shock etched on his friend's face. "Ah, Matthew . . ." He shrugged his shoulders and released Matthew's shirt. "I haf gone too fast, but I tell you this. You are a better painter than you know, Matthew Bradford! But I vill have it out of you. I vill have it out of your heart onto this canvas!"

Matthew stared into the electric blue eyes of the small, rotund figure standing before him, and his heart seemed to sink. "It's all been for nothing, all my study?"

"Not at all! Not at all! It is your apprenticeship! Now," Jan Vandermeer said, reaching forward to hug his friend with genuine affection, "now, we go to work and I teach you to paint, not only with the hands—but with the heart...!"

🜲   🜲   🜲

After two days of submitting to Jan Vandermeer's teaching, which was frenetic, to say the least, Matthew had just about endured all he could stand. It was with great relief that he received an invitation from Mrs. Esther Denham to have dinner with her that evening.

Matthew had been surprised, but he had written a note to Abigail, and obviously Abigail had prevailed upon her hostess to invite him. The note also included an invitation for Jan Vandermeer, whom Matthew had mentioned to Abigail.

When sunset came, Matthew put on the new clothing that he had purchased earlier in the morning. His britches were bone white and stuffed into jockey-type black leather boots. His shirt was made of cotton and linen, and the neck cloth made of pure silk, which he wound carefully around his neck, forming a bow. He put on his square-cut waistcoat, which was tan with stripes of darker brown, then slipped on the chestnut-colored frock coat. The tails ended at the back of his knees. He was interrupted as Jan Vandermeer entered and stared at him.

"Vell, there you are in all your glory." He walked around Matthew, studying him carefully, then punched him with a stubby forefinger. "You look vonderful," he said. "Now, if you drop dead vee won't have to do a thing except put a lily in your hand!"

Matthew laughed out loud, for he was now accustomed to the excesses of his friend. "Come along and get dressed. We've got to go."

Vandermeer stared at him. "Get dressed? You think I'm naked? I *am* dressed!" He was wearing a baggy pair of knee britches with a short waistcoat that buttoned up the front, only half the buttons were missing. Across his head, cocked at an odd angle, sat an old wig that had seen better days. The coat he wore was a glaring yellow with green-and-red stripes and a scarlet collar. Jan was obviously very proud of it, for he said, "This coat belonged to my father! I hope you like it!"

As a matter of fact, Matthew thought he looked awful, but thought, *Well, I can always tell Mrs. Denham that he's an artist, an eccentric one at that.* Aloud he said, "All right, come along. We'll get a good dinner out of this if nothing else."

The two made their way through the center of New York. In spite of its high population Matthew noticed that there was a rural air about the place. He even saw cows being driven through the streets to a common pasture west of Broadway. Pigs and chickens were a common sight along the road, which was simply a muddy thoroughfare. There were no sidewalks, and he later learned that the streets had to be cleaned by the householders. The street-lighting was also done by the citizens. One householder in every seven hung out a lantern before his residence, and six of his nearest neighbors shared with him the expense of keeping the light burning.

"This is the place, I think," Matthew said, stopping in front of a sturdy house of Dutch pattern on Williams Street near the corner of Wall. The house they paused before was as rigidly rectangular as a barn. It had no projecting wings, or bow windows, or frills of any kind. However, it was well proportioned, and the bricks used to build it were of various colors—yellow, brown, blue, and red arranged in different designs. The decorative brick gave the house a certain air of lightness and charm.

"This is a Dutch house!" Vandermeer announced. "I've seen many like it in Antwerp, back at my home!"

"Well, Manhattan was settled by the Dutch, and there's still a lot of Dutch people here," Matthew said. "Come along."

As they mounted the little porch, which Vandermeer called a stoop, Matthew felt an excitement at seeing Abigail again. They knocked on the door, and it was opened almost at once by a Negro woman wearing a gray dress with a white apron and a white cap.

"Yes, sir?" she said.

"My name is Matthew Bradford. This is Mr. Vandermeer. I believe Mrs. Denham is expecting us."

"Yes, sir, she is. Will you come in?"

As the two men entered, the woman took their hats and said, "If you'll come this way, Mrs. Denham will be right down. You can wait in the parlor." Matthew and Jan were ushered by the servant into a large parlor filled with fine old, dark furniture of mahogany and walnut. Along one side of the wall, two high windows allowed light, and a huge fireplace occupied one end of the large room. The sunlight touched a series of fine porcelain statuettes on the mantel, causing them to gleam richly, and at the other end a harpsichord with a small stool sat beneath a grouping of paintings.

Vandermeer went at once to examine the paintings, and turned, saying with some surprise, "Yah, these are good paintings! I'm surprised!"

"Why should you be surprised?"

"Most people buy a picture of horses jumping over fences and call it art. These," he turned to move his round, stubby hand in a sweeping gesture, "these are fine paintings. Mostly from England, I think."

They were examining the paintings when a woman with beautiful silver hair and quick brown eyes entered the parlor. She was in her middle sixties, Matthew judged, rather small boned, and carefully dressed in a pearl gray gown with delicate lace at the neck and sleeves. "Mr. Bradford? I am Esther Denham."

"I'm happy to meet you, Mrs. Denham. May I present my friend, Mr. Jan Vandermeer."

Vandermeer bowed deeply from the waist, and his eyes danced. Waving at the paintings he said, "Your paintings, they are very fine, Mrs. Denham."

Esther Denham smiled at the abruptness of the man. Her quick eyes took in the rather outlandish dress of the one, and the careful dress of Matthew Bradford, but she said only, "They were collected by my husband. He had quite good taste, I think."

"It was so kind of you to invite us, Mrs. Denham," Matthew said at once. "I've only come to New York recently, as Abigail may have told you."

"Yes, so she said. She and her mother will be down soon. I thought we might have an early dinner, then afterwards, we can come back in here and you can talk to us about painting. I understand you're a very fine artist."

Matthew flushed and shook his head. "Mr. Vandermeer is the expert. I'm only a pupil, I fear."

"Dot is right!" Vandermeer cried, nodding vehemently. "But one day he will surpass the master! You watch what I tell you!"

At that moment Abigail and her mother entered the parlor, and both men turned toward her. Matthew's eyes lit up, and he realized at that moment how much he had wanted to see her again. "Abigail," he said, going forward, "it's so good to see you!"

Abigail took Matthew's hand and smiled. "It's good to see you too, Matthew."

Matthew turned and said, "Mrs. Howland, I trust you're well?"

"I'm feeling better, Matthew. It's nice to see you."

Matthew said, "May I introduce my friend and teacher, Mr. Jan Vandermeer."

As soon as introductions were made, Mrs. Denham said, "I think we will go to the dining room now. I hope you two are hungry. We've prepared too much food, I'm sure."

Jan Vandermeer laughed loudly. "You ask two poor, starving artists if they're hungry? My dear lady, artists are always hungry, but it is good for us to suffer! Otherwise how could vee be artists?"

They moved into the dining room, which was furnished with a magnificent sideboard on which sat an array of silver trays and drinking vessels. The table was covered with a white cloth with candelabras on each end. Underneath it was a crumb cloth to protect the dark blue checked carpet beneath. As they sat down Matthew knew enough about furniture to recognize that the chairs were genuine Hepplewhite.

Mrs. Denham said, "I think we will have the blessing before the first course. Mr. Bradford, would you be so kind?"

Taken completely off guard, Matthew bowed his head and in a rather stumbling fashion asked the blessing. Of course, in his home he was accustomed to such things, but he had somehow not expected it of Mrs. Denham. He could not tell why. When he looked up he smiled at her and said, "That reminds me of my home. I don't think we ever had a meal in my life when my father didn't ask the blessing or ask one of us to do it."

"I'm glad to hear it, sir. Your father is a wise man."

The meal began with soup, which was then followed by fish, so fresh and white and flaky that it fell apart under the fork. Then there was a joint of mutton and also cuts of beef. Served with the tender meat were sauces, vegetables, which were crisp and well-done, and three different kinds of bread. They were served cider, which was evidently brought up from a cellar, for it was cool, and sparkling, and fresh. Finally for dessert there were several fresh fruits and custards.

During the meal Matthew had cast his eye whenever possible at Abigail. He was grateful for the presence of Jan, who dominated the conversation, having an opinion on everything that Mrs. Denham mentioned.

Abigail was wearing a pale green dress, and her hair was done up in a ravishing new hair style. She wore a pearl on each ear, and the rosy light of the candles brought a glow to her smooth skin. She said little, but Matthew was pleased that she seemed glad to see him, and he wished that he could enjoy the meal with her alone.

After the meal they went into the parlor, where Jan talked enthusiastically about the paintings. He admired the pictures, pointing out the flaws and the virtues of each. Finally he came to one, a portrait of Mrs. Denham herself, probably done ten years earlier.

"Now this is a really fine piece of work. May I ask the artist?"

"Gilbert Stuart, Mr. Vandermeer. He was a close friend of my husband's."

"Indeed, a fine, powerful portrait!" Vandermeer exclaimed. "He could compete against the finest of the Continent, I think!"

Abigail said in one of the few silences that Vandermeer permitted, "How is your family, Matthew?"

"Not too well, I'm afraid. There's some kind of an epidemic going around Boston. You're fortunate that you got out when you did."

"Oh, I'm so sorry to hear it!" Abigail said. She was sitting next to Matthew on one of the two couches in the parlor. Leaning forward, she touched his hand and said, "I hope it's not serious."

The touch of Abigail's hand on Matthew's sent a thrill through him. He wanted to take her hand, but did not. "My cousin, Clive Gordon, has come from Halifax to take care of them."

"Oh yes. His father is in the British army, isn't he?"

"Yes, he is, Mrs. Howland."

"How sad that families are pitted against one another in this terrible war. I hope it will soon be over."

"No, it will not be over soon!" Vandermeer announced in a voice as solid as granite. "Have you not heard about the meeting in Philadelphia?"

"What meeting is that?" Mrs. Denham inquired.

"The meeting of the Continental Congress," the artist nodded. "Everyone thinks they will declare this country independent from England!"

"It'll be a shame if they do," Abigail shook her head. "They could never stand against the full force of the English army. No nation on earth could. Why, England has the most powerful and trained army in the world—and the most powerful navy as well!"

Talk went around the table about the revolution, and finally Mrs. Howland excused herself and went to bed. Esther took Jan off to show him the different pictures in the house, and for a moment Abigail and Matthew were alone. Abigail said, "Come, it's stuffy in here! Let's go out to the garden."

"All right."

Matthew followed Abigail out through a pair of double doors and found himself in a delightful garden lit by a single lantern that shed its feeble light over the orderly rows. "This is beautiful!" he said. "Mrs. Denham must love flowers."

"I believe she does. She's a very fine woman."

Abigail moved closer to Matthew as they stood there speaking of the flowers, and knowing men as she did, it was simple enough for her to draw him on. Even as she did this she had a sudden thought of Nathan Winslow—how she had convinced him that she was in love with him— and the thought of that deception came with a painful start, which surprised her. She had never thought much about what kind of woman she was, but now that the world had fallen to bits about her she was forced to think. In the days since she left Boston, she had wondered over and over again how she could have become so despicable as to deliberately plot to entice a man to fall in love with her in order to manipulate him. Time and again she had almost decided it was more than she cared to do, but there was no other route of escape. She had no finances, no prospects. She and her mother were totally dependent upon the kindness of her aunt; therefore, she turned to Matthew and lifted her face, saying, "I've missed you, Matthew."

The slight touch of Abigail's body as she turned to him, the soft quality of her voice, and the faint perfume that was like an intoxicating drug seemed to draw Matthew Bradford. Almost without thinking he put his arms around her, drew her close, and kissed her. Her lips moved under his, and he felt her hands go behind his neck. There was an alluring quality in her that he had never known in any woman. She was a beautiful young woman, and her touch seemed to take his breath. Her lips were soft under his, and he held her almost fiercely, half expecting she would pull away. She did not, but held the kiss, adding the pressure of her own lips. When he lifted his head he said, "You are the loveliest thing I've ever known!"

"Thank you, Matthew." She moved back then as he reached for her, knowing that it was time to let him think about what she was and what he was. They went back into the house finally and met the others.

After the two men left, Esther said, "That's a fine young man. That artist friend of his, he's amusing, and I suspect a very fine artist."

Abigail responded, "Yes, Matthew comes from a fine family. They're patriots, of course. His older brother is with Washington here in New York."

"Have you known him long?"

"Yes, Aunt Esther, for some time. I've always liked him."

Esther Denham asked no more questions, but her sharp brown eyes had observed how the two young people had watched each other across the table. She was also aware of the flush on Matthew's face as they had come in from the garden and could pretty well tell what had happened. "Well," she said, "we will have to have him here again, and Mr. Vandermeer, of course."

Abigail gave her aunt a grateful look. "You've been so kind to us," she said. "I don't know what Mother and I would've done if it hadn't been for you."

Esther came forward and kissed the young woman on the cheek. "It's a delight to have you here. I was terribly lonely until you came. I hope you and your mother will stay a long, long time."

As she turned and left the room, Abigail suddenly felt a sense of distaste for herself. "What kind of a woman am I who can deceive a man so easily—and Aunt Esther, too. If she knew what was in my heart, she would throw me out at once." But she knew that was not true, for she had discovered quickly that Esther Denham was a woman of deep Christian character, and she could tell her aunt's faith was real and genuine. Turning, she moved across the parlor and went to bed at once. For a long time she lay there thinking of how odd her fate was, and for some reason she felt terribly discouraged and despondent as she thought of the future.

10

A Small Piece of Paper

AS SOON AS THE *Lone Star* anchored in the harbor, Clive disembarked and hurried to the Bradford household. When he knocked on the door it opened almost at once, and Daniel grabbed his hand, relief washing over his face. "Clive, my boy, I'm so glad you've come! Come in—let me take your bag."

"How are the sick folks, Uncle Daniel?"

"Not as well as I'd like." Daniel nodded toward the stairs. "Come along, I've kept a room on the second floor for you. You'll be staying here, of course." He moved up the stairs quickly and Clive followed him. When they reached the room at the far end of the hall, Daniel opened the door and waved Clive inside. He found a pleasant room containing a rather ornate bed with a canopy and a fine washstand with a china pitcher and basin on its polished surface. "Make yourself at home. You may want to lie down and rest," Daniel said. "I know it has been a hard trip."

"No, I'd really rather see my patients first."

Daniel nodded quickly. "Come along. I think they're all awake by now. I've kept them in separate rooms." He led the way to the next door, knocked on it, then opened it. "Sam! The doctor is here," he said as he entered the room, followed by Clive.

Sam, who was lying in bed, lifted his head and muttered, "Hello, Clive. Glad you came. I'm pretty sick."

"We'll have to see what we can do about that." Clive sat down on the chair beside the bed, gave Sam a quick examination, and said cheerfully, "We'll have you fixed up in no time! I've got some medicine I want you to take."

"Does it taste bad?"

"All medicine tastes bad! That's part of the reason it's good for you." Clive grinned. He took a glass, mixed a potion from the supplies he had

120

brought from Halifax, and watched as Sam gulped it down and made a horrible face. "You'll be coming around soon," he said. "You won't feel as bad as you do now."

"That's good," Sam muttered. "I hate to think I'd feel this bad the rest of my life!"

Clive rose and the two men left the room. Again Daniel knocked on the next door, and when a voice said faintly, "Come in," he opened it. The two men stepped inside, and Clive moved to where Rachel was lying in a single bed, just under a window. The light came in and touched her face, and Clive saw at once she had a gaunt look about her. Her features were swollen and she licked her lips almost painfully.

"Hello, Rachel," Clive said. He put his hand on her forehead, took her temperature, then examined her carefully. They were, of course, the same symptoms that Sam had, which he had expected. She was, however, feeling much worse, and although he spoke cheerfully to her and gave her encouragement, when he stepped out of the room he shook his head. "She's lost too much weight. She's got to eat more and drink more liquids."

"She can't keep much down." Daniel shook his head and bit his lower lip. "I'm worried, Clive, and Jeanne is the worst of all. She's across the hall here." He stepped to the door, knocked on it once, waited, and when there was no answer knocked again. "She's like that sometimes. Just passes out."

Opening the door, Daniel stepped aside and showed Clive into the room. It was decorated with a feminine touch with yellow curtains and delicate ornaments on top of a chest alongside the wall. Clive, however, did not notice this. He stepped up immediately to bend over the young woman who lay in the bed. Jeanne's face was pale, and her breathing was very shallow. "Jeanne—" he said quietly. She did not move, and he put his hand on her forehead, noting that she had a higher fever than either Sam or Rachel. He picked up her limp arm, felt her pulse, then turned to Daniel. "Has she done this often?"

"Almost every day she has trouble like this. I wanted to send for Dake, but, of course, he couldn't leave his unit." Daniel looked at the young man and wanted to ask questions, but he refrained until the two had stepped out into the hall.

"What do you think, Clive? What is it?"

"It could be cholera," Clive said, "or half a dozen other things. These plagues are all about the same. I'm glad you sent for me, Uncle Daniel. They do need quite a bit of care."

Daniel drew a deep breath and expelled it. He shook his head. "I'll be your nurse. You just tell me what to do. I'll do the praying and you do the doctoring," he said, attempting a smile. He knew as well as Clive the dangers of such sicknesses as these, and as the two men stood there quietly speaking of treatment for the patients, it took all the faith that Daniel Bradford had to believe God for three miracles.

🜚   🜚   🜚

Clive entered the room to find Jeanne sitting in a chair beside the window and said at once, "You shouldn't be up, Jeanne!"

Jeanne Corbeau Bradford smiled up at the tall, young physician. "You know what I've been thinking about, Clive?" she said, ignoring his gentle rebuke.

"I don't know—about what?" he said. He took his seat on the bed facing her and noted with relief that her eyes were clear and she seemed to be free from fever. The past few days had been difficult for him, especially when treating Jeanne. He had to remind himself constantly that thinking of the past was futile now. Yet even as he sat there, memories came flooding back as he thought of the days in the woods that he had spent with Jeanne and her dying father.

Jeanne was wearing a blue robe over a nightgown, and her curly black hair was cropped rather close. She had strange violet-colored eyes, the most beautiful Clive had ever seen. He remembered how he had been almost shocked when he had seen them. "What were you thinking of?" he asked, to drive the thoughts of the past away.

Jeanne smiled and cocked her head to one side. "I was thinking about how I found you so sick in the woods, and *you* were the patient then and *I* was the doctor. Do you remember?"

"Yes, I do," Clive said rather shortly.

Surprised at the brevity of his reply and the tone of it, Jeanne said, "What's the matter, Clive?"

"I just . . . think we'd better not discuss those days."

Jeanne understood at once. She knew she had hurt this man by her choice to marry Dake, yet great affection for him still remained and always would. Now she put out her hand and he took it. "You and I would never have been happy, Clive. You're going to be a great doctor and have a practice in London. You'll be among great society people. That's not for me," she said simply. "I like the woods. I like to go out in the morning and see where the deer have come up close to the cabin. I still like to hunt and to fish. It's the sort of thing you could do, but you would never feel yourself fulfilled."

Clive understood with part of his mind that Jeanne was right. He had always known this. Even when he had felt most in love with her he knew there was a dark foreboding in his mind about their future together. He was not a woodsman and liked his nature tamed—a cultured, cultivated garden perhaps, with all the flowers in neat orderly rows. He liked his hedges neatly trimmed and all in order. Jeanne, on the other hand, liked the wilderness, the wild tangles of the deep woods—the free running rivers that cut serpentine paths through the land. Clive thought of their differences for a moment, then smiled, "Perhaps you're right, Jeanne." He hesitated, then said, "Are you happy?"

"Very happy. I found a good husband, and we'll have a good life together when this war is over." She smiled gently and said, "And you'll find a wife who knows how to dress and do all the things that the wife of a famous surgeon in London must do."

The two sat there talking for a while, and from that moment on Clive felt a release in his spirit. All the sadness and grief that had been burdening him since Jeanne had chosen to marry Dake seemed to fade. It gave him a lighter look at life, and all that were in the house noticed that he seemed to be more cheerful than when he first arrived.

　　　　🜍　　　🜍　　　🜍

"Go to Philadelphia?" Micah was surprised. He looked up from the forge where he had been working on the latest attempt to create musket barrels and stared at his father. "What in the world is in Philadelphia? We're too busy here at the forge!"

Daniel had a sheet of paper in his hand. "I wrote to Benjamin Franklin in Philadelphia about a month ago. You know what trouble we've been having with this firing mechanism. I don't think we're ever going to get it right. Well, everyone knows Dr. Franklin is the most able inventor in the Colonies." He held the letter up and grinned. "I just wrote to him and asked if he would help. The letter came just this morning. He says for me to come and we'll talk about it."

"I doubt if you'll be talking about muskets, Pa," Micah said, shaking his head. "They're having that big meeting of the Congress, aren't they?"

"Yes they are, but Dr. Franklin says for me to come anyway. I don't know how that man does all that he seems to get done! He invents things, is into politics up to his ears, and runs his printing business. I don't think there's another man on this continent like him, or in Europe either for that matter. Anyway, I can't leave with a house full of sick people, and I can't leave the foundry either. So I want you to go and talk with Mr. Franklin."

Micah considered his father's request for a moment. It was typical for Micah to take his time, for he was methodical in all things, quite unlike his twin Dake who threw himself into any adventure impulsively. Finally, Micah nodded. "I suppose that would be best, Pa. When should I leave?"

"Right away! As soon as you can. I think it'd be quicker to travel by horseback rather than take the coach, but you can be the best judge of that. You'll need to take plenty of money for the trip. I'll go by the office and get it."

Daniel returned to the office and obtained the cash for Micah's journey. He was about to return to the workshop when he heard a knock at the door. "Come in!" he said. When the door opened, Cato, the butler for the Fraziers, stood there. "What is it, Cato?" Daniel asked.

Cato, a tall, distinguished black man, said, "It's Mr. Frazier, sir. He's taken a turn for the worse. Miss Marian wants to know, will you come?"

"Of course. How did you get here, Cato?"

"I rode one of the horses, sir."

"Come along, then. My horse is already saddled. I'll go with you."

"Yes, sir!"

Daniel delivered the cash to Micah and shook his hand, saying, "I think you ought to leave right away, son. Write me as soon as you get to Philadelphia."

Impulsively he hugged the young man, and then turned and walked away. He mounted the fine buckskin mare that was his favorite, touched her with his heels, and said, "Come on, Caesar!" The horse left the stable yard at a smooth gallop, and Cato followed on his horse as best he could.

When they arrived at the Frazier home, Cato said, "I'll take care of the horse, Mr. Daniel."

"Thank you, Cato." Daniel ran up the steps and knocked at the door. It was opened almost instantly by Hattie, the cook. "Miss Marian say for you to go up to Mr. John's room, sir."

"Thank you, Hattie!" Daniel quickly moved down the hall to the end, where he knocked on the door and entered when a voice indicated, "Come in!" Stepping inside he saw Marian leaning over her father, and moved to stand on the other side of the bed. "I came as quickly as I could!" Looking down he said, "How are you, John?"

John Frazier was not an old man, only sixty, but bad health had drained him of his vitality. His eyes were sunk back in his head, and his skin had the texture of pale clay. "Glad—to see you, Daniel," he wheezed.

There was a rattle in his chest, and alarm rose in Daniel. He had known of Frazier's poor health, but this bout seemed worse. Looking across at Marian he said, "Have you called the doctor?"

"Yes, he's been here once, and he's coming back later this afternoon.

You sit down and talk with father. I'll go make him some tea and broth. He's hardly eaten anything."

When Marian left the room, Daniel sat down and for a time spoke quietly, trying to encourage Frazier. In truth, he was worried, for he had great affection for John Frazier. Frazier had taken him in to the foundry when he'd had little to offer except the strength of his hands and the willingness to work hard. Now, he was half-owner, and for all practical purposes had complete authority. John had never questioned anything he ever did at the business, and the two had become very close friends.

Frazier lay quietly, seeming to labor for breath. Finally after a time he opened his eyes and looked up and whispered, "Daniel, I must talk with you." He took another deep breath, held it, and expelled it, then moved his hand in a helpless gesture. "I may not live, Daniel." When Daniel started to protest he shook his head. "I'm like an old animal; I know I'm going to die. I don't fear death, but it's Marian I'm worried about."

Daniel leaned forward to catch the words, which were very faint. "What can I do, John?" he asked quietly.

"Leo will get all the property when I'm gone. That's the law. Women have no protection." He hesitated and then reached out his hand. When Daniel Bradford took it he squeezed it with surprising force. "You must help her when I'm gone—protect her, Daniel."

The man's words brought a sense of uncertainty and doubt to Daniel. He shifted uneasily, then shook his head. "She has a husband, John."

"No!" The word came explosively, and John's grip tightened on Daniel's hand. "Leo will destroy her! You know what he is better than anyone. You must help her, Daniel!"

"Of course, I'll do what I can. You know that, John."

"You must do everything! I can't tell you how, but I've known for a long time that you two love each other—oh, I know it hasn't been a worldly thing! You're both honorable Christians. I can see it in your eyes, there's no guilt nor shame—" The sick man paused for a while; he had lifted himself in his vehemence and now lay back, seemingly exhausted. "Promise me, Daniel," he whispered.

Daniel saw that his friend was slipping into some sort of coma or sleep, so he leaned forward. "I promise, John. I'll do everything I can for her!"

When Marian came back into the room with a tray, she saw her father asleep. Daniel rose and said, "I think sleep might be the best for him."

Marian stood there, trouble in her eyes. "He's very ill," she murmured. Then looking up to Daniel she said, "Did he say anything?"

Daniel hesitated, then the basic honesty that was in him came forth. "He asked me—to look out for you."

Marian's eyes went to her father. She loved him dearly and knew that she would not have him for long. "That's like him," she whispered. "He's always put me first." Then she looked back, and even in her sorrow there was a tremulous smile on her generous lips. "And will you look after me, Daniel?"

"As well as is in my power, Marian." He did not say more, and the two turned away from the moment. Their emotions were deep. These two felt things strongly, but the barrier of Leo Rochester stood between them, and they knew better than to remain on dangerous ground.

🔔　　　🔔　　　🔔

Micah Bradford reached Philadelphia on the twenty-eighth of June and found America agonizing over independence. It had been months since Thomas Paine's *Common Sense* had swept across the Colonies, but as the summer heat came to Philadelphia, Congress could not quite bring itself to declare the Colonies an independent nation no matter how hard John Adams pushed and shoved. It teetered on the bank like a swimmer afraid to plunge into a raging torrent.

At this point in history, King George III of England made perhaps the greatest mistake of his reign. Parliament had voted to raise an army of fifty-five thousand men to come to crush the rebellion in America, but the men of England did not rally to the cause. Among the officers of the Royal Army and Navy there was much sympathy for the Americans. The war against America was not popular with the citizens of England. They felt, in effect, they were fighting against themselves—for these, after all, were Englishmen.

King George, faced with failure of his own people to rise to the occasion, went looking for hirelings. He found them among the principalities of Germany. Eventually some thirty thousand German mercenaries were hired, most of them from the Hesse-Cassel regions, who came to be called Hessians. Britain agreed to pay all the expenses of the Hessians as well as thirty-five dollars to their prince for each soldier killed, twelve dollars for each one wounded, and over five hundred thousand dollars annually to the Hessian government. With this last act, George III convinced most Americans that there was nothing left to do but cut the umbilical cord and declare their independence.

As Micah arrived in Philadelphia he noted at once the excitement everywhere. He had no trouble at all locating the home of the famous Benjamin Franklin, and although he rather doubted his welcome, he was pleasantly surprised. Knocking on the door of the yellow brick, two-story house in the center of town, Micah was ushered into the parlor by a diminutive servant and found Benjamin Franklin unable to rise.

Franklin, sitting in a chair, his right leg on a cushion, looked over his spectacles and said, "Good day, sir! You find me unable to rise to the occasion. You are Micah Bradford, I take it?"

"Yes, Dr. Franklin. My father has written you—"

Franklin waved his hand. "Yes, I'm very interested in your father's proposal." He winced as he moved his foot and muttered, "Blasted gout, what a time to be laid up! Sit down, Mr. Bradford, I have something that you'll be interested in!"

Micah sat down, and Benjamin Franklin nodded to the servant, saying, "Bring that folder over on the desk, Simon!" When he had it safely in his hand he opened it and said, "I've been doing some work on this firing mechanism for the muskets. I think I have come up with something very interesting." He started to rise and then cried out in pain. "Oh well, perhaps you will come and look over my shoulder!"

"Of course, Dr. Franklin!" Micah rose with alacrity, and soon the two men were pouring over the drawings, clear and meticulously executed on the sheets within the folder.

"This ought to work splendidly!" Franklin said. "I hope it will be of some use to you and your father!" He frowned then and handed the folder to Micah. "Take it home with you!" He added as an afterthought, "If I'm not mistaken, General Washington is going to be desperately in need of muskets very soon."

"How do things look with the Congress, if I may ask, Dr. Franklin?"

Franklin scowled. "You may ask, but I am afraid I have no easy answer! Adams wants the Colonies to be unanimous in their stand against England, but some of the Colonies are holding out, I'm afraid. New York, Pennsylvania, South Carolina, and Maryland are all on the fence. We must bring them in!" he exclaimed. "Will you have tea?" he interrupted himself. For the next thirty minutes Micah Bradford enjoyed the privilege of listening to perhaps the greatest mind in America speak freely about the problems of revolution and independence. Franklin was apparently speaking without any intention of stopping when the servant came in and said, "Mr. Adams is here—Mr. Sam Adams, I mean, Dr. Franklin."

"Have him come in!" Franklin said. His house was open to all visitors, and when Samuel Adams entered, Micah stood up at once.

Sam Adams said, "Why, Micah, I didn't know you were in Philadelphia." He came forward and offered his hand. Samuel Adams, the shabby, intense, master propagandist of the revolution was not handsome, but he had an intensity unmatched among men. His brother, John

Adams, was cultured, highly educated, and an aristocrat in every sense, but plain Sam Adams had been the spark that had ignited the revolutionary fervor. He had swayed Boston, played upon it like an instrument, bringing on the reaction of England, who sent General Gage and an army to quiet the firebrand.

"It's good to see you, Mr. Adams. I've just come from my father to talk with Dr. Franklin about our plan to build muskets."

Adams small eyes glowed with revolutionary fervor. "Fine—! Fine, my boy! We're going to need all the muskets we have!" He turned to look at Franklin and said, "Are you ready to go, Doctor?"

Franklin groaned and looked at his servant. "Bring the sedan chair to the door, Simon!" he said. He got to his feet, fumbling for his crutches. At once Micah leaped forward and handed them to him.

"Here, sir, let me help you!"

"Thank you, young man!" Franklin made his way painfully to the door, and the two men followed him. Two men carrying a sedan chair were there to meet him, and Franklin, groaning, got into the chair and said, "I'll be a little bit slower than you, Sam. You tell them I'll be there!" He turned his eyes and said, "You'll be around, will you not, Mr. Bradford? I'd like to talk some more to you about this factory your father's going to start."

"Yes, sir, I can stay as long as you please."

Sam Adams took Micah's arm. "If I remember right, you're quite a scholar! I need a scribe for the next few days. Could I press you into my service?"

"I'd be happy to serve any way I could, Mr. Adams."

"Come along!" Adams said impatiently, and he practically hauled Micah along the streets, headed for Independence Hall.

☫   ☫   ☫

Micah Bradford never forgot those first days in Philadelphia, when a new nation was birthed. Every day Franklin was carried in a sedan chair to the State House by two paroled convicts, and was helped inside by Micah, who had an opportunity to see the new government in action. He noticed that there was an irresolute air about this Second Continental Congress. It approved what was called the Olive Branch Petition, which appealed directly to George III against Parliament. It was an effort at peace but was doomed from the start. The king refused to receive the petition and instead called on Parliament to put a "speedy end to these disorders by the most decisive exertions." The news that England had hired German mercenaries to quell the rebellion stunned even the moderates, and they realized that they were engaged in more than a family feud. "Nothing is left now but to fight it out," said Joseph Hewes of North Carolina.

An effort began to set forth the position of the Colonies in a formal document. The committee to draft a declaration was formed, and Thomas Jefferson was chosen to do the actual writing. Micah was standing close beside the small group, along with Sam Adams. Jefferson, a tall, red-headed man, looked at John Adams and said, "You really ought to do the drafting, Mr. Adams!"

"Oh no!" said Adams.

"Why will you not? You ought to do it."

"I will not!"

"Why, sir?"

"First, you are a Virginian, and a Virginian ought to appear at the head of this business. Second, I am obnoxious, suspected, and unpopular. You are very much otherwise. And finally my third reason; you can write ten times better than I can."

Thomas Jefferson was perhaps the most remarkable man of that congress. He was indeed a fine writer, although a poor orator. He had a high voice and stammered considerably. Nevertheless, he was the right choice to draft the declaration. His document was based on George Mason's famous Virginia Bill of Rights, which, in turn, relied almost entirely on John Locke. When Jefferson submitted his draft to Adams and Franklin for their criticisms and suggestions, forty-eight changes were made. Adams was deeply impressed by the language of the declaration. Franklin proposed the most changes.

Micah was rather amused at the witty explanation that Franklin gave Jefferson, who was somewhat chastened over so many alterations.

"I remind you of a hatter," Franklin said, his eyes twinkling, "who was about to open his shop. He made a sign that read, 'John Thompson, Hatter, makes and sells hats for ready money,' but his friends declared 'hatter' superfluous because there was a picture of a hat on the sign. 'Makes' was not necessary, because the buyer should care less who made them. He also didn't need 'ready money' obviously because no one bought hats on credit." Franklin's lips turned upward in a smile. "Only, 'John Thompson sells hats' was left, and these words also vanished after it was argued that 'sells' was redundant because no one gives hats away, and 'hats' was not needed because of the picture. So, nothing was left but the name. So you see, my dear Mr. Jefferson, my changes are not quite so radical as these."

Mr. Jefferson took the changes in good grace, and the Declaration of Independence was complete. Jefferson read it aloud in his high-pitched voice. "We hold these truths to be self-evident, that all men are created equal, that they are endowed by their Creator with certain inalienable rights, that among these are life, liberty and the pursuit of happiness."

Micah heard them read and thrilled to them, despite his own uncertainties about revolution. "By George," Micah Bradford murmured. "That says it complete! What I've always thought life should be like— life, liberty, and the pursuit of happiness." He found himself stirred by the Congress and by the great men he watched and heard speak in great ringing words, and he found himself more and more in sympathy with what these men were trying to do.

T   T   T

On July 1, 1776, John Adams arose, confident that the vote on declaring the Colonies free and independent would pass unanimously. But a canvas showed that there were still only nine colonies in which a majority of the delegate supported the measure. Maryland had swung toward it, but South Carolina had defected under pressure from Edward Rutledge. While Delaware was evenly divided, Caesar Rodney, known to be a friend of independence, was home at the bedside of his ailing wife.

Standing close beside Sam Adams, Micah heard Adams say to Franklin, "We've got to get Rodney here! He can swing Delaware, and without Delaware we're lost! I'll send someone after him if you think best."

"Do so at once!" Franklin exclaimed.

That night a courier rode ninety miles to Rodney's home with a plea for him to return to Philadelphia the next day to cast his crucial vote. New York, its delegates still claiming their instructions were to oppose independence, abstained from voting. Pennsylvania, no longer similarly bound, nevertheless, was in opposition by a vote of four to three. The Quaker ruling class was responsible for this.

But Richard Henry Lee of Virginia persuaded Rutledge to drop his opposition if both Delaware and Pennsylvania voted approval. Next, a deal was made, which was typical of Adams. John Dixon and Robert Morris were persuaded not to take their seats officially the next day. Pennsylvania would thus be in the affirmative three votes to two.

On July 2, Congress convened again. Franklin was there, his gout-swollen foot propped up on a stool. Jefferson was pacing the floor, his face drawn with the strain. John Adams and others could hardly bear the tension. Rain lashed the windows, and all hope seemed to be gone, then finally a cry came out, "He's come! There's Rodney!"

Almost every delegate except Franklin came to his feet as Caesar Rodney entered the hall, spattered with mud and soaked to the skin.

He had a cancer sore on his small, round face that was hardly bigger than a large grapefruit, and he was livid from his hard ride.

"We can do it!" Franklin whispered. "Now we can do it!"

Rodney's arrival put Delaware into the affirmative column. Afterward Pennsylvania followed suit, and South Carolina came back aboard. Although New York still abstained, the Colonies' assembly notified Congress on July 19 that it now favored independence unanimously.

On July 4, all the delegates to Congress—except John Dickinson—approved the Declaration of Independence. John Hancock, as president of the Congress, signed first with a great bold flourish that was to make his name synonymous with the flamboyant signature. He declared loudly, "There, I guess King George will be able to read that!" One by one the others all signed. Radicals, moderates, and conservatives all united in their determination to form a free and sovereign new nation.

Micah was standing beside Sam Adams, and he saw tears running down the older man's face. Adams had fought for this for years, and now he whispered, "Under God we will have a new nation. . . !"

11

BETRAYED?

AND SO THE COLONIES had a Declaration of Independence—but paper declarations do not win wars—armies accomplish that. Though the Second Continental Congress had proudly declared their independence, the entire revolution was in a state of flux.

George Washington, listening to very bad advice, had sent Benedict Arnold with a small, makeshift army to capture Quebec. The quixotic notion that Canada could be easily conquered, the leaders found hard to shake off. The fortress city of Quebec had cast its shadow on a generation of American colonists, and it seemed plausible that they might seize it and add it to their own territory.

On the last day of the year 1775, Arnold and his ragtag army fought their way through bitter winter weather and, in a raging blizzard, launched surprise attacks on the city, but Montgomery, the commander of the French forces in Quebec, was killed and Arnold wounded. A counterattack on the leaderless American forces turned the tide. Throughout the bitter winter Arnold clung to his lines around the city, but spring brought heavy reinforcements of British troops and ended all American hope for a great northern victory.

At the same time that American survivors of this foiled invasion were trickling back to Fort Ticonderoga, the British admiralty dispatched an expedition against the southern colonies. Sir Peter Parker led an impressive force of ten fighting ships, plus transports, for Sir Henry Clinton's twenty-five hundred troops. Parker and Clinton decided to attack Charleston, the South's leading port. Guarding the channel into that harbor was a log-and-earth fort on Sullivan's Island commanded by Colonel William Moultrie. On June 28, 1776, the great ships closed in and unleashed a furious cannonade. The fort, however, made of palmetto logs and sandy earthworks, simply absorbed the shots and shell. The fire from Moultrie's guns gave Parker's fleet a fearful pounding. That night, after suffering a painful wound, Sir Peter Parker withdrew, and a great American defensive victory gained two years of peace for the South.

Thus the score was one to one, a victory apiece for the British and their American cousins. Now, like a game of chess, the moves would begin, and the game seemed uneven. On one hand was England, the empire, the most powerful nation on the face of the earth with the mightiest navy and the largest army; on the other hand stood a group of disunited colonies divided by politics, religion, and sometimes enormous distances, with no standing army and no navy at all.

The British political scene at this time seemed to balance out any disadvantages the Colonies faced. George III was not only hated by everyone in the revolution, but his popularity even among his family and subjects waned. George III was not born in the happiest of homes. Queen Caroline, the wife of George II, said of her son, "My firstborn is the greatest liar and the greatest beast in the whole world, and I wish, I most heartily wish, he was out of it!" Her greatest solace on her deathbed was, "I shall never see that monster again!"

On October 25, 1760, George II died, and young George became King of England. A queen was found for him at once, a young German lady named Charlotte. They settled into a happy domesticity, and George started trying to act like a king. He loved nothing better than mingling with his subjects as "Farmer George." He believed, absolutely, in the divine right of kings—which was unfortunate, for that particular doctrine was on the verge of going out of favor. By the time the war with the Colonies came, he had surrounded himself with a group of close friends whose advice and influence would sink all the empire's efforts to conquer the Colonies.

The prime minister throughout the revolution was Lord North, a fat, amiable man who hated trouble. While he was at Oxford his tutor told him, "You are a blundering blockhead, and if you were set in the office of prime minister, you would be exactly the same!" North admitted later, "It turned out to be so!"

The actual conduct of the war was primarily in the hands of George Germain. He had been born Lord George Sackville and was a proud and arrogant man who had once been sentenced to death by a court-martial for cowardice. By contrast with Lord North, who was liked by even his political enemies, Lord George was disliked even by his political friends.

The leadership of the army was weak, but the condition of the most powerful navy in the world suffered also. Commanding the British naval forces, Lord Sandwich, first Lord of the Admiralty, was a bit of a rake—a tall, shambling, weather-beaten man who looked as if he had been hanged and cut down by mistake. Seeing him walking afar off, an acquaintance said, "I am sure it is Lord Sandwich for, if you will observe, he is walking down both sides of the street at once." Sandwich was fairly capable, at times, but the British fleet had been badly neglected since the end of the Seven Years War.

Opposing the British forces was George I—George Washington of America. The burden of independence fell upon his shoulders, and this tall, quiet man came into his position as commander in chief with many good qualities and a few bad ones. He was incapable of fear, everyone reported, and he did not always fight wisely, but always bravely. He had experience on the frontier, and by the time the revolution exploded he had married a widow, Martha Dandridge Custis. He was one of the wealthiest men in the Colonies, and his chief interest was his plantation at Mount Vernon. On leaving for the First Continental Congress he had made his gesture. He was a gambler by vocation and knew the odds of war, and he made the decision to risk everything he owned on the Continental Army, such as it was. Although the Declaration of Independence was signed, the British had dispatched the mightiest expeditionary force in history toward the Colonies. Sir Peter Parker brought his beaten men back from Charleston, and General Howe awaited the sign to move toward New York. There was tension in the air of the English-speaking peoples, and no one knew what to think of the situation—of the sudden longing for freedom and independence that had exploded in the thirteen colonies of America.

🛡   🛡   🛡

While the British prepared to strike against New York, and George Washington's untrained forces prepared to receive them, Katherine Yancy tended to her father and uncle in Halifax. True enough, she was conscious of the great movements that were stirring. The warships at the harbor were constantly being supplied with stores from the mainland, and James Steerbraugh hinted several times that he would soon be leaving with the fleet.

Katherine had become very fond of the tall, young lieutenant. He had been helpful since Clive had left, but Katherine missed Clive. She was somewhat shocked at how much, indeed, she missed him. She did find time to go, more than once, to the Gordon home, but her uncle grew steadily worse, and she spent much time searching for good food that might help him regain his health.

On July 6 she received a distinct shock. She had gone around the small shops, gathered some fresh vegetables, what little fruit was to be had, and made her way to the prison, which actually was an old ware-house. There were no windows in the sides, and light filtered through only the front and the back where two panes each had been cut into the ends.

The entrances were guarded by red-coated marines who had learned to know Katherine. One of them greeted her as she approached that morning. "Good morning, Miss Yancy!" He hesitated, then said, "I'm sorry, I have bad tidings for you."

At once Katherine thought of her uncle. "Is it my uncle Noah? Is he taken bad?"

The marine shifted nervously and did not meet her eyes. "I couldn't say, miss. You see, your father and your uncle were taken back to the *St. George* just early this morning."

Katherine stared at the marine without comprehension. "Back to the hulks! But why?"

"I don't know, miss."

"Who ordered it?" Katherine demanded.

"I have no idea, miss. You'll have to ask the officers."

Katherine went at once to the headquarters, where she learned that James Steerbraugh was gone for two days. She asked to see General Howe, and was told that he could not see her at the present. She waited all day at the headquarters, and finally when the sun was almost set, the sergeant came out and said, "General Howe will see you now, Miss Yancy."

Katherine entered the general's office and demanded directly, "General Howe, why have my father and uncle been moved back to the ship?"

Howe looked at her with some surprise. He had been in meetings for the past several days, and his mind was completely taken up with the hundreds of decisions that had to be made before the fleet left Hal-ifax. "Why, I'm certain I don't know, Miss Yancy! I hadn't heard of such a thing! There must be a good reason for it, though."

"My uncle is in very poor health!" Katherine said. "I beg you, General. Let them be returned to the prison!"

General Howe ordinarily was a kindhearted man, but he was tense, for he had received orders from London that seemed to him impossible to carry out. His nerves were on edge, and he said sharply, "I'm sorry, Miss Yancy, but I cannot undertake to fulfill your request. It's possible that all the prisoners have been returned to the ship because the fleet will be sailing soon and they must, of course, go back with us."

"But you may not leave for days or even weeks!"

"I cannot discuss this matter with a civilian! Excuse me, I'm pressed for time!" Howe swept by the young lady. He felt sorry for her, but this was one minute detail that he felt his officers could better handle, and he fought down an irritation at this interruption.

Katherine felt helpless as the general left. She knew that there was only one thing possible, and she steeled herself to do it. *I'll have to go see Banks*, she thought. *And I'd rather die!* She made her way to the prison again and asked the same marine who had informed her of the change, "Could I see Major Banks?"

"I'll see, Miss Yancy." The marine left and soon returned to nod at her, saying, "Yes, you may go right in. You know where his office is, I believe?"

"Thank you, Sergeant."

As soon as she entered Banks' office, she had harsh memories of her last visit here when he had put his hands on her. Banks was sitting at his desk and looked up with what seemed to be surprise.

"Well, Miss Yancy, we meet again!"

"Major Banks, why have my father and my uncle been moved back to the *St. George*?"

"Why, I only heard about it myself this morning."

"Were they moved there by your order?"

"Oh, dear, no!" Banks got up and approached Katherine. He seemed to be relatively sober and said, "It was none of my doing, I assure you!"

"But you're in charge of the prisoners!"

"I have been forced to accept the assistance of Mr. Gordon. I think you know that!" There was a bitterness around his tiny, pursed lips and he said, "It was his father, the colonel—and he has interfered in my department—not for the better, I'm afraid. Your 'friend' Clive has asked Colonel Gordon to speak to General Howe, and he did, I'm sorry to say."

Katherine could not understand what the officer was saying. "What does that have to do with my father and my uncle?"

"Why, they were moved back to the hulks by Mr. Clive Gordon's request—his order was in his father's name, but it was his doing."

"I don't believe it!" Katherine spoke before she thought. "He wouldn't do that!"

"No? I assure you he did. Look—" Banks turned, walked back to his desk, opened the drawer, and pulled out a piece of paper. "Here is the order! It was here when I arrived this morning."

He handed the paper to Katherine, who quickly read it. "Have the prisoners, Amos and Noah Yancy, removed from the base prison back to the *St. George*." It was signed, "Clive Gordon."

Katherine stared at the sheet of paper, then lifted her eyes. "I can't understand this!"

Banks reached out for the paper, saying, "I must have that for my records!" Taking it, he put it back in the drawer, then turned to face her. "I'm afraid you don't know the young man's reputation! It's not very good where women are concerned. I think he was toying with you!"

Katherine found this completely unbelievable. She stared at the major and said, "Why do you say that?"

"Why, it's a matter of common record! He's been known to chase women before."

Katherine's head was swimming. She could not believe what was happening. "You could reverse his order, couldn't you?"

"No, oh, dear me, no! You saw what happened when I crossed Mr. Gordon. He threatened me with a duel. He's a hotheaded chap as well as a womanizer, and if I did this I would be crossing the colonel, his father."

Katherine stood there, her mind numb. She tried to think of something to say, but nothing came. Finally she said, "Major, could I have your permission to visit my father on the *St. George*?"

"Why, as I've always said, Miss Yancy, I want to be helpful! I'll give you a pass, of course, then later we can meet to discuss some better arrangements."

It sounded like something all too familiar to Katherine, but she accepted the pass that the surgeon scribbled out. As he handed it to her, he patted her shoulder and said, "Don't feel too downhearted! Many young women have been deceived by handsome young men before. You go along and see your father, and I'll speak with you later to see if . . . if the visits can be continued."

Katherine left the prison feeling like a trapped animal. She could not understand why Clive Gordon would do such a thing. She made her way at once to the docks, where she obtained a passage to the *St. George* with one of the fishermen.

When Lieutenant Smith saw the pass, he said, "I'm sorry to see them come back. They had to carry the old gentleman aboard. He was unable to walk."

Katherine allowed herself to be escorted to the cabin that had become familiar to her on her previous visits. She clasped her hands tightly together, trying to make sense out of it. When her father came in, she saw at once that he was troubled. "Father!" she said, going to him and putting her arms around him. He looked tired and worried. "Why has all this happened?"

"We weren't told anything, Katherine!" Amos Yancy said. The two sat down in the hard chairs while they spoke. "I'm worried about Noah! He's worse. I don't think he can stand life down in the hole."

"Why did he do it?" Katherine burst out.

"Who?" her father asked in bewilderment.

"Clive Gordon! The surgeon tells me it was by his orders that you were brought back!"

Amos Yancy was too tired to think straight. He was worn down by the long imprisonment, and now worry for his brother clouded his mind. "I don't know, my dear. We must simply trust God."

The two visited for a while and finally Katherine rose and said, "I'll try to get you moved back, but General Howe won't listen to me, and I don't think Major Banks will either. I'll do the best I can for you, though."

"I'm sure of that, daughter."

Katherine left the *St. George*, and as soon as she stepped ashore she stood there uncertainly. There was nothing really she could do, and for a long time she walked along the rocky shore seeking desperately to find some way to help her father and her uncle.

The sky was gray that day, and a storm was blowing up far out at sea. She saw dark clouds rolling along majestically, but with a menace in them. The gulls followed her, crying harshly as they swooped nearby looking for scraps. She ignored them and tried to pray, but she was not very successful. God seemed to be locked away somewhere from her. The heavens were brass, and her pitiful attempts to call on God seemed to be vain words, even to her.

Finally she turned homeward and thought about Clive. "I was wrong once before about a man," she said, thinking of Malcolm, her former fiancé. "I put my trust in him and he failed me. Now, here's another one I shouldn't have trusted." She was not thinking too clearly, for bitterness welled up inside her toward Clive. She made her way back to the inn, but it was dark and she went to bed at once.

For two days she went back and forth to the ship, each time receiving worse news from her father about his brother.

On the third day she had just risen and gone downstairs when she saw the tall form of James Steerbraugh. He caught her eye and came to her quickly. Removing his hat, he asked, "May I see you, Miss Yancy?"

Fear rose in Katherine and she said quietly, "Yes." They took a seat at one of the tables. There were no customers there, and even the innkeeper had stepped into the back room.

"I have bad news for you, I'm afraid." The fine eyes of Steerbraugh were filled with compassion, and he said, "It's your uncle. He passed away last night. I just got word and I came right here."

Katherine was flooded with memories from her childhood. "I remember riding on his shoulders," she said quietly. "He loved children, and he spoiled me hopelessly. He was such a good man, and to die like a dog in the bottom of that foul ship. . . !"

Steerbraugh could say nothing to this. He asked, "Would you like to go to your father?"

"Yes, I would!"

The two made their way to the ship, where Katherine was soon speaking with her father. Amos seemed almost calm. It was as if a burden was lifted. He said once while they were talking quietly, "He was so ready to go, Katherine. Almost the last thing he said to me was, 'I'll be seeing my Lord Jesus soon. I'll tell Him you'll be along one day.' " He looked at Katherine and nodded. "It's a good thing, daughter. There was no hope for him really."

"I know. It's just—" Tears came to her eyes and she dashed them away. "It's just that I'll miss him so!"

"Aye, so will I." He looked at her carefully, then said, "Now, listen to me, daughter. There is something you must do. You must take Noah home for burial."

"No, I must stay with you!"

"You can do nothing for me, but you owe this to Noah! I would do it if I could, but since I can't it's up to you."

They talked for some time, and slowly Katherine began to see that this was the way it would have to be. "All right, Father," she said. "I'll make the arrangements."

♯   ♯   ♯

The arrangements were difficult, and if it had not been for James Steerbraugh, Katherine would have been helpless. She found him a friend, indeed, and he took care of all the details. He came to her at the end of the second day and said, "Miss Yancy, I've taken care of everything. The ship will be leaving tomorrow. It will stop at Boston. Your uncle's body has been embalmed and placed in a casket."

"I'll pay you, of course, all the expenses!"

"Don't speak of that! I'm glad to help. I'm just sorry it's come to this."

"You've been so kind, not like—"

When she broke off, Steerbraugh blinked with surprise. "I'm not like who?"

"Not like your friend Clive Gordon." Steerbraugh tried to speak, but she said, "No, I don't want to talk about it!" She put her hand out, and he took it at once. She squeezed it, saying, "Thank you so much for your many kindnesses! I'll be on the ship tomorrow. I don't know if we'll meet again, but I'll never forget you, Lieutenant."

The next day at noon the freighter, with the unlikely name of *Blue Skies*, pulled out of Halifax headed for Boston. It was loaded with supplies that would be purchased by the patriot cause, but Katherine was not thinking of that. She was thinking, as she stood in the bow watching the gray water part and the white bubbles that clung to the sides of the old freighter, *I wish father were with me!*

She thought then of her uncle down below and of the loss she had suffered. Finally she thought of Clive Gordon, and her lips tightened. *I'll never trust another man as long as I live!* she thought with more bitterness than she'd ever known. She knew that was wrong, for she had seen the courtesy of James Steerbraugh, but she was not herself. Betrayal twice in a row had been too much for her, and she stood there holding the rail until her knuckles grew tight, thinking of how she had given her trust and admiration to a man who had turned against her.

12

"HE'S A MAN, ISN'T HE?"

LEANING BACK IN HIS Windsor chair, Clive Gordon surveyed the Bradfords that had gathered at the breakfast table and felt a glow of satisfaction. Daniel, of course, sat at the head of the table with Micah on his right hand, directly across from Clive. These two, naturally, were strong and healthy, but it was the other three Bradfords who brought a special pleasure to the young physician. Sam was shoveling pancakes down his throat so fast that there was some danger of choking, but he washed them down with huge drafts of milk. Beside him, Rachel, her cheeks having regained their glow of health, was eating eggs and ham with obvious relish. Across from her sat Jeanne, wearing a very attractive green dressing robe. She was faring well with a large bowl of mush over which she had poured a liberal dose of molasses.

"Well, I wish all my patients would recover as well as you three!" Clive said after taking a sip of the strong coffee in his mug. "That's what a doctor likes to see."

"That's what I like to see, too!" Daniel said. His face was tanned and he held a piece of pancake speared on the end of his fork. Pausing before he put it into his mouth, he looked fondly around the table and said, "You've done a fine job, Dr. Gordon! I'm going to recommend you to all my friends."

"They won't be able to afford him!" Micah grinned. He looked across the table at Clive and said, "The first thing a successful doctor does is raise his fee so that he doesn't have to fool with common folk like us, just the aristocracy!"

A laugh went around the table, and Clive took it good-naturedly. He had become very fond of these American relatives of his and was look-

141

ing forward to seeing his own family so that he could tell them about how well he had fared with them.

It was a pleasant breakfast, with light streaming in from the window to the left of the room and through the Dutch door with the top swung open. The smell of the new earth that had been broken up for a garden floated in from the outside, and it was cool and pleasant in the cheerful kitchen where they had gathered around the circular table for their morning meal. Finally Micah began to speak of the meeting in Philadelphia. He held them spellbound, tossing around names such as Thomas Jefferson, John Adams, John Hancock, and, of course, Benjamin Franklin.

Finally Sam interrupted to say, "I should've gone with you! I would have if I hadn't been sick! Dr. Franklin's an inventor like me!"

Micah grinned broadly. "Well, at least his stoves don't blow up like some of your inventions do!" Then when he saw irritation cloud his young brother's brow he said quickly, "You know I was just teasing! You and Dr. Franklin would get along very well, I think. He's a tinkerer if there ever was one—just like you!"

Mollified, at least momentarily, Sam speared the last morsel of pancake with his fork. He shoved it into his mouth, and Rachel said, "Sam, don't take such big bites! You never taste anything! You're like a snake. You gobble things down as if someone's going to take it away from you."

Sam paid his sister no heed whatsoever. "What does it mean, Micah, the Declaration of Independence?"

Micah's brow furrowed, and his mild hazel eyes grew thoughtful. He ran his strong hand through his straw-colored hair and, as was customary, thought for a moment before he spoke in a gentle drawl. "I suppose, Sam," he said finally, with regret tingeing his tone, "it means that we'll fight a war to separate ourselves from England."

Sam picked up the glass of cider, drained it off, and set it down firmly before looking at Clive. "What does that mean to you, Clive? Does it make you mad like it does old King George?"

"Sam, don't be impudent!" Daniel said sharply.

But Sam shook his head and shrugged. "Well, Clive's an Englishman, isn't he?"

Daniel Bradford said firmly, "So am I, Sam, and you heard what I said. We'll have no more discussion of this!"

Clive at once spoke up. "I suppose we'll have to discuss it; everybody else is in the Colonies—and at home in England, too." He looked at Sam and said, "Frankly, Sam, I think England is making a terrible mistake!"

"You do?" Sam's eyebrows lifted. "Well, why don't you do something about it?"

Clive laughed abruptly. "You mean I should go home and walk into the palace and grab King George III by the scruff and tell him, 'Now look, George, you have to stop that foolishness over in the Colonies, you hear? It's got to stop!'"

Laughter went around the table and Jeanne said, "But surely there's somebody over there to tell the king what an awful mistake he's making!"

"I'm afraid not! All his advisors are fools except for William Pitt, and George won't listen to him." Clive thought about the morass of English politics and said, "It's so simple when you think of it. North America, this country America, is the most valuable possession England has, and because she wants to collect a few pounds in taxes she's throwing it all away. Why, if she would be reasonable and accept America as Americans on equal terms, a kingdom could be forged that would keep Europe in peace for generations. France or Spain wouldn't dare attack if America and England united. America with all her resources, and England, with her powerful armies, would be an unbeatable combination."

Daniel listened carefully as the young man spoke. Finally he said with sadness marking his voice, "I'm afraid you're right, Clive. England's too bullheaded to listen, and it's going to be a long hard war. I wish your father were somewhere else, in India perhaps."

"So does he, Uncle Daniel!" Clive shrugged. "But a soldier goes where he's ordered, you know that."

"Yes, I know that. Still, it's a tragedy, and I shudder to think about Dake being in a battle with his blood kin on the other side. It's hard on your family, I know."

Rachel saw that the conversation had taken a turn that saddened Clive and her father, so she changed the subject abruptly. "I've been thinking about the Yancy family you spoke of. The young woman whose relatives you helped." She looked at her father and said, "Do we know them, Pa?"

"Yes, we do. Didn't you see Katherine at the wedding?"

"I don't know. If I did, I don't remember ever seeing her. Have I met the Yancys before?"

"Yes, we all met them when George Whitefield had the meeting here, remember? Everybody came, and we ate once at a tavern with several families who were attending the meeting, including the Yancys. You were very young then, and Sam there was no more than a baby, still crawling around." Daniel laughed at Sam's reaction and said,

"They were Congregationalists, I think."

"That's right!" Clive said with interest. "Katherine mentioned that. You do remember them?"

"Now I do! You had some talk with her father, didn't you, Pa? You were talking about the sermon and how Whitefield was different from any minister we had ever heard."

"Yes. I really enjoyed talking to Amos Yancy," Daniel said. "He was a tall, well-set fellow with brown eyes and curly brown hair. And his wife's name was Susan."

"That's right!" Clive said, excitement touching his eyes. "Well, this is interesting! I'll have to tell them when I get back to Halifax."

"I remember Katherine, now," Rachel continued. "She was about my age, I think. We sat together at the inn and talked about boys, if I remember. Both of us were just learning they were different from girls." She grinned roguishly at her father, who winked at her. "She was a pretty girl. I was envious of her! She still is I take it, cousin Clive?"

Clive was embarrassed and said merely, "You don't have to be envious, Rachel. You're every bit as attractive as Katherine!"

The breakfast ended, but later that morning Clive came upon Jeanne in the garden. She was sitting on a wooden bench that Sam had built, and Clive asked, "May I join you, Jeanne?"

"Of course, here, sit down!" She had changed clothes and was wearing a sky blue dress, and she wore no bonnet on her head. Her short, black, curly hair that Clive had always admired formed ringlets that framed her face, and her large violet eyes, as always, attracted him. "I don't know some of these flowers. I know these—they're primroses. And we call these four-o'clocks."

Clive picked one of the small blossoms—long tubes with a fragrant smell. "Why do you call them that?"

"Oh, because they open about four o'clock and don't close until the next morning." She named several more flowers, then Clive mentioned the ones that grew in England that he liked particularly.

A brown thrasher alighted in a hedge, twitching his tail and staring at them with bright eyes. They laughed at his antics and finally began talking about their experiences in the past. Clive began, for he had been somewhat troubled about his romance with Jeanne. Finally he said, "I suppose, Jeanne—what I'm saying is I made a fool out of myself over you! I can see now that Dake's the husband you need, although you'd be a prize for me or any other man."

Jeanne listened to him quietly, then hesitated only for a moment. "I think you're very interested in Katherine Yancy, aren't you, Clive?"

"What makes you think that?" Clive demanded rather defensively.

He picked up a stick and tossed it at the brown thrasher, which flew off ten feet, then came back arguing vociferously at the interruption. "I find her attractive, of course; she's a very pretty young woman."

"I think it's more than that!"

Clive shifted uncomfortably in the seat. She had touched on a sore spot with him, and finally he turned to her and said in a half-ashamed tone, "I guess I must be a faithless man, Jeanne. You're right, I am attracted to Katherine. Here a short time ago I was in love with you—or thought I was, and now I think I'm in love with her. I must be a womanizer!"

Jeanne reached over and put her hand on Clive's. Squeezing it she said, "You're not a womanizer, far from it! You're a gentleman in every sense of the word."

"Then, why don't I know when I'm in love?"

"I think it's hard to know love, Clive!" Jeanne tried to frame her thoughts. She was not an eloquent young woman, but things were very simple to her. She loved her husband, Dake. She loved the out-of-doors, and she loved God. Now, trying to explain the complexities between men and women was suddenly difficult for her. Finally she said, "I think part of the love between a man and a woman has to be—well, *admiration*. I always had such an admiration for you."

Clive looked at her with astonishment. "Well, that's what I felt for you, Jeanne! I think I admired you more than any woman I'd ever seen. You were so strong and handled hard things so well. That was what always impressed me about you."

"I think this is what attracts you to Katherine Yancy, isn't it? You said so before."

"Why . . . I believe that's right! She *is* a strong woman. Not many could have done what she's done." He began to talk enthusiastically about Katherine's struggle to help her father and her uncle. Finally he said, "It's hard for me to tell. She's very attractive, and a man is drawn to that. Good looks aren't everything, but they certainly don't hurt. It's what she is that has drawn me to her, I think. Is that love, do you think, Jeanne?"

"I think it can be part of it. Are you going to see her again?"

"Yes, I'm going back to Halifax right away, probably the day after tomorrow. There's a ship leaving then. I'm concerned about her father and uncle. Neither of them is in good condition." He rose and said, "It will be hard to leave here. You and the Bradfords have made me feel like part of the family."

Jeanne rose and said, "You are part of the family, Clive." Looking up at him she smiled and said, "I'm glad we've had this talk. I think it might have helped clear up something in your mind."

He leaned down suddenly and kissed her on the cheek, a brotherly kiss. "Yes it did! I feel much better now, *cousin* Jeanne. You are a discerning young woman."

The two men who walked along the streets of Boston, headed for the foundry operated by Daniel Bradford and John Frazier, could be mistaken for nothing else but clergymen. Both wore the customary suits of solemn black, broken by the whiteness of the stocks at their throat, and both had a serious look on their faces. Asa Carrington, at fifty, was the older of the two. He had black hair and eyes, was no more than medium height, but was strongly built. He moved quickly, purposefully, this pastor of the Methodist Church of Boston, and when he spoke his voice was deep and full. "You'll like Boston, and your new church is a fine one! I'm glad you've come, Devaney."

Reverend William Devaney, six inches taller than his Methodist friend, was the new pastor of the Congregational Church in Boston. He was a tall man, angular, no more than thirty years old, and there was an innate dignity in him. He had dark blue eyes, dark blond hair, and rather craggy features. "It will be quite different from the small village where I've been pastor for the past four years," he said. He looked at his new friend and said, "It's kind of you to introduce me around, Asa."

The two men had become close friends, and it had been helpful indeed for Devaney to get an introduction to the city of Boston. The Methodist pastor knew everyone, and Devaney had already met the mayor of the city council, and now he said, "I understand the Fraziers are staunch members of my church, although I've not met them yet."

"Well, John Frazier is an invalid. He has only the one daughter as I mentioned, Lady Marian Rochester, married to Leo Rochester."

"What sort of people are they?"

Asa Carrington hesitated, but only for a moment. "You'll find Marian Rochester to be an outstanding member of your church."

Noting the omission of the husband, Reverend Devaney looked at his companion. "And her husband?"

"Well . . . Sir Leo is not a church man. I tell you no more than is common knowledge. He's not a man that is admired. Oh, he's rich, of course, but has a bad reputation for gaming, gambling and—well, other things."

Devaney was an astute young minister and knew that "other things" probably meant consorting with women; however, he did not press the issue. He stored the facts in his mind and said, "Is that the foundry ahead?"

"Yes, it's owned jointly by John Frazier and by one of the members of my own church, Daniel Bradford." He hesitated again and said, "William, I hate to plunge you into wheels within wheels, but the situation is—well, *complicated*."

"Complicated how?"

"There are rumors around that Daniel, who came to this country as an indentured servant for Sir Leo and has worked his way up to half-owner in this factory . . ." The Methodist preacher hesitated, then said, "I'm not one to bear rumors, but there are some about Marian Rochester and Daniel Bradford."

"That's unfortunate."

"There's nothing to them, I'm convinced!" Carrington said quickly. "You know how rumor mills are; every city has them. I just tell you this because I know you'll hear it, and I want to assure you I'm convinced Daniel Bradford is an honorable man, and Marian Rochester is a woman I cannot presume to praise too much. She's put up with a terrible life from her husband, and now her father is dying. She has to rely on someone, and Frazier's very fond of Daniel, not only as a business partner, but he sees him as a son. Come along, I'll introduce you."

The two ministers entered and found Daniel working at a forge with his son, Micah. After the introductions were made Daniel said, "I'm happy that you've come, Reverend Devaney. It's been hard on the Fraziers not having a pastor, although our own pastor has been good to visit them."

Devaney was favorably impressed with the Bradford men. He spoke carefully to them of the Fraziers, of his having to make adjustments, all the time studying Daniel Bradford's face. What he saw pleased him, for there was a basic and inherent honesty, almost nobility, in Daniel's face. He could not imagine such a man to be involved in anything scandalous with another man's wife.

After a time Devaney said, "I begin my new duties on rather a sad note."

"How is that, Reverend?" Daniel inquired.

"A funeral, I'm afraid."

"Oh, you've had a loss in your church family?" Reverend Carrington asked. "That's not the best way to start, is it? Anyone I know?"

"I don't know them personally, of course. A gentleman named Yancy. I've met the family. The funeral is tomorrow."

"I am acquainted with some Yancys—but they have been in Halifax."

Devaney stared at Bradford. "Well, it must be the same family. This man's name was Noah Yancy. He died in Halifax, and his niece, I understand, who was there, brought the body back."

Daniel quickly questioned the minister, and as soon as they left he said, "I've got to go tell Clive about this, Micah! You can get by without me for a time."

Leaving the foundry he walked quickly home. It was too short a distance to even bother with a horse. He found Clive out in the garden in the backyard, where he was speaking with Rachel and Jeanne. "Clive!" he said, "I've got some news for you! Not very happy news, I'm afraid."

Clive rose at once, asking quickly, "What is it, Uncle Daniel?"

"Was the name of the man you treated in Halifax, Amos Yancy's brother, Noah Yancy?"

"Yes!" Seeing his uncle's face rather troubled, he said, "What is it? What's happened?"

"I'm afraid he died, and Katherine has brought the body home." He quickly told how he had heard the news from the new minister of the Congregational Church.

"I must go at once! This is terrible!" Clive said as soon as Daniel finished.

"Do you know how to get to the Yancy place?"

"No, but I'll find it!"

"I think you should go by the Congregational Church. The minister told me he was going back. In any case, someone can help you under these conditions. Take my horse—the mare!"

"Thank you, Uncle Daniel!"

As Clive left, Daniel said sadly, "Too bad! It bothered Clive; I could see that."

Jeanne said, "He was just talking this morning about going back to see if he could help the two men." She hesitated, then added, "And he was anxious to see Katherine, too."

꽃   꽃   꽃

Katherine had arrived at Boston only two days earlier, and that late at night. The previous day she had spent taking care of the affairs and comforting her mother, who was deeply grieved over the loss of her brother-in-law. Susan had been very attached to Noah, with a deep affection for him, and now it seemed her nerves could not stand the strain.

Katherine had taken over everything, including making the funeral arrangements. She had stayed at the church most of the morning, greeting friends of the family who had come by to offer their condolences, and had finally left at two o'clock in the afternoon. She had found her mother asleep, and she, herself, was weary and drawn. The trip had been hard on her, for it had been a rough crossing and she had been sick for the first part of the voyage, unable to eat. The strain of worrying about her father was always with her, and she went into the kitchen to fix a cup of tea. After fixing the tea, she sat there wearily, her mind clouded with thoughts. She heard a knock at the door, and since the servant had gone to the market, she rose and moved to open the door, assuming that it was another neighbor who had come to offer help.

When she opened the door she stood there absolutely dumbfounded, for it was Clive Gordon who stood there wearing a dark blue suit, his hat in his hands, and his eyes fixed on her.

"Katherine, I just heard about your uncle! I'm so sorry."

Katherine could not think for a moment. She had wondered how she would react if she ever saw Clive Gordon again, and it was worse than she had anticipated. She stared at him coldly, bitter thoughts flashing through her mind, but all she could really remember was that he had failed her. Coldly she said, "Mr. Gordon, I have nothing to say to you!"

Clive stared at her with astonishment. "Why . . . why, Katherine, what do you mean by that?"

Katherine's voice was as cold as polar ice. "You killed my uncle, and you will probably be responsible for the death of my father! I hope I never see you again!" She shut the door abruptly and turned and put her back against it. Her limbs were trembling, as were her hands, and tears of anger sprang to her eyes. She ran out of the hallway, ignoring the knocking on the door and the sound of Clive's voice pleading. She went to her bedroom, fell across the bed, and tried to stifle the sobs that rose in her breast.

🦁   🦁   🦁

Rachel stood outside the small red-brick house, and when the door opened she asked quietly, "Miss Yancy?"

"Yes, I'm Katherine Yancy."

"My name is Rachel Bradford. I believe we met once some years ago!" Rachel saw the doubt in the young woman's eyes and said, "It was at a meeting when George Whitefield came to Boston. Our two families met at the Pigeon Inn. You and I sat together and talked about the meeting. I've never forgotten it, though it was a long time ago."

"Oh, I do remember that! Won't you come in, Miss Bradford."

"Thank you!" Rachel entered the house and was escorted to the parlor, where the two women sat down. "I've come to offer my condolences on your loss, Miss Yancy."

"Thank you, it was kind of you to come—especially on such a brief acquaintance and so long ago."

Rachel had talked to Clive and had been shocked at the utter bewilderment and pain that she had found there. She had listened carefully, but saw that Clive was only confused by Katherine Yancy's behavior. "I thought I'd done the best I could for her, but she acts like I'm a murderer!" he had said. He had been as one stricken, and Rachel had decided to take it upon herself to make a visit. Now as she sat there, she knew she had to be absolutely honest. "I wouldn't have come on such a slight acquaintanceship, but I've come on behalf of a relative of mine."

"A relative, Miss Bradford?"

"Yes, my father's sister is Lyna Lee Gordon, and her son is Clive Gordon." Rachel saw the shock touch the eyes of the young woman and said quickly, "I've been very ill recently, along with my younger brother and my sister-in-law. My father sent for Clive to come and care for us. He stayed with us until we were all well."

Katherine sat there listening in a state resembling shock. She had known that Clive was going to treat his family in Boston, but to see the young woman before her brought everything back clearly.

"I'm afraid I have nothing to say about your cousin!" she said briefly.

"Would you mind if we talked about it? Clive is very distressed!"

"I have nothing to say about Clive Gordon!" Katherine said. She felt a moment's pain at the thought of the loss of her uncle, and somehow she had tied his death inextricably to Clive Gordon. She said, "If he hadn't put my uncle back on that prison ship, my uncle would be alive today!" She did not really know if this were true, for her uncle had been very ill even in the prison inside Halifax. But bitterness had gripped her, and she had linked Clive Gordon and Malcolm Smythe together as men who could not be trusted.

"I can't believe that my cousin would do anything dishonorable!"

Furious anger rose in Katherine and she said bitterly, "He's a *man*, isn't he? And if he's a man he can be unfaithful!" She stood to her feet, saying, "I'm sorry, and I thank you for coming, but I cannot discuss Clive Gordon!"

Rachel saw the hopelessness of remaining and she said, "I offer the sympathy of my family, my father, and my brothers."

"Thank you!"

The words were brief, and Rachel had no choice but to leave.

☖   ☖   ☖

The funeral was well attended, but Katherine was not really aware of the crowd. She did hear some of the sermon by Reverend Devaney. She believed with her head all that he said—that there would be a time when all the righteous would come forth out of the grave, and her uncle would be one of them. But that was dry doctrine to her. All she knew now was bitterness, that he was dead, and that nothing could bring him back.

At the cemetery the body was lowered into the grave, and Katherine stood there listening as the Scriptures were read. She was conscious of the blue sky overhead, the birds reeling about in wide circles, the smell of the fresh earth, and of spring, but it meant nothing to her.

Finally she lifted her eyes and saw Rachel Bradford standing, waiting to speak to her. Forcing herself to be polite she said, "I thank you for coming by. It was kind of you, Miss Bradford."

Rachel said, "I'm sorry for your loss." She hesitated, and then said quietly, "Clive has gone back to his family."

Katherine didn't answer, and finally Rachel moved away.

Later that afternoon, when the grave was filled in, Katherine came back to the cemetery, drawn there by some strange impulse. She stood over the grave, raw and red, a mound that covered one whom she had loved dearly. Bitterness came to her. It was mixed up somehow with a fear for her father. *He may die too!* was the thought that was constantly with her.

She thought of Clive and of all the Scriptures she had heard about forgiveness. She thought about something that Rachel had said during her visit, that bitterness can only destroy. She knew it was wrong, and yet somehow she could not put away the anger and the bitterness within her. She lowered her head and tears ran down her cheeks—yet she could not find a gentleness in her for Clive Gordon—and she knew she never would forgive him.

PART THREE

—

FIGHT FOR LONG ISLAND

August—September 1776

13

Abigail and Matthew

THE WORN OAK DESK was piled high with maps of every sort, and light from the small window threw a pale illumination over the one that had gained dominance on top of the stack. Standing behind the desk, Colonel Henry Knox allowed his large gray eyes to run over the lines that delineated the streets of Manhattan. Knox's left hand was braced against the table as he leaned over it supporting his ponderous bulk. He weighed over two hundred and fifty pounds and swelled the fabric of his pale cream waistcoat. The blue frock coat with the golden epaulets, the wide white collar turned down, was buttoned tightly just under the white ruff of lace at his throat. Knox's other hand was kept on his hip, just under the edge of the frock coat. He had been shot there in a hunting accident and lost several fingers, so he usually kept it half hidden.

Henry Knox was one of those men who loved war even though he was not a soldier—at least not at first. He had been a successful bookseller in Boston, but had delighted in stories of war, and had become an expert in the history and use of artillery. His hobby had become his profession when he had been hastily added to George Washington's staff and sent to Fort Ticonderoga to bring back cannon to Boston. Henry Knox might not have had a military background, but then neither had anyone else in Washington's ragtag army.

Knox's quick eyes ran to and fro outlining the problem before him with a keen, analytical mind. He studied the shape of Manhattan Island, and a sense of foreboding rose in him. "It's nothing but an island!" he said, noting that the boundary of one side constituted the East River, and the other side the Hudson River. Instantly he knew that the mighty warships of King George's navy could not be prevented from sailing up either side and pounding Manhattan with its cannons.

A knock disturbed the colonel, and looking up with some irritation, he barked, "Come in!"

When the door opened and a young man entered, however, a pleased smile turned the corners of Knox's lips upward, and he at once moved around the desk with a great deal of grace, which some heavyset men possess. "Micah—" he beamed. "Come in!" He extended his hand, shook Micah Bradford's hand, pumping it enthusiastically. "I just received your letter yesterday! You made good time! Here, sit down. There's some of this cider left. Let me pour us a drink. We'll toast your new service in the Continental Army!"

Micah Bradford was very glad to see Henry Knox. The two had been good friends for a long time. Micah was the reader of the Bradford family and had haunted Knox's bookstore since adolescence. The huge bookseller had taken to the young man, and the two had spent many happy hours together talking of books and poring over the latest volume of poetry or history.

"It's good to see you, Colonel Knox! My father sends his best wishes!"

"Ah, yes, and how's the musket factory coming along? I'm very interested in that—but I'd be more interested if he would begin to manufacture cannon!" Knox bustled around pouring the clear cider into two pewter mugs, then motioning for Micah to take one, he took the other. He held his glass out, which Micah touched with his own, and beamed. "To a happy military career for my young bookworm!"

Micah took a long drink, then shook his head. "Not a very long career. Only ninety days, Colonel."

"Well . . . well, we're grateful for that! Right now we need every man we can get to hold this place."

"You think it's going to be difficult?" Micah asked, setting his mug down.

"I think it's going to be *impossible* if the British send as many ships as I think they will."

"What does General Washington say about this?"

Knox shrugged his burly shoulders. "He's very sensitive to the desires of Congress. He says that Congress wants New York held, and His Excellency is determined to do so if possible."

"What's so difficult about it, Colonel Knox?"

"Why, it's completely indefensible! Come here, I want to show you something." Knox drained the remains of the cider, slammed the mug down, then moved back behind the desk. "Look at this!" he said, pointing a blunt finger at the outlines of New York. "We can be surrounded, cut off, and annihilated. That's what's the matter with it! I wish we could leave and make our stand somewhere else."

For some time the two men spoke of the battle that was to come, until a knock on the door interrupted them. When Knox barked out a command to open it, a young lieutenant came in at once, his eyes glowing with excitement. "Colonel Knox, the British fleet—it's beginning to arrive!"

Knox frowned and shook his head. "I wish they'd given us another month to fortify the city. Come along, Private Bradford, we'll have a look at the lobsterbacks and their ships!"

As the two men made their way down toward the harbor, Micah asked, "How many troops do we have for the defense of the city?"

"Counting every man jack of them, about nineteen thousand."

"Why, that seems like a great many!"

"Not enough, and they're not trained! Almost all of them are infantry—and half of those are militia," Knox scowled. "They're poorly armed, poorly equipped, and poorly trained." He glanced over and said, "Your brother Dake is here, isn't he?"

"Yes, sir! He's signed up for the duration with the regulars, the Continentals."

"Well, they're the best of the troops. If anything will save us, it will be the Continentals."

As the two men moved toward the docks, they noted the soldiers digging furiously, throwing up barricades. Knox stopped twice to give directions to the officers in charge. Finally they reached the dock and stared out over the water. Micah was shocked at the number of sails that covered the gray ocean. He said nothing, and it was Knox who began counting the masts out loud. The count went on for some time, and he finally said, ". . . forty-four, forty-five. I guess that's the lot of them, but there'll be more to come!"

There was a grimness on his round reddish face, and he shook his head. "By the time they all get here we'll have our hands full."

Sir William Howe had arrived with only three ships, but soon forty-five more appeared, and soon after eighty-two more. Howe had brought with him nine thousand three hundred men from Halifax. They landed on Staten Island and set up camp. Soon Sir William Howe's brother, Sir Richard Howe, appeared from England with another hundred and fifty vessels and more troops. Next came Sir Peter Parker with Clinton's expedition to Charleston—fresh from failure, and burning to wipe it out. A month later, Colonel William Hotham arrived with thirty-four more ships, twenty-six hundred elite troops from the Guards Brigade, and eight thousand Germans.

By the time they were all ready, the British forces mustered thirty-two thousand men under arms—horse, foot, and artillery—supported by twelve hundred guns from the warships, and ten thousand sailors. By then, so many transports and lesser vessels had arrived that they whitened the water.

It was the biggest and most expensive expedition that Britain had ever sent overseas. They had spent the staggering sum of eight hundred and fifty thousand pounds to organize and supply it. The Americans were now facing the most powerful armada ever assembled under the British empire!

† † †

Abigail Howland had fallen into a comfortable pattern during her brief stay in New York. After the hardships of the siege she had endured at Boston, her aunt Esther's house seemed to be an island of paradise. She loved the house itself, which was well proportioned and built following the Dutch fashion, one of the narrow ends of the house facing the street. On the warm summer evenings it was the custom for everyone in the neighborhood to sit outside, and even though the drums of war were sounding, there was lively singing and front-door parties that Abigail thought very pleasant.

The house itself had four rooms on the ground floor—a parlor, a dining room, a library, and a kitchen. Above, on the second floor, there were six bedrooms, and over them was an attic used by the servants. There was a cellar for the storage of household supplies, and just outside the kitchen door, a woodshed—a dark, roomy place in which a whole winter's supply of wood for heating and cooking could be kept.

On the roof there was a cupola—a sort of covered balcony that could be reached by the stairs. Already Abigail had found this the most pleasant place to stay in the cool, cobwebby hours of the morning. She had come up now to sit there with her aunt, and the two watched as the street below began to come to life with the morning activity.

"It's so different with all the soldiers here," Esther Denham said quietly, looking down as a troop passed, followed by a caisson and cannon rumbling over the cobblestones. She was wearing a light tan dress cut in a simple fashion, and wore a white bonnet, even indoors, as was customary with her. Her silver hair peeped out from under it, and she turned to smile at her guest. "You came at a very busy time, Abigail," she said quietly. "Ordinarily things aren't quite this busy in New York, but then we didn't have a war going on."

"I suppose I'm used to it, Aunt Esther," Abigail answered. She looked down on the narrow street below and thought about the difficult months she had spent in Boston uncertain of their future. Turning to her relative she smiled. "It's been so good to be here. Mother and I were in a bad condition back in Boston."

"It's been good to have you. I've been lonely these recent years. It's nice to have company again."

Esther Denham was a widow and had only one living daughter who lived in Pennsylvania. She was married to a merchant in Pittsburgh, and Esther had not seen her in over a year. There was a wistfulness in her face as she said, "I miss Aileen and my two grandchildren very much."

"Have you ever thought about going to live with your daughter and her family?"

"No, that wouldn't do! They have their own life, and this is home to me. I've spent almost my whole life here in this house. It would be too hard for me to leave it."

The two women sat there speaking quietly. Below in the kitchen, the servants were getting breakfast ready, but just now there was a quietness in the cupola, and it was pleasant to sit there with no responsibilities, nothing to do. At least it was so for Abigail. She had started coming up early in the morning only a few days earlier, invited by Esther, who had said, "I always begin my day there. Just a quiet time, just me and the Lord."

Abigail had been put off by the reference to God, but she had joined the older woman out of a desire to start the day differently. She had expected to be preached at, but it had not been like that. Esther had simply read one of the psalms and had made a few comments on it, then had bowed her head and prayed a brief prayer. Relieved, Abigail had joined her, and now as she sat there she was thinking how unusual it was for her to join anyone in what amounted to a religious exercise. She did not like church—what she had seen of it—and avoided it whenever possible. It had been necessary to make a show of appearing at the services, for her family had been rather strict about this.

Now Esther opened the Bible on her lap and without comment read a portion of the Psalms. It was the thirteenth psalm and it began, "How long wilt thou forget me, O Lord? Forever? How long wilt thou hide thy face from me?"

The words caught at Abigail, and she listened more carefully than was usual for her. When Esther closed the Bible and Abigail observed, "That's not a very happy chapter, Aunt Esther. It sounds like the psalmist is complaining to God."

"I'm sure that's true. That's one of the things I find attractive in the psalms. David and the others who wrote these songs were very honest. Sometimes they seemed to be downright angry at the Lord—as in this one. You can almost imagine," Esther said with a smile, "David shaking his fist and shouting, 'God, are you going to leave me like this forever? What's wrong with you?'"

The thought intrigued Abigail. "I never thought of that. He doesn't sound like a very holy man."

"David was a man after God's own heart," Esther said quietly. "But he was a man not only of great passions but of unbridled ones sometimes. He wept, he cried, he laughed, he danced, he loved God with all of his heart, though he often failed Him."

"Why did God love David so much?"

"I think because David loved Him so deeply. Secondly, I think because he was a great repenter."

"That's a strange thing to say—a great repenter."

"It's true enough, though. David sinned greatly, but the instant he recognized it he turned from his sin and cried out to God. I think that's something all of us need to learn, don't you?"

Abigail hesitated. She could not well agree with her aunt honestly, for she had never denied herself anything. In all truth, she had never been very sorry for anything she had done. Thinking back quickly she remembered how sorry she was that she had been caught on several occasions—but the thought of being sorry for the sin itself was a novel idea to her. "I suppose so," she said noncommittally, "but it doesn't sound like David was getting along with God."

"No, at this point I think he was not," Esther nodded. She let the silence run on and seemed to be meditating thoughtfully over the words on the page. She ran her fingers over the lines again and said, "That's clear from the second verse: 'How long shall I take counsel in my soul, having sorrow in my heart daily?' Those aren't the words of a happy man!"

"I don't understand it. I thought God's people were supposed to be happy."

"There's a difference I think, Abigail, between happiness and joy."

"Oh? I thought they were the same."

"Not really. Happiness is that good feeling we have when everything is going right—when we're not sick, and when we have plenty of food, a roof over our heads. When things are going very well, then we have this feeling of happiness."

"But what is joy, then, Aunt Esther?"

"I think that's the experience we have in our hearts when things go completely wrong—and still, we are not disturbed in our hearts. It is like happiness—but it is not dependent upon outward circumstances. I think that's how the martyrs could endure the flames; even though God had taken away everything in this world that brings happiness, He had given them the joy of His own presence in their hearts when they faced death."

Abigail listened carefully as her aunt spoke, but it made little sense to her. She finally was glad when her aunt closed the Bible and said, "I think we must pray for all the soldiers who will soon be fighting." She bowed her head and prayed a simple prayer. She ended by saying, "And bless Abigail, Lord. Touch her heart in a very special way and lead her in the way that is right, and I ask this in the name of Jesus. Amen."

Abigail was not at all sure of her feelings concerning this prayer—so personal! Something was stirring within her at the reading of the Bible. She could not explain it, but ever since she had begun reading with her aunt there had been a restlessness in her. More than once she had decided not to come again, but there was something in her aunt's calm assurance that intrigued her. Now she said, "Tell me some more about our family."

"You were so interested in them that I brought you a letter. This is from my mother, Rachel Winslow Howland. It was written to a friend while Rachel was in prison in Salem waiting to be tried for the crime of witchcraft."

"That was all such a long time ago. It's hard to believe in those things anymore."

"It was real enough for them. Gilbert Winslow was there, and he was an old man at that time. Let me read you some of what your grandmother says." She took up the piece of single sheet, handling it carefully, and read:

My dear Emily,

It appears that God may be about to take me out of this world. Five others from the prison were executed yesterday for witchcraft. One of them a very elderly woman, two very young men. The judges are sparing no one, and I am prepared to hear their judgment. I write these words to let you know that my faith has not been shaken. God is here in this dirty, foul prison. It is as though He had lit a lamp in my heart and lighted the dark places. If I go to be with the Lord God tomorrow, I will meet my Beloved. It will be a celebration for me, and I wanted you to know how glorious it is to be able to face death with joy. He has given this joy to me unexpectedly. I always was afraid of death, even the thought of it—but now that it is here, I feel the presence of the Lord Jesus Christ in my heart, and I go to meet Him with victory in my spirit.

Your friend,
Rachel Winslow

After Esther put the letter down carefully in her lap, Abigail shook her head. "I don't see how anyone could face death like that. I couldn't!"

Esther began to speak of the power of God to calm troubled spirits. Finally she said, "I'm not sure that I have dying grace now, but I don't need it. God gives us grace as we need it, not when we don't." She sat there quietly and asked finally, "What about your spiritual condition, Abigail? Are you at peace with God?"

Abigail was shaken by the simple, direct question as she never had been by any sermon. Somehow Esther's words brought a sense of fear, for she knew that she was not at peace with God. Almost abruptly, in order to shut off the feelings that were raging through her, she said, "God has no use for me!"

"You're wrong there, my dear!" Esther said quietly. "God so loved the world that He gave His Son, and you're part of the world. He loves you. We have the cross of Christ to prove God's great love." She began giving her own testimony on how she had found God.

Abigail was glad when the servant came to announce that breakfast was ready. She arose at once and went down the stairs, determined not to come back and listen to more of her aunt's preaching. It had frightened her and stirred things within her heart that she could not explain. "I know why I've come here," she said. "I'll do what Leo asks, and then I won't have to stay in this place any longer. . . !"

🔔   🔔   🔔

Abigail slipped into the new dress that her aunt Esther had insisted on buying her. It was a formal gown of watered silk taffeta in the empire style. The neckline was quite low, and the small dainty sleeves stopped at the same level as the necktie. She admired the rose satin ribbon that bound in the sleeve and the neckline, and looked down to the bottom of the skirt decorated with four flounces of lace, topped by rows of tiny silk ribbon florets. She slipped her feet into her satin slippers, picked up her fan and her bag, also made of satin, and wrapped a paisley stole around her shoulders. She took one quick look into the mirror, admiring the necklace that her aunt had insisted she wear, a double strand of pearls with a large rose quartz, and earrings of rose quartz to match.

Leaving her room she encountered her mother, who said, "My, what a beautiful gown—and you look so well in it!"

"It is beautiful, isn't it? And so nice of Aunt Esther to buy it for me. We had such fun shopping!"

"Oh, I forgot to tell you! A letter arrived by post yesterday. I put it on the card table in the hall."

"Thank you, Mother. I'll take it with me!"

"Where are you going this time? You and Matthew have been very busy for the last week. I think you've been somewhere every day and most of the nights."

This was true enough. Matthew had appeared and invited Abigail to spend an afternoon with him nearly a week ago. Since then he had been back every day enjoying several meals with the family and attending church with them two days earlier on Sunday.

"I think we're going to his studio or his apartment that he shares with his friend," Abigail said. "I'll tell you about it when I get back!"

She moved into the hallway, picked up the letter, and stopped abruptly. She recognized Leo Rochester's handwriting. For a moment she was tempted to return it, for she did not want to read it. Nevertheless, she knew that it must be done. Opening it quickly, she scanned the lines:

> My dear Abigail,
>   I have been waiting anxiously to hear from you. I am anxious to hear how our project is going. Also, I inform you, that if you need more funds, write me by post and I shall see that they are supplied. I am sure you are making progress, and I will expect to hear good news from you very soon.
>
>   Leo Rochester

Abigail slipped the letter into her reticule and left the house. The coach was waiting, and she gave the address to William, the driver, and then got inside. As the carriage rolled along over the cobblestones, she paid little attention to the activities on the streets, for she was thinking of Leo Rochester and their "project."

It had seemed logical enough, and possible enough, back in Boston—this convincing Matthew to do what Leo Rochester wanted. After spending a great deal of time with Matthew, however, Abigail felt less certain. She had learned to like him immensely, far more than she had ever thought she might. There was an openness and an honesty, yet a sense of humor that made Matthew a charming and delightful companion. He had spent the more recent years in England and kept her amused with countless, interesting stories of which he seemed to be filled.

I wonder if I can do it? she thought as the carriage pulled up in front of a building.

"Here we are, miss," the coachman said. Jarred out of her thoughts she got out of the carriage and said, "You needn't wait, William. I'll take a carriage home."

"Yes, ma'am!" William spoke to the horses, and the carriage pulled away.

Abigail looked at the building, then started up toward the door. She heard her name called and looked up to see Matthew leaning out of the window.

"Stay right there!" he yelled. "I'll be down to escort you up!"

Abigail smiled at his exuberance and realized that his yell had introduced her to the neighborhood. A small detail of soldiers laughed at her, and one of them said, "You better come and go with us, missy! We'll show you a good time!"

Abigail could not help smiling as the sergeant dressed the man down. *Soldiers are the same everywhere*, she thought. It had been the same in Boston whenever she went out on the street. Everywhere she had gone, she was constantly accosted by the British troops.

The door opened and Matthew came out at once. He was wearing a simple black broadcloth coat with white knee britches. His eyes were alive with pleasure and he reached out and took her hand. "Just on time!" he said. "Vandermeer and I have been planning for your visit. Come upstairs!" Matthew talked incessantly as he led her up the stairs. When they reached the top, he opened the door and ushered her into the apartment.

Vandermeer, who greeted her at once, was well dressed, as far as he was concerned for the visit of Abigail Howland. He had heard much about the young woman and had dredged up a colorful waistcoat, containing all the hues of the rainbow, and a pair of baggy trousers that were much the vogue in Holland, though seldom seen in England. His round moon-face beamed and he said, "Ah, Miss Howland, so happy to see you again! Just in time for tea and cakes!"

"We'll be going out to eat later on," Matthew said as he led her to a table covered with a rather ancient white tablecloth.

Jan began pouring the tea and gave neither of his companions time to speak. "You haf completely captivated our young friend, Miss Howland. I think he will never make an artist until he stops thinking so much of you!"

Abigail had liked the Dutchman from the first. There was an openness and a cheerfulness about him that could not be withstood. Smiling at him she asked, "Can't a man court a woman and be an artist at the same time, Jan?"

"I do not think so! Art takes everything!"

"What about yourself, Mr. Vandermeer? You do not have a sweetheart?"

Vandermeer found this amusing. He gestured enthusiastically with his hands and spoke in explosive bursts as was his custom. "I haf a million sweethearts, but they are all on canvas! Look at this!" He ran across the room, ripped a canvas from a stack, and came back holding it up. It was a portrait of a young peasant girl, apparently painted on the Continent. She was pretty and had a roguish expression on her face. "Here! Is she not beautiful?"

"Very pretty! Was she your sweetheart, Mr. Vandermeer?"

"It does not matter what she was. Whatever she was," Jan exclaimed almost violently, "she is not like this! In fifty years, she will be old and white haired and stooped, and perhaps with no teeth! But this one here on the canvas, ah, she will be just the same, yes?"

"I suppose so!" Abigail laughed. "But you can't cuddle up to a piece of canvas in a frame!"

"You are romantic!" Vandermeer grinned. "Most young ladies are!"

"I rather agree with Miss Howland, Jan," Matthew said quickly. "Flesh and blood is better than cold paint!"

Vandermeer held the picture up and shook his head. "You will never be an artist until you get that idea out of your head!" he exclaimed. "Everything changes but art. It always remains the same!"

"I don't think that would be good if people remained the same," Matthew said. "It's natural enough to be young, and naturally we grow old. Would you always have us stay sixteen years old?"

For nearly an hour the philosophical argument about youth and age and life went on. Abigail found herself, without difficulty, entering into it. It was refreshing to be listened to, able to talk in the company of men and be respected—which had not always been the case. Some men she knew had no respect at all for a woman's judgment. Looking over at Matthew she was impressed at how different he was from most other young men she knew. He was completely different from his brother Dake, and from Daniel Bradford. Now that she knew the truth about his birth, this did not come as a great shock.

However, he was not like Leo Rochester either. As the two men continued to fire barrages of arguments at each other she thought, *He looks like Leo somewhat, but there's a goodness in him that Leo doesn't have.* She thought he must have gotten that from his mother, and finally when the argument was referred to her she pulled her thoughts back together and laughed. "I can't settle all of your arguments. I think you both are pretty foolish anyway."

"You are right! All artists are foolish! Ve haf no sense at all in a practical way!" Vandermeer admitted, laughing at his own shortcomings.

Later on in the afternoon the three of them went for a walk throughout the city, then returned for a brief meal that Vandermeer fixed. He was actually a good cook, and the leg of mutton was expertly done with spices that he would not reveal. After the meal, Matthew said, "I must take our guest home, Jan."

"You must come back many times!" Vandermeer said, smiling as he shook the hand that Abigail offered him. "Matthew is a foolish young man, and it will take both of us to get him reared properly! You will teach him about love, and I will teach him about art!"

After the two had left, they went to a park and sat down for a time. It was a quiet place, giving the impression of being out in the open countryside. For a time they sat and talked, and then Abigail said regretfully, "It's getting dark. I must be getting back, Matthew!"

"I suppose so!" Matthew said rather grudgingly, then turned to her. "Stay just a while longer!"

"Well, not for long," Abigail said. She was aware that Matthew was very vulnerable in many respects. His years on the Continent had not made him into an accomplished ladies' man, as it might have many. There was an innocence in him, and she knew she had gained some power over him. Again she thought of Leo's note, and when Matthew suddenly reached out and took her in his arms she yielded herself to him.

As he kissed her she was suddenly confused by several things. She had been kissed before, naturally, and was not inexperienced in love. Nevertheless, there was something in his embrace and in his kiss that was somehow different—or at least so it seemed to her. There was a response in her as his arms pulled her closer, and his lips sought hers with passion. She gave herself to him, but at the same time she was aware of a disturbance within her own heart. *I'm doing this just for money*, she thought with a stab of disgust. *That makes me little better than a prostitute!*

Suddenly she pulled away, confused by her own thoughts, and stood to her feet.

"What's the matter? Have I offended you, Abigail?"

"No . . . no, you haven't, Matthew, but I think it's better that we go home now."

"As you say!" He found a cab, and the two rode quietly back to the Denham house.

When he walked with her to the door after the carriage stopped, she put out her hand and said, "Good night! It's been delightful!"

"Will I see you tomorrow?"

"If you like!" She smiled then and turned and entered the house. When she went to her room, she undressed quickly and put on her nightgown and got into bed. She sought sleep for some time, but it did not come. Her thoughts were ragged and wild, and she almost cried aloud as she thought, *What else do I want! I was ready to marry Nathan Winslow just to have security. Now all I have to do is nod and I'll have Matthew. He'll have a title someday. I'll be Lady Abigail Rochester!*

But these thoughts did not please her. Restlessly, she turned and buried her face in the pillow, trying to blot out the thoughts of what she had been and what she was now. Somehow, even in the midst of this, she was conscious of the quiet voice of her aunt reading Scripture to her, and this was even more frightening.

For the first time in her life Abigail felt completely and totally helpless. She was a self-sufficient young woman, able to manage her own affairs—or so she thought. But as she lay in bed, memories came to her that she hated—things that she had done, how she had used people. And for the first time in her life Abigail Howland prayed a sincere and earnest prayer. It was short and came out almost in the form of a cry, "Oh, God—don't let me be so awful!"

14

A Dream Out of the Pit

AFTER MICAH LEFT to serve with Colonel Knox in New York, Daniel Bradford found that he had to work twice as hard at the foundry. He had not known how much Micah had taken the burden from him, until at the end of the first week he had found himself red-eyed from lack of sleep and unable to think clearly as he went about his work. He rose before dawn and by noon had done a full day's work. Snatching a bite of food as he could, he doggedly moved through the rest of the day and often did not get home until well after dark. Rachel scolded him, and Albert Blevins, the tall sour-faced bookkeeper in the foundry, told him bluntly one afternoon, "You're going to kill yourself, Daniel, if you don't learn how to take some rest!"

Looking up from the piece of white-hot iron that he had been pounding with a sixteen-pound hammer, Daniel blinked and found that his throat was so dry he could not speak. He put the glowing iron on an anvil and pounded it into shape, then dipped it into the barrel of water. The water reminded him that his throat was dry, and he moved across and lifted a bucket, drinking directly from it thirstily. The water ran over his chin and down the leather apron he wore, but he did not heed it, so delicious was the drink, even though it was tepid.

Blevins watched all this with a jaundiced eye. He had been with the Frazier Ironworks long before Daniel came, and at first he had been skeptical of the new partnership. He was devoted to John Frazier and had been afraid that the younger man would edge his master out. However, through the years he had been satisfied to see that Daniel Bradford's devotion to Frazier was second only to his own. Now he was anxious that Bradford would put himself into a state of exhaustion and said

168

with a snappy tone, "Go home, Daniel! Take a long bath, crawl in between some clean sheets, and sleep for twenty-four hours!"

Looking across the smoky blacksmith shop, Daniel grinned wearily. "You're worse than a mother hen, Albert! Hard work never killed anybody!"

"Where did you ever get a crazy idea like that? Hard work has killed more people than wars. It just takes a little longer than a bullet to do it!" He came across and put his hand on Daniel's chest and shoved him. He was a frail man, and Daniel was sturdy, thick with muscle, and he could not move him. Doubling up his fist he struck him hard in the chest and said, "Go home! Spend some time with your son and daughter! Go out and get drunk. Do something besides work!"

"I don't think the last would answer," Daniel shrugged. Weariness struck him like a club, and he suddenly realized it was hard just to keep standing. "But I think you're right. I may come in late tomorrow."

"Good! That's showing some sense!"

"Have you heard from John today?"

"I got a note from Mrs. Rochester. She says the doctor was there, and he's not any better."

"I think I'll stop off on my way home." Then seeing the glint of disapproval in Blevins' eyes he said, "Just for a few minutes, I promise!"

"I know what your promises are worth like that. You'll sit there and talk with him for two hours!"

"Not that long, Albert. He's not able to talk that much." He looked over at the tall, thin man with the cadaverous face and shook his head. "I'm concerned about John, and so are you."

Blevins held Bradford's glance and nodded. His lips going tight, he said, "He's not doing well, Daniel. Go by and see him. Your visits cheer him up a great deal."

It was over an hour later before Daniel walked up and knocked on the door of the Frazier house. Again he was surprised at how tired he was. "Must be getting old," he muttered. "I can remember the day I could work like a mule for a week." He was still a strong man, he knew, and at forty-six could work most of his younger employees into the ground. He was thinking how age comes up, sneaking around the corner, and touches you instead of announcing itself.

When the door opened, Cato stood there, his teeth grinning. He bowed jerkily and said, "Yes, sir, Mr. Bradford. I'm glad you come!"

"How's Mr. Frazier, Cato?"

Cato reached out and took Daniel's hat and shook his head sorrowfully. "Not too well, I'm afraid. He's awake though. You can go right up."

"Is Mrs. Frazier with him?"

"No, sir! She's gone to see the Williams family down the street. They lost their little girl day before yesterday."

"I'm sorry to hear it. I was hoping she would pull through."

"Yes, sir, we all was hoping that, but she didn't make it. The funeral will be tomorrow I 'spect you will want to go."

"Of course. I'll go on up then, Cato."

"When you come down I'll have a bite fixed for you to eat. I 'spect you ain't had no supper yet."

"Don't bother, Cato."

"It ain't no trouble, sir. You visit a while with Mr. Frazier. It always helps when you come to see him."

Daniel nodded and went at once to the sick man's room. He found John Frazier sitting up reading in bed. He looked, in fact, better than he had the last time that Daniel had come, and he said cheerfully as he entered, "Well, if you keep improving like this, you'll be out chopping wood!"

A slight smile tugged at John Frazier's lips. He knew Daniel always put the best face on things and put the book aside. "Sit down, Daniel. Tell me what's been happening at the foundry! How's the musket enterprise going?"

Daniel sat down and for some time chatted with Frazier. He studied the older man without seeming to, noting that Frazier's color was somewhat better. He did not mention Frazier's sickness, for there was nothing to be said about it. He enjoyed the talk, for he had always had a special affection for John, and was grateful to him for giving him a start in a growing business.

Frazier enjoyed the visit too, but after thirty minutes he seemed to tire. "I just can't seem to gain any strength, Daniel, but the doctor has got me on a new medicine." He reached over and picked up a brown bottle and grimaced, pulling his lips back to show his distaste. "It tastes horrible! I think Dr. Bates thinks that the worse the taste, the better the medicine."

"Bates is a good man!"

"Yes, he is. He's done all he can. Well, go along. You look tired, Daniel."

"I think I will. Blevins was telling me I need to take it a little bit easier."

"So you should. You'll wear yourself out if you don't slow down. I remember," Frazier said with a sad look in his eyes, "when I could work like that. Enjoy it, Daniel, it'll soon be gone." Then he caught himself and laughed shortly. "There I am talking like a prophet of doom—but you mind Blevins. He's got a lot of wisdom in that skinny skull of his."

Daniel shook the frail hand and said, "Let's have a prayer before I leave."

Frazier looked up quickly. "That would be good, Daniel!" As Daniel prayed, John held to the strong, powerful hand with both of his as if to draw strength from it. A fleeting thought came to him—not a new one, for he had it often: *If only Marian had married Daniel.* When the prayer was over he whispered, "Thank you, Daniel, that helps a lot."

"Good night, John." Daniel left the sick man's room and went down the hall. He turned into the kitchen where Cato was sitting on a stool, holding a cup of something.

"Yes, sir, Mr. Daniel, you set yourself right down here. I done got some pork chops cooked up, and some of Lucy's fresh baked bread, and some of them field peas you like so much."

Suddenly hunger struck Daniel like a club, and he sat down and fell upon the food that Cato set before him, washing it down with long drafts of fresh milk. At some point Cato warned him, "Don't eat too much! We got fresh apple pie, just like you like, Mr. Daniel!"

Daniel pitched into the pie and finished it off with a cup of hot black coffee with three heaping spoonfuls of sugar in it. Leaning back he shook his head. "That's the best meal I've had in a spell, Cato! Thanks a lot!"

"You're welcome, Mr. Daniel!"

Daniel rose and left the kitchen, but as he turned into the hall he encountered Leo Rochester. He stopped abruptly and said, "Hello, Leo."

"Hello, Bradford."

Rochester was wearing a dark green dressing gown over what appeared to be some thin clothing. His hair was mussed, and there were dark circles under his eyes. "I couldn't sleep," he muttered. He shook his head, pulled his shoulders together, and said, "Come into the study." Without waiting for an answer he turned, and Daniel followed him down the hall. They turned into the walnut-lined study, where two lamps burned over the mantelpiece, casting an amber light over the desk and the horsehair furniture. "You want a drink?" Leo asked, picking up a bottle from the desk.

"No thanks, I've just eaten, and it's late!"

"Sit down!" Leo said. He, himself, turned and dropped into a chair, poured a drink, and held it up to the light, examining the amber color of it. "The doctor tells me," he remarked, "that I'm not supposed to do this!"

"Better listen to your doctor."

Leo lowered the glass and looked over it at Daniel. "I never was much for listening to advice," he said, then downed the liquor. His shoulders shuddered as the jolt of the alcohol hit him, and he leaned back in the chair. "I guess I look like death warmed over," he remarked, a sarcastic tone in his voice.

"You don't look very well, Leo. You've been having some kind of trouble. What is it?"

Leo Rochester considered the broad shoulder, the deep chest, and the thick neck of Daniel Bradford, and for a moment envy ran through him. He had always been envious of Daniel Bradford, not just of his strong body—but more of the spirit that the man had. Now, his own physical problems had stripped him of much of his own strength, which had been considerable. He locked his fingers together and leaned back into the chair. "I don't want to talk about myself. How's John?"

"Not too well. Have you talked to Dr. Bates lately?"

"Marian has. She says he doesn't hold out a great deal of hope. John's just wearing out."

"Yes, I think you're right, and unless God intervenes I fear he won't last."

His remark caught at Leo Rochester. He leaned forward, placed his elbows on the table, and locked his fingers together. Placing his chin on them he considered Bradford with a speculative look in his blue eyes. His brown hair had fallen over his forehead, but he did not notice. A silence fell across the room, and Leo seemed unaware of it. From somewhere out in the hall a large clock was ticking, counting off the moments in a sonorous fashion. Leo finally said thoughtfully, "You really believe that, don't you, Daniel?"

"Believe what, Leo?"

"That God's interested in us!"

"Yes I do!"

"Why should He be interested in a bunch of creatures like the human race? There's not much to us, Daniel, even the best of us."

"I disagree, Leo." Daniel's voice was calm. He was accustomed to Leo's poking fun at his religion and had long ago refused to let it bother him. "I think you know better, really. What about your own father? He was a good man, and you know it!"

Leo suddenly grinned. "You would bring him up! I could bring up a thousand men who are not what they ought to be—but you're right about my father. He was a good man! I can't deny it."

"I shouldn't think you'd want to!"

Leo was caught in some sort of inner turmoil. He had hated Daniel at times, but still there was something in the man he was drawn to. Ever since Daniel was a mere boy, he had tried to shake Bradford's rocklike Christian convictions. He had treated him shamefully, almost in an inhuman fashion, and still Bradford refused to strike back. Leo leaned back and said, "I've been thinking about the past a great deal. You and I have been tied together in rather strange ways, haven't we, Daniel?"

"Yes, we have."

"Do you remember those times how I lied to you and Lyna and made you both think the other was dead? Does that still grate on you a little bit, Daniel?"

"Not anymore." Daniel shook his head and added, "I hated you when I first found out about it, but that's gone now."

"Nice to be able to think like that . . . to forgive. I don't find it so easy."

"It's not easy for any of us!" Daniel sat back and looked at the ravaged face of the aristocrat before him. Dissipation had marked Rochester's face with coarse lines, and there was disillusionment in the eyes that were now sunk back into deep sockets. He had watched Leo destroy himself for years, and there had been times, as Leo too had admitted, that Daniel hated Leo. Now, however, he felt a strange compassion come over him, and he said, "God's not like we are. For some reason that I can't understand, and perhaps no one else, He *is* love. And, therefore, He forgives. I think we've got to grasp that about God even if we can't understand anything else."

"And you really believe the things these Methodists have been spouting about—that you must be born again?"

"Yes, I do! A man is naturally bad. That's why the Scripture says, 'All have sinned, and come short of the glory of God.' "

Leo considered this, then reached out suddenly and poured himself another drink from the bottle. He held it for a while and then downed it, shuddering again. "I'll agree with that. We've lost the glory of God, all right—if we ever had any! Go on, tell me some more," he said.

There was a jeering note in Rochester's voice, but Daniel took him at his word. For some time he sat there telling how Jesus Christ had come into his heart. How that since that time he had been different. He spoke slowly, deliberately, and in the background he heard the clock ticking out in the hall. It was the first time Leo had ever listened to him, and the thought came to his mind like a white-hot iron, *Why, he's dying!* Bradford was astonished at that but then he thought, *Men die every day, women and children, as well.* Leo Rochester had been a part of his life for so long that he had become a fixture—although one that he had to learn to endure. Now, looking at the weakness of what had once been strong hands, and noting the color of Rochester's face, Daniel somehow knew that this was his opportunity.

He spoke slowly and calmly, quoting many Scriptures, and finally when Leo did not speak he said, "We've never talked about these things, have we, Leo?"

"No!"

The brief word was enough to reveal some of the condition of Rochester's mind. The fact that he would listen, Daniel understood, was almost a miracle. He said, "I think it's good for all of us to stop and think about God. I wish I'd done it earlier. I wish you would now, Leo."

Leo Rochester was strangely quiet. He sat there listening as Daniel spoke about man's need for God and pressed the question upon him. But finally Leo brusquely said, "Good night, Daniel!"

Daniel hesitated. He wanted to say more, but he saw the adamant look in Leo's face. Rising, he said quietly, "It's been good to talk with you, Leo. Maybe we can do it again sometime."

"I said good night!"

There was a sharpness in Rochester's voice, and Daniel shrugged and left the room. Leo sat there for some time after the door slammed. He poured another drink and was about to lift it to his lips when Cato crept inside and said, "Can I do anything for you, Mr. Leo?"

"No! Good night, Cato!"

"Good night, sir."

Leo sat there holding the glass. It gave forth shimmering amber light as it reflected the lamps burning on the mantel. He did not drink it, however, but sat there quietly. His heart seemed to beat strongly enough, but he knew that was an illusion. Sooner or later it would either quietly cease to beat or would explode with one massive burst. Fear came to him then, which was something he could hardly bear. He had never been afraid of anything, but now he knew that this was something he could not buy and something he could not arrange.

He thought again of the words of Cato—*Can I do anything, Mr. Leo?*

It was as if the words had been spoken aloud, and he whispered huskily in reply, "No, Cato—nobody can do anything for me!"

T   T   T

Leo Rochester was not the only person in the Boston area who was suffering from an attack of fear. Katherine Yancy had gone to bed early, for she had been sleeping poorly recently. She wanted to go back to Halifax to find her father to do what she could for him, but everyone said that the British would be leaving there and moving back to New York. She was afraid that she would get there only to find that the fleet had sailed, bearing the prisoners away. Every day she had gone down to the harbor, noting that many ships were beginning to gather there, mostly men-of-war, and, of course, there was no way to contact them.

Katherine had eaten a light supper and gone to bed just after dark, but she had tossed restlessly until finally troubled dreams began to come to her. Usually she slept dreamlessly and awoke instantly refreshed and ready for whatever the day might bring. However, now she tossed and turned and muttered. Sometimes she came almost to the surface of consciousness and was aware of herself. Several times she almost decided to get up, but then dropped back off again into that part that lives just below the consciousness.

Finally she began to feel an ease, but just as she did, a cry came to her in her dream. It seemed to come from nowhere, and she felt herself wandering through a dense and thick woods. The branches reached out and grabbed at her hair, and briars tore at her hands and ripped her clothing. She did not know where she was, and the darkness frightened her. It was not an ordinary darkness. It was even darker than the darkest midnight down in a coal mine where no light can ever strike. She found herself crying out and whimpering with fear, for she suddenly remembered as a child she had been afraid of the dark.

The cries that she heard seemed to come from up ahead, and there seemed to be a tiny glow of light in that direction. Stumbling over the broken ground, her feet aching from rocks that cut her feet, she felt herself bleeding as the thorns struck her face. Fear rose in her, for she could not see, and the only sound was an unseen man's voice crying for help.

Finally the light grew brighter, and eagerly she pressed forward. The walking seemed to be easier and she was aware of huge, old trees that towered over her with trunks as large as small houses. Out of the darkness she sensed a presence of evil around her. She looked around and saw red eyes gleaming with a malevolent burning fire. Frightened, she stumbled forward toward the light.

The light seemed to swell, and suddenly she was aware that the land before her fell suddenly away. She halted abruptly and moved forward until she came to stand on the edge of a tremendous precipice. The land fell away down . . . down . . . down, but she was not looking far below where it ended with craggy rocks like teeth along the bottom of the tremendous canyon. Her eyes were fixed on a man who was hanging from a ledge not five feet away. Her first thought was, *He's falling. I've got to help him!* She moved forward and knelt, saying, "Reach up, let me help you!" She could not see his face because he kept it turned away, but his cries seemed to be fading. She called again, "Let me help you—!"

And then he looked up, and she saw in her dream that it was Clive

Gordon. His fingers were torn and bloody as he held on to the cruel stones. His face was contorted with the effort of simply hanging on, for if he released his grip, Katherine saw, he would fall to his death. He looked up at her saying nothing, but his lips formed her name—*Katherine!*

Katherine knelt there on the precipice, looking down into Clive's face. The wind was rising from somewhere, keening and howling behind her, and she felt the red eyes glowing as they burned in the darkness behind her. She was frozen in time and space. How long she knelt there in the dream looking down at the agonizing features of the man below, she could never tell.

Then Clive whispered, "Help me, Katherine!"

And then Katherine felt hatred well up inside her, bitterness like a bile in her throat. She clenched her fists together and shook them, suddenly crying out, "Go on and die—you deserve it!"

And then—Katherine awakened with a jolt. She was whispering, "No, no, no!" And suddenly her whole body ached, for she was tense in every muscle. Throwing the cover back, she stood up and found that her legs were trembling, as were her hands. She held her palms on her temples and moved over to stare out the window. The moon was shining mildly and she saw it reflect on the street outside, but she could not remain standing and collapsed, falling to the carpet on her knees, holding to her head and rocking back and forth.

She was horrified. The dream had torn at her and shaken her, and now she recognized that it was somehow more than a nightmare. For a long time she knelt there rocking back and forth, and finally she whispered, "Oh, God, forgive me, forgive me...!"

T T T

A pale sun was beating down on the waves as Katherine reached the docks and stared out over the sea. She had been up for hours, walking back and forth in her room, still shaken to the depths of her heart by the nightmare that had come to her. She had dressed and fixed breakfast for her mother, then left, unable to carry on a conversation. As she stood on the dock watching the British ships dot the green water with their white sails and their tall masts, looking much like a forest, she did not know why she had come here. For a long time she simply stood and watched the soldiers as they worked on the fortifications and thought of the battle that was to come.

She was more concerned, however, about the battle that took place in her own soul. Katherine Yancy was a spiritual woman. She knew what it was to pray, and since childhood had been taught the things of

God from both her father and mother. Now she seemed to have had a horrifying look into the depths of her own heart—and it was like looking into a bucket full of crawling, slimy things—ugly and hideous!

She thought again of how she had cried out in hatred and whispered hoarsely, "It was only a dream!"

But somehow she knew that it was a dream that held a meaning, and the meaning was connected somehow with her treatment of Clive Gordon.

"Why, hello, Miss Yancy!"

Quickly Katherine turned and found Rachel Bradford standing regarding her. "Hello, Miss Bradford!" she said rather stiffly. She remembered the last time she had seen Rachel at the funeral and how coldly she had treated her. Shame came to her, and she dropped her head. Finally she lifted her eyes. "Miss Bradford, I must apologize for the way I spoke to you at my uncle's funeral."

"Don't speak of it, Miss Yancy!" Rachel said at once. "It was a hard time—and still is, I'm sure."

"I thank you, but my behavior was unforgivable."

Rachel noted something different in the young woman's demeanor. It was hard to explain, but the last time she had seen Katherine Yancy there had been a burning anger in her eyes. Now, however, Katherine was somehow broken. "Could we walk together for a while?" Rachel asked quietly. "I like to walk and look at the sea."

"Why, yes, of course. . . ." Katherine said at once. Part of her wanted to refuse, and yet she felt so bad about the way she had behaved to Rachel Bradford that she knew she must somehow make it right.

The two women strolled along the harbor. The fishermen were bringing in their catches, and the two women watched, although both of them had seen it many times before. They talked about the war, and Rachel informed her about Micah's enlistment in the army. "So I have two brothers now with General Washington!" she said.

Katherine wanted desperately to say something about Clive Gordon. Already she knew that somehow she would have to deal with her attitude, and the thought had come to her that perhaps she could write him a letter. It would be a difficult thing to do, but she knew that somehow she would have to deal with her feelings toward him.

"I suppose Mr. Gordon has gone back?"

"Why, as a matter of fact, he hasn't!" Rachel answered.

Instantly Katherine turned to look at the young woman. "You mean he's still in Boston?"

"I don't have very good news, I'm afraid. You know the sickness that affected me and my brother and sister-in-law? Well, we've all recovered, but Clive came down with it just as we were getting well."

"I'm . . . sorry to hear it!"

Rachel blinked with surprise. This was not the same attitude she had sensed in the young woman before. "He's not doing very well, and I'm worried about him. So is the doctor."

Abruptly Katherine stopped and turned, and when Rachel did the same, she noticed that Rachel looked tired, almost exhausted. "You look very tired, Miss Bradford."

"Please call me Rachel. Yes, I am tired. Several people have come down with the sickness in our neighborhood—dear friends. Those of us who are well are trying to nurse them as best we can. Since Micah has left, it's been very difficult."

Katherine thought only for a moment, then she spoke impulsively. "If you would tell Mr. Gordon—" She broke off abruptly and bit her lip. She could not bring herself to say anything more, and finally said, "I must be going home. Good afternoon, Rachel!"

Rachel stared after her, mystified and puzzled. Finally she turned and made her way home, wondering what was going on in the mind of Katherine Yancy. *She's changed so much*, she thought as she made her way along the half-deserted streets. *I wonder what's happening to make her seem so different?*

ᛏ ᛏ ᛏ

Katherine arrived at home, cooked a lunch for her mother, and then finally went out to sit in the garden. Plato came to throw himself at her feet. He looked up at her with his big eyes, and she leaned over and ruffled his fur. He growled deep in his throat and Katherine said, "I wish my problems were as simple as yours, Plato. As long as you've got something to eat, and aren't hurting, and get a little attention now and then, that's all you require, isn't it?"

Plato suddenly reached out and took her hand between his huge jaws and squeezed slightly. It was a trick he had done from the time he was a big-footed mongrel puppy that her father had brought home. He had soon become Katherine's dog. Now suddenly she fell down beside him and hugged him hard. Plato looked somewhat surprised and moved to lick her face. For some time she sat there hugging the huge dog, then finally she left him and went inside.

All afternoon she thought about her dreams, and when twilight came she put her coat on and said, "Mother, I'm going out!"

"When will you be back? It's getting late!"

Katherine hesitated, then said, "I may stay the night with a friend. I'm not sure. James and Jewel will be here if you need anything." These were the servants that came on a part-time basis—Jewel to take care of some of the cooking, and James to chop the wood and do the man's work.

"All right, dear!"

Leaving the house, Katherine went at once across town, coming to stand at last before the door of the Bradford home. She took a deep breath, knocked, and saw the surprise wash across Rachel Bradford's face as she opened the door.

"Why, come in, Miss Yancy!" Rachel said.

"You may as well call me Katherine!" Stepping inside, Katherine suddenly found it difficult to say what she had come to say. Taking a deep breath, however, she straightened her shoulders and said, "I've come to help, if I can, Rachel."

"Help? Why, help in what way, Katherine?"

"I can see you're very tired. You're barely over your sickness yourself." Katherine hesitated for one moment and then said, "I want you to let me help with the house—and with nursing Clive Gordon."

Shock came then to Rachel Bradford, but she concealed it as well as she could. Of all the things she had expected, Katherine's sudden appearance and sincere offer to help took her aback. However, she smiled and said, "How kind of you, Katherine!—and I will not say no! Come along, we'll sit and talk about it awhile."

The two women went into the parlor and sat there for some time talking. Finally Katherine could not keep silent. "I may as well tell you. I have been perfectly horrible to Clive. We were very close in Halifax. I grew upset with him, and have been very bitter, but I want to make it up—if he'll allow me."

A smile touched the soft lips of Rachel Bradford. "I think he'll be very glad to see you. Come along. I think he's awake."

As Rachel rose and turned to leave the room, Katherine stood up and followed her, but she dreaded the scene that was to come. She knew that deep down inside she still resented Clive Gordon for what he had done to her uncle, but she had come this far and now she prayed, *God help me to go as far as I have to go. I can't stand another horrible dream like the one that's been haunting me.*

15

God Isn't Far Away

GENERAL WILLIAM HOWE'S BROTHER, Admiral Richard Howe, arrived off the coast of New York after a three-month's voyage from England. His fleet consisted of a hundred and fifty ships with a reported fifteen thousand reinforcements aboard for his brother, General Howe. Howe's secretary, a man named Ambrose Serle, described his emotions upon arrival after the tedious voyage in his journal:

> This morning, the sun shining bright, we had a beautiful prospect of the coast of New Jersey at about five or six mile's distance. The land was cleared in many places, and the woods were interspersed with houses, which, being covered with white shingles, appeared very plainly all along the shore. We passed Sandy Hook in the afternoon, and about six o'clock arrived safe off the east coast of Staten Island. The country on both sides was highly picturesque and agreeable. Nothing could exceed the joy that appeared throughout the fleet and the army upon our arrival. We were saluted by all the ships of war in the harbor, by the cheers of the sailors all along the ships, and by those of the soldiers along the shore. The soldiers and sailors may have been cheering the arrival of Admiral Howe's fleet, but even more they were giving vent to their happiness over the fact that that very day at noon the British warships the *Phoenix* and the *Rose* had forced their passage up the Hudson in despite of all the batteries.

When the heavily armed ships passed up the river, the cries of the unhappy Americans rent the air. General Washington was disgusted with the spectacle of his soldiers. He observed a number of them walking along the banks of the Hudson gazing at the ships as if they were at a show of some kind. Washington was not known for outbursts, but during this period some of his staff observed that he was unhappy enough to give vent to his rage.

Admiral Richard Howe, unlike his pleasure-loving brother, was a generous and liberal man. He was a Whig who had hopes of inducing the Americans to see the folly of their ways. He had also arrived in New York empowered to offer peace terms to the Colonies in hope of preventing a full-scale revolution. His first step was to send Joseph Reed, who had returned to the army as adjutant general, a letter. Reed did not reply; instead he forwarded the letter to Congress. Two days later, after his arrival, Admiral Howe decided to arrange an interview with Washington, the American commander in chief. What followed was a comedy of manners.

Lord Howe sent a flag of truce up to the city. He also sent the captain of his flagship, the *Eagle*, with a letter to the commander in chief. He was met by Colonel Henry Knox and Colonel Reed. The captain said, "I have a letter from Lord Howe to Mr. Washington."

"Sir," said Colonel Reed coldly, "we have no person in our army with that address."

"Sir, will you look at the address!" the officer said.

Reed looked at it, and it was simply addressed to George Washington, Esquire. "I'm sorry! No sir, I cannot receive that letter."

"I am very sorry," the officer said, "and so will be Lord Howe, but any error in the superscription shouldn't prevent them from being received by General Washington!"

Colonel Reed then said, "You are sensible of the rank of General Washington and our army?"

"Yes, sir, I am! I am sure my Lord Howe will lament exceedingly this affair, as the letter is quite of a civil nature and not a military one! He laments that he was not here a little sooner."

Knox and Reed simply refused to receive a letter that did not acknowledge their commander in chief as General Washington. They bowed and left the captain of the British navy standing there. But Lord Howe was a persistent man. He tried once again two days later, but the peace talks came to nothing, as everyone quite expected.

General Washington had worries of his own—for the sails in the harbor were as thick as the wings of birds of prey. Moreover, sickness decimated his ranks. To oppose an enemy force that now exceeded thirty thousand, Washington now had but ten thousand five hundred men in the posts around New York, and about three thousand seven hundred of these were sick and unfit for duty.

Shortly after this, forty more ships arrived to bolster the British force. Washington was perplexed at the enemy's failure to attack. He deemed it wise to send his headquarters' papers to the Congress at Philadelphia for safekeeping. He finally came to the conclusion that rainy weather was postponing the attack, or else the enemy was awaiting still more forces.

The weeks of waiting ground sharply on the nerves of the British troops, but they availed themselves of daily amusement offered by Staten Island, a land of Tories. The Hessians arrived and were spoiling for a fight. In fact, the entire British army seemed confident that the disorderly, untrained troops of America could not stand against them. Every soldier was eager to teach the colonists a lesson they richly deserved.

🔔　　🔔　　🔔

Abigail Howland could not remember a time in her life when she had been so utterly confused of mind. She continued to meet with Esther in the mornings, saying little, but listening as her hostess quietly read from the Scripture and drew lessons from it that Abigail had never considered. She had always thought Christians dull and hypocritical, but she could not claim this for her aunt. She had learned well the generosity of the older woman's heart, and her reputation among the servants and the neighbors was impeccable. Everyone knew that Esther Denham was a woman of godly character—this Abigail could not deny.

One Sunday she went to church with Esther, as had become the custom with her and her mother. She sat there in the high-back pew listening as the preacher spoke on a rather alarming subject, "Prepare to Meet Thy God."

It was, however, not a hell-and-brimstone sermon such as Abigail had heard a few times. The minister, a tall man with steady brown eyes who wore the vestments of a man of the cloth as if he had been born to it, said in the midst of the sermon, "These words usually are accompanied by warnings of the pits of hell and the fate of the unbeliever. I would have you hear them this morning as a gentle call from a loving God. He is calling you to prepare. That is why Jesus Christ came into the world, to prepare a way for those that do not know God so they can find Him. And now that that way has been prepared through His blood, the only preparation we can make is to confess ourselves unable to forgive our own sins and free ourselves from them, and to look to Him to do that."

For some time the minister spoke of turning from sin and turning to God. He quoted liberally from the Scriptures, and Abigail, by the end of the sermon, was totally miserable. She could not understand what was happening to her, and that afternoon she kept to her room, unable to keep her countenance before her mother or her aunt.

Finally after the sun went down, she went to supper and managed, though with great difficulty, to keep her turbulent spirit from showing. Carrie Howland remarked on how much she enjoyed the sermon, and Esther said eagerly, "Yes, it was a fine sermon, wasn't it? Reverend Johnson is such a gentle, loving man. It's so good to see a man like that proclaiming from the pulpit."

Abigail said nothing as the two women continued to discuss the sermon. She excused herself as soon as possible and went to bed early.

The next morning she arose, dressed, and at ten o'clock Matthew came to take her out for a drive. As usual they drove by the harbor to take a look at the fortifications and the excitement of the soldiers. She had never seen so many different colors and kinds of uniforms in her life, and she remarked on this to Matthew. "Why don't all the soldiers have the same kind of uniforms, I wonder?"

Matthew answered, "I think it's because they come from different states. Each state chooses its own uniforms. Colorful, isn't it?"

"It must be very confusing. All the British wear the same color uniforms, don't they?"

"I think not! The Jaegers, for example, wear green uniforms, I'm told. And the Black Watch, the Scots regiment, wear kilts!"

"Kilts—you mean like little skirts? How funny!"

"I'm told they're not very amusing! They're called the 'Ladies From Hell,' they're so fierce in battle," Matthew remarked. They were driving along, looking out over the ocean, and he turned, suddenly stopping, and took her by the arm. "Look at that! It's a beautiful sight, isn't it, Abigail?" He swept his arm to where the armada of ships formed out in the harbor, looking like a forest of bare trees. The sails were all furled, and they could see, even at this distance, some of the British sailors as they moved about the decks. "I'd like to paint that, but it would be hard."

"Jan would ask you what it would all mean!" Abigail said. From the several times she had been in the company of the Dutch artist, she had absorbed some of his theories concerning art. "According to him, every painting has to mean something."

"I'm not sure he's right about that!" Matthew shrugged. "Some paintings just *are*! If you paint a picture of a dog, it's because people like to see pictures of dogs. It doesn't have to mean anything."

"Jan would have your head for that!" Abigail said. She looked up at him and smiled slightly. She made a fetching picture there in the morning sunlight. She was wearing a pale apricot dress and a straw hat with a wide brim, as was the fashion of the day. Her complexion was flawless, and there was something in her hazel eyes that expressed the light that lurked within her. She made a most attractive picture to young Matthew Bradford.

He looked at her suddenly and, without preamble, said in a husky voice, "Abigail—"

Caught by his tone, Abigail looked at him. "Why, what is it, Matthew?"

"Marry me, Abigail!"

Abigail was aware of the sound of the lapping of the waves on the piers, and of the harsh cries of the sea gulls far down the beach. She was aware, as well, of the hard blue sky above and the dark green of the sea. They met in a line straight as a knife's edge out of the horizon. Something inside her said, *This is what you've always longed for! Now it can be all yours—money, position, everything. . . !* The thought came to her strongly as a physical blow, and she knew that a few days earlier she would have at once accepted Matthew's proposal.

Now, however, she found herself hesitating. When she said nothing, Matthew took her arms and looked into her face, saying, "Marry me, Abigail, I love you! I want you to be my wife."

Abigail opened her lips to say, "Yes, I will marry you"—but somehow the words would not come. She was confused and knew that somehow her confusion resulted from the days she had spent in Esther Denham's company. She had become dissatisfied with what she was—the deceit she was carrying out—and she remembered suddenly the words of Paul Winslow, *I've seen the hard beauty on the outside, but deep down there's another Abigail Howland, a better Abigail.* Desperately she sat there trying to think, wondering at herself for hesitating, but somehow she could not make up her mind. Matthew was speaking, and she heard him say, "We can take Leo's offer, after all he is my real father; I believe that. It was hard for me to accept at first. It wouldn't mean that I wouldn't love Daniel and the family any less, but it would open up a whole new world for me—and for you, Abigail."

"Matthew!" Abigail said, struggling for words. "We haven't known each other very long." It was not what she wanted to say, but she looked up at him and could only add, "A couple ought to know each other better than we do!"

Matthew shook his head stubbornly. His hands tightened on her arms and he said with force, "I know I love you! All that matters is, do you love me? Do you care for me at all, Abigail?"

Abigail could not meet his gaze. She dropped her head, thinking of Leo's offer that she had so eagerly accepted back in Boston. She had, in effect, agreed to betray this man who stood there with love in his eyes, and on his face, and in his voice—to betray him for money. Now she could not bear the moment any longer. "You will have to give me time to think," she whispered. She managed to lift her eyes and say, "You're such a fine man, Matthew, but this is too important to decide right now!"

Matthew did not speak for a moment, then he nodded. "I see you're not certain about me, but you will be, Abigail!" He smiled then and looked suddenly very handsome as the wind blew his hair, and she was conscious of the fact that here was a man that she could love. Strangely enough, she had never thought about the long-term side of marriage. Always it had been pleasure for a moment, and security. Now those two things somehow did not seem as important, and she turned the moment away by saying, "Let's go to the park."

"All right, but I promise you, you're not going to have any rest. I love you, Abigail, and I'm going to marry you!"

🦁   🦁   🦁

For two days Abigail listened as Matthew continued to press his case. More than once she decided to accept his offer. Once she even got out a sheet of paper and started to write to Leo of what had happened— but somehow she could not bring herself to do it. She became nervous and even irritable, and finally her mother said, "I don't know what's the matter with you, Abigail! You ought to be having the time of your life with a fine young man like Matthew, but you're as snappy as I've ever seen you!"

Finally, in desperation, Abigail decided to talk to Esther. She could not talk to her mother. They had never been intimate, and even now she did not feel comfortable speaking of something like this to her. She waited until the next morning when the two went to the cupola for their usual morning tea and time of quiet conversation. Abigail waited until Esther had finished reading the psalms and said the prayer, then before she could change her mind said almost desperately, "Aunt Esther, there's something I have to tell you!"

Turning to her niece with some surprise, Esther said, "Why, what is it, child?"

Abigail hesitated for only one moment, then she began. "You don't know me, Aunt Esther. All you know is what you've seen since we've been here—but I'm not what I seem."

"I think few of us are."

"*You* are!" Abigail said. She bit her lip, then straightened her back as if she were marching in front of a firing squad. "I'm going to tell you what kind of a girl I've been. . . ." She began to speak with an effort,

185

going back to her childhood, and for the first time in her life she confessed things that she had known about herself. She spoke of her selfishness, how she had cheated her way through life, how she had learned to manipulate people when she was little more than a child. She seemed to hear her own voice as if it belonged to someone else speaking of what a terrible young woman she had grown into. Finally she related how she had had an affair with Paul Winslow and how she had betrayed him to snare Nathan Winslow when the tide of politics changed suddenly. Finally she said, "I came here under false colors, Aunt Esther. Leo Rochester hired me to come to be nice to Matthew Bradford. He wants something from him, and he thinks I can help him get it."

Finally Abigail ceased. Her hands were clenched around the handkerchief that she had pulled at as she related her story, and her lips were drawn tightly together. She dropped her head, and there was a moment's stillness, then she looked up and there were tears in her eyes. "That's what kind of terrible woman I am, Aunt Esther!"

Esther's voice was filled with compassion. "Why are you telling me all this, Abigail? You didn't have to."

"I don't know!" Abigail shook her head and dabbed at her eyes with the handkerchief. She almost never cried, and was somehow resentful and ashamed that she was crying now. It hurt her pride. Straightening up, she stared out at the street below for a long time. "Matthew asked me to marry him two days ago," she finally said, then turned to look at Esther with a tragic expression. "It's what I've always wanted. He'll come into a fortune. I can't tell you about that now, but I could have everything I've always wanted."

"Do you love Matthew, Abigail?"

The question seemed to disturb Abigail tremendously. She stood up suddenly and began to walk about the cupola wringing her hands and keeping her face turned away from Esther. Finally she stopped and turned to face her aunt. "How can I know?" she asked in desperation. "I came here to betray him for money, and now he says he loves me— and I believe he does! It would be so easy just to say yes, but somehow I can't do that!"

"Come and sit down. I want to talk to you, Abigail," Esther said quietly. She waited until the young woman came, then said, "You may not know what's happening, but you've been very unhappy lately, and I've watched you."

"I've been *miserable!*"

"I think it's the Spirit of God striving with you, Abigail. That's the way it happens. We will never come to God as long as we are happy and content. It's only when we become discontented and know something is wrong that we begin to reach out to Him. I think God has been touching you, stirring your spirit—Christians call this sort of thing *conviction*. It simply means that you are becoming aware of what you are, and God is doing it!"

"Why is He doing it? Why doesn't He leave me alone?"

"Because He loves you, and He wants to make something much sweeter, and finer, and nobler out of you than you have ever been."

At once Abigail thought of what Paul had said about a better woman being deep inside of her. She shook her head and whispered, "I can't go back and redo all the things that I did that were wrong. I can't, Aunt Esther!"

"You can't undo the past, but that's the part that Jesus plays. He takes us where we are and forgives all of our sins, and then He gives us the power to live a good and holy life. We could not do it ourselves."

"I can't believe it. God's a million miles from me!"

"God isn't far away! The kingdom of God is within you, Abigail. Jesus said, 'I stand at the door and knock. If any man will open the door, I will come in.' I'm going to ask you to do that right now!"

Abigail stared at her aunt with shock and disbelief. "Ask me what, Aunt Esther?"

"I'm going to ask you to open the door of your heart and let Jesus Christ come in."

"I don't know what you're talking about!"

"Jesus said, 'You must be born again.' By that He simply meant that you must become a different person. Just like a baby is a brand-new human being. All old things will pass away. You will be a new Abigail, a sweeter, finer woman than you've ever known possible. That's the work of God to make you like himself. . . ."

When Abigail failed to respond, Esther continued, "Abigail, did your father ever tell you much about your grandmother, Rachel?"

"No, not really. He just said she was a foolish old woman who died with nothing to show for her life."

"Well, Saul was wrong about that. I'm sad to say that I agreed with him for many years. Your grandmother was one of the finest Christian women you could hope to meet. We've already talked about the struggles she faced living in the Plymouth colony. She always stayed true to her God, no matter how difficult the circumstances. She even faced down an Indian to save someone's life.

"She took after her grandfather, Gilbert Winslow. He was one of the original pilgrim settlers that landed at Plymouth Rock in 1620. He was acting as a spy for the Crown at the time to gain information about the actions of the 'feared' separatists, the pilgrims. He was converted after coming to America and became a wonderful preacher. He had pretended to be one of the pilgrims and had fooled many of them before he was converted, including your great-great-grandmother, Humility Cooper Winslow. Our family, the house of Winslow, is filled with many men and women of strong faith in God. It pains me to have to say that for a long time I was not one of those. Saul and I both went in different directions from what our parents wished.

"I still remember how your father and I used to mock our cousins, William, Mercy, and Adam, for their beliefs. It wasn't until after I was married that I began to see the futility of striving for things of this world like money, power, and position. My husband, George, and I had worked to amass a small fortune, before we lost everything in a bad business venture. It was then that I remembered everything I had been taught by my parents. I encouraged George to attend some church services with me. We were both wonderfully and miraculously converted in a revival service. We then began to live for the Lord, and through His infinite mercy, He saw fit to restore our fortune, which we always tried to use to help those less fortunate. I think God wanted to see if we would still serve Him after getting our money back, and I can thankfully say that with His help we remained true to our commitment to Him.

"Abigail, I am not proud that it took me so long to come to the Lord after all He had done for me, but I am thankful that He forgave me even after all the times I had mocked Him and those who chose to serve Him. Please don't waste more of your life like I did. Accept Him now. He is always ready and willing to open His arms of mercy and forgive His lost children."

For over an hour Esther spoke softly, answering questions, reading Scripture, quoting many verses from her heart. When Abigail became frustrated and almost angry, Esther patiently would bring her back to the thought of giving her heart to God.

Finally Abigail said, "I don't understand any of this, Aunt Esther! I'm tired, and I don't know what to do!" Then suddenly she began to weep in earnest. All of the pressures, all of the fears, and all of the anxieties suddenly burst over, and she simply wept. She was aware that Esther had come and put her arm around her, and she turned to the older woman and clung to her as a child clings to its mother. The storm in her heart continued for a long time, and finally she drew back and drew a shaky breath. "I don't know what to do, Aunt Esther! Tell me— help me. I can't go on being what I have been!"

"Then it's time to be what you have never been—a child of God. Let me read you a few Scriptures, and then we're going to pray." She read several passages from the Bible, speaking of turning from sin, and of the blood of Jesus, and finally she said, "We'll pray now. Abigail, you must speak to God in your heart exactly as if He were here. As I pray, you call upon the Lord, and He will enter and do a work in you."

Esther began to pray, and Abigail prayed, too—not aloud, but in the depths of her heart. She never remembered all that she said. She was sure it was not eloquent. She did remember once crying aloud with her voice, "Oh, God, help me, I'm such a wicked girl! Help me to be good, in Jesus' name!"

Soon it was over, and Abigail found herself completely drained. She had wept in deep repentance for all the things that had led her so far from God. But now her face relaxed, and she could feel the tremendous tension give way to a deep inner peace. She looked at Esther with wonder in her eyes and whispered, "I feel so . . . so *clean*, Aunt Esther!"

"Yes, I can see that! There's a difference in you. You're at peace with God now." She kissed Abigail and said with joy and tears in her own eyes, "Didn't I tell you?"

"Tell me what, Aunt Esther?"

"Didn't I tell you that God isn't very far away? Now you've found Him, and you must never turn Him loose. Be obedient to Him."

"I don't know how."

"I will teach you, and the Holy Spirit will teach you. That's what He's here for."

The two women sat there for a long time, and finally they rose. Abigail knew, as she left the cupola, that her life would never be again what it had been before!

16

A Man Can't Erase the Past

THE ATTACK CAME WITHOUT WARNING, even without a hint. Leo Rochester had risen from his bath and was putting on his clothes. Sitting on the bed, he drew on first the white stocking that came up over his knee and had reached down to pull the second over his toes. He had pulled the stocking up over the heel, and it fit so snugly that he grunted as he gave it a firm tug.

Somehow that tug seemed to have pulled something loose inside his chest, for he felt a pain that started somewhere deep inside—a dull ache that he had learned to recognize with dread.

Loosing the stocking, he straightened up and sat on the side of the padded Windsor chair, his face pale, and his eyes wide with shock. The pain seemed to swell inside him as if he had swallowed some kind of monstrous seed that was now exploding into growth. It pushed at the walls of his chest, and the throbbing of his heart was like a mighty engine churning in his ears. He held his breath and prayed that it would go away, but it did not. A tiny needle-sharp pain began at the top of his left shoulder. It increased in magnitude, feeling as if someone were shoving a white-hot stiletto into his flesh. It moved down to his biceps, then his forearm, and then his fingers, so that the whole arm was one seething mass of agonizing pain. Gasping, Leo fell back on the chair, closing his eyes. The pain gnawed at him, but even as he sat there, it began to recede. It took the same route that it had taken. First his fingers were freed from the agonizing grip and became numb. Next the whole arm was numb, and the throbbing in his chest mitigated somewhat. He grew nauseated and thought that he would vomit. Swallowing hard, he sat very still and waited for it to pass.

190

Finally, his brow damp with perspiration, he drew his right hand shakily across it and took a cautious breath. He had the familiar sensation that something in his chest was made of fragile glass and that a sudden movement would shatter it into a thousand shards, destroying everything within him.

Finally the nausea left, and he became aware that, at least this time, he was spared. He rose, and as he did so, his left arm seemed to flop like a lifeless member. Standing in the middle of the room, he tried to lift it. He grunted and strained with all of his might, but all that he achieved was a slight twitching of the hand and a slight bend at the elbow.

"It can't go on like this!" Rochester muttered. He had put his sickness out of his mind as best he could, although he knew it was just lurking, waiting to attack him. Now he stood there uncertainly, and finally, for lack of anything better, he bent and managed to get the stocking up over his knee with his right hand. But as he looked at the rest of his clothing, he knew they were too much for him. Standing, he moved to the door and called out, "Cato—Cato. . . !"

The servant had been just down the hall polishing silver, and he arose at once. He moved swiftly down the hall, where he found Sir Leo standing in the doorway of his bedroom. "Yes, sir?" he inquired. "Can I help you, Mr. Rochester?"

"Come in here!" Leo said quickly. When he stepped back, and after Cato entered the room, Rochester said, "I've got to have help. I've injured my arm. Help me get my shirt and britches on!"

"Why, yes sir, Mr. Rochester!" At once Cato went to the heavy clothes press and said, "You want this shirt, sir?"

"Yes, and those dark gray britches."

As Cato was assisting Rochester to dress, he asked, "How did you hurt your arm, Mr. Rochester?"

"I took a fall from my horse! It'll be all right."

Finally Rochester was completely dressed, including the small waistcoat that Cato had been obliged to button. He slipped on his frock coat and reached out for the tricorn hat and put it over his head. He hesitated one moment, and then said, "Cato, make a sling out of something. Something to put my arm in so it won't be giving me any trouble." He assisted Cato in picking out a square of cloth and making a neckerchief. When it was tied around his neck, he put his arm in it and nodded with some relief. "There, that'll do until it gets better! Go tell High Boy to bring the carriage around. I want to go to town."

"Yes, sir!" Cato said, then left for the stables.

Leo left the house walking very carefully and climbed awkwardly into the carriage using his one hand. He seated himself with a sigh of relief, and soon after the door slammed he stuck his head out. "Take me down to Jefferson Avenue, High Boy!"

"Yes, sir, I'll do that! Get up there, you hosses!"

Forty minutes later Leo was climbing the stairs to the office of Dr. Henry Settling. He entered the narrow reception room and found, to his relief, that there were no patients there. It was too early in the morning, he supposed, and he called out, "Dr. Settling!"

Almost at once the door opened and Henry Settling came out. He had apparently been about to leave, for he had on his street clothes, which consisted of a dark brown suit and a frock coat that he had not buttoned. He held his hat in his hand, but when he saw Rochester, he immediately put it down on a table and said, "Sir Leo, you just caught me. I was just about to go out. Come in!"

Leo stepped into the inner office and once again noted how crowded it was with rows of cabinets containing the paraphernalia and instruments of the medical trade. He was usually slightly disgusted by the acrid smell of chemicals, but this time he did not notice it. "I've had another attack," he said bluntly. "Worse than the others. . . !"

Settling, at once, took off his coat, saying, "Sit down here, and let's have a look at you!"

"I can't use my left arm too well," Rochester said.

"Let me help you with it."

With the physician's assistance, Leo managed to get out of his coat, and soon sat with his shirt off before the doctor. This time the examination was more thorough; Settling took so long that Leo grew irritable. Settling was listening to his chest for what seemed to be an interminable time, and Leo finally demanded, "Well, what's wrong with me?"

Settling straightened up and stroked his Vandyke beard. A careful light had come into his light blue eyes, and he spoke slowly. "You had another attack. I'm sure you must realize that."

"What does that mean?"

"I'm afraid it's not good news, Sir Leo." Settling said, "Let me help you get dressed." As he helped Leo fasten his clothing, he spoke in a moderate tone. Settling was used to delivering bad news, as all doctors have to be. He never liked doing it. It was the one part of being a doctor that he would have assigned to another if that had been possible, but he had learned to recognize fear, for it became almost palpable in many people. Settling saw it there now in Leo, so strongly that he could almost smell it. Behind the eyes of the aristocrat lurked a mindless, screaming fear that had to be imprisoned as a madman in a cage. He spoke soothingly, but he was aware that Rochester was not at all fooled by his bedside manner. He finally said, "Your condition is not as good as it was when you first came here."

"Well, I know *that*!" Rochester tried to move his arm and found that he had regained some use of it. "My arm's better now!" he remarked. "What happened to it?"

"It often happens with heart problems. You have some kind of a stoppage in your blood stream, I would think, and when that's shut off you lose the use of one of your arms. Hopefully, you'll gain the use of it back completely."

Leo flexed the arm again and decided to leave it in the sling until he regained better use of it. Awkwardly he struggled back, and Settling moved forward to help him get it in a comfortable position. Then Leo turned and faced the doctor squarely. Though the fear gnawed inside him, Leo Rochester was no coward. He was an utter realist who prided himself on looking things straight on, taking the facts as he found them. "Am I going to die, Settling?"

Settling did not hesitate a moment. He had been asked this before by patients and had a stock answer. "We've all got to do that, Sir Leo."

"I don't want any of your blasted philosophy!" Leo snapped harshly. "I mean, am I apt to drop dead before I get back home?"

For one minute Settling hesitated, then said, "I can't give you the answer to that. I've known men in worse condition than you who have lived many years. They took their problem as a warning and did all they could to modify it. I've already told you that it depends to a great extent on how well you take care of yourself."

Something left unsaid in the physician's words caught at Leo. "So I notice that you say that I won't drop dead."

"That's always a possibility. I've known men who've never had a pain in their lives. Young men, apparently healthy, who suddenly, without cause, died of a massive heart attack. I wish I could give you guarantees, Leo, but there are none in this life."

"Well then, give me your sermon again on how to take care of myself." Leo listened as the doctor repeated his instructions about diet, staying away from strong drink, and getting plenty of rest. It was, he knew, the same speech the doctor had delivered to many people. Finally he asked, "What would be the risk in taking a sea voyage?"

"A sea voyage? Where do you want to go?"

"I'd like to go to England."

Settling shrugged. "I see nothing against it as long as you don't hit a storm at sea, or run into something unexpected. Are you planning on leaving right away?"

"I'm not sure."

"See me before you go, and I'll do the best I can to get you some tonic."

Leo left Dr. Settling's office, got into the cab, and said, "Drive around by the city hall, High Boy!" He settled back again, and when the carriage stopped, he got out and went into a small red-brick building across the street from Boston's city hall. He was greeted there by Dawkins, the family lawyer, a short fireplug of a man with flaming red hair—what was left of it—and spent an hour in the inner office going over business. By the time he had emerged, it was nearly noon. He got back into the carriage and said, "Take me home, High Boy!"

"Yes, sir! Get up there, you hosses!"

T   T   T

Dinner had been a quiet affair, and Marian was pleased that her father had been able to come downstairs to the table and eat. "It's so good to have you here, Father," she said. "Here, try some more of these beans. Hattie made them especially for you! She knows just how you like them."

John Frazier smiled and accepted another spoonful of the beans that she placed carefully on his plate. He speared a few with his fork, put them in his mouth and chewed them, then nodded, "Hattie always could make the best beans in the world! I wonder how she seasons them?"

"I don't think she'll tell anybody that!" Marian smiled. "It's her secret formula." She was wearing a pale yellow dress with light green trim, and her hair fell down her back in a most attractive fashion. "She's got a surprise for dessert, too!"

John Frazier was enjoying the meal tremendously. He did feel better, and these days he seized times like this eagerly. Looking around he said, "I always liked this room. I remember when your mother and I were building the house, we had some rousing arguments over the wallpaper."

"Who won?" Marian asked, knowing his answer.

"Oh, she did, of course! She always knew how to have her own way out of me—exactly as you do!" He looked over at Leo, who was sitting across the table, his arm still in a sling. "I'm sorry about your arm, Leo. I've never known you to fall off a horse before."

Leo looked up from his plate, for his thoughts had been far off, and he caught only the last part of Frazier's words. "It isn't serious," he murmured. "I'll probably take it out of the sling tomorrow."

"Did you go see Dr. Settling?" Frazier inquired.

"Yes, I did. He's not concerned about it."

"Good man, Settling," Frazier said. He had become somewhat of a connoisseur of doctors since his illness, and for a while spoke of the virtues of Leo's physician. Then he inquired, "Have you heard any news of the action in New York?"

"I don't think the battle has started yet," Leo said. His brow furrowed and he shook his head. "I don't think the colonists will have much of a chance against King George's army. I understand it's a formidable array of force that General Howe will command." He spoke for a while about the revolution, but his mind was obviously not on it. He got up finally and said, "I'm going to read for a while in the study. I'm glad you're feeling better, John."

"Why—thank you, Leo." Frazier watched as his son-in-law left the dining room, then turned to face his daughter. "Leo's looking very poorly, isn't he, Marian?"

"Yes, I'm glad he went to see the doctor." She was fairly certain, however, that whatever he had done to his arm, it had nothing to do with falling off his horse. He had lost weight, and there was a lifelessness about him that was foreign to his character. "I think he's more ill than he lets on."

"He was always such a big, bluff, strong fellow," Frazier murmured. The thought came to him, *What if he should die before me?* But he put it aside, saying, "Well, at least you're healthy, and I've never seen you looking prettier, Marian."

"Why, thank you, Father," Marian smiled. She rose and came over, then bent down and kissed him. "You sit right there. I'm going to get you some of that custard that Hattie worked so hard on."

She left the room and soon returned with a cut-glass deep dish, which she set before her father. Handing him a silver spoon she said, "Now, you start on that, and I'll get some for myself."

The two sat there enjoying the custard, and finally Frazier sat back and sighed with pleasure. "It's been good, coming to the table and sharing a meal with you and Leo."

"It's been good to have you! I'm praying that you'll get well and get out of that bed again." There was a longing in Marian, for she loved her father dearly. She thought back again to the days when he had been strong and lively; they seemed almost like a dream now, but she did not let him ever see the doubts that came to her. "Now, do you feel up to a game of checkers?"

The evening passed, and finally, when her father retired to his room, Marian returned to the parlor. She sat there for a while reading, then was surprised when she looked up to see Leo enter. Putting the book aside she asked, "How does your arm feel?"

"Well enough." Leo sat down across the room from her on one of the couches. He was silent, and there was a heaviness in his manner. Finally he said, "I went to see Dawkins today. I made some arrangements with him."

"What sort of arrangements, Leo?"

"Oh, just things that need to be taken care of. The deeds to some of the lands I bought last year in Virginia. I had to have him write letters—oh yes, I made a new will."

Marian's head lifted at this. She made no comment, except to say, "What was wrong with the old one?"

"I've never been satisfied with it." Leo crossed his legs and stared down at the soft satin slippers that he wore for comfort in the house. He touched one of them and ran his finger along the seams, then looked up abruptly. "I made sure that you'd be well cared for if anything happened to me."

Marian flushed slightly. It was the first time he had ever said anything about the possibility of his death to her, and she knew that it was not accidental. "I hope," she said quietly, "that I never have to think about that."

Leo straightened up then and gave her a direct stare. "Marian, do you love Daniel Bradford?"

Instantly Marian grew fearful. "Leo, we've talked about—"

"I'm not accusing you of having an affair with him!" Leo said quickly. "You've assured me often enough that you haven't."

"And do you believe me?"

Leo slowly nodded. "Strangely enough I do. I think I always have." He smiled suddenly at a thought that touched him. "I think Bradford's too much of a holy man to try to steal another man's wife."

"Don't mock, Leo!"

"I'm not mocking," he said, shrugging his shoulders. "I'm just thinking what I've always felt. He's always been that way, ever since he was a boy—and I've had a wry sort of admiration for him. Oh, I've hated him at times and wanted to kill him when we were younger, but that's all over now!"

"I'm glad to hear that, Leo!" she said quickly, hoping he would not press her further on the matter.

"I asked you if you loved him."

"I don't have any right to love him, Leo, nor he me—but that's not an answer." She hesitated, then said, "It's difficult to explain. I've always admired Daniel. The very qualities that you've made fun of, I've found very—well, attractive. He's honest, he's been faithful to his wife, he's a good family man." Suddenly she looked straight at him and said,

"I think I admired him most because he never did try to take advantage of me!"

"If he had tried, would you have surrendered?"

Marian Rochester had a streak of honesty that ran broad and was strong as an iron bar. Without blinking she said simply and plainly, "I don't know, Leo."

Leo Rochester stared at her and finally grunted, "Well, that's honest enough for me!"

"I'm married to you, Leo, and as long as we are alive I'll be your wife."

Leo Rochester found this statement interesting. It was simply a restatement of the marriage vows, but he was thinking more deeply these days than he had in the past. He sat there quietly, considering his wife and knew that her beauty was little less than it was when he had first seen her. Now, at forty-one, she was still the same tall, well-shaped dark-haired beauty he had married. A pang came to him, not physically, but thoughts of what might have been. Slowly he got up and said, "You wouldn't have given in to him, not you!"

"I'm glad you think so, Leo."

"You're too much like him. You're a puritan to the heart—just like he is. The two of you are a pair." He turned and left the room, and she heard his footsteps as he moved down the hall. She sat for a long time, wondering at the strange scene that had passed. A sense of foreboding came to her, and she considered her life, how it had been, but did not permit herself to think of the future. The clock ticked out in the hallway, and she slowly picked up the book and began reading again.

🦁 🦁 🦁

Clive Gordon had been asleep, but a sudden jerking of his tall body brought his head in contact with the hard maple headboard. The solid *clunk* sounded loud to his own ears, and he grunted aloud and reached up to touch his head.

"Clive, are you all right?"

The voice came from his left, and he turned quickly to see a figure outlined there. He could not see the face, for the lamp was behind the woman, forming a golden aureole around her head. He squeezed his eyes together and shook his head, which aggravated the ache that came from the blow he had taken. He opened his lips, which were dry as toast, and croaked in a voice that he did not recognize. "Where—who—?"

A cool hand touched his forehead, and twisting in the bed, his body was wet with sweat. He felt that his skin was tight and dry, so hot had it become. "Water," he croaked again and tried to lick his lips. The woman left, and he heard the sound of water pouring from one vessel to another, then she was back again. He felt an arm under his back, pulling him upward. "Sit up," the voice said. He felt the cool glass against his lips and gulped thirstily. He was trembling so much that his teeth chattered against the glass, and some of the water ran down his chin and dripped onto his chest. Reaching out he grabbed at the glass and turned it upward, for it was the most delicious thing he had ever tasted.

"Be careful, you'll strangle yourself, Clive! Wait just a minute, and you can have more."

Clive felt the hand on his back. He could speak more clearly now and asked, "Rachel, is that you?"

"No, it's not Rachel."

Clive lay back down and watched as the woman turned her back. She returned to the washstand where she poured water from a pitcher to fill the cup. When she turned again he saw her face, and shock washed over him. "Katherine!" he whispered.

Katherine moved and helped him up again. His flesh felt hot beneath the thin shirt he wore, and the shirt itself was soaked and damp. She said quietly, "Drink this!" She waited until he gulped the water down, then still holding him said, "I'm glad you're awake."

"Katherine, what are you doing here?"

"Helping Rachel," she said quietly. "Your nightgown is soaked." She put the glass down on the table, then felt his forehead. "I think your fever has broken some. It's been so high, we've all been afraid for you."

"How long have you been here?"

"I just came tonight. Now, we've got to get you a dry nightshirt on. Can you sit up?"

"Why . . . yes."

Clive was not thinking clearly. He sat there while she tugged the nightshirt upward, pulling the sheet up over his lower body, then said, "Lift your arms." When he obeyed, he felt the shirt go over his head. He shivered, for suddenly the room seemed cold. Staring with fever-bright eyes, Clive watched as she removed a nightshirt from the chest against the wall, came back, and said, "Now, lift your arms again." When he obeyed, she slipped it over his head, and then said, "Now, do you want to lie down?"

"No, let me sit up!"

Katherine put a pillow behind him, then moved away. Drawing up a chair she sat down and looked directly at him. "You've been very sick. I'm sorry."

Clive could not believe what was happening. The sickness had come on him slowly, and he had remembered how he had thought to fight it off, but then the high fever had come, and it had been a nightmare. Now, waking up to find Katherine taking care of him was a distinct shock. He said nothing for a long time, and neither did she. Finally she leaned forward and asked, "Clive, are you awake enough to understand me?"

"Why, of course. My head is beating like a drum, but what is it?"

Katherine had prepared herself for this moment. She had always known that she would have to do it, and she saw that even now he was not in complete control of his faculties. "I wanted to tell you," she said with some hesitation, "how I'm sorry I treated you so badly." He started to speak, but she shook her head and cut him off. "I don't know why you did what you did, but you were kind to me in Halifax and to my father and uncle, and I'm grateful for that."

Actually Clive was understanding very little of this. He was dizzy, and his head ached, and a chill was coming on. He began to tremble, and he could not make sense out of what Katherine was trying to say. He stared at her with a lack of comprehension, and then sickness came upon him.

Katherine quickly helped him lie down. He shook so violently it frightened her, so she began to put covers on him. As she sat beside him she thought, *I've told him how I feel*. She knew she would have to tell him again when he had recovered, but somehow it would be easier now.

🦁   🦁   🦁

She had gone to sleep sitting in the chair, and now she woke up with a start, for she heard him calling out. "Clive—" Her neck ached, but she ignored it as she rose and bent over him. "Are you all right?"

Clive muttered and threw his arms about. He was, she saw, having some kind of a nightmare. He was mumbling something she could not understand.

Leaning forward she whispered, "Clive, wake up. You're having a nightmare." But he was too deeply caught by the dream. She heard him say, "We'll get you out, Amos. I'll get you out of here. . . !"

The words caught at her. He was speaking her father's name, promising to get him out. It had to be a dream of the time when he had helped them in Halifax, and suddenly she was glad to know that at least in his dreams he was still faithful! She stood over him and listened as he mumbled over and over again, speaking of some of the things that she recognized. She heard her own name called more than once, and finally he dropped off into a fitful sleep. She stood there looking down on his thin face outlined by the yellow gleam of the lamp. He seemed very young, and she could not see the traces of deceit she had blamed him for. Finally, she took her seat again and sat there until dawn watching him and thinking of what had happened between the two of them.

🜂   🜂   🜂

The next morning, at ten o'clock, Clive awoke. His fever had broken and his eyes were clear. He called out, "Katherine!" but when someone came to the door he saw it was Rachel. At once he asked, "Was Katherine here last night, or was I having a nightmare?"

Rachel came over and put her hand on his forehead. A smile touched her broad lips and she said, "Yes, she was here. She's gone home now, though. How do you feel?"

Licking his lips and taking stock of his condition, Clive said, "Much better. The fever is gone—although it was bad last night. It happens like that sometimes, doesn't it?"

"Yes, it did with me! Could you eat something?"

A ravenous hunger suddenly arose in Clive and he said, "Yes, anything!" As she started to leave the room he said, "Is she coming back . . . Katherine, I mean?"

"Yes, she said she'd come back to help take care of you tonight."

Clive slept most of the day, but he ate several times, and by the time the shadows were beginning to fall, he was feeling much stronger. He managed to get out of bed and put on a robe that belonged to Daniel Bradford. Since he was six feet three and Bradford was somewhat shorter, it did not fit him well, but he was able to take a few shaky steps back and forth and laughed aloud. "I'm going to make it!" he said with satisfaction. He had not been at all sure of that, for he had seen others go down and not recover from whatever this sickness was that ravaged Boston.

He was sitting in the chair staring out the window when he saw Katherine approach. He straightened up and watched as she moved to the entrance and was admitted by Rachel. Turning to face the door, he waited expectantly. Soon enough it opened, and when the two women came in, he ignored Rachel, saying, "Katherine!" But then he could think of nothing else to say.

Katherine was embarrassed as well, but seeing this, Rachel said, "Sit down, Katherine. I was about to bring his supper in. I'll bring yours too, and you can eat together. Move that table, will you?"

"All right, Rachel."

Glad to have something to do, Katherine moved the table over and then pulled the chair across from Clive. "How are you feeling?" she finally asked.

"Much better!" He stared at her so directly that she blushed. "I thought I was having a dream last night."

"You did have a dream, several of them," Katherine said. "Do you remember any of them?"

"A dream? I remember some nightmares, and being so hot I thought I was going to catch on fire. Then I woke up and there you were."

"Do you remember what I said to you?"

"Not very much."

"Then I'll have to say it again." Katherine was more at ease now. She had spoken to him about this once, although he didn't remember it. "I treated you shamefully when you came to Boston. I think I hated you, Clive."

Clive shook his head. "I never understood why you were so angry."

Katherine looked at him, tilting her head to one side. It was an attractive way she had. She studied him carefully and saw nothing but a genuine bewilderment in him. "Don't you really know why I was angry?"

"I haven't the foggiest idea!"

"When you left Halifax," Katherine asked, "did you leave any orders concerning my father and my uncle?"

"Why, no! What sort of orders do you mean?"

Suddenly Katherine saw that he was telling the truth. There was a bewilderment in him that she could not mistake. "I went to see Major Banks at the hospital and discovered that my father and my uncle had been moved back to the hulks."

"Back to the hulks? Why, that's impossible!" Incredulity showed itself plainly on Clive's face. "I can't believe it!"

"I went to see Major Banks—" Suddenly Katherine hesitated, for looking back she saw clearly what had happened. Slowly she said, "He showed me an order that he said was written by you. It ordered my father and my uncle back onto the *St. George*."

"I never gave such an order! I never wrote it, Katherine!"

"I . . . I see that now, Clive. It was all Banks' doing!" Anger flared through her, not at Banks, but at herself for being beguiled by the man. "I was a fool to believe him. I've never seen your handwriting, so I didn't question it, and he kept it. He must've written it himself!"

"I see why you were so angry," Clive said. "Anyone would be."

But Katherine was shaking her head almost violently. "I can't *believe* I was so foolish! I never believed anything he said before, and I never trusted him. Somehow it just never occurred to me that a man would do a thing like that!"

"He's a bitter, vindictive man, Katherine," Clive said.

The two sat there, and suddenly Katherine could not meet his eyes. "I'm . . . I'm so sorry, Clive."

He reached across the table; her hands were folded on it clenched tightly together. He took them, pried them apart, and held one of them in his own. "Don't grieve yourself," he said, and gentleness ran through his tone. "All the evidence pointed against me." .

The touch of his hands on hers was warm, and she remembered how it had been with him before. How she had admired him and trusted him, and how kind he had been to her and to her relatives. Tears came to her eyes, and she whispered with bitterness, "I was hurt by a man once. Do you suppose I'll go on distrusting every man I meet?"

"You can't live without trust, Katherine, and you won't. It's not in you to be like that."

Startled, she looked up and met his eyes. Most men she knew would have been at least victorious to have been proved right. Many would have even been harsh and condemnatory, but she saw nothing of this in Clive Gordon. He was smiling at her now, and suddenly a heavy weight lifted from her shoulders. She whispered, "You're so kind, Clive!"

His hands tightened on hers, and he lifted them suddenly and kissed one hand. She flushed and dropped her eyes. She could not speak for a moment, for the fullness in her throat. Finally, she looked up and found that somehow all of the anger and bitterness had dropped away from her. Blinking her eyes to clear them of the tears, she said softly, "Will you let me start all over with you, Clive Gordon?"

Clive looked at her, then kissed her hand again. "We'll both start over," he said, his eyes warm and confident.

17

DISASTER FOR HIS EXCELLENCY

FINALLY, EVEN THE CAUTIOUS General William Howe was ready to make the advance, the first step against the conquest of New York. On the twenty-first day of August 1776 British officers began loading troops onto the ships at Staten Island. They swung east to Gravesend Bay, where they were well out of the range of Washington's cannons. A great thunderstorm interrupted briefly, but the complicated maneuver went smoothly. The British troops were ferried ashore in seventy-five flatboats, eleven bateaux, and two galleys, all built specifically for this invasion.

The landing made a splendid sight. The vessels spread acres of white sails to dry in the bright sunlight that followed the storm. Long Island glittered, the hills and fields a bright green. By noon fifteen thousand men with all their arms and supplies were landed, and rank after rank of brightly arrayed British regiments advanced smartly in time to the beat of the drums and the tinkling of the fife. The British objective was the American position on Brooklyn Heights.

Brooklyn's defenders, less than eight thousand in all, occupied a series of posts on a broken ridge nearly two miles in front of the main fortifications of the village. Despite being outnumbered, Washington's troops had an advantage in holding higher ground than the British. Once again the British, as at Breed's Hill, would have to march up a hill into the guns of the Americans.

General George Washington had faced the problem of how to stop the overwhelming troops of England with foreboding. Finally, he had entrusted the command of his troops to an Irishman from New Hampshire, General John Sullivan. Then Sullivan was replaced, by the order of Washington, with Israel Putnam. Between the two of them they arranged a forward line along a bluff overlooking Flatbush where the British were camped. The Heights were broken by several roads and passes, and the Americans carefully guarded the three western ones. Jamaica Pass, on the east, was left guarded only by a small picket.

Early in the morning General Howe called his officers together. When they were standing before him he said, "Gentlemen, we are ready to do our duty!" He had stretched a map of Long Island and its environs out on a table. "You see here, our adversary has put their line across this area. Here is the battle plan. The Hessian troops will mount noisy demonstrations against the western end of the Heights, here near Gowanus Bay and the two center passes. Meanwhile, Lord Cornwallis and Sir Henry Percy, with ten thousand men will sweep to our right. You will fight your way through and come around behind the rebels." Howe looked up with satisfaction in his eyes. "We will trap them, I believe, gentlemen. Are there any questions?"

Sir Henry Crutan said with exultation, "We shall have them, General. The war will be ended here today!"

"It very well might! Washington, I'm told, is a fox hunter," Howe said, and a smile lifted the corners of his lips. "We shall drive the fox to cover, and then take him, and this little demonstration among the Colonies will be over. We can get back to being Englishmen as usual!"

♜   ♜   ♜

Dake Bradford was on the left flank of the American line. He stood there beside Silas Tooms, and his heart beat faster. "I keep hearing firing down to our right," he said.

Tooms nodded, his jaw tight with tension. "I reckon that's right. They're hitting Sullivan hard down that way." He stared out into the morning across the fields, expecting to see the red flash of troopers. "I expected them to hit here before now," he said, a puzzled look in his eyes. "I wonder where they are?"

Thad Mobrey, a sixteen-year-old who had joined only the day before, said, "Let 'em come. We'll stop 'em, won't we, Sergeant?"

Tooms gave Mobrey a look of disgust. "Just be sure you don't turn and run, Mobrey, when you see the lobsterbacks coming!"

"Run!" Mobrey said and laughed loudly. He shook his musket and said, "That'll be the day when Thad Mobrey runs from a bunch of lobsterbacks!"

The tension built as the firing on the right grew louder. Dake grew thirsty but discovered there was no water to be had.

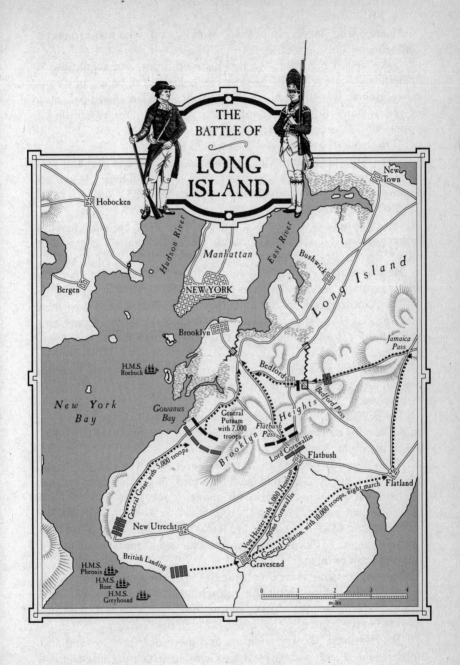

THE BATTLE OF

LONG ISLAND

Hobocken

Hudson River

Manhattan

East River

New Town

Bushwick

Long Island

Bergen

NEW YORK

Brooklyn

Jamaica Pass

H.M.S. Roebuck

Bedford

Bedford Pass

New York Bay

Gowanus Bay

General Putnam with 7,000 troops

Brooklyn Heights

Flatbush Pass

Lord Cornwallis

Flatbush

General Grant with 5,000 troops

Flatland

Von Hester with 5,000 Hessians joins Cornwallis

General Clinton, with 10,000 troops, night march

New Utrecht

British Landing

H.M.S. Pheonix

H.M.S. Rose

H.M.S. Greyhound

Gravesend

0   1   2   3   4
miles

"Here, Dake, have a sip of this!" Mobrey said, who had brought a canteen.

Dake sipped the water, washed his mouth out, and swallowed it gratefully. "Thanks, Thad!" he said. He looked at the young boy curiously. Mobrey was slight, not over five six or seven, and had a pale mop of yellow hair. He looked about fifteen years old. "You're a little bit young for this, aren't you, Thad?"

"I'm sixteen," Mobrey said. "That's old enough!"

Dake thought of Sam, who was the same age as this boy, and was suddenly very glad that his younger brother was not here. He started to answer Mobrey when a yell went up from his left.

"To the rear, the Redcoats, we're flanked!"

Instantly, Tooms whirled and narrowed his eyes. He was chewing tobacco and spat it out on the ground. "There they come!" he said quietly. "They've got us boxed."

He was exactly right. Howe and his troops had mousetrapped the whole position, and now the trap was sprung!

The American officers did what they could. They pulled their men into line, but Howe simply rolled up their left flank. Dake, Tooms, and Mobrey stuck close together while falling back, but Dake saw that it was hopeless.

The ground was almost totally covered by impenetrable brush woods. The greater part of the American riflemen could not defend themselves.

The British line marched on inexorably, and finally when the militia could stand it no longer, they broke and ran despite the officers' desperate attempts to get them to stand.

"They shouldn't have run," Thad Mobrey said. His face was pale, but his lips were tight. He had loaded his musket, and he peered across the field that was now covered with smoke. "Look, I never seen no soldiers like them. . . ."

Tooms and Dake looked up, and it was Tooms who said, "That's the German Jaegers." His voice was grim and he said, "Our boys will never stand in front of them."

The Jaegers came marching through the drifting mist of the morning, their green uniforms blending in with the trees and bushes. Their drums played a steady cadence, and their bright bayonets dipped and sparkled in the sun's rays that broke through the smoke.

"It's Hessians!" the cry went out and the farmer boys, young and untried, stared with wide eyes at the Germans with an aching fear.

They tried to make a stand, but it was a thin little ragged line. Suddenly they heard the drums of the Redcoats coming from behind them.

Dake whirled around and yelled, "They're coming from the other direction!" He sighted his musket on a tall German and pulled the trigger. The rifle kicked and he saw his man go down. Frantically he reloaded.

"We can't stay here!" Thad Mobrey said, his voice trembling.

"Take it easy, son!" Tooms said. "We'll get out of this."

But men were streaming by, mostly young farm boys who had never fought in any battle before, except for the few who had been at Breed's Hill. Overcome by fear and panic, they threw down their muskets and ran. The officers pleaded with them, trying to stop them, but they blindly dashed away. Thad Mobrey stood, and, trembling, his face began to twitch. Dake said, "We'll handle it, Thad—" but Mobrey threw his gun down and started to run. Dake started to run after him, but Tooms grabbed him and pulled him back.

"You can't stop him, Dake! Come along, they're making a little stand over there."

But Dake was watching as the Americans ran away. He saw that they were trapped. The Germans were yelling and laughing as they ran after the fleeing men. The Germans were yelling, "Yonkee! Yonkee!" and then Dake saw Thad trapped and flanked by two groups of German Jaegers. Thad turned to run, stumbled, and a big German came forward and held his gleaming bayonet high. He rammed it into the boy's back and laughed as he did so.

Dake only had time to see the boy writhe like a cut worm as the Jaeger yanked the bayonet out and plunged it in again and then again.

"Let's go, Dake!" Tooms said.

Dake blindly obeyed, and the two found themselves fighting for their lives. It went on for hours between the wooded lines that tried to hold in the American base fortification.

General Sullivan was found in a cornfield trying to hide, but he was captured by three blond Germans who dragged him to his feet and hauled him off. General Sterling was also captured, and still the fighting went on. Only on the American right, where the Maryland and Delaware Continentals, the best-furnished troops in the army, fought, was there anything like success, but by early afternoon the battle was all over. More than three hundred were killed, and a thousand Americans were captured. British and German losses were less than four hundred.

The British were exultant, for they were now directly in front of the American fortifications on Brooklyn Heights. All they had to do was make one more push, and the army of General George Washington would be gobbled up—and the American Revolution would end!

As the wounded, exhausted American soldiers struggled back, Dake found himself wondering if it had all been in vàin. He and Silas Tooms had survived, along with most of their squad, but it seemed hopeless. "I don't see how we can stand another attack, Silas!" Dake panted glumly. He looked around at the gruesome wounded, many twitching with pain, and some dying even as he watched. "They're going to hit us one more time, and then we'll be done for!"

As George Washington, from his vantage point, looked over the ghastly scene, he noted the British converging on an open plain below. *They make a rather beautiful sight*, he thought, *British in red, Hessian regulars in blue, and Jaegers in green*. They fanned out like the spokes of a multi-colored wheel, almost like a rainbow. They had stopped firing and ignored Washington's feeble cannon fire. It was the largest army Washington had ever seen gathered together in one place, and he watched as the preparations for the final charge were being made.

"Now they will attack!" Washington said grimly to Knox, who was standing by his side.

Micah had served as Knox's aide throughout the battle, and now he saw that Washington's face was grim and unrelenting. He glanced down below at the thousands of red and blue and green coated soldiers, admiring the way they marched in perfect unison. But then he heard Washington say with a note of relief and incredulity in his voice, "Look, Knox, they're not going to attack!"

The big man stared at the British forces, and whispered, "What is happening, sir?"

"General Howe has decided not to attack, not today anyway, unless it's a trick. Perhaps he's going to try a sneak attack tonight under cover of darkness."

"I don't think he'll do that, sir. A frontal attack and he'll have us."

Washington suddenly became all action. "Double the sentries! Rum and water for every man! The men must return to their formations, and all must be fed."

Micah was kept on the run then, for Knox utilized him, as he did every man he had, in getting the guns pulled into position. Washington moved through all the encampment, and it was a miracle how he was able to pull the army of wounded and terrified men together again.

Down below, the officers of General Howe were perplexed and angry. Howe had called off the attack, and Clinton and Cornwallis both pleaded with him to make one more effort.

"Sir!" Cornwallis said urgently. "They are waiting for us! They're in our hands. All we have to do is attack and we'll finish this thing once and for all!"

But General William Howe had a long memory. He was thinking of how at Bunker Hill, the British troops had marched up into the guns of the Americans and had been cut to pieces. True enough, the army in front of him seemed to be beaten, but he knew that the Americans, like a wounded bear, could turn, and he could not spare any more men. Some might ignore the fact that it took a year to train one British soldier and cost hundreds of pounds to get him to this point, but he could not afford to do so. Besides, he was a careful man, one who could analyze the situation carefully.

Pointing upward to the hill he said, "Look there, gentlemen, there is the enemy. Over there is the East River and there is the Hudson. Our ships can pull in and cut them off. In the morning we will send the ships in, and we will gather them up."

General Clinton disagreed. "I wish we would go now, sir, and finish it off!"

But Howe said, "The men have been marching for sixty-seven hours under a sixty-pound pack. They have fought a battle for six hours, running up and down hill, and they are exhausted. In the morning they will be fresh. We will attack in the morning!"

So the British sat down to rest, and the shattered and frightened Americans began pulling themselves back together again. Washington took command and wasted no time on attempts to fix the blame for their defeat. It was obvious to him that the battle had been lost by Sullivan's failure to hold Jamaica Pass, but he did not give the slightest hint of the serious predicament that he and his tiny army were in. Instead, by his powerful physical presence alone, he inspired new courage in his men. He moved throughout the camp, overseeing the construction of a new fortification, visiting guard outposts, speaking encouragingly to his men in the trenches. Finally he looked up, his attention broken by a roll of thunder and a bank of dark water bearing clouds that moved over Brooklyn and Long Island. A thought began to form in his mind, and he withdrew to his camp, letting it take form.

Morning had worn to midday, and now midday into a rainy, humid afternoon. Dake found Micah, and the two brothers embraced each other. Micah cried out, "I'm glad you're all right, Dake. I was afraid for you!"

Sergeant Silas Tooms stared at the two men. "Well," he said, "I must be seeing double. I guess I lost my wits after that last battle."

"This is my twin, Micah," Dake grinned. "This is Sergeant Tooms, Micah."

Tooms studied the faces of the two young men, so identical, and then said, "Well, you'll have somebody to talk to when they put us into a prison camp."

"It won't come to that!" Dake argued.

"Tell me why it won't!" Tooms spat out. He pulled his hat off, and water ran down his face in rivulets. He was a hard-bitten man, tough in bone, muscle, and mind. Now he looked around and said, "They got us boxed. Look, troops over there—over there, and over there!" He swung his arm around and said, "And over there, nothing but water! The lobsterbacks have got us!" He put his hat on again and shook his head dourly. "I reckon that's why that British general wasn't anxious to attack. He can take us anytime he wants to."

Washington's staff felt about the same way. General Putnam came over, and when Washington asked how many men they lost, he said, "I don't know, but we're hurt sore." He studied Washington, marveling that a man could be composed with such staggering odds outnumbering him. *It'd be better*, Putnam thought sourly, *if he had cursed and raved a little bit at what's happened*. Aloud he said, "It'll be dark soon, sir. They may attack again."

"They may," Washington agreed.

"We're in no condition to resist another attack, Your Excellency."

Washington turned his cold gray eyes on Putnam. He said in a hard tone, "If they attack, we will fight again!"

"Yes, sir!"

Washington walked back and forth, his mind moving from one possibility to another, and rejecting them one at a time. "There must be something, even now when things seem to be at an end!" He knew that the men were all watching him, and through the gathering dusk he could see the hundreds of white faces of the soldiers waiting—expecting him to do what seemed impossible. Slowly it came to him that there were only two alternatives. The first was to surrender, and something in him longed to give up, to get rid of this cowardly rabble he called his army, to go back to Mount Vernon and Martha. This was the obvious way, but he never allowed it to rise in his mind, but put it down firmly.

The second alternative was to fight. He could gather his troops together, and when the British attacked at dawn, they could all die for their country. He knew that the officers, men like Henry Knox and Israel Putnam, loved the thrill of danger. They would follow him into utter defeat, but he knew that the fight would not even be glorious. The army would turn and break at the first British charge, and nothing would be accomplished. The revolution would be lost.

One other thought kept nibbling at his mind, and he allowed it to surface. *Retreat*. Retreat would save his army—at least for a time. If he could get the men away, he had a chance—and America had a chance. But retreat seemed to be the only alternative that was utterly impossible.

"Retreat!" he said aloud, and his mind fluttered like a bird in a cage. He looked up at the dark sky, swept the confusion of the stricken battlefield. The only thing that stopped them from deserting now was the cold waters of the river that lay at their backs. "Retreat!" he said half aloud.

It began raining in earnest as he walked through the camp. He reached one of his officers, General Mifflin, who was, at thirty-two, his youngest general. The young man had not been in on the battle yesterday, and now he spoke carefully. "I'm sorry that we took such losses, sir."

Washington nodded. "We will fight again!" he said.

"Yes, sir, of course!"

Washington and Mifflin walked slowly along, speaking to the men from time to time. Washington noticed that boats were sliding back and forth across the East River. As he always did, he admired the men who rode, as he admired all men who did things well. Observing more closely, he saw they maneuvered the boats with such skill that he said, "They know about boats."

"Yes, sir, they do!"

They know about boats. Washington studied the men in the boats. They were leather-skinned, long-faced Yankees, and there was a uniformity in the blue jackets and stained oilskins most of them wore. This was the one thing that his army lacked for the most part. At least these men skillfully, easily maneuvering the boats were one of a kind. "Who are they?"

"They're part of Glover's regiments. Marblehead fishermen, I think. Maybe they can't fight, but they certainly know boats. They been fishermen all their lives."

Washington's mind leaped at the statement. "How many are there?" The rain was pouring down now, and when Mifflin said six or seven hundred, he suddenly knew what had to be done. For ten minutes he paced in the pouring rain.

Putnam, who was old and tired, came down the slope to join them, and Mifflin glanced at him past the big man. Putnam finally said, "I don't think they'll attack today. Why should they fight in the rain when they can sit in their tents and wait for the weather to clear?"

Suddenly Washington lifted his head, and there was a light in his gray eyes they had not seen. "We won't retreat, gentlemen. We are going to bring over reinforcements, and we're going to take our sick and wounded back to New York!"

"Back across the river, sir?" Mifflin asked in confusion.

"Yes!" Washington pointed to the Marblehead fishermen. "I want

211

you to get every boat on this river, everything that floats. I want boats brought down from the North River, every fishing boat you can lay your hands on, and I want every one of them brought to the Brooklyn shore."

The men looked at him and Mifflin said, "But what for, sir?"

"We're going to withdraw to Manhattan."

"The entire army, sir?"

"Yes, the entire army."

The Marblehead fishermen all had the look of men of the sea. They marched with a sailor's rolling gait. True enough, they wore cocked hats to the line, along with short blue jackets and loose white trousers. They spoke a language all their own, the language of the sea, of storms, sails, and ships.

Stocky John Glover, their colonel, was on hand on the dark night of August 29, and he was jubilant that he and his men were on the water again. They had taken charge of the small boats that Washington had collected. Now they brought them bobbing up to the Brooklyn Ferry Landing. Men bent beneath loads of baggage and equipment, marching silently down to the waiting boats. The army began to come like phantoms, silent, words softly spoken and whispered even. The rain came down in torrential sheets, for which they were all profoundly grateful. For a while it seemed they could not make the crossing, the tide was so strong—then suddenly the wind veered to the southwest and subsided.

Washington had visions of thousands of panic-stricken men fighting madly into the boats when the order to retreat was given. When his officers mentioned this, he had said, "You won't tell them. Order certain regiments to be relieved, one by one. Let them think the rest are holding the line."

And strangely enough, and miraculously enough, this was the way the massive retreat happened. When Washington moved later down to the waterfront, he was amazed by the number of boats the Marblehead men had gathered. They came out of the murk of fog and rain, in an endless stream driven by the wind, commandeered by laughing fishermen. The laughter sounded strange to Washington. He had not heard much of that lately. As the boats came in, Glover had them moored and beached and stripped of all gear; then he ordered them to wait.

Knox came to ask, "Sir, what about my guns?"

"Spike them!" Washington said.

"Where are we going to find more guns if we spike these?"

Washington said nothing, and Knox argued, "An army fights with guns!"

Washington turned his eyes on the big man. "An army is men. We'll get more guns, Colonel."

"Yes, sir!"

It was astonishing how well the scheme worked. Throughout the night, every regiment, when it was told to leave, thought that it was the lucky one, that they would not have to bear the brunt of the English attack. Slowly they all made their way down into the boats, and when it was close on morning, the fog began to lift. The British had not caught them, which was a miracle in itself. One ship, up the East River, would have revealed the whole scheme, but they had not come.

George Washington waited until all the boats were loaded. Knox was sitting in one of the boats as it rocked with the swell of the tide. His eyes were on Washington, who was marching along the shore. Knox said to Micah, "He won't leave until the last man's loaded."

Micah Bradford watched George Washington as he advanced. "That's right, he won't." His heart suddenly was filled with devotion for the big man as he approached. *I did the right thing*, he thought, *joining with General Washington*. He watched as Washington stepped in and sat down.

"We're ready to go," he nodded to the sailor.

The tiller man finned it off, and his oars scooped at the water. The boat glided out into the river, and Micah saw with astonishment that George Washington was already sitting limply, his head on his chest. He was asleep!

Knox said, "Well, Bradford, he's still got his army. We'll see now what he can do with it. . . ."

18

ONE BRIGHT STAR IN THE HEAVENS

MICAH ACCOMPANIED COLONEL KNOX after they disembarked from the boats of the Marbleheaders. They were the last of the whipped and exhausted troops to arrive on the East River shores and stagger through the narrow streets of Manhattan. The weather was unseasonably cold, and the fog sent a chill through his bones as he accompanied the colonel through the groups of wounded that lined the streets.

"The surgeons are going to be busy, sir!" Micah murmured.

Knox cast his glance at the surgeons moving among the scores of wounded men. "You're right!" he said shortly. He shook his head and muttered, "It never should have happened."

Hundreds of wounded now lay in rows through which the two men made their way. Micah winced as he saw bloody heads and the stumps of severed arms and legs being stuffed into canvas sacks. It was a gruesome sight, and he said, "War isn't really very glorious, is it, Colonel?"

"Not this part of it."

The two men made their way toward headquarters. The moans of the sick and dying were an anthem of pain that made an accompaniment to the clash of the guns being moved and the rattle of iron wheels on the cobblestones. Micah noticed, with a sense of cynicism that was not his custom, that there were few citizens lining the streets to see the fighting heroes home. When Micah and Knox reached Washington's headquarters, which were in Richmond Hill, they found the small group of officers gathered in the comfortable house. It was a massive framed building with a portico supported by two ionic columns decorated with carved pilasters. From the second floor, out of a railed balcony, one could see for a great distance.

The meeting began when Israel Putnam said, "Sir, we must evacuate Manhattan immediately!" Putnam was stout and strongly built, with a remarkable head of bushy white hair. Now he shook his massive head, saying, "It's impossible for our forces to defend sixteen miles of coastland!"

Washington, himself, was confused. The disaster at Brooklyn had shaken him, but not a man knew it, for he kept his usual calm demeanor. "Congress has ordered that New York be held at any price, at all hazards!" he said firmly.

After some discussion the generals all agreed that the obvious military decision was to move north into the rough, hilly northern end of Manhattan Island. Washington pointed at the map, saying, "Nine thousand troops will withdraw to Harlem Heights. Five thousand will remain in the city proper, and we will strengthen Fort Washington and Fort Lee." There was some talk but little argument, for Washington's officers had learned to give their advice and counsel and then wait for His Excellency, General George Washington, to speak.

After Washington had left, Knox said to General Greene, "I think he'd be calm if the sky fell in on him."

Greene, the tall, balding ex-Quaker, nodded slowly, "I think it *has* fallen on him."

🛡️　　🛡️　　🛡️

For three weeks Washington watched the army of General Howe, expecting each day that the attack would come. Howe, however, did little. He went back to Staten Island and waited, planning his next move. Washington had spent the time trying to plan for the defense of New York. He could not bring himself to give it up, and in the midst of his confusion committed himself to one of the worst military decisions he made during the entire revolution. He left some of his army in the city at one end of Manhattan, and some of it he posted up in Harlem at the other end. The weak part he put in the middle, using his poorest troops in the most critical place.

On the night of September 14, British frigates crept up the East River and anchored off Kip's Bay. The shore was held by several regiments of Connecticut militia who had scratched out only a shallow ditch along the water's edge. The leader of the Connecticut troops, a Major Gray, was disgruntled, as were his men. They were tired and angry, and confident that nothing could happen to them. Most of them slept during the night, which was as black as ink. The East River was hidden in the murky darkness. At some point someone said, "There be someone out in that river!"

"Shall we give them a volley?"

"What for? They can't see us."

When the gray of dawn lit the eastern skies, the Connecticut men saw four mighty ships of the line anchored prow to stern with broadside spacing them, guns rolled out, and gunners standing by. The sun broke through the mist and cast an enchanting halo about the ships of war, and the Americans stared in horror and astonishment.

Then on the British deck pipes began to twitter, and wide flotillas of marines began to move toward the shore. Major Gray gave a hoarse command, but no one heard an American musket fire, for at that moment one of the British officers cried, "Fire!" and an inferno of round shot and grape shot struck the Connecticut men. The poor patriots never saw the ships of the line again. A solid wall of smoke formed in the river. They tried to run, but their weapons were ripped from their hands by the solid blast of grape that rained down on them. They tried to rise up, but the shells tore them to pieces. They tried to crawl to their friends, and saw that their friends were lying dead.

Finally they did what frightened men will do. They began to run. They left the belching guns behind them, but they saw columns of men marching in close order, and someone cried out, "Hessians!"

The big guns had ceased their fire, but the decisive shout from the Germans rang out, "Yonkee! Yonkee! Yonkee!" They plunged away, these men from Connecticut, but knew that they were doomed as the Hessians marched forward, crying, "Yonkee! Yonkee! Yonkee!"

The town of New York was clustered tightly on the southernmost tip of Manhattan Island. It was full of crooked little avenues and ordinarily was a bright, cheerful town. Israel Putnam had been assigned by Washington to defend the city itself, but the general was awakened from a sound sleep by a young man named Aaron Burr, who burst in, saying, "They've landed!"

"The British?"

"Hessians, too, on both sides of the Island!"

"How many?" Putnam demanded.

"I don't know—thousands!"

Putnam shook his head. "They couldn't have landed!" he insisted. "If they have, we're caught like rats in a trap!"

"They're on both sides of the Island coming toward the middle. We've got to get through before they close the door."

Putnam thought for only one moment, then nodded. "Get the men together. You'll have to lead us out of here, Burr!"

"Yes, sir! We've got to hurry or we'll wind up in a filthy British prison!"

🦁   🦁   🦁

Washington had been awakened by the crashing of the guns. He had leaped to his horse and recklessly driven the animal, clearing a wall with a bound, then a brook, then a fence. He saw the army coming toward him, running and straggling. Pulling in his horse, he tried to talk to them, but there was no recognition in their blank eyes. They swarmed past him, ignoring his commands. "I'm your commander. I'm your general! Get behind the stone walls and use your guns!"

But the men swarmed past him like rabbits, and Washington knew a moment of rage. He drew his pistols, but the guns misfired. He flung the pistols at them, then drew his sword. Riding among them, he struck at them with the flat of it, begging, pleading, but they ran on. Still, Washington rushed across the field like a madman, his voice raging.

Then he paused helpless. He braced himself in the saddle, and looking up he saw the column of the British marching smartly only a few hundred yards away. Yet he didn't move. He felt that he was dead, and wondered vaguely why he could still hear and see. The British were only a hundred yards away now.

"Come away, sir, please!" General Mifflin was beside him, along with others begging him to retreat. "Please, come away, Your Excellency!"

Washington slowly turned his horse and rode away in front of the advancing British troops.

🦁   🦁   🦁

The long column crawled over the road like a scarlet snake. General Howe rode at the head of the column, he and his aides all mounted on white horses. All around them were evidences of the Americans' headlong flight: old bayonets, knapsacks, muskets, hats.

They rode on and the heat increased. Their beautiful pressed, colorful uniforms became limp and wet. They were herding a long group of American prisoners, clusters of dirty, frightened boys, and one of Howe's officers stared at them, saying, "Stubborn beasts!"

Howe felt no hate. He simply wanted to end this stupid war so that he could return to England. It was almost over now, he knew.

One of his officers said, "We can have them all before night, General. They're probably ten thousand."

"A good catch," Howe nodded, taking off his hat and wiping his brow.

"Yes, sir, but we must hurry!"

"Oh, there's plenty of time."

"Well, of course, sir, but a few of them are across the Island. We could cut them off, you know."

"I suppose. You know I'd give my soul for a drink." He pointed to a pleasant Georgian house set back off the road. Two colored servants were occupied in taking down wooden shutters, and he asked idly, "Do you suppose they'd offer us a drink?" Without waiting for an answer, he started his horse for the house and the staff followed him.

Several ladies sat in front of the house, but they rose to greet the British officers. General Howe swept off his hat, and all three ladies were impressed by his good looks. One was blond and blue-eyed, with hair like combed flax. They were all quite pretty.

"My dear ladies, I wonder if we could prevail upon you for water. William Howe at your service."

"Your Excellency!" the three ladies said and dropped very graceful curtsies.

"I am Mrs. Murray. This is Miss Van Clehut and Miss Pinrose. Please, gentlemen, come into my humble house."

Howe and his officers dismounted and followed the ladies into the house. They were all relaxed, and by tea time Howe had finished his third bottle of claret.

"But we are rebels, you know," Mrs. Murray said roguishly.

"Bosh, there are no more rebels," General Howe smiled genteelly.

There was some talk of the war. All the time General Clinton was urging Howe to get on with the battle. However, Clinton was persuaded to give them a little music, so he sat down at the clavichord, playing and singing very well indeed. The hot afternoon passed as pleasantly as any late summer afternoon. Finally the clock struck five, and Howe looked outside. "Well, dear me, I've lost track of the time! We must be on our way. Thanks, Mrs. Murray, for your gracious hospitality."

And so the afternoon passed, and Mrs. Murray's tea party kept General Howe busy. Mrs. Murray was a devout patriot, but did not really know what a service she was doing for her country and for General Washington. While the British generals enjoyed their afternoon tea, George Washington and his ragged troops passed north and found refuge behind the lines at Harlem Heights. There Washington worked ceaselessly, under a driving rain that almost drowned his poor half-dressed men. He was thinking, *We've got to do something to put a spark of light in the men. They must have some sort of a victory! They can't go on fighting, and retreating, and losing. There's got to be one bright star in the heavens for them to look to!*

That bright star came on September 16. A Colonel Knowlton and his rangers, about one hundred twenty of them, made a valiant foray against the British. Knowlton was a favorite of his superiors and the idol of his men. Erect and elegant, he was a tall, handsome man in his late thirties.

Knowlton and his rangers stood off nearly four hundred light infantrymen for half an hour; then they heard the squeal of bagpipes, which warned them that the famous Black Watch regiment was hard on its way. Knowlton ordered a careful retreat. As jeering scarlet lines poured into the valley, Washington came up to stand beside Knowlton just as a British bugler stood up in full view and blew the fox hunters' call that always announced the end of a chase, for it meant, "The fox has skulked into his den."

Exhausted and his nerves on edge, Washington felt the sting of disgrace. Rage suddenly brought color to the face of Washington. It was an insult to the Virginia aristocrat to hear the hunters' call.

He turned to Knowlton and said, "Knowlton, are you afraid?"

"No, sir, I'm not afraid of anything on the green earth!"

"Could you take a party down to that valley and come in behind those—fox hunters?"

"Yes, sir, I can do it!'

"Then try it! Take a regiment with you, some Virginia men and Major Leitch."

As soon as Knowlton left, Washington turned and said to General Mifflin, "I want a frontal attack in that direction!"

Mifflin nodded and turned away, glad that he was given a chance to show that he was not afraid either.

Knowlton led his men and the Virginians through the hills. Soon they encountered the enemy, for a German officer spotted them. *"Was ist das?"* the German cried. Then the cry, "Yonkee! Yonkee!" went running down the line of Jaegers. The Germans advanced and a blaze of musketry crashed into the faces of the Americans. Knowlton fell dying, but as his lieutenant stooped beside him, he managed to say, "Tell the general I wasn't afraid."

In the meantime, Mifflin had led two hundred Massachusetts men head on into the fray. They started across the valley, and Washington spurred down toward him. They watched as the men attacked, and then suddenly from the right came another sound of musketry.

"It's Putnam coming up with another five hundred!" Washington cried. There was a crashing sound and he saw Knox and young Micah

Bradford coming with their light field pieces. The men, seeing the reinforcements, scrambled over the stone wall and charged the British infantry. They forced the British back, and Washington followed, yelling and laughing, as they routed the enemy.

The single column of British light infantry had expected no opposition whatsoever. Now, they faced what seemed to be a screaming mob of lunatics. The column gave way, and then—for the first time British regulars forgot their guns. They threw them down and turned in retreat.

"We did it!" Micah gasped, turning to General Knox, who was watching the British troops run away. "We stood up against British regulars!"

Knox could not speak, he was so moved, and then General Washington came up. His face was alight with joy, and he said, "Well, this was one bright star in the heavens!"

☦   ☦   ☦

Not a drop of rain had fallen in New York since the stormy night when the American army had retreated to Harlem Heights. It was very dry now, indeed, and practically the only pure drinking water to be found in New York was in the Collect Pond, north of the Commons. All the rich families purchased pure spring water from peddlers who hauled it in carts and stopped at their back doors.

Most of the houses in the city were wooden, and most roofs were shingled with cedar. They had been baked by the blistering summer sun and now were dry as toast. Many of the trees that had long shaded the city streets had been cut down by the troops, both British and American. There were many wretched dwellings in the city, and in narrow lanes and in filthy, crooked alleyways the poor made their homes in log huts with dirty floors and rickety wooden tenements of three or four rooms.

On Friday afternoon, September 20, a hot wind began to blow from the southwest and increased until it was almost a gale force. As darkness fell, the winds whipped the branches against the windows and tossed dry leaves and blew dust into the eyes of those who made their way along the darkening streets.

In the dark hours of the night somehow a fire started. Many of the New England soldiers were eager for the city's destruction. General Greene had reminded General Washington that two-thirds of the property in the city was Tory owned. Militarily it made sense to raze the city. Why willingly hand over comfortable quarters to the enemy when you were quartered in leaky tents in Harlem Heights?

Somehow several fires started simultaneously in the crowded

downtown streets. One began in a house of prostitution on the wharf near Whitehall Slip. It spread immediately to an adjacent tavern, burning through the flimsy wooden structures. When it hit the kegs of hard cider and sawdust, it sent both buildings up like exploding bombs. The explosion scattered blazing sparks to the tinder-dry roofs of the dwellings next door. Soon another fire broke out in the Old Fighting Cocks Tavern on the Battery, then in a crowded inn on Broadway called the Whitehall.

All of the church bells had been carried away by the retreating population, so there was no way to spread the alarm except by women's screams. Fire companies—all volunteer—soon arrived, but they were disorganized and undermanned. The engines and pumps were out of order, and water itself was in short supply.

Soon women and children rushed out of burning houses to watch helplessly as flames leaped from roof to roof. Soon a wall of fire moved hungrily up the entire Island. It sucked the air from the narrow streets and alleyways, and rickety tenements went up like kindling. Showers of sparks fell everywhere, and men and women formed almost useless bucket brigades.

Horses trapped in their stables shrieked in fright. Some broke free and stampeded through the streets. Some people trying to flee ran barefoot through the fire, beating at the sparks that fell from the sky and ignited their hair and nightdresses. A warehouse full of guns and gunpowder on Stone Street blew up, turning the immediate neighborhood into an inferno.

Matthew Bradford was awakened by the sound of people crying. He jumped up, shouting, "Jan, something's happening!" The Dutchman came out of his bed, and the two ran to the window. "The city's on fire!" Matthew cried.

Jan stared blankly at the street, then nodded slowly. "We must get what we can out of here! Never mind the clothes. Take the paintings."

The two men took the best of their paintings and left the building just before it was swept by a solid sheet of flame.

"Jan, I've got to go see about Abigail! Those women are all alone in that house, and it's right in the pathway!"

"Ya! I will go with you!" Vandermeer nodded.

The two men made their way to the Denham house, and not too soon. They piled their paintings in the front yard and rushed up, where they were met by a frightened Abigail. She had been watching the fire advance, and even now it was next door.

"Oh, Matthew!" she cried. "I'm so glad you've come—and you, too, Jan!"

"We've got to get out of here!" Matthew said. He glanced at the fiery wall that was even now catching the house on fire and said, "Where's your mother and Mrs. Denham?"

"Aunt Esther's gathering her valuables."

"There's little time for that!" Vandermeer said. "But I vill go help!"

The three of them rushed inside, and soon were all engaged in helping Esther Denham gather her priceless family paintings and photographs and letters.

"We can't take any more. The house is on fire now!" Matthew cried.

But Esther begged for just a little more time. She had the servants gathering her family silver, and then the cry came, "The porch is on fire! We've got to go!" Jan had come in and picked up the bag. "Come, Mrs. Denham. Nothing's worth losing your life for!"

Esther stood looking around the room that had been her life for so long. Soon it would be nothing but ashes, and she hesitated for one moment.

Abigail came over and put her arm around her. "Come along, Aunt Esther," she said quietly.

"All right, Abigail."

The two women got as far as the porch. The others were already outside when suddenly Esther remembered. "Oh, I forgot my mother's portrait!" She rushed back inside before anyone could stop her.

"Matthew, go get her!" Abigail cried. She looked up and saw that the entire top of the house was on fire and in danger of caving in.

Matthew dropped the sack he was carrying and, without hesitation, dashed back into the house. The smoke was so thick it burned his eyes, and he called out, "Esther—Esther, where are you!" He got no answer, so he dashed into another room—just in time to see the ceiling begin to cave in. He also saw Esther Denham, who was evidently blinded by the smoke, groping her way across the room.

An ominous creaking came from overhead, and suddenly without warning, the beams gave way. The whole upper floor seemed to fall in, and Matthew saw one of them, a heavy timber, strike the elderly woman. It merely grazed her shoulder, it seemed, but it knocked her to the floor. It was on fire, and quickly he leaped forward, pulled off his coat, and smothered the blaze that licked at her clothing. Picking her up, he forced his way blindly through the smoke. The fire was crackling and roaring behind him, and he barely managed to make it out of the house before the whole structure collapsed.

Abigail came forward. "Matthew, are you all right?"

"Yes, but Esther was hurt, I'm afraid! Let's get away from the house." He carried the injured woman out into the street, and then paused.

"We've got to get her out of here!" he said.

Esther began to move her head and open her eyes. She was dazed, but quickly her wits returned to her. "Abigail!" she cried and reached out her hand.

"Yes, Aunt Esther, what is it?"

"Is the coach out of the carriage room?"

"Yes, it is!" Abigail had seen one of the servants bring the coach around to the street, so the horses were already hitched to it.

"We must go to Boston!" she said.

"Boston?" Abigail was amazed. "Why would we want to go to Boston?"

"I have a house there. Just a little place, and no one's living in it." Esther Denham looked at the house that had been so precious to her and shook her head. "There's nothing left here."

"But you're hurt, Aunt Esther."

"Get your mother, we must go! There's nothing left here in New York!"

Matthew said quickly, "That might not be a bad idea, Abigail. I'd better go with you! It wouldn't be safe for you to travel alone."

"Ya!" Vandermeer said. "I vill also go! We can paint in Boston as well as New York!"

It was decided, and the carriage and the extra wagon made its way down the streets. The houses were blazing on each side, and Esther sat huddled close to Abigail, who had her arm around her shoulder. She had not been badly injured, but the thought of losing her home and all her treasures made her turn and look back.

Abigail knew her aunt was hurting and she whispered, "I'm sorry, Aunt Esther, but you lost everything."

Esther Denham turned and the light of the blazing fires illuminated her fine-boned face. "I haven't lost everything," she whispered quietly. "I still have Jesus, and I'm looking for a city that has better foundations than a little village like New York!"

The small procession moved out of the city, and finally onto the country roads. They made their way along quietly. Matthew and Jan drove the wagon behind, which contained the few possessions they had been able to salvage. Neither of them said anything, but as they looked back they saw the sky lit with the fires that were consuming the city.

"Well, I suppose Howe will have the city, but it will be nothing but ashes," Matthew remarked.

"Ya, that is so!" Vandermeer agreed.

As the flames leapt into the sky, lighting it up, Esther Howland Denham looked back once more—then said goodbye to earthly possessions.

PART FOUR

THE FALL OF FORT WASHINGTON

October—November 1776

19

BACK TO BOSTON

THE DEVASTATING FIRE THAT LEVELED over five hundred houses in New York had an unexpected side effect. Many victims of the inferno left the city seeking refuge with relatives in the outlying districts, and some even migrated to other states. This exodus soon caught up with the small band that Matthew led. The first day they were passed by wagons loaded with furniture salvaged from the fire. Some rode horses, carrying only what they could stuff into saddlebags. As they watched this rather grim flight Matthew shook his head. "It's going to make things a little bit harder, Jan."

"Why's that?" The roly-poly Dutchman was not a man to worry past the next meal. However, it was going on toward dark, and this was becoming a concern for the artist.

"I think it's going to make it harder to get a place to stay at night," Matthew nodded. Looking up at the sun he said, "We can travel for maybe another three hours; then we'd better find something."

"Ya, but in the meanwhile I will see what we can find to eat! Pull over under the shade of those trees, Matthew!" When Matthew obeyed, the Dutchman jumped in the back of the wagon and began digging through the pile of boxes, bags, and assorted plunder. Lifting up a basket he said, "Aha, now ve will haf a picnic!" He leaped to the ground, walked back to the carriage, and lifted up his hand. "Now, ladies," he beamed, "I invite you to join me for a little banquet!" He assisted Abigail and her mother to the ground, and then said, "Mrs. Denham, would you like to get down and walk a little?"

"You know, I really think I would." The falling beam had grazed Esther Denham's left shoulder, and she had such difficulty using her left arm that Abigail had fixed a sling for it. Nevertheless, with the sturdy Dutchman's help, she got down out of the carriage and arched her back, sighing with relief. "This is good, Jan," she said.

"Come mit me!" he said, and led her over to the shade of the tree. "This time I will be the host!" As the ladies walked around stretching their cramped muscles, Vandermeer laid out the food that he had hastily stuffed into a large basket on his last trip into Esther's house. Ruefully he wished that he had salvaged more, but he made the best of it. "Come," he called, "ve will have our little banquet!" The others came to stand before Jan, and he put his eyes on Mrs. Denham, saying, "I will ask the blessing, no?" Without waiting for permission he bowed his head and asked a most proper blessing. When he looked up and found Matthew staring at him with surprise, he said, "You did not think Jan could do that? I tell you my father and my mother were fine Christians! I would hope some of it rubbed off on me! Now, we have baked chicken, pickles, French bread, and a meat pie. Here, let me help you, Mrs. Denham!" He sat down beside her and, to the amusement of the other women, treated her like a child. Since she could use only one hand, he cut her food into small pieces and put it onto a plate, also seeing that she had plenty of the cider, which he had brought in a large stoneware jug.

"You're a very fine host, Jan," Esther said, staring at him. She was exhausted, and the pain from her injury nagged at her, but she did not let it be known. "I'm glad to hear that you come from a Christian family."

"Oh, ya, mine uncle he was a *predicator*—that is a preacher. My parents thought they would make a minister of me, but such was not to be!" He sighed heavily and shook his head. "Now I am a simple painter and a disappointment to my parents!"

Esther put her hand out on his and said quietly, "You're not a disappointment to me, Jan."

Jan's face flushed, but then he smiled. "Maybe I'm not a complete failure." He glanced over to where Matthew and Abigail were sitting off to one side and said, "That pair, they would make a fine couple!"

"I think they might. Abigail just recently found her way." Esther thought of Abigail's past and studied the girl's face. "She's such a beautiful girl, and her life's been wasted up until now."

"Matthew, he is foolish with love for her! I never saw such a lovesick duckling!" He chuckled deep in his chest and said, "He dreams about her whether he's asleep or awake, but that is the way it should be between young lovers, ya?"

"Ya, indeed!" Esther smiled, continuing to watch the pair as they talked and enjoyed their meal.

After the meal they rested for a time, lying on quilts and blankets that Jan and Matthew had pulled out of the wagon. It was indeed refreshing, but then they loaded up, pulled out, and rode for another three hours. Finally they came to a small village and Jan said, "I will go see about rooms at that inn."

Matthew waited until Jan came back and noticed that he was frowning. "No room for us in the inn?" he asked.

Jan looked at him. "You know the Bible, too! Well, they say they will make places for us, but it will not be pleasant."

The innkeeper was an enormous woman who did not believe in bathing often. The aroma from her sweaty body was forceful enough to make Matthew blink when he drew near to her. She had a strident voice that would stop hair from growing, and she negotiated the prices in a bullying way.

"We've got plenty already stopping here, so if you want to stay you'll have to pay for it!"

"We'd be glad to pay," Matthew said quickly. "Do you have a room for these ladies? My friend and I can manage anywhere."

"They'll have to share it with some others. You ain't the first to get here, you know!" The woman was taller than Matthew, and her fingers were like miniature sausages. Her nails were bitten to the quick, which accounted for them having no dirt under them, but the dirt seemed to be everywhere else. Her dress had almost lost its original color by food that had been allowed to dry across her massive bosom. She wiped her runny nose with her sleeve and said, "The women can have the room downstairs. You and your friend, the Dutchy, can bunk with the fellers upstairs!"

None of the women had ever had such an experience as they had that night. The small room had three beds in it, so there was barely room to walk between them, and there were already five other women in the room. The stench of unwashed bodies seemed to fill the place, and Mrs. Howland's face grew very pale. "I believe I'd rather sleep out in the wagon," she murmured.

Abigail agreed with her. "We'll stay here tonight, but tomorrow we'll have to find something better." She bargained with the other tenants so that the three of them had one of the beds, and somehow they made it through the night—despite the fact that one of the women snored so loudly that there was little chance of a sound sleep.

Up in the attic the men fared little better. Their bedfellows were every bit as unwashed and prone to snore as those below. However, they made the best of it. Corn-shuck mattresses were their lot, placed on the hard boards that composed the floor. Matthew shook his head doubtfully. "This is pretty rough, Jan. I hope the women are better off."

"I don't think they will be! Bad on them, although it doesn't matter so much for us! Ve must do better tomorrow!"

They arose at dawn and shuddered at the cold, greasy pork chops that were offered for breakfast. Instead, they made the main part of their meal on hot mush with butter and salt, which they washed down with a great deal of the strong tea that their hostess sloshed out of a huge urn.

During the days that followed, Matthew learned to begin looking for an inn early. More often than not, he managed to find an acceptable place for the women, while he and Jan slept in the wagon, or under it if it happened to be raining. The roads were bad, and several times Matthew wished that he had arranged for a sea voyage—but the die was cast and they made the best of it.

On the last night of their trip, just outside of Boston, they found a respectable inn with good accommodations for the women. The cooking, too, was better than usual, and after the evening meal Abigail and Matthew stepped outside. Ragged skeins of clouds were scudding across the gray skies above. The smell of burning leaves brought an acrid odor to them, a smell that Matthew always liked. He leaned his back up against a big oak tree and stared upward, thinking of what might be coming, then turned to look at Abigail. "It's been hard on you!"

"Harder on mother and Aunt Esther," Abigail said. She was wearing a gray dress of simple cut, which now was sadly in need of washing, but there was no chance for that. Even in this rather worn garment she made a fetching picture. She was not wearing a bonnet, and her hair cascaded down her back. She reached up and touched it and made a face. "I'd give anything to wash my hair!"

"We'll be in Boston tomorrow; you can do it then. It looks pretty to me, though." Matthew stepped closer to her and ran his hand over her hair. "I'd like to see you all dressed up in a beautiful gown, and wearing diamonds, at a ball. We'll do that someday."

This had been Abigail's dream once, but now she was disturbed to find that that sort of thing did not matter too much to her. "That would be nice," she murmured. She turned to study Matthew, examining his face rather curiously. He was not a large man, though taller than average, but hard living had pared him down so that he seemed to be almost gaunt. He was wearing butternut trousers, a white shirt with fluffy sleeves, and a leather vest cut off at the shoulders. He wore brown stockings and scuffed leather shoes with pewter buckles. His hair was light brown and blew with the wind, and as always, the light of quick intelligence shone in his blue eyes.

He looks like Leo, Abigail thought with a sudden start, *but he's not like him—not really*. She had thought much about Leo Rochester and his offer to her, and as the days had gone by, Abigail had become more and more aware that she had been wrong to accept it. She had spoken once to Esther about how she grieved over her past. Her aunt had said quickly, "You can't go back to the past. God has forgiven you for all of that. Now what you must do is live for Jesus Christ today! The past is gone forever, Abigail!"

Her aunt's words had comforted her then, but now as she looked at Matthew and saw that he was considering her with an admiring light in his eyes, she was confused and wondered if she ought to tell him of Leo's plot. She almost did as they stood there. The impulse came to her abruptly, lingering on her lips. Matthew saw that she was about to say something and waited—but at that instant Jan came out of the inn and joined them, speaking jovially of their safe arrival in Boston.

And so the moment passed away. Afterward, Abigail wondered what it would have been like had Jan not come out of the inn at exactly that moment.

🦁   🦁   🦁

"Well, I guess we just about made it, Jan." Matthew Bradford drew a sigh of relief as he pulled the team up in front of the red-brick house that set back from the streets farther than most. The horses were willing enough to stop, for Matthew had driven them hard for the past four hours, anxious to get the women into shelter before nightfall. A cold wind was sweeping in from the west, and Matthew glanced up at the threatening skies. "May be snow in those clouds," he muttered, "but we're all right now!" He turned the team into the narrow lane beside the house and, reaching the carriage house, jumped to the ground. Moving back to the buggy, he looked up into the wan face of Esther Denham and said quickly, "We're all right now, Esther."

Esther Denham had been hanging on to the seat as the buggy had bounced over the rutted roads for the past few hours. Her face was set and pale, but she had not complained. She looked at the house and asked, "Where is this, Matthew?"

"Why, this is my home," he said. "Here, let me help you down."

"We can't all pile into your home like this unannounced!"

Matthew laughed. "We're not much for formalities around here. Unless father's taken in a lot of extra company, there'll be plenty of room. Come now, let me help you down." Matthew helped the elderly lady down, and when she staggered slightly, put his arm around her. "Can you help your mother, Abigail?"

"Of course!" Abigail leaped to the ground, then turned to her mother. In truth, she herself was exhausted, but she had youth and strength on her side. "Come along, Mother, we'll soon have you into a nice comfortable bed." She helped her mother to the ground and followed Matthew as he led Esther to a door on the side of the house.

Jan had immediately begun to unhitch the horses and soon had both teams inside the small barn. He found the feed bin, gave them a generous portion, then hung the harness up before turning to go to the house. When he stepped inside the door, he called loudly, "Hello!"

Matthew appeared at once, with a young woman by his side, and said, "Come in, Jan!" He waited until the Dutchman was inside and said, "This is my sister, Rachel. Rachel, this is Jan Vandermeer."

Rachel smiled and offered her hand. Jan took it and bent over it with a flourish, kissing irrepressibly. She smiled at his exuberance and said, "My brother's told me so much about you."

"And I haf much to tell you about him!" Jan smiled broadly.

"Come along," Matthew grinned. "I'll show you where you'll be sleeping, Jan! You'll have to share a room with me."

Matthew turned and led Jan to a room on the second floor pleasantly furnished with a trundle bed. Matthew nodded at it. "Did you ever see one of these?"

"See one? It was a Dutchman who invented trundle beds! I vill take the bottom part!"

"We'll let the ladies get all cleaned up. My brother Sam has invented a newfangled kind of bathroom," Matthew said. "You have to heat the water outside, then it comes in through pipes."

Jan was interested in such things and followed as Matthew went outside. There was a large iron tank next to the house with a firebox underneath. Quickly Matthew built a small fire, fed it steadily until it grew larger, then turned to say rather wearily, "Well, that's all there is to it! There'll be hot water soon." He rubbed his face, the stubby bristles rasping under his fingers. "I'd be glad to get a bath and a shave!" he said. "It's been a rough trip."

Inside, Abigail and her mother were in the large bedroom that Rachel had shown them to. It was actually a master bedroom, the largest of the six in the house. "Pa would want you to have this!" she had said. "He sleeps wherever he is when he gets tired. Sometimes I wake up to find him on the floor in the parlor with a book beside him."

All of the women had protested, but Rachel had smiled. "Abigail can sleep with me. We have a guest, Mr. Clive Gordon, in one bedroom, but we'll make out fine, won't we, Abigail?"

Abigail was not prone to argue. The trip had worn her down, and she could not but express her gratitude to Rachel.

After the unpacking was done, Rachel led Abigail to the special bathroom, where she gestured toward a large copper tub. The two older ladies had already washed their faces and collapsed into bed, but Abigail had mentioned that she'd love to have a full bath. Now, as Rachel explained the apparatus, Abigail looked curiously at the tub and at the plumbing that young Sam Bradford had installed.

Rachel leaned over, turned a valve, and suddenly water began trickling in from the pipe. Steam began to arise at once, and Rachel laughed at the astonished expression on Abigail's face. "This is my brother's invention. Sam is a specialist in them, I suppose you might say! Here are the towels, and we always place this rug on the floor so when we step out we won't get water on the carpet. . . ."

As soon as Rachel left, Abigail removed her soiled clothing and lowered herself gingerly into the hot water, then gave a sigh of relief. She had filled the tub almost full, and now lay completely submerged in it. It was an exquisite sensation, and she closed her eyes and allowed herself to enjoy the pleasure of the moment. After she had soaked for fifteen minutes, she sat up and picked up the bar of scented soap that Rachel had left and soaped herself completely. After this she washed her hair, then rinsed it. Stepping out of the tub she pulled the metal flange away and saw the water begin to form a small whirlpool as it drained away. This fascinated her. She also saw, with chagrin, that she had left a line of dirt in the tub. Quickly she grabbed a small towel and washed it out.

"It looks like pigs have been bathing in this!" Abigail laughed to herself. Toweling herself off, she put on the clean undergarments and the dress that Rachel had furnished, then left to go back to the bedroom. With a feeling of exceptional good will, Abigail sat there beside the window drying her hair, brushing it and combing it. When her hair was finally dried she fixed it quickly, pinning it up. Just as she finished, Rachel entered to say, "Pa's home, and supper's ready. I bet you're starved!"

"I could eat anything!" Abigail nodded. "The food's been just *awful* in the inns where we've stayed."

The two young women left the bedroom, went down the hall, and Abigail was greeted by Daniel Bradford. "Well, Miss Howland," he said, "I'm very glad to see you!"

"It's so good of you to have us, Mr. Bradford. I trust we won't be an inconvenience for too long."

"Don't be foolish!" Daniel shook his head and smiled. "We're always glad to have company. You've met my son Sam?"

Abigail advanced at once to the young man who was watching her carefully. He had auburn hair and was rather strongly built, and at the age of sixteen looked extraordinarily like his father. "Sam, I must thank you for your invention. It was lovely having a hot bath! I think you're a genius!"

Sam grinned suddenly and winked at her. "I've always thought so myself. Maybe you could sort of spread the word around with Pa here, and the rest of the family!"

A laugh went up from the others who had gathered at the table, and Daniel Bradford said, "Well, let's sit down and see what kind of a cook that daughter of mine is!"

"Mrs. White cooked most of it, Pa!" Mrs. White was the house-keeper, and just as Rachel spoke she entered the dining room bearing a large tureen of soup that gave off a delicious odor.

"And what's that, Mrs. White?" Daniel asked.

"Turtle soup! Sit down and eat before it gets cold!" She was a short, broad woman with crisp brown hair and decisive ways. "Hurry up, now! I'll bring the rest of it after you've said the blessing—and make it a short one!"

Laughter filled the room again as Matthew said, "She's the real head of this household. The rest of us just mind her!"

Daniel said, "Clive, I believe you've met Miss Howland."

Clive Gordon had risen when Abigail came in. "We've met before, at an officer's ball when I was here in Boston. How are you, Miss How-land?"

"It's good to see you, sir, and how are your family?"

"Very well, I trust."

"Mr. Gordon came to doctor us all and got sick himself," Sam an-nounced. He seated himself firmly and said pertly, "Remember what Mrs. White said about the blessing, Pa. Make it a short one!"

"A longer blessing wouldn't hurt you any, boy!" Daniel said with a smile that pulled the corners of his lips upward. He bowed his head and said, "Lord, we thank thee for this food. Amen."

The brevity of the blessing caught Sam off guard, and he sat there for one minute before realizing it was over. His head flew up, and his eyes blinked with shock. "Well, Pa, you didn't have to make it that short!" Then he immediately held his soup bowl out and filled it with the large dipper.

"Make yourselves at home," Daniel said. "Just watch Sam, and you'll see our expert on good manners around here!"

They all laughed, for Sam was slurping his soup energetically and noisily. He paused long enough to say between bites of the fresh bread that had been served with the soup, "The Chinese say that you're supposed to eat food real noisy when you're a guest to show that you enjoy it."

"You made that up, Sam Bradford!" Rachel said indignantly and looked over at their guest and shook her head. "He's always making things up! When he doesn't know something he just makes up a story!"

During the course of the meal, which everyone was enjoying, Esther said, "I hope I'll be able to move us all into my house. I haven't been there in many years. It was rented out for a time, but not lately."

"Where is it, Mrs. Denham?" Daniel inquired.

"Over close to the older Catholic church, St. Luke's."

"I'll find it tomorrow, Mrs. Denham," Matthew said, "and get you moved in as soon as possible."

Clive listened as talk ran around the table, and finally he excused himself and went to his room. After he left, Mrs. Denham looked at Daniel and said, "He is your nephew, sir?"

"Yes, his mother is my sister. His father is a colonel in the British army in New York now." There was a sadness in his tone, and he shook his head. "Not an easy thing to think I have two sons there with Washington. They may be facing my brother-in-law in battle at this very moment."

A silence went around the table, which Matthew finally interrupted, "Well, come along into the parlor." The group moved in there, where they had a pleasant enough evening. They were all tired, however, and went to bed early.

🆃   🆃   🆃

The next day Matthew rose early and went at once to locate the house. He found it easily enough, then went to the foundry, where he found his father already at work. "It's a mess, Pa!" he said. "I think the Redcoats stationed some of their men in there during the occupation. All the windows are broken out, and the furniture is wrecked—they left it practically a garbage dump!"

"We'll have to fix it quickly!" Daniel said decisively. "You take Sam and whoever you need from the foundry to get it cleaned up. Buy new furniture if you have to."

Matthew nodded and said, "That's what I expected you'd say, Pa. Poor lady—she lost almost everything in the fire."

"Did you see your brothers while you were there in New York, Matthew?"

"No, I didn't. I asked about their units, but they were always up in the north part of the Island. Have you heard from them?"

"Nothing lately, of course. We're all concerned about them and I know you are."

Matthew hesitated, then asked, "Have you seen Leo, Pa?"

"Yes, as a matter of fact I have. I was out to see John not long ago. I stayed a little bit late, and Leo and I had quite a talk." He studied Matthew carefully and asked, "Have you given any thought to Leo's proposition?"

Instantly Matthew looked up, his eyes locked with his father's, and he hesitated uncertainly. "I . . . I haven't thought about it a great deal." Defensively he added, "I've been studying hard with Jan, and then the fire came, and trying to get the women here—" He broke off uncertainly, then shrugged his shoulders. Weariness swept across his features, and he finally said, "I just don't know, Pa—it seems like I can't make up my mind. I wish things were more simple." Bitterness ran through his words, and he turned and stared out the window at the men who were unloading a wagon. The scene did not seem to interest him, and he turned back to say, "I'll have to think about it a great deal."

A great pain came to Daniel Bradford then. He loved this boy, no less than he loved the children of his own blood. He had loved his mother, and he saw her now in Matthew. Seeking for some way to make the choice easier, he said evenly, "Whatever you do will make no difference in the way I feel about you, Matt. I hope you know that."

Matthew could not speak for a moment. "I know that, Pa, and it wouldn't make any difference about the way I feel about you either—but when a man changes his name—I don't know, it frightens me a little bit to think about it for some reason."

"You'd still be who you are. Nothing's going to change that. You pray about it, son, and do what you think is right." For a time Daniel stood there gazing at this young man who was going through such a difficult time. Finally he added, "You could do a lot for people with the money. I don't deny that. And your years in England have given you a sympathy for that country that none of the rest of us have."

"Don't say that, Pa!" Matthew said quickly. "I don't want to be classed with those who are coming to take over. I'd like to see America a free country!"

Daniel smiled and slapped Matthew on the shoulder. "I think you will see it, but it's going to be a long, hard struggle. I worry about Micah and Dake in the army—and soon Sam will be in there." He hesitated, then added, "I think I've got enough sons in this fight. Maybe the best thing would be for you to go back to England and finish your studies."

Matthew shook his head hesitantly. There was an uncertainty in him that he had lived with for months, ever since Leo had first told him the truth about his birth. Finally he said wearily, "I don't know, Pa. We'll just have to see."

✠ ✠ ✠

Matthew found that the house took more work than he'd thought, but between what he did with Sam's help and several of the workmen, they put Esther's house back in good condition.

Sam took a special delight in it, and when they went to get the ladies two days later, Sam gave them a tour through the dwelling. He pointed out all the work they had done, and when he had finished he said, "I hope you like it, Mrs. Denham."

"Why, Sam, it's perfectly wonderful. It looks better than it did years ago! I'm very much afraid I'm going to have to give you a reward."

Sam perked up at once, expecting money. Esther came over, reached up and pulled his head forward, and kissed him on the cheek. When she saw the chagrin in his face she laughed aloud, reached into the reticule tied to her wrist by a small chord and pulled out a gold coin. "There, Sam, that's a little bit more substantial than a little old woman's kiss!"

Matthew helped Sam carry in all of the belongings that they had brought from New York, and when it came time to leave, he said, "You'll need a man around here, maybe two men. Anything you want, I'll be handy and so will Sam."

"Where is Jan?" Abigail asked curiously.

"Oh, he's found a little romance of his own at the Elkhead Tavern, a little barmaid there that he's romancing. She's about a foot taller than he is, which makes it a little bit hard." The thought of the two together made him laugh, and he said, "We'll go visit them soon. You'll enjoy Jan's courtship, Abigail!"

"All right, that'll be fun!"

When the two left, the women moved through the house, and it was Esther who said, "I don't know what we would've done without them!" She looked curiously at Abigail and said, "Have your feelings about Matthew changed?"

"I don't know. I'm afraid I don't know myself, Esther."

"Well, don't you worry one bit," the older woman said. Then she brightened up and said, "But you will know yourself. I know things are going to be fine with you and him."

✠ ✠ ✠

Two days after Abigail and her mother had moved into the house with Esther, Leo came to the front door. Abigail answered the door and

237

found him standing there, a heavy overcoat covering him down to the tops of his boots. The temperature had dropped, and the threat of snow was in the air. "Oh—come in, Leo!" she said quickly.

Rochester entered and removed his hat. When he turned to her, she was shocked to see how drawn his face was. He had lost so much weight that when he took off his coat she noticed how his clothing hung on him. He had always been so well tailored that his appearance came as quite a shock. However, she only said, "There's a fire in the small parlor. Come, and you can thaw out."

"Thank you, Abigail." He moved to the parlor, asking, "How's your mother?"

"She's doing very well." Abigail turned to him and motioned toward one of the overstuffed chairs in front of the fire. When he sat down she poked the fire logs and sent up a swarm of sparks, then turned and said, "We got here just in time, it seems. It would've been terrible to have been caught out on the road in weather like this. I think it's going to snow."

"Yes, I think it might." Leo's voice was idle, and he sat there staring into the fire wordlessly.

"I'll get you something hot to drink, tea perhaps."

"That would be nice."

Abigail moved into the kitchen where she found the other two women working on supper. "It's Mr. Rochester," she said. "Come in and meet him, Aunt Esther."

"Oh, not now, I'm not properly dressed!" Esther protested. "Perhaps later."

Abigail took one of the trays, and after the water was boiling on the stove, she made the tea, then moved back into the parlor. Setting the tray on a small table, she poured the tea and passed one of the cups to Leo.

"Thank you," he said and sipped at the tea.

Abigail said, "I've been meaning to send you a note, but since we got back it's been all I could do to keep the house running." She expected him to comment, but he said nothing.

Finally Leo looked up and said, "I suppose you've heard, I've been ill?"

"Yes, Matthew told me. Have you seen him since we got back?"

"No, I haven't. Is he here?"

"Not yet, but he should be anytime. He usually comes in about this time of the day." She sipped her own tea, then struggled to find some way to communicate with Rochester. He would not, she understood, be sympathetic with her new desire to lead a better life. He was not a man

238

of God, and had little sympathy for things of the Spirit. She remembered suddenly how once at a party they had made fun of a raw preacher, and shame washed over her as the scene came back before her eyes. She sat there sipping tea, talking about how they had gotten settled, and how fortunate they were that Mrs. Denham had had a place to flee to in Boston after the fire.

Finally, Leo looked up at her. He set the teacup down and said, "I have been expecting to hear from you about your progress with Matthew." He waited for her to answer and when she did not, he said, "What's the matter? He *is* in love with you, isn't he?"

"I . . . I'm not sure, Leo. He seems to care for me."

"Well, what's the problem? Has he asked you to marry him?"

"Yes, he has, but—"

"Why haven't you told me this?"

Abigail looked at his face and saw that his eyes were sunk deeper in his head. She noticed also that he had difficulty using his left arm. All this came to her while she desperately tried to find an answer to his question. Finally she said simply, "I can't go through with our agreement—I just can't!"

Leo stared at her with incomprehension. This was his last hope! He knew that his health was growing worse constantly, and if ever he was to have his way with Matthew, it would be through this girl. Anger now touched him when he realized the thing he wanted the most was being dashed by her stubbornness. "What's the matter with you, girl?" he asked roughly, gesturing impatiently with his right hand. "Long as I've known you, you've wanted money, position, and fine clothes. Now, it's right in your grasp. What is it? Don't you like Matthew?"

"Oh yes, I do! I like him very much, but I can't marry him just to— well, just to get the money!"

"It never troubled you before!" Leo said shortly. "What's gotten into you?"

Abigail drew a deep breath, and then said, "Something happened to me in New York. I know you're going to laugh, but I was converted while I was there, Leo." She tried to say more but realized that anything else would be superfluous. She sat there and saw shock, amazement, and then scorn sweep over the craggy features of the tall man. Before he spoke, she knew what he would say.

"So, you're becoming another one of these puling Christians! Well, what's wrong with that? I guess he's probably a Christian himself, isn't he? His father's practically a saint—the whole family is. That ought to make things even better."

"I . . . I just can't—"

Suddenly she broke off at the sound of the door slamming, and she heard Matthew's voice calling out. "It's Matthew!" she said. "Please don't say anything to him about—what we've talked about!"

Matthew suddenly appeared at the door and said, "Abigail, I wish—" He turned and saw Leo and said quickly, "Why, I didn't know you were here, sir!" He came quickly and offered his hand. He was shocked at how Rochester had deteriorated in the period since he had seen him last. He tried to allow none of it to show in his face. "I'm glad to see you. May I have some of that tea, Abigail?"

Abigail said, "Yes, of course!" She poured him some and then said, "I'll let you two talk."

After Abigail had left the room, Matthew spoke rapidly. He was nervous and hardly knew what he was saying. Leo sat there and listened to him quietly, trying to digest what he had just heard from Abigail. He inquired finally, "How have your lessons gone with Vandermeer?"

"Oh, very well, sir! He's a fine painter, and I'm learning a great deal. He's here with me, did you know?"

"No, I didn't know that. Why haven't you come to see me?"

"Well, I had to get Mrs. Denham and Abigail and her mother settled. The house was a wreck." He went on to explain how he and Sam and some of the others had put the house together and said, "I was coming by tomorrow. I should have sent you a note, I know."

Leo said without preamble, "I want you to give me an answer, Matthew." He struggled for a moment about what he wanted to say next. He hated speaking of his own health, but now there was no way out. "I've—not been feeling well."

"I'm sorry to hear that, sir. You've been to the doctor?"

"Yes, they're a worthless lot! I've never been one to think a great deal about the future—but according to the doctor, it's time for me to be thinking seriously about taking care of myself."

Matthew could not think how to answer that. He heard the wind blowing against the panes, sweeping around the eaves of the house, carrying dead leaves that rustled crisply. Finally he said, "You really should. You're not looking well at all."

"What's your answer, Matthew? I don't have time to waste." He glanced toward the door and said, "What about Abigail. Are you fond of her?"

"Yes, I am. I've asked her to marry me."

"You could take better care of her if you had money. Her mother's a widow now. She's going to need care, too."

"I can't let that be a factor, sir."

Never had Leo Rochester felt so helpless. All he wanted lay here within his grasp! He felt again the fragile beating of his heart. He had begun to imagine it was skipping beats, but he was not sure if that were actually so. As the fire crackled, and the leaves swept around outside the house, all punctuated by the ticking of a clock on the mantel over the fire, he realized he was powerless to gain his ends. Finally he looked up and said, "I can do no more, can I?"

"I really don't think so, sir. I must have a little time."

Leo's thin lips grew tight. He stared at this son of his, thought of his life for a minute, and finally got to his feet. "I must go." He let Matthew go with him to the door and help him on with his coat. He settled his hat on his head, then looked at Matthew Bradford and said almost desperately, "Time is just what I don't have, Matthew." He turned then and left the house. The door closed behind him, and he looked up at the sky that was beginning to show tiny flakes of snow. It was a long winter coming on, he knew, and he felt in his heart that the coldness of it had already touched him.

20

LIFE IS MORE THAN ART

AFTER THE DEFEAT that Washington suffered at Brooklyn Heights—then later on the Island of Manhattan—many felt he should be replaced as commander in chief of the American forces.

As if in answer to this desire, General Charles Lee descended upon the beaten army that languished on the island. For weeks his coming had been anticipated. Mr. Lee, his supporters pointed out, was everything that the commander in chief was not. They told of how he had repulsed a British attack on Charleston. They wrote about his military history in Europe, and insisted that the Continental Army would not have been beaten in Brooklyn if General Lee had been there to lead them. Soon some were pushing all the blame for every mistake onto the shoulders of Washington of Virginia. And Washington agreed with many of the comments. He knew, only too well, that as a military man, Charles Lee was everything that George Washington was not. He had a deep and sincere reverence for Lee and had constantly written him telling him of his confidence.

Lee was now coming to Harlem, but many of Washington's officers did not share their commander's evaluation of the skinny general. Knox fairly bristled with dislike for Lee, General Putnam sneered openly, and General Nathaniel Greene proclaimed that he would not trust Lee to command a squad!

When Lee arrived at the encampment on Manhattan, those who had not seen him were astonished by the man. He brought a dozen dogs with him, yapping at his heels, and his appearance was not impressive. He was tall and extremely skinny. He spoke with a high-pitched voice, blinking his eyes rapidly, and had a nasal drawl. He seemed to have an affectation of seeing only what he wanted to see, whether the object was a hundred yards away or right under his nose.

For all his mannerisms and ugliness, Lee was a good soldier—far more experienced than anyone else in the American army. He had been born into battle, and all of his forty-five years he had never known any other life but the army. He did not fight for a cause, but because soldiering was his trade, he accepted the admiration that came from some as if it were his due.

Lee had not been at headquarters for more than two hours before he demanded a counsel of war. The officers came without eagerness into the dining room of the Morris house, which Washington had made his headquarters. They were taken aback by Lee's sprawling in the commander's seat at the head of the table. Washington stepped back in the shadows, effacing himself as Lee began to speak with a corrosive expression. "Blast it all!" he said. "We must get out. There's no other way to it! This place is a filthy trap, and if those lobsterbacks only had sense to put a ship up the river, they'd have us already!"

"We've held them for weeks!" Putnam growled.

"There's no way in the world to take Fort Washington!" Greene pointed out.

"Oh, you simpletons!" Lee drawled. "Ten soldiers could work and drive you out of here in an hour!"

They wrangled and almost came to blows shaking the frail table. It even came to the point where they were speaking of duels and challenges, calling each other names. Lee had only one answer for all of this. He called them, "Simpletons!"

Coming out of the shadows, Washington said quietly, "General Lee is right! Sooner or later we'll have to leave New York and retreat. Perhaps we'll try to hold Fort Washington and Fort Lee. I don't know yet, but when I went away from home I thought it would be for a little while." He hesitated and a quietness settled on those gathered in the room. "But it will not be for just a little while, gentlemen. We will be gone from our homes for a long time." His voice grew more firm and he said, "We will retreat, if we have to, over the mountains. Why, there's a forest there that's twice as large as Europe itself! Someday we will become an army, and then we will not run away anymore!"

In the days to come Washington had to repeat those words to himself many times. "We will not run away, we will not run away, we will become an army." And he tried to make an army. He took what measures he could conceive of, patching the ragtag organization together, lecturing, advising, scolding, and pleading. All the while Lee drifted through the camp like a guest of honor telling endless tales of his experiences on the battlefields of Europe. And the Yankees loved it—some of them. They loved his cleverness and his obvious hints about who would be the commander in chief in time to come.

243

Men deserted by tens and twenties and fifties. When some of them were brought back, the commander in chief grimly ordered them to be whipped until the blood ran in rivulets down their backs. Day after day there was a steady plague of mutiny, desertion, thievery, and complaint. And all the time, the entire army waited for the British to come—as they surely would.

🔔   🔔   🔔

Winter began to close its icy grip on Boston, and as Katherine Yancy came into the house, her face was ruddy with the touch of the cold wind that was whipping across the streets. Slipping out of her coat and gloves, she went to the kitchen and put the parcels of food on the table. The fire was going down in the stove, so she rekindled it, thinking quickly of the menu for the day. After the fire was burning sufficiently, she heated water and made tea, then she put together a bowl of mush, added butter and salt, and putting it all on a tray she moved out of the kitchen and to the room that her mother was occupying.

When she went in she found her mother still in bed. "Get up, Mother!" she said. "I fixed you some fresh mush." Susan Yancy had been ailing for some time. The doctors could find nothing specific wrong with her, and she had tried not to complain. Now she got stiffly out of bed and let Katherine assist her as she put her arms through a warm wool robe.

"You shouldn't be cooking breakfast for me. I don't eat that much," she said.

"Sit down, Mother," Katherine said. "Try to eat all this if you can. It will be good for you. I'm going over to the Bradfords' this morning. I'll fix you something for lunch and put it on a tray."

"How is the young man?" Susan Yancy inquired as she sat down and began to sip the steaming tea.

"He's doing very well, but I'm really going over to see Rachel this morning. We're going to put some things together for the children at the orphanage."

After she had seen that her mother was comfortable, Katherine left for the Bradford home. When she was welcomed in by Rachel, she said, "It's getting colder all the time. I shouldn't be surprised if we didn't have snow this week!"

"Come into the kitchen. We'll sit down and talk for a while." Rachel smiled. "Your nose looks like it's frozen."

The two young women went into the kitchen. They had become close friends, and Katherine had been able to come over often. For a while they spoke of the small things that occupied the lives of women who keep house, and finally Clive walked in the door. He was thin, and the traces of his illness showed in the hollows of his cheeks, but there was a clear look in his blue eyes, which lit up at once when he saw Katherine. "I thought I heard you, " he smiled. "How's your mother?"

"Not too well, Clive!" Katherine admitted. "She just doesn't seem to be able to get her strength back."

"This has been a bad time for Boston!" Rachel shook her head. "I can't think of a house that hasn't had someone down sick."

"Maybe I ought to set up practice here!" Clive grinned. He took his seat at the table with them and accepted the cup of tea that Rachel poured and put before him.

"You might get plenty of patients, but no one has any money!" Katherine shrugged. "The town's not the same since the occupation."

Clive did not respond to that. There was still an awkwardness between the two of them, which neither of them had been able to overcome. Since their reconciliation, the two had become close, but there was always the matter of the revolution between them.

Now as Clive sat there looking at Katherine's cheeks, which were reddened by the cold, he admired her features again. He especially liked the way her eyes crinkled when she laughed. Her eyes almost disappeared, and he had said once, "I don't see how you can see anything when you laugh; your eyes are closed!" There was a goodness and a fullness about this girl that he had found only in Jeanne Corbeau, and now he sat there comparing the two women. As Katherine and Rachel talked he suddenly felt foolish, as he often did when he thought about Jeanne. He could not get it out of his mind that he had been too quick to make up his mind that he was in love. He knew now that Jeanne had married the right man, and he was happy for her.

"Well, I've got to clean the house. You two sit here and talk for a while," Rachel said briskly.

When Rachel left the room, Katherine gave Clive a critical look and said, "You look stronger. How do you feel?"

"Much better! It's nice to be taken care of. Rachel's a good nurse, and I'm fortunate to have been here when I got sick."

"Have you heard from your family?"

"No, the mails aren't running too regularly. The last letter I got, they were fine." He hesitated, then said, "They mentioned you—how much they missed you."

Katherine dropped her head, unable to meet his eyes for some reason. "You have a fine family," she said.

They talked for a time and finally Katherine said, "I must help Rachel. We're getting a few things ready to take to the orphanage. We'll have to be gone most of the morning collecting them from the neighbors."

"I wish I could go with you, but I have an errand of my own. Through the mail, of course." He sounded mysterious, and when she asked him what it was, he merely shrugged his shoulders and said, "Oh, just something I'm involved in."

He rose when she stood up and came over to stand beside her. She looked up with surprise. She always liked to do that—look up at him. She had always thought herself too tall for a woman and for years had stooped to make herself seem shorter. Her father had said roughly, "Stand up, girl! God made you tall and strong; now thank Him for it!"

It gave her a feeling of femininity to look up at a tall man, and she rather liked it. A fleeting thought crossed her mind that this may have been part of her problem with Malcolm Smythe, but she put it aside as foolishness. *He's fine looking,* she thought, noting his regular features. She liked his hair, which was red and rather long now. *I've got to give him a haircut,* she thought, and then wondered at herself for considering such a thing. *It's as if I've taken him over.*

"I've been thinking about our time in Halifax, Katherine. We had good times there."

"Yes, we did, Clive."

He said no more but suddenly reached out and took her hand. He held it, looking down at it for a moment, then squeezed it and left the room abruptly.

Katherine stared after him, then said aloud, "Well, I wonder what that was all about!" Then she turned and left the room herself, her mind filled with the errands she and Rachel must attend to.

☩   ☩   ☩

"Are you warm enough, Esther?" Matthew Bradford had stopped by early Sunday morning at the request of Esther Denham. She had asked him to take her to church, and he had been pleased to do so. He had ushered her to his buggy, and now he tucked the blanket around her, adding, "I felt some snow earlier. It might be falling fast by the time church is over."

"I'm fine, Matthew," Esther said. She looked back in the rear seat where Abigail and Jan Vandermeer were sitting. The two of them had grown to be great friends. Vandermeer had been a good influence on the whole family. He was filled with enthusiasm and seemed to wake up every morning shouting, filled with plans, his clothes smudged with the paints that he constantly worked with. She turned and said, "I've missed going to church."

"Well, you'll hear a good preacher this morning. I haven't been as faithful as I should, but as far as preachers go, I think Reverend Carrington is top drawer!"

"I must have good preaching!" Jan insisted from the backseat. He reached forward and slapped Matthew on the back so hard the young man wheezed. "Good preaching should be like good art—strong, powerful, and lots of it!"

Matthew spoke to the horses, and by the time they reached the church, tiny snowflakes were stinging their cheeks, getting somewhat larger. He stopped in front of the church and leaped out and helped the ladies down. Then he drove around to the side of the church and tied the horses to the hitching post, noting that the crowd would be small today. When he entered the building he heard Jan's booming voice. Reverend Carrington was standing in front of the round-bodied Dutchman, smiling slightly.

"I expect a good sermon, Reverend!" Jan exclaimed. His blue eyes were crackling with excitement, and he said, "I like my art and my preaching strong! Let us haf the full gospel, sir!"

Reverend Asa Carrington was amused by the man. "I'll do my very best, Mr. Vandermeer! It will be good to know that at least one member of the congregation won't fall asleep!"

"Asleep in church? You point them out, and I vill wake them up!" Vandermeer nodded vehemently. He turned around to see Matthew, then said, "Come, we get seats up front where we can hear the good minister!"

Reverend Asa Carrington was a fine minister. Abigail sat listening to the sermon, drinking it in. She had discovered since becoming a Christian that the Bible, which had always been a dead book to her, had now suddenly come alive. She had discovered also that there was a special pleasure in listening to preachers—some of them at least. She had heard Asa Carrington before, and as he spoke that morning on "Christ in you, the hope of glory," she thought how different things were for her. It came to her that the last time she had been in this church, she had sat beside Nathan Winslow. Her face flushed as she remembered, with shame, how she had tried to trap him into a marriage simply to escape from difficult circumstances. But that soon passed, and sitting between Matthew and Esther, she enjoyed the sermon thoroughly.

Matthew was very much aware of the young woman at his side. He had watched her carefully since first meeting her, and was firmly convinced that he was in love with her. Now there was a pride in him as he saw her fresh beauty, and the thought came to him, *I think she's the most beautiful woman I've ever seen!* Looking across the room, he saw his own family sitting together as they usually did—at least part of them. He missed Micah and Dake, and from the look on his father's face, he knew that same thought was in him.

After the sermon was over, they returned to the Bradford house, where they ate a lunch of cold chicken, cuts of beef, and bread baked the previous day. Rachel heated up a huge pot of beans, and as they sat around the table, Daniel and Jan discussed the sermon.

Daniel Bradford liked the Dutchman—as they all did. He was amused at the interpretation that Jan put on some of the pastor's remarks, and finally said, "Were you converted at a young age, Jan?"

"Converted? I'm not converted, Mr. Bradford!"

The remark brought the attention of all of them, for Jan certainly gave the impression that he was a converted man. When he saw their surprise, he spread his thick hands out and said, "I am going to be converted one day, but I haf never done it yet!"

Matthew exclaimed, "Why, I'm surprised, Jan! I thought you were a Christian."

"I am making up my mind!" Jan said. He began to tell them how he had been brought up in a Christian home, but had gotten far away from God. "I went to Paris, and if a man wants to get away from God, that's the place to do it!" he said explosively.

"But what are you waiting for?" Daniel asked with some bewilderment. "You know the gospel. And you obviously are aware of the dangers of waiting to become a Christian."

For once Jan Vandermeer was speechless, perhaps for the first time since Matthew had known him. He sat there saying nothing for a time; then he said, "You are right, no doubt, Mr. Bradford! Many are fools like me who let their opportunity pass until it is too late!"

Abigail was sitting on Jan's right. She turned and there was affection in her large eyes. "I know what you mean, Jan," she said. "I got far away from God, too. So far that I was afraid that God wouldn't have me!"

Jan turned to her, interested in her remark. "You could not haf been such a sinner as I was!" he declared firmly.

Abigail could not speak, so full was her throat with emotion. She was aware of Matthew's eyes on her, and the shame of how she had tried to deceive him was cutting inside her like a sharp razor. She could not find words to answer, and it was Matthew who said quietly, "I think men are greater sinners than women!"

Abigail glanced up quickly, catching Matthew's eyes. It was a kind thought on his part, and she at once felt a warm glow at his thoughtfulness.

After the meal they went into the parlor, where they enjoyed

Rachel's singing. Finally, they had a visitor. Katherine Yancy came in, and everyone noticed how Clive, who had said very little during the meal, at once became very animated.

"Come in! Come in, Katherine!" Jan boomed. "Now we will hear you sing!"

"Oh, I'd rather not!" Katherine said, but the Dutchman would not be put off. He led her over to the harpsichord, practically plunked her into the seat, and gave her no choice. "Now sing!" he commanded.

Katherine laughed and shook her head. Vandermeer's manner was abrupt, but she rather liked it. She sang two songs, and then refused to sing more, despite Vandermeer's urging.

When she took her seat, Clive crossed over to sit beside her as the others listened to Vandermeer speak with great authority on everything under the sun. Clive turned and surprised her by saying, "I'm going to be leaving soon."

Quickly Katherine glanced at him. "Why, you're not able to travel, Clive!"

"Something important has come up. I got a letter today that could be very significant." He saw the question in her eyes and said, "It's something that I must do." He hesitated for one moment, then said, "Katherine, you've become very important to me!"

Suddenly Katherine knew a start of agitation. She had learned that this tall Englishman had a way of putting his heart into simple words. Looking at him, she saw that his eyes were intense, and that he was waiting for her reply.

"Clive—" she said hesitantly. "You mustn't—you mustn't feel too strongly about me!"

"Why not? Is it the revolution?"

"Well, yes!" Katherine said.

"Revolutions come and go, but love is forever!"

Katherine looked up quickly. It was strange the way he had put it, but she said at once, "But the revolution is here, and you and I are divided by it. The Bible says that two must agree or they can't walk together." She looked over quickly and noticed that the others were paying them no attention. "You mustn't think about me like that, Clive! You'll be going back to England, and I must stay here. I couldn't be happy in England."

Clive Gordon did not answer. For a time the noise of the room floated over them, but they were intensely aware of only each other. Finally he said, "Katherine, I know you trust God, and now I want you to learn how to trust me!"

It was an enigmatic remark that Katherine could not fully grasp. She saw that there was something in his eyes that she could not quite ex-plain. During his illness she had learned to take care of him, almost as if he were a child, but now he was no child, but a tall, strong man. And he was saying something to her that she could not grasp. She was thank-ful when she heard her name spoken.

"You must settle an argument, Katherine!" Jan boomed. His voice always dominated the room, and he said, "Which is more important, art or life?"

Katherine was still thinking of the strange statement that Clive had made and stared for a moment, trying to put Jan's words into focus. "Why, I think life is more important, of course."

"No, you are not correct! You sing well, but you do not understand art!"

"Look at that picture!" Jan waved his hand at a picture of a young girl. "There she is! Who is that young lady, Mr. Bradford?"

"Her name was Amy Templeton. She was a good friend of ours years ago. She grew up with Matthew. You remember, don't you, Matthew?"

"Of course," Matthew said. "A sweet girl. It's a shame she died so young."

"Ah, she is dead! That is too bad, but there is the picture!" he said. "So she is not gone at all!"

"But that's only a picture!" Katherine said. "I don't know the girl, of course, but a picture is not as good as having a person."

Jan got up and began to pace the floor. He was wearing a mis-matched suit that consisted of a coat of a strange yellowish color, trou-sers of a faded plum tint, and a shirt that should have been thrown away, as it had traces of crimson paint on the collar, but none of this mattered to Vandermeer. He walked over to the picture, gesticulating wildly, and said, "Art is for the purpose of freezing things so that they will stay the same! This young girl was captured by the artist's brush on that day! Now, it is sad that she is gone—but there she is!"

Katherine listened as Vandermeer went on speaking with great en-thusiasm. When he paused slightly she said, "But life isn't like that, Jan. Things change! We wouldn't want things to always remain the same. If that were true, a baby would always stay a baby, and as sweet as babies are, we want them to grow up. That's part of life."

Vandermeer loved to argue. He said, "Of course, they must grow up, but when the artist steps in he will take just a tiny part of life, and he will fix it so that it will never change! That young girl—look at the eyes how they glow, and the lips how soft they are, and the hair! See how the artist has caught her there at a moment so that she will never change! That is why Matthew must paint you very quickly, Abigail!"

He turned to the girl and said, "As beautiful as you are, young lady, I regret to say one day that your hair will grow silver, and the beautiful form will not remain so!"

"That wouldn't matter to me!" Matthew said. "I've already painted a portrait of Abigail—though you could do better." He thought of what Jan had said, then shook his head in disagreement. "That's just part of love, Jan. You love people when they grow older, just like you do when they are younger—even more, I think."

Abigail turned to look at him quickly but said nothing.

Katherine, however, was aware that something seemed to be wrong with Jan's thinking. She argued for some time with him, and the Dutchman chortled with delight. He did not seem to care whether he won or lost the argument. It was the lively discussion itself he liked.

Finally Katherine said firmly, "I like your paintings, Jan, but we have to grow up!"

"Ah, but growing up means pain. You have no idea how much pain I went through growing up! I still see men and women everywhere, and they give each other pain, even when they say they love each other!"

"That's better than being frozen!" Katherine said firmly. She thought for a moment, and then feeling Clive's eyes upon her, she said quietly, "Life is more than art!"

Finally the meeting broke up, and as Katherine was leaving, Clive came to take her hands. "This is goodbye for a while. I'm afraid I may not see you again for a time." He smiled at her, adding, "I liked what you said to Jan. You are a very wise woman, Katherine—and a beautiful one, too."

Katherine's lips turned upward in a smile. "Perhaps you'd better have Jan paint my picture. According to him, I'll soon be a tottering old woman, and all that will be left will be a picture of me as I am now."

"That's not a bad idea, his painting your picture—but I liked what you said about life being a process." He held her hands for a moment, then suddenly raised them and kissed them. "Goodbye, Katherine! You'll be hearing from me."

Katherine left the house, wondering at the strangeness of the conversation. As she made her way home, she seemed to feel the pressure of Clive's hands on hers, and she wondered at the strength of her feelings for the tall, young Englishman.

21

LYNA HAS A DREAM

THE *PORPOISE* LEFT BOSTON, its hull packed with salted cod. Clive Gordon had been fortunate in securing a place on the small freighter. He had heard that it was going to touch in New York to deliver part of its cargo to the British quartermaster in Howe's army, and Clive had at once gone to the captain.

"We're not a passenger ship, Mr. Gordon," the doughy Captain Millford told him brusquely.

"I realize that, Captain Millford, but I very much need to get back to my family in New York. Just put me anywhere. I promise I won't interfere with your passage!"

Millford had reluctantly agreed, and Clive had made the journey in relative comfort. The sea was calm, but the snow that had been threatening Boston came floating out of an iron gray sky the first day out. He had stood in the bow watching the flakes, some of them as large as shillings, as they fluttered down. They disappeared as soon as they touched the water, and as he stood there he was mindful of the brevity of human life. His sickness had not frightened him, but it had made him keenly aware of how fragile life was.

The prow of the *Porpoise* rose and fell, and as Clive held on to the rail he thought steadily of Katherine. An image of her face formed in his mind, and he was amazed at how clearly he could recall every feature. He could also recall practically every conversation he had ever had with her, and he found pleasure in going over them repeatedly. It had been more of a shock when she had turned on him than anything that had ever happened to him, and now he knew a moment of gratefulness that they had resolved their differences.

The snow did not last long, and by the time the *Porpoise* pulled into the harbor at New York, the weather had turned somewhat better. He said goodbye to Captain Millford and clambered down the side into the small dory that bobbed over the tops of the waters as the oarsman sent it toward the shore. Stepping out on the dock, he looked around and was taken aback by the large number of soldiers that he saw. The Redcoats were everywhere, and he could tell there was an excitement in their behavior. He was still somewhat weak from his sickness, so he motioned to a carriage, which pulled up beside him at once.

"Yes, sir, gov'nor?" the cabby asked alertly. He was a muscular man wearing a multicolored wool coat, and a soft-brimmed felt hat pulled down nearly over his bright blue eyes.

"I need to go to army headquarters."

"Get right in, gov'nor!" The cabby said, "Take you there in two shakes of a duck's tail!"

Twenty minutes later Clive dismounted from the carriage, paid the driver, then turned toward the large building that was obviously some kind of a headquarters. The British flag flew at the top of a staff that was mounted on the second story, and as he went up the steps he stopped in front of one of the two guards who were standing guard with their muskets. "I'm looking for Colonel Gordon. Can you tell me where I might find him?"

"He's right inside, sir, on the second floor."

Clive mounted the steps slowly, though he was satisfied to find that he had regained most of his strength. He still was conscious that he had lost weight, but he knew that he could gain that back. When he reached the second floor, he tried the first door, and was informed that Colonel Gordon was at the end of the hall. Moving down, he opened the door and stepped inside. He saw a familiar face and smiled. "Hello, Corporal Cummings!" he said. "Is my father here?"

Corporal Cummings, a diminutive young man no more than twenty, had looked up with surprise from the papers scattered on the desk in front of him. "Why, yes, sir, Mr. Gordon! He'll be glad to see you!"

"Does he have someone with him?"

"No, he doesn't. I think you could just go right in!"

"Thank you, Corporal!"

Clive advanced to the door behind the corporal, which led to some kind of inner office, knocked, and then stepped inside. He smiled at his father, who looked up, and Clive saw the astonishment sweep across his face. "The bad penny back again, Father!"

"Clive!" Leslie Gordon leaped to his feet, stepped around the desk, and came at once to give Clive a mighty hug. "Where in the world have you been? How are you? Are you over your sickness?"

Clive laughed. "Well, I'm fine—if you don't crush me!" He smiled at his father and said, "I'm very well. I just got in. I probably smell like fish—that was the cargo."

"Sit down! Sit down, my boy! Your mother will be excited to hear this. Have you been home yet?"

"Not yet. I wanted to come and talk to you first."

"Well, we have been concerned about you. It was a pretty bad sickness, I take it?"

"Not very pleasant, but God brought me through it. It's been a sad time in Boston. Quite a few have died."

"How are Daniel and his family?"

"Completely recovered." Clive took his seat and leaned back in the hard-back chair. "Micah and Dake are in the army with Washington. I suppose you knew that?"

"I knew about Dake. I thought Micah hadn't made up his mind about this war, what to do about it."

"I suppose he has. At least he's signed up for ninety days."

The two sat there talking for some ten minutes, then Leslie Gordon leaned back and clasped his hands, studying his son carefully. "What about Katherine Yancy? Is she all right?"

"Well, yes, sir, she is." He hesitated, for he was not at all certain how his father would receive the news that he had come to give him. To put the matter off he said, "How is the army positioned?"

Leslie Gordon's face clouded. "We should have ended this thing before! We had them whipped, but General Howe called off the attack. Nobody knows why."

"What's the situation now, sir?"

"We're getting ready to move out in a day or two, I expect. The men are ready to end it. They want to go back home to England." The long features of Colonel Gordon grew sad, and he shook his head thoughtfully. "I'd like to go myself, and I suppose you're ready to go, too?"

"Well, I'm not sure," Clive said carefully. "I've been thinking a lot about that."

Instantly his father understood that this reluctance of Clive to leave America was connected with the young woman who had become such a vital part of his life. He almost reminded the young man that it had not been long since he had been just as interested in another young woman, but he restrained himself. "This would be a good country once we put this rebellion down—when things can get back to normal."

"I really came back with an idea, sir." Clive hesitated, then said, "I'd like to do something for Amos Yancy."

"Ah, you're still there, are you? Well, I don't think you need worry about it. Once we bag Washington's army, there'll be an armistice, and

I'm sure all prisoners will be released."

"I hope so. Is there no way he could be released now?"

"Not that I can think of at this point. The general is too busy to even approach him with it."

Clive thought about that for a moment, then said, "I suppose so. I think I'd better get home and see Mother."

"Good! She'll fatten you up a little bit. You've lost weight."

"Will you be home later?"

"Of course—that is if we don't decide to attack, but that's not likely for a few days. Go on now! Tell her I said to kill the fatted calf for the prodigal!"

Clive left, and as his father had known, Lyna Lee Gordon overwhelmed him. She and Grace hugged him until he had to protest, "You're going to break my bones! Give a fellow room to breathe, will you?"

They welcomed him home, along with David, who was equally glad to see him. Clive was tired after his long journey, but that night after the others had gone to bed, he and his mother sat talking before the fire for some time. He had always been able to talk about himself with her, and now he did not realize how much of himself he was revealing.

Lyna sat there looking at this tall son of hers, thanking God that he had survived the illness. She was well aware of how often Katherine Yancy came into the thread of his dialogue. She was a discerning woman, and her son was very precious to her—as were all of her children. *He looks so much like Leslie*, she thought. *And he's like him, too. Naive and he doesn't know very much about women.* She thought of how in her attempt to escape from a lustful master, she had disguised herself as a young man and entered into the service of Leslie, then a young lieutenant. She had fallen in love with him while he had no idea that she was a young woman. *When he did discover it, however*, she thought suddenly with a smile, *he certainly made up for lost time.* And now this young son of hers, who looked so much like his father, was falling in love, too. She listened as he told of the misunderstanding that had come between him and Katherine, and then how he desperately wanted to help Katherine's father gain his freedom.

Finally, Clive stopped and looked surprised. "I always did talk to you too much!" he laughed, half embarrassed. "Don't you get tired of hearing all of my problems?"

"No, I never do!" Lyna looked at him as the fire threw its reddish reflections across his face, making his craggy features seem even more pronounced. She was apprehensive, for she knew the gap that existed between those loyal to the Crown and those fighting for their freedom.

She also knew from her acquaintanceship with Katherine Yancy that there was little likelihood that the young woman would ever join herself to a man who was loyal to the Crown.

Finally she said quietly, "Katherine's a fine young woman. You think a great deal of her, don't you, Clive?"

"Why, yes I do. Do you like her, Mother?"

"Very much!"

"How do you think I could help her father? I thought about it, and there seems no way."

"We'll pray about it. With God all things are possible!" Lyna said. She rose then, kissed him, and went to bed. Clive sat before the fire for a long time after that, and as he had seen Katherine's face in the sky on the ship, now he seemed to see it in the flames of the fire. Finally he got up and went to bed, remembering his mother's words, *We'll pray about it*. He smiled and muttered, "That's what she always says."

🕇   🕇   🕇

Lyna was tossing on her bed, half asleep, half awake. Leslie had left early before dawn. He had whispered to her, "You sleep as long as you can. No reason for you to get up." He had kissed her, then left, and she had dropped off back into a deep sleep. For some time she lay there sleeping quietly, and then she began to dream. In the dream she remembered again how she had met Leslie. The dream came to her in sharp, clear fragments, some of which were frightening, and others were very joyous. She did not dream often, and it disturbed her somehow when she did.

Finally, that part of the dream ended, and other images began to form in her mind. It was not a clearly oriented dream, and the chronology of it seemed all wrong. She threw her hands up over her head, striking the headboard, and this seemed to pull her out of the dream. But, as such dreams are, she lay there for some time neither sleeping nor fully awake, and still the figures appeared. She seemed to see Clive's face, tense and drawn—and then the face of the young woman that he was in love with. Others came, and a voice seemed to speak, but she could hardly make out the words.

Finally she awoke with a start and sat upright in bed. She had been wearing a cap, but it had come off in her tossing, and her hair was falling down her back. She sat there trying to put the pieces of the last dream together, for somehow she felt that it was important.

Oh, God, help me to know the interpretation, if there is one!

She prayed this prayer, feeling somewhat foolish. She had never had a dream that meant anything. She had heard of others who had, and, of course, knew well the Bible stories of those to whom God spoke in dreams. Now she sat there quietly praying and waiting as she had learned to do when she was uncertain. Slowly the dream began to fall into place, and astonishment came to her. She sat there for some time, and then finally threw the covers back. Quickly she dressed and went down to the room that David shared with Clive. She knew that a cannon shot in the room itself would not awaken David, so she stepped inside and moved over to where Clive lay sleeping on one of the single beds. "Clive," she whispered, "get up!"

Clive was a light sleeper. His eyes flew open, and when he saw his mother he was startled. "What is it—is something wrong?"

"Get dressed, I have something to tell you," Lyna said quietly. She turned and left the room, going into the kitchen, where she stirred the fire from the ashes that she had banked the night before. Soon it was burning cheerfully, and she began to move about pulling together the materials for a breakfast.

Clive came in, his face troubled. He was stuffing his shirt down in his breeches and came to her at once. "What is it, Mother? Is something wrong with Father?"

"No, nothing like that." Lyna said, "Sit down, Clive, I want to tell you something." She waited until he was seated, then came over to stand before him. "I don't put much stock in dreams. I don't have many dreams as a matter of fact—but I had one early this morning that I think has a meaning."

Clive's interest was caught. He had never known anyone who had a dream that actually meant something. "What sort of a dream was it?" he asked.

"It was about you, Clive," Lyna said. She reached up, touched her hair, then shook her head. "It wasn't very clear at first, then it came to me sometime early this morning. I think the sun had already begun to come up, but I wasn't fully awake."

She began to describe the dream to him as best she could, and found it very difficult. Clive listened, and finally he said with puzzlement, "I don't really see that it means anything. Naturally you were interested in me and in Katherine and in her father."

"I think I know what it means." She came over and pulled her chair closer. Her eyes were bright and her lips were parted with excitement. "Here's what I think it means, Clive. . . ."

🛡   🛡   🛡

"Well, Clive, you're here bright and early this morning. I didn't expect to see you!"

"Father, I want to talk to you. I have a favor to ask."

"Well, of course!" Leslie stood up at once behind his desk, for he saw Clive was tense. "What is it?"

"I want you to arrange an exchange, sir."

"An exchange—what sort of an exchange?"

"I want you to get Amos Yancy's release in exchange for one of our men held prisoner by the Americans."

Leslie stared at Clive and wondered what had brought all this on. "That would be very difficult," he said. "What made you think of such a thing?"

"Actually, it was Mother who thought of it." Clive hesitated, but he knew his mother would certainly tell her story to his father when he got home. "Mother had a dream this morning, and that was what she saw in the dream. She saw all of us, me and you and Katherine and her father, and then she saw me bringing a man out of the American lines. Then she dreamed that you unlocked a door and Amos Yancy came out of a cell."

"Your mother dreamed that?" Leslie was genuinely surprised. "She doesn't dream much that I know of."

"No, but she says she thinks it's more than just a dream." Clive's face was intense, and he asked with an earnestness in his voice, "It could be done, couldn't it, sir?"

"Well, there *are* exchanges made all the time. Usually it isn't too complicated, but now with a battle shaping up, it would have to go through certain channels of command. And how do you know the Americans would exchange one of our men for Yancy?"

"I don't know that, but I'm going to find out. I can't think of any other way, so I'm going to believe in Mother's dream or vision, or whatever it was."

"Well," Leslie said, troubled by what he had heard, "I'll do what I can, son, you know that. But it will take a miracle."

Clive suddenly smiled. "Well, Father, there are precedents, you know." He turned and walked to the door. When he got there, he looked back over his shoulder. "You start getting the paperwork. I'm going to talk to the Americans."

"You're going over to the American lines?"

"Yes, that's what I'll have to do!"

"But you might get shot! They're not very careful who they shoot at. They're expecting us to attack at any time."

"I'll be careful!" Clive shut the door, and left his father standing alone in the room. He made his way out of headquarters, his mind buzzing with the plan. It wasn't a plan, really, but he knew it was something he had to do. He made his way to a livery stable, and when the hostler came to meet him he said, "I want to rent a horse."

Ten minutes later he was mounted on a fine gray mare. He rode north, headed for the lines that his father had mentioned the previous day. He had no idea of how he would get through his own lines, and certainly none of how he would cross over to the American side without getting shot at. All he knew was this was something he had to do.

22

"A Man in Love Does Very Strange Things"

THE HARSH OCTOBER WIND was sweeping across the Heights where the American army stretched out waiting for the British attack. Overhead a flight of noisy crows split the air with their harsh calls, then settled down on a cornfield and pecked at the stalks.

Dake watched, without interest, as the birds darkened the sky, then fell to the ground. Turning to Micah, who had come from his position with Knox's guns to visit, he said, "I wish they'd come on. I'm tired of this waiting!"

Micah wore a heavy blue woolen coat that reached to his knees, and he had procured a fur cap that came down almost over his ears. It was like one he had seen Benjamin Franklin wear once, and he rather fancied it. "I wish I had some mittens made out of fur to go with this cap," he murmured. He blew on his hands, which were rough and bruised from handling the guns of Henry Knox, then followed Dake's gaze down the hill. They could see the British sentries moving faintly, the red of their jackets making colorful splashes against the specter gray of the earth. He pulled off his cap and rubbed his head for a moment, then pulled it back on. "General Knox says he doesn't know what they're waiting for. They could have hit us anytime."

"I wonder what General Washington thinks?"

"I don't know. Nobody knows that, I guess."

The two stood there talking quietly, stamping their feet from time to time to get the circulation going, and Dake suddenly slapped his hands together in an impatient gesture. "I'd hate to die at a time like this!"

"A time like this?" Micah stared at Dake with surprise. "What do you mean by that? Anytime is a bad time to die!"

Dake was wearing the makeshift uniform of the Continental Army. It wasn't much, but he felt a little pride in the difference between it and those worn by the militia. He ran his finger along his musket, lifted it, and sighted it down the hill. The range was too far, of course, and he put it down, then turned to say, "I guess you're right. There aren't many times when a man wants to die, but it's just—"

Suddenly Micah smiled, "You're thinking about Jeanne."

"Yes!" Dake flashed a grateful smile at this twin of his. Though they were far different in many ways, still there was a link that bound them together. And sometimes they seemed to know what the other was thinking. "I want to take care of her. I want us to have children, and then grandchildren. I'm looking forward to being a crotchety old grandfather someday!"

Micah laid his hand on Dake's shoulder. "You'll make it, Dake," he said gently. He received a shy smile from Dake, then said, "I got to get back. We're going to have more practice with the guns—not that we ever shoot them; not enough powder for that." He turned and walked away, saying over his shoulder, "Don't get into any trouble while I'm gone."

Dake grinned, then turned to look back down the hill. For the next two hours he entertained himself by passing along the lines. Someone had brought up some beef, and he helped make a fire and boiled the meat. After it was done, he and Sergeant Tooms took their portion, lay it on a slab of thick brown bread, and moved over to sit down on the log of a fallen elm tree.

"I don't see why we're hanging around here," Tooms complained. He bit off a portion of the beef, chewed it thoroughly, then swallowed it. "If it was me, I'd get this whole army off of this island quick!"

"Maybe you're right!" They had gone over the argument many times, and Dake had no inclination to argue further. He was aware that something was happening down the hill. In the distance he saw a horseman break out of the English camp and move slowly toward the American lines. "Look at that! Maybe he's coming to surrender the army!" he grinned.

Tooms finished his beef and bread, and then stood up. Grasping his musket he said, "Let's drift over and see what's going on."

The American sentries down the way had seen the solitary horseman leave the British lines. Their sergeant said, "You all primed, men? We may have to shoot that limey out of his saddle just to teach him a lesson."

"He ain't wearin' no uniform, Sarge!"

261

"Well, he's a spy then. We ought to shoot him anyway!" a continental said.

"Shut your mouth!" Sergeant Oaks said. He was a tall, weather-beaten man from Delaware, and now stood up to get a better view of the horseman. "I don't know what he is! Maybe he's bringing a message over! Anyhow, I'll talk to him. You fellows get back to your post! I'll handle this."

Clive Gordon had kept his eyes on the line of American soldiers along the top of the ridge. He had encountered some difficulty passing through the English line, but had had the forethought to bring a pass from his father. That had scarcely been enough, but he had simply talked his way into passing through the lines. Now he saw a tough-looking sergeant and half a dozen Continental soldiers spread out awaiting his arrival. As soon as he got close, he pulled his horse up and said, "Good afternoon, Sergeant!"

"What's your business!" Sergeant Oaks snapped. "This is no place for a civilian!"

"I'm here to see General Washington!"

A laugh broke out among the soldiers, and a short, stubby one with a full beard said, "You're gonna have tea with him, limey?"

"I have business with the general." Actually Clive had no hopes at all of seeing General Washington, but he had thought by showing a little audacity it might make his case stronger. At least he might get to see one of Washington's lieutenants.

"Well, you ain't going to see him! Turn around and get back there!"

Clive did not move but stepped off his horse and came forward, leading the animal. "It's highly imperative that I see someone in authority!" he said. "I have urgent business."

"You got any papers?"

Clive shook his head. "None that would interest you."

The sergeant stood there arguing, and Clive's heart sank. It was fairly clear he was not going to be admitted. He had stiffened himself for resistance, intending to get himself arrested if necessary, when suddenly, to his surprise, a voice said, "That's all right, Sergeant Oaks, I know this man."

Oaks turned around to see who spoke and instantly said, "What are you doing here, Private Bradford? Get back to your place!"

But relief washed over Clive as he saw Dake Bradford. "He'll vouch for me!" he said. "We're relatives!"

Oaks looked at the tall Englishman doubtfully. "That can't be!" he said.

"Yes, it is!" Dake said easily. He carried his rifle in the crook of his arm and nodded his head toward the civilian. "This is Clive Gordon. He's my cousin. His mother is my father's sister." He did not ask what Clive was doing there but turned to the sergeant and said, "I'll be responsible for him, Sergeant!"

"Well, he'll have to leave his arms here."

"I'm not carrying any weapons, Sergeant."

"All right then, but, Bradford, you go right to the lieutenant. He's supposed to handle things like this!"

"All right, Sergeant, I'll do that!"

Turning, Dake walked away, and Clive quickened his pace until he caught up with him. "I'm glad you came along!" he said as soon as they were out of earshot. He looked along the line and saw that every soldier seemed to be eyeing them with curiosity. "I guess you don't get many visitors around here—not from our side!"

Dake said, "Not many." Then when they had passed through a grove of trees he pointed over to where a group of tents had been set up. "We'll have to go see the lieutenant. The sergeant will check on that." He turned to face the other and asked directly, "What are you doing here, Clive?"

Clive had considered what he might say when it came down to it and had decided that simplicity was the best thing. "I want to get a man exchanged, a prisoner in the hulks."

"One of our men?" Dake spoke sharply. "Why would you be interested in an American prisoner?"

"He's the father of a friend of mine."

"What's his name?"

"Amos Yancy."

"Yancy? I don't know any Yancys."

"I thought you might. The family's from Boston. Your father knows them slightly, and Rachel as well."

"Who are they?"

Clive stood there in the cold wind explaining who the Yancys were, and he saw skepticism on Dake's face. "Why are you so suspicious, Dake?"

"Because you're an Englishman. Your father is a colonel in the English army. I can't understand why you'd be so anxious to get an American out of prison."

Clive hesitated only momentarily, then he made a helpless gesture with his hands. "Well, to tell you the truth, Dake, I'm in love with his daughter."

Dake stared at Clive unbelievingly. It had not been that long ago when the two of them had been fiercely competing for the attention of

Jeanne Corbeau. Dake had been rather shocked when Jeanne had chosen him. Clive Gordon had money, education, was a doctor, and had a fine career ahead of him, while Dake had a job in a foundry. Now he asked, "What do you mean you're in love with her?"

Instantly Clive knew what Dake was thinking. "I don't mind saying it, Dake," he grinned sheepishly. "I've said it myself. I thought I was in love with Jeanne, but I see now that I wasn't. I talked to her about this not long ago."

"You talked with Jeanne?"

"Yes, I went there to take care of your family. You heard about that? Jeanne was very sick, as were Sam and Rachel."

"I did get a letter from Pa about that."

"Well, I got sick after they got well, and Jeanne helped take care of me." He shook his head and said, "I can see how it would never have been good for me to marry Jeanne. I'm a city man, and she loves the out-of-doors. Besides, she's so crazy in love with you I wouldn't have had a chance."

Dake grinned suddenly and felt much better. He had thought wildly for one moment that Clive had come here to tell him some bad news about Jeanne. Relieved that his family and Jeanne were doing fine now, he said, "I'm glad we got your approval, cousin!"

"You've got a fine wife there. She's worried about you, though."

"Well, I'm worried about myself." Dake looked back toward the hill and shook his head. "What's this girl's name?"

"Katherine Yancy."

"Well, why did you come over here?"

"Dake, I've got to have a man, an English soldier that you've captured to trade for Amos."

Dake looked at him and began to laugh. "I swear, Clive, I thought Sam could come up with the most harebrained schemes in the world, but this beats all! You want to ask our officers to give you an Englishman so you can trade him for an American? Why, they'll never do it!"

"They might. I've got to try! Amos is in bad shape, Dake. I don't think he can live much longer if he doesn't get out of that foul prison ship! I know! I know—!" He put up his hand as Dake started to speak. "We're the ones that began making prisons out of leaky old ships, but that's none of my doing, and I'm against it!"

Dake stood there listening while Clive pleaded his case. The more he listened, the more he was certain that it would never work, but a scheme began to form in his mind. "I'll tell you what," he said, "there's one man that can do you some good."

"And that man is?"

"Colonel Knox."

"Is he your officer?"

"No, but Micah's serving under him. Come on, we'll go let Micah in on all this, and he can get you in to see the colonel."

"What makes you think Knox would listen more sympathetically than some others?"

"From what Micah says, it's just the kind of thing he would listen to. He's a great big fellow. He knows guns better than anybody in our army, but more than that, Micah says he's downright romantic!" A wry grin twisted Dake's lips, and he shrugged his broad shoulders. "It looks like it's going to take somebody romantic to listen to your proposition. Come on now!"

♦ ♦ ♦

"Let me get this straight," Micah said, "you want me to get Colonel Knox to release a prisoner that we've taken so that we can give him to you, so that you can take him back over the line and trade him for an American that we don't know, and that we may never see?"

Clive stood before Micah and shrugged helplessly. "I know this all sounds crazy, but it's all I can think of to try. Armies do trade prisoners. They're exchanged all the time!"

"Yes, but it takes a mountain of bookwork, and the lobsterbacks aren't going to be interested in making any trades. They're more interested, right now, in wiping us out."

"Will you at least take me to see Colonel Knox so that I can ask him myself?"

"Oh yes, I'll do that. That won't be hard. Come along!"

Micah led them through the camp to a line of guns that the men were drilling with. Micah walked up to the colonel and said, "Colonel Knox, could I trouble you for a few moments?"

"What is it, Corporal Bradford?"

"There's a man here, an Englishman, that I would like for you to hear. Actually, he's my cousin."

"Your cousin?" Knox was wearing an outlandishly colorful uniform. He favored such things, and now as he turned he looked enormous as he eyed the tall Englishman standing beside Dake. "Is that your cousin there?"

"Yes, sir! I must warn you, he's a little bit romantic."

Knox's eyes twinkled. He kept his maimed hand inside his coat, but his interest had been captured. "Well now, we shall see about that!" He moved across the ground lightly, for he was very agile despite his large size.

265

"Colonel Knox, this is my cousin Clive Gordon. His father is Colonel Leslie Gordon of the Royal Fusiliers."

"Indeed, and you are not in the army yourself, Mr. Gordon?"

"No, Colonel, I'm a physician. I appreciate your taking time to speak with me. I have a rather audacious request."

"I see! Well, let's have it!"

Clive immediately plunged into an explanation, speaking rapidly. He even rose to heights of elegance when he spoke of the poor condition of Amos Yancy and the terrible conditions of the hulk where he was kept prisoner. He finished by saying, "I have come on the hope that you would exchange one of the English soldiers for this man."

"And why have you done all this? Is he a relative?"

Instantly Clive recalled Dake's word about Knox being a romantic. "I'm in love with his daughter, sir." He embellished the story somewhat, telling how the two had met. Finally he said, "I know this sounds foolish, but a man in love does very strange things."

"Indeed, so I've heard, and do in part believe," Knox said. He laughed and his huge belly shook as he said, "I did some foolish things myself when I was your age, Mr. Gordon."

"Do you think there's any chance at all, Colonel Knox?"

Knox thought hard for a moment. "It would be very difficult. Every time we try to trade one of their men for one of ours, they make impossible demands. They want us to give them a captured general for every private that they have. The trades are supposed to be equal, that is a lieutenant for a lieutenant, a private for a private."

"This man was probably not even in the army! He was at Bunker Hill in the first action. I think he was just part of the local militia."

"That makes no difference. He's been treated as a soldier!" Knox said rather brusquely. His mind was racing, for he was a quick-witted man. He studied the young man carefully and liked what he saw. He had had many friends among the British officers in Boston, General Gage being among the best. Many of them were unhappy with the way England treated America, and this young man was not in the army.

The three men stood there waiting, and finally Knox made a sound of surprise. "Ah," he said, "a thought comes to me! We took a lieutenant captive a week ago, a Lieutenant Harrison. I've spoken with him, and it seems he's one of General Howe's aides."

Hope came to Clive at once and he said, "Are you thinking perhaps you could exchange him for Amos Yancy?"

"I think it might work. I will have to cut some corners and see that some papers are burned. Actually, we can't use the fellow. He just clutters up our way. He's nothing but a clerk. He won't be doing any fighting, I found that much out. Yes," he said pensively, "I think it might do." He studied young Clive Gordon and said, "Come along, I will see what can be done."

"Thank you, Colonel!" Clive hurried off with the colonel, and Dake and Micah stood regarding them.

Micah pulled off his fur cap, tossed it up in the air, and caught it. He grinned, saying, "Well, Clive is right about one thing."

"What's that?"

"A man in love does do very strange things!"

🛡   🛡   🛡

General Howe had just finished his dinner and was in a rather good mood. He looked across at Colonel Leslie Gordon, who stood facing him, his son Clive at his side. Leslie had said when he had entered, "Sir, this is my son Clive. I think you may have met him."

"Yes indeed! He's done some fine work helping our surgeons!"

Clive said, "Thank you, sir. I don't want to take up much of your time. I believe you have an aide, a Lieutenant Harrison."

"Yes." Howe's face fell. "A very fine young man—a distant relative of mine by the way. Too bad, he was captured last week."

"Yes, sir, I know. I've been across the American lines. They're willing to exchange Lieutenant Harrison."

"Indeed! That would be excellent!" Howe's face grew puzzled. "May I ask how it happened that you were in a position to negotiate such an exchange?"

"I have a friend, a young woman, whose father is in the hulks. You may remember the name Amos Yancy."

Howe's brow furrowed. "Yes," he said hesitantly, "it is familiar, but I don't recall."

"You may remember that the surgeon and I had some difficulty over the man. I had him taken off the hulks, and then Major Banks had him sent back."

"Oh yes, I do remember. Unfortunate affair. I remember the young lady, too. Very attractive, very attractive, indeed! What is this you're proposing?"

"It's very simple. Colonel Knox, who is in charge of such things, said he will exchange Lieutenant Harrison for Mr. Yancy."

Howe looked at the young man, his mind working quickly. He was a ladies' man himself, and every bit as romantic, in one sense, as Henry Knox. A smile tugged at the corners of his lips and he said, "I believe such an exchange would be mutually beneficial. You may work it out with my adjutant." He put his hand out and said, "I am grateful to you for your service. Have you considered, perhaps, a commission as a surgeon in our own army?"

Clive hesitated. "It's a possibility, sir. My father and I have talked about it."

"Well, I hope you decide to join. We need fine young men like you. My thanks again for your help! Take care of it, Major Burns."

As soon as the visitors were gone, Howe turned to a tall colonel who had been waiting patiently. "Well now, that's a relief. I'll be glad to have Harrison back."

"Yes, sir, he'll be most welcome. Now, have you decided about the attack?"

"The day after tomorrow if the weather is fine." Walking over to a map he said, "We will take the men here"—he pointed to a spot on the upper end of the Island—"and land them, then come around behind the Americans. You will accompany General Cornwallis, advancing upward."

"We'll have the men trapped. There's no way for them to go."

"Exactly! Well, Colonel, it'll all be over soon."

🛦   🛦   🛦

Amos Yancy looked up when a voice said, "Come along, Yancy!" A hand seized him and pulled him to his feet. His bones ached, but he withheld the cry of pain that leaped to his lips.

"Where are you taking me?"

"Don't ask questions, just come along!"

Stumbling as the burly guard pulled him across the floor and through the massive oak door that slammed behind them, which was locked by a sentry, Yancy shivered in the cold. But that was nothing new. He shivered all the time. He had chills and fever, and knew that he could not last much longer. Every day the cry, "Throw up your dead!" echoed, and he had helped to deliver the bodies of some of his best friends out on the deck for burial in the sea, sewn in a canvas sack with a cannonball at one end. It was midafternoon, and the sun was not bright, but after the darkness of the hold, it almost blinded him.

"Come along there, pick your feet up!"

Doing his best to keep up with the guard, Amos wondered what could be happening. He hoped briefly that perhaps Katherine had returned. He had given up, almost, thinking about that, and had resigned himself to die.

"In here, step lively!"

Stepping inside the cabin, the door slammed behind him. There stood the captain of the *St. George* and a tall man whom he had seen

He stared at him, squinting until finally he made out the features. "Dr. Gordon!" he said.

"Yes, I'm glad to see you, sir, and I have good news."

"Good news?"

"Yes!" Clive had come aboard the *St. George* with the papers signed by General Howe himself. The captain had been shocked but pleased. "You've worked hard enough to get this one off," he said. "I'm glad of it. He's in poor shape, I'm afraid, as all of them are."

Now Clive came over to stand beside the smaller man. He was emaciated and was trembling through the thin shirt that he wore. "You're going home, Mr. Yancy," he said quietly. He saw the head snap back and unbelief wash across Yancy's face. "Yes, it's true enough. You've been exchanged for an English prisoner, but you can't go like that. Here, I brought some warm clothes for you."

His mind reeling with unbelief, Amos Yancy allowed the tall doctor to help him put on the warm woolen clothes. They felt so good after the rags he had worn, and finally he murmured in a whisper of wonder, "I can't really believe it!"

"You will. We'll stop at an inn and spend the night. You can have a warm bath. We'll get you shaved—then we'll head for Boston in the morning." He smiled and said, "You'd like that, I know."

Amos was silent for a long time, it seemed. Slowly it began to sink in, and he trembled, not from the cold, but from relief. "That will be good, Doctor!"

Clive took his arm. "We'll take it slow. You'll be with your wife and daughter soon, and you'll be well, too."

Amos Yancy reached out and touched Clive Gordon on the chest to assure himself that this was real. He smiled tremulously and whispered, "God has delivered me, my boy—that will make me well!"

🜊   🜊   🜊

Howe's plan to attack should have worked. There was, as a matter of fact, nothing to keep it from working. It was fairly simple. He sent a large force through the East River into the Sound, and a flanking attack on Westchester. All the British troops had to do was to dismount from their boat, march overland, and form a line of battle. The poor, ragged troops of Washington would be trapped. They had an enemy advancing from their rear, and they could not run forward because Cornwallis and the other half of the army was positioned there.

It should have worked—but it did not.

The boats crept up the East River under cover of night. It was a foggy night, and they did not land at the planned destination, but in a soggy, swamplike area where the troops had to dismount and wade through the cold water. It was not an auspicious beginning, and almost accidentally their flanking movement had been spotted. A young boy had seen them land and passed the word along to some of the sentries, who at once went to General Washington. Washington had not expected a flanking attack. He went to study his map, and no way of escape occurred to him. He was caught; there was no way to escape—except one. A faint possibility began to grow. He thought slowly, *If I were to pick up this army and move slowly and deliberately, there would not be a mass retreat with my men losing their heads. If I could get them packed together, men crowding each other, and know that there was a solid rear guard behind, it might work—but first someone has to hold off this flanking attack.*

He put his finger back on the map at the spot where it might be held. The Delaware and Maryland troops had held once at Harlem Heights against unfavorable odds. They might hold again. Suddenly he thought of the Marblehead fishermen who had brought them off from Brooklyn, across the East River. He had been impressed with them then, how they moved slowly, methodically. He had seen them with oars in their hands, and he wondered how they might fare with muskets.

"Send for Colonel Glover!"

Shortly Colonel Glover entered, a man of Washington's age. He had very light blue eyes, and his lips seldom broke into a smile. There was a Yankee air about him, and he spoke in a nasal voice but moved with a certainty that Washington liked.

"Colonel Glover, your men can handle boats, but can they fight?"

Glover stared at his commanding officer. "Yes!" he said simply.

Washington liked that single word, that one monosyllable, for it had the confidence of granite from the cliffs in Vermont. Washington pointed at the map. "The British have landed here. I want you to hold them until I get the army past them. Can you do it?"

Again Glover looked at the map, and again he said, "Yes, Your Excellency."

"It may take a while to get the whole army out of here. We'll have to do it slowly, and in order. I don't want the men in a panic." Again he asked, "Can your men hold them?"

And again Colonel Glover looked Washington full square in the eyes. "Yes, sir!" he said.

They shook hands, and Washington smiled then for the first time in a long while. "I'll give you some extra men from the Continentals," he said. "A few that will serve as the rear guard once the army has made its way out."

T T T

Dake was one of those selected to join the Marblehead fishermen in their attempt to stop the British. He and Tooms were tapped by their lieutenant and soon found themselves joining Glover's men. They had three tiny field pieces with them, and finally Glover found a spot that suited him. They settled behind the stone walls and primed their muskets. Glover called his officers together, and Dake was close enough to hear his instructions.

Glover lit a pipe and nodded toward the sun that was rising over the Sound. "The British will be coming from there." He seemed to be through with his instructions, but he added, "We will wait here until the army of His Excellency passes by. Now, any questions?"

There were no questions and the men went at once to prepare themselves for the onslaught. Dake watched as they loaded the cannon, and was shocked at what he saw. They loaded the cannon, not with shot, but with rusty nails, bits of wire, old iron bolts, broken horseshoes, even pieces of glass and parts of pewter pots and pans. A cold chill ran down Dake's spine, and he turned to look at Tooms who had come to stand beside him.

"I never saw anything like that, Sergeant," he whispered.

"Me neither!" Tooms grinned as if amused. "That'll give the Redcoats something to think about when they meet a cannon full of that." They moved up and down the line and discovered that the fishermen had all sorts of weapons, none of them standards. They were not riflemen, but carried huge, wide-bore muskets that were stuffed with the same rusty nails, old wire, and any sharp bits of metal they could find. They went about their task as they would have gone about baiting hooks back on their ships in Cape Cod. Then they began to wait calmly for the enemy to make its move.

The sun came up, a blinding orb of red, and metamorphosed the Sound into what seemed to be a sea of blood. The British began marching in. Dake heard their fifes playing a fine high tune before he saw them. Then they came into sight, their drums beating, their shakoes swaying, and their glittering bayonets punctuating the morning air. If they knew the enemy lay ahead of them, they did not show it. They had been drilled for years, and as they marched forward every foot was in step, every line perfect.

Dake glanced down the line of fishermen and readied his own musket. He saw the three cannons, their mouths open as if hungry for the feast that awaited them, and again a chill ran down his back as he thought of the sweepings of the blacksmith's floor, the nails, and the broken glass that lay in the bellies of the loose guns.

When the British line was less than thirty yards away, the fishermen let go. The guns belched with a mighty roar, and the muskets went off. Dake saw the man he aimed at driven backward, and knew he had hit him squarely in the heart. For a moment smoke obscured the field, but as it cleared he saw the horrible scene unfold before him. The whole field was full of men squirming and screaming on the earth, their bodies riddled with rusty nails and bits of broken glass.

"Load again!" Glover's voice came down the line.

Surely they won't come back, Dake thought. His hands were sweaty, despite the cold, as he loaded the musket, then looked up.

"They're coming again!" Tooms exclaimed.

The British came again, straight and precise, as if nothing had happened. They stepped over the bodies of men bleeding and squirming, and once again were wiped out by the terrible rain of steel and glass.

All morning they attacked the position of the Marblehead fishermen, but Glover's men held them off. It was glorious—and it was murder. The rusty nails and bits of metal of the fishermen cut the Redcoats to bits. Only three or four of the fishermen had died, but by late afternoon, more than five hundred British and Hessians lay on that bloody field.

And then General Howe called it off, for he could not stand seeing his troops cut down so brutally.

Thus, the army of Washington was protected by a group of fishermen who held the skies up while the Continental Army of George Washington passed northward, leaving New York behind for the British.

23

END OF A MAN

FOR NEARLY A WEEK Abigail had been severely pulled emotionally. Her newly found walk with God had wrought a profound change in her spirit. She found this demonstrated most dramatically in her inability to go any further with Leo Rochester's proposition to use her to gain Matthew as his son. The nights had passed interminably as she tossed and turned, unable to sleep as she considered the enormity of her problem. She lost weight, and both her mother and Esther questioned her concerning her well-being. She had put them off as long as she could, but finally on the morning of October 19, she arose almost ill from struggling with the problem.

Wearily she got out of bed, moved across to the washstand, and began to prepare for the task she dreaded. Pouring the tepid water out of the ceramic pitcher into a bowl, she washed her face, holding the cloth in place to soothe some of the lines out. Her eyes were gritty from lack of sleep, and she felt totally unequal to the scene that she knew she was facing. Slowly she donned a simple light green dress without paying any attention to the style, worked lackadaisically at putting her hair up, and then chose a warm cloak and a wool bonnet. Snow had fallen two nights before and now lay six inches deep over the countryside.

Moving out of her room she was glad that neither Esther nor her mother had risen. She left a note on the kitchen table, weighed it down with a light blue china sugar bowl, then moved out of the house.

The sun was already rising, and the brilliance of its reflection on the snow blinded her for a moment. It seemed a magical world that she moved through. The sharp edges of the houses and the shops that she passed were rounded into smooth curves, and all the ugliness of the street litter was now concealed and camouflaged by a pristine whiteness of the blanket of snow that covered everything. A fanciful thought came to her as she tried to find a carriage to take her to the Rochester home. *It's so much easier to cover up a dirty city with snow than it is to hide something horrible in your life!*

A carriage finally came along and stopped for her. Gratefully she got in, instructing the driver to take her to the Frazier home. Leaning back, she noticed that the fresh snow that had fallen throughout the night had caused the carriage to move along silently. She missed the clip-clopping of the horses' hooves and the noise of the iron-bound wheels bouncing over the rough cobblestones. It was a smooth, silent ride, and only the sibilant hissing of the wheels passing over the snow broke the silence.

"What will I say to him?" she murmured aloud and shook her head fearfully. She was determined to free herself from the agreement she had made with Rochester—but how to do this without angering him she had not yet determined. Now, as the carriage moved along past house after house, glittering with its gleaming mantle of snow, she began to pray. She longed for the faith of her aunt Esther, but she knew that she did not have it yet. Finally, all she could pray was, "Lord, I don't know what to say, but I know this is the right thing to do! So help me to get through this, please. . . !"

By the time the carriage had stopped in front of the Frazier house, she had achieved some measure of serenity. Stepping out of the carriage, she searched through her reticule, found a coin, and passed it along to the driver, who touched his hat and said, "Thank you, mum!" then spoke to the horses, which quickly stepped out and the carriage moved off.

Turning quickly and lifting her head with determination, Abigail made her way up the long walk that led to the house. She stepped up on the stoop, reached out and grasped the brass knocker, giving it three sharp raps. The sound seemed to echo in the silence of the frozen morning, and for one moment she was tempted to turn and flee. The door opened, however, before she could move, and a tall black man, wearing a black suit, white stockings, and a ruffled white shirt, asked, "Yes, miss. What may I do to help you?"

"I would like to see Mr. Rochester, if I may. My name is Miss Abigail Howland."

Cato hesitated, saying doubtfully, "It's a little early, ma'am, but I know Mr. Rochester's up. If you'll come in and wait in the parlor, I'll ask if he will see you."

"Thank you very much."

Cato took the young woman into the parlor, where he indicated a couch. "I just made the fire, miss. You best warm yourself. You may have to wait a time until Mr. Rochester gets dressed and comes down."

"I'll be fine—thank you very much!"

Cato left the parlor at once and made his way to Leo Rochester's room. He knocked on the door, and when a voice answered sleepily he stepped inside. Rochester had already risen and was sitting in a chair wearing a dark blue robe and a pair of matching slippers. "What is it, Cato?" he asked.

"There's a young lady to see you. She says her name is Miss Abigail Howland."

At once Leo became more alert. "Miss Howland, is it? Well, go tell her I'll be down in twenty minutes!"

"Yes, sir, I'll tell her that."

As Cato left the room, Rochester rose immediately. He'd had a restless night, but that had become commonplace now for him. He had already shaved, so he threw off the robe, tossing it across the bed, and dressed as quickly as his limp arm would allow in a pair of dark brown knee britches over tan stockings. He slipped into a white shirt but ignored the tie. It was very cold, so he put on a double-breasted waistcoat of a brown hue, then over this a frock coat that he did not button. He pulled on a pair of velvet slippers, gave his hair a few strokes with a brush, then left the room. He made his way to the parlor, his heart beating rather irregularly, he thought. This also had become commonplace, so he ignored it. Entering the parlor he saw Abigail sitting on the couch across from the fire. He smiled, saying, "Well, my dear, you're early this morning!"

"Yes, I know I am. I should have waited until later." Abigail stood at once and looked apprehensively at Rochester.

"Well, sit down, my dear. You needn't stand!"

"I . . . I have something important to tell you, Leo," Abigail said with some hesitation. Her face was rather pale, and she swallowed hard, trying to remember her resolution. Finally she said, "I have some news that you won't like, I'm afraid."

Leo blinked and stared at her, his good humor vanishing. "What is it?" he asked harshly.

"I've come to tell you that I . . . I can't go through with what I agreed to do—about Matthew."

Leo knew a flash of blinding disappointment. He knew that he was a sick man, and he also understood that his only hope of gaining Matthew's consent to become a Rochester lay with this girl. He was not a praying man, but he had thrown his spirit with all his force into willing Abigail to do as he asked. Now as she stood before him, pale of face, and with lips trembling slightly, a blind, unreasoning anger suddenly rose in him. This had happened to him many times during his life, but not so much in recent years. It had happened once when Daniel Bradford, only a boy, had crossed him, and he had thrown himself with a blind fury in an attempt to kill Bradford with his bare hands.

His voice was shrill as he ground out, "You're a fool! You gave me your word—and I demand that you do what you promised!" The girl began trying to speak, but Leo moved forward, took her shoulders, and began to shake her. "I won't be frustrated by a pious hypocrite like you!" he said furiously. The rage that crept up in him was like water from a dam that had broken. For weeks and months he had gauged everything in life by this one thing, and now he was being frustrated by this pale-faced girl who did not realize the enormity of what she was doing. He began to curse, and the impulse to slap her came strongly.

Abigail tried to speak, but he was too strong for her. There was a maniacal glaze in his eyes as she had never seen before, and she began to fear for her safety. "Please . . . please, Leo, don't—" But it was no use.

Leo was shouting now and shaking her violently. The rage that had come to him was like a red tide that rose, possessing him entirely, and he forgot everything except that he must make this girl do what he demanded.

Abigail put her arms out to push him away, and as she did, she became suddenly aware that Rochester had stopped shaking her. His hands were still on her arms, but his face suddenly turned pale as ashes. His lips opened, and he seemed to be gasping for air. Then with a hoarse cry he put his hands together over his chest, his eyes closing.

"Leo—what is it?" Abigail cried out.

Leo tried to speak but could not. He could only garble syllables, for the pain that had risen somewhere in the middle of his body was like an explosion. It shattered the frail tendrils of his nerves, and he felt the pain run down his left arm as it had before. But this was much worse than the last time—it was worse than anything he had ever known. He staggered forward blindly, thrusting his hands out.

Abigail tried to catch him, but Rochester toppled like a tree. His knees suddenly could not support his weight. He fell forward, and Abigail tried vainly to hold him. He was a tall man, however, and his weight was too much. She collapsed under his weight, and both of them hit the floor. "Leo!" she cried. "Is it your heart?" She saw him nod, and then his eyes rolled backward in his head, and he began to kick convulsively.

Abigail struggled to her feet, then ran at once to the door, calling, "Help! Somebody, help. . . !"

At once Cato appeared, his eyes wide with shock. "What is it, miss. What's wrong?"

"It's Mr. Rochester. He's having an attack. He needs a doctor!"

Cato stood immobile for one minute, then he said, "You go wake Miss Marian. Tell her I'm going to get the doctor. I'll be back as soon as I can!"

"Which is her room?"

"Upstairs, first door on the left!"

Abigail wheeled instantly and dashed to the stairs, scarcely aware of the slamming door as Cato left the house. She took the stairs two at a time, turned to her left, and rapped hard on the door, calling out frantically, "Mrs. Rochester—Mrs. Rochester. . . !"

"Yes!" came a voice from within. "Yes, what is it!"

"It's your husband. He's very sick!"

Almost at once the door opened, and Marian Rochester stood there wearing only her gown and a nightcap, but she was totally awake. "Where is he?" she demanded.

"Downstairs in the parlor!" Abigail said. "I came to talk to him. We were talking, and he had a terrible attack of some kind!"

"We have to send for a doctor!" Marian said at once.

"Cato's already gone. He said he'd be back with him as soon as he could get here."

"I must go to him!"

Marian paused only to get a robe, and Abigail followed her down the stairs. They rushed to the parlor, and Leo lay where she had left him. Marian fell on her knees and pulled his head up to her breast. She pushed his hair back, saying, "Leo! Leo, can you hear me?"

There was no response except for a mild fluttering of the eyelids.

Abigail stood there helplessly. She had the horrible thought that it was her visit that had brought on the attack. Unsteadily she whispered, "Is there anything I can do, Mrs. Rochester?"

"If you can pray," Marian whispered, holding Leo's head tightly, "you can pray that God will spare him."

The silence seemed deafening in the room, it was so thick. Only the sick man's hoarse breathing, rapid and irregular, broke the silence. The two women watched Leo's face, which was now twisted into an agonizing expression, and both of them prayed for Leo Rochester.

T　　　T　　　T

Daniel had not been at the foundry for more than half an hour when Cato came rushing into his office. He gasped hoarsely, "Mister Daniel, it's Mr. Rochester! He done had a bad spell!"

For one moment Daniel Bradford could not speak. His first thought was, *If he dies, he'll die lost without God.* Aloud he said, "Is he alive?"

"Yes, sir. I took the doctor there, but Miss Marian said I was to come and tell you."

"I'll come at once, Cato!"

"Yes, sir, I got the carriage outside."

Twenty minutes later the carriage pulled up in front of the Frazier home, the horses covered with froth, for Cato had driven them hard. "I'll take care of the horses. You go on in, Mister Daniel!"

"All right, Cato!"

Daniel sprang from the carriage and ran to the front door. He did not knock this time, but opened it and stepped inside. He saw Marian standing with Dr. Settling and moved toward them at once. "How is he?" he demanded without preamble.

Settling tugged at his Vandyke beard, his eyes hooded and serious. "Not good, I'm afraid, Mr. Bradford. He's had a massive heart attack."

Daniel cast a quick look at Marian, noting that her face was as pale as he had ever seen it. She was holding a handkerchief in her hands, which she tugged at nervously.

"I'm glad you came, Daniel," she whispered.

"Is there anything I can do?"

Settling shook his head. "There's not much anyone can do in a case like this—except wait and pray."

Dr. Settling told them the details, at least as well as he knew them. "You're aware that he's had these attacks before?"

"No," Marian whispered, "I never knew that. He never said a word."

Settling gave her a surprised look. "But you knew he was ill?"

"Oh yes, I could see that—but he never said anything about heart attacks!"

"How long has this been going on, Doctor?" Daniel asked. He listened as Settling outlined Rochester's case, and when he was through Daniel said, "Isn't there any treatment, some sort of medicine? There must be *something*!"

Dr. Settling bit his lower lip nervously. He did not like to lose cases, but he had a premonition that he was going to lose this one. He had been worried about Leo for some time, and now he said in a weary tone, "We doctors can't do much. We can set a broken bone, we can bleed a man or a woman—but there's so much we can't do. Sometimes there's nothing we can do."

"And you think that's the case with my husband?" Marian asked directly, her face pleading as she turned to him.

Settling knew something about the marriage of this woman and Leo Rochester. He was aware of how Leo had mistreated her and was amazed to find that she still had this kind of compassionate concern. "I'm sorry, Mrs. Rochester," he said slowly, "but unless God does a miracle, your husband cannot live."

The words seemed to hang in the air. Settling shook his head and said, "There's nothing I can really do here. I'll go take care of the rest of my patients, then I'll come back as soon as I can."

"Thank you, Doctor."

As soon as the doctor left the house, Daniel said, "I think I'd better go get Matthew."

"I believe that would be best, Daniel. Leo's thought of little else these past days."

"I'll get back as soon as I can. Will you be all right alone?"

"Abigail Howland is here with me. She's sitting beside Leo now. Do you want to see Leo before you go?"

"No, I think it might be better if I go as quickly as possible." He left unsaid what was on his mind—that Leo might die at any moment. He looked at Marian, then said quietly, "I'm sorry about this, Marian."

"So am I, Daniel."

🦁   🦁   🦁

Marian heard the door slam and heard Cato's voice. "That must be Daniel and Matthew," she said to Abigail. The two women rose and went out of the bedroom where they had been sitting beside Leo. The sick man had not spoken a word, but he was conscious from time to time.

When they stepped outside and moved down the hallway toward the two men, Daniel asked quickly, "Is there any change?"

"He's conscious, but only by fits and starts," Marian said. She looked at Matthew and said quietly, "I'm glad you could come, Matthew. I know Leo will want to see you."

Matthew had been deeply shocked by Daniel Bradford's news of Leo's sickness. At first he could not believe it, but then he remembered how badly Leo had looked physically over the past few weeks. The two had gotten into a carriage and returned at once to the Frazier house. Now that he stood before Marian, he found it difficult to speak. "I can't believe it's as bad as Pa says."

Abigail said nervously, "I'm glad you've come, Matthew. He did ask for you once when he woke up."

"Yes, he did!" Marian nodded. "Come along, he may be awake now."

The four of them made their way down the hall and turned into the room. Two high windows on one side allowed the bright midmorning sun to throw pale bars of light across the bed, falling across Leo's face.

They were so bright that Matthew could see the small motes dancing in them, but he was staring at Leo, whose lips were pale as clay. He saw that the sick man's eyes were closed, and for one sickening moment he thought Leo had died—but then the eyes fluttered open, and Matthew moved quickly to stand beside the bed.

"Do you know me, sir?" Matthew was the eyes flutter again, then open, and recognition come to them. "I'm sorry to find you so ill—but we must hope that you'll get better."

Leo Rochester was living in a strange world, one such as he had never known. He had awakened in bed, not knowing how he got there, and then it all had come rushing back. Now he was conscious of voices, of people moving, of the light that broke across the gaily colored quilt filled with reds and blues and yellows—but it was as if he saw through another man's eyes. Nothing was clear. The pain was still with him, that much was definite—but it was numb now, not sharp and keen and piercing as when it had knocked him to the floor.

He studied Matthew's face, striving to put everything together, then he whispered, "I'm glad you've come—Matthew."

"Is there anything I can do?"

Leo did not answer, indeed, did not seem to hear. His eyes were fixed on the face of the young man who bent over him. Finally he whispered, "You're very—like me, did you know that, Matthew?"

The remark brought a flush to Matthew's face. Flashing memories came to him of how he had first become aware that Leo was his father, so far as blood was concerned. Memories of how he had raged when he had discovered that Leo had forsaken his mother. He thought also of how for weeks he had been struggling with the offer of Rochester to make him his son, according to law—to hand him, as it were, a fortune, a title, and all that this world could afford. These thoughts came, not singly, but as bright flashes of scenes that struck against his mind. And now at the reminder that he closely resembled Leo, all of his thoughts coalesced on the one fact that he had not yet ever acknowledged Leo in any way whatsoever.

Awkwardly he reached out and picked up the hand that lay limply on Leo's chest. He held it and saw Leo's eyes grow suddenly surprised. "I am very like you, sir!" he said. "My mirror tells me that."

Leo felt the pressure of the young man's hand on his, and it moved him greatly. He was still not completely clear in his mind, but he knew that the face of that young man before him had goodness in it. There was honesty there, integrity, and for one moment bitterness came as he thought, *He got that from living with Daniel Bradford.* But then that thought passed away and he said, "You're not like me inside. That's . . . a good thing."

Matthew could not answer for a moment, but he was tremendously moved. He knew that this man was his closest link in blood in the world. He had half brothers and sisters, but this man—for all his faults—was his father. This was the man who had given him life. Matthew kept his hold on the limp hand and tried to think of something to say. It all seemed very inadequate now, and finally all he could do was murmur, "I'm sorry that I didn't have more time with you, but perhaps we shall yet. We must be hopeful."

Leo listened to the words but shook his head slightly. He himself recognized that he was a dying man. For some time he lay quietly, clinging to the hand of his son, and then his eyes dropped and he seemed to pass into a restless sleep. When Matthew tried to withdraw his hand, however, Rochester held to it tightly. Seeing this, Marian came over and, moving a chair closer, whispered, "Sit beside him, Matthew. He needs you now."

🗡 🗡 🗡

"Is he any better, do you think, Doctor?"

Marian had stepped outside with Dr. Settling, who had returned to examine Leo. It had been a long day for her. Twilight had come, and now the sun was going down, and there had been little change in Leo Rochester's condition. Marian kept her eyes fixed on Dr. Settling, looking for some sign of hope, but try as she might, she could not discern one ray in the gray eyes of the doctor.

"You must prepare yourself, Mrs. Rochester," Settling said gently. "I do not think he can last the night. His heart is shattered. I don't know what's keeping him alive now."

Marian stood quietly, taking in the doctor's words. She had expected no better news, and as he gave his advice about how things might be done, she realized that he was preparing her for the worst.

"Thank you, Doctor. I'd better go be with him."

"I think that would be best—he could go at any second."

Marian moved back inside and saw to her surprise that Leo was awake, and that Daniel had seated himself across the bed from Matthew. They made a strange tableau, these three men. She looked from one face to another, thinking how strange it was that Bradford and her husband had been drawn together in this final scene. Her gaze went to Matthew, and she noted the grief and uncertainty on his face, then she drew closer.

"We talked about this before, Leo," Daniel was saying quietly.

"About how a man needs God, and there's no better time than the present for any of us."

Leo seemed to be more alert and aware than he had been for the last two hours. He turned his head to study Daniel Bradford, and his voice was muffled by the pain. "I've lived a hard life, and an evil one in many ways."

Daniel said, "A man can change."

Leo Rochester had to struggle to form the words. "A deathbed repentance? No, I will not do it!"

"There's nothing shameful about that, Leo," Daniel said quietly. "You must have heard many times how as Jesus died, one of the thieves beside him on the cross didn't find it so. You remember? He said, 'Lord, remember me when you come into your kingdom.' Jesus told the thief, 'This day shalt thou be with me in paradise.'"

Leo's eyes were dim, and his features seemed to be collapsing, but stubbornness still dominated him even as his spirit was fleeing. "No—no!" he gasped. "That . . . would be the coward's way—to live for the devil all your life. Then when you're losing it to turn to God—and beg!"

"Leo, please listen to me!" Daniel leaned forward and there were tears in his eyes. "All of us have to beg. We're *all* beggars before the throne of God. Only His mercy saved any of us. There's no difference between you or anybody else. The Scripture says that all have sinned. We may not all have sinned alike, but we've all sinned. That's why Jesus died. . . ."

As Daniel pleaded with Leo to turn to God, Abigail stood behind Marian back in the shadows of the room. The lamp was lit now, and the light cast its golden gleams over the tableau before her. She was frightened, for she had never seen anyone die. She was more disturbed, and almost sick, at the thought that she might have been responsible, at least partly, for Leo Rochester's condition.

Once hours before, when his mind was clear, Rochester had put his eyes on her. Matthew had been sitting beside him, and Abigail had thought, *He's going to tell Matthew what I've done.* But Leo had only studied her carefully, giving her an enigmatic smile, then glanced at his son and said nothing.

Now Abigail watched as Daniel seemed to struggle, almost physically, to bring this man into the knowledge of God. She prayed as well as she knew how, and she could hear Marian praying over to one side, but it all seemed to be for naught.

Leo lingered on for nearly an hour. Finally they saw that he was adamant. He spoke in a hoarse whisper, his voice broken, his lips barely moving, "Daniel, I've always . . . hated you . . . for being what I . . . could never be!" He studied Daniel through dimmed eyes and shook his head. There was a bitterness in his lips, and he could say no more.

He turned to Matthew, and Matthew reached out with both of his hands and enclosed one of Leo's. Then Leo said, "You will have every-thing—even a title—if you want it. You can be Sir Matthew Rochester—or you can turn from it."

Then his eyes moved to Abigail. He seemed to see her alone, and he motioned to her with his head. Marian saw the girl stand back and said, "He wants you, Abigail."

Abigail started, then moved forward. She was trembling as she came to stand over Leo, who whispered, "Bend over—"

Abigail put her ear down to his lips that barely moved. She could not imagine what he wanted to say to her. She was aware that Matthew and Daniel Bradford had moved back, and then the hoarse whisper came. Rochester spoke in broken tones, but Abigail heard the words clearly: "Marry him, Abigail—keep your mouth shut—never tell him of our—arrangement. . . ."

Abigail waited, but he said no more. She straightened up and saw that death was coming. As she stepped back, her heart ached for this man who had never valued anything except the things of this world—and was now losing everything.

Marian stepped forward and fell on her knees. "Leo!" she whis-pered. "Leo!" She could say no more, for her throat was tight with grief.

Leo Rochester was almost gone, but he came back for one brief mo-ment. He opened his eyes and tried to speak. Finally he said, "Marian, you . . . have been . . . faithful."

Those were Leo Rochester's last words. He closed his eyes, his body arched, and he seemed to fight for breath. He grasped Matthew's hand with a sudden surprising strength—and then his grip relaxed. His breath was expelled—and then he lay absolutely still in the finality of death.

Sick at heart, Daniel rose and walked blindly to the window. More than he had wanted anything in a long time, Daniel had wanted to see this man, who had harmed his family so much, find God. But Rochester had gone out into eternity without knowing Jesus Christ.

He turned back to see that Marian was crying. He wanted to reach out and touch her—but that would not be fitting. He took one last look at Leo Rochester and saw the face that had been so tense now relaxed.

Matthew stood beside the bed looking down at the face of his father. It all seemed unreal somehow, and finally one thought came to him: *I found you—and now I've lost you!*

24

THE SWEET AND THE BITTER

THE DEATH OF SIR LEO ROCHESTER had been a shock to many in Boston. He had not been a popular man, in one sense, for he had few close friends. He had, however, been a powerful and a wealthy man—and when death takes one of these, the world sits up and takes notice.

Those who had spoken most plainly about Rochester's faults while he was alive now mitigated their statements—at least in public. The news of his death meant a loss of income to some, such as the gamblers and the loose women of the town that had been beneficiaries of his wealth. They would certainly miss him in a pecuniary fashion!

Other more respectable people, such as his lawyer, his boot maker, his tailor, and those who served him in one fashion or another, would also miss the income that his death produced.

But there were others who were sincerely regretful, and one of these was Daniel Bradford. He'd gone over and over in his mind his history, remembering how Leo had caused him to be thrown into a dank and horrible prison in England when he was an innocent man. He also could not forget that for many years he had served Rochester as an indentured servant—also against his will. Despite himself, he remembered Leo's cruelty to Holly Blanchard, the young woman Daniel had married to give her child a name. Nor could he forget the cruelty toward Marian Rochester.

Still, for all of this, Daniel Bradford was deeply filled with regret. He had tried to comfort Matthew, explaining, as best he could, his own feelings. He saw that Matthew was more disturbed and fragmented by Leo's death than he was himself.

"It's natural enough that you should grieve, Matthew. For all his faults, he was your father, and I have to believe that he wanted the best for you. We didn't always agree. As a matter of fact, we rarely did—but I think as far as you were concerned, he was honest."

"He wanted a son more than anything else," Matthew said bitterly. "I could have at least been more understanding!"

"You can't torment yourself with what might have been! It was a hard thing for you to decide, and who knows, if he had lived you might have done exactly as he had wanted. In fact, you still could."

"Take the name of Rochester?" Matthew looked up. The two were standing alone in Daniel's office speaking quietly. It was after hours, and the two remained to talk. Matthew stared at Daniel and said, "I couldn't do that."

"You could if you think it's right. Personal things would be out of the way now. You mustn't stop on my account," Daniel said bluntly. "I know that's been on your mind."

Matthew nodded slightly. "It has. I'd have a new name. I wouldn't be Matthew Bradford, I'd be Matthew Rochester."

"Rochester is a good name. Your grandfather, Leo's father, was a fine man. I remember him well." He paused as memories from the past came to him, then said, "I think that's what Leo wanted—to see the virtues of his own father somehow come to pass in you."

Matthew was caught by this, for he had not considered it. "I never thought of that," he muttered. "Anyway, I can't think about it now. The funeral's tomorrow. I'll need more time."

"Certainly, that's only natural. But I just wanted you to know, Matthew, that this will be your choice. I'll love you, and you'll always be my son in my mind, no matter what name you call yourself. You'll still be Matthew to me!"

"Thank you, Pa," Matthew whispered, and suddenly he wished that his father would put his arms around him as he had when he was a small boy.

As if sensing this, Daniel moved forward. He grasped Matthew and hugged him hard. Matthew was slighter of form, and as he felt the strong arms of this man go around him, he thought of the thousand things that Daniel Bradford had done, how he had always been faithful, honest, and loved him without reservation. He felt tears beginning to rise and quickly shook his head. Stepping back he said, "I'll think about it, but I'll talk to you, Pa, before I do anything."

Katherine Yancy had not been well acquainted with Leo Rochester, but when she heard the story from Abigail of how the man had died without God, it had disturbed her. The two women had talked about it, and it had been to Katherine that Abigail had finally revealed her fears. She spoke of how she had agreed with Leo to try to sway Matthew, not sparing herself.

"I . . . I agreed to make Matthew fall in love with me," she said stiffly, pain in her eyes. "I've not been a good woman, Katherine, and that was one of the worst things I've done."

"That's in the past," Katherine said quickly. "You're a Christian now, and that's all put away. And besides, you couldn't go through with it, could you?"

"No." Abigail shifted nervously in the chair she sat in, then added, "But, Katherine, I can't help feeling guilty over the fact that he had his attack over the news I gave him." She related how upset Leo had become that morning when she refused to do his bidding. When she finished, she looked up with some sort of sorrow in her eyes. "I feel I should have done it differently."

"You couldn't help what happened." Katherine comforted her as well as she could and finally said, "I think you should talk to your aunt Esther about this. I think she'll tell you that you have nothing to reproach yourself for."

"What about Matthew? Should I tell him what I did?"

Katherine almost spoke out, but then said, "It's easy for an outsider to make judgments, but I can't do that. I can't tell you what to do—but I believe God will tell you. We'll pray that you have understanding and wisdom, and when you do, whatever you do, it will be right."

Later that morning, after Abigail's visit, Katherine had moved about the house wondering if she had given good counsel. She wished she could have said more, but somehow there seemed nothing more to say. She was totally in sympathy with Abigail Howland. She had heard of the girl's bad reputation before, but Katherine was a firm believer in God's power to change people. Besides, she saw something new in Abigail that was pleasing to her. Abigail had a determination to go on with God, and all morning as she worked, Katherine prayed for the troubled young woman.

Just before noon, a knock sounded at the door. She called out, "I'll get it, Mother!"

Moving to the door, she opened it and stared speechless at the two men who stood there.

"Well now, daughter, you didn't expect to see me, did you now?"

"Father!"

Katherine threw herself forward, and her father caught her in his arms. Amos Yancy was smiling and patting his daughter on the shoulder, for she was weeping. He said, "Now, now, that's no way to take on. It's all over now. I'm home!"

Katherine pulled back and stared at him. "Pa!" she whispered. "How—" When Amos saw that his daughter could say no more, he turned her around, still keeping one arm around her. "There he stands, daughter. I believe you've met this young man?"

"Clive!" Katherine said and put her hand out. "Did you do this?"

Clive Gordon had been amply rewarded by the sight of the girl he loved so much in the arms of her father. "Well, I've done what any man would do," he shrugged finally.

"Amos!"

Amos looked up and saw his wife and rushed toward her. "I'm home, Susan!" he said.

Clive stepped forward and stood beside Katherine. The two watched as Amos and Susan Yancy embraced. Clive looked down to see the tears flowing down Katherine's face, and his own eyes were a little misty. He had gotten to know Amos Yancy very well on their trip from New York, and now as he watched the reuniting of this family, a sudden feeling of joy and pride came to him.

Katherine turned to him with wonder in her eyes. Her lips were tremulous, and she looked up into his face. "Clive, how did you do it?"

"I think the Almighty did most of it," he answered. He looked back at the couple who were still holding to each other. "They look very good together, don't they?"

"Yes, they do."

Katherine could not speak, her throat was so full, but she reached up and put her hand on Clive's shoulders, then she pulled him down and kissed him on the lips fully. "Thank you," she whispered, "for me, and for my mother, and for my father. Thank you so much, Clive Gordon!"

Amos turned to see his daughter kissing the tall Englishman, and he squeezed his wife and turned to wink at her. "Well now," he said, "could a man and his doctor get a bite to eat in this house?"

There was an instant bustling as Susan and Katherine pulled the two men into the kitchen, sat them down, and began rattling pots and pans, building fires, and making tea. It was a time of loud talk, and Susan Yancy came often to stand beside the chair her husband sat in, to touch his cheek, to smooth his hair back, to hold his hand.

Katherine was much the same, and finally after Susan had taken Amos off to put him to bed to rest, Katherine turned to Clive, saying, "How can I ever thank you?"

"Well, I can think of several ways," Clive grinned.

Katherine stared at him, and then shook her head. "You're a head-strong, willful man, Clive Gordon."

"That I am, and a man like me needs a headstrong, willful woman like you, Katherine Yancy!"

Katherine grew serious. She came to him, took his hand, and suddenly raised it with an odd gesture and kissed it.

"Oh, Katherine, you don't have to do that!" Clive protested, his face flushed.

"You've done so much, and I know you care for me, but—"

"Do you care for me?"

"I do, very much!" Katherine turned from him and walked over to the window. She stared outside at the sleigh that was sliding by in the snow, not seeing it really. She turned to him then and said, "Clive, we're so far apart."

"I know," he said. "I'm English and you're American."

"That's a big gap. Very big, indeed. This war's going to go on. Plenty of blood is going to be spilled on both sides. How would you feel if your father were killed by an American?"

"I would be grieved no matter whose hand killed him," Clive said evenly. He came to stand beside her. As he was very tall, he looked down, and then he reached out and touched her hair. Very gently he said, "It seemed impossible to get your father out of that prison, but I found out that with God, all things are possible. You know my mother had a dream in which God told her how to get your father out?"

"And I had a dream that showed me what I was so that I could forgive you."

"So God's speaking in dreams and visions, I suppose," Clive said. "But now you and I will have to believe that no matter how difficult circumstances get, we love each other. Somehow—someday, God will put us together."

"Do you really believe that, Clive?"

Clive Gordon took the young woman before him in his arms. He held her close, kissed her, and then said simply, "I believe it, do you?"

Then Katherine Yancy, who a very short time ago had determined never to trust a man, suddenly knew that this was one man she could trust her heart to forever.

"Yes, Clive," she whispered, "I believe that somehow it will happen."

🔔　　　🔔　　　🔔

The funeral of Leo Rochester was simple. The pastor had a difficult job, for he knew that the man who lay in state in the walnut coffin in front of the church had not been a man who had faith in God. Such times were always difficult, and Reverend Devaney, the pastor of the Congregational Church, did the best he could. He spoke for some time about the mercies of God, and mostly quoted Scriptures. As he looked out over the congregation, his eyes filled with compassion as they fell upon the widow dressed in black. He noted also the strong, stalwart form of Daniel Bradford, and recalled what the Methodist pastor had said about rumors concerning the two. Devaney was a man who had learned to believe what he saw, not what he heard, and he saw genuine grief in the face of Marian Rochester.

After the sermon was over, the congregation moved out to the small graveyard where a grave had been dug. The casket was lowered, and Devaney read more Scripture. The wind was moving slightly, swaying the bare black limbs of the trees overhead. The trees seemed to stir with the promise of life sometime in the far and distant spring. Overhead a ragged flight of blackbirds moved across the slate gray sky, and the gravelly sound of their voices came faintly to those who stood beside the open grave.

Finally the service was over, and people filed by to murmur words of consolation to Marian Rochester. She received them all with grace and dignity, the veil hiding her face for the most part.

Finally she turned, and Daniel Bradford longed to go to her—but he had more wisdom than that. He was glad to see Abigail Howland accompany her and said to Matthew, "I'm glad Abigail is staying with Marian for a while. She'll need someone. She shouldn't be alone."

Matthew nodded silently. He had been very quiet all day long, and he paused to take one look at the grave, then turned and walked away. Daniel wanted to go after him, but realized that this was one time that Matthew needed to be alone. Sam came up to stand beside him and said through cold lips, "Matthew sure feels bad, doesn't he, Pa?"

"Yes he does, Sam."

Sam asked directly, "Pa, was Mr. Rochester really Matthew's pa?"

"Yes, he really was."

Sam could not take this in. He shook his head finally and said, "That puts Matthew in kind of a bind, doesn't it?"

"I suppose it does." Daniel thought it might be good to prepare Sam, and he said, "He may be taking the name of Rochester."

"Why would he want to do that?"

"Well, Mr. Rochester didn't have any sons, Sam, and he wanted his own name to go on. He left most of his property, I understand, to Matthew, and a request that he take the name Matthew Rochester."

"Well, I don't think he ought to do it, Pa."

"You're very young, Sam. You know a lot of things now, but you won't be quite so sure of them before you're much older."

Daniel's voice was sharp, and Sam looked up with surprise. "Are you mad at me, Pa?"

"No! No, Sam, I'm not. Come along, we'll talk more about it at home."

T   T   T

Abigail knew that sooner or later she was going to have to tell Matthew the truth, and finally when he came to her two days after the funeral, she knew that it could not be put off any longer. She had stayed with Marian for these two days, and the two women had grown very close. Katherine Yancy had come by bringing Clive Gordon, and Abigail could see the way the wind blew in that direction. She and Esther had discussed it, and Esther had said doubtfully, "I don't see how they could ever marry. He's English and she's American."

"I know, but I'm just praying that God would put them together. They're so much in love."

Now, at three o'clock in the afternoon, Matthew came striding up to the door. Abigail had seen him out the front window, but she let him knock. She went to the door and admitted him, and saw at once that he was feeling much better than he had been during the funeral. "Come in, Matthew," she said.

"Hello, Abigail!" He smiled and reached out and took her hands. "My hands are cold!" he said.

"Come into the parlor. We've got a fire there and I just made tea. We've got some cakes that Mrs. Rochester and I made this morning."

The two moved into the parlor and Matthew sat down. He seemed much calmer now, but still there was a restlessness in him, and he asked, "Where is Mrs. Rochester?"

"She's gone out to do some business with the lawyer, I believe."

"How is she holding up?"

"She's very grieved over the loss of Mr. Rochester, but she's going to be all right."

Matthew seemed to be preoccupied with some thoughts, and his talk for some time was disjointed.

Finally he shook his shoulders together and said with dissatisfaction, "I didn't come here to eat cakes or drink tea, Abigail! I came to get you to marry me. You know I love you."

At that moment, Abigail knew exactly what she had to do. A great fear rose in her, but she fought it down and said quietly, "I have something to tell you, Matthew."

"Of course, what is it?"

"You may have heard some things about me, about the way I lived. I've been a selfish, thoughtless woman, and I want to tell you all of it."

"Do you mean about—?"

"Wait, let me tell you everything, Matthew. It's not pleasant, and I don't like to say these things, but I want to be perfectly honest with you. Will you listen until I'm through, and then you can say anything you please?"

"Why, of course, Abigail!" Matthew was somewhat shocked at the soberness of Abigail's tone, and he saw that her eyes were totally serious. He had been in a state of shock since the funeral, and still was to a great extent. He had one thing on his mind now, which was to carry out the wishes of Leo Rochester. He had made up his mind to that. He had also made up his mind to marry Abigail, and now he was curious as to what she might say. He knew, of course, that she had had an affair with Paul Winslow. That was common knowledge. He had thought that through in his mind, and now was sure that he harbored no unforgiveness or ill will because of it. Now he leaned forward and listened carefully as she told him the details of her life.

Abigail did not spare herself. She spoke clearly and evenly, though it almost tore her heart out to have to go over what she had been. She was fairly certain that he was aware of her behavior with Paul Winslow; nevertheless, she recounted it, and said, "I was very wrong, but God has forgiven me for it."

"And so do I. We'll put it behind us, Abigail!" Matthew said eagerly. "And that's what—"

"But that's not all." And now Abigail did hesitate. "I have to tell you that after the British left Boston I was destitute, my mother and I. She wasn't very well, and I was terrified. I didn't know what to do." She went on to speak for some time about her fear and uncertainty, and finally took a deep breath and went right to the heart of the matter.

"Just when I was most afraid, Matthew, I had a visitor. Leo Rochester came to me and said he had a proposition. Can you guess what it was?"

"No, I can't!"

"As you know, he wanted more than anything else for you to agree to take his name and to be his son."

"Yes, I know that, but what does that have to do with you?"

Now that the moment had come, for one instant everything in Abigail cried out for her to say anything but the truth. But she knew if she did, her whole life would be a lie. Taking a deep breath she said, "He wanted me to make you fall in love with me." She saw Matthew's face suddenly grow stiff, and his cheeks seemed to grow pale. Still she continued, "He gave me money to go to New York with my mother to live. We were going anyway to live with Aunt Esther, but he insisted that I try to influence you to get you to do what he wanted."

It was suddenly very hard for her to go on. Abigail saw the pain in Matthew's eyes and whispered, "I know this hurts you, but I must tell you. I took the money, and I came to New York with that in my heart, to make you fall in love with me, and to get you to do what Leo wanted."

Matthew seemed to be struck dumb. He stared at her in disbelief. Such a thing had never occurred to him! He had been attracted to Abigail long before he had found her again in New York. He thought of all the times they had had together, and there at that place, how she had filled his life with joy. Even as he thought of it he grew suddenly angry and said coldly, "So, that's why you were so ready to spend time with me?"

"Matthew—" Abigail began, but the whole truth was needed. "That was the way it was. I'm not proud of it, but I had to tell you." She was about to say that she had changed, and that her feelings for him had changed, but he gave her no opportunity.

Matthew Bradford was not in a sound, logical state. He had been distressed for some time over finding out the secret of his birth, a shameful secret it seemed to him. And then the strain of trying to decide whether or not to take Leo's offer had been bearing upon him hard. Then came the sudden death of Leo Rochester, and all hope of making an objective decision was gone, for the dying man's last request now lay heavily on him. In other circumstances he might have been cool and thoughtful, but now as he looked at Abigail, all he could think was, *She used me! She doesn't care a thing about me!*

Slowly he rose to his feet and said stiffly, "Thank you for telling me! It was kind of you!" There was a bitterness and a wry cynicism in his tone. He saw that his remarks hurt her and he said, "I will not impose on you any longer, Abigail. Obviously, you don't have to keep up the charade anymore."

"Matthew, it's not like that!" Abigail said. "Please, let's talk. . . !"

"I don't see that talk would help!" Matthew was gripped by an anger, such as he had never known. He turned and walked stiffly to the door and out of the room.

Abigail sat there hearing the door slam, and then tears came to her eyes and she began to sob.

She never knew how long she stayed there, sitting on the couch, her face buried in her hands. She was dimly aware that a door had closed, and she heard Marian say, "Abigail—?"

And then Abigail felt a hand on her shoulder, and she turned to Marian and suddenly threw her arms around her and began to weep afresh.

Marian Rochester held the trembling, weeping girl, and, like a mother, stroked her back and murmured comforting sounds. She made no attempt to discover what the trouble was at first, but finally Abigail began to speak. Marian listened to the choking sobs as the girl repeated what had happened, and then Abigail said, "Oh, Marian, I've lost him forever now!"

Marian said quietly, "Abigail, you've been faithful. You have done what you thought you should do, what God would have you do."

"But he doesn't believe me! He thinks that I didn't love him, that I was just after Leo's money."

"You know that that isn't so. It may have been once, but you wouldn't have told him if money were the only thing that mattered."

For some time the two women sat there, and Abigail's sobs began to grow fainter. Finally she groped in the pocket of her apron and found a handkerchief. She wiped her eyes and swallowed hard. "I'll never see him again—or if I do, he'll hate me. You should have seen the look in his eyes."

Marian Rochester had endured a life of sorrow and grief herself—living with a man who did not love her. And now her heart went out to this young woman who had thrown herself on God's mercies—and now it seemed that it all had been in vain. She tried to pray and ask for wisdom and finally she said quietly, "Abigail, you have been faithful. Now you must wait for God to be faithful. He never fails, not once, and someday you will look back and thank Him that you were honest, that you didn't shrink from doing this thing. God will honor you for it."

Abigail looked into the eyes of Marian Rochester. Hope was a cold, dead thing in her. She could not sense the presence of God. She realized now that she did love Matthew Bradford, that she had for some time, but he had looked at her with hatred, disdain, and bitterness. She knew she could not wipe that out from her memory, that expression on his face and the tone of his voice. She tried to believe the words of Marian Rochester, but it seemed impossible.

"I'll try to believe, Marian," she whispered finally. "But it's so hard."

Marian put her arms around the girl again and held her close. "It's always hard to believe God when the waters are deep and the night is dark," she whispered, "but somewhere, on the other side, you will find this God of ours never fails!"

25

WE'LL FIGHT AGAIN?

GENERAL HOWE WAS DISGRUNTLED when he discovered that the remnants of Washington's Continental Army had moved once more out of his grasp. Howe pursued doggedly, however, and on October 21, he found the Americans were digging in at White Plains. It took Howe another six days to reach this position. He prepared for a full-scale attack, deploying his whole army in the open before the eyes of the American troops. The next morning brought a confused fight. British and German troops drove the Americans off Chatterton's Hill, the right-flank anchor of their positions. Again some militiamen panicked. Some of the regulars did well, while others retreated prematurely. The British did not fare much better.

The Battle of White Plains was a confused and disorderly affair. Grant, the British general, contemptuous of American soldiers, suffered far heavier losses than was necessary. By the time the hill was finally taken, Howe decided to wait until morning before finishing the job. In the morning, however, it was raining heavily, and by the time it stopped, the rebels were gone again to another, and better, position three miles back. At this Howe gave up in disgust and returned to Manhattan.

George Washington never understood why Howe failed to deliver the blow that would have finished his army. Neither did anyone else ever understand. Some of Washington's officers made the wry remark that "General Howe is the best general we got in the American army."

Washington now was watching his men desert almost by the hundreds. His army had been split into three parts, one at Fort Washington in New York, one across the Hudson at Fort Lee, and the third part in Westchester. Washington went about his task as though he had won a victory. He inspected the regiments, and he wrote letters to Congress.

Among his officers and men he never showed anything less than total and absolute confidence.

On November 12, Washington rose one bright, cold morning and wished that he were back at his home at Mount Vernon. He loved the life of a country gentleman, and not a day went by but what he thought of the time that he might be permitted to return. For a while he went about examining different units and thinking about what General Howe's next strategy would be. One thing he knew, that somehow he would have to get his men out of Fort Lee and Fort Washington. They were strongly built forts, but he did not know if they could be held against the enemy's attack.

The next day he went to Fort Lee and discovered, to his amazement, that instead of beginning to withdraw the troops from Manhattan Island, Greene had reinforced them. He faced the handsome, young Quaker alone and said, "Nathaniel, what sort of insanity is this!"

"Sir, we can hold that fort!"

Washington had great confidence in Nathaniel Greene, and he did long to see Fort Washington defended, as Congress wished it to be held. After a moment or two he said, "Tell me the truth, Nathaniel, not what you think I *want* to hear. Can that fort be held?"

"Sir, we can hold it forever!"

"Never mind forever. Can you hold it for a month?"

"Yes, sir. Give us a chance and we can hold it!"

Three days later, General Washington received a message that General Greene should know the state of affairs at Fort Washington. At once the commander in chief mounted and made his way to the edge of the high cliff overlooking the Hudson River and Manhattan. From the direction of Fort Washington came the dull boom of a cannon. "Where is General Greene?"

"Across the river, sir."

"And General Putnam?"

"He's at Fort Washington, too, General."

Finally, unable to contain himself, Washington decided to cross the river. A boat was found, and he sat in the stern until they were halfway across the river. He heard the creak of oarlocks and called out, "Who's there?"

"General Washington, is that you?"

It was Nathaniel Greene, and the two men at once discussed the situation.

The geography of Manhattan was not complex. It was a finger of land, about two miles in width and fifteen miles long. The defense of this panhandle had been obvious to Washington. It seemed to be made for defense. What Washington did not know, what none of the American officers knew, was that General Magaw, who had been placed in charge of the defense of Fort Washington, had been betrayed. An American had gone to General Howe's headquarters and given him the complete plans of the fort. And now Howe, anxious to redeem his reputation, sprung the trap. British and Hessians had landed and surrounded the fort. As they did, the defenders fell back, often wounded, and out of ammunition.

As the two men sat in the boat discussing the seriousness of the situation, a furious roll of cannons split the air. "Get us to shore!" Washington commanded. As soon as the boat touched the shore, he leaped out. Instantly he saw a guard of Redcoats and long files of red-coated soldiers climbing up the path to the fort. The path that Greene and Magaw had assured Washington would not be taken!

Washington suddenly heard the cry of the big green-clad Jaegers calling out, "Yonkee! Yonkee!" And then they saw American soldiers fleeing in a panic from the Jaegers. Washington and Greene stared in horror as the Pennsylvania troops were flanked. They were pinned against the trees and driven screaming into the river, and there was no way for the officers to help as the Hessians began to shoot them, laughing all the time.

There was never really a question of defense. As Washington watched numbly, almost three thousand men of the American army and mountains of precious supplies fell into the hands of the British. The Hessians swarmed in from the south, others from the eastern approach, and red-coated troops marched up from the river. Soon it was all over, and Washington watched silently as the American flag was hauled down, and the British flag went up in its place.

🔔　　🔔　　🔔

"And now Fort Lee is all we have left."

Dake Bradford stood beside Silas Tooms in the middle of Fort Lee, both bitter about the loss of Fort Washington across the river, and Tooms shook his head. "It was a foolish thing to try to hold these forts. The worst mistake George Washington ever made or ever will make! Three thousand of our fellows are on their way to prison camps. All those supplies, cannons, guns, ammunition of all kinds, uniforms—all gone!"

Dake swallowed hard, for it was a defeat that was hard to take. He was talking quietly with Tooms when he saw Knox stride across the open ground inside the fort. Behind him was Micah, and Dake went to him at once. "What's happening, Micah?"

"General Knox wants to take all the supplies out of the fort."

"Well, that makes sense," Dake said. "We've lost everything over in Fort Washington."

Micah looked over his shoulder. "I don't think there's time. The general says there isn't."

General Washington was facing Knox and General Greene, and Greene said bitterly, "There are reports of six thousand British soldiers. They've crossed the Hudson, five miles north of here. They are already coming to cut us off."

Instantly Washington demanded, "Evacuate the fort!"

"How can we evacuate, Your Excellency? We have no wagons, nothing to haul the supplies off."

"Never mind the supplies. Evacuate the fort!"

"But all the cannons, the provisions, what are we going to do?"

Washington's temper flew out suddenly. "General Greene, evacuate the fort and leave everything!"

"Sir, tomorrow we can have horses for the cannon."

General George Washington stared at him, his eyes flashing. "You heard my order! Right now!"

Greene began to yell commands. Knox came to where Dake and Micah stood. There were tears in his eyes and he said, "We've got to leave the cannons! We'll have nothing!"

Micah said, "Colonel Knox, we'll get them back."

"My beautiful guns!" Knox was mourning. "How can I leave them?"

Micah saw that the man was seemingly incapable of leaving the cannons and said, "Sir, we have to go—General Washington commanded it!"

Knox straightened up. "Yes, Corporal Bradford!" He stared around at men who were running and said, "Come, we must join them, we must not be taken!"

Washington fairly drove the men out of Fort Lee. He drove them as a cattle herder drives stock. When they fell or stumbled, he roared at them and whipped them with his quirt.

Dake and Micah were in that race, and even as they left Fort Lee and everything behind, Washington stopped and looked back to see the British Redcoats entering from the other direction.

General Greene came over to stand behind him. "Well, they have it, sir."

Washington said slowly, "You know, General, the symbol of Britain is the lion."

"Yes, sir, I know."

"There's a verse of Scripture that says that we shall tread upon the lion. It's in the ninety-first Psalm." Washington seemed to grow still.

297

"I've always liked that psalm. As a matter of fact, I've memorized it. Do you remember how it begins?"

"I don't believe so."

Washington quoted softly, "He that dwelleth in the secret place of the most High shall abide under the shadow of the Almighty." He continued to quote the psalm, word for word, and he paused and said, "The devil quoted part of this once to Jesus. Do you remember? It says, 'For he shall give his angels charge over thee to keep thee in all thy ways. They shall bear thee up in their hands, lest thou dash thy foot against a stone.'"

"Yes, sir, I do remember that."

"It's the next verse that I like, verse thirteen, 'Thou shalt tread upon the lion and adder: the young lion and the dragon shalt thou trample under feet.'"

The shouts of the British soldiers who had taken the fort came to them on the thin air. There were shouts of exultation and triumph, and Washington looked around and saw the beaten fragments of his army. He was quiet for a moment, and then he said, "One day, with God's help, we *shall* tread upon the lion. Your eyes will see it."

"Yes, sir! We shall indeed see our cause come to victory."

Micah and Dake were watching the British also. Dake said, "Well, they whipped us again!"

"No, they just took the fort—we're not whipped!"

Dake stared at his twin with surprise. He had not known the inner toughness of this brother of his. Micah had always been soft-spoken, thoughtful, but now there was a light in his eyes that revealed a determination that lay within him. "You're getting to be quite a bear cat!" he grinned. "You really think we can whip all those Redcoats?"

Micah nodded slowly. "With God, all things are possible. I believe God has put His hand on this land. He has a purpose for America. We'll fight again!"

"Well, let's get on with it, then," Dake said. He picked up his musket, slapped Micah on the back, and said, "Come along, brother. Tell me more about this purpose God's got for America."

🔔   🔔   🔔

Ten days after Fort Washington and Fort Lee fell, Daniel Bradford was alone. He had stayed at the foundry until dark, and finally sent the workmen on home. He and Blevins, as usual, had quarreled, saying that he would stay until the work was done, but Daniel had clapped him on the shoulder and said, "No, go on, Albert. We'll start again Monday."

It was late on Saturday, and after Blevins left, Daniel moved to his small office and sat down, looking at the drawings on the table before him. He had struggled hard with the problem of how to make a musket that could be produced for the troops of Washington. It was harder than he thought, and for a long time despair came upon him.

He had almost dozed off when a sound suddenly came to him. His head snapped up, and he was shocked to see Marian enter through the door.

"Marian!" he said, rising at once. "What are you doing here this time of the night?"

Marian did not answer. She was wearing a long royal blue cloak, and she removed it, putting it down on one of the chairs. She pulled off her felt cap, and her dark auburn hair fell down her back. She shook her head, and it caught the light of the lamps, giving off a reddish tint.

"You're working late," she said. It was not what she intended to say, but she needed time to catch her breath and to think.

"I know." He motioned toward the drawings. "I've been trying to put everything together so we can turn out the muskets, but I can't figure out how to do the rifling." He talked for a while about how to do the mechanism. "Nothing seems to work."

The two stood there for a while, and she shivered with the cold.

"Here, I've got tea! It's probably not very hot, but we can heat it up on the fire."

"That would be good."

Marian watched as he stirred the fire up and heated the water, talking about unimportant things. Finally when the tea was made, he poured it, and the two sat down in front of the fireplace and sipped at the rich, strong brew.

Daniel finally said, "I'm worried about Matthew."

"So am I," Marian said. "Has he said anything to you about Abigail?"

"He won't talk about her. Has Abigail said anything else?" Marian had shared with him the part of the story of how Abigail had confessed to Matthew that she had betrayed him and how he had stalked out angrily.

"He's young. He'll come around," Daniel said quietly. "Do you think he loves her?"

"I know she loves him!"

A log on the fire suddenly shifted and sent a myriad of sparks up the chimney. The crackling made a cheerful sound, and Daniel suddenly turned to look at the woman beside him. She met his gaze and he once again thought how beautiful she was. Her green eyes seemed enormous. Her heart-shaped face was the most attractive he had ever seen.

Finally he said, "You shouldn't be here, Marian."

"Because people will talk?"

"Yes, exactly that!" He stood up, and she stood up with him.

Daniel could not take his eyes away from her face. He whispered, "Years ago, when I was just a young man, a young woman came to the farm where I was an indentured servant. I took one look at her and I thought, *That's the most beautiful woman I've ever seen in my life!*"

"Did you think that about me, Daniel?" Marian's voice was a mere whisper, and she looked up at him, her lips parted slightly.

"I still think so—I always will."

Marian had come to see Daniel after spending several days wondering what her life would be now that Leo was gone. She had walked for miles in the cold streets of Boston, thinking, and had spent many more hours shut up in her room, unable to free herself of the questions that had come to her.

Suddenly she looked at him and put out her hands. He took them with surprise and found them warm and strong. He wondered at her impulsiveness, and he remembered that with one exception he never allowed himself to be alone with her after her marriage to Leo Rochester.

"Daniel—?" Marian hesitated then looked into his eyes. "Aren't you ever going to come to me, Daniel?"

"It . . . wouldn't be proper."

Marian increased the pressure of her grip, and there was an intensity in her that he had never seen before. "Do you love me?"

"I can't speak of that!"

"I realize you couldn't speak when I was a married woman, but I have no husband now."

Suddenly Daniel Bradford was aware of her as a woman in a way that he had not allowed himself to be. There was an intense femininity in her lips and her eyes, and he could only say, "It's too soon."

"We've wasted so many years, Daniel. We can't waste any more!"

She moved against him, something she had never done. Reaching up, she put her arms around his neck and pulled his head down. "I love you," she whispered, and then she kissed him.

Her lips were soft, and they moved under his. His arms tightened about her, and as she put herself against him he felt stirrings that he had fought against for years begin to rise up and to seize him. He was intoxicated with the smell of her hair, the touch of her soft form against his. She held him firmly, and when he increased the pressure of his lips she met him freely, fully. She withheld nothing, and he knew that this was her declaration of love in a way that she had never made before.

Finally, Marian pulled her head back and said, "We can wait a year to avoid talk—or we can have each other to love and cherish right now, very soon!"

Daniel found his hands trembling, and there was a weakness that he had not known was in him. More than anything under the sun, he wanted this woman, and he knew the courage it had taken for her to come.

"I should have been saying this to you, Marian! I shouldn't have made you come to me."

"It doesn't matter," she said quietly. She let her hand rest on his cheek, and they were quiet for a time, resting in each other's arms. Finally Daniel put his hand on her hair, letting it run behind her head. He kissed her again gently as if it were a seal of his love, and then he said, "We must talk to your father."

"Yes, and to your children. They'll be shocked."

"So will everybody. People will talk. Are you sure of this, Marian?"

"I'm as sure that I love you as I am that the sun rises in the east."

And then he kissed her again. He held her tightly, and she put her face against his chest. She could hear his heart beating loudly. His strong arms about her felt so protective, and she closed her eyes and whispered, "I wish the two of us were alone somewhere in a strange land with only each other. Then we wouldn't have to worry about what people thought. We could just love each other!"

"It can't be like that, Marian." Daniel pulled back and took her hands. "We have a country. There's a terrible war on, and we have a part to play in it. We can't hide from any of that."

"I know. I was just dreaming, I suppose."

"I like a woman who dreams," he said.

He smiled suddenly, and Marian thought how much younger he looked than he had in years. His eyes were clear, she saw, hazel eyes with just a touch of green. She studied his thin face, high cheekbones, a broad forehead, and then she smiled with him. "What a handsome bridegroom you're going to make, Daniel Bradford!" she whispered.

He laughed suddenly, picked her up easily, and spun her around the room, then sat her down after she was breathless. "Come along, woman, I'm going to take you home."

The two left the foundry. He held her hand in the carriage, and they were intensely aware of the love they had restrained for years. When they arrived at her house, he walked with her to the door, then said, "Good night, sweetheart. I'll see you in the morning."

She took his kiss, then whispered, "Good night."

He walked away and got into the carriage. Marian stood watching him until he was lost in the darkness. Still, she stood there, her heart full as she thought of the love she had for this man.

Finally she looked up at the stars where they twinkled and said aloud in a voice of wonder, "Mrs. Marian Bradford . . ."

Then she laughed like a young girl and threw her hands up in a wild gesture toward the stars. She spun around in a happy dance, then turned and walked up the steps and opened the door. Pausing for a moment, she took one look up at the spangled stars overhead. Then she smiled and closed the door, whispering softly, "Marian Bradford . . ."

SONG IN A STRANGE LAND

BOOKS BY GILBERT MORRIS

THE HOUSE OF WINSLOW SERIES

★　★　★　★

1. *The Honorable Imposter*
2. *The Captive Bride*
3. *The Indentured Heart*
4. *The Gentle Rebel*
5. *The Saintly Buccaneer*
6. *The Holy Warrior*
7. *The Reluctant Bridegroom*
8. *The Last Confederate*
9. *The Dixie Widow*
10. *The Wounded Yankee*
11. *The Union Belle*
12. *The Final Adversary*
13. *The Crossed Sabres*
14. *The Valiant Gunman*
15. *The Gallant Outlaw*
16. *The Jeweled Spur*
17. *The Yukon Queen*
18. *The Rough Rider*
19. *The Iron Lady*

THE LIBERTY BELL

1. *Sound the Trumpet*
2. *Song in a Strange Land*

CHENEY DUVALL, M.D.
(with Lynn Morris)

1. *The Stars for a Light*
2. *Shadow of the Mountains*
3. *A City Not Forsaken*
4. *Toward the Sunrising*

TIME NAVIGATORS
(For Young Teens)

1. *Dangerous Voyage*
2. *Vanishing Clues*

SONG IN A STRANGE LAND

GILBERT MORRIS

BETHANY HOUSE PUBLISHERS
MINNEAPOLIS, MINNESOTA 55438

Song in a Strange Land
Copyright © 1996
Gilbert Morris

Cover illustration by Chris Ellison

Published by Bethany House Publishers
A Ministry of Bethany Fellowship, Inc.
11300 Hampshire Avenue South
Minneapolis, Minnesota 55438

Printed in the United States of America.

Library of Congress Cataloging-in-Publication Data

Song in a strange land / Gilbert Morris.
    p. cm. — (The Liberty Bell ; bk. 2)
ISBN 1-55661-566-3
I. Title.   II. Series: Morris, Gilbert. Liberty Bell ; bk. 2.
PS3563.O8742S66   1996   813'.54—dc20   96-4432
                                                             CIP

To Terry McDowell—My Editor

It takes many people to make a book—and without their work I'd be pumping gas at a filling station!

Terry, you are one of those unsung heroes who made this book possible, and I'd like to shout my thanks from the housetop. For all your beyond-the-call-of-duty labor, your fine sense of the *right* word, and your unfailing good humor and patience, I can no other answer make, but thanks—and thanks—and ever thanks!

(And your dear wife is a sweetheart, too!)

GILBERT MORRIS spent ten years as a pastor before becoming Professor of English at Ouachita Baptist University in Arkansas and earning a Ph.D. at the University of Arkansas. During the summers of 1984 and 1985 he did postgraduate work at the University of London. A prolific writer, he has had over 25 scholarly articles and 200 poems published in various periodicals, and over the past years has had more than 70 novels published. His family includes three grown children, and he and his wife live in Orange Beach, Alabama.

CONTENTS

PART FOUR
Guns Over Boston
Winter 1776

PART ONE

—

A House Divided

April–May 1775

1

Encounter in Boston

SAM BRADFORD HAD VERY FEW OPPORTUNITIES to boss his older brother Dake around, therefore he made the most of his present opportunity. Sitting in a chair outside their home with his bandaged right leg stuck stiffly out in front of him, he gestured with a locust walking stick, saying preemptively, "Hurry up, Dake! Put some more wood on the fire. . . !"

Dake Bradford, at the age of seventeen, disliked taking orders from *anybody*—especially from a brother who was two years younger. He had wheat-colored hair and hazel eyes; only a small scar on his left eyebrow made it possible for anyone to distinguish him from Micah, his identical twin. Micah, however, would never have spoken as impulsively and with such a sharp temper as Dake, who snapped, "Is that all you've got to do—sit there and give me orders? I've got half a mind to throw you and this blasted 'invention' of yours into the bay! It's probably going to blow up and kill somebody, anyway."

"No, it's not!" Sam ran his fingers through his rebellious auburn hair, fixing his electric blue eyes on Dake. His five-foot seven-inch frame was strongly built, giving promise of great physical strength—but it was his constant fascination with machinery and making things work that set him apart from his brothers. Now he grinned suddenly, the elfin humor that lurked in him popping out. "You've got to do what I say, Dake, because I'm a wounded veteran."

"I've gotten worse scratches from picking blackberries than you got from Lexington," Dake snorted. Nevertheless, a smile twitched the corners of his broad lips as he looked at his younger brother. It was hard to believe that it had been less than a week since he and Sam and their father, Daniel, had stood on the Green at Lexington and heard the whistling of British musket balls and seen men die. Sam had taken a minor wound in his upper leg and had been glorying in it ever since. Lifting

11

one eyebrow, Dake said sarcastically, "I guess now you'll be wanting a pension—but if Pa hadn't carried you out of there, you probably would've gotten a British bayonet in your belly."

"Why don't you just get that fire going?" Sam interrupted. Staring at the odd structure just outside the wall of their red-brick house, his face grew animated. "It's going to be great!" He nodded with an air of certainty. "Why, Benjamin Franklin himself couldn't have thought of anything better than this!"

Staring doubtfully at the iron monster, Dake shook his head. "This is going to a lot of trouble for just heating water," he muttered. "What's wrong with the old way we did it? It was good enough for me."

"Well, maybe *you* like to go outside and build a fire under a pot, then try to pour water into buckets to carry into the house, but not me. Look," Sam argued, "with this iron casing protecting the fire, now we can build the fire up even when it's raining. That way we can heat all the water we need for washing, cooking, and taking baths—and never have to tote those blasted buckets again!"

Dake grinned rationally. "Sam, I don't remember that you were ever one for taking baths. Seemed like Pa had to tan you just last year for gettin' dirty as a pig."

A red glow tinted young Sam's cheeks and he shot up out of his chair, hobbling over on his walking stick. "Well, if you won't do it," he complained, "then I'll do it myself!"

"No, sit down," Dake commanded. "I'll fix this infernal machine—but it looks like foolishness if you ask me." Picking up several sticks of wood, he thrust them into the fire that was burning in the lower part of the iron structure. It was, he had to admit, a clever idea. He stepped back and studied it, remembering how Sam had first carefully drawn out all the designs on paper. Then the two of them had built it in the foundry that their father owned half interest in with John Frazier. The water heater was a fairly simple structure—merely a square firebox built of iron that rested on a brick foundation. A fire inside the box heated water, which was contained in a large steel barrel mounted over the firebox. "Are you sure this contraption will work?" Dake asked.

"Of course, it'll work!" Sam waved his stick at the water heater, speaking didactically. "That pipe at the bottom will carry the hot water into the house. Part of it will go to the kitchen, and then it forks off to that copper bathtub Pa built."

"I still think it'll probably blow up and kill somebody," Dake muttered gloomily. Nevertheless, he was fascinated by his younger brother's ingenious mind and grudgingly admitted, "I don't think there's another house in the Colonies that has built-in hot water." He stroked his chin thoughtfully and shook his head. "For some reason it doesn't seem natural to me." As the fire began to crackle and the sides of the firebox glowed with a cherry color, the two brothers watched with growing interest. Though they had their usual sibling conflicts, these Bradfords were a tightly knit family, closer than most.

Suddenly Dake found himself staring over Sam's shoulder toward the direction of Cambridge, thinking of the hundreds of volunteers who had swarmed to Boston after the Battle of Lexington and Concord.

Catching his gaze, Sam had no trouble interpreting his older brother's thoughts. "I bet there must be ten thousand patriots out there. Boston's surrounded now, isn't it? We'll give those lobsterbacks all the trouble they ask for! When are you going to join up, Dake?"

Dake was thinking of the militia that had rushed from New England to join the swelling ranks of the fledgling Continental Army. He longed to join them, and every night he stared at the red campfires that surrounded Boston and glowed like fiery eyes. "I'd like to go right now," he admitted. "But I have to wait till Pa says it's all right."

The two were startled when a shrill whistle went off. "There, it's boiling," Sam announced with satisfaction. "I put that whistle at the top so that the steam can blow off if it gets to boiling too hot. This way it won't blow up. Come on, let's go in and see how she works."

"Wait a minute! You'll hurt that leg," Dake cautioned. "Here, let me give you a hand. Lean on me." He put his arm around Sam's waist, and the boy hopped along beside him as they moved up the steps and entered the house.

As soon as they were inside the kitchen, Sam said, "Rachel will want to be the first to try this bath. She's been pestering me about it all week." He continued to hop along energetically as they turned down the hall floored with hard pine that gleamed warmly in the late afternoon light filtering in through the window. Lifting his voice he yelled, "Rachel. . . !"

A door flew open and a young woman stepped out. "What is going on? What are you yelling about, Sam?"

"Well, it's all ready," Sam announced proudly. "Come here and I'll show you. Move along, Dake!" Urging his brother, he hopped down the hallway, stopping at a door and shoving it open.

The room he entered was no more than eight feet wide and ten feet long. It appeared to have been added almost as an afterthought by the original builder of the house—probably for supplies. Now it had been cleaned out and the dominant object in the room was a rectangular copper bathtub that rested firmly on a foundation of red bricks. Sam was almost bursting with excitement. "Look—you get in there and turn this handle—you see?" He reached out and turned a short handle control-ling a valve that was attached to the end of a pipe which came in di-rectly through the wall.

For a moment nothing happened and Dake said in disgust, "Why, it's not going to work. I told you it was a foolish idea."

"Sure it is! It just takes a little while for the pressure to get it here. Look—there it is—see?" He pointed.

The three watched as a small trickle of steaming water began to pour out of the small pipe. Sam stuck his finger in it and drew it back quickly. "Yow! That's hot! Feel it, Rachel."

The young woman reached over tentatively and touched her finger to the water and smiled. "Oh, that *is* hot!" She turned suddenly and grabbed Sam in a powerful hug. "You're a genius, Sam! If you never do another thing in your life—I will love you forever for this."

"Well, let's see how it works first. I promised you could be first, Rachel," Sam said, stepping back.

Rachel stared at him. "Well, you're not going to stay and *watch*!" she exclaimed. "Is that all I do—just turn this handle here until the tub is full?"

Sam nodded confidently. "That's all. And look—you see that cork in the bottom of the tub? That leads to a pipe underneath that drains the water out. When you are through, you just pull it and it will drain out into the yard."

Rachel's eyes gleamed at Sam's invention. "A hot bath!" she sighed. "You two get out of here! I've got to get ready for that ball. You can take a bath after I get through, Dake," Rachel said, tossing a teasing smile at her brother.

"Not me," Dake said loftily. "I don't hold too much to bathing. I think it weakens a fellow."

Rachel quickly shooed them out and moved down to her bedroom, returning almost at once wearing a heavy robe. Stepping inside the room, she saw that the water was already three or four inches deep in the bottom of the copper tub. Carefully, she turned the handle. After dribbling for a moment, the water finally stopped. Slipping off her robe, Rachel hung it on a peg on the wall, then picked up a cake of soap. It felt odd being completely undressed—for there were few opportunities for bathing in a tub like this in any of the houses in the colony. Now, however, she stepped over the edge of the tub and found that the water was too hot. She waited impatiently until it was bearable and then slowly eased into the tub. Settling herself down carefully, she sighed ecstatically, "Ohhhhhh, that feels so *good*!" For a long time, she lay there basking in the hot water and washing her face and neck. Finally she sat up and began scrubbing herself heartily. This was a pure delight. The soap that she had bought in a fancy shop downtown had come all the way from England. It had a delicious, sweet fragrance to it, unlike the strong lye soap they used for cleaning most things in the house.

For a long time she soaked, thinking, *I can do this anytime I want to now!* Rachel was a fastidious girl who hated dirt of any kind, and the luxury of soaking in a tub of hot water with fresh clean-smelling soap was a pleasure such as she had rarely known. She would have loved to enjoy it longer, but she had to hurry to get ready for the ball at General Gage's tonight.

Reluctantly, she sat up, pulled the cork, and watched a tiny whirl-pool form as the water was siphoned away down the small drain. Fascinated by this new experience, Rachel watched till the last of the water disappeared with a slight sucking sound. Stepping out of the tub, she quickly toweled herself off and then slipped into her robe again. Barefooted, she walked down the hall, noticing before she left that the room was full of steam. She got back to her room and glanced at the small mantel clock that sat on a cherrywood shelf over her dressing table. Not wanting to be late for the festivity, she wasted no time in pulling out the clothes that she planned to wear to the ball. She slipped into a pair of drawers that reached to her knees, then donned a vest. Over this, she put a new type of chemise with a gathered silk bandette. It had shoulder straps of elastic knitted webbing that crossed in the back. Her petticoat came next and then the stays.

After this she turned to the dress itself. Carefully she lifted it from the bed and put it on. It was a new dress that she'd plagued her father to buy for her for some time, made of shimmering green satin with an empire waistline. The bodice was gathered lightly above and below the bosom. The full, clinging skirt had a row of satin swag near the hemline, and she fastened a satin belt with a delicate silver broach in the center. Turning to the full-length mirror, Rachel admired the sleeves which were gathered at the top with three rows of puffed satin shirring. She touched the collar of starched lace and then picked up a shawl made of white lace. Sitting down, she slipped on a pair of green satin shoes with ties around the ankle, then picked up a bag made of the same satin as her dress and a small hat trimmed with lace that she fastened in her dark red hair. Standing in front of the mirror, a smile of satisfaction and approval reflected back from a very attractive young woman of sixteen with a heart-shaped face, very much like her mother's had been. She had gray-green eyes that looked frankly at whatever she saw. "Well," she said aloud, "I suppose you'll do to go to a party with a bunch of British officers." Turning, she left her bedroom and walked into the din-

15

ing room, where her brothers were waiting for her.

Dake was wearing plain breeches made of dark cotton material. He'd already put on his coat with claw-hammer tails. He looked strong and rather handsome, she thought, but Sam caught into her thoughts.

"Wow, Rachel, you look real nice," he said, his eyes filled with admiration. Then he looked with disgust at Dake. "Why do you have to wear that old suit? Why don't you dress up?"

"I'm not dressing up for a bunch of British officers!" Dake snapped.

Micah, Dake's twin, who was sitting at the table, put down the book he'd been reading. "I'm surprised you're going," he remarked quietly. He also had wheat-colored hair and hazel eyes, but spoke much slower—with a drawl. He was a gentle young man, much like his mother—as his father had often told him.

Dake looked at him, saying, "I want to see what they look like. Who knows? I might have an opportunity to say a thing or two about what they need to be doing—which is getting out of this country."

Rachel spoke up quickly, wanting to head off another heated argument that often took place between Dake and Micah. "Where's Pa?"

Dake turned to her. "He sent word he couldn't be here. Something came up that he needed to take care of, so Matt and he will meet us at the ball."

"All right," Rachel said. "We'd better go; I wouldn't want to be late."

"Don't forget, when you get back, I want to hear all about it," Sam said as he hobbled closer and sniffed at her. "My, you sure smell good! Where'd you get that fancy perfume?"

"None of your business." Rachel smiled as she gave him another hug. "The bath was lovely. I'm going to bake you the best cake you've ever had, Sam, and you can have it all to yourself." She laughed at his expression of utter joy, then turned, saying, "Let's go, Dake."

The two of them left the house and proceeded down the street. It was twilight and the sun ducked behind the building to their left, casting bold shadows on the ground. As they moved along the streets, they noticed that there were few people stirring about.

"Funny how people have been staying off the streets since the battle," Dake remarked.

"Yes, but there was a lot of trouble with the troops. Some of the soldiers were treating civilians very rough. Martha Hanshaw was terribly insulted by two British soldiers just day before yesterday."

"Did they hurt her?" Dake demanded quickly.

"Not really, but they frightened the wits out of her," Rachel said as they continued on their way.

Dake's face glowered, and he said, "They'd better not try anything tonight. There's nothing I'd like better than to start another battle with them!"

Rachel glanced at him with a worried look. "We don't want any trouble, Dake. I'm sure it will be all right."

The ball was being held at a fine two-story mansion which had belonged to the governor at one time. General Gage had taken it over as his general headquarters. Fortunately, it was only a twenty-minute walk from the Bradford house. They passed soldiers more than once and a few of the townspeople who dared venture out at night. An air of tension hung over the darkened streets, or so it seemed to Dake and Rachel as they walked along. They were almost halfway to General Gage's headquarters when six soldiers came stumbling out of a tavern just ahead of them.

Quickly Rachel said, "Let's cross the street, Dake."

Dake stared at her. "Cross the street? What for?"

"We don't need to have any trouble with those soldiers," she said worriedly.

"This is my town, not theirs," Dake said defiantly. "Come on."

The soldiers were wearing the flamboyant dress of His Majesty's troops, red jackets with white facings and white shiny breeches, whitened with clay piping. From the sound of their raucous laughter, it was obvious they had been drinking.

"That's a likely-looking wench. . . !" one of them said as Rachel and Dake drew near.

Dake pulled to a sudden halt, as if he'd hit the end of a rope. Turning around, he leveled a cold gaze on the drunken soldier. "Keep your filthy mouth shut if you can't say anything better than that!"

The soldier was a thickset man with a beefy red face. He had smallish eyes and a catfish-thin mouth that now broke into a sneering smile. "Well," he said, "listen to the Yankee." He stepped forward, adding, "That's mighty big talk for a tadpole like you." His eyes moved over to Rachel, and he said, "Now, sweetheart, why don't you come in and we'll have a drink together."

"I told you to keep your mouth shut! I don't expect any manners out of a lobsterback. It's the way you were brought up, I expect," Dake said, his anger starting to rise.

Dake turned to go, but his caustic remarks had insulted the soldier, who happened to be a sergeant. The man's face suddenly flushed with anger, and he stepped in front of Dake. "You watch your own mouth or I'll shut it for you!" he said threateningly, raising a hamlike fist.

Rachel saw Dake's eyes turn steel cold. She grew nervous, knowing that one of his problems was that he was not afraid of anything. Some might have construed this as valor, but it also evidenced a lack of common sense that knew when to avert danger. He was scarcely aware—as was Rachel—that the other soldiers had formed a circle around them. They were grinning, she saw, like hungry wolves as they circled their prey. "Let's go, Dake. Don't talk to him," she whispered.

Suddenly, the sergeant reached out and grabbed her arm, saying, "Just come in and 'ave one drink, sweetheart. You'll find out wot a *real* gentleman is like."

"Take your hands off her!" Dake's hand instantly shot out and caught the sergeant in the chest. It drove him backward a few steps.

He grunted and then stared at the bold young man in amazement. He'd lost five of his squad on the long march back from Lexington, and several others were so badly hurt that they might not survive their wounds. He was typical of the British soldiers. They were furious at the cowardly Americans who had chosen to shoot at them from behind trees and fences instead of meeting them out in the open in a pitched battle. Now the pent-up anger broke out in him, and he stepped forward, snarling, "I'll show you!"

The man's fist came around in a vicious swing, but Dake deftly stepped under it. Dake then planted a tremendous right-hand blow that landed squarely on the sergeant's mouth, the force of which drove him backward so that he fell down full-length on the street.

Looking up, he yelled, "Well, get 'im! Don't just stand there!"

Dake whirled and shouted, "Get out of the way, Rachel," but he had no time to say more, for the five soldiers concerted their attack. If there had not been so many, they might have done better instead of getting in each other's way. Dake took several blows, but he was a fiercely strong young man, and his patriotic anger burned in him against these drunken lobsterbacks that had insulted his sister. He struck one soldier far below the belt, and felt a wicked satisfaction to see the man fall down, groaning as he rolled in the street. Right then a vicious blow caught him in the ear, driving him to one side. He staggered and whipped a long left hand that exploded in the face of a tall, thin soldier. It struck the man directly on the nose and blood spurted down instantly, covering the man's uniform.

Rachel began to cry aloud for help, but the sergeant who had risen to his feet reached out and grabbed her. "Just be quiet," he hissed. "He asked for this and now 'e's going to get it!"

There was never any question about the outcome. Dake was strong and quick, but there were too many opponents. One thickset soldier grabbed him by the coat while another struck him at the same time, high in the temple. Dake felt hands clawing at him, and he struck out, again and again, trying to fight them off. But blow after blow smashed into him from all sides. He felt himself going down and knew if he fell they would kick him to death or beat him beyond recognition. Wildly he fought on, his fury saving him for the moment.

Terrified, Rachel continued to cry out for help. The sergeant's hands were like steel bands on her arms and she could not break free. Suddenly, she heard a voice cutting out over the cries of the soldiers.

"What's going on, Sergeant?"

"Wot's it to you?" The sergeant, holding Rachel tightly, turned to face a very tall young man who had suddenly appeared out of nowhere. "Get on with you, or you'll get more of the same."

"Please help us," Rachel said. "Go, get help!"

The young man drew himself up to his full height, which must have been six feet three inches. He was lean, with long arms and legs, and wore a very fashionable suit. He looked, as a matter of fact, like a dandy. He wore a single-breasted suit with decorative buttons. The jacket had swallow-tails, with the tails dropping below knee level. A frilly sort of cravat adorned his neck, and his trousers were a lightweight, shadow-striped wool. He gave the soldiers, who had momentarily stopped pummeling Dake, a look out of bright blue eyes. "Turn that man loose!" he snapped. He had reddish hair, a strong tapered face, and an imperious quality in his voice—as of a man who expected to be obeyed.

The sergeant sneered at him and stepped forward, drawing back his large fist, ready to smash the fellow who had interrupted them. "You men, beat that fellow to death if you want. I'll take care of your lordship 'ere."

Not an ounce of apprehension appeared in the stranger's blue eyes. "I see you're from the Royal Grenadiers," he said calmly.

"Wot's it to you?" The sergeant drew his fist back and stepped forward, a grin on his meaty lips. "I'll teach you to mess in affairs wot don't belong to you. . . !"

"Colonel Gordon will have a stern word to say to you, Sergeant. He has strict orders about stirring up trouble with civilians."

"Wot do you know about Colonel Gordon?" the sergeant demanded suspiciously.

The well-dressed newcomer had very broad lips, which now turned up slightly as he said, "Quite a bit, I expect. He's my father."

Instantly, the sergeant dropped his fist and swallowed hard. "Why . . . you see, sir," stammered the sergeant, "this here civilian . . . he attacked us."

"That's a lie!" Rachel exclaimed. "We were minding our own business and these drunken swine insulted me and attacked my brother!"

The tall young man turned to her and said, "I assume you're Miss Rachel Bradford?"

Rachel was amazed. "Why, yes. How did you know my name?"

"My father sent me over to accompany you and your father to the dinner at General Gage's." He bowed slightly and said, "My name's Clive Gordon."

Dake jerked away from the grip of the soldiers. His face was battered and bleeding, and his clothes were torn. "Well, you can tell your father—and General Gage for that matter—what a bunch of *swine* he's got in his army!"

Clive Gordon blinked with surprise. "And your name is?"

"This is my brother Dake. My father and my brother Matthew have been delayed."

"Well, come along, Mr. Bradford," Gordon said. "We'll get you cleaned up. That's a nasty cut you've got there."

But Dake shook his head adamantly. "I'm not going to eat with any British officers." Then he glared at the sergeant. "And I'll be ready to take this up anytime you want. If you'll meet me like a man, we'll see. . . !"

But the sergeant had his eyes fixed warily on the tall form of Clive Gordon. "I hope you won't have anything to say of this to the colonel, Mr. Gordon."

"I think you'd better learn to keep your men in hand, Sergeant. I'll let it slip this time." Clive turned to Rachel and Dake and said, "I'm sorry this happened, and we'll do our best to get you cleaned up."

But Dake had turned away, saying gruffly, "I'm not going to any party!" and had stomped off, his back held indignantly stiff as he headed back down the street.

Gordon turned and said, "Would you rather go home, or will you let me escort you to the party, Miss Bradford?"

Rachel's breath was still coming rather rapidly, but she was a courageous young woman. "No, my father's expecting me." She hesitated, then said, "Thank you so much for what you did, Mr. Gordon. If you hadn't come along just now, I'm afraid to think of what they might have done."

"It was nothing really. Oh, you can call me Clive," Gordon smiled. "After all, we're cousins."

"Why, that's right!" Rachel exclaimed. "It's difficult to remember that I have cousins." She referred to the fact that her father, Daniel Bradford, and his sister, Lyna Lee Bradford Gordon, had been separated for many years, each thinking the other was dead. Only recently had Colonel Leslie Gordon brought his family to Boston from England, where

Lyna and Daniel had encountered each other at a similar dinner occasion.

As children they had been extremely close, a bond formed out of the hardships they had had to face together when left as orphans in London so long ago. Then the shock of discovering each other after years of grieving for the other's death was washed away amidst tears of joy that night.

Rachel took Clive's proffered arm and said, "Come along then, cousin, and escort me safely to the party."

"On your way, Sergeant," Clive said, waving his walking stick at the soldiers with an imperious gesture. "And mind what I say. Any more rude behavior like this and I'll report you and your men." Ignoring the sergeant's frown, Clive looked down at Rachel. "I must say, it is good to have relatives, especially such attractive ones. Come along now. You'll be the belle of the ball at General Gage's dinner party!"

🇹 🇹 🇹

Colonel Leslie Gordon straightened and stared at himself in the tall, full-length mirror beside the oak-framed bed. He was, at the age of forty-nine, still very youthful in appearance. Tall, well-formed, with reddish hair and blue eyes, he wore the uniform of the Colonel of the Royal Grenadiers, which consisted of a scarlet uniform coat complete with brass buttons and epaulets, dark breeches, a sword belt, and knee-high leather boots. He glanced slyly at his wife, who was sitting at a small dressing table, and said, "I don't understand it."

Lyna Gordon turned her gray-green eyes on her husband. At forty-three, her hair was still the color of dark honey, and her oval face, wide-edged lips, and fair, smooth skin were the envy of many a younger woman. "Don't understand what, dear?"

"How you ever persuaded a handsome chap like me to marry you. By George"—he shook his head, gazing at his stunning reflection with admiration—"I *am* a handsome rascal!"

Humor caused Lyna's eyes to crinkle till the pupils were almost invisible. "You may be handsome, but you're certainly not overendowed with modesty, Colonel Gordon," she remarked, carefully applying a small amount of rice powder to her fair cheeks.

Gordon laughed heartily and came over to stand behind his beautiful wife. Bending over, he embraced her and planted a firm kiss on her neck. She squealed and pushed at him ineffectively. "Stop that! You'll ruin my hairdo."

"Be glad you've got a husband to ruin your hairdo," he said. "Think of all the poor widows and old maids who are sleeping cold without a handsome husband to pester them to death." He kissed her again, then straightened up and slouched across the room. Leaning against the wall and shifting his shining saber slightly, he watched as Lyna continued applying the rice powder; then he said idly, "It will be interesting having Daniel and his family at the dinner party tonight. I don't know how it will work out, especially with Dake and his support for the Sons of Liberty. Daniel says he's a regular fire-breather!"

Lyna closed the lid on the small case that held the rice powder, then stood and turned around. "How do I look?" she said, flashing her husband a demure smile.

Lyna was wearing a light blue formal gown of watered silk taffeta. The neckline was somewhat low and the small dainty sleeves stopped at the same level as the neckline. Both sleeves and neckline were bound in dark blue satin ribbon, and the bottom of the skirt was decorated with four flounces of lace, topped by a row of tiny wine-colored silk ribbon florets. A single strand of pearls adorned her shapely neck and her earrings were of rose quartz.

"You look beautiful, as always," Leslie said. Then a sly humor came to him. "You should! That dress cost as much as *three* of my dress uniforms!" He came to her then and wrapped his arms around her and held her close, looking down into her lovely face. "You're worth it, though." He leaned forward and kissed her and her arms went up around his neck. When he drew back, he smiled wickedly. "We'll take this up at a more . . . ah, *opportune* moment, Mrs. Gordon. Now it is time to go to dinner."

They left their bedroom, stopping by the parlor to say goodbye to their seventeen-year-old daughter, who was not feeling well and had decided to remain at home. Grace Gordon had the same dark honey hair and gray-green eyes as her mother. David looked up and said pertly, "If you have anything good to eat, bring some of it home, will you, Father? I'm starving to death around here!" At fifteen, his five-foot ten-inch frame was lean and his appetite was prodigious.

"I'll smuggle you something out in my pocket." Gordon smiled and winked at his son.

The two left the house and got into the carriage. Gordon was pensive, saying as they drove down the street, "I'm worried about Daniel and his family. I imagine it's not very pleasant for them to be cooped up in Boston with the enemy."

"What's going to happen, Leslie?"

"I expect there will be a battle. At least that's what General Gage says."

"Well, I hate to think about it. I know Daniel will be caught in the middle of it." She had talked with her brother since Lexington and found that he had determined to pledge his loyalty on the patriots' side. "Now," she said, "after finding each other after all these years, I can't stand the thought of losing him."

She held tightly to Leslie's arm as the horse clopped down the street at a sharp pace. "I can't bear to think of you going into battle either. I wish we'd never come to this place!"

Leslie Gordon had somewhat the same feeling. "It's going to be a bad time," he said slowly. "A terrible mistake has been made in England, Lyna. These are *Englishmen* over here. Daniel was born in England, and now he is being forced to fight. I'd do the same, I suppose, if I lived in the Colonies." He sighed heavily and said, "Well, we'll pray that some sense will come to the prime minister and His Majesty. It's not very likely," he admitted, shrugging his shoulders. "But, I suppose, miracles do happen. . . ."

2

"To His Majesty, King George the Third...?"

THE EFFORT OF CARRYING THE TWO MAMMOTH buckets upstairs caused the muscles in Cato's ebony arms to bulge. Each bucket held three gallons of water, which he had just drawn from the pump outside the kitchen door. Reaching the top of the stairs, he turned to the third door on his right and entered. A leviathan blue enameled washbasin sat on the mahogany washstand. Carefully, Cato filled it with the clear water, then left the room. He passed Marian Rochester's door, tapped on it, and said softly, "Miss Marian—? I've fixed your bath."

"Thank you, Cato."

Marian was wearing a light green cotton robe, and her hair was covered with a towel as she left the bedroom and went directly to the dressing room. Stepping inside, she moved toward the washstand—but for one moment stopped and looked around. *It's been a long time since I grew up in this room,* she thought. Memories came flooding back from her past—poignant scenes from her childhood. Gone was the small trundle bed she had slept in as a child, and indeed all of the familiar furniture. Her first bedroom had been converted into a dressing room, but her eyes fell on the handsome toilet set and she instantly thought of the Christmas so long ago when her father had proudly presented it to her mother. It had been the last Christmas gift her mother had received, for she had died the following May. Marian reached out and touched the handsome toilet articles. They were all pink with a delicate gold band— the washbowl, pitcher, slop bowl, soap dish, brush dish, sponge dish, tumbler, two glasses, and a water bottle—all still as colorful as she remembered them.

A smile creased her lips as the memory of that Christmas morning

24

floated out of whatever realm holds dear that sort of treasure. All of the articles had been spread out under the decorated tree in the parlor, and the small slop jar, which had been cast especially for her, she had found irresistible. While her parents were looking at the rest of the items, she had put it over her head—and then discovered she could not get it off! Marian glanced around the room, smiling at the childhood memory. She noticed again that the wallpaper was the same as it had been when she was a girl. It was filled with exotic Turkish scenes: a river flowed all around the walls of the room, its banks covered with moss and minarets; just over the oak chest to her left, a beautiful Turkish house perched on the bank, its steps leading down to the water; at the foot of it an elegant lady lounged on a pleasure boat with purple awnings and thick soft cushions.

Marian reached out and touched the wallpaper, remembering the time she had been very ill with a fever. She had awakened in the middle of the night and had seen the lovely Turkish lady. In her half-sleep she had wished that she could get out of her bed and step into the boat— and sail off to some land where the world was as beautiful and colorful as in that wallpaper.

Marian's lips tightened and she shook her head. It was not good to think of the past. She had a tendency to do this—seeking refuge from the difficulties of the present by thinking back on better days. Removing her robe, she laid it across the wing chair upholstered in dark blue fabric, turned and stepped onto a piece of waterproof floor cloth that the maid had placed before the washstand—a two-yard square piece of green cloth—and began her sponge bath.

At forty, Marian Rochester still possessed the beauty of a much younger woman. She had rather pale skin, except for her face, which was tanned to a golden glow from the heat of the summer sun. Bending over the tremendous washbowl, she dipped her face in it, enjoying the coolness of the water. Quickly, she sponged off her face, neck, and then her hands and arms, enjoying the refreshing sense that the water brought to her. Then straightening up, she began immersing the sponge in the washbowl and squeezing it over her shoulders. As the water ran down her body, she worked up a lather with a cake of white, sweet-smelling soap. Under her feet, the green toweling soon became saturated, and she replaced it with another one, throwing the wet one into a slop pail. As she continued her bath, she suddenly looked up and thought, *Why couldn't water be put into some sort of pot overhead so that it could run down over you as you bathe? We do that when we water flowers.*

But regretfully she knew of no such device and soon finished her bath, toweling off and slipping into her robe. When she got back to her bedroom, she put on the dress that she had selected to wear to General Gage's party. Slipping on her underclothes, then the decorated petticoat, Marian struggled into the gown, which was really an open robe with a closed bodice. It was a wine-colored dress made of silk. As she looked at herself in the mirror, she muttered, almost carelessly, "It will do for General Gage, I suppose. . . ."

She sat down in front of the dressing table, arranging her hair and applying a small amount of makeup. As soon as she was satisfied with her finishing touches, she picked up her coat and left the room. Going down to her father's door at the end of the hall, she knocked first and then stepped inside.

"Well, you're ready to go, I see." John Frazier was sitting in a chair beside a small table on which burned a sinumbra oil lamp, designed to cast no shadows. Laying down the book he'd been reading, he rose to his feet with effort, smiling as he did so. "You look beautiful," he said quietly. "I'm sure all the gentlemen will be impressed."

Marian came over and kissed his cheek tenderly. He looked so frail and ill that it troubled her, but she did not let her concern show. "I'll try to be back early."

"Don't trouble yourself; just have a good time, Marian." His eyes grew cloudy with doubt. "Will Daniel be there?"

"I understand that he will."

"Ask him to come and see me tomorrow if he has time." Even this much seemed to tire him. He kissed her, then sat down and watched as she gathered her skirt and left the room.

As she descended the stairs to the lower part of the house, Marian was assailed by troubling thoughts. *He looks worse almost every day. I wish the doctors could find some way to help.* She found Leo waiting for her impatiently in the parlor.

"Are you ready at last?" he said tersely. He was wearing a blue velvet jacket with claw-hammer tails and brass buttons. His knee breeches were a pale gray, and on his feet he wore a pair of polished black slippers with silver buckles. "Come along," he snapped.

She followed him out to the carriage, and when they were settled inside, he leaned out and ordered, "Be quick about it, Rawlins."

"Yes, sir!" said the driver as he jerked the reins and they started off.

The carriage rolled over the streets and almost at once Leo turned to Marian and said caustically, "I suppose you're happy that you'll get to see your lover tonight."

"Daniel's not my lover, Leo." Marian's voice was weary, for since the day Leo had come home to find Daniel Bradford embracing her in the library, her husband had given her no rest. She had paid dearly for the small indiscretion. Whether or not he knew that she spoke the truth about her present relationship with Daniel, she could not say. Leo was extremely bitter about the incident. Even if he believed her, she knew his innately cruel nature would never allow him to admit it.

"I come home to find you in another man's arms and you expect me to believe that it was all a matter of friendship?" The way he emphasized the word *friendship* with a sneer on his thin lips was in itself an insult. Leo Rochester had had many mistresses and affairs, both here and abroad. Since his marriage to Marian, he had violated his marriage vows countless times. It was a libertine age when men were forgiven for such things, but women—never!

"Have you thought about my offer?" Leo asked suddenly.

Marian turned to look at him. He was still, at forty-six, a handsome man. He had light blue eyes and brown hair. Though he was somewhat overweight and dissipation lined his face, women still found him attractive. He smiled at her and she noticed that one tooth did not match the others. She didn't know that it had been knocked out by Lyna Bradford, Daniel's sister, years before at Milford Manor in an attempt to escape from his unwelcomed advances one night when he had been drinking.

"What offer are you talking about, Leo?" she asked calmly.

"Why, I'm surprised you've forgotten, my dear," he said with sarcasm. He leaned back, picked up the gold-headed cane that he customarily carried, and stroked the figure of the lion's head that adorned the top of it. "It seems so simple, if you'd just listen to reason. I want a son— and you're obviously not capable of bearing a child."

Again came the cruel twist of words that caused Marian to flush and drop her head in shame. She did feel guilty, for he had told her of numerous offspring outside of their marriage that he himself had sired, while she had never conceived.

"Now I've found one—but you and your friend Daniel are standing in the way."

Quickly, Marian looked at him. "Matthew is Daniel's son," she said quickly.

Leo reversed the cane and slapped the wall of the carriage sharply. "He's *not* Daniel's son—he's *my* son! All you have to do is look at him to see."

Unfortunately, Marian could not answer this. Matthew Bradford *was* the exact image of what Leo had looked like as a young man. The lad had the same brown hair, the same blue eyes, and even the same posture as Leo.

She had never heard the sad history of how Holly, Matthew's

mother, had been a servant in the Virginia estate of the Rochesters. After being raped by Leo, Holly had run away, willing to bear her disgrace alone. Daniel had felt great pity for her and had gone after her. In the end he had married her. The child that had been born, as far as anyone knew, was Daniel's. But Leo Rochester had recently learned the truth and was now determined to claim the boy as his son.

"He's not a child, Leo," Marian said as calmly as she could. "He's been reared in Daniel's family, and that's all he knows. You can't just rip him away from there and expect him to become what you want." Anger shot through her as she turned and faced her husband. "What do you want to make of him?"

"I want him to have his true heritage. What will he have being the son of an ironmonger? Nothing! But I could legally adopt him. He would be the owner of Fairhope, and he wants to learn to paint. I could get him the best teachers, take him to England, Spain, France. Do you think Bradford has the means to do this?"

Marian knew it was useless to argue with him and finally said, "You can't do it, Leo."

Leo Rochester leaned back, and there was a glint in his steely blue eyes. "We'll see what I can do and what I can't do!" His words held an unspoken menace, and an unpleasant smile twisted the corners of his lips upward. "We'll see what I can do," he repeated softly.

🔔   🔔   🔔

"I guess we're pretty late," Daniel said, a rueful frown creasing his face.

"I'm surprised you wanted to come to this party, Pa." Matthew Bradford had been taken by surprise when his father had invited him to attend General Gage's party. Knowing his father to be a patriot, Matthew had assumed that he would not want to spend time with the British general who had been sent to subdue the Colonies. "Why are we going?" he asked curiously as they mounted the steps of the two-story mansion that sat well back off the street.

Daniel Bradford shrugged his broad shoulders. He was one inch over six feet, and his one hundred and ninety pounds were evenly distributed. He had a heavy, strong upper body from years of iron work, and was smoothly muscled. His wheat-colored hair and eyebrows reflected the hazel eyes, which at times had just a touch of green. They were penetrating eyes that at times could see beneath the countenances of people in a discerning manner. His hard youth on the streets of London had taught him much about what people were like. His fair skin was burned to a golden color, and with his high cheekbones and broad forehead he looked somewhat like a Viking. His chin was prominent and thrust forward with a cleft. On the bridge of his nose, an old scar from a forgotten fight made a faint white line.

"I guess I'm still hoping that this fight will be resolved without more bloodshed," he said evenly.

"I hope you're right, Pa," Matthew said.

They were met in a spacious foyer by a lieutenant, who took their hats and names. "Good evening, sir," he greeted Bradford. "Your daughter arrived only a few minutes ago, escorted by Clive Gordon. The general said for you to come in at once, but your daughter asked me to let her know when you arrived." The tall man excused himself, and a few minutes later reappeared with Rachel at his side, followed by Clive Gordon.

Daniel greeted his tall nephew. Then he turned to his daughter and asked, "Rachel, where's Dake?"

"Pa, Dake and I ran into some trouble with some drunk soldiers on the way. Uncle Leslie had sent Clive to escort us, and he came along right then and helped us out."

"Sir, it was nothing serious," said Clive, noticing Daniel's look of concern. "Dake got roughed up a bit. Since I was there to escort Rachel at my father's request, Dake decided to return home."

"Why, thank you, Clive," said Daniel. "It seems I am in your debt."

"Don't mention it, sir. Glad to have been able to help. Please, come in. I'm sure the general is waiting to see you."

They entered an enormous room built by a man who had been accustomed to expansive rooms in England. Looking up, Matthew noted that the unusual chandelier had been imported. The large room was filled with the aroma of spices and rum. A sumptuous buffet was laid out on a long mahogany side table, covered with an array of meats, breads, fruits, and sweets. Clive escorted Rachel to the buffet table.

Glancing quickly to one side, Daniel saw a small group of uniformed officers standing around a silver punch bowl and conversing. Moving across the room, with Matthew at his side, he stopped a few feet away. When the officers turned to face him, he said, "Good evening, General Gage. I'm sorry to be late."

Thomas Gage, large, handsome, and congenial, waved his hand, dismissing the apology. "Not at all, not at all, my dear Mr. Bradford! We're happy that you could attend my little party tonight."

General Thomas Gage had been sent to America by King George the Third to clamp a tight lid on the rebellious activities of the Colonies. It had been Gage's troops that had precipitated the Boston Massacre in 1770. The Sons of Liberty had been warned that Gage had come to destroy their freedom. The Tories, of course, joyfully welcomed him, rejoicing that their sovereign king had finally sent them a man who could make the Yankee Doodles dance. However, there was nothing in Gage's broad features to indicate that he had any such idea in mind. The general had written a letter only the night before explaining the explosive situation—but he was certain that George III would never understand the political cauldron that was beginning to boil so far from English shores.

Leslie Gordon stood to one side taking little part in the conversation. He listened as the officers probed at Matthew and Daniel in an attempt to get them to commit themselves to the typical Tory position. All of them, however, seemed to be aware that Daniel Bradford was not inclined to do so.

Finally, Colonel Gordon said, "Come—your sister is waiting to see you, Daniel." By sheer power of will, he pulled Daniel and Matthew away from the small audience of officers and piloted them across the crowded floor to where Lyna Lee was sitting. She arose at once and held her hand out.

Daniel pressed it, then smiled. "You look beautiful, Lyna," he said.

"Thank you, Daniel." She glanced over at the officers. "Were you being interrogated by the staff?"

"A little, I think—but that's understandable."

Matthew asked suddenly, "Is it true that General Gage plans some sort of military revenge to pay us back for Concord and Lexington?"

Leslie Gordon's face grew long and he shook his head. "We're all sitting on kegs of gunpowder—my countrymen and you colonists, too. We've seen it all before. Just one shot started the Boston Massacre, and it happened again on that green field at Lexington. Some fool pulled a trigger and another fool shot back." A dour expression darkened his handsome face as he continued. "I'm not sure that we're going to be able to head this thing off, but, God willing, we will try."

They were unable to speak for long because General Gage called out, "Now—to the table," and led them into the dining room. Daniel and Matthew found themselves seated across the table from Paul Winslow and Abigail Howland, and next to them sat Leo Rochester and Marian.

Paul Winslow was a young man who portrayed a neatness both in feature and figure. He was of average height and not massively built, but there was a depth to his chest that hinted of strength. He had a handsome face, his dark hair smoothed in place like a cap. His eyes were large and brown. The planes of his face smoothly joined to form a pleasing picture alongside Abigail, whose brown hair was set off by the elaborate gown that flattered her figure.

It was a splendid dinner served on beautiful pink and white English china. The heavy silver glowed under the candlelight, and crystal vases overflowed with fresh flowers that were pink, white, and lavender. The servants set out platter after platter of food: roast squabs stuffed with spring mushrooms, braised leg of mutton, asparagus, creamed oysters and lobster meat dressed with Hollandaise sauce, onions and cheese, and tureens of rich turtle soup.

"Well, this sort of meal won't be available very long," Paul Winslow said. "Now that the rebels have us cut off, we'll be lucky to have beef and potatoes once in a while."

Rochester turned to look at Winslow. "Why, sir, it can't last that long. A rebel in arms—that's all we have to face. Don't you agree, Daniel?"

Daniel knew that Leo was only baiting him, and was also keenly aware that others were listening, waiting for him to make his position clear. He took a sip of the rich soup, swallowed it, and then said, "Time will tell, Leo."

Abigail Howland had been speaking to Matthew about painting. She was a beautiful young woman indeed—and something of a flirt. "I've been thinking of having my portrait painted, Mr. Bradford," she said. "What are your charges for such a commission?"

Matthew smiled abruptly. "My rates are much lower than they will be in the future—after I become famous."

Leo leaned forward, his eyes intent. "Mr. Thomas Gainsborough is one of my good friends, Matthew," he said. "Did you happen to meet him while you were studying in England?"

Matthew gave him a startled look. Gainsborough, probably the most famous artist in England, was an idol of his. "No, sir, but I would give my right arm to do so!" he said fervently.

"Well," Leo smiled as he spoke, focusing his attention on the young man, "there's no point in losing your arm. Thomas would be very happy to look at your work if I ask him to. I think he owes me that much. After all, he did two commissions for me."

Matthew stared at Rochester. He was well aware of the antagonism between the tall Tory and his father. He remembered the night that Leo Rochester had come to their house and pulled a pistol, apparently intending to shoot Daniel Bradford. It had been an aborted attempt, but Matthew remembered how Rochester had stared at him most strangely. He had not seen him since, but now saw that there was a burning interest in the tall nobleman's eyes. "Well, Sir Leo," he said, "perhaps not my right arm, but I would give a lot to meet Mr. Gainsborough."

"Do you plan on returning to England?" Leo asked casually.

Matthew had been planning something very much like this, for he wanted to return and continue his studies in art. He glanced at his father and saw anxiety in the hazel eyes that were now fixed on him. "Why, my plans aren't formulated, but it's possible."

"I may be going myself," Leo said. "If it happened that our voyage coincided, I would be happy to take you to meet Thomas."

Marian sat quietly and wondered how much of this was true and how much Leo was fabricating. She, of all people, was well aware that the plots Leo wove in his mind were tenuous, and that he would tell any lie or do anything necessary to serve his own interests. Though he had spent a great deal of time and money on many pursuits, she had never seen him set on anything so intensely as having Matthew Bradford become his son. Without appearing to, she lifted her eyes and saw the edged pain on Daniel Bradford's face as he listened to Leo talk to his son. Others might not see it, but she knew him well enough to know that the conversation was indeed very painful for him.

After the meal was over, General Gage invited all the gentlemen into another room to smoke. The language grew much rougher, as it always did without the ladies' genteel presence to restrain it. There were rather coarse jokes and a great deal of drinking. Matthew found himself seated next to Leo, who made amusing comments on the characters of some of the officers present. There was something about Leo Rochester that fascinated Matthew. He was not usually so quick to be drawn to someone he didn't know, or there was something in Sir Leo that caused him to hold off—a determination to weigh the character of the man before allowing him to get close. He was puzzled about this interest that he felt in Rochester, and knew that it had something to do with his father. He could not, however, fathom what that might be.

General Gage finally began to talk about the military situation. "Gentlemen," he said, "a toast!" He raised his glass high and said, "To our brave men who gave their lives for the sake of England."

They drank this toast and then Lord Percy, who had led the relief column to rescue the British on the way back from Concord, raised his glass and said, "And to His Majesty, King George the Third!"

Daniel Bradford suddenly realized that every eye was upon him. This was the test! Without thought, he raised his own glass and echoed the toast. "To His Majesty, King George the Third."

A look of satisfaction spread over the face of Thomas Gage, and when he had drunk the toast, he said genially, "Well now, what have we here? It was an unfortunate event, that business in Concord, but it's not too late if sound men will come to the bargaining table."

Lord Percy looked at Matthew and Daniel, saying impetuously, "You've just drunk a toast to King George, so I suppose that satisfies our questions about your politics, Bradford."

The man's comment ignited a stubbornness in Daniel. It was always there—a streak that would not allow him to bow his head. It had begun in England years ago, and it had brought him some hard knocks over the years. Now he looked over at Leo Rochester, who was smiling slightly, his eyes gleaming. "I drink to the health of the royal sovereign, but I will also drink to the lives of my fellow Americans who died at Concord."

Daniel's sudden toast presented a predicament for the officers gathered around. They could not well drink to the enemy who had slain their own men. Though the silence was but a few seconds, the intent was clear, and it was Rochester who quickly spoke up. "I see you do not share all of your father's convictions. Is that true, Matthew?"

Matthew Bradford hesitated. "I'm not a political person, Mr. Rochester. I'm an artist."

"Paul Revere is an artist of sorts," said Major John Pitcairn of the Royal Marines. "Yet, he is an avid follower of the Sons of Liberty. I think the time has passed when a man can hide behind any title, be it artist, clergy, or politician."

The man's challenge was plain. Matthew put his cup down slowly and said, "My father and I do not agree on this matter. I feel that the problems of America can be solved without bloodshed."

"Well said—very well said!" Leo exclaimed.

A silence fell over the room, and Daniel realized that he had been tried in the balance and found guilty. "If you'll excuse me," he said, "I must be going home. Are you coming, Matt?"

Matthew hesitated. "Yes, sir, of course."

The two men left and Rochester looked over at Colonel Leslie Gordon. "Your brother-in-law seems to be somewhat confused in his loyalties, Colonel," he said smoothly.

Gordon stared at the man, feeling an instinctive dislike. "There are many of his opinion, sir," he said and turned and walked away.

Later that night, Clive, who had spent most of the evening with Rachel and had missed the conversation that had taken place in the smoking room, asked his father about it.

"It's going to be hard for Daniel," Leslie said slowly, shaking his head.

"Do you think he'll actually join with the rebels? His daughter is a lovely girl. I'd hate to see them on the wrong side of this thing."

Lyna spoke up at once, "Daniel has never dodged a fight in his life. I doubt that he'll dodge this one."

"I fear that you're right," Leslie said. He straightened his shoulders

33

and then said, "I'm going to be gone for a while."

"Where are you going? You can't get out of Boston," Lyna protested.

"Oh, there are ways to do that." He hesitated, then said, "This is all very confidential. General Gage has asked me to go to Fort Ticonderoga. We still hold that fort, and there's a good supply of cannons there. He wants me to go check the defenses to make sure the rebels don't make a raid on it."

"Ticonderoga? I'd like to see that part of the country," Clive said. His eyes brightened at the thought of it. "I think I'll go along, if you won't mind my company."

Leslie smiled. "I'd be glad to have you, but it could be very dangerous. If they capture us, we'll both have to spend the rest of the rebellion in a cold and damp prison cell somewhere."

"Oh, we're too smart for that," Clive smiled. "I'd really like to go along with you, Father."

"Very well. Be ready at dawn." Leslie put his hand on the shoulder of his tall, young son. "We'll have plenty of time to talk," he said. "And decide about your career. Mine," he added rather sourly, "it seems has already been decided. I've been sent here to fight in a war I don't believe in against people that I respect." Then he forced a smile. "But as a physician you can go anywhere. That's why I was glad you chose to be a doctor rather than a soldier."

Lyna at once came and stood beside Leslie and put her arm around him. "You have a noble profession," she said. "If there are evils in high places you are not part of that. England would not survive if it weren't for men like you."

"Well, then, I'm a hero." Leslie smiled at her, then turned to Clive. "We'll be up at four and be on our way. Don't oversleep!"

3

A Matter of Honor

GENERAL GAGE'S DECISION TO VERIFY THE MILITARY readiness of Fort Ticonderoga was sound, but the matter of carrying it out was going to prove to be a little difficult. Colonel Leslie Gordon had served the king in Europe, but the rugged wilderness of America presented a number of challenges. It was a simple enough matter to obtain an accurate map of Germany, or France, or Belgium, but the maps of the Colonies were scarce and highly inaccurate. It would not be possible to stop at a courthouse or a military post for instructions as to the whereabouts of Ticonderoga, for a thick forest lay between Boston and the isolated fort. Ticonderoga was situated at the southern end of Lake Champlain. This meant that Leslie and Clive would have to make their way across hundreds of miles of rough wilderness where there were no roads at all, not even bad ones. They would have to cross four rivers and face the possibilities of chance encounters with hostile Indians who still occupied some of this area and were willing to kill to defend their hunting grounds.

Eager for the adventure, Clive was up before dawn. He dressed hurriedly, then came downstairs and found that his mother had risen and already fixed a hearty breakfast. Coming over to her, he kissed her cheek, saying, "You shouldn't have gotten up this early."

Lyna had a worried expression but quickly replaced it with a forced smile. "I can't very well send my men off on a long journey without a good breakfast," she said. "Sit down and eat. I'll call your father."

Clive sat down and soon his father appeared dressed in full uniform. "Are you going to wear that uniform, sir?" he asked. "You might get captured by the rebels."

"If I do, I won't be shot for a spy. And you'd better be sure to carry your papers to prove you're a civilian, Clive." Sitting himself at the table, Leslie surveyed the steaming bowl of battered eggs, the platter of

35

fried bacon, and the fresh bread still warm from the oven. Smiling at Lyna, he said, "I imagine this will be the last good meal we'll get for a while. Sit down and let's eat." He asked the blessing slowly, requesting safety for the long journey and for those who were left at home.

The two men ate all they could hold, but Lyna picked at her food, saying little. Finally, when they rose to go, she took Leslie's kiss and clung to him for a moment. "Keep safe," she whispered. Then turning to Clive, she reached up and put her arms around his neck. He was so tall that she felt like a child. Stepping back, she said, "It seems impossible that I held you in my arms once—and you're still like a baby to me in some ways."

"Mother!" Clive was embarrassed as always when she referred to things like this. Laughing awkwardly, he said, "I'll bring you back a bearskin. You can make a rug out of it and put it beside your bed so your feet won't get cold."

The two men left the house and rode to headquarters, where they went at once to the colonel's office. Leslie collected the few maps he had acquired and a waterproof leather case. He spread one of the maps out on the table, calling Clive over to look at it. "It's a long way that we have to go, Clive," he said soberly. "I hear these Berkshire Mountains are rugged and a steep incline, and the valleys are deep and twisting. There are no roads at all for much of the way. I'm glad we're not trying to make this in the dead of winter."

Clive stared down doubtfully at the map, which actually was a rudimentary sort of affair. "I don't see how this is going to help us much," he muttered. "Seems to me that our first obstacle is getting out of Boston without any trouble. But once we do, how do we find our way?"

"I've already made arrangements in Boston. We won't waste our time trying to find our way through the rings the rebels have thrown around the city. It's too dangerous that way."

"How do we get out, then?" asked Clive, looking up from the map.

"I've arranged to have us taken on a ship. At least we still control the sea. We'll be set ashore about twenty-five miles north of Boston." He stared at the map again and said, "If we head west we'll run into the Hudson River and can follow it up north almost to Lake George. Once we reach Lake George, it won't be hard to find the fort. See here?" he said, pointing to a spot on the map. The two men studied the map briefly, then left the office and headed for the stables, where they found three horses and three pack animals waiting for them.

"I picked the best animals for you, sir," the corporal said as he led them outside. "They're well fed and I've packed some extra grain for them. They're good horses, all of them."

36

"Has there been anybody here asking for me?"

"Yes, sir, there has. Oh, here he comes now," said the corporal.

Leslie looked around to see a stocky man dressed in buckskin and carrying a long rifle approaching them. The buckskin had fringes on it, and on his head was a cap with the tail of an animal dangling down his back. The man's ruddy face was burned by the sun, and his eyes had a continual squint, it seemed. When he slouched up and stood in front of Gordon, the man turned and spat a stream of amber tobacco juice to the ground and nodded.

"I'm Thad Meeks," he said. "Supposed to guide you to Fort Ticonderoga."

"I'm glad to see you, Meeks. This is my son, Clive. Do you understand the mission?"

Meeks pulled his hat off and twirled it around his finger. His unkempt hair was brown, streaked with white. His age was difficult to say, but Leslie placed it at a little less than fifty. He was surprised that their guide was an older man, for when he had made his request he assumed that he would get someone from the army. He knew, however, that few of his fellow officers and regulars were acquainted with the vast expanse of the West. The man's age hinted of experience, and his rugged appearance already showed that he was no stranger to the harsh wilderness they would have to traverse to reach the fort.

"Wal, Colonel, the general said my job was to get you to Ticonderoga and back with your hair on."

Clive grinned, taking an instant liking to the man. "Do you think that'll be a hard job, Thad?"

"It's all in the Lord's hands," Meeks said plainly. "It's all been decided—doing what God's laid out for us to do."

"Well, you're a Calvinist, I see." Clive was amused at the man's position—that whatever is to be will be.

"That's the way I see it." The stocky guide grinned amiably. "Sure saves a lot of worrying about things. I got shot about a year ago by one of them pesky Mohawks. Soon as I got knocked to the ground and saw that I wasn't going to die, I thought to myself, 'Well, Lord, I'm sure glad *that's* over.' "

Leslie Gordon found the man amusing and said, "Let's hope the Lord has laid it out that we do get back with our scalps. Are we ready to go?"

"Thar's the sun," Meeks nodded. "I done helped the corporal load the supplies on them animals. Can't take enough grub with us to get us all the way to the fort, but I reckon we can knock down a deer or maybe some ducks on the way."

"Very well, let's be going," said Gordon.

The three men mounted and rode down to the wharf. There they found a small transport schooner with one sail waiting for them, and soon the horses were loaded and secured. They sailed out of Boston Harbor under a brisk wind, then headed north. By the time they arrived at their destination north of Boston, the sun was high in the sky. The ship pulled into a natural harbor with a sloping bank, and three of the sailors helped them get their horses ashore. Leslie thanked them and then the three men mounted.

"Well, let's mosey on," Meeks said. "We ain't gonna get no place sittin' here." He looked ahead at the ground as it lifted away from the shore, and his eyes began searching the tree line.

"What are you looking for, Thad?" Clive asked curiously.

"Don't do no harm keeping an eye out for them pesky Injuns."

Mischief rose in Clive and he asked innocently, "If the Lord's determined that we're going to get attacked by Indians, it'll happen, won't it?"

"Maybe so, but it may be that the Lord's planned it for me to keep a lookout for them varmints. Hard to know the ways of the Lord. All a man can do is keep his powder dry and his eyes open. I'd advise you to do the same, sir."

The three men moved ahead quickly and soon entered the dense forest that stretched endlessly ahead of them. As they followed the narrow, twisting road, Leslie's mind raced, trying to anticipate the challenges that might lie ahead. He wondered what condition the fort was in. Such speculation was useless, of course, but his success in the military was because he was a man who carefully thought out his plans before forging ahead unprepared. Glancing at the stocky figure of their guide riding alongside him, Leslie smiled. *Maybe Thad's right*, he thought. *Maybe the Lord's already got this whole adventure planned out—but men must do their part....*

☩   ☩   ☩

Several days on the trail had hardened Leslie and Clive, although the beginning of their journey had been difficult. Neither one of them was accustomed to the long hours in the saddle. They grew saddle-weary and were ready each night to fall into their blankets after a quick meal. On the fourth day of their travel, however, as they pulled up just before dark under a stand of towering trees, Clive felt much better. He glanced at the small stream which flowed in a meandering fashion, saying, "Maybe I can help with the cooking, Thad."

"I'll go out and see if I can knock some fresh game down," Meeks said as he tied his horse and pulled out his rifle. "A bit of fresh meat roasted over a fire would go down pretty good." He left the two men to make camp and disappeared into the thicket.

He had not been gone over ten minutes when Clive suddenly straightened up. "I heard a shot," he said. "I hope Thad brought down a good, juicy deer."

Meeks came back in no time carrying not a deer but a wild turkey. "Ought to taste pretty good," he remarked. "I'll shuck the feathers off this fellar while you get the fire made." He moved away from the campsite and soon feathers were flying. He came back by the time Clive had the fire going and held out the plucked bird to him. "Ain't nothin' much better than a wild turkey. 'Course I'd like to roast it in an oven along with some sweet taters and corn bread—but out here we can't have everything." The odd theology that marked the mountain man popped out as he added, "Shore was thoughtful of the Lord to have this here turkey in that thicket jest when I came along."

Clive's eyes sparkled with amusement, but he only said, "Amen, Brother Meeks!"

The meal proved to be very satisfying. They roasted the entire turkey, and after they ate their fill, Meeks wrapped the rest in cloth, saving it for their noon meal the following day on the trail. Night had closed in around the camp, and the stars overhead began to twinkle against the black, velvet sky.

"How is it that you're willing to serve King George, Thad?" Leslie asked finally as they sat around the fire. He knew many of the mountain men were on the patriot side, and this made him curious about their guide.

"Well, I ain't really got no dogs in this fight, Colonel. My entire family got wiped out by the Indians, and I ain't never found another woman. We was so far out in the mountains that we didn't even know there was a war brewing up, except with the redskins. What do you think this war's going to come to?"

It was a question that Leslie Gordon had asked himself a thousand times—and found no satisfactory answer. "I'm not sure," he said moodily. "On one hand, there's the king of England three thousand miles away. If he thinks of the Colonies at all, it's just a small part of his vast empire. Then there are the colonists themselves. As with all men, they're the center of their own world."

"They're strange people, aren't they, Father?" Clive said. "They're like Englishmen in so many ways—yet not like us."

"It's because of all this." Leslie waved his hand around, indicating the dark forest that seemed to spread out endlessly. "They came to this country seeking a new life and freedom. When they got here, they discovered a land that's so big it's frightening—and so far away from London and the king that they had to govern themselves. They've had a taste of ruling themselves, and once a man does that, I suppose, he'll never be satisfied with anything less."

"But there has to be some form of government," Clive protested. "After all, as I understand it, the whole thing started over taxes that the Crown imposed on the Colonies, but there have to be taxes, too. Why do they object so much to paying them? Most of it goes to pay for the war England waged against France that saved the colonists' necks! Otherwise, they'd be French subjects and would be forced to accept the Catholic Church—and pay for it. You'd think they'd show a little gratitude!"

"They don't see it like that, Clive. Talk to your uncle Daniel sometime. He can give you the colonial side of it, but it's beyond me," he said finally.

"Well, now," Meeks said slowly, "who's going to win the war?"

"Everybody says that England will. We have the largest standing army in the world, and the colonists don't have a professional army at all. You don't win battles with inexperienced militia."

"I heard they done pretty well fighting you folks on the way back to Boston after Concord."

"But how many battles are fought like that?" Leslie shrugged. "Our forces had to stay on the road and the colonists shot from behind fences and trees. In a real battle, Thad, you move massive troops of men. The rebels could never stand before a mass charge of professional soldiers. They don't have the leadership for it."

Leslie listened as an owl cried plaintively somewhere off in the forest. It seemed to strike a responsive note in him, bringing the depression that had settled on him since the military disaster on the road from Concord. He disliked the war intensely and wished he were back in England—anywhere but in this forsaken place! Now that Lyna had found her brother Daniel, whose political loyalty was firmly on the side of the Sons of Liberty, it was even more depressing. Finally, he said, "I don't see any good ending for it." With that he rose, walked over to his blankets, and rolled into them, leaving the two men alone staring at the crackling fire.

"Guess we all better settle in. We have a long ways to go, so I want to be up and on the road before daybreak," Meeks said. He studied the young man across from him. "You ain't in the army. How come that?"

"Well, I decided I wanted to be a doctor when I was just a child."

"A doctor—well now, I don't have much time for that breed, but they're good for lopping off an arm or setting a broken bone, but not much else."

Clive was not insulted, since it was a common enough opinion. He smiled, his white teeth flashing in the dancing firelight. "A pretty good description of the medical profession, Thad," he murmured. Then he moved across to his bedroll, wrapped up in his blankets, and drifted off to sleep almost instantly.

Thad Meeks sat there staring into the flickering yellow flames. He was all alone in the world, having lost a wife and two children in Indian attacks. Now he wandered aimlessly across streams, down in the deep wooded valleys, and sometimes on the high crest of the mountains. His only clock was the rising and the setting of the sun. He had no plans for making anything out of his life—other than simply to live through each day. Meeks had been converted to faith in God at a late age. He could not read the Bible, so his theology was very simple, picked up from a few teachers and preachers who had instructed him. Now he glanced over at the two Englishmen and thought of the task before them. It was merely a job to him, for which he would be paid. As he lay down and wrapped his blanket around him, he muttered, "I don't see what all the fuss is about. All this happens when you get too many people crowded together. . . !"

☙   ☙   ☙

Thad Meeks seemed to know the woods as well as Leslie Gordon knew his own house. Ignoring the rudimentary roads that threw up huge clouds of dust in the summer, and no doubt were frozen troughs of mud during the winter, he avoided the more commonly followed trails, and instead turned due northwest. They crossed the Connecticut River, and on April 29 they reached Fort George, a small post on the southern end of Lake George. At the northern end of the lake was a short, narrow strait that opened up to form Lake Champlain. Fort Ticonderoga stood on the western shore at that narrow point. The three travelers reached the fort shortly before dusk. As they passed through the gates, they were met by a soldier wearing the uniform of a lieutenant.

"Lieutenant James Felthim, sir," he said as he stared at them incredulously. "I'm a little amazed to see you here, Colonel."

"I'm Colonel Leslie Gordon of the Royal Grenadiers in Boston. This is my son, Clive." He turned to indicate the guide. "And this is our guide, Thad Meeks. We would appreciate it if you could have our animals cared for, Lieutenant."

"Of course, Colonel." Felthim turned to give orders to a sergeant, then said, "Come inside. You'll be wanting to see Captain Delaplace."

The lieutenant led them inside the fort, where they found Captain William Delaplace, who was as shocked to see them as the lieutenant had been. "Well, sir," he said. "We don't get too many visitors. We're cut off from civilization way out here, of course."

"You are a bit out of the way, Captain. Here are my instructions from General Gage." Removing the packet from his waterproof case, Leslie handed them over, saying, "Briefly, the general wants to be sure the fort's in a state of readiness in case of a surprise attack by the rebels."

Captain Delaplace took the papers, stared at them briefly, then shook his head. "I'm afraid I have no good report for you to take back to General Gage. We're in poor condition here, sir."

"What seems to be the trouble, Captain?" Leslie inquired. He had noted after a cursory examination on the way to the captain's office that the fort was dilapidated. There was none of the sharpness and exactitude that he was accustomed to in the Royal Grenadiers.

"Why, we've been stripped of most of our men," Delaplace said. He was a short, slight man with an unhealthy pallor on his face—the look of a chronically ill individual. He was nervous, also, for he was well aware of General Gage's hard usage of officers who did not come up to his expectations. "We've no more than forty men now in the command, and at least half of them are down with some infernal sickness."

"Sickness?" Clive straightened up, gleaming with interest. "What sort of sickness, Captain?"

"The flux of some kind—fever—who knows?"

"My son is a physician," Leslie Gordon said quickly. "Perhaps he can be of some help."

"A physician! That's exactly what we need. Our own surgeon was transferred out six months ago. We've had no medical attention since then, except what we can give ourselves." He looked over at Lieutenant Felthim. "Lieutenant, if the doctor would be so kind as to look at our poor fellows, I would appreciate it."

"Of course, I'd be happy to," offered Clive.

At once, Lieutenant Felthim broke out, "Excellent! Come this way, Doctor."

As soon as the lieutenant had led Clive out of the room, Leslie turned to the captain, saying, "Now then, perhaps I could have your full report, and I'd also like to inspect the fort."

"Certainly, Colonel." The captain spent the next thirty minutes laying out the matter of supplies, men, and problems to the colonel. It was a bleak report, and when he had finished, Delaplace spread his hands wide in a resigned gesture that seemed habitual with him. "We're practically helpless at the moment, Colonel. Why, a force of thirty well-armed men could take us by surprise and easily overcome the fort!"

Alarm bells started to ring in Leslie Gordon's mind. He said little, for he realized the captain's assessment of the situation was alarmingly true. *Obviously there has been a grave mistake,* he thought. *To strip this place of its fighting force is inviting an attack.* Aloud, he said, "I'm sure you've done the best you can, Captain. Soldiers have a hard time of it, don't we?" said Gordon, trying to encourage the man.

Grateful for Colonel Gordon's obvious understanding, Delaplace put his hand over his forehead. He *had* done the best he could, but he was also well aware that General Gage might not see the bleak situation as understandingly as Colonel Gordon. "Come along," he said wearily. "I'll show you the defenses we have laid out."

Later that night, Captain Delaplace and Lieutenant Felthim entertained their visitors at a supper in the officers' quarters. It was a simple meal, for food supplies were dangerously low. "We had one of the last of the sheep slaughtered, so the mutton should be good," Delaplace said. "And the wine is my own. I had it shipped out to this wilderness all the way from France."

"A fine meal," Colonel Gordon said. He could sense that the captain was nervous and anxious for his approval. "We've been eating roughly for the last few days, although our guide is a good hunter. Perhaps he could go out and bring in some game."

"That would be most helpful, sir."

The colonel turned to his son and said, "What about this sickness, Clive? What do you think it is?"

"I'm not sure, sir," Clive admitted. He had spent several hours checking the men, who were pathetically glad to see him. He'd brought a full kit of medical supplies along with him, and had dosed most of them, uncertain whether it was the correct amount. But Clive had discovered that oftentimes a patient needed the assurance that a doctor was treating them. Even if the treatment was not the best, at least it encouraged them to know they had received some medical attention. "I'm fairly sure that it's not the plague," he said.

"That's good! It's been on our minds!" Lieutenant Felthim exclaimed with obvious relief. "I've never seen anything like it, Doctor! A man's fine one day and the next day he's as weak as a cat, with fever and the flux."

"Can you do anything for them, Doctor?" Captain Delaplace asked quickly. "As you can see, we're down to half strength here."

"I'll do the best I can, but it might take a little time to get them back on their feet. They're all pretty weak."

Colonel Gordon put his cup down and stared at the three men around the table. "Time is the one thing we do not have, I'm afraid," he said gently. "I'll have to leave in the morning. It may be possible, Captain, that General Gage could spare some men to shore up your defenses here."

"I think it must be done, sir."

"I agree, and I think once the general is appraised of your situation, he will agree as well. I will advise him to send some troops immediately. Think what it would mean if the rebels took over this fort!" He shook his head and his lips drew thin with displeasure at the thought. "Ticonderoga is the gateway to Canada. Just imagine what the rebels could do with all these cannons!"

The three officers talked rapidly, and finally it was decided that the best military procedure would be if General Gage could send reinforcements. "It's a hard trip back without rest. Can you make it, sir?" Lieutenant Felthim asked.

"I think I shall have to—and I have a good guide," Leslie assured the captain.

"But what about my men? I'm concerned about them," Captain Delaplace spoke up quickly. He put his eyes on Clive and said, "Six of them have already died, and others are likely to if they don't get a doctor's care."

Clive looked at his father and said quickly, "I believe it might be better if I stayed here, sir. I can do some good, I think."

"But how would you get back to Boston?"

"It can be taken care of, I'm sure," Captain Delaplace said quickly. "As soon as the men are able, we can find a guide who will bring your son back to Boston."

"Or it may be," the lieutenant said, "that you will be sent back with the reinforcements."

"I doubt that it will be that quick." Turning to his son, he said, "I'm not sure about leaving you here, Clive."

"Oh, it will be all right, Father. It'll be a good chance to practice my profession. It's a matter of honor, I think, to heal the sick, and this is my real chance to do so."

Later that night, Leslie talked at length with his son in the room they shared. They were stretched out on their beds, talking quietly. "I think I will rest up tomorrow," he said, "but I must get back as quickly as possible. I'm not entirely happy about leaving you here, Clive. It could be dangerous."

"Why, I'll be as safe here as I would be in Boston. I really want to do this, Father."

"Well, the decision has to be yours to make. You're a man now, so you'll have to decide before I leave."

Leslie rested the next day, but on the following day, May 1, he mounted, along with Thad Meeks, early in the morning. He looked down at Clive, who had come to wish him a good journey. They had eaten breakfast together early, and now streaks of gray light were appearing in the east as the colonel prepared to leave. "Are you sure you want to do this, Clive? There's still time to change your mind."

"No, sir, I'll be fine," Clive said cheerfully. He looked over at Thad and said, "I believe it's God's will, Thad."

Meeks knew that he was being teased, but he said strongly, "If it is, then you'll do it. We need to get going, Colonel, if you're in as much hurry as you say."

"Goodbye, Clive. God keep you."

"Goodbye, sir. Don't worry." Clive watched them as they headed off, leading the pack horses, then he turned back toward the infirmary, thinking of ways to help his patients.

☩   ☩   ☩

Exactly one week after his father and Meeks had left to go back to Boston, Clive was mounting his horse. He thought with satisfaction of how the men had greatly improved during the last week. "I'm not sure it was my doing," he said out loud to himself. "It was probably some sort of sickness or fever that would have passed even if I hadn't been here." He knew, however, that at least two of the men would probably have died, and felt a swelling satisfaction that he had fulfilled his promise as a doctor.

James Felthim had come out to see him off, accompanied by Captain Delaplace. Felthim said, "Are you sure you want to do this and don't want to stay awhile longer? We could always use a doctor."

"No, I really need to get back to Boston, Lieutenant."

Captain Delaplace said, "You've been a great mercy and blessing to our men. But I worry about you making the trip alone."

"I won't have any trouble getting to Fort George if the path is plainly marked. From there I can get a guide. I may go on down to Albany by boat, and then head to Boston."

"It's a long way, and you're not accustomed to the country."

"I'll stick to the main trails and the river. I'll be all right, sir."

"Well, we can only express our thanks from myself, the lieutenant, and from the men." Delaplace walked over, reached up and took Clive's hand. His eyes narrowed and he said, "You're not looking too well. You look a little flushed."

"Oh, it's nothing," Clive said carelessly. "I feel fine." He shook the hands of the two men, then turned and took the road that led to Fort George. The truth was that he had a little fever, but nothing serious. He was pleased with himself as he rode along, satisfied that he had done a good job of caring for the men. When he made a dry camp at noon and ate some of the beef and bread that the cook had packed for him, he discovered that he had little appetite. "Fever's up a little," he said to himself. He bathed his face in the cool stream where he had paused for a drink and felt better. However, by the time he made camp that night, he was feeling much worse. He felt so miserable, in fact, that he made no fire and cooked no meal. He tried to eat a little of the beef, but felt nauseated. *I've got to do better than this!* he thought fuzzily. He rolled in his blanket, but it soon became interminably hot, and he knew that his fever had risen. He tossed most of the night, rising the next morning feeling weak and listless. It was all he could do to saddle his horse and get on. Leading the pack animal, he slumped in the saddle, his head swimming.

Clive's fever climbed steadily, and by three o'clock he was sicker than he had ever been in his life. He knew he had to reach Fort George, but from time to time he almost fell out of the saddle. Clive allowed the horse to pick its way along, and he concentrated on merely hanging on. His fever was raging, and he knew he had made a mistake leaving Ticonderoga. Finally, he fell asleep in the saddle. For a while, subconsciously he was able to keep his balance, but the horse put a hoof in a hole and Clive was thrown roughly to the ground. He awoke in confusion, hearing the sound of his horse breaking into a run. Clive struggled to his knees and saw the two horses disappear down the trail, then nausea took him. He vomited so violently that it nearly tore him in two. Struggling to his feet, he wiped his pale face, now hot with fever. He staggered down the trail, calling for the horse, but only the sound of his voice echoed back to him. By then night was beginning to fall, and he finally fell full-length at the base of a tree, raging with thirst and his stomach in great knots of pain. The darkness continued to close in, and he tried to rise, but could not. And then it was totally dark, and Clive Gordon was as alone as he had ever been in his life.

4

JEANNE CORBEAU

FEEBLE LIGHT FROM AN EARLY-MORNING SUN filtered through the single window of the log cabin, bathing a young woman with soft golden beams. Jeanne Corbeau held a pint-size brown glass bottle up to the small window and squinted carefully at the contents. "Nearly half gone," she murmured. "I'll have to go back to the settlement soon and get more of it."

Turning from the window, Jeanne set the bottle on a rough pine table, then moved to the open fireplace, where a black pot was suspended over a bed of glowing coals. Quickly, she stirred the mush, then with an efficient movement took boiling water from a small kettle and made tea. A single candle set on the mantel cast its amber light over the sparse hand-built furniture of the room. The young woman carefully spooned some of the mush onto a tin plate, then added a spoonful of sugar and a little milk from a copper can. *Milk's getting blinky—but it's all we have.* Straightening up, she put the tin plate of mush, a mug of steaming tea, and the brown medicine bottle on a tray whittled out of a white pine slab. She moved to the door which hung by leather hinges on the left side at the back of the cabin. The doorway was low and narrow, and as she stepped inside she said in French, "Papa, some breakfast for you."

The small bedroom Jeanne entered was illuminated by an oil lamp that sat on a roughhewn table beside a bed made of black walnut. The only other furniture in the room was a chest alongside the wall and a trunk with a rounded lid at the foot of the bed. Rough clothing hung from several pegs driven into the walls, and a blue enameled pitcher and a colored picture of Jesus pinned to the otherwise bare wall lent the only tints of color to the room.

The man lying in the bed was awake. His eyes were sunk back into his head, and his cheeks were thin and drawn. Struggling to a sitting position, he looked at the tray that the girl was holding, then said in French, "Not hungry, daughter."

"You've got to eat something, Papa," Jeanne answered firmly. She set the tray down, then picked up the tin plate of mush and a large pewter spoon. "Try to eat some of this. I've made some tea."

As Pierre Corbeau took the tin plate with a sigh, Jeanne noticed how thin his arms were. A pang of grief stabbed her heart as she remembered how strong and muscular her father's arms had always been. She'd seen him paddle a canoe for ten hours at a stretch, the corded muscles of his arms and neck firm as rock. Now they were shrunken, and the thin blue veins were plainly visible.

"Try some of the tea. I made it the way you like," she urged. As his mouth twisted with pain, she saw that he could not eat.

"I can't eat anymore," Corbeau whispered hoarsely, handing her the untouched plate. He tried to drink the tea, but a spasm of pain racked his body, making his hands shake so violently that some of the tea slopped over on his chest. Jeanne quickly picked up the medicine bottle, poured a spoonful of it into the spoon, then offered it to him. "Here, take this, Papa—it will make you feel better."

Corbeau obediently swallowed the medicine, blinked at the bitter taste, then took another swallow of tea. He had been a strong man all of his life, and the suddenness of the illness that had hit him months earlier had left him defenseless and as weak as a baby. He had always been alone in a sense, except for the time when he had married young Mary Carter. He had brought his young bride to the remote mountains to make a life, but they had known only a brief happiness. She had died when their only child, Jeanne, was three years old. Since that time, Corbeau and Jeanne had lived alone. He was a lonely man, missing his wife terribly, but his love for her had been so great that he had never thought seriously of marrying again. Perhaps it was because he was afraid of losing another love—but in any case he had spent the last fourteen years pouring his love and devotion into his daughter.

Jeanne sat beside the sick man for a time, and soon the medicine took effect. She rose, saying, "I've got to go run the traps, Papa. Will you be all right here alone for a while?"

"Yes—"

"I'll put some food on the table and lots of tea. I'll be back as soon as I can, but it'll probably be dark by the time I do."

"Be careful," he whispered weakly.

"I will." She leaned over, kissed his cheek, and ran her hand over his hair, which seemed to have grown dead and lifeless during his sickness. Her hand lingered there for a moment, and he looked up and managed a smile.

"A hard job, taking care of your papa, eh, Cherie?" He used the term of endearment for her that he had used when she was a small child, and a spark of liveliness lightened his dull eyes. "I'm so much . . . trouble for you. . . !"

"You're no trouble at all," she whispered quickly. The name that he gave her, "Cherie," brought back poignant memories of her childhood. She had known no life but this simple cabin, hidden far away from the settlement. She and her father had lived isolated from the mainstream of the world. The only contact with others in the settlement was when they needed some supplies or went in to trade the furs they trapped. Pierre had taught her to read, and she practically knew their small library by heart. Now, however, she felt a fear gripping her heart, for she knew that he was growing weaker with each passing day. What she would do without him she did not allow herself to think, for he had been her life for as long as she could remember.

Quickly she left the room and moved about the larger living area, seeing to it that he was left with food and fresh drinks of tea, but she was sure he would not eat much. She stepped to the door of the small bedroom, saying as cheerfully as she could, "I'll be back as soon as I can."

Corbeau looked at her, thinking how much she had grown up—almost overnight it seemed to him. She had been a good child while his wife was still alive, and after her death, Pierre had taken care of his daughter the best he could. At times he had had a hard time and felt inadequate to properly train her, for he had known little of the finer things a mother could have provided for her. Jeanne had grown up more like a boy, accompanying him on the traplines, on hunting trips, and on the journeys into the deep woods that he sometimes made for no good reason other than to enjoy the immensity of the untamed land. He loved to wander and travel, and was proud when even during her adolescence she grew strong, loving the woods and outdoors as much as he did.

Now, as Corbeau studied Jeanne, he realized she was no longer a child. She had short, curly black hair that she kept cropped because it was less trouble. Her face was oval, as her mother's had been, and she had a tiny mole, like a beauty mark, on her left cheek very near her lips. He studied the high cheekbones, the wide lips, and noted again the delicate little cleft in her determined chin. It was much like his own mother's had been—and like his own. She was not tall, but even wearing the buckskins as she did most of the time, he saw that his daughter, at the age of seventeen, was very attractive. *She's grown into a beautiful young woman*, Pierre thought. *But she doesn't know it yet. . . .*

A pang of sudden anguish gripped him as he thought, *What will she do when I'm gone? How will she live here all alone?* He felt suddenly depressed that he had not raised her in the company of other people. Her only acquaintances were lone hunters, men who occasionally stopped by their cabin on their trek over the mountains. Their rare visits to villages in the settlement had not been pleasant to either of them. The tiny villages—most of them being composed of only a half-dozen families—offered nothing in the way of entertainment. Jeanne had shown little inclination to spend time with the married women there, and the young people were sometimes unkind to her, making ribald remarks about her appearance.

Jeanne left the sick man's room and moved to the stone fireplace, where she plucked down the long rifle that was held by pegs over the mantel. Quickly she checked her powder and shots, then put some food in a leather bag that she slung over her shoulder. Leaving the cabin, she went to the small shed. Two horses lifted their heads as she approached. She slipped a saddle on one of them, speaking gently as she did so. "Come on, Charlemagne. You're getting fat and lazy! You need some good exercise." She checked to be sure she had bags to bring the game back, then stepped into the saddle with the ease and grace that few men possessed. Charlemagne humped his back, for he was a spirited horse. She merely laughed and slapped him on the neck. "You feel good, do you? We'll see how you feel after a hard day's work!"

She left the shed with a worried frown creasing her forehead. She hated leaving her father alone while he was so sick—but there was no alternative. The traps had to be run, and she had waited much too long already. The trapline was strung out in a large semicircle, mainly following the creeks where animals went to water. As she moved along the trail, her eyes darted back and forth. They were never still. Pierre had taught her to be on the alert whenever she was alone in the deep woods. There was always danger lurking in the woods, not so much from wild animals, although there were panthers that often screamed like women, but the Indians were never to be trusted. Pierre had formed friendships with some of the tribes, but there were always wandering Mohawk, who were dangerous and looking for a chance to vent their anger at those who were taking over their land. The white hunters, too, whether French or English, were rough men, especially where a lone woman as young and pretty as Jeanne was concerned. Those in the surrounding vicinity knew Pierre and were not likely to harm his daughter, but there were others who were as wild as the game they hunted in the rugged mountains.

Jeanne reached the first trap after an hour's ride. The game around the cabin had been trapped out, so they had to throw a wider circle. The first trap was empty, so she baited it quickly, efficiently, and set it out. Mounting Charlemagne, she then moved on to the next. There she found a mink, the highest-priced furbearer of all. Jeanne dismounted and tied up the horse to a small sapling nearby. Pulling a short club out of one of her sacks, she advanced slowly, hating what she had to do. Ever since she was a small child, she'd always felt sorry for the animals, and her father had laughed at her—for none of the mountain men felt any pity for the game they trapped or hunted. But as the mink, which was trapped by one foreleg, looked at her, Jeanne had a stab of remorse; nevertheless, it had to be done. With one quick, hard, short blow, she broke the animal's neck, then quickly removed the dead animal from the trap. Putting the limp, furry body into the sack, she tied it on behind the saddle and swung up again.

All day she traveled hard, until the twin sacks behind her were cumbersome and heavy with the bodies of the animals. She would have a hard day's work skinning them and putting them on stretching boards when she got back. All through the day her mind drifted back to the lonely cabin where her father lay sick.

She kept time by the sun. Now as the sun dropped behind the mountains, casting dark shadows across her path, she realized that she had stayed out longer than she had intended. "Come on, Charlemagne," she urged. "We can still make it home, even though we have to ride in the dark."

The horse surged forward, and Jeanne rode hard until the trails grew dim in the darkness. Afraid to run the horse full speed for fear of being knocked off by an overhanging branch, or his breaking a leg by stepping in a hole, Jeanne pulled him down to a slow walk. She was peering ahead into the darkness when a sudden movement made her sit up alertly in the saddle. Having carried the gun across the saddle, she now lifted it, her finger on the trigger and her thumb on the hammer. There were bears big enough to kill a man in these mountains, and at first she thought that's what it was. But then a whickering sound came to her and she realized it was a horse.

Replacing the gun in the leather scabbard, she urged Charlemagne forward and found a saddled horse with a pack animal tied on to his saddle with a long leather thong. "What are you doing way out here?" she said. Lifting her head, she listened carefully but heard nothing.

"Anybody out there?" she called. Silence came echoing back, and she shook her head, puzzled. Quickly, she moved forward and, stooping down, grasped the bridle, then proceeded down the trail leading the two animals. She stopped occasionally to listen, for she had decided that the rider must have fallen, or else the horses had run away, leaving their owner stranded. From time to time she called out, but no one answered. It was almost totally dark now, and she halted and listened again. She thought she heard something and called out, "Anybody there?"

"Here—over here. . . ."

Cautiously she stepped off the horse, tying his reins to a sapling beside the trail. "Where are you?" she called. There was no sound for a moment, then she heard a thrashing.

"Over here—" came the sound of a weak voice.

Jeanne moved forward and found a man who was struggling to get to his feet. She knew instantly that he was either hurt or drunk or sick, for he staggered and fell to his hands and knees again.

"Are you hurt?" she cried, running forward. She bent over him, and when he straightened up, she saw by the last flickering rays of light that he had a long face and was dressed in an English fashion—not like a hunter in buckskin. His lips tried to form words as he licked them.

"Water—" he finally managed to say.

Jeanne had a water bottle tied on her saddle. She sprang to fetch it at once. When she came back to him, she found that he had fallen back, lying full-length on fallen leaves. She uncorked the top of the water bottle and gently lifted his head. He seemed unconscious, and she said, "Try to drink a little." She was encouraged when he did swallow some of the water, but when his eyes opened, she saw that they were not focused completely. She put her hand out and touched his forehead. "You have a high fever," she said in French.

He stared back at her, saying, "Sick, I'm so sick. . . !"

Realizing that he was British, she said in English, "Wait here, I'll fix a place for you." Her English was not as good as her French, but he seemed to understand her and lay back.

Quickly Jeanne made a decision. *I'll have to keep him here tonight. It's too dark to go on.* She returned to the pack animal and brought back plenty of blankets and even a piece of waterproof canvas. She was glad for her father's training, for he had taught her never to go out on the trail unprepared. She made a bed quickly and thought, *Fire! We've got to have a fire.* Starting a fire would be no problem, for the woods had been dry. When she had fixed the blankets, she dug through the thick leaves and found some small dead limbs. Fortunately there was a downed tree not far away. Walking over to it, she dug into the heart of it and pulled out

some of the crumbly, rotted pulp—dry punk. Quickly she arranged the
punk and, reaching into the pouch on her back, pulled out her powder
horn. She carefully scattered the powder in a thin trail over the punk.
Then reaching into another bag, she pulled out a piece of flint along
with a small piece of steel. She struck expertly, igniting the powder with
a spark, which led a small line into the punk. It caught at once into a
tiny blaze. She sat there, squatted in the darkness, nursing the small fire
patiently by blowing on it and feeding it small leaves and one twig at
a time. She finally muttered, "Catch—why don't you catch!" As the
smoke then boiled up thickly, she continued to fan the small blaze with
her hand, blowing it until she had it going. She nursed it with larger
branches until it was blazing well enough for her to risk leaving it.

Moving back to where the man still lay, she tugged at his clothing.
"Sit up," she said in English. "Come over to the fire." She watched and
saw his eyes slowly open, and he muttered something, but she didn't
understand his mumbled words. He was a big man, taller than almost
any man she had ever seen. He was too large for her to do more than
urge him to his feet. Slowly, he began to shake his head and fall to his
knees. He swayed and would have fallen, but she said, "Hold on to me.
Come, you must get up." She staggered under his weight as he came to
his feet and leaned against her. "Come now—over here." She led him
to the blankets by the fire, and he collapsed on them immediately. She
put the blankets over him, and when he murmured, "Water," she gave
him more to drink. Then he lay back and instantly was unconscious.

Jeanne had seen men with high fevers before. Her father had suffered through one a few years back when he had fallen into the river
during the winter. She knew that this man would have to sweat it out
too. Going back to the pack, she found more blankets and wrapped
them around him. Soon perspiration was flowing down his flushed
face. She sat beside him, wiping the sweat away with a piece of cloth.

After she fed the fire so it wouldn't go out, she went to a creek to
replenish the water in the bottle. Finally, resigned there was nothing
more she could do, Jeanne sat down cross-legged beside the fire, and
from time to time looked at the still face of the man she had found out
in the middle of the forest. He had reddish hair, as well as she could
tell, and there was a certain strength in his face. She could not guess his
age; not more than twenty-five, she supposed. He was clean shaven and
well dressed. "He must have come from Ticonderoga," she murmured.
"But why would he leave, as sick as he is?"

The night passed slowly, and she worried about her sick father being
left alone. Finally, she managed to sleep some with her back against a
tree. "I'll have to get him back to the cabin tomorrow," she said aloud.

The sound of her own voice seemed to startle her and she looked around, but nothing stirred in the woods.

Shortly before dawn she woke and threw the blankets back. Going over to the man, she found that he was still asleep. Putting her hand cautiously on his forehead, she shook her head—the fever was still raging. Rising, she took her knife and went into the woods. Selecting two tall saplings, she cut them down and dragged them back to the camp, where she formed a travois. She had made one before when game was too big to pack on horseback. It consisted merely of two sticks with the ends fastened to a horse and the other ends allowed to drag on the ground. She formed a bed out of the blankets, fastening two cross sticks to keep the saplings separated. She knew that the man was too sick to walk, so she brought Charlemagne closer to his side.

"Come—you must get in here," she said. She watched as his eyes fluttered open and his lips formed incomprehensible words. He was only semiconscious, and it took all her strength to drag him onto the travois. She tied him on with rawhide strips under his arms so that he wouldn't fall off. He seemed worse than the previous night, and so she quickly packed her things and swung into the saddle. She led the man's horses behind her and traveled as steadily as she could.

As she slowly made her way toward home, weariness caught up with her. Working the trapline the previous day had tired her out. The concern over her father had been enough, and as she rode along she thought, *Now I'll have two sick men to take care of.*

🦌　　🦌　　🦌

Somehow there was a coolness that he had not known. He had been trapped in a burning furnace that had left his lips parched and his eyes scalded. At times he felt a coolness on his face, but then it would go away and the raging fever would return, sapping him of strength.

His mind roamed back to his past, and he remembered fragments from his childhood in England, but they were wild and disjointed. He remembered once how his father had taken him on the Thames and they had seen the Tower of London off in the distance. This seemed to dissolve, and another memory surfaced, sharp and clear. He had fallen and gashed his knee. Running inside, he had found his mother. He remembered how her eyes had turned fearful at the sight of his bleeding knee, and he had said, "It's all right, Mother, I'm not going to die." She had laughed at him then, taken him upon her lap, and cleaned and bandaged his knee with her gentle hands. He had been no more than four, but the memory was vivid in his mind for a moment. He even remembered that she had been wearing a light blue dress with tiny flowers on the collar.

Soon that memory faded too, and new faces appeared—some of them he didn't seem to recognize—and finally vague sounds came to him out of the silence. From the depths of the stupor he realized that someone was speaking to him and that it was not a dream.

Opening his eyes, he blinked against the bright lamplight that blinded him. As he turned his head away, he heard a voice with a gentle accent saying, "Are you awake?"

Carefully, he opened his eyes to slits and saw the thin outline of a girl's face bending over him. He blinked and tried to speak, but his throat was raw and scratchy and his lips as dry as dust. "Water," he whispered hoarsely.

"Here."

At once he felt a hand lifting his head and holding a tin cup to his lips. Suddenly a raging thirst seized him and he gulped noisily, spilling much of it on his chin and throat. It was delicious, and he managed to say huskily, "More!" This time he watched as the young woman poured water from a pitcher into the cup.

"Can you sit up?" she asked.

He tried and was astonished at how weak he felt. Nevertheless, he struggled to a sitting position, and when she handed him the cup, he used both hands to steady it. "I'm as weak as a kitten," he murmured.

"You've been very sick."

Clive looked at the young woman and was shocked to see that she was dressed in buckskins, much like those that Thad Meeks had worn. There was no mistaking her for a young man, for he looked into the smooth, oval face of a very attractive girl. Her hair was short-cropped, very black and curly, and her eyes were strangely colored, almost blue-violet, he decided. "How did I get here?" he whispered.

"I found you in the woods. You were passed out, with a high fever."

"My name is Clive Gordon, and it seems I owe you my life. Thank you."

She smiled and said, "You must rest and get your strength back."

There was an accent to her speech, and he had been in France enough to recognize the quality of it. "Are you French?" he asked.

"Yes—and English, too. My name is Jeanne Corbeau. I live here with my father." She moved suddenly and put her hand on his brow. "Your fever is nearly gone, monsieur," she said. "I thought for a while you were going to die. You've had a high fever."

"I can't remember much. How did you get me here?"

"In a travois. You've been unconscious for almost three days. Are you hungry?"

At the question, Clive felt a sudden sensation of hunger. "Yes," he said, "I guess I am."

"I'll get you something." The young woman rose and moved quickly to the fireplace. Using her knife, she hewed off a piece of meat from a large chunk that hung on a spit. Placing it on a plate, she took a fork and cut it up into bite-size portions. Then dipping some hot mush out of another bowl, she put it beside him. "I'll get you some bread," she said.

"Thanks. Thank you very much." Clive took the plate and found that as sick as he was, he was able to eat. He knew he needed the nourishment after such a high fever. Now he understood what so many men back at Fort Ticonderoga had suffered.

She returned soon with bread and a cup of tea, then pulled a stool up and watched him as he ate. "How do you feel?" she asked.

Clive swallowed a small bite of food and then nodded. "I feel weak, but I think I'm going to live."

"That is good," she said. "You'd better not eat too much or you'll get sick."

"Where is your father?"

Jeanne cast a quick glance at the door on the far side of the room. "In the bedroom. He . . . he is very sick," she said.

Something in the tone of her voice caught at Clive, and though his head was not clear, he recognized trouble when he saw it. Looking into her eyes, he saw pain there and asked quietly, "What is it, Miss Corbeau? What's wrong with your father?"

"I . . . do not know. He was always such a strong man, always! He could do anything in the woods—run farther than anyone and lift more weight. But a few months ago, he began to get sick. He started to complain about his stomach, you know?"

She had odd pronunciations, coming from her use of French, he supposed. He chewed slowly, then drank some of the tea. "I'm sorry to hear that. Have you had a doctor check him?"

Jeanne stared at him. "We live alone, and the only village around is far off to the east, and they have no doctor there."

Clive held the cup of tea and tried to think. "I am a doctor, Miss Corbeau."

Jeanne Corbeau stared at him as if he had announced that he'd come from the moon. "You are a doctor?" she whispered. "Thank God! He must have sent you here!"

Clive thought at once of Thad Meeks' firm conviction that all men

56

are moved by God. Clive was only a nominal church member, having none of the warm personal relationship with God that his parents had. He had seen it in their lives, though, and now he managed a weak smile. "I'm not so sure about that. My father is an officer in the British army. We had come to Fort Ticonderoga on a military mission. He left a week ago and I was to follow, but I got sick, as you can see."

Jeanne Corbeau was not a young woman given to excessive displays of emotion, but suddenly tears sprang to her eyes. She was astonished at her strong emotions, for the last time she had cried had been when she was a very young girl. Embarrassed, she turned, bit her lip, and dashed the tears away. When she had gained a measure of control of herself, she turned back and said, "It must have been the good God who sent you. No doctor has even been in this part of the world."

"I'm not sure I can help him, but I'll do what I can," Clive said. Suddenly he felt a wave of weakness coming on and his hand trembled. "I'm not very strong. Maybe . . . tomorrow—"

She took the cup and eased him back, seeing that he was passing out. His breathing was regular, and he no longer had the fever. "Tomorrow you'll be better," she said.

The next morning, Clive did feel better. He woke up hungry again, and Jeanne fed him. "I've got to get up and try my legs," he announced. He swung his legs over the cot that was too short for him, and she came to him at once. "Be careful, monsieur, be careful! You'll be dizzy."

Clive laughed then, but when he stood up the whole room seemed to turn upside down. He grabbed wildly, and she half supported him. "I'm as weak as dishwater!" he exclaimed.

"Just be still for a moment and you'll be all right," Jeanne encouraged him. She held on to him, aware of his great height. She, herself, was only of medium height, and he seemed to tower over her. As he held to her, she was suddenly conscious of the strength of his lean body, and a flush tinged her face. He had, she saw, long fingers as well as long arms and legs. Finally, she asked, "Are you still dizzy?"

"No, I'm all right now. Thank you." Clive straightened up and held on to the wall. "I didn't mean to fall all over you, Miss Corbeau. I think the dizziness is gone now."

"Come and sit at the table and rest a bit. I'll fix you some hot tea, and then perhaps you can look at my father."

As she moved about fixing the tea, Clive found out a little about their lives. There were apparently no neighbors for miles around. The two lived out in a remote area of the densest woods he had ever seen. From her simple manner and speech he was able to discern that the girl was practically untouched by civilization. Though she was not like any of the young girls he knew, he was also very much aware of the natural beauty of the young woman, despite the buckskin clothing she wore.

Finally, after drinking two cups of very hot tea, he took a deep breath and said, "If you'll bring the bag in that was tied on to my horse—"

"It is here. I brought it inside along with your other things when we first arrived." Jeanne moved quickly to the corner of the cabin and brought him the bag. "I will carry it," she said. "Let me see if he's awake."

She moved to the door and opened it carefully. Stepping inside, she saw that her father was awake and saw him smile as she moved to the side of his bed. "Papa, the man I found—he's a doctor. He can help you."

Pierre stared at her incredulously. "A doctor—here in the woods? How can that be?"

"I believe God sent him," Jeanne said. Just then she heard the door open and turned to see Clive Gordon, who was forced to stoop, coming through the low doorway. Jeanne thought he was accustomed to this, for he was a very tall man.

"Papa, this is Clive Gordon, the man I told you I found in the woods."

Pierre raised his eyes to stare at the tall form in the bedroom. "Pleased to meet you, sir. You're a fortunate man to have had my daughter come along when she did."

"Yes, sir, I was. Well, Mr. Corbeau, I'm sorry to find you ill."

Jeanne shoved a chair over and said, "He's been ill himself, Papa. Sit down here, Doctor." She pushed him into the chair, set the bag at his feet, and then stepped back and waited.

Still slightly dizzy, but feeling stronger, Clive examined the older man. What he found was not encouraging. He could tell that Corbeau had once been a very strong man, but was now stripped down to nothing but flesh and bones. After questioning him, Clive discovered that Corbeau had developed a tremendous pain in his stomach that grew worse each day.

"It feels like it's stripping the flesh off my bones, Doctor Gordon," Corbeau said. His gaunt and sunken eyes were fixed on the face of the young physician. Pierre had given up any hope of recovering, and now he asked quietly, "What is it, do you think?"

"I'm not sure, Mr. Corbeau. I have something here that will ease the pain. Then we will see what we can do."

Pierre Corbeau's lips turned up into a smile. At Clive's slight hesitation, Pierre recognized that the young doctor had little hope to offer him; then the smile faded and he nodded. "Thank you. That will be helpful."

Clive stayed for a moment asking a few more questions, then said, "I'll be back to visit with you fairly often. Right now I'm beginning to feel a little shaky myself." Rising to his feet, he grabbed his bag and left the room to go back and rest.

Jeanne came over and straightened her father's blankets. Her eyes were bright with hope. "He's a doctor. He will help you, Papa."

Pierre reached out an emaciated hand and took her by the arm. "He will do what he can, but we're all in the hands of the good God," he said faintly. He lay back then and closed his eyes as Jeanne quietly slipped out of the room.

As soon as she closed the door behind her, Jeanne instantly went to Clive and asked, "What is it?"

He turned to her and started to give her the blunt truth, which was that her father was dying, but when he saw the hope in her violet eyes and the tremulous movement of her lips, he found it hard to put the matter so bluntly. Still, he owed it to her to be honest. "He's very ill, Miss Corbeau—you know that."

"Yes, but perhaps you can do something, Doctor?"

"There's so little that we doctors can do," he said gently. An enormous pity for the girl welled up in him, for he realized that she was very vulnerable.

"But you will stay? You won't leave?"

"Yes," Clive said, "I'll stay." He was experienced enough to know that he was not committing himself to a long stay. He knew that Pierre Corbeau did not have long in this world. And after all, the girl had saved his life. He smiled and put his hand on her shoulder. It was firm and warm beneath his touch. "I'll stay for as long as you need me, Miss Corbeau," he promised.

Her lips moved slightly as she said, "Thank you, Doctor," and turned away from him. She had been alone for most of her life—but now she had someone to help with her father. She turned suddenly, put her eyes on him, and whispered, "I'm glad the good God sent you!"

5

"I Don't Need a Man?"

"AH, THIS IS *GOOD!*" Pierre breathed softly. He looked around at the tall pines which were gently swaying in the afternoon breeze, then leaned back with a sigh in the chair that sat just outside the front of the cabin. It was Clive's third day at the Corbeau home, and he had regained his strength almost miraculously. Carrying Corbeau outside from his bedroom had been like carrying a small child. Clive had been shocked at the thinness and fragility of his patient. From what Jeanne had told him, Clive knew that at one time Pierre Corbeau had been heavily muscled and strong. Now, however, his arms and legs were like sticks wrapped loosely with skin and stringy flesh. It had been Clive's idea to bring Corbeau outside, and when he had mentioned it, Corbeau had nodded eagerly.

"I don't know where Jeanne went," Clive said, sitting down in the other kitchen chair he had brought from inside the cabin. Glancing out at the trackless forest that surrounded the cabin like an ocean of green, he shook his head. "I'd get lost out there in ten minutes!"

"She will not get lost—not *Ma Petite*," Pierre said with a smile. His face was sunken in now, and his eyes seemed enormous in their dark cavernous sockets. "She knows every foot of this ground for fifty miles around."

There was pride in the sick man's thin voice, and Clive studied him carefully. Even in the brief time that he had cared for this man, Clive's medical experience and instinct told him that there was little time left for Pierre Corbeau. Something terrible was feeding on him, and there was nothing medical science could do for him. Clive had not said as much, but the two men understood each other well. Corbeau, from the first, had smiled and taken the pain-killer that Clive had given him, but had not once expressed hope of recovery. Once Clive had said fervently, "I wish there were something I could do for you, Mr. Corbeau."

Corbeau had studied the tall, young physician for a long time. "I am in God's hands, monsieur," he said. "It is as the good Lord wills—and it now seems to be His will for me to be with Him."

Leaning back in the chair, Clive rested his long frame and tried to think of some way to speak to Corbeau about the end that lay before him. There was a quietness and a peace in the man that puzzled Clive. Most men, when they faced death, were wary, afraid, or even bitter— or a hardened combination of all three. Corbeau had an almost placid air about him as he sat in the chair looking at the trees. A fox squirrel descended from a large fir, perched impotently on a limb, and barked at them, as if they had invaded its space.

"He might be good in a soup, that one," Corbeau smiled.

"Yes, but I couldn't hit him. I'm not much of a shot," Clive admitted.

"Your father, he is a soldier?"

"Yes—a colonel in the British army."

"Why are you not with him?" asked Pierre.

"I decided a long time ago that I would be a doctor. Soldiering is not a life that I would like."

"I suppose it is hard—little money and much risk."

"All very true, but it's not so much that," Clive replied thoughtfully. "A man can learn to endure hardness. My father has, and I suppose I could, too. But it seems to me that a man can do more than spend his life waiting for a war. That's what soldiers do, because in peacetime they are useless. They're an embarrassment to the government, and the public doesn't really care about them. With nothing to do, they spend their time drinking and carousing. Back in Boston, it has stirred up the general populace like a hive of angry hornets. It only makes the tension worse between the patriots and the British soldiers." He smiled bitterly, then shook his head. "But you let the first shot in a war come and then it's different. Then they are all heroes and everyone comes to applaud and shout as they march down the street with the drums pounding and the flags flying, but after the parade—there's nothing but danger and chances of getting your arm or leg blown off facing death."

"This war—what did you say it's about?"

"It's about one group of men, here in the Colonies, who want to rule themselves. There is another group of men in England who think they should remain loyal to the authority of the Crown."

Corbeau smiled briefly. He had taken a large dose of the laudanum Clive had given him and spoke slowly, his eyes slightly glazed over with the effect from the narcotic. "Me—I think I'd like to be with those who want to rule themselves." His eyes ran around the small clearing and the towering trees, then looked up at the blue skies overhead, where white billowing clouds rolled slowly by. "I've never liked to be told what to do. A man who has lived under tyranny likes his freedom. That's why I came to this place. Me and my dear wife, and then Jeanne was born. We live here and do as we please. Nobody bothers us. I don't even like to go to the settlements. Too many people! I think it is better that a man is not cluttered up by too many people."

"You may be right, Pierre. I grew up in the middle of thousands of people, and sometimes I feel so crowded that my head is going to explode. That's one thing about America—it's certainly not crowded! A man can always move on deeper into the forest if he doesn't like his neighbors, but I'm the sort of man who needs people. Most of us do." He examined Pierre curiously. "Don't you have any family, Pierre?" The question was not accidental. He had already been thinking about what would happen to Jeanne when death finally took her father, and had been intending to ask the man before it was too late.

Pierre shifted in the chair. He lifted a skeletal hand and scratched his forehead, then dropped it again into his lap. It fell like a stick, as if life had already drained from it, and his voice was slightly thickened as he said, "I have one half brother far away in Canada. I wouldn't know where to find him." He hesitated, then said, "I have one sister. She lives about fifteen miles west of Ticonderoga, but she is an invalid. I get a letter once in a while, then Jeanne answers it. We used to go to see her once or twice a year, but I have not seen her in three years now. Jeanne likes Ma Tante very much."

Clive considered the man's words. An aunt who was an invalid did not sound too promising as a guardian, but it might be the only alternative. "Ma Tante is her name?"

"In French that means 'my aunt.'"

"What about close friends? You've been here a long time—surely you must know some people by now."

"I know many hunters who pass through these mountains. They are like I am, some very ruthless, some wanting only to wander, going where they wish. A few I know in the settlement—but we're not close. I've thought of this often lately," he said slowly. "Maybe living so isolated out here has not been a good life for Jeanne. For me, for a man, it is all right—but for a young girl, I am not happy now about Jeanne."

The two men talked for a time, and by the time Jeanne came out of the woods, striding like a man and carrying her rifle lightly in her left hand and a brace of rabbits in her right, Clive's fears had been realized. *They have nobody,* he thought. He got up to greet the young woman as she approached them. *What in the world will happen to Jeanne when Pierre dies?* Aloud, he said, "Well, rabbit for supper, I see."

"Yes, fat, juicy ones!" Jeanne's face glowed from the exercise. She was a picture of health and moved as easily and quickly as a cat. There was nothing feminine in her actions, but there was in her appearance. She leaned the rifle against the cabin, tossed the rabbits down, and came over to kiss her father on the cheek. "Ah, you're outside," she said. "A beautiful day, Papa."

Pierre studied her for a moment and appeared to be ready to say something, but the drug had taken hold of him. "You had a good hunt?" he mumbled.

"Yes, Papa," she said, seeing that he was drugged. Soon Pierre asked to return to his bed. As Clive carried him inside and put him into bed, she waited outside the cabin.

When Clive stepped outside he saw that she had taken her hunting knife and was already skinning the rabbits. She did it so efficiently in two or three swift motions that he shook his head in admiration. "I don't see how you do that. I've tried to skin a few, but sometimes it's like skinning myself."

Jeanne held up one of the naked carcasses, and her white teeth flashed as she smiled. "By the time you skin two or three thousand, like me, you learn to do it well and fast." She continued to dress the rabbits, and then she looked up and said, "He is no better, is he, Doctor Gordon?"

"Jeanne, I wish you'd call me Clive. After all, you saved my life. I don't think we need to be quite so formal. I've been calling you Jeanne since I got here."

Jeanne flushed slightly. "All right—Clive." The rabbits were quickly cleaned, and she picked them up, saying, "I have to wash them off before we can cook them." She moved to the creek that held the cabin almost like an elbow. It was very small, no more than a foot or two across, but it was fed by a spring and was very cold. She washed the dressed rabbits, then her hands. Finally she came back to him and said, "I'll make some rabbit soup. Papa always likes that. Maybe he can eat some."

Moving inside the cabin, Clive watched as Jeanne quickly stirred up the coals and laid a few sticks on them that she kept for such purposes. The flames burst out almost at once, and within a few minutes she had a good fire blazing. Everything she did was efficient and well done, with no wasted energy. *She's learned how to live in this place without conveniences*, he thought. Most women he knew wouldn't be able to handle this. They wouldn't know what to do without their household accoutrements.

She hung one of the blackened pots over the fire and put one of the rabbits on to boil and the other on a spit. "This one's for us. Roasted rabbit, I think, tastes much better."

"Let's fix some tea," he said. "That's one thing I miss about England. The tea's much better there."

Fifteen minutes later, they were seated at the roughhewn table drinking tea. Jeanne's short, curly hair was glossy and lent a piquant air to her face. Her hands, he noticed as she sipped the tea, were strong and tanned to a golden color. As her lips curved around the cup, he was impressed again with the smoothness of her complexion and the beauty of her features.

"What do you do with yourself, Jeanne, when you're not setting the trapline or hunting?"

The question caught her off guard. "Why, I treat the furs. They have to be scraped and stretched. Sometimes I make furniture for the house—and I have a little garden behind the cabin that I have to keep the deer and coons out of."

"But what do you do at night in your spare time when you can't be out hunting or working?"

"Oh, I don't know." She seemed embarrassed by the question. Suddenly she looked up and smiled, and her eyes grew bright. "I read."

"You like to read?" he said, surprised at her answer.

"Oh yes. I have many books. Come, I will show you."

He had never been in her little room, which was no more than ten by ten and had evidently been added to the original cabin. As he stooped and stepped inside, she pointed proudly. "See—Papa put a window in just for me. When it rains I can lie here on my bed and read." She turned, motioning to a small bookshelf fashioned out of hand-hewn boards. "There, you see, I have many books."

Turning, Clive saw that the bookshelf contained some twenty or thirty books, mostly old and extremely worn from use. Stepping over, he picked one up and saw that it was a book by Daniel Defoe. "*Robinson Crusoe*," he smiled. "I've read this one. Do you like it?"

"Oh yes. That's one of my favorites." Her face glowed and she said, "He was a wise man, Mr. Crusoe, to make a life for himself out of nothing on a desert island. He would have made a good woodsman here in these mountains."

"Yes, but he got pretty lonely, though," Clive suggested. He handled the book carefully, for it was almost ready to fall apart. The pages had been worn thin, and as they talked about the story, Clive realized she had practically memorized it.

Finally, she picked up a different book, and her brow furrowed. "This one I do not understand, nor like."

He took the book she handed him and glanced at the title. "Why, this is *Clarissa!*" He had read the long novel by Samuel Richardson and had not particularly cared for it either. He glanced at her, asking, "You didn't like it?"

"No, it is silly, I think."

"Silly? I thought it was a little boring, but why do you say silly, Jeanne?"

"Why, this woman—she's always being chased for page after page after page." Jeanne shook her head in an explosive manner and slapped her hands together with disgust. "She is chased by this man all through the book. Why didn't she leave? That would have solved everything."

"Leave? Where would she have gone?" asked Clive, trying to suppress a smile.

"Anywhere!" Jeanne insisted. "She could have gone where he could not have followed her."

"That's not so easy in England—or maybe even in America," Clive said. "A woman doesn't have many options."

"I would have left, I promise you!" Jeanne exclaimed. Her cheeks were slightly flushed, and Clive could see that she'd been upset and angered by the book.

"The fellow who's chasing her is quite a villain," he said, speaking of the character in the book who had pursued Clarissa relentlessly. "But Clarissa didn't have much of a chance. If she'd gone somewhere else, some other man might have been after her. A woman was rather helpless in those days—even in these days for that matter."

"No, I am not helpless," she said vigorously.

Clive smiled. "I don't think you are," he said. "But there aren't many women like you—none that I know, anyway." His assertion startled her, and he saw that it troubled her for some reason.

"I am not like other women?" she asked, her voice tense and defensive. "Why do you say that?"

"Oh, I just meant that most women can't do all the things you do," Clive answered quickly. "You've been brought up to take care of yourself in a hard place. Most women let men do the hunting and things like that."

"I would not be any different." Jeanne seemed troubled by the thought and turned to show him the rest of her collection of books.

After a few minutes they returned to the table by the fireplace and sat down for another cup of tea. Clive said, "Your father is not a great reader."

"No, he reads the Bible and that is all, I think. I tried to get him to read *Robinson Crusoe*, but he said it was all make-believe and not true.

65

But he knows the Bible, I think, almost by heart."

"Is he a Catholic?" Most people of French descent in this part of the world were Catholic, and Clive expected the girl to say yes. However, she shook her head.

"No—we have no church here. When we go there is a Methodist mission, but it is fifty miles away. We do not go often. Are you a Christian?" she asked abruptly.

"Why . . . I'm a member of the Church of England," Clive said, taken aback by her question.

"What is that? Is that like Methodist?" she asked, puzzled at his response.

Clive laughed. "The leadership of my church would be offended if you said that."

"They do not like Methodist?"

"They say the Methodists are—enthusiastic—that they shout and carry on and that they have extreme views." Seeing she seemed genuinely interested, Clive went on to expound to her the differences between the Anglican Church and the growing movement led by John Wesley.

When he'd finished, she said simply, "Why cannot everyone just be Christians? Why do there have to be so many differences?"

"Many have asked that very same question, but none have answered it," he said regretfully. "Are you a Christian, Jeanne?"

"Oh yes," she said. "My father, he has taught me all my life, and I gave my heart to God when I was only twelve years old."

This was only one of the many talks that Jeanne and Clive had over the next few days. The young woman would often disappear mysteriously into the woods and come back with food, or berries, or roots that she stored in a small shed, along with the smoked meat. She felt easier in his presence and questioned him incessantly about city life.

One day she said, "Come—we'll go hunting. We'll see what kind of a shot you are."

Clive went willingly, and the two walked quite a distance into the thick forest. Jeanne led the way, and he followed closely behind, stopping when she stopped to listen or glance at tracks on the ground. He was amazed at the things she noticed that had not drawn his attention. He had watched with admiration as she picked almost instinctively where her feet would fall, knowing which stone would roll, which branch would give and crackle, and the kind of underbrush that would give way. She avoided these without effort, while Clive seemed to stumble along behind her like an awkward cow.

Finally they moved into a stand of large fir trees that rose above the forest floor and almost blocked out the sun. The secluded spot was dim and deathly still, and it seemed the ground underneath their feet was spongy and damp. There was a quietness that reminded Clive of the time that he had stood in Westminster Cathedral late one night, and the silence had seemed to be almost a palpable living thing. The solemnity and grandeur in these tall trees in the deep woods impressed him.

Finally, she led him to a stream that wound itself tenuously through the heavy woods. It gurgled and purled at their feet. Standing on the edge of it, she said, "Here—see that?"

He looked down at the ground but saw nothing. "What is it?" he inquired curiously.

"Don't you see it? Look—deer tracks," she said, pointing to the moist soil near the edge of the stream.

Leaning forward, Clive stared at the footprints. Finally he stood up and said, "I guess so, but I wouldn't have seen them if you hadn't pointed them out to me."

"They're fresh," she said. "It's always easy to get a deer here. Come on." She led him to a concealed spot behind some bushes and turned to him, saying, "Now, you have to be absolutely still and you will see."

It was, Clive discovered, one of the most difficult things he had ever tried to do. To remain absolutely still was more of a challenge than he expected. The girl stood there as if frozen. Her head did not move, and the rifle held in her hands was as still as if it were made of marble. He himself was tormented with an itchy nose, and his foot went to sleep almost at once. Determined not to be outdone by a mere slip of a girl, he stood there as immobile as he could! After a few minutes he began to notice things he would not have noticed otherwise: a white flower that was dangling from a branch not ten feet away. It was as beautiful as any he had ever seen, though he did not know the name of it. A slight movement caught his eye, and without moving his head, he glanced around and saw a mouse that had tiny white feet emerging from a hammock of grass—obviously its nest. Soon, four baby mice came trundling out. They apparently did not see the figures that loomed over them, and for a time Clive enjoyed watching the mice nurse and roll and play, while the mother would sit up frequently, her whiskers twitching and her tiny round eyes alert.

Finally, without warning, a magnificent buck stepped out into the small clearing near the stream not fifty feet away. His large antlers swung from side to side, and he was poised to spring away at the first sign of danger. Jeanne whispered, "Shoot, Clive!" He swung his rifle up, and the deer, catching the sudden motion, wheeled. Clive fired but knew with a keen sense of disappointment that he had missed. Two seconds later, Jeanne's rifle barked, and the buck fell midstride to the ground. He was up again almost instantly and disappeared, crashing into the thick brush. "I missed him clean, but I think you wounded him."

"Yes, he won't go more than a hundred yards," Jeanne said confidently. "He's a nice one, too." She followed the tracks of the deer by the scarlet drops of blood that she pointed out to Clive along the track. Shortly they found the large deer, like she said, less than a hundred yards away.

"How in the world will we haul him back to the cabin?" Clive asked, looking at the size of the large animal.

"We could go bring a pack horse back, but this time I think we'll just dress him out and take what we can carry."

Again he was impressed at how comfortable she felt in the middle of this wilderness. As efficient as any man, Jeanne dressed the deer skillfully as Clive watched. The knife she used must have been as sharp as a razor, and she knew exactly how to remove the hide and slice between the joints. It was, he thought, as easy for her as it was for a city woman to shop for a new dress. Finally, loaded down with the quarters and the liver, which she said her father loved, they started back to the cabin. Knowing that Jeanne had to take two steps for each of his one, he was embarrassed that she had to stop and wait for him at least once. His pride was ruffled, and he muttered, "It's because I've been ill." Deep within, he knew that was not so. A lifetime of this kind of arduous activity had strengthened the young woman till she was the equal of almost any man he knew, the superior of most.

When they arrived, she said, "Will you wash the meat off? I want to go see how Papa is."

"Of course," said Clive. He carried the meat to the small creek and proceeded to wash it.

When he was finished, he moved it to the front of the cabin. Not knowing what to do with it, he carried it inside and put it beside the fireplace. His legs were a little stiff after the long walk.

He went over to one of the chairs, sat down at the table, and thought about the situation. *I've got to get back soon. Mother and Father will be worried about me. I don't know whether to go back to the fort or press on to Boston. I guess Boston would be the best.* Jeanne came out as he was considering this, and he asked, "Is he awake?"

"Yes." Her face was drawn up tight and she seemed pale. She walked over to the fireplace and stared down unseeingly at the quarters of venison that he had placed there. She did not speak for quite a while, and Clive grew concerned.

"Is he in a lot of pain?" he asked quietly.

"Yes, he is." Jeanne turned and there was torment in her eyes. Her lips were drawn into a taut line, and she was fighting desperately to keep back the fear and anxiety that rose in her. "Can't you do *anything*?" she asked. "He's dying."

Clive lowered his head and gritted his teeth. He had been through this moment before with families of patients who were approaching their end. As always there was nothing easy to say, but somehow it was different with this young girl who had pulled him back from the brink of death alone in the forest. Somehow, in this short time he had grown close to Pierre. At the same time he was deeply impressed by the dying man's dignity and courage in the face of such an agonizing death. Lifting his eyes, Clive studied her for a moment, then said quietly, "There's nothing anyone can do, Jeanne. The finest doctor in the world wouldn't be able to help. It's his time to go."

His words seemed to strike her like a blow. She had fought against letting this realization come into her heart and mind. Somehow she had hoped and prayed for a miracle, but each day her father had continually grown weaker and weaker. The intense pain squeezed him like a large steel trap and had become almost unbearable. Without a word, she turned and ran from the small cabin. Clive did not hear the sound of her feet as she moved outside and into the woods, but he knew how soundlessly she could walk. He expected that she had gone out to weep in private, not wanting him to see her overwhelming grief. Suddenly he raised a fist and struck the table with a powerful blow that rattled it and knocked the teacups to the floor. One of them broke, but he ignored it.

"Blast!" he exclaimed. "Blast it all! Why did it have to happen to these two?"

T   T   T

The yellow light of the single candle illuminated the gaunt face of Pierre, making his stark, ravaged features even more pronounced and harsh. Jeanne leaned forward, smoothing the dry hair that had once been lustrous from her father's forehead. She had sat beside him now for hours, saying very little and watching his face. For a while she had read his favorite Bible passages to him, and he had listened as always, but then he drifted off into a comalike trance. This is what frightened her—that he might slip away and never turn his gentle eyes of love on her again.

Finally, she laid the Bible on the table, rose stiffly, and left the small bedroom. She was surprised to find Clive Gordon still seated at the table. The oil lamp had been placed on the shelf behind him, illuminating the book that he was reading. He glanced up quickly.

"You're up late," she said.

"I couldn't sleep." Clive closed the book and looked at it. His eyes were gritty from lack of sleep, and he said, "I've never read this one before. I suppose you've read it many times."

Jeanne looked at the book, which was a collection of sermons by George Whitefield, the famous evangelist. "Yes, I have."

"I've heard a lot about Whitefield. He was a great friend of Benjamin Franklin, they say."

"We heard him preach once," Jeanne said. "I've never forgotten it. It was the only time I've ever left here, other than to visit my aunt a few times. My father had heard so much about Whitefield that he wanted to hear him preach. I was only twelve years old, but we traveled all the way to Philadelphia."

"People say Whitefield preached to thousands, and that he had a voice like a bell. I've heard that people fell down to the ground when he preached—at least that's what his enemies said about him."

"It's true enough. I saw it for myself," Jeanne said, looking at Clive.

The thought disturbed Clive. He was actually a straitlaced young man, rather provincial in his ways. "It's not seemly," he said, "for people to fall down in church and writhe on the ground."

"This wasn't in church—it was outside. You couldn't have gotten that many people in a church, because there were thousands of them."

Clive questioned her closely about the great evangelist and found that her memory was sharp down to the smallest detail. Finally, he said, "It sounds—uncivilized to me. I don't like it much. I'd rather experience my religion nice and organized and inside a church like it ought to be."

"Isn't God outside?" Jeanne demanded sharply. From their talks she had noticed that Clive Gordon was rather stiff and had some strange ideas about things. Now she discovered that he had his views on religion nicely boxed and labeled. From his comments she sensed that he preferred services to take place in a certain kind of building, and the ministers to have certain qualifications. And people had to react in a respectable fashion. She also saw that his ideas of God were far different from hers. She asked abruptly, "Is God real to you, Clive?"

"Why—" The question caught him off guard and embarrassed him. "I . . . I don't know what you mean," he stammered.

"I mean, has God ever spoken to you?"

"Certainly not! Well, except through his ministers, of course," Clive said, a bit uncomfortable about her probing question.

Jeanne was weary from the long hours of watching her father. "He's real to my father," she said, glancing toward her father's room. "And He's spoken to him too, many times."

Clive thought this was nothing but part of the love and respect that Jeanne had for her father. He smiled, saying, "I suppose we differ in these things." He changed the subject quickly, for the discussion of religion with this young woman was making him feel uneasy. Religion was supposed to be personal and private. Yet he had felt the same thing with Pierre. Pierre had asked some penetrating questions about Clive's personal feelings about God. Since Clive had few of these, he had tried to avoid the issue as much as possible. Now, however, he quickly turned and said, "Have you ever thought of getting married, Jeanne? How old are you—seventeen?" He saw her flush at the question and realized that she had never spoken of such things with him.

"Yes, I'm seventeen," she said.

"But what about getting married? Many young women are married by the time they are your age."

"I . . . don't think about it very much." The truth was that she had had none of the usual opportunities most young women her age had to meet eligible men. Those she had met were rough hunters, most of them either already married or confirmed bachelors. Her few visits to the settlement had been lacking in the sort of male companionship that most young women long for. She had scandalized some of the people by wearing men's clothing, and the rumor that had spread through the settlement was that she was "strange." There had been sneers and giggles from some of the young women in the settlement when she would appear with her father on rare occasions to purchase supplies. A few young men had shown boldness and made some ribald remarks to her but had been quickly rebuffed by her father. The only knowledge of love, courtship, and marriage she had all came from stilted novels that bore little relationship to real life. She was awkward and embarrassed with talk about it, and now the bright blue eyes of Clive Gordon made her uncomfortable. "I don't want to talk about this thing," she said abruptly. "I'm going to bed."

Clive was not surprised by Jeanne's reluctance to speak of such things. He had surmised that her knowledge of men was confined to a few rough hunters and her own father. *What's going to become of her?* Clive thought, drumming his fingers on the table. *She's afraid of love, and she's afraid of being a woman. . . .* He sat there for a long time and finally nodded his head. "I'll have to talk to her," he said. "She has to change. She can't go around wearing buckskins all of her life. She's got to find a husband. That's all there is for a woman in this world."

71

The next night Jeanne was roasting more of the deer she had killed. She had said little that morning, and obviously hadn't slept much, for her eyes had dark circles under them. Finally, Clive, who had slept poorly himself, rose and went to where she stood before the fire. "Jeanne," he said, "let me talk to you." He waited till she turned to face him. Then he took the cooking fork out of her hand and said, "Come over here."

"What do you want?" she asked, alarmed, as he took her hand and seated her at the small table. She thought he had something to say about her father, and her eyes grew wide with apprehension. She knew what was happening to her father, but somehow putting it into words made it more final.

"Jeanne," he said, turning to her and looking down at her from his great height, "you're going to have to—well, you're going to have to make some changes in your life."

"Changes? What kind of changes?" she said, looking up with eyes filled with fear.

"You can't stay out here by yourself. You've got to go where there are people."

"I don't want to hear this."

She stood up and started to leave, but he took her by her shoulders and said, "Listen to me, Jeanne. You must listen. You're going to have to learn a different kind of life. When your father is gone, what then?" This is what he had wanted to say to her for several days, and now he spoke earnestly. "I hate to speak of this, but you're going to have to make a new life for yourself. And to do that you have to make—well, you'll have to become different."

Her eyes were enormous as she looked up at him with a stiffness in her back. Jeanne was aware of his hands holding her shoulders, but she did not try to get away. "What kind of difference do you mean?"

"Well, you'll have to change the way you dress. You can't go around wearing buckskin all your life. Don't you even have a dress?"

"There's nothing wrong with the way I dress!" she said, annoyed at his words.

"Not for out here, but after all, it isn't very feminine."

"I don't care about that."

"Well, you *should* care." He grew a little more insistent. "You're a young woman, and you've got to start to think and act like one. You're going to *have* to find a husband."

Jeanne Corbeau stared up at him for a moment. Then she struck his hands away. "I don't need a man!" she said, her lips drawn thin.

Clive stared at her and blinked in surprise. "Of course you need a man," he said. "Every woman does."

But Jeanne shook her head and repeated, "I don't need a man. I can get along all by myself. And don't talk to me about this again!"

Clive watched her as she whirled and walked back to the fireplace. Her back was stiff as a ramrod, and he realized that her situation was worse than he'd thought. Somehow he had expected that she would agree, for it seemed so logical to him.

What he did not know was the fear of change that gripped the young woman's heart. Living off the land in this wilderness with the skills her father had taught her over the years was her life. She had never known any other life but the one she had. She feared exactly what he had spoken of—finding a man. That had lingered in her restless thoughts for some time now, but she had put it away, not wanting to face the necessity for making a decision. Jeanne was very much aware of his eyes on her, and she did not turn around for a very long time. When she did, she saw that he was still standing in the same place.

"You have to let people help," he said quietly.

There was a firm insistence in his voice, and she sensed also that there was a gentleness in him that she yearned to respond to; but stubbornly she shook her head and said tightly, "No, I don't need anybody." She moved past him and went back into her father's bedroom, leaving Clive standing there, gazing at the door with a rising sense of alarm.

"She's got to change," he said aloud. "She can't go on like this. . . !"

73

6

A QUIET PASSING

PIERRE CORBEAU LINGERED ON for only two days after Clive had attempted to reason with Jeanne. For the most part he lay unconscious, sometimes his breath so faint that Jeanne would lean over, holding her own and listening. The pain that had racked his body for days seemed to have left except for brief spasms. A silent truce existed between Clive and Jeanne. The difficult words that he had spoken about her bleak future had raised a wall—or at least he felt so. He said no more to her about what he felt she should do, for her grief had caused her to withdraw.

On Monday morning, Corbeau awoke suddenly. Both Jeanne and Clive were sitting beside his bed, keeping a constant vigil. The silence between them had thickened in the room, so that it was almost palpable. As they both listened to the raspy, irregular breathing of the dying man, Clive expected that each breath would be the last.

A mockingbird began to utter its peculiar call outside the house, a whirring sound that at times broke into a melodic song. It seemed incongruous—the happiness and joyfulness of the bird's singing filtering into the room where the two living sat in vigilance beside the dying.

Jeanne was physically exhausted. She had slept very little for two nights, and now an intense weariness caused her bones to ache. She was holding her father's thin hand in her own. It seemed cold, already lifeless. She patted it from time to time and made an inarticulate sound deep in her breast. As she watched her father slip from this world, her hopes seemed to die like a candle about to flicker out. She knew now that the end had come. When Pierre opened his eyes, she leaned forward and whispered instantly, "Papa, do you know me?"

"Yes, Cherie—"

His voice was almost inaudible, a mere wisp of air, but his eyes opened wider and he seemed to draw some strength from deep within.

74

His skin was waxen, but a touch of color suddenly appeared in his cheeks, and Clive leaned forward expectantly. *I don't see how he's held on this long*, he thought. *He can't go on much longer.*

Corbeau turned his head and studied the tall man, with a strange look on his face. With an effort, he whispered, "You have been good—may God bless you, my dear Gordon."

Somehow the words touched Clive deeply, and he felt his eyes mist over as he swallowed hard, forcing down the knot of grief that rose within him. Reaching over, he took the dying man's hand, squeezed it gently, and said earnestly, "I will do what I can for your daughter."

"Will you do that?" rasped the man.

"Yes, I promise, you have my word," Clive said, his voice choked.

Corbeau managed to squeeze Gordon's hand one more time, and then suddenly his chest began to heave. He turned quickly to Jeanne and in a faltering voice said, "Goodbye, Cherie. I . . . go to the good Lord—and to your dear mother. . . ."

Jeanne was leaning over, her face close to her father's, and she felt the last bit of strength leave the frail body. There was a relaxing, and it was as though he had simply dropped off to sleep. But there was a stillness in him that she knew was final. "Papa . . . Papa, don't leave me!" She threw herself across the dead man's chest and began to sob uncontrollably.

Clive Gordon had never felt more helpless in his life. He had been at the bedside of the dying before and had felt grief—but this time it was different. He felt somehow involved in it, so that the pangs of loss that the girl was suffering were joined to him. Awkwardly, after a time, he reached out and put his hand on her shoulder. "He's gone, Jeanne," he said quietly. When she turned her tear-stained face to look at him, he said, "I've never seen a man go to meet his God with more courage—or more dignity. He was a noble man, this father of yours!"

Jeanne stared at Clive for a moment; with trembling lips she struggled against the sobs that rose within her but managed to conquer them. Dashing the tears away, she reached out and began to straighten the thin arms across the chest.

"Let me do that," Clive said at once. He was glad when she rose quickly, as though released by his words, and almost ran out of the room. He sat beside the body of the man that he had learned to love in just a few days and wondered aloud, "If I went to meet God, could I go as easily as Pierre?" Then because he knew the answer to that, he shook his head and sat there for a long time, thinking about the fate that had brought him to this isolated cabin in the middle of the wilderness at such a time.

🛑   🛑   🛑

The two stood beside the grave that Clive had dug. He had asked Jeanne early the next morning where she would like to bury her father, and she had taken him to a small clearing not far from the cabin where a stone marked the final resting place of Mary Carter Corbeau. It was on high ground, surrounded by tall trees. "He always loved this place," Jeanne had said. "That's why he buried my mother here." Her face had been pale and tear-stained, and these were the first words she had spoken of her own will. "He came here often to sit and pray among these trees. He told me once that he felt very close to my mother in this place."

Clive had dug the grave and had washed and dressed the body in buckskins. He had fashioned a plain casket out of boards that he had found in the shed. It was not much, but he had worked all morning on it. Jeanne had come to look at it, and he could tell that she was touched by the dignity he was bestowing on her father. Finally, she had brought a blanket and put it in the bottom of the roughhewn casket. Clive then placed the wasted body of Pierre Corbeau inside. He was grateful for his restored strength, for he had lowered the casket into the grave by using some rawhide thongs, and then the two had stood over it. He stood there feeling helpless, a gentle breeze stirring the trees around them.

Finally Jeanne had bowed her head and said a short prayer over her father. It had been simple, and her voice had broken once, but she had collected herself and stepped back. She had looked at Clive, her violet eyes bathed in tears and her lips drawn into a tight line as she held control of herself. "Would you say a prayer too, Clive? He loved you very much. Even though you only knew him a short time, he saw something in you that he liked. I could tell."

Clive had never prayed before in public. He had read printed prayers aloud in church, but this was very different. A helpless feeling seized him, but he knew he could not deny Jeanne this simple request. Bowing his head, he said in a rather faltering fashion, "Oh, God, you knew this man and—he knew you. He was a good man; even I could see it in a short time. My Lord, you have taken him to be—to come to you. We commend him to you—until the resurrection." He searched desperately for something else and finally he added, "Bless this daughter that he loved so much—in the name of Jesus, Amen."

It had not been an eloquent prayer, but Jeanne cried softly, somehow touched by the heartfelt manner in which it had been spoken. She whispered, "Thank you, Clive," then reached for the shovel.

"I'll do it. Why don't you go for a walk down by the creek? I'll come along and join you later."

"All right, I think I will," she said, then turned and headed down the path toward the creek.

As soon as she was out of sight, Clive filled in the shallow grave, grateful that she did not have to hear the dreadful sounds of the clods falling on the top of the wooden casket. He worked hard and made a mound, thinking when he was through, *I need to make a marker of some kind for the grave. Jeanne would like that.*

Afterward he walked down the path and along the creek and found her sitting on a rock, looking down at the clear pool. The minnows in the clear water made silvery shadows, darting back and forth. He sat down beside her, wrapped his arms around his knees, and said nothing. She did not speak either, and it felt strange to him. For nearly an hour they sat there in silence, each engulfed in their own grief. He, for his part, could think of nothing to say, but he sensed that she was glad for his presence.

Finally, she rose and said quietly, "I will go fix us something to eat." She walked back up the path, and he quietly followed her back to the cabin.

Clive watched as Jeanne busied herself fixing a simple meal in the quiet cabin. One time as she was stirring the pot that hung over the fire, he noticed her looking toward the room where her father had lain sick for so many days. The sudden shudder of her shoulders and the tears that ran down her cheeks did not escape him. He too sat in silent grief for the man who, after losing his young wife had given all his love and devotion to this lovely daughter, who now was all alone.

When the meal was ready, they sat down at the small table and spoke quietly about incidental things. Clive wanted to say something, anything to try to ease her grief, but nothing came. As soon as they had finished, Jeanne gathered up the dishes and quickly washed them as Clive sat and silently watched the flames flicker in the hearth.

When she was done, she said, "Good night, Clive," and went to the privacy of her small bedroom.

Clive sat at the table for a long time. He picked up the Bible that had belonged to Corbeau, opened it, and tried to read the words, not understanding much of it for it was in French. Finally, he went to bed.

Jeanne heard his movements, for she had not gone to sleep. She lay awake for a long time, her fist against her lips to keep the sobs back. Finally, however, she rolled over, shut her eyes, and fell to sleep.

The next morning Clive was surprised to see Jeanne looking so well. He expected her terrible loss would have overwhelmed her and left her in bed for a while. Though sadness and grief had left their traces on her face, when Jeanne came out of her bedroom and stood before him there was something different about her.

"Good morning," she said quietly.

"Good morning, Jeanne. Did you sleep?"

"I . . . I slept very well."

She hesitated, and he knew that she meant to say more than this. Somehow, though, he sensed the shyness that came over her. *I'll have to be very careful*, he thought. *I can't rush her, but she can't stay in this place alone.* Aloud, he said, "I'd like to have some eggs for breakfast. Do you suppose those hens of yours have produced anything?"

"I'll go see," Jeanne said quickly. She went outside and, to her surprise, found three eggs. The hen clucked loudly in protest at her as she removed them, but Jeanne smiled and said, "You'll have to do it again, Amy. I need these." Going inside, she held them up and smiled. "Two for you and one for me."

"Sounds right," Clive said, glad for the note of cheer in her voice. "Maybe some of that bacon would taste good, too, and I think there are some biscuits left over."

They made an affair of fixing breakfast. Once, he made a remark that she found humorous, and he was amazed to hear her laugh. He stole a glance at her and could tell that something was on her mind that he could not understand. Again he purposed to give her the time she needed. After all, she had saved his life, and he had promised Pierre that he would do what he could to help her now that she was all alone.

They spent the day in a leisurely fashion. Jeanne went off later in the morning, to be alone, he supposed. He stayed inside and passed the time reading one of the tattered books from her bookcase—a novel by a man named Sterne—and wondered what in the world Jeanne got out of it. When she came back, he asked her, "Have you tried to read this book?"

"I think it's crazy. I couldn't even understand it. What's it about?"

"Beats me. I think the man's insane." The two read several more passages of *Tristram Shandy* and were amused at it together.

Late that afternoon, they went walking through the woods. He had intentionally avoided the path that led to the tall stand of trees where Pierre's grave was, thinking that it was too early for Jeanne to face that. They crossed the tiny creek, then followed it upstream for a distance, listening to the babbling of the clear, cold water.

Clive began hesitantly, "Jeanne, I've been thinking about you and what you must do." He saw her head lift and steeled himself. The last time he had tried to meddle in her business it had turned out badly, but he knew he had to try again. "You can't stay here alone. Oh, I know," he held his hand up to her quickly, "you can cook and hunt and do everything as well as a man. You're strong and quick and better than any man in the woods, I think, but it's no life for a young woman. There's no future in it. You need people."

"What . . . do you want me to do? I don't know anybody. My aunt is an invalid, and we haven't heard from my uncle in years. I suppose I could go try to get a job in the village, but I don't know how to do any of those things. All I know is the woods."

"I want you to think about something, Jeanne," Clive said carefully. "You don't have to answer right now." Ever since he realized Pierre had been failing he had thought about a possible solution, and was convinced that what he was about to say was right. "My mother and my sister would love to have you. My father and brother, too, of course. David's younger than I am, and you'd like my father. We have a nice house in Boston. I don't know how long I will be there, since I'll be busy doctoring, but I assume my father will be in Boston for some time. "

Clive was watching Jeanne's face, which was turned to him. Taking a deep breath, he said, "Why don't you come with me? Just call it a visit. It would be good for you to get away for a while. If it doesn't work, you could always come back." He put the matter to her as gently as he could, and he saw her drop her head. *I've hurt her feelings again*, he thought desperately. *Lord, I wish I knew how to talk to her!* "It was just a thought, Jeanne," he said hurriedly. "You don't have to make any decisions now."

Jeanne had been moved by his kind words and his generous offer. She lifted her head finally, the black curls framing her oval face. Her hair was so black it was almost purple, and her eyes were enormous. "Thank you, Clive," she whispered. She hesitated, then shocked him by saying, "I will go with you—at least for a visit."

"You *will*! Why, that's wonderful, Jeanne!" Clive's face grew animated and his tone expressed his happiness. "It'll take a day or two to get things arranged and then we'll go."

"All right, I'll do as you say," she said quietly.

All day Jeanne stayed busy. She felt that someday she might come back, but she had to take care of the animals now. They had only two pigs, some chickens, and a milking cow. She would take the horses with her, and she knew she could sell the other animals to Pete Tyler, who lived nine miles away—an old bachelor who didn't really need them but would be happy to take them off of Jeanne's hands.

The next day they drove the animals to Tyler's shack, which was located in an isolated hollow with a stream nearby. "You should have told me that Pierre died," the old man said. "I would have come to the funeral." He shook his head, saying, "He was a good man." He was a short fellow with dark eyes and a shock of rough, gray hair. "You going to be home, Jeanne?" He looked at the tall man beside her, his eyes questioning.

Jeanne said quickly, "I'm going to go visit some friends in Boston. Mr. Gordon's taking me. I appreciate your buying the animals, Pete."

As soon as Pete Tyler paid for the animals, Jeanne thanked him and turned to leave. She could tell that the man was hoping she would have stayed around. Riding in silence, she breathed a silent prayer for the wisdom of the dream and the kind man alongside her who was willing to help her face the changes that lay ahead. To remain alone in the cabin would eventually have invited trouble.

When they got back to the cabin, Jeanne spent the rest of the afternoon making final preparations to leave. After finishing the packing, she made a quick meal for them out of a pheasant she had shot on the way back from Tyler's. They spoke some about the long trip ahead of them, but then Jeanne washed the dishes for the final time and excused herself to retire early.

The next morning they boarded up the cabin. The horses were packed, and Jeanne felt ashamed at the pitiful baggage that she had. She owned only two dresses—one that she wore to work around the cabin, and another that she had worn the few times they had gone to church in a nearby settlement. And she had only enough personal things to fill one bag.

Before they left, Clive said tentatively, "Do you want to wear a dress, Jeanne?"

She looked at him strangely. "No, it would be hard to ride with a dress on. I'll put one on when we get to Boston."

Clive had a sharp, painful thought of what it would look like riding down the streets of Boston with a beautiful young woman dressed in buckskins, but he did not argue with her. All she had ever known was the hard life of the woods. He couldn't expect her to change so quickly. He decided he would best leave those matters to the gentle influence of his mother and sister. They would, no doubt, enjoy doting on her.

They left at once, and he talked a great deal to keep her occupied as they rode side by side. They had not gone far when they met a trapper on the trail from Ticonderoga. They talked for a few moments and then Clive asked, "Things all right at the fort?"

The traveler, a short, fat man with a bushy beard, shook his head. "You ain't heard? The rebels took the fort—some soldiers under the command of Ethan Allen and Benedict Arnold. Unless you got business, I expect you better not let them catch you. Ethan Allen's a rough one, so they say. Him and Benedict Arnold, they've got the Englishmen locked up in jail."

A shock ran through Clive, and he carried on the conversation in a desultory manner. He made an excuse to get away as soon as they could.

When they were farther down the trail, Jeanne turned in her saddle and asked, "What does that mean?"

"I guess it means that my father's mission was a failure. General Gage will be sorry to hear news of this."

They followed the main trails on the way back to Boston. It was on the night before they were due to arrive on the outskirts of the city that they were sitting by the campfire. They had cooked and eaten two squirrels that Jeanne had knocked out of a tree with shots from her rifle. Clive had been amazed at her marksmanship with the long gun, for she had shot them both in the head.

She'd smiled at him, saying, "It doesn't mess up the meat that way."

That night Jeanne had been rather quiet and he asked, "What's wrong?"

"I'm worried about what happens when I get with your people. What if I don't fit in, Clive?"

"Oh, don't worry. They're going to love you. You'll see, and you'll learn to love them, Jeanne."

"I don't know—" She looked at him plaintively across the fire. "I don't know *anything*, Clive! I don't know how to dress—or how to talk proper. They'll laugh at me!"

Clive rose to get a piece of wood. He tossed it on the fire and sat down beside her. "I don't want you to worry about this," he said. "It'll be all right."

She lifted her head and looked so sad that he put his arm around her and whispered, "Don't worry, Jeanne. My mother and my sister— they'll teach you everything. And you'll make friends—lots of them."

"But I don't know how—"

Suddenly, as her face was turned toward him, he was aware of how intensely feminine the curve of her lips was. Clive was not particularly known as a ladies' man, but there was an innocent sweetness in Jeanne that he had never seen in another woman. He reached around and pulled her close, whispering, "You're so sweet, Jeanne," then he kissed her.

Jeanne was taken completely off guard. His lips were on hers before she knew what he was doing. She remained still, feeling the strength of his arms, and there was a need in her that responded to him. Having lost the only person that mattered in life to her, here was one who was strong and who had helped when she had needed it. She was frightened at the feelings that rose in her at the touch of his lips on hers. She had only read about kissing in books, but there was a warmth and insistence that she did not understand. She did not understand, either, the strange emotions that she felt. She knew that these were not the impulses of a child, but of a woman.

She drew back then abruptly and said, "I . . . I wish you hadn't done that, Clive."

"It was just a kiss," he said, half ashamed of himself. He had been shocked at the softness of the young woman as she leaned against him, the velvet lips beneath his. Now he said hastily, "I shouldn't have done it—but I feel very close to you, Jeanne." He wanted to kiss her again, but he knew that wouldn't be wise. He got up, went around to the other side of the fire, and rolled up in his blankets.

Finally, after staring into the fire for a long time, Jeanne rolled into her blankets. She thought about what had happened, and knew that it would be a long time before she would be able to forget what her first kiss was like.

PART TWO

BATTLE FOR A HILL

May–June 1775

7

Too Many Generals

CLIVE GORDON HAD SPENT MOST OF HIS LIFE inside heavily protected structures: houses, churches, and college buildings. He had been protected from the outdoors for the most part, and on the journey from Ticonderoga to Boston, he had been amazed at the wealth of knowledge about nature that Jeanne Corbeau had filed away in her head. No matter what he pointed to, she knew the name of every bird, bush, and tree along the way! Now as they urged their weary animals forward, hoping to reach the outskirts of Boston before nightfall, Clive saw a clump of tall plants, some of them ten feet high, beside the road. They had purple-pink leaves, and the branches were loaded down with a dark purplish berry that a flock of birds were gorging themselves on.

"What sort of plant is that, Jeanne?" Clive asked, turning to glance at her.

Jeanne was still wearing her tan buckskins, for riding in a dress all that distance would have been impossible. Yet even after a long day's ride she appeared fresh. Casting one glance at the plants, she shrugged as she replied, "Some people call them pokeweed. Papa called them *garget*."

"Are the berries good to eat?"

"Some people like them. As you can see, the birds fill up on them. Ma Tante makes a remedy for rheumatism out of them. She calls them 'red-ink plant.'" Turning to him, she added, "The roots of the old plants are poisonous, but when the young shoots come up, you can boil them and eat them. They're very good with a pinch of salt."

"I wish I knew as much about plants and birds as you do."

Jeanne dropped her eyes for a moment. Being a natural rider, she moved instinctively with the movement of the horse. The sun had given a slightly golden tint to her skin, and her black hair glistened in the rays of the fading sun. After a time she said rather wistfully, "I wish I knew more about your kind of life."

Clive glanced at her, knowing that she was worried about what would happen when they reached Boston. "Don't worry, Jeanne. You'll pick it up in no time."

The two had been headed for the lifting hills that flanked Boston. Now as they drew closer, Clive grew somewhat apprehensive. "I hope that some *patriot* doesn't take a shot at us," he muttered. "Hard to tell what's happening since I've been gone—but I suspect these woods are full of patriot rebels."

By now the fast-falling darkness was casting long shadows across the road. Half an hour later as they were following the crooked road, they were stopped by a small band of men, all carrying rifles ready at hand. Instantly, Clive and Jeanne pulled their horses up short, and Clive called out quickly, "I'm trying to reach Boston before nightfall." He hesitated, then said, "My name is Clive Gordon."

A short, muscular man wearing a brown shirt and black breeches studied the two with a pair of steady gray eyes. "Why you headed for Boston?" His voice was high-pitched and rather gravelly—and he did not relax his stance or lower his rifle, which was pointed directly at Clive.

Clive thought quickly. The very fact that he was the son of a colonel in the British army was enough to get him into serious trouble. Hurriedly he said, "I'm trying to escort this lady to my parents' home. She just lost her father."

The eyes of the men had all been fixed, more or less, on Clive, but now they shifted to Jeanne—who flushed as she met the gaze of the leader. A smile touched the lips of the stocky man. He seemed ready to make a remark but apparently changed his mind. "We'll have to have more information than that," he said. "There's a war going on—and you both might be spies, for all I know."

"We'd better take them in, Matthews," said a tall, lanky individual. "Let the officers question them and decide."

The man called Matthews nodded. "I suppose that would be best. Come along."

Clive touched his heels to his horse. Jeanne moved her own mount close beside him, and they were quickly surrounded by the small group of patriots. There was little conversation, and when they had ridden no more than a quarter of a mile, Clive saw a camp on the crest of a hill. He found that he was sweating, for he could think of nothing more unpleasant than being accused of being a spy and thrust into a dank cell. As they approached, he saw that there were no men in uniform, but what appeared to be a leaderless mob. Some of them were wearing buckskins and carrying long rifles, while others were apparently farmers, carrying no firearms at all. He felt nervous around mobs, which this group appeared to be, for the lack of a leader often meant chaos and danger, for certain.

"Lieutenant, these two say they're headed for Boston. This woman has lost her father—or so this fellow says."

A man of average height wearing a blue shirt and black knee breeches came to stand before them. "You can get off your horses," he said briefly. "I'm Lieutenant Ascott. We'll have to have some more information, I'm afraid."

The lieutenant was an older man, in his early fifties, as far as Clive could judge. He waited until they had dismounted, then took their names, putting his interested gaze on Jeanne, who stood silently by the head of her horse.

"Do you know anyone that can identify you?" Ascott asked suddenly.

Clive realized the difficult predicament they were in. Suddenly, he thought of his American relatives. "Mr. Daniel Bradford is my uncle."

"Oh, well, that's good enough. Why didn't you say so?" Ascott remarked. "Dake would be your cousin?"

"Why . . . yes, that's right."

"He's right down the line. Follow me and we'll let him identify you," said Ascott.

With some apprehension, Clive followed the lieutenant. He glanced at Jeanne once, seeing that her lips were drawn together tightly, but she kept her silence. They walked not more than a few hundred yards, he judged, when a group of men around a fire roasting some meat looked up as they approached. One of them, he saw instantly, was Dake.

Lieutenant Ascott called out, "Private Bradford? Come here!"

Dake stood up, pushing the stick that held the meat he was roasting into the ground. Moving forward, he came to stand before the three and spoke at once. "Hello, Clive! What are you doing here?"

"This is Miss Jeanne Corbeau," Clive said quickly. "She's had a tragedy in her family, and I'm taking her to stay with my parents for a while. She just lost her father."

Dake glanced at Jeanne Corbeau, his hazel eyes narrowing. He took in the curly black hair, the striking blue-violet eyes, and the trim figure dressed in buckskins—and a smile touched his lips. But it disappeared at once as he nodded, "I'm sorry for your terrible loss, Miss Corbeau." He turned to his officer, saying, "How about if I accompany them into town, Lieutenant?"

"That would be best. They might run into some trouble along the line." Ascott looked at Jeanne and studied her for a moment, once again on the verge of speaking some thought. But he changed his mind, bowed his head slightly, and said, "Sorry about your trouble, miss."

"Come along," Dake ordered quickly. He led the pair down the road, and as soon as they were out of earshot, he turned to Clive, saying sharply, "What's going on, Clive? You could have been shot for a spy back there!"

"I'm not a spy and I'm not a soldier," Clive snapped. He could not say any more, for his father's mission to Fort Ticonderoga was not to be spoken of to Dake, for he was a loyal patriot and would have no qualms about relaying the information to his superior officers.

Dake walked along with the pair until they had come down out of the hills. He tried at first to get some information from them, but neither of them was saying much. Finally he stopped, saying, "You won't have any troubles from here on, I don't think." He was wearing a soft tri-cornered hat that he pulled off as he said, "If I can be of any help, miss, just say so."

"Thank you," Jeanne said. She looked intently at the husky young man and studied him carefully. *He doesn't look like a town man*, she thought. *He looks like some of the hunters who go over the mountains.* She found herself admiring the young soldier, but she turned at once as Clive walked away. "Thank you, Dake. I'll tell your family that I saw you," he called back over his shoulder.

T   T   T

"Mother, I think I hate making candles as much as I hate anything in the world!"

Lyna Gordon glanced over to where Grace was sitting in front of a large black pot suspended over the flame in the fireplace. It was very hot in the small room, and Grace's face was streaked with perspiration. She stared down at the pot that was boiling with a foul-smelling odor emanating from it, wrinkled her nose, and exclaimed, "It stinks!"

The preliminaries of drying out animal fat for candles was not pleas-ant, but it was a chore that had to be done in every household. "We have to have candles," Lyna shrugged. Moving to stand beside her daughter, she reached out and tucked a curl of Grace's dark honey-colored hair under the cap she wore. "Candles *are* awful, aren't they? They are ter-rible to make, tiresome to store, they put out heat, and the drippings spoil the tables—and they *do* smell bad."

"Can't we put some bayberries in this one or some spermaceti?" Grace asked. "I get so tired of plain smelly old candles!"

They worked for a time dipping the candles, then suddenly Lyna lifted her head as she wiped her brow. "There's someone at the door. I can't imagine who it could be—your father won't be home till later." Wiping her hands on her apron, she moved across the room. "I'll help you with the candles after I see who it is." Leaving the kitchen, Lyna made her way to the front door. Opening it, she blinked with surprise, and then exclaimed, "Clive!" She moved forward, put her arms up, and his arms went around her. "I'm so glad that you're back—we've been worried to death about you! Your father never should have left you."

Clive held his mother, shielding her from the visitor for a moment. All the way from Fort Ticonderoga he had wondered how he could present Jeanne to his family. It was all very well for him to agree to take the girl in, but after all, it was his parents who would have to bear all the responsibility of caring for her. More than once he thought he had been rash in making such an offer, but under the circumstances he had seen no other alternative. Now he kissed his mother on the cheek, straightened up, and stepped back.

"Mother, I have someone I want you to meet." He glanced back and saw that Jeanne had stopped short, about four feet back. Quickly he lifted his hand and motioned her in, and as she took a reluctant step forward, he said, "Mother, I'd like for you to meet Jeanne Corbeau— and this is my mother that I've told you so much about, Jeanne."

If Clive had entertained doubts of his mother's poise and calm spirit, they vanished at once. Not by one flicker of an eyelash did Lyna Gordon reveal the surprise that came to her. Ignoring the travel-stained buckskins and the rather masculine haircut of the young woman, Lyna said warmly, "I'm so glad to meet you, Miss Corbeau. Please, come in, both of you."

Jeanne had dreaded this moment from the time Clive had mentioned it. Heartily she wished she hadn't come! The busy streets of Boston had intimidated her. She had never seen so many houses, and as they had approached, she had been overwhelmed by the number and the neatness of them. They all looked like dollhouses to her, set up close to the street, many of them painted red, blue, or yellow. Most of the windows were outlined in white, and the mortar between the red bricks was painted white, also. Now that she stood facing Clive's mother, Jeanne's heart was beating rapidly—and she could not say a word to save her life!

Seeing that the girl was unable to speak, Lyna smiled and said briskly, "Well, you've had a long journey. You must be tired, and I know you'll want to clean up. Clive, I'm going to put Miss Corbeau in the small bedroom upstairs. You get some fresh water and bring it up so that she can refresh herself. Come along, Miss Corbeau."

Jeanne found herself being eased into the house and up the stairs as her hostess spoke pleasantly of other things. The young woman did not say a word, but when Lyna finally opened the door and stepped inside, Jeanne saw a room that was prettier than anything she had ever seen or imagined. As Lyna Gordon turned a lamp up, Jeanne took one quick look around, noting that the bedroom had a green rug that covered the floor, a bed such as she had never seen with four posters, two at each side, and a canopy and curtains made of a pretty white-and-yellow material. To the left stood a washstand with a blue enamel basin with tiny white stars and a pitcher to match. On the opposite wall a window was open, and a gentle breeze was admitting fresh air.

A large tawny cat with green eyes sprawled across the bed, and he studied the two women with an imperial calm. "That's Caesar," Lyna said. "I'll just take him out—"

"Oh no!" Jeanne spoke up quickly. "I love cats, Mrs. Gordon."

"Well, he thinks he owns the house," Lyna shrugged. "He'll take over your bed if you don't put him out at night."

Jeanne moved to bend over the cat. She stroked his thick fur, and when he turned his head to stare at her lazily, she smiled slightly. "He won't be any trouble to me."

"Good! Well, this will be your room, Miss Corbeau," Lyna said. "Just take your time. Have you been traveling all day?"

"Yes," Jeanne answered, glad to be able to say something to this beautiful woman so finely dressed. "We've been on the road for a week now." Something caught in her throat and she said, "I didn't want to come, but my papa—he died, and your son asked me to come and stay with you—just for a while."

"Oh, I'm so sorry, my dear." Lyna stepped forward and touched the girl's arm. "You did exactly the right thing—and so did Clive to invite you." Lyna felt compassion for the girl and put her arm around Jeanne's shoulder and squeezed it slightly. "I won't trouble you now, but later you must tell me all about it." She heard Clive coming up the stairs and turned to the door. He entered bearing a large wooden bucket of fresh water. "Put it in the pitcher, Clive." He obeyed and she said, "Now, you move along and let this young lady make herself presentable."

Clive nodded, relieved that his mother had taken the initiative. "I'll bring your bag up, Jeanne," he said, then left the room. His mother stepped outside with him and closed the door. When they reached the foot of the stairs, he turned and briefly told her the story. "I didn't know what else to do, Mother. She had absolutely no one, except for an invalid aunt and an uncle she hasn't seen in years."

90

"You did exactly right," Lyna said firmly. "Now, go get cleaned up. When your father gets home we'll have a good supper. I think perhaps your young friend will be hungry."

Clive smiled with relief. "I didn't know whether I did right or not, but it seemed the right thing to do. I couldn't leave her alone in that cabin in the middle of the wilderness."

"You've always been like that," Lyna said, reaching out to pat his arm. "Always bringing home stray dogs and kittens . . ." She caught herself and smiled. "Although I don't suppose I should say that about this young woman." She cocked her eyebrows and said, "I don't mean to be impertinent, but—does she *always* dress like that?"

"I think so," Clive shrugged. "She's been reared like a boy. You ought to see her stalk game in the woods! I'm afraid she knows nothing about social graces. You'll have to help her learn to dress—you and Grace."

"Yes, of course. Now—go get cleaned up. Your father will be home in an hour or two, then he can meet Miss Corbeau. He'll be interested to hear all that's happened since he left you at Fort Ticonderoga. She's the first young woman that you've brought home."

"Why, Mother, she's more boy than woman," he said. "But she needs help, and I thought you'd be glad to do what you could for her."

🐾 🐾 🐾

Jeanne waited until Clive brought her small bag back, but when she removed the few clothes she had, she discovered that they had gotten soaked at one of the river crossings. The dress was wadded up into a hopeless mess, and she knew she couldn't wear it downstairs. "Oh, I wish I'd never come!" she whispered, desperation drawing her up tightly. There was no help for the dress. Moving over to the washstand, she poured water into the basin and found a cake of the sweetest-smelling soap she had ever encountered. She used it to wash her face and hands, but still she dreaded going down wearing what she had on. As she stood there she heard a tap at the door. She moved forward, opened the door, and found Lyna standing there holding a beautiful blue dress. "This belongs to Grace, my daughter," she said. "You weren't able to bring many clothes, so I brought you this, along with some undergarments and shoes. You two are about the same size. You wouldn't mind wearing them, would you?"

"No. Thank you very much, Mrs. Gordon."

Hurriedly, after she closed the door, Jeanne stripped off the weather-stained buckskins and undergarments. She sponged off quickly, then put on the clothing that she had laid across the bed—discovering to her amusement that the huge yellow cat had settled himself squarely in the middle of them. She sat down and stroked his head, and at once he closed his eyes and a noisy rumbling sound filled the room. "Sorry, Caesar—but I've got to have these clothes." Carefully she retrieved them, getting a reproachful look from the emerald green eyes.

Jeanne had never seen underwear so fragile and marveled at the beautiful garments. When she slipped on the petticoat, and then the light blue dress over it, she felt very strange. The clothes were a good fit and the shoes, finer than any she had ever seen, fit her very well. A small mirror hung on the wall and she tried to see herself, but she could not get the whole picture. She felt strange in this fine room wearing the most feminine clothes she had ever had on in her life. She looked at her hair, which had neither been combed nor brushed. She ran her hand through it and shook her head almost in despair.

She found a comb in a drawer and did the best she could. Finally she moved over to where the cat watched her with indolent interest. Sitting down, she picked him up and buried her face in his smooth fur. "I wish I could stay here with you, Caesar," she whispered, dreading to leave the room. The cat dug his needle-sharp claws into her shoulder, and she laughed and put him down. He yawned hugely, exposing an impressive set of gleaming white teeth and a red throat, then settled down in her lap, ready for a long nap.

Thirty minutes later there was another knock at the door. When she moved to open it, she found Lyna there again.

"We'd like for you to come down and join us for the evening meal," Lyna smiled. "If you'd like to." She was able to cover her surprise at how well Jeanne looked in Grace's dress.

"Yes, thank you very much. That would be nice," Jeanne said.

Placing Caesar on the bed, Jeanne left the room and walked down the stairs. Lyna led her down the hall and then through a door on the right. When she stepped inside, the lights were brilliant to her, the lamps casting their reflection over the polished dark furniture, catching the gleam from the white tablecloth. But she had no time to look at the furniture, for a tall man, obviously Clive's father, had risen.

"Come in, Miss Corbeau," he welcomed. "I'm Clive's father. I don't think you've met my son, David, or my daughter, Grace."

David Gordon stared at the girl, intensely curious. His mother had earlier put her finger in his face, warning him, "If you ask *one* question or make *one* remark, I'll have your father cane you so you won't walk for a month, do you hear me!"

David had heard her and indeed was convinced. His natural curiosity bubbled over, but he merely said, "Happy to know you, Miss

Corbeau." But he was thinking, *She looks afraid. I wonder what she's scared of?*

Grace had been given the particulars of the girl's background, and Clive had been rather insistent in urging her to try to help. Now she smiled and said, "I'm happy to know you. May I call you Jeanne?"

"Oh yes, please!"

"Well now, everyone sit down and we'll have something to eat," said Lyna.

Jeanne found herself seated across from Clive and Grace, with David on her left and the Colonel and Mrs. Gordon at the ends of the table. When Colonel Gordon bowed his head and the others followed suit, she drew a sigh of relief. He asked a quick blessing and then said, "Now, Clive, while the rest of us eat, tell us what has happened since we last parted."

Clive was aware that his father was trying to put the young girl at ease and launched into the story at some length. He noticed Jeanne was able to recover some composure, and by the time Clive finished relating all that had happened in the last few weeks, he could tell she felt somewhat more at ease.

"I'm so sorry about your father, Jeanne," Leslie Gordon said gently. "But I'm glad that Clive brought you here. We are in your debt for what you did for Clive. If you hadn't come along out there on the trail . . ." Leslie paused for a moment and then continued. "We are most grateful. Please consider this your home for as long as you please." He hesitated, then a frown touched his face. "That may not be long if the patriots take Boston. We would all have to leave—the military, that is."

"Do you think that can happen?" Clive asked in astonishment. "Why, they're nothing but a reckless mob, Father!"

"I'm not as sure as I once was about this war," Leslie said. He glanced around the table and spoke for a moment about the military situation. Then he said, "But as long as we're here, Jeanne, you must give us a chance to show you what hospitality we can."

Jeanne swallowed hard and then said, "Thank you, sir, but I don't want to be a bother."

"Why, how could you be that, my dear?" Lyna spoke up instantly, a sweet smile on her face. "The first thing tomorrow, Clive, you'll have to take Jeanne on a tour of Boston."

"Why, of course," Clive said, once again feeling relieved that his family had taken the girl in without a question. He had expected no less, but it made him proud of all of them to see how they welcomed the young woman so warmly.

After the meal was over, Grace, who had been instructed by her mother, said, "Come along, Jeanne. We have a lot to talk about."

Jeanne rose and stood for one moment before Clive. She wanted to say something, but nothing came. Finally, she whispered, "Thank you—" and then she turned and moved away quickly.

Leslie watched Clive and saw how he kept his eyes on the young woman as she left to go upstairs with Grace. "Well, we didn't expect this, did we?"

"No, sir, we certainly didn't." He came and sat down again, his brow knitted in thought. "I honestly don't know what she'll do, Father. After all she's been through, we've got to do something to help her. She can't go back to living like an Indian back in the woods. It wouldn't be safe for her out there all alone."

Lyna's face was uneasy and she spoke carefully. "You must be careful, Clive."

"Careful? What do you mean, Mother?"

"I mean you've always been quick and impulsive. This young woman is not a stray kitten—and she mustn't be treated as one."

Clive stared at his mother with surprise. "Why, I had no intention of doing that. What do you mean? Shouldn't I have brought her here?"

"Yes, but you must be very gentle. I can see how she trusts you, and you must never violate that trust."

Clive flushed. "Why, Mother! I'm surprised to hear you say that."

"You're a young man and she's a young woman. She's very attractive, but she obviously knows nothing about the way we live—and probably not much about men."

"No, she doesn't want any men in her life. She made *that* clear enough."

Leslie Gordon stared at him. "How did that subject come up?"

To Clive's annoyance, his face grew still warmer. "Oh, I don't know. She hasn't had any experience, you're right about that, Mother. But you and Grace can teach her how to dress and act."

"We'll do our best. But still, I think she looks to you, Clive." Lyna hesitated, then smiled. "Be very tactful, Clive. She'll need all the kindness and encouragement she can get."

That was all that was said at the time concerning Jeanne. Clive and his father sat talking about Ticonderoga, and it was Leslie who remarked, "If we run the rest of this war as poorly as we did Fort Ticonderoga, then King George can say goodbye to the Colonies."

"It can't come to a full-scale war," Clive insisted. "They can't mount an organized army."

"Have you considered how difficult it is to get one English soldier from England to the Colonies? It takes three tons of supplies for one man for a year—food, uniforms, horses, wagons, and all it takes to keep him in the field. And those supplies have to come on ships—and our ships are spread out all over the world, and fighting at least one major war on the Continent. Every time we lose a man, that has to be done again. If these colonists unite, then we're in serious trouble, Clive." Leslie Gordon had spent much time pondering the situation, and he shook his head as he rose from the table. "We have pretty uniforms and we know how to march—but this is their country. At least that's the way they see it. If you try to take a man's country away, he doesn't worry about his brass buttons...!"

🨠 🨠 🨠

Clive enjoyed the next morning immensely. Jeanne had come down to breakfast wearing one of Grace's dresses that he recognized, but he did not dare mention it. Jeanne had said very little at breakfast, but evidently Grace had been able to make an inroad into the girl's reticence, for from time to time Jeanne would smile at one of Grace's remarks.

After breakfast they left the house. Clive took her through the market area—a vast open space set up with open wagons and stalls of vendors selling their wares. Live animals for sale added to the excitement—chickens squawked, ducks quacked, pigs squealed, and the voices of the hucksters scored the air as they cried out their bargains to passersby.

"Candles!—Wax at bargain prices!—Cabinet wares!—Lobsters!"

They moved along the streets in a leisurely fashion, and Clive halted in front of a dressmaker's shop. "Look!" he said. "That's the sort of thing a young lady like you ought to wear, Jeanne. Come on, let's go look at it."

"Oh no!" Jeanne said quickly. But he laughed and insisted, taking her arm and escorting her inside. The dressmaker met them, a smile on her face. She was a small woman with dark brown hair and lively gray eyes. "Would the young lady be interested in something?"

"That dress in the window? Would it fit her?"

"Oh yes, with a few alterations. Come with me—we'll see how it looks."

Despite her protests, Jeanne found herself in the back room, where the dressmaker helped her put on the dress. It was a delicate dove gray color with a marvelous shiny surface and white lace gathered around the neck and wrists. When Jeanne had tried it on, she was hustled out front by the dressmaker, who beamed, "Lovely, isn't she?"

Clive was surprised at the impact Jeanne had on him, for she did look lovely and he said so. "That's a very pretty dress. I think you ought to have it."

"Oh no, I couldn't do that!" Jeanne said quickly.

Abruptly Clive chided himself. *I should have known she didn't have enough money for that—and I can't afford to pay for it.* "Well, you have a birthday coming up. We'll see," he said, winking over her head at the seamstress.

She smiled at him and nodded, "Yes, but you'd better hurry, sir, it won't be here long."

They left the shop and continued to wander around the city. Their meandering took them along the docks, where he pointed out the British fleet. "Those are fighting ships in line," he said. He looked around and added, "A lot of whalers go out of here. They're not going out now, though, not until this trouble is over."

The codfish were piled high on the dock, and Jeanne glimpsed something floating near the wharf and asked, "What's that?"

"It *was* a whale. Now it's just a floating carcass." He made a face. "This air is pretty foul—rotten fish! Let's get out of here."

Afterward he walked her down past some of the shops. He saw many British soldiers turn as they walked by and cast an eye on Jeanne. Fortunately, she did not notice, and Clive was aware that she did not have that tendency to flirt that most young ladies had. *May be a good thing for a girl to be brought up like she has*, he thought. *At least she's not chasing every uniform that walks in front of her. . . !*

As they passed by a tavern, several British soldiers stood talking outside, and one of them made a remark loud enough for Jeanne to hear. It was raw and crude, but in her innocence she did not understand. She felt Clive tense beside her and looked up and asked, "What's the matter?"

"Didn't you hear what he said?"

"The soldier? I guess so, but I didn't understand what he meant." Her eyes looked enormous, framed as they were by her curly black hair. The small neat cap that Grace had furnished her sat pertly on her head. Jeanne looked back at the soldiers, who were laughing, and asked, "What did he mean?"

"Never mind," Clive said grimly as he grabbed her arm and hurried along.

When they arrived home, David was waiting. "Did you have a good walk?" he asked. Then without waiting for an answer, he said, "I want you to tell me about the woods and the Indians, Jeanne. I've never seen an Indian. Do they wear war paint? Do they wear clothes? Did you ever see a scalp?"

Jeanne felt a streak of humor surface. She took an instant liking to the fifteen-year-old and said brightly, "Oh yes, I've seen scalps. At one time the British offered ten dollars for every white person's scalp that was brought in."

Both David and Clive stared at her in disbelief. "They didn't really do that!" Clive exclaimed.

"Yes, they did. Papa and I saw an Indian bring in twelve scalps and collect his reward."

"Come on! I want to hear all about it," David said. Without ceremony, he seized Jeanne's arm and dragged her off, leaving Clive standing there. "Tell me about it! How do you go about scalping somebody?"

Clive shook his head and moved out of the foyer and found his mother in the parlor sewing. When Lyna asked where Jeanne was, Clive grinned. "She's telling David how to scalp people." At her look of surprise, he shrugged. "Well, that's what she's doing!" He sat down opposite her and said, "Mother, what do you think of her?"

"I think she's a very sweet young woman. She's a fine Christian, Clive—did you know that?"

"Yes, I did. Her father was, too." He related some of the details of Pierre's last days and then sat there quietly. "She knows God better than I do."

Lyna did not answer, for it had long been a prayer of her heart that this tall, handsome son of hers would learn to know God better than he did. He was a good man, not vicious, very generous, and ready to help anyone in need. But his religion was mostly formal, and this grieved both her and Leslie.

"Maybe you'll catch some of it from her—and she'll learn some manners from you. Did she make any mistakes today?"

"No, not really, but she would at a tea party. You have to teach her how to behave, Mother."

"I'm not sure that she wants to learn. She may not like our kind of life, Clive. You have to consider that." She watched her son's face, wondering what was going on behind those cornflower blue eyes that she admired so much. He said nothing more about the girl, but when he left, Lyna thought, *I wonder what he'll do with her and what she'll do with herself.*

🜚   🜚   🜚

On May 25, the *Cerebus* sailed into Boston Harbor carrying three generals sent to America to deal with the American crisis. The powers in London had decided that General Thomas Gage was incapable of dealing with the growing rebellion. The prime minister, Lord North, had finally chosen these three to squelch the uprising that was creating agitation in the British Empire.

Ranked along the rail, as the *Cerebus* pulled in, the three men stood looking out over the harbor. The senior of the three was forty-five-year-old William Howe—tall, dark, and an excellent soldier. He was a strict disciplinarian, respected as a tactician and well-liked by officers and men. He did enjoy the company of women, although he was said to be fond of his attractive wife—whom he had left in England. He had been a Major-General for three years, so his capacity to lead an army had not yet been tested in actual battle. Next to Howe in seniority was Major-General Henry Clinton. Clinton was an officer of severely limited talents, who had risen to his rank through the influence of powerful friends. The general was shy, diffident, with a sense of insecurity that made him appear quite touchy and suspicious. He was, in effect, a lonely, aloof, introspective man quick to take offense at the slightest provocation.

The third British general to arrive in Boston, John Burgoyne, had aristocratic connections. Fifty-three years old, he was believed to be the illegitimate son of a high-ranking nobleman. He had risen in the army by proving himself to be a successful and distinguished cavalry officer. He was even better known as a man about town and as a writer for the theater. He was believed by some to be a vain and vicious man—which was true to some degree.

As the three men stood speaking of the problem they faced, Clinton turned to his two fellow generals and said gloomily, "The whole affair seems to have been poorly handled so far. Here we are, the British army, pinned down in Boston by an undisciplined and leaderless rabble force! I think it's a disgrace!"

Gentlemanly John Burgoyne, as he was called by his troops behind his back, smiled expansively. "Well," he said, "now that we are here, we shall be able to make a little elbow room."

Unfortunately, his remark was heard by a corporal who repeated it to others. It was one of those chance remarks that becomes well known, and soon Burgoyne was to hear the cry "Make way for General Elbow Room" whenever he made an inspection.

The three generals looked at the dark, brooding hills beyond Boston. If they had been able to read the future, they would have perhaps stayed on the *Cerebus* and sailed back to England. Before it was over, the "small crisis" in the Colonies was to prove to be a graveyard for the reputation of British generals!

8

Memories Can Be Dangerous

THE HOME OF DANIEL BRADFORD had two parlors. The best parlor was rather aloof and ceremonial. It was located on the main floor in the front of the house just off the entryway. The furniture was rich and delicate; the walls and furnishing colors were cheerful and bright. A mixture of mahogany and walnut, the chairs were carved rather ornately and positioned along the walls and in corners. It was the day in which the floors in most houses were left with an open space in the center, which facilitated housekeeping, promoted an easier arrangement for tea drinking—and prevented people from tripping over the furniture in the dimly lit interiors.

Daniel passed absentmindedly through the larger parlor into the sitting room, or what the family usually called the "back parlor." Picking up a candle, he lit it from one that sat on the mantel and placed it on the cherry desk set along one of the walls. He stood there for a moment, as if he had forgotten what he was doing, and stared into the yellow flame of the candle. His mind was far away, but then he shook his heavy shoulders, set the candle on the desk, and seated himself in the leather-covered chair.

It was a comfortable room containing a Pembroke table with hinged leaves and a drawer. This piece served as a desk, a stand, a tea table, or even a dining table. Most of the furniture had casters mounted underneath so it could be easily moved. Against one wall a finely carved cherry bookcase reached almost to the ceiling. It had glazed doors, but Daniel had had them lined with pleated green silk to protect his collection of books from the rays of the sun. The carpet underfoot was very colorful, red-and-green checks with an intricate design. A beautiful and delicate sinumbra lamp rested on a low table. It had a handsome glass shade and had been designed to cast uninterrupted light. However, oil lamps required hours of laborious cleaning and maintenance if they were not to smoke or smell, so Daniel usually made do with a candle.

He leaned back in the chair, his large, square hands gripping the arms tensely, although he was not aware of it. His eyes fastened on the painting in a gold frame across from him—a portrait of Holly, his wife. Good thoughts about their life together formed, and he felt a sharp stab of loneliness touch him briefly. He found himself wishing—as he had so often—that Holly had lived. Their courtship had not been a wildly romantic affair. He had married her primarily because she was alone and pregnant and had no one to help—but also because God had given him the most direct word he'd ever had from the Lord to do so. When the baby had come, Holly had not told him the father's name. He had never asked—though he had strongly suspected Leo Rochester—and when the child, Matthew, was born, Daniel had taken him as his own. Only when Holly lay on her deathbed had she disclosed the secret she had guarded. "If I don't tell you, no one will ever know. . . ." She had related then how Leo Rochester had raped her, then had callously forsaken her to fare for herself.

A creaking door brought Daniel back to the present, and he shook off his thoughts and glanced up to see Dake enter. "Dake!" he exclaimed in shock, coming to his feet instantly. "What are *you* doing here?"

Dake grinned crookedly. "I live here, Pa. Don't you remember?" He came over and the two shook hands, then Daniel slowly seated himself, not taking his eyes from his son's face. Dake sat down in the rocking chair across from his father. Clasping his big hands over his knee in a familiar gesture, Dake began rocking slowly back and forth. There was an ease and relaxed air about Dake Bradford. He seemed to have no serious thoughts, although Daniel knew that he did. The lamp illuminated the wheat-colored hair and made the wide-spaced hazel eyes glow, almost like a cat's. He spoke impulsively, as was his custom. "What are you going to do about the militia, Pa?"

"I don't know."

"Pa, you have to decide *something*!" Dake pushed at the subject. It was his way to set his mind, then make a direct frontal attack. He was never contented to be still, to wait like his brother Micah could wait and see how time took its course. Ever since his childhood and youth, Dake seemed to have a driving energy about everything he did. He always had a purpose or goal he pushed himself to obtain. He stopped rocking, put his feet on the floor, then leaned forward, clasping his hands.

"Sooner or later, you've got to decide on this thing, Pa. Of course I've already made my decision."

"And if you're caught, you might be hanged for a spy."

Dake laughed, his white teeth flashing. "One good thing about not wearing uniforms. We don't have any, and they can't hang a man for coming to his own house. They can't prove that I've been up with the militia. . . ."

Daniel sat there listening as Dake spun out the tales of how the men were pouring in from all over the Colonies. With excitement glowing in his eyes, he mentioned units from Delaware, Connecticut, New Hampshire, and Rhode Island. "Why, I reckon we've got enough men right now to whip the British!" he exclaimed.

"It won't be like fighting along the road from Concord," Daniel warned quietly. "It'll take trained soldiers to defeat the British." Daniel knew whereof he spoke, for he had served in the army in England years ago. He had learned discipline, the handling of arms and—despite the many mistakes of the British commanders—he knew that the army of England was a formidable force to reckon with.

"What do you think Micah will do?" Dake asked suddenly.

"Hard to say. He's not quick like you, Dake."

"No, but I wish he were! We're going to need all the men we can get."

"Just don't let Sam go with you is all I ask."

"I know. He'd go in a minute. He's got something, that youngster has." Dake hesitated, then said, "Pa, you're going to have to make up your mind. Nobody can sit on the fence in this fight that's coming. If you don't fight for the patriots, you'll be against us."

"Is that what you think, Dake?"

Dake flushed. He hated confrontations with his father, and could not understand why Daniel Bradford did not leap wholeheartedly into the fray as other men had. He had no doubt of his father's courage—yet he could sense something was in the way. Finally he said quietly, "You know how I feel about you, Pa—but people won't let you alone. This country's going to be one thing or another—either the slaves of the British or free men."

Daniel looked at his son, sharp grief in his eyes. Life had been good since he had served his time as an indentured servant of Leo Rochester. He had hoped to live to an old age in peace, to see his grandchildren about his knees—but now he saw clearly that such was not to be. To the British Empire, the struggle of the Colonies against England was no more than a cloud the size of a man's hand. But Daniel Bradford knew as clearly as he knew his own name that soon the drums would sound, the cannons would boom—and men would lie torn and dead in obscured fields. The thought that this fine young son of his might be one of them was like a bayonet in his heart. Still—there was nothing he could do to prevent it. He was caught in the avalanche, as were others throughout the land, and there was no way of turning back.

❖   ❖   ❖

Marian leaned over and poured her father's tea. He seemed better to her today. There was some color in his cheeks, and he had chatted in a lively fashion with her while they had breakfast together. She worried about him, for although he was not old in years, his health had been very poor for some time. If it had not been for Daniel Bradford, she had long realized, the foundry and ironworks would have been beyond her father's strength.

John Frazier leaned back, reached for his pipe, and packed it with tobacco. Taking a taper out of a small bronze vase, he touched it to the candle flame beside him, then brought the tiny flame to the large bowl of brown tobacco, drawing slowly on the Meerschaum pipe. When it glowed a ruby color and tiny purple clouds rose toward the ceiling, he leaned back and sighed. "Tobacco's a comfort," he said. "I know it's a filthy weed and a bad habit, but I guess I'm too weak to break it."

"It's your only vice," Marian said with a smile. She was wearing a dark green dress that brought out the color of her eyes. Her dark auburn hair lay in waves, gathered at the nape of her neck and tied with a white ribbon. She was not dressed to go out, and leaned back comfortably, enjoying her tea. "Everyone ought to have one bad habit," she smiled mischievously. "Suppose you wanted to repent and you didn't have a single bad habit? Well, there it is," she nodded. "You'd be a moral pauper—not a thing to cast overboard."

John Frazier laughed at her. "Not a single sin to repent of? Well, I don't have to worry about *that*." He watched this daughter of his for whom he had such deep love. It was the bitterness of his life that she had married Leo Rochester. He held himself accountable for that, for he had encouraged the match. Looking back now, he realized that the mistake was his. *I should have given her more guidance—she had no mother,* he thought bitterly. *Too late now.* Aloud he said, "Leo's gone?"

"Yes," she said, staring into her cup of tea.

The monosyllable spoke volumes. Leo was usually gone, off on business. He made long trips to other cities—where he drank and gambled and wenched and made little secret of it. Frazier pulled his mind away from the subject of his son-in-law and began to speak of the revolution that was gathering strength amongst the Colonies. Although he was mostly confined to the house, he had a keen mind and read the papers avidly. Marian kept up with the political military aspects as well as she could. They talked quietly, and finally Frazier said, "I'm worried about Daniel."

"Why? Is something wrong?" she said, looking up.

"You know what will happen. He's a man of deep conviction about freedom. He'll never stay out of this fight."

"Has he said anything to you?" Marian asked, not meeting his eyes. They spoke on rare occasions about Daniel Bradford. Marian never knew how much her father suspected. It was true enough that she and Daniel had been drawn to each other since they had first met in Virginia. She had married Leo with great reservations, and after a few months, she knew that she had made the most terrible mistake a woman could make. Since then, every time she saw Daniel Bradford, something whispered, *This could have been my husband!* And he was in love with her—her heart told her that. Then she thought abruptly of the time that he had taken her into his arms—in this very house. Leo had unexpectedly returned early from a trip to England and had come into the library and found them. Since then her life had been all the more miserable, for Leo never let her forget it. His verbal abuse and sarcasm seemed to have no limits whenever he brought it up.

Seeing the troubled thoughts darken Marian's face, Frazier wanted to ask how it was with her. But he knew how much she was suffering. She was a sad woman with no children to lavish her love on, married to a cruel husband who was little more than a beast at times—and there was nothing at all he could do about it! He bit his lip, then said as lightly as he could, "I need to see Daniel. Would you get word to him to come by the house?"

Marian agreed and sent word by Cato, the slave who served as butler and head over the other servants. She went about her work that day saying little, but from time to time she would find herself eagerly awaiting Daniel's arrival. The futility of it all caught at her, and once she went into her bedroom and sat staring into the mirror for a long time. Tears did not help—she had found that out. Putting the best face on her marriage required all the strength she had. It was a shallow and bitter relationship she had with Leo. He had not desired her for years and often taunted her with the fact that she was cold and barren as a brick. Sometimes he boasted of his conquests among the women in the town, forcing her to listen as he talked. She would sit in silence, grieving at the cruel pain he seemed to enjoy inflicting on her. She knew that her marriage had worn her down spiritually and emotionally. Yet when her despair seemed the darkest, she never forgot those words that day in the carriage when she went to see how Daniel was after the battle at Concord. He had professed his love for her, but he was more committed to God and said he *must* honor her marriage to Leo. And so when the hard times came, she took refuge in being a good daughter, serving her church, and trying to do the best she could for those about her. Though Leo had broken every promise he had ever made to her, Marian committed herself once again to God and placed her broken heart in His arms of faithfulness.

Daniel arrived just before dark, and Marian took him to her father's bedroom, where John Frazier was eagerly awaiting him. He felt well enough to be up and dressed, so the three of them met in the small dining room. The mahogany dinner table had been rubbed with a brush and beeswax until Daniel could see his face in it. A fine damask tablecloth with embroidery representing a landscape with trees and flowers was spread on it by one of the maids, then the dishes and glassware were set in place. The handsomest Windsor chairs available were arranged, and soon the three were sitting there enjoying their meal. Cato came from time to time and refreshed their drinks from silver vessels set on top of the heavily carved mahogany sideboard with a serpentine front.

The meal consisted of poached turbot and lobster, a dish John Frazier loved more than any other. They ate buttered toast and muffins, eggs in little napkins, and crispy bits of bacon under silver covers. Afterward there were some delicious sweet cakes and a strawberry shortcake, which was Frazier's favorite.

The three adjourned to the parlor, where they sat for an hour while Marian performed on the harpsichord. She was an excellent musician and sang with a clear, pleasing contralto voice.

The two men leaned back in their chairs while watching Marian. Her father smoked the Meerschaum, sending little puffs of smoke up at intervals and tapping his foot in cadence to the music. From time to time, he would nod appreciatively. He had been in much pain during the past months, and at times like this it was enough that the pain was gone and that his daughter and Daniel were there. Glancing over at Daniel, he could not help the thought, *I wish that he were my son-in-law.*

Daniel was oblivious to the gaze. His eyes were fixed on Marian, who was wearing a plum-colored dress that caught the lights from the sconces bearing fragrant-smelling candles. The faint glitters of candlelight winked as she moved, reflecting from the dress and catching in the delicate pearls that adorned her luxuriant hair. Finally she turned around and said, "Now, no more for tonight."

She came over to her father and looked at him. "You're tired," she said.

"Daughter, it's too early. . . !"

"You always overdo," she chided. "Now, to bed with you. Cato—" she called. "Make sure my father gets his medicine." She kissed her father on the cheek, promising, "I'll stop in to say good night before you go to sleep."

"All right," Frazier grumbled tiredly. His eyes were drooping already and he was feeling some pain. "Come back tomorrow, Daniel. We didn't get to talk about the business."

"Of course, John."

After Cato had helped Frazier out of the room, closing the door behind him, there was a moment of awkwardness. "You take fine care of John. You're his life," Daniel said.

Color touched her cheeks. Any praise from him pleased her immensely. "Father enjoys your company so much. Tonight was good for him."

"Yes, he looked better tonight."

The conversation lagged, and both of them suddenly started talking at once to cover it up. Then Daniel asked, "Will you be going back to Virginia soon?"

"No. Father's not able for me to leave him just yet. I wouldn't feel at all comfortable leaving him when he's still so weak." She looked at him and asked, "Daniel, what are you going to do about this war?"

As always the mention of the war seemed to bring a cloud to Daniel. It was a subject that no man living in Boston could get away from. "I'm going to be drawn into it, I suppose. There's no way out. It's going to be bad here in Boston. Do you think you could take your father and go somewhere else? Savannah, maybe?"

"He'd never leave here," Marian said.

They sat talking for a while, then she got up and made tea. When she leaned over to pour it, he could see the clear, translucent quality of the skin on her cheeks and neck. He looked away quickly and made some inane remark.

Marian knew at once that her closeness had stirred him. She quickly moved away, and they talked for a few more minutes, but finally he arose.

"I'd best be going," he said. "I left some papers for your father to sign over there on the table."

"I'll see that he signs them." Marian rose and walked to the door with him. When they got there, she turned and said, "Do you ever think of the days when we first met—how you taught me to ride?"

Daniel smiled. "I didn't have to teach you much. You didn't think you had anything to learn."

"Wasn't I awful?" She laughed at the fond memory. "I've thought of that so many times. Those were happy days, weren't they, Daniel?"

"Yes, they were." He paused, then said slowly, "Those are good things to think about."

She looked up at him and said, "Remember—you kissed me once?"

"Yes, I did. I've never forgotten."

A silence fell between them. Her lips were parted slightly as she looked at him. She saw the wish in his eyes that she could not mistake. *He still desires me*, she thought. The realization brought color to her cheeks, but instantly she said, "Memories can be dangerous."

Daniel was struggling against the strong emotions that rose in him. She was fragrant, soft, and beautiful as she looked up at him with longing eyes. Her physical attributes were torturing him with desire—and yet he was as far from having her as a man could be. She had a husband, and to both of them that was the end of the matter. He said stiffly, "Good night, Marian," then turned quickly and left, settling his hat firmly on his head.

She watched him go. When he disappeared into the darkness, she turned back slowly, closing the door. For a moment she stood there, leaning against the door. Then she moved through the house, going to her father's bedchamber to attend to him, but her thoughts drifted back to the days when she had been young—before she had made her dreadful mistake.

🔔　　🔔　　🔔

"Well now, I find you here."

Matthew Bradford finished the stroke he was carefully making on the canvas that he had fastened firmly to the easel. The sun shone on the water, making him blink for a moment. He turned to find Leo Rochester, who had approached and was standing at his shoulder. "Hello, Mr. Rochester. Yes, I'm here making my smears again."

Leo had not come by accident. He had discovered that Matthew often came down to the harbor to paint the ships, the rough fishermen, the delicate nets drying, and the soldiers who paraded back and forth. He had come purposefully and now peered closely at the forms taking shape on the canvas. "That's very fine," he said quietly. "I'd give anything if I could do that. My father was a painter. Have I ever told you that?"

"No, was he indeed?" Matthew said, laying his brush down.

"Oh yes. He would have been a fine professional artist, but he didn't have the opportunity—or at least didn't take it." He stepped back and cocked his head as he stood at the painting. "I think you've caught the light on the water. I don't see how you do that."

"You ought to see some of the works by Flemish painters," Matthew said. "Those fellows *really* know how to paint light."

Leo stood there chatting as the warm sunshine beamed down. All around them they heard the usual sounds of men working and boats grinding against the wooden piers. For a long time, they talked about painting and art, and then Leo invited, "Come and join me for a bite to eat. Then I'll bring you back and watch you paint some more."

Matthew was indeed hungry, for he had left the house early that morning without eating. As soon as he had set up his easel by the harbor and got his paints ready, the hours seemed to fly by. Now, at the mention of food, his stomach growled, so he went willingly with Rochester. He really had no one to talk to about art and discovered that Leo Rochester was unusually well informed as they walked along. After a short stroll, the two sat down in one of the better restaurants in Boston, and Rochester spoke with him, relating witty and entertaining anecdotes of his encounters with the famous artists of England and Europe.

"I wish you could see my home in Virginia, Matthew. When I came over here," Rochester said, "I didn't bring much furniture—but, oh, you should see all the paintings we brought from Milford Manor, our old ancestral home."

"I'd love to see them."

"You would? Well, I think that could be arranged. Virginia's not so far from here."

Matthew stared at him with surprise, not thinking he was serious. "It seems a long way to me, sir."

The two looked up suddenly when a voice said, "Why, Mr. Bradford . . ."

Abigail Howland stood there smiling down at the two men, and as they rose, protested, "Oh, please keep your seats. I was strolling by and saw you through the window. I just wanted to see if you had decided to lower your rates so I could have my portrait done."

"At your service, Miss Howland," Matthew smiled. "My rates aren't very high right now. Shall I call on you?"

"Yes, please do," Abigail said. She smiled at the two men and then excused herself and moved toward the door of the restaurant.

"I understand that she's planning to marry Nathan Winslow," Leo said. "I don't understand why she would waste herself on a rebel. I hear that Paul Winslow is interested in her as well. I'll bet there is an interesting story surrounding those three. Pretty thing, isn't she?"

"I believe *interesting* might be an understatement, sir. And, yes, she is very pretty." Matthew looked out the window, then turned back to Leo and said, "I wonder if she's serious about the painting."

"Oh, she's serious enough. Pretty women always like to be painted, don't they?"

"Yes, they do." Matthew grinned back at the man across from him. "But they don't always have the money. Is her husband-to-be rich?"

"I don't think so. The Winslows, some of them, are fairly well off, but not Nathan. Now"—he leaned back—"what are your plans?"

"I suppose I have as few plans as any man in America," Matthew shrugged. And this was true enough. He could not settle his thoughts or desires, and he felt out of step with the rest of his family. He wanted to go back to England to continue his studies in art, but with the patriot uprising, he was hesitant to leave his family right now. He and Micah more or less agreed that the war was a tragedy that should have been averted and still should be. Dake, of course, and Sam were hotheads who would fight till the last drop of their blood was spilt. It was an uncomfortable situation at home, and he spent relatively little time there.

"What about Mr. Bradford? Will he join the patriots?" Rochester asked.

Quickly, Matthew glanced at the man across from him. This was a dangerous question. One did not ask such things in Boston, where the mere suspicion of being a patriot was enough to get a man thrown in jail. "He hasn't said what he'll do," Matthew said carefully.

"Good! I see you can hold your own counsel. I like a man like that," Leo smiled. "Quite honestly, I hope Daniel stays out of it. It's a losing cause. The colonists are in a terrible plight. If they lose against the British, they'll lose everything. And if they win, they'll be in worse shape."

"Worse shape? How can that be?"

"Why, they'll be gobbled up by some second-rate European power. It's happened before. They'll never be strong enough to stand against Germany, or France, or whoever comes along with a trained army. How unfortunate that this thing has happened!"

"What will *you* do, Mr. Rochester?"

"Oh, call me Leo. Why, I plan to have the best of all possible worlds," he said cheerfully. Rochester was charming when he chose to be. He had a powerful and persuasive personality and knew how to win people to his way of thinking. "I'll go to England when it gets too hot here. You've been there, you say?"

"Oh yes, I love it!"

"Ah yes, I can see why. And right across the channel is France, and not too far away is Italy. Have you been there?"

"No, but I'd give anything to go see the paintings there."

"Well, why don't you?"

"A mere matter of money."

Rochester said carefully, "Money is a problem—but it shouldn't be. Artists shouldn't have to worry about money. They give this world something that nobody else can. I think all good artists should be supported either by the government or by a rich wife—or a rich relative."

"I'd be for that—any one of the three," Matthew laughed.

"Yes, art is civilized, and true artists are citizens of the world." Leo began to speak of his plantation, finally saying, "I like Virginia better than Boston. They've got a tradition there, because those men are actually English gentlemen. George Washington, for example, is English—and nothing else to make of him. He's one of the richest men in the Colonies and likely to be dragged down by this horrible war. But Virginia is a wonderful place, so I suppose I'll stay there as long as the hotheads will allow me."

"And if you have to leave the Colonies?"

"Then England, France, and Italy." Rochester paused, saying finally, "Nothing I'd like better—but I've seen it all. It'd be nice to have a young fellow like you to show it to."

Leo knew when to fold his cards. He had planted a seed and now he said, "Come along. I want to see more paint on that canvas. . . ."

🜋　　🜋　　🜋

That night when Matthew got home, he found his father in his study. Matthew's cheeks were flushed, for he and Leo had stopped by a tavern and had enjoyed several drinks. Now as he threw himself into a chair, he began telling of the way he'd spent the afternoon. He was not astute enough to notice his father's face. Daniel Bradford said nothing as Matthew told him with great excitement of Rochester's interest in his art. "He's rich and wants to show me all of his paintings. You've seen them all, haven't you, when you lived there as his servant?"

"I wasn't in the big house too often, but yes, I've seen them. Fine paintings," Daniel said quietly.

"Leo wants me to make a trip with him to Virginia." Matthew's eyes were shining and he said, "Do you think that will be all right?" And then he added quickly, "He even thought when he goes to England that he might like to take me and introduce me to some famous artists he knows. He even mentioned about going to France and Italy." He spoke rapidly, more excited than he had been since he'd come home. Finally

Matthew said, "It would be a good thing, wouldn't it, Pa?"

As Daniel Bradford sat there in silence, listening to all Matthew said, it grieved him deeply. Everything in him longed to cry out against it. He remembered clearly how Leo Rochester had deceived Matthew's mother and had thrown her aside. He remembered the cruelty in Rochester, deceiving both him and Lyna into thinking that each other had died. There was nothing pleasant in his memory of his old master and he wanted to shout, "No, leave him alone! Stay away from him, Matthew! He'll destroy you as he has everything else that he has touched."

But he did not. He clasped his hands together, squeezed them tightly, and bowed his head. "I'm sure you would enjoy seeing the paintings at his home," he said quietly. Then he rose and said, "I'm tired. I think I'll go to bed. Good night."

Daniel went to his room, sat down on the bed, and buried his face in his hands. He was trembling. "I didn't think anything could do that to me," he whispered, looking at his hands. He'd used these hands once on Leo Rochester years ago, and now the same impulse to use them again came forcibly to him. "If he destroys Matthew, I'll . . ." He shook himself and his jaw hardened. "I can't think of that," he said quietly, his face set like granite.

9

When Cousins Disagree

ON JUNE 12, 1775, GENERAL THOMAS GAGE issued a bombastic proclamation in which he said, "The rebels, with a preposterous parade of military arrangement, affected to hold the army besieged." The arrangements may have been preposterous, but the siege was real enough. The straggling American army of some seven or eight thousand men stretched in a great semicircle from the Mystic River on the north through Cambridge and Roxbury to Dorchester. The opinion of some concerning this army was revealed in a letter from an anonymous British officer. He wrote, "There is a large body of them at arms near Boston. But truly it is nothing but a drunken, canting, lying, praying, hypocritical rabble, without order, subjection, discipline, or cleanliness; and must fall to pieces of itself in the course of three months."

The officer's opinion might have contained some validity, but General Gage knew that his position was precarious. He was boxed in by land and on sea, supported occasionally by Admiral Graves, who performed less than admirably. Gage also well understood that the American command, either of Dorchester Heights or Georgetown, would make his own position untenable.

In corresponding with Lord North, who guided the course of the war from London, Gage wrote a letter almost dripping with discouragement: "In our present state all warlike preparations are wanting. No survey of enemy country, no proper boats for landing troops, not enough horses for the artillery, no forage, either hay or corn, of any consequence." He went on to describe a very accurate picture of the battle tactics being employed by the rebels. "Their mode of engaging is by getting behind fences and every sort of covering. They fire, then retire

111

and load under cover and then return to the charge. The country for thirty miles around is amazingly well situated for their manner of fighting, being covered by woods and small stone enclosures."

Lord George Germaine, who had served as Secretary of State for the Colonies, gave a harsh judgment of General Gage. "I must lament that General Gage with all his good qualities finds himself in a situation of too great importance for his talents. I doubt whether Gage will venture to take a single step beyond the letter of his instructions."

Inside Boston itself the situation grew more difficult. After the engagements at Lexington and Concord, the population had declined from seventeen thousand to less than seven thousand civilians. Not all of those who remained behind were Tory. Some civilians stayed, like Daniel Bradford, to take care of their businesses. Those who did choose to remain in the city suffered the hardships of the siege and of exposure to the enemy. John Andrews wrote to his friend, William Barrell, of the difficulties that had already surfaced by this time:

"The British soldiers think they have a license to plunder the house and stores of everyone that leaves the town. Wanton destruction of property is common. Food grows scarce already. Now and then a carcass is offered for sale in the market, which we would not have picked up in the street, but bad as it is, it readily sells for eight pence lawful money per pound. Pork and beans one day and beans and pork another and fish when we can catch it. It has so far influenced many to leave, and others will surely follow."

🔔   🔔   🔔

Jeanne Corbeau was less aware of the tribulations of the patriots who remained in Boston than she might have been. The officers of Gage's army naturally suffered less, for they had first choice of such fresh food as could be found. And during the siege the British even carried on some rather gala affairs, including balls, plays, teas, and whatever sort of entertainment they might conceive.

Grace Gordon had made it her mission to make a social being out of the young woman who had stepped into her world. She had spent hours talking with Jeanne about her life in the woods and was appalled at how narrow it had been. Speaking to her mother, she had said, "She knows how to skin a deer and track a bear—but she doesn't know how to serve tea! And as for clothing and makeup and making herself attractive, she puts on whatever is at hand. But I'll soon change that...!"

Grace quickly discovered, however, that Jeanne was not as easy to educate in the social graces as she had anticipated. There was a wariness in the young woman that held her back. Part of this was a natural shyness mixed with a rather stubborn spirit. Jeanne herself was constantly uneasy in her new settings and spent hours longing to return to her old life.

"I can't stand these four walls much longer, Grace," she said one morning as the two sat together in the kitchen drinking tea. It was a clear day outside, and Jeanne rose to stare out the window. White clouds drifted across a hard blue sky in a leisurely fashion, and a brisk breeze stirred the tops of the mulberry trees outside in the small garden. Jeanne turned with discontent on her face. "I wish I were back home again!"

"I'm sorry you're lonely and bored," Grace said quickly. "But I've got a surprise for you."

"A surprise? What kind of surprise?"

"We're going to a party tonight. Not a ball, exactly—but there'll be some of the younger officers there and some of the leading Tories. I think you'll find them quite acceptable."

Jeanne instantly felt her heart sink. The social events she had already attended had only succeeded in making her feel clumsy and completely out of place. "I don't think I'd like to go, Grace," she said.

"Oh, Jeanne, you've got to go! I've got a beautiful dress that will be just right for you."

"I don't feel right. I feel like a doll for some reason," Jeanne insisted. "You dress me up and show me how to fix my hair, but when we're there, I can't think of a thing to say." She turned back to stare out of the window, adding disconsolately, "I don't have anything in common with any of those people."

"You will have. It takes time, Jeanne, but soon we'll have a dance, a real ball."

"But I can't even dance!"

"I'll teach you," Grace nodded firmly. "If you can walk through the woods as Clive says without making any noise, then you're graceful enough to learn to dance. Come on—I'll show you now." Grace stood up, grabbed Jeanne's arms, and walked her through the steps of a dance for a few moments around the stone floor of the kitchen.

Finally Jeanne stumbled and threw up her hands in frustration. "I'll never learn this, and I don't want to go to the party!" She whirled and left the kitchen unhappy and determined to stay home that night.

But Grace was not about to give up and enlisted Lyna's help. Together the two women persuaded Jeanne to go. At three o'clock, the two stepped out of the house and into a carriage. They made their way to Faneuil Hall, which General Gage used on occasion for social affairs. When they stepped inside, Jeanne almost shrank from the sight of the brilliant scarlet coats of the officers and the beautiful colored dresses of the ladies. The air was filled with the sound of laughter, but Jeanne longed to turn and flee.

"Come along—there's Father. Isn't he the handsomest thing!" Grace led Jeanne to where her father was standing with several officers.

Leslie Gordon greeted them with a smile. "Well, we are graced with your presence, ladies. Do you know these gentlemen?"

All the officers were wearing their finery, the scarlet coats, the glittering brass buckles, the epaulets on the shoulders of some. Most of them wore powdered wigs, except for a few such as Leslie Gordon, who preferred not to wear one.

Jeanne allowed herself to be introduced to the officers, and was aware that they were all curious about her. *They know I've been brought in out of the woods like a wild animal of some kind*, she thought rebelliously. *I wish I'd stayed home!* She resented being put on display, and despite the kindness of the Gordons, she was convinced that some people were laughing at her. More than once she caught stares from several ladies gathered in small groups.

"Come along, Jeanne," Grace said. "There are some young ladies that you need to meet."

The two young women moved across the polished floor of the hall to several long tables set up along the walls. The tables were covered with silver and pewter vessels filled with tea, ale, and other beverages. The cut-glass goblets filled by the servants glittered under the brightly burning chandelier overhead, and there was a carnival air throughout the hall.

"I don't believe you've met our guest, Miss Jeanne Corbeau." Grace introduced the girl to three young ladies, who greeted Jeanne with the same curiosity that she had seen in the eyes of the officers.

One of them was Abigail Howland. She was wearing a beautiful rose-colored dress and had her hair fixed in a rather ornate style. With a coy look, she remarked, "I understand that you come from our possessions in the west, Miss Corbeau." Abigail, along with the others, had gotten reports of the "country bumpkin" that Clive had brought home to live with his family. Abigail found Clive very attractive and had teased him about it. "Did you bring her home for a house pet?" she had asked. Now looking at the young woman, her countenance changed. She had expected less than Jeanne's trim figure in the light blue dress and the strange attractiveness of the short-cropped black hair. "Clive tells me you're quite a woodsman—or would that be woodswoman?"

The other young women hid their smiles—almost—and Abigail

asked with a glitter of amusement in her eyes, "Did you ever shoot an Indian, Miss Corbeau?"

Jeanne looked straight at Abigail, for she recognized the calculating stare in the eyes of the beautiful young woman. "No, I've never shot an Indian. Only animals that threatened me." There was an evenness in her voice, yet she held her chin high, and Grace knew at once that she was angry.

"When will the next ball be?" Grace asked quickly to change the tenor of the conversation.

"Oh, whenever General Gage sees fit. Now that General Burgoyne is here," Abigail said, "I'm expecting we'll have more of them. He's quite a man about town, you know."

Jeanne was as miserable at the affair as she had anticipated. Her eyes brightened when Clive came in. When he came over wearing a beautifully tailored brown suit with a frilly white shirt, his reddish hair catching the reflection from the chandelier, she thought of how handsome he was.

"Are you having a good time, Jeanne?" he asked, sipping at the glass of punch one of the servants had handed him.

"Very well, thank you," Jeanne said.

Her answer was so brief that Clive knew at once something was wrong. He glanced quickly at Grace, who shook her head with a slight motion, then cut her eyes to where the young ladies were sitting at the next table in the midst of a group of admirers. "Well, these social affairs can be rather tiresome," Clive said briskly. For the remainder of the evening, Clive stayed close to Jeanne so as to spare her from any more embarrassing moments. Whenever he would introduce her to anyone, she was polite enough but never entered into the conversation. Finally, when it was time to leave, Clive said, "I'll see you home, ladies." He left Grace and Jeanne waiting near the door while he went and expressed his thanks to General Gage for the invitation. When he returned, a servant had already brought around the carriage. As they made their way back to the house, Grace and Clive commented on the party, but Jeanne remained wrapped in silence, staring straight ahead. As soon as they arrived and entered the house, Jeanne excused herself and went at once to her room.

"She feels so . . . so out of place, Clive." Grace shook her head almost in despair. "I'm not sure she can be turned into a graceful young lady who would fit in at a ball, or meeting, or party like today."

"Of course it can be done!" Clive snapped with some irritation. "It'll just take time. If you were thrown out into the woods, it would take a while to teach you what she knows."

"I think there are more difficulties learning the things of civilization—and sometimes I think the dangers are worse than they are in the forest."

"What do you mean by that?"

"I mean, Clive, that people can be crueler than wild animals at times. I could've strangled Abigail Howland and her superior airs!" Grace had a temper that sometimes flared up, and now her gray-green eyes almost glittered as she clenched her fist and glared up at her brother. "Don't you have anything to do with that wench! You hear me, Clive!"

Clive grinned down at her. "Had no intentions of doing anything with her. She bores me to tears! All she talks about are balls, ribbons, dances, and dresses—but I suppose that's what most of them talk about. We'll have to do something for Jeanne, Grace," he said. "Maybe we can take her and introduce her to some of the more genteel women. You can do it, Grace, and I'll help."

♜ ♜ ♜

"There's a young man to see you," Lyna announced. She'd come up to Jeanne's room and stood in the door, a slight smile on her face. "Are you receiving visitors today?"

"A young man?" Jeanne turned to stare at Lyna. "What young man?"

"A relative of mine. Come along."

Most young ladies would have stopped to look into the mirror to see if their hair was brushed or if their beauty mark was in place or if their clothes were suitable. But it was typical of Jeanne Corbeau that she thought of none of these things. She moved down the hall with Lyna and down the stairs. When they got to the foyer, Lyna turned to her. "I believe you know my nephew, Mr. Dake Bradford."

Dake, standing beside the foot of the stairs, grinned broadly, saying, "I've come calling, Miss Jeanne. It's time you knew something about the respectable side of this family."

Dake was wearing a pair of butternut knee breeches and a leather jerkin over a white shirt with full sleeves. His corded neck looked very strong, and there was a depth of thickness to his broad chest that spoke of great physical strength. He had remained in Boston, for his officer had told him that he could be of more use in town by picking up information. "Not a spy exactly. Just see what you learn," the lieutenant had said.

"I've come to take you on an outing."

"An outing?" Jeanne blinked with surprise.

"Sure. Clive's been telling everyone what a great hunter you are, so

116

I thought we might go out and see if we can't bring in something for the pot."

Instantly Jeanne's eyes grew bright. "Oh yes, I would like that very much!" Then she remembered that she was a guest and turned at once to her hostess. "Will that be all right, Mrs. Gordon?"

"Why, I suppose so. But you be careful, Dake. I hear there's been an exchange of shots between our troops and the patriots."

Dake quickly nodded. "I'll be very careful, Aunt Lyna. I know the ground around here better than any man in the Colonies—every foot of it. Don't you worry. I'll bring her back safe and sound—and maybe with a nice fat brace of rabbits or a buck if we're lucky."

"I can't wear these clothes. Let me go put on my old dress." Jeanne turned at once and disappeared up the stairs.

Lyna smiled at Dake, but there was a worried look on her face. "Isn't it dangerous for you to be here, Dake? I mean, you could be accused of being a spy, I suppose."

"No, I'm just a plain ordinary citizen. I'm not very popular with you British types," he said. His smile creased his wide lips, and his teeth seemed very white against his tan skin. "It'll be all right, Aunt Lyna. One day it won't be, maybe, but for now it's safe."

"Very well. I'm putting her in your charge, but you understand that you must be on your good behavior."

"Why, Aunt Lyna!" Dake assumed an injured expression. "When was I anything but on my good behavior? Especially with young women." He saw her concern and assured her quickly. "From what Clive has told me about her, I thought she might like to get out into the woods. That's been her whole life as I understand it."

"I'm glad you came. She doesn't like parties too much, but I'm sure she'll have a good time with you. It will do her some good to get out of the house other than for another party."

Jeanne came down the stairs shortly, wearing the old dress that she had brought with her. It was a simple gray affair that was worn and without ornamentation, and she said, "You can't hurt this one, Mr. Bradford."

"Mr. Bradford's my father," Dake said cheerfully. "I'm Dake, and I suppose I can call you Jeanne."

"Yes, of course," Jeanne smiled. "Let's go. I'm ready to get outdoors."

Dake led her out of the house. He had brought two muskets with him and carried them both as they walked through town. As soon as they had turned off and entered into a copious woods, she said, "I can carry that musket." She took it, and he grinned to watch the familiarity of her touch.

"It's not loaded yet," he said.

"Let me do it," Jeanne said eagerly.

They stopped, and he watched as she expertly inserted the powder, the wad, and the shot, and prepared the weapon to fire. She threw it up and took a practice shot, and he saw that she was strong enough to hold it steady.

"Does it shoot true?" she asked.

"That's Father's gun. I haven't shot it much. This one is mine," he said. "We'll stop and take some more practice shots when we're a little farther out of town."

It was a brisk day with the pale sun slipping out from behind billowing clouds from time to time. They passed into a thick forest, and Jeanne relaxed as they walked along a rather secluded trail that wound between large first-growth timber. Finally they found an open spot, and Dake set up a target, which Jeanne struck with such ease that Dake whistled. "I never thought a woman could shoot so well," he said. "I'll have to look out or you'll best me."

Dake had not boasted when he'd told his aunt that he knew the territory around Boston. He loved the woods and had covered every foot of this ground at one time or another. Whenever the need for meat arose, it was his boast that he could bring in game at any time. "Just like a butcher shop to me—the woods are. Give me your order and I'll bring it in!"

As they walked along quietly, he noted that Jeanne had the traits of an expert woodsman. Clive had mentioned this, but Dake had not believed it completely. Now he saw that years of practice had made her as good at moving through the woods as he. For some reason this pleased him, and he enjoyed her company. They did not speak much for a time and finally he said, "See those oak trees up ahead? We'll find a bunch of squirrels there. Do you like squirrel meat?"

"Nothing better than squirrel stew," Jeanne said. Her cheeks were flushed and she wore no hat, so that her black, curly hair was blown by the breeze in a most attractive way. When she turned to him, he was again surprised at her eyes. He'd never known anyone with such striking blue eyes and found them intensely attractive.

"Thank you for bringing me," she said rather shyly.

"I know what it's like to want to escape into the quiet of the woods," he offered. "Come along now. I want to show you some favorite places where I like to hunt."

An hour later they had bagged six fat squirrels. To his chagrin,

Jeanne had shot four, while he, himself, shot only two. "You bested me that time, Jeanne," he laughed good-naturedly. "You're a fine shot!"

It was a compliment that pleased her. She suddenly thought of how much more at ease she felt in the woods with Dake than she had been with Grace and Clive at the party in Faneuil Hall. "I wish I didn't ever have to go to another party," she said abruptly. "I feel so awkward and ugly and out of place!"

"Why, that's not true!" Dake said with some surprise.

"I feel like it—which is the same thing."

"Well, you've got to stop feeling like that," Dake insisted. He'd put the squirrels in a game bag and swung it over his shoulder. "Come on, I think we might get a shot at a deer. Some roasted venison would taste pretty good for dinner." As they moved forward, they came to a brook that gurgled quietly in its banks. "They come here to drink pretty often. Maybe we can find some tracks." They continued down along the stream until Jeanne suddenly stopped. "There! That's a big one," she said.

Dake looked down and saw the large tracks and said, "You have good eyes, Jeanne. Fresh tracks, too." He turned around and said, "Let's get over there behind that stand of trees. I think we can get a good shot if they come back to drink."

They moved to the shelter of the glades to wait. Dake was interested to see if Jeanne could remain still, as a good hunter must over a long period of time. He was not disappointed, for Jeanne stood there in absolute silence, her gaze fixed on the spot where the deer might come to drink. They had not been there over fifteen minutes when a buck with a full rack of antlers stepped out of the deep woods and approached the water. He kept his head high sniffing the air for an enemy, then he lowered his head and began to drink. He'd come out farther from their position than either of them had anticipated. It would be a hard shot, but the only one they were likely to get. Dake reached out and touched Jeanne's arm. When she turned to him, he made the words with his lips silently, "You take the shot."

Jeanne smiled and in one smooth motion she flung up the rifle, held it steady as a rock for one instant, then pulled the trigger. There was a flash and explosion as she felt the rifle's impact on her shoulder.

"You got him!" Dake yelled. "Come on!"

They splashed across the brook and found the deer lying with his neck broken by the shot. "Fine shot!" Dake said. "Fine! Isn't he a beauty!"

Jeanne's face was flushed with excitement and her lips were parted as she said, "He is nice." She knelt down and touched the antlers and then looked up. "They're so beautiful that I hate to kill them."

It was a thought that would not have occurred to Dake. To him the deer was food, but he was pleased with this gentleness within her. "They are beautiful—but we have to eat. I'll tell you what—I'll come back with a pack animal and bring him in."

As they made their way back toward town, Jeanne talked more than Dake had expected. He saw that the trip had given her great pleasure, and he was glad of it.

When they arrived at the Gordon home, Jeanne burst in through the back door, where she found Lyna and Clive in the kitchen. "We got six squirrels and a deer," she said. Her eyes were flashing with excitement as she turned to Dake. "Oh, it was wonderful, Dake! Thank you so much!"

Clive stared at Dake. He had come in half an hour before and had been greatly disturbed when his mother had told him of Jeanne's expedition. Now he said sharply, "Dake, you shouldn't have taken her out there. You should have known better."

Dake was surprised at the sharpness of his cousin's words. "Why, there wasn't any danger," he said defensively.

"Of course there was! There's firing over the lines from both sides. A sergeant got clipped in the leg yesterday just walking along the lines. She might have been killed!"

Instantly Dake straightened up. "I guess I've got enough sense to stay away from places like that. After all, I know where the troops are. I took her to a safe enough place."

Clive shook his head stubbornly. "You shouldn't have done it," he repeated. "And I won't have it anymore."

A flush reddened Dake's neck. All of them saw a recklessness surface in him suddenly. He opened his mouth, saying, "Now, wait a minute—"

Lyna quickly interrupted. "Don't quarrel over this! Jeanne's safe enough." She tried to ease the tension that was mounting by putting her hand on Clive's arm. "Clive was worried—that's all."

Jeanne stood there, amazed at Clive's anger and protectiveness. He had never shown this side of himself to her. "I'm sorry, Clive," she said. "But I didn't really think there would be any harm in it. It felt so good to be back in the woods again."

His feelings ruffled, Clive said stiffly, "I don't think you ought to do it again. If you *must* go, *I'll* take you." He turned and walked out of the room, leaving an awkward, tense silence.

"I apologize for Clive," Lyna said quickly. "I'll go talk to him. He'll be all right. He was just concerned for your safety." She turned and left the room, leaving the two alone.

"I don't see why he's so mad," Jeanne remarked.

"You don't?"

"No, it was just a hunting trip."

Dake knew she was speaking the truth. Her years of seclusion in the wilderness had left her with an innocence that did not recognize what he and Lyna had seen at once—Clive Gordon was showing a possessive air about this attractive young woman. Dake would not speak out against his cousin, but said, "Clive's all right. He's just a little bit stuffy. We'll have to do this again, but we'll clear it with him first."

"Oh, I'd like to go again!"

When she turned to him, there was a freshness in her eyes and a clearness in her expression that pleased him. Dake had never been in love, but he appreciated the company of young women. Somehow he was drawn to the qualities in Jeanne Corbeau that he had not found in the powdered and pampered daughters of Boston society. He smiled and put his hand out. When she took it, he found her hand firm and strong, yet, paradoxically, soft and feminine.

"We'll go again," he murmured. "I'll go back and bring the deer in. Half for the Bradfords and half for the Gordons." He left, and after getting his horse, he made his way to the grove, dressed the deer out, and delivered half of it back to the Gordons' house. He did not see Jeanne, and when he got home, Micah asked him how the expedition had gone.

"It went fine," Dake said. "Someone needs to take Jeanne out some, so I guess I'm the lucky fellow." He grinned rashly. "Those British relatives of ours are all right, but they've sure got some uppity ways!"

10

AMERICA FINDS A GENERAL

WHEN THE SECOND CONTINENTAL CONGRESS began meeting in May of 1775, Philadelphia was swarming with militia. Already thirty companies had gathered for the war that had been declared. There were martial demonstrations in the streets, with riflemen volunteering for companies. But despite the ardor of its surroundings, the Congress moved slowly.

Some members of the body wanted to send "a humble and dutiful" petition to His Majesty to try to solve the crisis through diplomatic negotiations. Against these would-be petitioners stood John Adams. Adams was the cousin of the fiery Sam Adams who had touched the spark to the gunpowder in Boston. John Adams was more temperate, but also more of a politician. He was well aware that the most important single task that faced this Congress was the selection of a man to lead the fledgling army into battle.

Many sought this honor, including the immensely wealthy John Hancock. But John Adams had fixed his eyes on the one man he felt would not falter in the crucible that the country was about to enter. Day after day, Colonel George Washington sat in the Congress, his two-hundred-pound, six-foot three-inch frame upright in the chair. He wore a red and buff uniform, and he sat for hours wrapped in a mantle of silence, observing the proceedings. His silence disturbed some.

As the tall man sat there, his gray eyes fixed on the meeting, one of the Massachusetts members asked, "Who is he?"

"Him? Oh, he's a farmer from Virginia. His name's George Washington."

"He never speaks?" the inquirer asked.

"No, but he's one of the richest men in the Colonies."

Later John Adams told his cousin, "I think he's the man that we need at the helm. He knows how to keep a still tongue."

Sam stared at the tall officer. "Maybe he's got nothing to say."

"No, this man, Washington, is chairman of four military committees. Nobody's ever heard of him, but look at him! You can't ignore the man. They hear how much money he's got and they vote for him without even thinking about it."

"How much is he worth?" Sam asked.

"More perhaps than anybody else in this country. He can wear the uniform and he is an expert horseman."

"The North won't like it, but the South will!"

"But we've already got the North," Adams said. "Now we need the South. I mean, of course, Virginia. I'm going to nominate Washington."

Adams bided his time. He listened while talk ran around. Some argued that the commander in chief should be a professional, such as British-born Charles Lee, or Hancock, who burned to wear the honors of commander in chief.

On June 14, Adams rose and waited as the din of voices hushed to an expectant silence. John Hancock, sitting in the president's chair, listened hopefully as Adams began to describe his worthy candidate. After a moment, the words "a gentleman from Virginia who is among us and who is—George Washington of Virginia" shocked him. John Hancock's face went pale, and George Washington got up and left the room without a word. A swelling hum of voices grew—some shocked and some pleased—as Sam Adams rose to second the nomination. The next day, on June 15, Washington appeared and heard Hancock say, "The president of Congress has the order of Congress to inform George Washington, Esquire, of the unanimous vote in choosing him to be general and commander in chief of the forces raised."

George Washington rose and said slowly, "I do not think myself equal to the command I am honored with." He then declined to take any pay for his service and stated that he would keep an account of his expenses.

"And so, we have a general," John Adams announced. "Now we will see what he can do with this army, whose duty is to save America from England's tyranny."

Ⱦ   Ⱦ   Ⱦ

While Washington was being chosen by the Second Continental Congress, General Thomas Gage did very little in Boston. He did call a meeting of his fellow generals and tried to hammer out some plan to lift the siege of Boston. All three of the generals had been dismayed to learn that Gage's complaints about the fighting ground of America had not been exaggerated. Burgoyne pointed out, "We have a supply line three thousand miles long, and the chance for maneuvering in traditional European style is impossible in the wilderness."

"Agreed!" Gage said. "Still something must be attempted, gentlemen."

General Howe had been studying the map that was pinned to the wall inside Howe's headquarters. "I think the only thing to do is to attack Cambridge. Look!" he said, pointing at the map. "If the Americans control Dorchester Heights here overlooking Boston, then we're lost. We must take the initiative and attack!"

Howe had already been making his plans. He spoke swiftly and surely, pointing at the map as he laid out his strategy. "It seems fairly certain that as soon as we move, the Americans will immediately fortify one of these hills—either Breed's Hill, close to the shore, or Bunker Hill farther back. I, myself, will lead an amphibious invasion at Dorchester Point. Here to the right of Cambridge. General Clinton, you will land at Willis Creek to the left and secure the high ground at Charlestown. Then we will roll up the American flanks, converge on Cambridge—and serve a fast victory!"

Burgoyne and Clinton seemed pleased with the plan, but General Thomas Gage had seen maps and heard plans before. It was necessary of course that he seem positive, so he said bluffly, "At last we're ready to put these rebels back on their hill. Gentlemen, let's all propose a toast to our imminent victory." But in his heart lurked grave doubt, for the fierce struggle the patriots had put up on the road to Concord had shaken him. He, at least, had no illusion about the willingness of these men of America to lay their lives on the line and fight when their hearts burned for freedom from English rule.

🔔　　🔔　　🔔

Reverend Able Dorch of the Anglican Church of Boston looked around the dining room and felt pleased. He had long had a special feeling for Clive Gordon and his family, and had often taken meals with them. Now he paid special attention to the strangely attractive young woman who had apparently been added to the family circle. Colonel Gordon had discreetly informed him of the young woman's circumstances, and Dorch had been dutifully tactful.

"Well, my dear Mrs. Gordon, you have managed to set a good table in spite of our problem with the supply line," the minister beamed. He looked over the haunch of venison and nodded with appreciation.

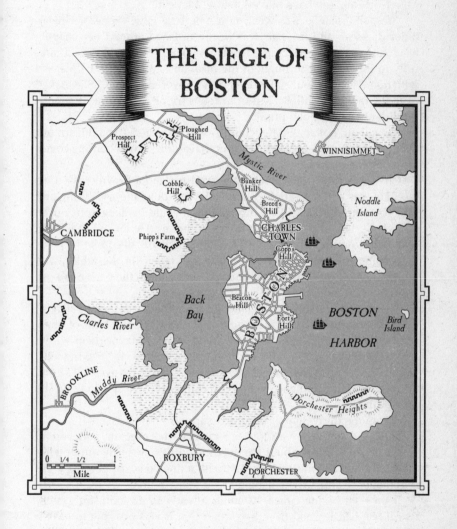

THE SIEGE OF BOSTON

Prospect Hill
Ploughed Hill
WINNISIMMET
Mystic River
Cobble Hill
Bunker Hill
Breed's Hill
Noddle Island
CAMBRIDGE
CHARLES-TOWN
Phipp's Farm
Copp's Hill
BOSTON
Back Bay
Beacon Hill
Charles River
Fort's Hill
BOSTON
Bird Island
BROOKLINE
HARBOR
Muddy River
Dorchester Heights
0   1/4   1/2   1
Mile
ROXBURY
DORCHESTER

"Nothing like well-cooked venison, I always say."

"You'll have to thank our guest for that," Clive Gordon said. "It was Miss Corbeau that brought down this particular bit of supper."

"Indeed!" Surprise washed across Dorch's face. "I congratulate you, Miss Corbeau. You have hunted before, I take it?"

"Yes, sir." Jeanne was wearing a pale rose gown—one of Grace's older dresses—and her hair was neatly brushed around her shapely head. She wore no jewelry at all and no makeup. She had listened carefully to the minister throughout the meal and appeared to be pleased with him. "That's about all I've ever done, Reverend Dorch." She looked over at Grace and smiled. "Miss Gordon is trying to teach me manners, but I'm not a very good pupil."

"Not at all, not at all!" Reverend Dorch protested. "You'll learn our ways soon enough—and I must admit that a skill such as hunting comes in handy these days."

Clive was sitting across from the minister, and a frown crossed his face. He was still not satisfied that Dake had done the wise thing and said so. "I tried to tell Miss Corbeau that it could be dangerous out in the woods," he said, sounding rather pompous. He looked at Jeanne, who had dropped her head. "It's for her own good, of course."

Sensing the tension that had suddenly fallen on the table, Lyna quickly spoke up, "If we're all finished, let's go into the parlor. We can have some singing."

They moved into the parlor, and although there was no harpsichord in the house, the Gordons were all fine singers. After an hour of unaccompanied singing, Leslie Gordon asked Dorch to favor them with a few thoughts taken from his sermon the past Sunday. "Yes, indeed," Dorch said. A warm humor flickered in his dark brown eyes. "It's good to have a captive audience here. Next Sunday, I'll be speaking on the new birth."

"From the third chapter of John, I suppose?" Lyna asked.

"Yes, indeed, Mrs. Gordon! 'Ye must be born again.'" Reverend Dorch began to speak about the doctrine of the new birth, quoting liberally. He was an entertaining man with a fine voice, possessing a gift for eloquence and an astonishing grasp of Scripture.

Jeanne sat beside Grace, listening intently to the minister's every word. She had learned from her father that it was possible to have a deeply personal relationship with God, but her own religious experience had only consisted of listening to what others said about God. She had talked with a few Catholic missionaries who had come through from time to time. She had seen the great evangelist George Whitefield preach once, and it had deeply impressed her—but had also left her full

126

of questions. A few other roughhewn evangelists had visited their iso-lated area. Offshoots of the Great Awakening, they had displayed more enthusiasm or zeal than politeness, and she was not sure what to make of them. She found Reverend Dorch to be most interesting, expounding on things she had often wondered about but had no way of searching out.

Before the minister left, he extracted a promise from Jeanne to attend services the following Sunday. Later, she asked Clive, "What did the minister mean about being born again?"

Clive was taken aback. "Why ... I'm not sure. It's in the Bible, though."

"My father knew God. I wish I knew God like he did."

"Maybe you ought to talk to the minister."

"No, I can't do that. He's a busy man."

Clive felt somewhat perplexed, for he didn't know how to help her on this matter. "I think that *is* his business, Jeanne. I'm sure he wouldn't be offended."

Jeanne turned to look up at him, a thoughtfulness growing in her eyes. "I think I will," she said. Then without preamble she asked, "Have you been born again, Clive?"

Clive had taken a blow once in a rough game with some compan-ions. He had been struck in the pit of his stomach and for a few mo-ments had been unable to speak or move or even breathe. Something like this happened to him right now. The question was simple and forth-right, and Jeanne looked at him out of innocent eyes—waiting for his reply—but he found that he could make none.

Jeanne saw that he was embarrassed and quickly put her hand on his arm. "I didn't mean to bother you," she said quickly, "but I'd like to know more about it."

Clive, for once, was anxious to be out of Jeanne's company. "Well, perhaps you ought to talk to Mother. She knows more about things like that. I think I'll go to bed early. Good night, Jeanne."

He left hurriedly and went to his room, amazed to find himself so shaken by such a simple question. He had heard the Bible read in church many times, and his mother and father read it constantly. He himself, however, had never been a reader of Scripture. He had read hundreds of medical books, and now somehow he vaguely regretted it. "I'll have to look into that. She may ask again," he murmured. Then he promptly forgot it and reached over to pick up a book on a scientific subject.

11

AN UNCERTAIN VICTORY

DAKE WAS TAKEN BY SURPRISE when Asa Pollard and Aaron Burr came running up all excited with their news. The three men had been fast friends ever since their childhood. Everything they had shared together in their experiences of adolescence and young manhood had formed a firm bond of friendship between them. Asa, a bony, cheerful young fellow, grabbed Dake by the neck playfully. "Get your musket, Dake! We're going hunting for lobsterbacks!"

Dake slapped Pollard's hand away and grinned. He liked the young man very much. "What do you mean by that, Asa?" he demanded.

"We just got word that the British are on the move," said Aaron Burr, a tall, thoughtful young man of nineteen, with gray eyes and a thatch of rusty red hair. "General Putnam's sent word out to all the volunteers to report for duty as soon as possible."

As Aaron spoke, quickly outlining the events of the day, Dake felt a surge of excitement begin to course through his veins. Ever since the road back from Concord, where he'd had his first taste of battle, he had waited for this moment to fight back against the hated lobsterbacks and drive them all the way back to England. When Aaron finished, Dake said quickly, "I've got to talk to my father. You fellows wait here."

Aaron said, "I wish he'd go with us. He has a lot of respect, your father does—and it would mean a lot more men would join if we could convince him to join the cause. Talk to him, Dake."

Dake hurried at once to his father's study. Without knocking on the door, he burst in, saying, "Pa, the British are moving! We've got to stop them."

Daniel Bradford looked up from the book he was reading. He closed it and tossed it on the desk, knowing that he could no longer sidestep the decision that had been hovering over him for weeks now. "What's happening, son?" he asked quietly.

128

"I guess Gage finally woke up to what he's got to do. They're going to move ships in and cover a landing and try to take Cambridge. Aaron and Asa are outside. They say the Committee of Safety found out all about it through their spy network. Word was they were supposed to hit Dorchester Heights, but now they're going to try and take Cambridge. General Ward and General Putnam are calling for every man that has a rifle to come and fight them off."

"And—you're going?" The question was useless, for Daniel saw the light of excitement in Dake's eyes. Slowly getting to his feet, he walked over to his son and said, "I've been thinking and praying about this for a long time, Dake. I've tried every way I can to stay out of this thing— but there's no way. I'll be coming with you."

Without thinking, Dake let out a shout and grabbed his father by the shoulders. "I knew you'd do it, Pa!" His eyes gleamed with exhilaration, and he added, "They can't stop us. We'll win, you'll see! I'll go get Micah."

"No, let him alone. He wouldn't go anyway. His mind's not made up on this thing, and whatever you do—don't get Sam all stirred up. I've made Micah promise to keep his eye on him. I've dreaded that something like this might be coming. Well," he said, taking a final look around the study, "this might be the last time you or I will see this place. It's been a good home."

At his father's stark remark, Dake stopped still and an odd look crossed his face. The thought of death somehow had not occurred to him. "Why, of course we'll be coming back," he said indignantly. In the exuberance of youth and the excitement of the moment, he had put the possibility of death somewhere far from his mind. But now that his father had voiced it, the thought troubled him. "Well," he said, "a man's got to do his duty."

"That's right, Dake, but he's also got to remember to answer to God. What about you? Are you ready to meet God?"

Dake suddenly felt awkward and embarrassed as his father stared at him intently. He was not a man of God, and did not like to be questioned about it. His father was a devoted Christian, but he had put the matter off, and now dropped his head and murmured, "I guess not, Pa—you know that. But I've got to go anyway."

Daniel was saddened by his son's response, but he said no more. The two left the house, joined Aaron and Asa, and made their way through the streets of Boston. They saw a few soldiers, but not as many as usual. They went at once to the outskirts of the city, where they found General Israel Putnam meeting with General Artemas Ward.

Putnam was fifty-seven years old, a huge man with a bear's body, a voice like a bull, and a great, round, owlish head. To his advantage, he had military experience. At one point in his military career, he narrowly missed being burned at the stake by Indians. He had also been a prisoner of the French during the French and Indian War. On this night, he was standing in front of a fire with a group of men as more volunteers joined the growing patriot army. In his hands were a set of fine horse pistols that he was admiring. He smiled as he looked at them, for they had belonged to Major John Pitcairn, who had lost them on the road back from Concord.

As soon as Putnam saw Daniel approach, his eyes lit up. "Bradford!" he said. "You've come to join us, then?"

"Yes, General. It's been a hard decision to come to, but I can do no less."

Putnam nodded with pleasure. "We need men like you, Daniel Bradford! You've had some experience, I understand, in military matters."

"When I was a young man in the British army."

"Well, that's more than most of these fellows have had." Putnam waved his hand at the soldiers that were milling around, then turned to the tall, older man on his right. "You know General Ward," he said. "We've been trying to pull everything together." He quickly explained the military situation to Daniel. "We know the British are going to attack Charlestown by making a landing. We're waiting now for Colonel William Prescott. He's supposed to arrive here with twelve hundred men, and we're going to need every man jack of them!"

"And you—you're now Sergeant Bradford," Putnam grunted.

"Why, I'm not ready for that," Daniel protested.

"You're older than some of these fellows. We need older men with some experience to hold them together when the fighting gets tough. Come along and I'll introduce you to your squad."

So it was that Daniel Bradford found himself a sergeant in the fledgling army that was to face the British forces the next day. The men who had gathered about him were of all ages and wore no uniforms. Included among them were his own son Dake, and Dake's comrades, Asa Pollard and Aaron Burr. Daniel gathered them round and said, "You'll not hear any speeches from me. Any one of you could probably be a better sergeant. I say let's stick together and drive the British back into the sea."

"That's the way to talk, Sergeant!" Asa Pollard exclaimed. He held his musket up in his scrawny hand, and his grin flashed as he said, "We'll get the lobsterbacks!"

The men moved about almost aimlessly, waiting for Prescott. He arrived with his force at about nine o'clock that night. Prescott was a farmer from Pepperell and had fought so well at Louisbourg during the French and Indian War that he had been offered a commission in the British army. But he returned to his plow—until Lexington and Concord had roused him. He was a lean, sharp-spoken man with light blue eyes, as practical and careful as Israel Putnam was impetuous and rash. He brought with him Colonel Richard Gridley as his engineer.

The force that he'd brought with him looked much like the men already there. Most of them were dressed in homespun that was dyed in the tan and brown colors of local oaks. They wore wide-brimmed farmer hats, and the majority of them clutched hunting muskets in their hands. Some of them carried old Brown Besses from the Colonial Wars, and Daniel even saw an ancient Spanish Fusee as they marched through the town's deserted streets and into the hills beyond.

When they reached the hills, the leaders immediately began to argue. They were searching for Bunker Hill, the height they were to occupy, but found three hills. Moulton's Hill, the lowest of the three, was quickly ignored. There remained Breed's Hill and Bunker Hill to its rear. Breed's Hill could be defended more easily, but for a time Prescott held out for Bunker Hill. Gridley, the engineer, maintained that the hill they stood on, Breed's Hill, was the best one to fortify. It took them an hour to convince Prescott that this was the best strategy. As soon as the decision was made, Gridley marked out lines for a redoubt, one hundred sixty feet long and eighty feet wide, and gave the order "Dig!" The farmer-soldiers may not have looked like soldiers, but they knew how to dig! They sent the dirt flying in a fashion that would have exhausted a British soldier within an hour. Daniel joined in and listened to Dake, Asa, and Aaron making jokes as the dirt flew high. The young men were lighthearted, and to them this was another kind of game, like the fox hunts they had often engaged in. As they threw themselves into preparing to defend the hill, Daniel thought, *They won't think it's a game after the shooting starts!*

🛡   🛡   🛡

If the American generals had their disagreements, the British staff had far more. As General Gage called his council of war, General Henry Clinton aggressively pointed at the map spread before them.

"Look," he said loudly, "it's very simple. We can land five hundred men at the neck and seal off the Americans' escape—then our ships can battle them into submission to the water."

It was a very good plan, one that the Americans had not thought of, and it would be a tremendous opportunity for the British to obtain a decisive strike. General Thomas Gage pondered for a moment, then re-

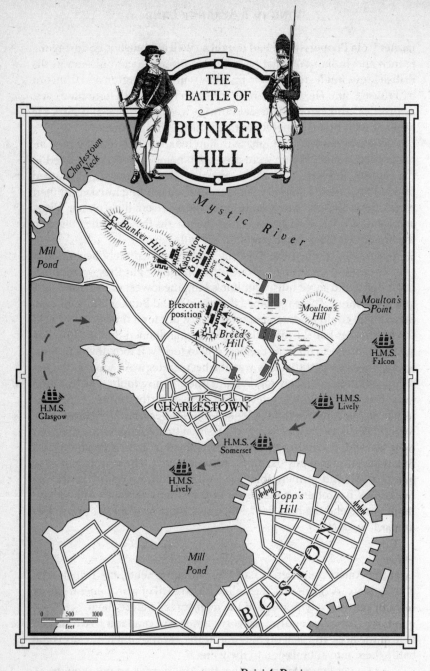

THE BATTLE OF BUNKER HILL

Charlestown Neck

Mystic River

Mill Pond

Bunker Hill

Knowlton & Stark fence

Prescott's position

Breed's Hill

Moulton's Hill

Moulton's Point

H.M.S. Falcon

H.M.S. Lively

CHARLESTOWN

H.M.S. Glasgow

H.M.S. Somerset

H.M.S. Lively

Copp's Hill

Mill Pond

BOSTON

0   500   1000
feet

(1) American Redoubt
(2) Gerrish
(3) Putnam
(4) Pre-existing British Redoubt

British Regiments

(5) Marines
(6) 47th Infantry
(7) 5th Infantry

(8) 38th, 43rd, and 52nd Infantry
(9) Grenadiers
(10) Light Infantry

marked, "We must remember, General Clinton, that we do not know how many troops the enemy has at this point. To put five hundred men between two enemy forces would be a very dangerous tactic."

"I agree," General Howe said instantly. He, himself, was an expert in amphibious warfare, whereas Clinton was not. "There's very little equipment for such an operation. What if our ships cannot get up the Mystic River?" He did not mention that there was another reason for not following Clinton's plan—a feud had sprung up between Admiral Graves and Thomas Gage. The admiral's ships were the only means of transporting meat from the harbor islands and seacoast towns, and Admiral Graves had brought in cattle to Boston, charging an astronomical guinea a pound for the meat. This had inflamed Gage, and the two had fought so strenuously that Graves now had shown a lack of enthusiasm for any plan proposed by the general.

Clinton pouted, for he never enjoyed having his will questioned. "If we don't follow my plans," he said, putting a finger on Breed's Hill, "we will have to make a frontal assault. An army as small as our force simply cannot stand heavy casualties."

"I agree," Gage said at once. "But the Americans must be chastised. We must maul them badly, and what better way to crush them than by routing Yankee Doodle on a battlefield of his own choosing. Look— we'll land our troops here." He touched the map at the tip of the peninsula, Moulton's Point. "You see, for half a mile from the water's edge to the American position, there's no cover available for an ambushing force. If they send out a large body of troops, the guns of the fleet will open up on them and destroy them. We'll land there and send a column of light infantry along the shores of the Mystic to turn the Yankees and get around their rear." He smile grimly. "Nothing demoralizes raw troops more than the terrifying knowledge that the enemy is behind them and has cut them off. Once they're routed, General Clinton will join and we will assault Cambridge, probably tomorrow."

Considerable discussion continued among Burgoyne, Clinton, and Howe, with Gage's strategy finally carrying the day. Clinton had one last objection. "What if the Americans choose to fight inside their fort?"

"Very unlikely," Howe shrugged. "The hill is open, but if they do, we will take them. They've never met trained troops. The hill is easy to climb and will be a simple matter to carry. That's it, gentlemen," he said brusquely.

He sent the order at once and Admiral Graves' flagship, the *Lively*, opened up on the American redoubt. "That ought to do it," he said. "We'll soften them up and then we'll make our landing." Gage was pleased with his strategy and was already composing in his mind the letter he would send to His Sovereign King George the Third, outlining the glorious victory of His Majesty's troops in America. . . .

T   T   T

"Take cover! Take cover!"

Prescott drove his men into the shelter of the six-foot walls of the redoubt. The sudden roar had risen from the ships in the harbor, and soon cannonballs came whistling down on the fort. Daniel reached up and pulled Dake back. The young man had been staring up with curiosity and had protested, "Why, they can't hit anything with those balls." At the same time, a ball smashed a keg of water, sending it flying. Beside it, a keg of rum stood undamaged. Asa Pollard jumped up and cried out, "We can't let them blow our rum to bits! I'll get them!" He had taken three steps when Colonel Prescott called out sharply, "Get back in this redoubt!"

But Asa ignored the officer's order. Without looking back he strode out the front of the fort. All the men were watching, and Dake could not believe what he saw unfold before his eyes. His friend did not get far, for right then the sound of a cannon blast ricocheted across the water and Pollard was stopped dead in his tracks, struck down by a cannonball.

"Asa!" Dake screamed and stood up to go after him. He felt the iron hand of his father grip his arm and jerk him back.

Prescott, however, jumped up and called for two men. He had been in enough battles to know that fear could spread among the men faster than any other emotion and paralyze them.

The sergeant asked in a quavering voice, "What should we do, sir?"

"Bury him!" snapped Prescott. He was deliberately curt and watched his men warily as they weighed his order.

"Without prayers, sir?" the sergeant asked.

"Without prayers," Prescott ordered. He knew that he had to calm the men as they carried the body of the young man away. Otherwise, the troops might panic. He walked along the parapet, exposed to the enemy guns. "It was one in a million shot, men," he shouted out. "See how close they come to hitting me." But they didn't come close and Prescott gave a huge sigh of relief. He put the soldiers to work plugging the holes in the patriot line, extending it down toward the Mystic River that the British general so confidently expected to find open.

The shelling continued unceasingly, and at ten o'clock the American artillery reached the redoubt. Prescott and the other officers stared at it grimly. "Only four guns," Prescott whispered. "Little four-pounders up against King George's twenty-four-pounders." General Ward, he knew, had larger guns, but the lieutenant who had brought them said General Ward refused to relinquish them. *They're going to wipe us out*, Prescott thought to himself. *These guns won't help!*

Colonel Prescott didn't realize that all the British fire was falling short. The ships could not elevate their guns high enough to reach the fort without drawing to a distance that would put them out of range. The rebels' battery was simply too far away. The British balls were falling, then bouncing and crashing over the hillside like log pins.

Dake stood beside Aaron Burr, the two of them seized with anger at what they had just witnessed. The death of Asa Pollard had suddenly changed the nature of the thing. "They killed him," Dake muttered, a murderous look in his eyes. "They'll pay for that!"

"I'm glad he was a Christian," Aaron answered slowly. "The two of us got saved the same summer. Do you remember? I thought you were going to be saved that night, too."

Aaron's statement was another reminder—much like his father's— of the barrenness of his own soul. And the sight of his friend's mangled body painfully brought home the cruel reality of the nature of war to Dake Bradford. One moment Asa had been alive, breathing and enjoying the air, the sky, and all the beautiful things that the world had to offer. Then suddenly, in his impulse and anger to stand up against the enemy, Asa was robbed of life in an instant by a fluke cannonball. He was dead, cold, and gone forever. Staring death in the face shook Dake something fierce. Not for one moment had he ever questioned the existence of heaven and hell. But as he stood there watching the men carry his friend to a shallow grave that had been hastily dug, he realized how thoughtless he had been to ignore the state of his soul.

In a daze he turned and looked down at the harbor. The white puffs of the cannons made a rather pretty sight, and the whistling of the balls sounded in the air, and Dake knew that he had been foolish. He started to say something to Aaron, but some of the men, realizing that the cannonballs were simply rolling up to them, had left the protection of the redoubt. Many of them had spent all their lives on farms and knew nothing about war. They had never seen cannonballs before. When one of them rolled straight up to the redoubt, several men gathered around it, and one man picked it up and pretended to throw it. "I wish I could heave it back at you!" he yelled down toward the harbor.

Aaron and Dake, seeing that there was no danger, moved out from the cover of the redoubt. Even Daniel came out to watch. Colonel Prescott came to stand beside him. "This is all very well," the colonel said, "but when the charge is made, we will have to see that the men stand firm and hold their position. They've never seen bayonets brandished in an attack before."

The two men watched from time to time as a cannonball would roll in and come crashing through. The men were even starting to make a game out of it.

And then it happened! One of the solid shot struck with much more force. Aaron Burr, who couldn't imagine the weight of the iron as opposed to the nine pin, leaped forward to stop it with his foot. It struck him and he fell to the ground, uttering a shrill cry. The men gathered around him and Dake took a deep breath, for Aaron's leg had been mangled below the knee. "We've got to stop the bleeding!" he said, and they did what they could for the wounded young man.

Colonel Prescott ordered him carried back to Bunker Hill, where there was a field surgeon ready to tend to the wounded.

"You'll be all right," Dake said. But he knew that Aaron Burr would not be all right. Already the loss of blood had drained his friend's face white. Even if he did recover, he would never run through the hills like before.

When Dake came back and stood beside his father, his face ashen, Daniel murmured, "Two of your best friends shot down. I'm sorry, son."

Dake gave him an odd glance. His lips were drawn tight and his hazel eyes held a gleam of anger. "I'll make them pay for it, Pa—see if I don't!"

T   T   T

It took General Howe six hours to gather his force of twenty-three hundred men for their water-borne trip. The orders forced Colonel Leslie Gordon to work feverishly, for as the orders read, this was to be a military pageant. Every belt had to be white with pipe clay, every boot properly blackened. The generals were determined to parade their disciplined troops in full uniform as they defeated this fledgling army of rebellious patriots.

When they were finally on their way, Gordon was dismayed. The order added that each man should carry a full pack, which weighed an incredible one hundred twenty-five pounds. "How can veteran officers expect a man to fight with such a weight on his back?" Gordon demanded indignantly. But he was under command and made no formal protest.

Prescott and Putnam seized upon the six-hour delay to strengthen their redoubt, and back on Bunker Hill, Israel Putnam was everywhere—getting units ready and stiffening the spines of the reluctant. Twice he rode over to Charlestown to ask for reinforcements. And twice

General Ward refused to grant him his request. Finally, Ward sent out the New Hampshire regiments of John Stark and James Reed. Colonel John Stark was the true commander of this force of about twelve hundred frontiersmen. They were splendid sharpshooters but had little ammunition. They had been issued two flints apiece, a gill of powder, and a pound of lead cut from the organ of a Cambridge church. Men with bullet molds made musket balls, and men without them hammered out slugs of lead. When they reached the battleground, the site of the proposed battle, Prescott sent Stark to cover the fence that ran down to the Mystic River. Stark took his men and positioned them behind a barricade built of stone, the sharpshooters waiting for the British to attack. Colonel Prescott looked out to see Joseph Warren wearing white satin breeches and a pale blue waistcoat laced with silver, his blond hair carefully combed. The physician had been appointed a Major-General, so Colonel Prescott offered him command.

"I shall take no command here," Warren said. "I came as a volunteer with a musket to serve you."

He moved and took his place in the line with the rest of the men and stood looking down alertly at the shore below, where General Howe had begun to muster his men.

As the British troops, making an impressive sight in their scarlet uniforms, began to form, Prescott, fierce and burly, rode up and down the lines on a magnificent mare, roaring the words that would become immortal, "Don't fire until you see the whites of their eyes!"

🜂   🜂   🜂

Leslie Gordon kept his eye on General Howe, who had divided his soldiers between himself on Moulton's Point and Sir Robert Pigot on the left at Charlestown. Pigot's orders were to storm the redoubt, while Howe was to break through the breastwork and rail fence and position his men behind the Yankees. The British commander had relaxed, laughing and joking with his staff, preparing for the attack. Suddenly he heard cries and angry shouts. Turning, he saw five terrified soldiers being driven by a group of their fellows. "What's this?" Howe demanded impatiently.

"Deserters, sir! They broke out of the ranks and ran for the American lines," said an officer.

A steely look came to Howe's face. He stared at the white-faced men and said in a barren tone, "Any man who shall quit his rank on any pretense shall be executed. You knew this?" When they nodded dumbly, Howe snapped, "I would like to hang all five of you! But we need men." He pointed to the two men in the center and said, "Hang those two."

The two were dragged to a nearby oak, which was full of beautiful green buds blossoming. A sergeant formed nooses from the ends of two ropes, then threw them over a sturdy, low-hanging branch. The men were hoisted into the air, the noose tightening around each neck. The British soldiers stood grim-faced as they saw the men hanged, a warning to others who had thoughts of deserting their lines.

Howe turned from the tree and took his place at the head of the ranks. "Behave like Englishmen! I shall not desire one of you to go a step farther than I myself will go at your head. Let the artillery commence firing!"

When nothing happened, a lieutenant came running up, his face pale. "Sir, the wrong ammunition is in the side boxes! Someone brought twelve-pound balls instead of the six-pounders."

"No artillery, then. Well," Howe exclaimed, "we shall have those rebels anyway!"

Right then word came that American snipers in the houses of Charlestown had begun firing at the Redcoats. "Burn the town!" Admiral Graves gave the order. The ships in the harbor and the batteries began showering Charlestown with red-hot balls and iron balls filled with pitch. Charlestown caught fire to the great delight of John Burgoyne, who stood watching with Henry Clinton. Soon Charlestown was one great blaze with whole streets of houses collapsing in a great wall of flames. The hiss of flames and the crash of timbers could be heard everywhere.

That took care of the resistance on the left, and on the British right, Howe changed his formation. He drew up his light infantry and put them in columns of four along the Mystic Beach, three hundred and fifty of them. They were to break through the Yankee flank and attack the enemy from the rear. Howe's main body then began marching toward the breastwork at the top of Breed's Hill.

The patriot soldiers watched anxiously from their positions as the British troops moved toward them, an impressive mass of military might in their striking red uniforms. Colonel Stark stepped out from behind the stone wall and drove a stake into the ground forty yards away. "Not a man's to fire," he yelled, "until the first Redcoat crosses that stake!"

The attack commenced. Leslie Gordon had a moment's swift pride in his men as they marched up that hill against the silent breastworks of the rail fence. His grenadiers wore tall bearskin hats that did not keep the sun out of the men's eyes. He, himself, stumbled in the thick grass that reached to their knees. Men began to gasp under the burning sun, and the weight of their packs pulled them backward.

Along the Mystic Beach, Howe's favorite troops were led by the Welsh Fusiliers. When the Fusiliers marched past John Stark's stake, the wall ahead of them suddenly exploded with a thunderous volley of gunfire. The Fusiliers were decimated! Great rents were torn in the attacking column, but they were brave men and experienced in the art of war. They ran on, while behind the fence Yankee sharpshooters with empty muskets gave way to men with loaded ones and the volleys crashed out, striking down man after man of His Majesty's army. The Tenth Regiment was called upon. With swords waving, the officers knew that surely there could not be a *third* volley! But once again the lines of scarlet, with steel-tipped bayonets glimmering in the sun, met a third volley—and that destroyed them. Ninety-six dead British soldiers were left sprawling on the blood-clotted sands.

In effect, if Howe had known it, his plan was wrecked at that moment. He did not pause, however, but sent two more ranks of men up the hill to attack the breastwork in the rail fence. "Come, men!" he shouted. "Show them what the British soldiers can do!"

Leslie Gordon was part of that red line of heavily laden soldiers advancing toward the rebels. They stumbled on grass, past clay pits and apple trees, and fell over jagged rocks, climbing over low stone walls and fences. As Leslie moved forward, his lips grew thin, for he knew that behind that fence lay men with muskets ready to fire. The fact that they held their fire warned him. *If they had been nothing but farmers*, he thought grimly, *they would have fired as they pleased. But they're going to let us get close, and we'll just have to take it.*

No sooner had he thought this than flame and smoke belched forth from the walls. On both sides of Gordon, tightly dressed ranks of red and white were instantly transformed into little packs of stunned and stricken men. "Forward, men!" he cried. "That's their volley—we have them now!"

But even as they moved forward, the American weapons continued to spit death, and the men in red spun and toppled or staggered away streaming blood. Every man in Howe's personal staff was either killed or wounded, and it was a wonder that General Howe, who was in the forefront, had not suffered even a scratch. The British soldier was capable of enduring tremendous punishment, but not this kind of slaughter! The call to retreat rang out, and Leslie began moving his men back down out of range of the terrible muskets that continually blazed from behind the wall.

The barrel of Daniel's musket grew hot, for he had fired again and again. And when the British retreated, a shout of exaltation went up among the American lines. They had met and beaten the finest troops in the world with little cost to themselves. Colonel Prescott went among them praising them and reminding them that the battle was not over. He did not tell them that a steady trickle of American deserters had drained his forces and the redoubt was down to one hundred fifty men.

There were many men back on Bunker Hill, but Artemas Ward refused to send them. Israel Putnam stormed among them, sometimes beating reluctant soldiers with the flat of his sword. But his efforts got only a few men to follow him back to Breed's Hill—and worse, he returned with no ammunition for the men who had held off the British advance.

A quarter hour after the first bloody repulse, Howe attacked again. The light artillery rejoined the main body. They all were to attack the rail fence, while Pigot and Howe threw all they had against the redoubt and the breastwork. As they moved forward, Pigot depended mainly on Major John Pitcairn, but when they approached within a hundred yards of the Yankee fort, the fire burst forth and Pitcairn sank to the ground, mortally wounded. His son had been wounded also and held his bloody forearm, crying, "I've lost my father!"

It was reported that the marines echoed his cry, with one difference. "We have lost our father!" they said.

Gordon saw his men being scythed to the reddened earth and heard Howe calling out, "Bayonets! Give them bayonets!" But an incessant fire ruined that plan. The British Light Infantry was riddled. Some companies of thirty-eight men had only eight or nine survivors after a volley of fire that came forth from the redoubt. A few had a scant four or five. And for the second time, General Howe sounded the cry for retreat.

"We're not going to make it. We can't fight without ammunition," Prescott raged. He had received two companies of reserves, but for every man he got, he lost three. Most of the men had enough ball to repulse a third assault, but little powder remained for another reload. "Break up the cannon cartridges!" Prescott demanded. "Distribute their content."

Prescott stood and watched as the British reformed their lines. "They're going to come again," he said. Daniel, who was standing close enough to hear him, nodded with agreement. "Yes, I think they will, Colonel. And we don't have any more ammunition."

As the Redcoats marched up the hill again, Daniel said to Dake, "You have to admire their courage—they just won't quit."

"Neither will we," Dake said grimly. His face was black with the powder, and he gripped his musket, ready for the charge.

Howe hurled himself up the hill once again, and this time the Redcoats reached the ditch and the American musket fire slackened. From three sides the British came and still the Americans fought. Dake grasped his bayonet and knocked down a British soldier who came at him with a bayonet. All up and down the line, the Americans were fighting as best they could—bare-handed or with clubbed muskets. Some of them actually tore guns out of the hands of the regulars, but it was a losing battle.

"Give way, men!" Prescott shouted. "Save yourselves!"

But Dake fought on. A bayonet caught his coat and tore it to tatters but missed the flesh. Finally the patriots fought their way out of the trenches and gave way. As Daniel joined the retreat, he looked down and saw a tall figure, his breast bloodied. Dr. Joseph Warren, one of the most influential patriots in America, lay dead.

It was on the retreat that the Americans suffered most of their casualties. They fought bravely and well, and when they finally fell back on Bunker Hill, Colonel Prescott organized a formal retreat.

The British claimed a victory, but as William Howe looked over the bloody battlefield, he whispered under his breath, "Another such 'victory' like this and England is undone!"

12

MATTHEW AND LEO

THE BRITISH WERE SHOCKED AT THE CASUALTIES they had incurred at the campaign they now referred to as the Battle of Bunker Hill. Out of two thousand four hundred men engaged, one thousand fifty-four had been wounded, and two hundred twenty-six of them had been killed. British regulars had never suffered such losses at the hands of what the general called "a rabble in arms."

General William Howe had not been wounded physically, but the damaging effect on his confidence as a leader was perhaps even more telling. From that point onward, he was never able to forget the bloody tabloid that took place on the hills overlooking Boston where his men were slaughtered. Howe had formed his whole military personality after James Wolfe, as daring a man who ever lived. After the Battle of Bunker Hill, however, Howe turned overly cautious and time after time would draw back from throwing his forces into the fray of battle. Indeed there were some who would say that General William Howe was the best general that *America* ever had!

The American casualties were fewer—about four hundred and fifty—with one hundred and forty killed. Though the battle had been a tactical victory for Howe and England, Henry Clinton wrote in his diary, "A dear-bought victory; another such would have ruined us!"

The sense of shock that ran through the British army was beyond description. One of Howe's own officers blamed Howe for allowing his men to fire as they advanced, and for bringing them up in lines instead of columns: "The wretched blunder of the oversized ball sprung from the dotage of an officer of rank who spends his whole time dallying with the schoolmaster's daughter. God knows he is old enough. He is no Samson, yet he must have his Delilah."

As for Gage, Howe wrote to Lord Barrington, Secretary of War, "The loss we have sustained is greater than we can bear." Gage did not know

142

it at the time, but because of his lack of decisiveness he was on the threshold of being replaced by the general who had done the fighting at Bunker Hill. But most of the British soldiers realized that Bunker Hill was one battle that should never have been fought.

After the battle, the British strongly fortified Bunker Hill and then Breed's Hill, and remained in full possession of the peninsula. The patriots backed away from the peninsula but continued to strengthen their army, encircling Boston, so that their lines reached all the way around to Roxbury.

And then—the armies settled down to a time of inactivity. It was as if they had fought themselves out in one brief, gory, cataclysmic struggle, and now they lay panting. The British looked up at the hills where the fires of the newly fledged army blinked at them like the eyes of an animal ready to attack. The patriots looked down from their positions encircling Boston, waiting for the opportunity to come that would enable them to rout the British and drive them away from the city.

T   T   T

The bodies of the dead British officers were carried off the field for burial in Boston, but ordinary British soldiers were interred where they had fallen. All through the night the groans of wounded and dying men could be heard on the slopes of that hill. It was not until the next day that the last of them were removed to the hospitals in Boston. Soon the hospitals were so crowded that many of the wounded had to lie out in the courtyards.

From the moment the wounded began arriving, Clive Gordon had thrown himself into helping the British surgeons. They were extremely grateful to receive his help, and for several days he worked long and grueling hours to save the lives of those who had been wounded. Late one afternoon one of the surgeons stopped him, saying gently, "Dr. Gordon, you're a young man, as I once was. May I give you an older man's bit of hard-earned advice?" The speaker was a tall, gray-haired man, Major Andrew Chumley, a fine doctor Clive knew and admired.

"Why, of course, sir, I would appreciate it."

"If you keep this up, you're going to wear yourself out," Dr. Chumley said gently. "I commend your passion for trying to help these poor fellows, but some of them are going to die, and there is nothing you, nor I, nor the finest surgeon in London can do that would make any difference. This is going to be a bloody business here, and we must learn to spend ourselves carefully."

Clive looked across the ward where every bed was occupied by a wounded man. "It's hard not to feel sorry for the poor fellows, Dr.

Chumley," he said quietly. "I hope I never get to the point where I don't feel that."

Chumley saw that his advice was not welcomed and shrugged his thin shoulders. "You will come to such things by and by with a more clinical spirit. It is the only way for a physician to survive. When one man dies, my boy, we can feel great compassion and our hearts can break. But when five hundred men die, or five thousand, as I have seen on the fields of battle, they become—well, mere ciphers—and that's the way it must be. We cannot help those who *might* live if we spend our time on those who *can't* live." He smiled grimly and said, "But you must learn this for yourself. No physician can communicate it to another. In any case, you have my gratitude and that of the general for the valiant work you have done." He hesitated, then asked, "Would it be a possibility—"

"That I might volunteer as a regimental doctor?" Clive had expected this question, had in fact already been asked by another of the staff doctors. "I have not made up my mind about this. I had thought of going into private practice, but count on me to do all that I can, Major Chumley."

On the third day after the battle, Clive returned home late and took his seat at the table while his mother set a plate of food before him. "You're looking thin," she scolded. Reaching out, she brushed his hair back from his forehead as she had done when he was a small child. "Your hair never would lie down," she smiled, then went around to take her seat again.

Grace asked, "Have you been treating the wounded again, Clive?"

"Yes, it's a difficult thing. Some of them just give up and die. Two of them did this morning, in spite of all that I could do."

Leslie stared at his son and muttered, "It should never have happened."

David turned quickly, his lean face intent on his father. "Why is that, Father? Soldiers have to fight, don't they?"

Very seldom did Leslie Gordon bring any criticism against his superiors, but for some reason that evening he seemed to be different. Lyna, indeed all of them, had noticed that he'd said little. They had assumed that he was tired from the reorganization of the regiment. Now, however, it was clear that his spirit had been dampened by the sorry affair.

"It was a slaughter—a useless slaughter!" he said. He spoke quietly, but there was a bitter edge to his voice that he had never used when speaking of his superiors. "The only hopeful thing I can think of is that our generals might realize that this senseless battle is a turning point in the history of war."

"Why's that?" Lyna asked quickly.

"Because the patriots refused to play according to our 'rules,'" Leslie said, biting off each word. "Our men are trained to load and fire on the orders of their captains. The forward line fires while the rear one loads. If the Americans had done that, we would have subdued them easily. But for whatever reason, probably lack of discipline, they refused to fire volleys after the first one. They loaded and fired, every one of them, as fast as they could. That is what slaughtered us—that steady, relentless fire without intervals between volleys."

Suddenly, Leslie Gordon seemed to realize that his words of criticism were not appropriate. He straightened up, passed his hand across his forehead in a weary gesture, then shook his head. "I shouldn't be talking like this. It isn't proper." He attempted a smile, which was a rather pitiful one, and looked around the table at his family. "We'll do better another time," he said, though the look on his face belied the words he spoke.

After the meal was finished, Clive got up from the table and paced the floor restlessly. He looked suddenly at Jeanne and asked, "Have you been out today?"

"Just out in the garden a little."

"Come along and we'll take a walk."

Without hesitation, Jeanne rose, plucked her shawl off the hall tree, and stepped out the door he opened. The air was still, and the smell of honeysuckle, which clung to the fence and partially hedged the side of the house, was rich and strong and sweet. "I love that smell," she said as they made their way down the cobbled streets. "We always had honeysuckle back home."

Clive noted that lately she was able to talk more about her home without much grief. "Do you think about home a lot?" he asked finally, turning to look at her. The moon was bright and silver and as round as a dinner plate in the sky. It seemed her face was washed by the argent moonlight, and it outlined the clear sweep of her jaw and the high forehead and cheekbones.

"I think about it all the time, Clive," she said quietly. "After all, it's the only world I've ever known. This," she waved at the buildings that huddled about them almost like ancient listeners to their conversation, "is all so strange to me. Sometimes I think I'd give anything just to see a mountain or hear a panther scream in the night."

Clive made no answer for a time. Finally he said, "Someday I'll take you back there for a visit." He had not forgotten how much she had liked going out with Dake and now made another apology for it. "I'm sorry I made such a nuisance of myself for refusing to let you go hunting with Dake Bradford. I shouldn't have done that."

Jeanne didn't answer, but a smile touched her lips. She had known that her going with Dake to hunt that day had bothered Clive, and now she said gently, "It's all right, Clive. I just didn't know you would be so worried about me."

The two reached the harbor and stared out at the ships, which were lifting and settling on the gentle swells. A wedge-shaped cone of light seemed to run down from the moon to the shore. "The old Norsemen used to call that 'the whales' way,'" Clive said, "Pretty, isn't it?"

"Yes, it is."

For a while they stood talking, the only sound the gentle lapping of the water against the dock. Once, far off, a watchman called out that all was well. Finally Clive said, "I've thought about going to England. Would you like to go there?"

Jeanne turned to him. "What would I do in England?"

"Oh, I don't know. I'd just like for you to see it, I suppose." He shrugged his shoulders and laughed shortly. "You can't go, of course. I'm not even sure I can."

"Are you going there to live?" Jeanne asked curiously. "I thought you were going to stay in this country."

"Well, the Colonies are not really my country. I guess England's where I belong. My father's been assigned here, and I came to be with my family. We never thought it would be for long, and I still hope it isn't. I think one day we'll all go back when this trouble is settled."

"What's it like in England?" Jeanne asked.

"Green. Everything is green in the spring—and the flowers are so red and yellow and orange that it almost hurts your eyes." His voice grew soft and his eyes were dreamy as he described the fall and springtime of England. "I wish you could see it," he said finally.

"I'd like to," Jeanne answered quietly. "But I doubt that I ever will." She felt uncomfortable at that moment and added, "I'd hate to see you go. I'd miss you, Clive."

"Would you?"

"Of course. Why would you doubt that?"

"I don't know," Clive said. He looked up at the moon and didn't answer for a moment. "That old moon," he finally said, "looks down on so many things. He looked down on Anthony and Cleopatra once."

"Who were they?"

He smiled and shook his head. "Just a pair of foolish lovers. Or maybe all lovers are foolish. Anyhow, the old moon's seen a lot, and I suppose it will be seeing a lot more." Suddenly he took her hand and held it. "I haven't forgotten when I woke up in your cabin." Her hand was soft and strong and warm in his. He squeezed it and shook his head. "I thought I was looking up into the face of an angel."

Jeanne's lips curled up and she pulled her hand back and ran it through her short, cropped hair. Clive could see the tiny mole very near her lips and the tiny cleft in her chin that somehow made her look strangely stubborn, even in the moonlight. "I'm no angel, Clive. You'll find that out if you know me long enough. Come," she said, "we'd best get back."

T   T   T

Through all Marian Rochester had suffered in her unhappy marriage, she had learned how to read her husband very well. She was totally aware in the days following the Battle of Bunker Hill that something was preoccupying him. She had long ago discovered that it was useless to try to share his life. She had not done that for several years. In fact, she knew Leo had purposely distanced himself from her. She did, however, make honest attempts to keep their relationship at least on a civil level—which Leo did not particularly care to do. It seemed he constantly enjoyed tormenting her and causing her pain—and she was well aware that it was because she had not given him a son. Even his seething anger against her for her feelings for Daniel Bradford stemmed perhaps from this.

Leo Rochester was a self-absorbed man who loved getting his own way. He had been a vicious child, striking out at whoever crossed him, and rarely had he been corrected by his doting parents. As a young man he had grown, if possible, even worse. Daniel Bradford had felt the weight of his anger and cruel revenge—and more than once he had felt the slashing blows of Leo's riding crop. Totally selfish and completely amoral, Leo took what he wanted, never spending one moment's regret for those who were hurt by his selfishness.

Now, late one afternoon, he sat in a tavern, where he had been drinking steadily for some time, and thought of Matthew's mother—Holly. Time had so blurred his memory that he could not even recall her face. She had been a young servant girl in his house, much like the other pretty young girls he had defiled. The difference was that when he had gotten her pregnant, Daniel Bradford had married her—out of pity, he supposed. Leo was not capable of thinking in terms of such sacrifice. He could recall clearly enough his attack on the girl. She had resisted with all of her pitiful strength. Until his recent discovery, it had never once occurred to him all those years that Daniel Bradford's firstborn son, Matthew, was actually his own flesh and blood. Ever since he had learned it, however, his mind had chased ideas and plots and schemes, searching for a way to gain Matthew as his own son to carry on the Rochester name.

He drank slowly out of the goblet that the innkeeper had put before him and then set the cup down and stared into the red wine that lay deep within it. He'd offered what he thought was a reasonable proposition. He'd said to Bradford, "I want a son and you want my wife. Why shouldn't it be? Divorce is expensive, but I can afford it."

It had been to Rochester a perfectly reasonable and logical solution to the problem, and he sneered now as he thought about how Bradford had rejected his suggestion out of hand. He thought then of Marian, who loved Daniel Bradford. "No doubt of that," he muttered. "She loves him—and she never loved me!"

For some time he sat there growing more and more drunk. It was happening to him a lot these days. He suddenly thought, *I've got to stop drinking so much.* He paid his bill, flinging the silver on the table, and walked unsteadily to his carriage. When he got home, he found Marian coming down the stairs from attending to her father.

"Hello, Leo," she said, pausing at the bottom of the stairs.

Rochester stopped and stared at her with glazed eyes. "Aren't you going to ask where I've been?"

"No, I'm not."

The brevity of her reply irritated Leo. "I've been getting drunk. That doesn't shock you any longer, I suppose. You've seen me drunk often enough."

"Leo, you're drinking too much."

He cursed her and flung his hat and coat to the floor. As he passed her, he reached out suddenly and grabbed her arm. He was almost too drunk to stand, but now he leered down at her. "You're my wife. Suppose I claim my husbandly privileges."

He had no intention of doing so, for somehow the fact that she was in love with Bradford had taken away what little desire he had had for her. "What do you say to that?" he grunted.

"You'll do what you please," Marian said calmly, although inside she was shrinking. She had not let it show in her face, but his ill manner and the touch of his hand gave her a crawling sensation. In the eyes of the law, she was still his wife—really his property according to many authorities, to do somewhat more than he would for his dog or his horse, but certainly not his equal.

Leo blinked his eyes, and his lips grew thin. "If I were Bradford, you'd love it, wouldn't you?"

Marian shook her head. "There's nothing between us," she said calmly. "I've told you that before."

He shoved her backward so that she stumbled, then turned and walked to his room. He flung himself on the bed fully dressed and passed out. But sometime before that, he muttered, "I'll have my son. I'll have him no matter *what* it costs!"

T   T   T

Matthew had not been particularly surprised when he received an invitation from Leo Rochester. The invitation had been sent by one of Sir Leo's servants, inviting Matthew to meet Leo at the home of John Frazier. Twice before he had had dinner with the man and had found him to be an interesting dinner partner. Leo was very engaging in conversation and knew much of the arts, of which Matthew was eager to learn more. Matthew was also aware that his father had no use for Sir Leo and had puzzled over it. He had never known his father to be antagonistic toward very many, but whenever the subject of Leo Rochester came up, his father's aversion for the man showed in his eyes, although he refused to say much.

Matthew had mentioned the invitation to his father, and since Frazier was his father's partner, he said, "Why don't you come along? I'm sure it would be all right with Sir Leo."

"No, I think not."

The brevity of his father's answer was an indication of his feelings, and Matthew shrugged and said no more. He had dressed for the occasion, wearing a pair of new doeskin breeches, a new frock coat, and a hat that he had purchased at a shop he'd fancied.

When he arrived at the Frazier house, he was greeted at the door by Cato, the butler, who said, "Come in, Mr. Bradford. Sir Leo is waiting for you in the library."

"Thank you." Matthew followed the servant to the library, where he found Sir Leo sitting at a large walnut table reading a book. "I'm a bit early," Matthew said, reaching out to take the older man's hand.

"That's fine. We'll have time to talk before dinner. Sit down. I want to tell you about an occasion that you'll be interested in. I was at the Buckhouse once," he said when the two were settled, "and we had an unusual visitor—Sir Joshua Reynolds. You've heard of him, I suppose?"

"I rather think so! He was the first President of the Royal Academy and one of my teachers."

"What a privilege indeed! A magnificent painter and fine fellow he is too. Well, Sir Joshua came in . . ."

For over an hour, the two men sat talking, Leo speaking in a way both witty and knowledgeable on many subjects. It was not all an act—he was interested in the arts and was himself a dabbler in music, being a modest performer on the violin. He played the boy skillfully and finally said almost regretfully, "Well, I suppose we have to eat. Come along. Maybe after dinner I can tell you more about some of the painters I've encountered from time to time."

The dinner was pleasant. Matthew was pleased to see Marian again. Her father, however, was unable to come to the meal. Matthew noticed that Marian had almost nothing to say, unlike their last meeting when he had spent a lively evening in conversation with her at a dinner with his family. *She's so quiet tonight,* he thought. *I hope she talks more than this when she and Leo are alone together.*

Finally when the meal was over, Leo led his young guest back to the library. Matthew sat down, and Leo had Cato bring a bottle of wine. They talked for almost an hour, and finally Matthew exclaimed, "You know, Sir Leo, this has been a fine evening for me!"

"You don't get to talk much about painting at home, I suppose?"

"Well, they're not really too much up on it. Not that they should be. My brothers are all good foundry workers. I never was worth anything at that."

Leo turned his light blue eyes on the young man who sat across from him. He let the silence continue for a moment, then rose and went to the window. He stood there looking out for a time.

Matthew shifted in his chair, uneasy at how quiet the older man had become. "Is something wrong?" he asked finally.

Leo turned, and his jaw was set in a determined fashion. His eyes were half shut as he studied Matthew Bradford. "Yes," he said slowly, "I'm afraid there is something wrong."

Matthew blinked with surprise. He stood to his feet and said, "I hope I haven't done anything."

"I'm afraid I'll have to confess that you have given me a great deal of a problem, Matthew."

Matthew was shocked. "Why, sir, I can't imagine—!" He racked his brain trying to find something that he had done or said. "What is it? What have I done?"

Leo put his hands behind his back and planted his feet squarely. "I have something to say to you," he said quietly.

Something in his tone captured Matthew's full attention. He had learned to admire Leo Rochester to a certain measure, although he had heard certain rumors about him that were far from complimentary. But as for himself, Matthew had seen a man who appreciated his art and talent and had never shown him anything but a generous spirit in the few social contacts they had had recently. "What is it, Sir Leo?"

"I have fought with myself against revealing to you what I'm about to say," Leo said slowly, almost ponderously. He dropped his eyes for a moment and stared at the pattern in the carpet and then lifted them. There was a light in his eyes that spoke of the excitement that lay deep within him. "Matthew, I don't know any way to say what I have to say, except to be forthright and tell you the truth."

"The truth? What truth are you referring to, sir?"

Rochester took a deep breath, wondering if he was overplaying his hand. Still, he'd tried everything else, and now, being a gambler, he risked everything on one card.

"Matthew, you've never been told the truth, but I will tell it to you now." He hesitated for one moment, then said, "I'm your father."

"I beg your pardon?" Matthew stared at Leo Rochester, certain that he had misunderstood. "What does that mean?"

"Well, it means that when I was a young man I was very foolish. Your mother was a servant in my house. She was a beautiful young woman and I behaved very badly toward her. I must tell you that. She was in no way at fault. She was a good woman. I misled her—and I've never stopped grieving over that." This lie came easily to Leo Rochester. He had planned his speech carefully, and now as he saw the unbelief flare in Matthew's eyes, he almost panicked. "Believe me, I never once knew that your mother was expecting a child."

"I don't know what you're talking about!" Matthew exclaimed. He swallowed hard and shook his head. "You must be making this up— but I can't imagine why!"

"I can imagine how shocking all this must be to you. I wish there were some way to make it easier for you. But there is only one way I can convince you of the truth."

"It's not the truth!" Matthew said. "Daniel Bradford's my father."

"If it *were* the truth," Leo said incessantly, "would you accept it?"

"I don't have to answer that because it's not so. You're lying to me! Why are you doing this?"

"Will you let me show you one thing?"

Matthew's head felt light and his hands were trembling. Somehow he knew that Leo Rochester would not have made such a claim unless he'd felt he had some hope of convincing him. "Show me what?" he said.

"Come over here, Matthew." Leo had planned for this moment. He'd had a large mirror placed on the wall, and now he moved to it and turned back to say, "Come and stand here for one moment."

Matthew felt like an actor in a play. Somehow the scene lost all sense of reality. "It's not true! It's not!" he whispered vehemently. Nevertheless, he reluctantly moved to where Leo stood before the mirror.

"Now, just stand beside me and look into the mirror."

Matthew looked at the two reflections clearly outlined in the mirror before him. "Well, what does this prove?" he asked.

"What does your father look like?" Leo asked suddenly.

"He's tall and very muscular. He has very light-colored hair and hazel eyes."

"And your brothers are just like him, aren't they?"

Abruptly Matthew realized the truth of that. It was not the first time he had thought of it. Dake and Micah were both younger versions of their father. Sam, it was true, had hair that was more red, his eyes were bluer, and he was not yet very tall. Nevertheless, the shape of his face, his shoulders, his walk, all were exactly that of his father, Daniel Bradford.

"They all look like your father. I've seen it," Leo said. "But what about you? Look at you—you're slender, not at all tall like your father— you have light blue eyes and brown hair. And your hair grows exactly like mine. As a matter of fact, I have a portrait at my home in Virginia, a portrait of myself when I was just your age." He turned and said, "Matthew, if you saw that painting, you would say, 'There I am!'"

Matthew felt as if the world had suddenly changed more in the last five minutes than in all of his life. Everything in him rebelled against what he was hearing. Yet, when he stared at his reflection in the mirror, he saw exactly what Rochester meant. *I do look like him!* he thought. *He must have looked exactly like me when he was my age!*

Nevertheless, he turned and shook his head, saying, "No! It's not true. You're not my father. You can't be!"

Leo then spread his hands wide and shook his head regretfully. "I had no idea, as I said, that your mother was expecting a child. I've always wanted a son. Now"—a grimace twisted his lips violently—"it is apparent that my wife will never give me one. She's barren, and I will *never* have a son."

He turned again, and his eyes practically consumed the young man. "The first time I looked at you, Matthew, I knew you had my blood in you. We look alike, we Rochesters. My father, his portrait as a young man, looks just like you—and his father. We have a family likeness. I have the pictures in Virginia of all my forefathers. You come and look at them and you'll see that you're a Rochester."

"I . . . I can't believe it!" Matthew said, backing away from the mirror.

Leo then played his trump card. "There's one way I can prove what I say."

"Prove it, then!" Matthew said defiantly.

"Go home and ask your father."

Matthew stared at Rochester. He saw no doubt on the face of the man who made such an astonishing claim—and the man's confidence shook him more than anything else.

"I will!" he said. "I'll . . . I'll go ask him."

"Fine! Daniel will tell you the truth. He will also tell you that I was an evil man—and that I misused your mother." He bowed his head then and shook it sorrowfully. "And he will speak the truth. I can never be more sorry for anything in my life than for that. But I can't change the past."

"Why are you telling me this?"

"Because you are my hope of immortality. I don't believe in God, but I believe that we put ourselves into our children. That's immortality! We can only live in them." It was a private belief that Leo had never spoken of before, but now as he said it to his son he felt it deeply. He added, "I'm doing it for my sake. I want a son and I want to give him the things a Rochester should have. I want there to be a man bearing my name and bearing a son with my name. And I will not deceive you, Matthew. I am a selfish man—but that's not all." Leo hesitated, then said, "It will be good for you to be my son. I can give you a career that you could never have without me. I can take you to England. I have the money to do it. It would be my privilege to watch you develop as an artist. Why should you not be a member of the Royal Society? There are worse men and lesser talent in that group."

As Leo continued to speak, Matthew listened and then held up his hands. "I don't want to hear this!" He stared defiantly at Leo Rochester and said, "I don't believe you, but my father has never lied to me."

"No, and he won't lie to you about this. Go to him, and when you can, after the shock is gone, come back and talk to me."

Matthew left the Frazier house and went straight home. His mind was spinning, but he knew what he had to do. When he entered the house, he walked at once to the study, where he found his father, as he often did, reading the Scripture.

"Why, hello, Matt," Daniel said, then saw something in his son's face. "What's the matter?" he asked quietly.

Matthew stopped before him and licked his lips that were suddenly dry. "I have to ask you something."

"Yes, what is it?" asked Daniel as he closed his Bible.

Matthew could hardly frame the words. "Are . . . are you my father . . . my real father, I mean?"

Slowly, Daniel stood. He moved from behind the desk and went over to stand in front of the young man. "I've always tried to be a good father to you," he said gently.

"That's not what I mean."

"I know. Leo Rochester has spoken to you, hasn't he?"

Matthew pleaded with his eyes and finally said, "He's lying, isn't he? He's not my father."

Great temptation came then to Daniel Bradford. He knew there was no evidence that Leo could produce to prove his claim. Only Holly had known the truth. The two of them had been married and the child had been born with Daniel's name. In the sight of the law there was nothing Leo could do. Still, he knew that he had no choice but to speak the truth.

"I had hoped that you would never ask this question. I would never have mentioned it, because your mother would not have wanted it."

Matthew swallowed hard and for a moment could not speak. Finally, he said hoarsely, "It's true, then? He *is* my father?"

"Yes, it is true." Daniel put his arm around Matthew and felt his son's body quake. "This is terrible for you. I wish to God that you had never learned it. It makes no difference to me. You're as much my son as Dake, or Micah, or Sam. I mean that with all my heart."

Matthew looked up at the man he'd called his father and saw the truth in his eyes. For one moment he was overwhelmed as he thought of all the care and love he had received from this man. He said, "I know that, sir, and nothing will ever change that."

Tears suddenly glittered in Daniel's eyes, and he said, "Good! We understand each other, then."

Matthew felt the weight of his father's embrace and said slowly, "Tell me all of it. I need to know."

The two sat down and for the next hour Daniel related the history of the young man. When he saw that Matthew was shaken to the very fiber of his being, he spent much time encouraging him and reassuring him. Finally he said, "You understand that Leo Rochester is a totally selfish man. I hate to speak against him, but he was unjust to your mother. I'll say no more. I assume he wants you to become his son legally?"

"I don't know," Matthew said. "I don't know what he wants." He stood up, his back stiff. "I wish I'd never heard of him!" He walked out of the room and left the door open. Daniel stared blankly after him, then finally went back and fell on his knees behind his desk. He prayed as hard as he'd ever prayed in his life for this son of his who had suddenly had his life turned completely upside down. "Oh, God," he prayed, "he's going to need you more than he ever has. Don't let him fail!"

PART THREE

THE GUNS OF TICONDEROGA

June 1775–January 1776

13

DESPERATE VENTURE

TWO WEEKS AFTER THE BATTLE OF BUNKER HILL, George Washington, the new commander in chief of the Continental Army, arrived to take command. Washington was described by one man as tall and muscular, straight as an Indian. His bluish gray eyes, beneath prominent brows, had a way of holding men motionless. He always wore well-cut uniforms, and upon encountering him for the first time, being gripped by an extremely large, rough-skinned hand, strangers often found his appearance formidable, even forbidding. Yet friends spoke of his generosity as a host—the pleasure he took in barbecues and picnics, his fondness of dancing, playing billiards and cards, gambling, and going to the theater. He was an enthusiastic and skillful horseman who enjoyed hunting and shooting and considered farming the most delectable of pursuits.

George Washington wrote his wife immediately after being appointed commander in chief: "You may believe me, my dear Martha, when I assure you in my most solemn manner that, so far from seeking this appointment, I have used every endeavor in my power to avoid it. Not only from my unwillingness to part from you and the family, but from a consciousness of its being a trust too great for my capacity. But, as it has been a kind of destiny that has thrown me upon this service, I shall hope that my undertaking is designed to answer some good purpose."

As soon as Washington arrived in camp outside Boston, he was made aware of the appalling condition of his command. Discipline among the men was lax or nonexistent. Officers were treated with little respect. Drunkenness and malingering were common. Provisions were scarce and ammunition so low that for a time no man had in his possession more than three rounds. The camps were filthy and perfunctorily guarded by sentries who frequently strolled away from their posts before they were relieved—and sometimes even went over for a chat with the enemy.

Even worse than all of these things, the troops had been enlisted only until January or, in some cases, earlier. Washington was faced with the imminent dispersal of an army only too anxious to return home as soon as possible. Many men indeed did wander off to their farms, and several were never seen in the camp again. The camps to which Washington rode outside Boston presented a most strange appearance. Some were made of boards, some of sailcloth, others of stone and turf, brick or brush. The countryside was cut up into hastily built forts and entrenchments. Orchards were laid flat with cattle and horses feeding on choice mowing land.

One visitor recorded, "The army is most wretchedly clothed and is as dirty a set of mortals as ever disgraced the name of soldier! They have no women in camp to do washing for the men, and they, in general not being used to doing things of this sort, and thinking it a rather disparagement to them, choose to let their clothes rot upon their backs rather than wash them. Their diet consists almost entirely of flesh from which springs those malignant and infectious disorders which run rampant through the camps."

🔔　　　🔔　　　🔔

On September 26, 1775, *H.M.S. Scarborough* dropped anchor in Boston Harbor. Aboard her were papers from Lord North that brought to a close the end of the military career of General Thomas Gage—at least in America. Within three days after the news of Bunker Hill reached London, the decision to replace him was made. Thomas Gage turned over his affairs to General Howe, packed his papers, and on October 11 set sail for home. The man who stepped into his place was the idol of his troops, "a man almost adored by the army and one with the spirit of a Wolfe who possessed the genius of a Marlborough."

Life for the British was not pleasant in the months that followed. Inside Boston many of the soldiers were unable to get into warm quarters. In even worse shape, the men and officers in British posts outside the town were plagued by the bitter winds and snows of winter, which brought utter misery. Quartered in bleak huts and tents the regiment shivered, and even the officers found their duties severe. Inside the city itself, the crowding of more men into town increased disorder among the civilian population.

A general order from the military command continued the depressing picture of a cold, miserable city in wartime: "Thomas MacMahan and Isabella MacMahan, his wife, tried by court martial for receiving stolen goods. MacMahan to receive a thousand lashes on his bare back with a cat-o'-nine-tails, and said Isabella MacMahan to receive a hundred lashes on her bare back at the cat's tail and to be imprisoned for three months." A thousand lashes could kill a man and only a portion thereof had been known to do so. The same court found Thomas Owen and Henry Johnson guilty of robbing a store. They were offered to "suffer death by being hanged by the neck until they are dead."

Despite the dismal conditions, the officers in the city found a light side to their bleak existence. One of them wrote home, "We have plays, assemblies, and balls, and live as if we lived in a place of plenty." He went on to tell of one interesting drama: "We are to have plays this winter, and I am enrolled as an actor. General Burgoyne is our very own Garrick, the great London actor."

☘   ☘   ☘

Throughout the long months of the siege, Jeanne found herself very unhappy. It was not that food became more scarce, as did firewood, for she was used to cold and a sparse diet. She was a sensitive young woman and very much aware of the harsh spiritual and emotional tensions that pulled the city apart. The British troops grew more cruel in their treatment of the remaining patriots. Some soldiers went so far as to pull down fences and even houses for firewood. The order was given that all old houses in every part of town could be pulled down for this purpose. During her walks, Jeanne watched as one fourth of the town was either pulled down or destroyed.

Dake remained with the troops camped outside of town, so Jeanne did not spend much time with him. Clive had attached himself to a local physician and kept his days busy with the inhabitants who fell ill; he also served as an apprentice assistant to the surgeons of the regiment. There was so much sickness spreading that Jeanne saw little of him.

In Clive's absence, Jeanne had spent considerable time with David Gordon and had grown very fond of him. He taught her to play chess, and although she never managed to win a game, she enjoyed the time she spent with him. One long winter afternoon when rain was falling steadily so that any outdoor expedition was damp and unpleasant, the two of them sat in front of a meager fire in the keeping room—the term often given to the parlor. After he had beaten her three games, she threw up her hands, saying, "I can't play this game!"

"Let's make popcorn, then," David said, and at once the two busied themselves popping corn over the small fire. They sat back afterward eating the white, blossomlike delicacy, and David suddenly gave the young woman an abrupt grin. "Have you ever had a lover, Jeanne?"

"Why—!" Jeanne felt her face flame, and she stared at the young Gordon, scandalized at his bold question. She was so startled that she could not think of a sharp enough reply. Finally she glared at him, saying, "You—you're awful, David Gordon! What a rude thing to say to a girl!"

David popped another morsel of corn into his mouth, chewed on it thoughtfully, then shrugged his shoulders. He had a square face, dark brown hair that curled crisply, and he was very lean. "I don't see what's so awful about it. Happens all the time."

Jeanne could not help a quick feeling of fondness for the young man, despite his audacious conversation. "It's none of your business!" she said. "And it's not the sort of thing a young man should say to a young lady!"

"Well, I haven't had a lover or a sweetheart," David admitted. "Oh, I did kiss Molly Barnes two or three times. Wasn't much fun, though."

Jeanne smiled, shocked but intrigued by the bluntness of the young man's conversation. "Why wasn't it fun?" she asked. She herself had been kissed only once—by David's older brother, Clive. That experience was confusing, but she kept her thoughts to herself. She wondered if boys experienced similar feelings.

"Oh, she's a skinny thing. No meat on her bones. I like a girl to have a figure. Like you!" he said calmly.

Once again Jeanne could not keep the flush from rising to her cheeks. She sputtered for a moment, then laughed aloud, "You are the awfullest boy in the world!" she said. "Don't talk about such things anymore."

David raised one eyebrow. "I don't see why not. After all, that's what's going to happen to both of us. I'm almost sixteen and you're seventeen—practically grown up. I tried to get Clive to tell me what it's like to court a girl, but he won't tell me anything."

"Has he . . . courted many girls?"

"Oh, I suppose so. He's a good-looking fellow. I wish I were as tall as he is. Never will be, though. I'm more like Mother. Worst luck!" He chewed thoughtfully on the popcorn, then asked, "Who do you like the best, Clive or Dake Bradford?" When she looked startled, he grinned. "Both of them are sweet on you, aren't they? I guess you know that. You could take your choice. I wouldn't if I were you," he said. "Make 'em jealous of each other. I'd like to see 'em get in a rousing fistfight over you."

Jeanne threw her hands up. "I don't know what to say to you!" she cried in exasperation. "You have the worst ideas I have ever heard. I'm going to get ready for the play and you'd better, too. It's getting late."

☥ ☥ ☥

All of the Gordons were attending the play that evening. It was to take place in Faneuil Hall and was called *The Blockade of Boston*. Faneuil Hall had become one of the landmarks of the Colonies, and General Burgoyne had been the leading spirit in providing entertainment by putting on dramas there.

When the Gordons arrived, they found the place filled with officers and regular soldiers. The officers, of course, were all seated at the front. Clive held to Jeanne's arm, leaning over to whisper, "It's packed in here tonight!" Looking around at the mass of Redcoats and listening to the laughter and giggling and loud talking, he shrugged. "It won't have to be a very good play. Anything's better, I suppose, than sitting in a cold house or a lonely barrack."

"I've never been to a play before," Jeanne said. "What's it like?"

Leslie Gordon, who was on the other side of the young woman, grinned. "Well, it's not like this, I'm sure. But perhaps it'll be an experience for you. You don't often get to see a British general act in a farce."

Shortly after they found their seats, the curtain went up and the comedy started. Jeanne was fascinated with it all. All the actors were dressed in outlandish costumes. The one called "George Washington" had adorned himself as a farmer. He spoke loudly and ungrammatically and was, overall, a farcical character indeed.

Once Clive reached over and took her arm and held on to it, whispering, "I don't think Washington's quite as bad as they make him out to be."

Jeanne was very much aware of his hand on her arm, which he did not remove immediately. Thinking of what David had said, she stole a glance, admiring Clive's handsome appearance. He had dressed well for the evening, wearing a suit of brown corduroy that set off his tall figure. His auburn hair glowed under the chandeliers that studded the ceiling, and she was not unaware that many of the young women in the audience had cast secret glances at him.

The play had just ended and the curtain was about to fall when one of the actors came rushing out dressed in the character of a Yankee sergeant. He began waving his arms frantically and calling for silence. As the audience hushed, he cried out, "The alarm guns have been fired! The rebels are attacking the town and they're at it tooth and nail over at Charlestown!"

A round of laughter went up from the audience and the actor's face flushed. "This isn't part of the play! The rebels are coming!"

Suddenly a silence fell on the audience, and General Howe rose, saying, "All men report to their units!"

Leslie Gordon leaned over and said, "Clive, see that the ladies get home safely, you and David." After a short word with the general, he went out at once and formed his men, who moved out immediately. Upon getting to Charlestown, he discovered that there had been an attack, but not of any serious consequence.

As Clive escorted the family home he said lightly, "I don't think it's anything serious. They wouldn't dare attack full strength."

"I'm not sure about that," David piped up. "They may be better soldiers than we think."

Later that night, when everyone had gone to bed except Clive and Grace, the two talked for a while. The house was cold and Grace had donned a heavy cotton robe over her clothing. She made an attractive picture with her dark honey hair and gray-green eyes, and Clive took a moment's pride in her. He was twenty-two and she was seventeen, a five-year difference in their ages that had not allowed them to be particularly close. When he was a young man, she had been an irritating younger sister at times. Grace, on the other hand, had adored Clive and had tagged along whenever she found a way. Now the two of them drank cups of steaming hot cocoa, and it was Clive who said, "I don't know why I'm hanging around, Grace. I'd planned to go back to England and start a practice."

Grace looked at him calmly. She was a young woman gifted with a keen sense of discernment. A slight smile turned the corners of her wide lips up and she said evenly, "I know why you haven't gone back."

"You don't either."

"Yes, I do. You're interested in Jeanne."

"Why, that's . . . that's ridiculous!" Clive was flustered and, to cover his feelings, took a sip of the cocoa. It was so hot it blistered his tongue and throat, and he almost gagged. Yanking out his handkerchief, he wiped his lips and set the cup of cocoa down on the table. "Why, that's ridiculous!" he said adamantly. "She's just a child!"

"She's my age, Clive. A seventeen-year-old young woman. That's what she is," Grace said. "And I don't blame you. She's a very attractive girl."

"Oh, I . . . I suppose so," Clive muttered. He picked up the cocoa and blew on it cautiously, then looked across the cup and smiled at his sister. "You've done a good job with her, you and Mother. At least she's learned what not to wear. She did come out with some odd combinations when she first got here, didn't she?"

"I like her very much, Clive," Grace said, "but I'm worried about her. What's going to happen to her? She doesn't have any family. What

164

would happen to her if we had to leave this place? What would she do, and where would she go?"

"I don't know," he said finally, frowning, for he had entertained some of the same thoughts and had no answer. "Good night! I'm going to bed."

Grace smiled, for she knew that her words had disturbed him. She knew more about this tall brother of hers than he realized. He had never shown any serious interest in any one woman, but ever since Clive had returned from Fort Ticonderoga, Grace saw that the girl from the backwoods somehow had been able to draw an attention from him that he had never shown to another.

🔔　　🔔　　🔔

When Dake saw his father among a group of militia gathered outside the hills of Boston, he was surprised to see him. Washington, he knew, had asked his father to stay at the foundry in Boston. "You can be of more use there, Bradford," Washington had said, "than you can out here in the hills. When the action starts, we'll need every able-bodied man to fight. You can get your musket and join us then. But, until then, do your best to hang on to your foundry. God knows we're going to need all the equipment we can get before this war is over."

"Hello, Pa," Dake said, coming closer. "I'm surprised to see you here!"

"General Washington sent for me. He wanted to know how things were going in Boston."

"Well, what's happening there?" Dake asked. He looked around at the shoddy barracks and said in disgust, "Better than here, I think."

"It's pretty rough, Dake, but it can't go on forever," Daniel said. "Come over to my horse. I've got something for you in the saddlebags. Your sister sent some food you might like."

"If it's not alive and wiggling, I'll eat it," Dake grinned. He accompanied his father to the horse, where Daniel pulled a leather sack off and started to remove the contents.

"Don't pull that out here!" Dake warned quickly. "I'll have to share it—but just with the men in my barracks. I'll bring this sack back."

"It's a cake and some smoked meat." Daniel looked at Dake and asked quietly, "It's pretty rough out here. You think you can stick it out?"

"Sure I can," Dake said quickly, a pugnacious light in his hazel eyes so much like his father's, "but like you say, Pa, it can't go on forever."

"The general's having a staff meeting with his officers. I think something's in the air, but he's not saying what it is. I wish you could come home with me." It was a rare personal remark, but Daniel had missed Dake. In a way, he had felt closer to him than any of his other sons, although he would never have said so. Dake's flare for life and that streak of fiery independence reminded Daniel of his own youth.

"Come on and meet the men in my barrack, Pa. Then you can fill me in on what's going on at home."

There was rejoicing in the shack when Dake pulled the cake and the meat out of the sack. Dake divided it evenly among his fellow soldiers.

Afterward the two men walked around the camp, and Dake told his father about the morale of the army. Dake had been shocked to discover that war had not been one battle after another with flags flying and bullets whistling. After the one engagement, there had been nothing but cold and discomfort and waiting. "Lots of the men have gotten discouraged and have quit and just gone back home," he confessed. "I can't blame them too much, but it makes it hard on those of us who stay."

"They'll come back when the action starts," Daniel remarked. "I'd like to be here with you, but the general thinks I'm of more use in town right now."

"What about Matt? Has he gone back to England yet? That's what he's going to do, I guess."

"No, he hasn't. I'm worried about him, Dake. He seems upset—can't find himself."

"He's not tough like me and Sam, is he? But then, Micah's not either. Has he decided that this war's a bunch of foolishness?"

"Micah hasn't made up his mind. He'll come around, son. So will Matt, I'm sure."

Later, as Daniel made the ride back to Boston, he thought of Matthew. Lately, he had sensed some sort of wall between the young man and himself, as if Matthew could not allow him to come close. *It's Leo,* he thought. *He's spending a lot of time with Matt.* The thought grieved him, and he felt helpless. As he rode along toward the besieged city, he prayed silently and surrendered the matter of Matthew and Leo to the Lord.

☂   ☂   ☂

By the time winter had set in, Washington's army had dwindled to about ten thousand men. Washington's every attempt to persuade the regulars to stay on failed, and even he lost his temper and wrote of the "dirty mercenary spirit" of the men upon whom he'd counted. In truth, the men had enlisted for eight months and thought that they had served long enough. They had suffered enough of the deplorable conditions in the makeshift camps and wanted to return to their homes. Now it was somebody else's turn to come support the cause.

Fortunately for Washington, thousands of men in the Massachusetts and New Hampshire militias came to fill in the gaps left by those who had returned home. However, the new arrivals had no intentions of staying long either, but at least they gave Washington time to recruit men and build his army.

Actually, Washington might well have attacked at this time. The condition of the British army was dreadful. Smallpox was rampant among the men, and food supplies were extremely low. Howe, who had assumed command after General Gage returned to London and was supposed to provide leadership, was more interested in the charms of blond Betsy Loring, whose complacent husband condoned the illicit liaison. When Washington heard of the farce *The Blockade of Boston*, he took advantage of the night most of the officers were gathered for the comedy by raiding Charlestown on opening night. One light moment had come when a few British officers who had been dressed as women in the play were seen rushing to battle in petticoats.

Shortly after, an idea to break the gridlock of power held by the British appeared from a most unexpected source. Henry Knox, the Boston bookseller who had become Washington's artillery chief, met with the commander in chief and proposed a most audacious scheme. Washington listened carefully as Knox laid out his plan. "Sir," the enormous man said, excitement beaming from his round face, "if we had the guns, we could mount them on Dorchester Heights and the British would be stalemated. They would either leave or be destroyed."

Washington had thought of this possibility long ago and now shrugged his shoulders. "But we have no cannons, Colonel Knox!"

"But we do have, sir," Knox insisted and, at the look of surprise in his commander's face, smiled happily. "Well, not *here*, of course, but there are plenty of cannons at Fort Ticonderoga. I propose that you send out a regiment and bring those cannons back here."

Washington was intrigued with the idea but shook his head. "In the dead of winter? I'm afraid it would be an impossible undertaking. You know what that country's like! Hundreds of miles of woods and deep valleys, and the very few roads there are will be bogged down with snow or knee-deep mud for the next few months."

"It would work if we load the cannons on sledges, hitch up teams of oxen, and drag them over the mountains. We'll put them on boats when we get to the river if they're not frozen. Sir, it can be done!"

Desperate to push back the British, George Washington finally agreed to the big man's persuasions. His generals, however, warned that it was foolish and impossible. But Washington needed a miracle—and the only miracle in sight was the seemingly impossible one proposed by the chief of artillery, Henry Knox. Willing to take full responsibility and the risk, Washington gave the order, then put Knox and his brother in charge of carrying out the daring expedition. He also sent some of the best men he had available to aid in what he knew would be a terrible struggle to drag the heavy guns through the mud and snow and frozen rivers.

Dake Bradford had known Henry Knox for some time. He had frequented his bookstore and Knox lived not far from his home in Boston. When Knox asked him to volunteer for a difficult mission, Dake, happy for any chance to be freed from the boredom of the camp, agreed at once.

🔔   🔔   🔔

Early one morning, Rachel finished her work and decided to pay one of her frequent visits to see Jeanne and invite her for the evening meal. When Rachel arrived, Grace opened the door.

"Hello, Rachel, please come in. I was just putting on some water for tea. Have a seat in the kitchen and I'll go get Jeanne."

"I came to invite Jeanne for the evening meal," Rachel said. "Sam has brought in some fresh game, and he has been after me to make him some more donkers."

"I'll go tell Jeanne you're here. I'm sure she will enjoy getting out."

A few minutes later, Jeanne came into the kitchen. "Rachel, what brings you here so early?" she asked.

"Oh, with a houseful of men, I guess I needed someone to talk to. And I'd like you to come and eat with us tonight."

"Oh, I'd like that."

As they sat down at the table with cups of steaming tea in front of them, Grace entered with a letter in her hand.

"Jeanne, this just came by post. Mail is very uncertain here."

Rachel watched as the girl opened the letter, almost fearfully. When Jeanne lifted her eyes, there was such trouble in her face that Rachel demanded instantly, "What is it, Jeanne? Bad news?"

"Yes, it's Ma Tante—my aunt, I mean. She's very ill. She wants me to come to her."

"Where does she live, Jeanne?"

"West of Ticonderoga."

"But there's no way to get there in the winter, I'm afraid," Rachel said sympathetically. "Certainly not by yourself."

"Oh, Rachel, I have to find a way to go to her," Jeanne said.

Rachel looked at the troubled young girl, then finally said, "Jeanne, maybe there is a way. But you have to promise me not to say a word to anybody. You too, Grace."

Both girls looked at Rachel, puzzled at what she meant. As soon as they gave their word, Rachel went on. "I wasn't supposed to know, but Dake can't keep anything from me. He's being sent on a secret mission to Ticonderoga to bring back cannons. I'm sure we could get Sam to take a message to him and see if he could convince them to let you accompany them."

Jeanne gasped and said, "Oh, Rachel, would you? Do you think it would work?"

"I don't know, but we can try. I'll talk to Sam this afternoon, then when you come for dinner tonight, you can give him a note for Dake."

As soon as Rachel left, Jeanne went to her room and paced the floor for a long time. Finally, she fell on her knees and begged God to make a way for her to see her aunt. Ma Tante had been the person closest to being a mother to Jeanne after her own mother had died, and now the young woman longed to go to her aunt. She wrestled in prayer with God as she seldom had before.

☩   ☩   ☩

During the meal that night at the Bradfords', Sam piped up and said, "Pa, I wish I could go to Ticonderoga with Dake. When will I be old enough to be a soldier?" He had heard his father that morning speaking quietly to one of his friends about the mission to Ticonderoga. Being a rather outspoken young man, he could not keep it to himself.

At once Jeanne looked up and saw that Daniel Bradford was disturbed. "Ticonderoga? Is Dake going there?"

Daniel glared at Sam. "It's a military secret—but some people have big mouths." He shrugged in disgust. "You may as well know. Henry Knox is leading an expedition to Ticonderoga to bring back the cannons that are there. Dake's going along."

Jeanne said no more, but after the meal was over she went at once to Sam. "You've got to help me, Sam," she said. "I must get this note to Dake."

At once Sam saw a chance for an adventure. "Why, I can take it for you. It won't be anything for me. I'll be right off. I'll be back before Pa even knows I'm gone."

Jeanne hated to deceive Daniel Bradford, but her need was urgent. Handing the note to Sam, she watched as he took it and was off at a dead run.

✠   ✠   ✠

Dake was surprised to see Sam when he showed up at the barracks—and he was even more surprised to read the contents of the note from Jeanne. Sam, of course, had been wild to spend time with the soldiers. Asking one of his friends to keep an eye on Sam, Dake hurried off to speak with Colonel Knox. He was fortunate in finding Knox alone in his quarters and said, "Sir, I have a special request to make."

"A request? What's that, Bradford?"

Awkwardly, Dake explained the situation, how that Jeanne Corbeau had come to Boston, brought there by his cousin, the son of Colonel Leslie Gordon.

"I've met Gordon. Seemed a decent chap for an Englishman. What's the problem?"

"Well, the young woman's only relative is very ill, and she wants to go to her. She lives not too far west of Ticonderoga. I'm wondering, sir, if we could be an escort for her."

"Oh, I don't think that would do at all," Knox protested. "This is strictly a military expedition, and it could be dangerous."

Dake could be a persuasive young man when he chose, and he threw his whole heart into it until finally Knox threw up his hands in defeat. "All right, but I'm warning you. It's going to be a long, hard trip, especially getting those cannons back here. But mind you—you're totally responsible for her."

Dake went at once and found Sam. After scribbling a quick note, he gave it to his younger brother. "Help her all you can," he said. He explained what Jeanne had on her mind, and Sam agreed to bring her back through the lines when he got word that the expedition was ready to leave.

"Pa will tan your hide if he catches you running around these hills," Dake grinned.

"Aw, this is nothing," Sam said boastfully. "You just wait till next year. I'll be right here carrying a musket with you, Dake."

✠   ✠   ✠

Jeanne was not certain whether she should tell the Gordons her problem or not. She knew she had promised Rachel not to say anything, but she felt horrible about deceiving Lyna. It was a complicated affair, seeing that she would be accompanying a group of "enemy" soldiers. She did not, of course, feel free to speak of the trip, yet she had to go. Finally, she decided to be honest with Lyna. She approached her and told her the complete truth. "I can't tell your husband because I'll be going with the Continental soldiers." She explained how she had learned of the mission from Rachel. "But I have to go, Mrs. Gordon. I have to see my aunt. She's all I have left."

Lyna bit her lip. "Very well," she said after a time. "I see that you must go, but Leslie must never know. I think we'll have to tell Clive. It would only be fair. After all, he's not a soldier, just a civilian."

Clive had listened in shock when the two women had come and told him of Jeanne's intention to travel to see her aunt. Angrily he said, "Why, it's impossible! You can't do it, Jeanne!"

"She has to! Can't you see that, son?" Lyna said quietly. "Suppose I were ill and you wanted to come to me. Wouldn't you do anything you had to?"

Clive remained quiet, for he saw the truth of his mother's words. "But it's so dangerous," he said. He argued briefly and then said, "If you have to go, then I'm going with you."

"Why, they'd never take you! You're a Tory," Lyna exclaimed.

"I'm not anything!" Clive shook his head. "I'm just a doctor. We can tell the Americans I'm going to take care of your aunt, Jeanne, which is exactly what I'll try to do."

Jeanne looked at him doubtfully. "They might accuse you of being a spy and arrest you and lock you in a prison!"

"Well, they'll just have to do it, then," Clive said. He thought of the mountain man Meeks and his theology. "If they do it, they do it, but I don't think they will. When are we leaving?"

🕱   🕱   🕱

Dake stared at Clive angrily. "You can't go and that's final! You should have had better sense than to come here, Gordon!"

"I'm here as a civilian on an errand of mercy to a dying woman," Clive snapped. He had accompanied Jeanne and Sam through the lines and now stood outside Colonel Knox's tent. The colonel was standing there staring at the tall Englishman. Doubt clouded his face and Clive saw it.

"Sir, I've been honest with you. It's true my father is Colonel Leslie Gordon in the king's army—but I am not a soldier. I am not even a political partisan, to tell the truth. My intention is to return to England and become a doctor, but until I do I feel obligated to help this young woman."

"I can see that, sir," Knox said, "but—"

Desperately, Clive interrupted, "You see, Colonel Knox, this young woman saved my life." He related the story of how Jeanne had found him dying in the forest and had saved him from a terrible death, nursing him back to health. "I have a debt of honor to pay, Colonel. I am sure you can understand that."

Knox found the notion romantic, and being a highly romantic man himself, he shrugged his massive shoulders. "Very well, but I must warn you, you'll be under constant surveillance until we reach Ticonderoga. We can't have you sending messages back to the Tories. Not that I think for a moment you would." He turned to Jeanne and smiled. "I can see how you would be inclined to help such a lovely young woman to whom you owe so much." Then he turned to Dake and said, "Private, it will be your responsibility to keep an eye on these two. I am sure you will."

As Knox disappeared into his tent, Dake shook his head. "This is a mistake."

Instantly Jeanne said, "Clive just wants to help, and maybe he can do something for my aunt. Try to understand, Dake."

It was a tense moment, but then Clive broke it by saying, "I understand your feelings, Dake, but really, this has nothing to do with the army. I don't care if you bring a million cannons back. All I want to do is help Jeanne's aunt and make sure she's safe."

Dake stared at the tall young physician and seemed to mellow, at least partially. "All right," he said, "but I'll have to do what the colonel says, and keep an eye on both of you."

After Dake turned and walked away, Jeanne looked up at Clive, a smile turning her lips, "Thank you, Clive. I know this is hard for you, but I'll never forget it."

"Well," Clive said, feeling relieved now that the difficulties were over, "it won't be a vacation trip. It'll be hard in the middle of winter, but we'll make it, Jeanne."

"Yes, and by God's help you can do something to help Ma Tante."

14

A Man Can Change

MARIAN WAS SURPRISED WHEN SHE OPENED the door to find Matthew Bradford standing there. She thought he looked somewhat awkward and ill at ease, but she merely smiled, saying, "Why, Matthew, come in!"

Matthew stepped inside, removed his hat, and said quickly, "I hope I'm not intruding, Mrs. Rochester."

"Not at all. Leo isn't here, however. I believe he won't be home until tomorrow."

"I . . . I didn't come to see your husband." Matthew bit his lip, shifting his weight nervously.

As he stood there seemingly speechless, once again Marian was aware of the startling resemblance the younger man bore to her husband. The same blue eyes and hairline, the same sweep of the chin, and even the set of the ears were all very much like Leo. She let none of this show on her face, however, seeing his awkwardness, but inquired gently, "Is something wrong?"

"Well, if you have a few moments, I would like to talk to you, Mrs. Rochester."

"Certainly. Come into the back parlor." Leading the young man to the smaller of the two parlors, she gestured to one of the Windsor chairs and, when he had seated himself, asked, "What is it?"

Matthew Bradford had been a guest at their house twice for dinner. Each time Marian had said very little and excused herself to retire early. Since she was aware of what Leo was trying to do, she felt rather uncomfortable around the young man. Perhaps she was afraid that she would say too much.

"Well, the thing is, I suppose you know—that is, I mean, I suppose your husband's told you that I'm his son." The words came hard to Matthew. They sounded weak and artificial and stilted. He felt foolish as he sat there, but for the past few weeks he had been moving around in a daze. By this time he had accepted the truth of Leo Rochester's confession. His father had not denied it, of course, and he had the evidence of his own appearance whenever he gazed into a mirror. "I wanted to talk to you about . . . what I should do."

Marian hesitated. "Are you certain I'm the one you should talk to?" she asked gently.

"I've almost driven myself crazy thinking about it." Matthew leaned forward, clasped his hands, and stared down at them intently. "It's been quite a shock, as you can probably suppose."

"Yes, I know it must have been. You had no idea at all that Daniel was not your real father?"

"None! Oh, of course, I didn't *look* like the rest of the family—but I supposed I took after my mother or one of her ancestors."

"A very natural thing, I'm sure."

"But, it's so . . . so *strange!*" He got up and began to pace the floor nervously, his slender face taut with anxiety. "Have you ever been walking along, Mrs. Rochester, on level ground and stepped into a hole you didn't know was there?"

"Yes, of course I have."

"Well, that's what it's been like for me. My life was fairly well planned out. I'd thought to go back to Europe, England probably, and continue my studies in painting. Now, all of a sudden, it seems the ground just opened up—and I fell in this awful hole that I didn't dream of."

"Have you talked to your father about it?"

"Yes, he says it's true."

"He didn't have to do that," Marian said.

"No, but I knew he'd tell me the truth. He always has. That's what makes it so hard in one way. He's been such a good father to me and to the other children, of course. There never has been a better one, and somehow I feel I'd be a traitor to him, failing him somehow, if I recognize Mr. Rochester as my real father. That was my first impulse—to tell your husband to forget he ever saw me."

"And what did he say?"

"He didn't really argue, but I've seen quite a bit of Mr. Rochester lately. Naturally, I've been curious about what he's like. But now I know he *is* my father and I have his blood in my veins." Matthew hesitated, then lifted his eyes to her. "That's why I came to see you, Mrs. Rochester. I want you to tell me what kind of a man my father really is."

His forthright question caught Marian off guard and agitated her. She dropped her eyes at once and lost the composure that seemed habitual with her. Her hands moved nervously on the fabric of the couch she sat on, and finally she said rather nervously, "I don't think you should ask that of me. I don't think I can answer it. It wouldn't be fair for me to speak of it."

"But why shouldn't it be—unless, of course, you have something to tell me that you're afraid of."

He had touched on the very center of Marian's reticence, for she knew better than others that Leo was the most selfish and cruel man she had ever known. He had beaten her physically more than once, and his verbal and emotional abuse had become almost habitual with him. She longed to warn this young man to stay as far away from Leo Rochester as he could—but still something kept her from it. "I can't tell you what you wish to know, Matthew," she said, her voice low and guarded.

Matthew gazed at her intently, studying her carefully. He did not speak for a moment, and the only sound in the room was the steady ticking of the Seth Thomas clock perched on the mantel. The awkward silence stretched out for what seemed an eternity, until finally, he sighed and said, "I suspected some of it, of course. I've heard tales of your husband, ma'am. I wouldn't want to even repeat them to you."

"You mean that he has other women?" Marian asked abruptly, her cheeks suddenly flushed. "I've known that for years, and of course it's been a hardship on me."

Her pain embarrassed Matthew, and he rose at once, saying, "I didn't come to be a bother. I see now I shouldn't have come at all. I beg you'll forgive me, Mrs. Rochester."

Marian rose and walked with him to the door. She handed him his hat, then something prompted her to say, "I can't speak as plainly as I'd like, but I will say one thing—"

"What's that, Mrs. Rochester?"

"You have a wonderful family. Daniel Bradford is a fine man and loves you very dearly. I would think twice, if I were you, before doing anything that would threaten that very precious relationship that many young men would love to have."

Matthew studied the woman's face. He had heard rumors, of course, that his father was in love with her. They had known each other for years. His father had been an indentured servant to Leo when they had met at Fairhope, and she a wealthy young woman. As Matthew looked at the heart-shaped face, the steady green eyes, the smooth complexion, he could understand how any man could be drawn to her beauty. And there was a depth of honesty in her that he saw in few people. In that brief moment, he realized that there was something more sinister to her husband's faults than she was willing to say, but he honored her for keeping her silence. It showed a loyalty that few people possessed.

"Thank you, Mrs. Rochester. I won't trouble you again with this matter."

"God be with you, Matthew," Marian said. She watched him as he turned and moved out of the house, walking down the street. Somehow there seemed to be a sadness about him that pulled his shoulders down and slowed his steps. As she closed the door, she turned and leaned against it, weary suddenly of all the bitter pain and suffering Leo Rochester had brought into her life. She had cried herself out over her bad marriage years before—but now she bore a poignant grief that came from knowing that all was lost and could not be restored. Slowly she straightened up and moved away from the door, trying to put the incident out of her mind.

🔔 🔔 🔔

Matthew wandered through the streets of Boston for some time thinking of his visit with Marian Rochester. He was almost unconscious of the soldiers who patrolled the streets and the tradesmen in the remaining stores who struggled desperately to stay open despite a lack of stock. Children, as usual, were playing in the streets, and once a large, mangy dog came out of an alley and approached with fangs bared. "Go on, bite me!" Matthew said aloud. The dog, however, only barked at him, then turned and slunk away.

When Matthew returned home, he went straight to his room and sat staring out the window silently. He was tired of his own disturbing thoughts and weary of the sleepless nights ever since Leo had talked to him that day. He remembered England and how pleasant it had been studying with his teachers, the joy of learning his craft. As he sat there, Micah came in and said, "Hello, Matthew." Without an invitation, Micah sat down on the stuffed chair beside the window and waited silently for his brother to speak.

Matthew looked up and saw the sympathy on his brother's face. Micah was so different from Dake! Dake was the man if you needed action, but Micah was the thoughtful one who could sense when someone needed to talk.

"Have you decided what to do yet about Leo Rochester?"

It was unlike Micah to speak so directly, but there was real concern in his strong face. He weighed exactly the same as Dake, one hundred eighty pounds, and was exactly the same height, an even six feet. The wheat-colored hair, the hazel eyes were the same also. But his speech was different. Whereas Dake spoke impetuously, often irresponsibly, Micah ordinarily was slow to speak. His voice had a slight drawl. He was gentle, like his mother. He was also a devoted Christian and seemed to have a wisdom beyond his years.

"No, I haven't, Micah," Matthew answered. He straightened up, shrugged his shoulders wearily, then ran his hands through his brown hair. "I wake up every day thinking I'll make up my mind now, but as soon as I do, I stop and wonder if I've made the right decision."

"It's hard for you, I know," Micah said quietly. "Have you talked much to Pa about it?"

"Hardly at all. I can't bear to look him in the face when I think of saying I might take another father. Could you do that?"

"I'm not sure. We do what we have to," Micah said. He was relaxed and there was an air of introspection about him as he began to speak. "I think it's a little like having a bad accident, the thing that's happened to you."

"An accident?"

"Yes. Remember the time I fell off the wagon and hurt my back? It all happened so quickly. One minute I was healthy and strong, able to run, and then I turned a flip and lit on my neck, and it was awful. Everything changed. You and Dake had to carry me into the house. I was confined to bed for two months. I couldn't do anything. You had to bathe me and feed me. And the worst thing was," he said thoughtfully, "as far as anyone knew then, was that I might have to stay in that bed for the rest of my life."

"I remember that. It was a hard time for you." Matthew had spent a great deal of time with Micah during his convalescence, reading to him, trying to encourage him. He smiled faintly, saying, "You got over it, though!"

"Yes, I did, and that's what I'm saying. You'll get over this, Matt. It's painful right now, but time has a way of making things a little bit easier."

Matthew was encouraged just to be talking with his brother. He rubbed his chin and said thoughtfully, "You may be right. But this is a little bit different. That was a physical thing. It's harder when you deal with—well, people."

"*You'll* be the same," Micah said instantly. "Suppose you do become Leo's son—I guess he wants to adopt you legally?"

"I'm sure that's on his mind. He said he wanted someone to carry on the family name. He doesn't have any sons or brothers, and he's the last of the Rochester line."

"Well, you'd still be Matthew, wouldn't you? You know what Shakespeare says, 'A rose by any other name would smell as sweet.' I'd just have to call you Matthew Rochester."

"It's more difficult than that and you know it, Micah."

"I suppose so. It's always easy for one to make light of another's troubles." Micah thought for a moment, then said, "I don't think you ought to punish yourself like this, if you can help it, Matthew. What's your real feeling about Leo Rochester?"

"He's not a good man, I can tell you that much."

"Why do you say that?"

"Why, common gossip. He's a womanizer and drinks too much. He's not a kind man either."

"He hasn't mistreated you?" asked Micah, concern in his voice.

"No, because he wants something out of me. But watch his servants sometimes when he's around. They cut their eyes at him as if they're afraid they'll get a blow at any moment. No, he's not a good man." Matthew hesitated, then said, "That bothers me more than anything else. I have some of him in me. I'm his physical son, at least."

"Well, you don't have to worry about that," Micah said and smiled. He reached over and clapped his broad hand on Matthew's shoulder. "You haven't got a mean bone in your body, Matt. I've known you all my life—you're just not that sort."

His words encouraged Matthew, and the two sat there talking for a long while. Finally, Micah got up and impulsively reached out and gave Matthew a quick hug. "You're all right, brother. You've got a family here no matter what tag the world puts on you. I'll be praying for you, but you knew that already."

Micah left, and Matthew sat there thinking of all that Micah had said. *Maybe he's right. I'd be the same, no matter if I were called Bradford or Rochester.* Deep down in his heart, however, he knew it was not that simple a matter. There were questions that had to be answered before he made his decision.

"I'll make that trip to Virginia with him," he muttered abruptly. "That way I'll get to know him better. It'll help me to make up my mind."

🔔   🔔   🔔

"Rachel, you're going to have to stop taking so many baths!"

Daniel had entered the kitchen where Rachel was roasting a hen on a spit. She straightened up and looked at him with surprise. "Why? Why should I do that?"

Daniel Bradford had a special love for this daughter of his. She was, of course, his only daughter—and that always makes a difference to a father. He saw in her some of her mother, whom he had learned to love after marrying her—out of pity more than anything else. Rachel had a heart-shaped face, exactly as her mother had. But the rest of her was a strange mixture of his other children.

"We're running out of firewood," he laughed, reaching out to touch her red hair. It was a glorious red, not your carroty red nor even a dark auburn, but a fiery red which he knew she had hated when she was a child. "Besides, as Dake says, it weakens a person to bathe more than once a month."

"Oh, Dake! He just talks like that," Rachel sniffed. She turned to the chicken, prodded it with a knife, and nodded with satisfaction. "I'm making your favorite supper tonight, Pa."

"Good. Groceries have been a little thin lately. Is there any tea?"

"Sit down. I'll fix us both a cup."

Bradford sat down at the table and relaxed. He loved sitting in the kitchen, talking with Rachel or with Mrs. White, his housekeeper. She was gone for the weekend and he missed her cheerful conversation. Rachel set the water to boil, and soon she sat down and the two enjoyed their tea together.

Finally, Daniel said, "Has Matthew told you he's going to Virginia with Leo Rochester?"

Rachel was more like Dake in one sense, more prone to speak her mind frankly than her brother Micah. Anger flashed in her eyes and she snapped, "Well, he doesn't have any business going off with him!"

Her sudden burst of anger startled Bradford. He looked up and studied her for a moment, then shook his head. "You've got to look at it from Matthew's standpoint, Rachel."

"No, I don't," she said almost bitterly. "Why'd that man have to come along, anyway?"

She had been informed finally by her father, as had the other children, of how he had married Holly, knowing that she was pregnant, how he had grown to love her and Matthew, of course. It had been hard for him to speak of those times from so long ago. They had been buried in his past all these years, but he felt strongly that his children had deserved a truthful explanation.

"I know it's been a terrible shock for all of you—Matthew most of all."

"I don't like that man. Leo Rochester isn't a fit companion for Matthew."

"Why do you say that?" asked Daniel, surprised at his daughter's perception.

"I've never liked him. I've always felt sorry for his wife. She's such a beautiful woman, and you can tell he abuses her."

"You don't know that—!" Daniel started to protest.

"Of course, I do. Just look at them sometime when they're together. You'd have to be blind not to see what a selfish, arrogant man he is, and what a fine noble lady Mrs. Rochester is."

"Well, I can't speak to that, but try not to be impatient with Matthew. This has all been such a shock to him. He's going through a bad time, Rachel, and he needs all the support from his family he can get."

"His family! He shouldn't even be thinking about leaving his family! Do you suppose it's just the money? Rochester's rich, you know."

"No, it's not that. Suppose you suddenly discovered that I wasn't your father. Wouldn't you be interested in knowing your real father?"

A startled look leaped into Rachel's eyes and she said, "I *am* your daughter, aren't I, Pa?"

The real fear that came to her revealed how deeply his casual remark had frightened the poor girl. "Yes, of course," he said, leaning forward, taking her hand. "We're two of a kind, you and me. But you see how frightened you are just to think about such a thing?"

"Pa, you scared me something terrible. I guess maybe I can see how badly Matthew has been shaken by all of this." She bit her lip and ducked her head. "I'm too quick to judge, Pa. I always have been. Dake and me are just like a pistol on full cock."

"And Sam's the worst of you all," Bradford added with a smile. "But you've all got good hearts, so if you're here when Rochester comes for Matthew, try to be as good-mannered as possible."

Rachel had opportunity to put her father's word to the test, for two days later a carriage drew up in front of the house and Leo Rochester dismounted and was admitted at once.

"Good morning, Miss Bradford," he said to Rachel, who had come to meet him. "You're looking well."

"Thank you, Mr. Rochester." Rachel managed a smile of sorts, then said, "If you'll wait in the parlor, I'll go call Matthew. I think he's ready to go." She started to leave, but he spoke her name and she turned to face him. "Yes?"

"I hope you don't feel too badly toward me."

His remark caught Rachel off guard. She had formed a firm opinion that he was an arrogant man, but his manner now seemed different. He had pulled his hat off and stood before her with an odd expression on his face. Somehow, although he was heavier and his face was deeply lined, she knew instantly that he must have looked exactly like Matthew when he was a young man.

"I realize how difficult this must be for you—for all your family," Leo Rochester said quietly. "I'm sorry for it."

His apology surprised Rachel, and she hesitated for a moment before saying, "Nice of you to say so, Mr. Rochester. It *has* been a strain. It would be for anyone, I suppose." She knew that this man had tried to shoot her father and that there was bad blood between them. Now she knew the reason why, or so she thought. "I hope you know what you're doing, Mr. Rochester," she said, holding her head high. "It's a dangerous thing to try to change people."

"And you're thinking I'll bring something bad into Matthew's life?"

"You're asking him to become something completely different. That's always dangerous, isn't it?"

Leo Rochester cocked one eyebrow. He was wearing a fine suit of a light tan color with a frilly white shirt. He was a clever man and had learned to judge people well. "You are an intuitive young woman, I see. I can promise you that I want only the best for your brother. I hope you believe that."

"I'll try to, Mr. Rochester," Rachel said. "I'll get Matthew now."

Rochester waited in the room and was not too surprised when Daniel Bradford entered along with Matthew. "Ready for our journey, Matthew?" he said pleasantly. "Hello, Bradford."

"Hello, Leo." Daniel's tone was spare, and he kept his true feelings well hidden.

"I'm all ready," Matthew said. He turned to his father and there was a slight hesitancy to his manner. "Goodbye, sir. I expect to be back in a few days."

"Goodbye, Matthew." Daniel shook his son's hand, and then Matthew turned to embrace Rachel.

"Take good care of everything," he said. "But then, you always do."

Turning, Matthew moved out of the house quickly, accompanied by Rochester. When they got to the coach, however, and Rochester stepped in, Matthew said, "While the servant's loading my bags, I want to have one more word with my father."

"Of course."

Matthew turned and almost ran back to the house. He found his father had moved out of the foyer, and he caught him in the hall. "Pa!" he said.

Bradford turned, surprised. "Yes? You forget something, Matthew?"

Matthew, now that he had his father's attention, hardly knew what to say. He felt awkward and stood there almost helplessly.

"Yes, what is it, Matthew?"

"I . . . I wanted to say goodbye a little better," Matthew said. "We've had our differences about the war and all that, but I want you to know, Pa—" He felt a lump rise in his throat as he thought of the multitude of kindnesses this man had shown to him. "I want you to know," he said huskily, "I . . . love you very much." He stepped forward and embraced Daniel Bradford. He felt the strong arms around him as he was held tightly. They stood there for one long moment, and then Matthew stepped back and cleared his throat. "Goodbye, Pa. This is something I have to do, but I'll be back soon."

He left the house, and when he climbed into the carriage, Leo Rochester asked pleasantly, "Got your goodbyes all said, Matthew?"

"Yes, I suppose so."

"All right. We go to Virginia, then. . . ."

🕆   🕆   🕆

Matthew loved Fairhope. He'd never been in Virginia, and he found the rolling hills surrounding Leo's large estate very appealing. It was entirely different from the hustle and bustle of the crowded streets in Boston, even different from the exotic activities of England and France. The place had a genteel quality.

Leo, of course, lived at the top of the pyramid. The success of the plantation was clearly evident by the apparent opulence in which Leo lived. The wealthy planters controlled their world, and everyone beneath them more or less existed to serve their desires.

It has been a good visit, Matthew thought as he returned from a ride with Rochester, and he said so. "It's a beautiful home," he said, glancing at the white pillars of the two-story mansion. The house was painted white with blue shutters, and a long portico stretched across the front, supported by white columns, with a circular driveway that led through the green grass. The weather was cold, but the exercise had been pleasant enough.

"I'm glad you like it," Leo nodded, pleased with the remark. He'd made it a point to ride around during the last few days so as to show Matthew how extensive his land holdings were. "I knew you would. Tonight you'll have to be at your best behavior. We're visiting the Hugers."

"Quality folks?" Matthew smiled at Leo.

"Practically own the whole of Virginia. All that the Washingtons and the Lees don't own. Fine people."

The two dismounted, and their horses were taken instantly by two stable hands and led into the large stables that housed Leo's fine horses. As they stepped inside, once again Matthew found it difficult to move around in the house, for everywhere he turned esquisite paintings hung on the walls. He stopped before one, a portrait by Gilbert Stuart.

Leo paused to watch the young man. "That's your grandfather, Edmund Rochester," he said easily. "You'd have liked him—and you look almost exactly like him. He was older there, as you see. It's like looking at yourself, isn't it?"

"What kind of a man was Gilbert Stuart? Did you know him?"

"I met him several times while he was painting the portrait. Come along, we'll go into the library, and I'll tell you what I know about him."

It had been this sort of personal acquaintance with famous artists that enchanted Matthew. Leo had moved freely in artistic circles in England. His home, Milford Manor, had been a haven for artists, particularly painters, and he seemed to have met every important painter that ever set foot in England. Now, as the two men sat there before the fire sipping strong tea out of exquisite china cups, Leo suddenly asked, "Matthew, tell me. Have you really liked it here? Do you like the house, the plantation?"

"Who wouldn't like it? It's all magnificent. More than I had imagined."

Leo hesitated, then said slowly, "I must admit, part of it is due to your foster father. Daniel came with me from England as an indentured servant. I didn't know a thing about horses or plantations—or how to run one, but he did. What he didn't know, he was quick to learn. I'm very grateful to him for all that he did to make this place prosper."

Such remarks Leo made about his father—about Daniel—confused Matthew, but he was pleased at the tenor of it.

"I've met several who remember him. Not many are left, though," Matthew said.

"No, there's been a big turnover in the last twenty years."

Matthew hesitated. "Sir, is there anyone left, that you know of, who knew . . . my mother?"

Now it was Leo's turn to feel an awkwardness. "Very few. You might try Haywood—Samuel Haywood. He works on a plantation up the road. He was here, as I recall, about that time. Not many more, though." Leo said no more but studied the face of the young man who sat across from him. "We get along well, you and I, don't we?"

Matthew nodded, then smiled suddenly. "You're on your best behavior, aren't you, sir?"

Leo stared at him, then burst out in a strained laughter. "By George! You have me there!" he exclaimed. He shook his head, saying, "Yes, I am on my best behavior. I want you to like it here. I want you to like me. That's natural, I think."

"I suppose, but if I did . . . do what you ask me to do, I suppose I'd see the other side of you."

Leo's face grew serious. He twirled the cup in his hand and sat there silently. "A man can change," he said solemnly.

Somehow Matthew was touched more by those few words than by anything that Rochester had done. "Yes," he said quickly, "we can change."

🛡   🛡   🛡

They arrived early evening at the Hugers', where Matthew spent a pleasant evening meeting the cream of Virginia gentility. When they discovered he was from Boston, they fired questions at him concerning the British troops there and, of course, the condition of the Continental Army under the command of George Washington.

"Now, don't pester him," Leo had interceded quickly. "No politics tonight." Grabbing Matthew by the arm, he led him to the large study where they could sit and not be bothered by so many of the men who were interested in the state of affairs back in Boston.

"It's true in Virginia, as it is everywhere, we're all looking for labels. A man's either a Tory or he's a patriot. That doesn't leave any middle ground."

"Well, there really isn't, is there, sir?"

"I think there should be. I'm opposed to the war—but I don't hate those who are fighting it. I believe it'll bring great harm and trouble upon those who rebel against authority." He grimaced and said, "I'm not a moralist, as you know, Matthew, but after all, we must have government—and we are Englishmen here." He looked at the young man and said, "I know your family feels differently. Perhaps we'd better not speak of it. But you see, you and I can sit here and discuss it easily and reasonably. We don't have to fight even though we might disagree."

There was something rational and calm about Leo Rochester's manner; nevertheless, Matthew felt that it wasn't that simple a matter. He did not argue, however, and the two rose and went back and enjoyed the party for the rest of the evening.

🛡   🛡   🛡

It was three days later that Matthew encountered Samuel Haywood. He had ridden to the plantation where Haywood was the manager and found him to be an elderly man in his eighties with the hale, healthy appearance of a much younger man. When he introduced himself as Matthew Bradford and mentioned that his father was Daniel Bradford, Haywood's eyes opened wide with surprise.

"You tell me that! I remember your father well! Sit down, young man, and tell me all about him."

Matthew was glad to find an old friend of his father's. The two sat there in the kitchen and drank hot cider. For a good hour Matthew told the elderly man all about his family and how they had fared in Boston since his father left Fairhope years ago. Finally, Matthew put the question he'd come to ask. "Did you know my mother, Holly Blanchard?"

"Why, yes—but only slightly. I can tell you she was a fine young woman, a servant at Fairhope, of course."

Matthew did not know how to ask his next question. He wanted to find out the truth of the matter about Leo Rochester's treatment of his mother, but he soon discovered that Haywood knew little. Finally, he rose and said, "Thank you. It's been fine speaking with you, sir. I'll give my father your good wishes."

"Do that! Oh, by the way. I had a thought just now." The old man's eyes grew small as he pondered. "You might talk to Mrs. Bryant. She was one of the servants in the house back then. I think she might have known your mother fairly well."

"Mrs. Bryant?"

"Yes. She's crippled now with arthritis. She lives with her daughter and her family." He gave Matthew instructions and said, "She'll be happy to see you. Doesn't get much company these days."

"Thank you, sir."

Matthew mounted his horse and rode off to see Mrs. Bryant. Following Haywood's directions, he found the house easily enough and was greeted at the door by a strong-faced woman of thirty. "I'm looking for a Mrs. Bryant who once worked as a housekeeper for the Rochesters years ago."

"That's my mother."

"My name is Matthew Bradford. I would like to see your mother, if I might."

"Of course, she's always glad to receive company on her good days."

Mrs. Smith led the young man into a parlor set off from the kitchen. There was a small fire burning in the hearth, and nearby sat an elderly woman dressed in black in her chair. She was small and frail, and her hands were terribly twisted by arthritis. But her eyes were quick and sharp, and when Matthew introduced himself, she at once said, "I never expected to see you, sir. Please sit down. It's a pleasure to meet you!"

"I'll fix tea for you," Mrs. Smith said and left the two alone.

Matthew at once began speaking with Mrs. Bryant. "I don't expect there are too many people around who knew my mother. As you know, she died some years ago, but I understand you were the housekeeper at the time."

"I knew her well. She was a fine, sweet girl. Came from the country, she did. Knew nothing at all about fancy big houses when she came to work at Fairhope. I spent quite a bit of time training her. She learned

185

quick, though, and was a hard worker."

Mrs. Bryant rambled on about how she and Holly had worked so well together. Matthew listened carefully. The old woman was garrulous enough, and finally he risked asking the question. "Did you know of the trouble that she had?"

Instantly the wrinkled face turned to him, and Mrs. Bryant stared sharply at his face. "You know about that?"

"Yes, I do."

"A terrible shame it was, what happened. She was such a fine, sweet girl. No one could mistake her for anything else. And your father, Daniel Bradford, he's a saint, he is!"

"He was kind to her, then?"

"What else is it to marry a girl bearing another man's child?"

"You know the father? Was it known who the father was?"

For all her talkative attitude, Mrs. Bryant suddenly fell silent. She studied the young man carefully. "There was only one it could have been. Never spoken of it all these years."

Matthew swallowed hard and said, "Was it Leo Rochester?"

"Yes. She never said so—but I knew it. He had troubled young servants before. He was a wild young man when he arrived from England. He ruined many a girl. I tried to get your mother to speak of it, but she never would. But every time I mentioned his name, she'd turn pale."

"Did he ever offer to marry her?"

"Him? Leo Rochester? Why, she was naught but a plaything to him! He cared no more for her than . . . than a child cares for a toy that he's broken. He threw her aside. Never gave it a thought!"

Matthew had his answer. In that moment, he made a firm decision in his mind. He made the remainder of his visit as pleasant as he could, then said, "I'll tell my father I saw you."

"Daniel Bradford was a fine young man. You must be very proud of him, and I'm sure he's proud of you."

"Yes, he has been a fine father. Thank you for your time, Mrs. Bryant." Matthew bowed and then left the room. Finally, his suspicions about Leo's character were confirmed by someone who had known him. He rode slowly back to Fairhope and went at once to speak with Leo Rochester.

As soon as Rochester saw Matthew's face set and angry, he stood up from the chair where he had been sitting. "What's the matter?" he asked with alarm.

"I've been talking with Mrs. Bryant." Matthew had watched Rochester's face closely as he spoke the name and saw the subtle change that took place. It was very slight but noticeable. "You didn't want me to talk to her, did you?"

"She's an old woman, not well," Leo said hesitantly.

"Don't lie to me," Matthew said bitterly. "You *knew* what she'd tell me—about the way you treated my mother."

For all of Leo's ability to scheme and manipulate people, he had not anticipated this. Nevertheless, he instinctively knew better than to deny the charge.

"I've already told you, Matthew. I was a fool back then."

"You got my mother pregnant, then threw her away!"

"That's not true. I didn't even know she was pregnant. Had no idea under the sun. I'm not defending myself—but at least you must believe that."

Matthew stared at the man, not knowing what to believe. He knew that Leo Rochester was capable of deceit. He had learned enough of his reputation to know that, but there was a distress in Rochester's face that he had never seen before—almost pain.

"You swear that?" Matthew said abruptly.

"I swear it! I'd pledge my everlasting soul on it!" Leo said fervently.

Matthew remained rigid, and Leo came over to him, saying, "A man can't go back and change the mistakes of the past, but sometimes he has a chance to change the present, sometimes even the future. Believe it or not, Matthew, that's what I'd like to do! I wish I could go back and make it right with your mother—but that's impossible. I don't know if you can ever forgive a young man's folly. You know that I'm not a good man. I mistreated your father and your aunt and, most of all, your mother. All my life, I've been quick-tempered, impulsive, and had the power to hurt people, and I've used it." He hesitated, then said again, "But a man can change, Matthew! I want to change, and I want you to change."

"Change how? What would you have me become? In all but blood, I'm Daniel Bradford's son."

"I would not try to separate you from Bradford. Naturally, you'll always have respect and admiration for him. You would not be the fine young man you are if you felt any differently."

Matthew was softened by the man's compliment. "What do you want to change in me?"

Leo took a deep breath. "I want to see your pictures hanging in the Royal Palace. I want men to look at them and say, 'That's one of Rochester's paintings.' I want my name to go on in you. That's all I've wanted since the first moment I saw you."

Matthew listened as Leo spoke. Part of him still seethed with anger from what he had just learned from Mrs. Bryant, but yet there was a quality in Rochester that he had not seen before. He could not tell if the man was acting or not. Finally, he said, "I . . . I'm going back to Boston. I need time to think."

"Of course, Matthew." Leo knew better than to argue, but he did step forward and put his hand on the young man's shoulder. "It's only wise to do that. Just remember this; I'm not trying to take Daniel Bradford out of your life. I'm trying to add something to you—something I think you yourself desire. If a man has a gift like yours, he has no right to withhold it. As many people as possible should benefit from it."

Although Leo did not know it—that had been Matthew's theory of art for a long time. Now he stared at Leo Rochester and finally nodded. "I'll leave in the morning—and I'll think about what you've said."

15

Colonel Knox's Cannons

COLONEL KNOX LED HIS PARTY OUT OF THE HILLS that surrounded Boston, and all that day they made their way along the roads with little difficulty. The weather grew increasingly colder for the next several days, but it stayed dry and Knox was grateful for that. Muddy patches of road began to freeze during the night and would not thaw out until the middle of the following day, which made the traveling somewhat easier. They crossed the boundary between Massachusetts and New York, and Jeanne remarked to Dake, who was riding at her right hand, "They look just alike, don't they?"

Dake grinned at her. "A boundary line's pretty artificial, Jeanne," he said. "Men get together and decide that this part of ground will be Massachusetts and this part will be New York. But it really doesn't make all that much difference."

Clive, who was riding on the other side of Jeanne, listened as the two spoke cheerfully along the way. He had been very much aware of the fact that ever since they'd left Boston, not for one minute had he been left alone. While not actually a prisoner, the constant scrutiny made him feel like he was the closest thing to it, and it had soured him somewhat. "Never should have come," he murmured under his breath.

"What did you say, Clive?" Jeanne turned to him quickly.

"Just wondering how much farther we're going to have to go today."

As it happened, the force pulled up less than an hour later and set up camp. Jeanne made herself helpful by joining the cook, who welcomed any assistance he could get. "I ain't no cook anyway," he grunted the first time Jeanne had offered to help him. "Be lucky if I don't poison half the men in the command."

Jeanne had laughed and had proved to be a valuable member of the crew.

That night as the men gathered around to eat, Knox was jovial. He winked at a tall, young officer across from him, saying, "Now, Winslow, this is more like it—having a real cook."

Nathan Winslow smiled at Jeanne. "I have to agree with Colonel Knox, Miss Corbeau. I thought for a while we were going to have to shoot the cook. But this here meal is real fine." Nathan was a tall man at six feet three inches, with auburn hair and startling light blue eyes. He turned to another of Knox's aides and said, "How about that, Sergeant Smith? A little of that tastes pretty good, doesn't it?"

Sergeant Laddie Smith was the smallest of the soldiers, and he kept to himself mostly. He had a pale, smooth face and looked to be not much over sixteen. "Yes, it's fine," Sergeant Smith said. Looking over at Jeanne he added, "I'm glad you came along. It's sure nice to have someone who knows how to cook. Makes things a lot easier."

Laddie was glad for Jeanne's companionship on the trip, even though she could not reveal she was really Julia Sampson in disguise.

"Mr. Winslow, weren't you at Lexington?" asked Dake.

"Yes, I remember meeting you there in the thick of it. Wasn't your father with you?"

"Yes, he joined me and my brother. Didn't I see you carry your brother Caleb off the field? How is he?"

"I'm sorry to say he died shortly after," said Nathan. Quickly turning, he said to Colonel Knox, "How're we gonna get those cannons back?"

The talk ran around the campfire for some time about the ways and means of moving the cannons back over almost impassable roads. Jeanne got up and began to pick up the dishes, and to her surprise, Dake offered her a hand.

"I can't cook," he said cheerfully, "but I can do this." They worked together and Dake said, "Let's go down to that creek to wash them. We may have to break the ice."

"All right," Jeanne said, and the two gathered up the rest of the tin plates and made their way down to the creek. It was about a hundred yards away from the camp, and in the twilight, with the sun gleaming redly over the horizon, they stooped and used sand to scour the plates.

As they worked, Dake spoke cheerfully, and finally when they had completed the job, Jeanne started to go back, but Dake said, "Let's sit here and watch that old moon sail by. Nothing to do but go to bed—or listen to all the officers make big plans that won't ever work out."

Jeanne smiled and sat down beside him on the bank. "What do you mean the plans never work out?"

"Nothing does in an army that I can see." Dake put his hands around his knees and rocked slowly back and forth. "I think they know that, too. The officers spend all that time arguing and making big plans, and then as soon as the first shot's fired, they throw the plan out the window and it's us men that have to make the thing work. It's easy enough to move a pin on a map, but when that means a man's got to crawl under fire up a hill to gun emplacements—well, that's a different story."

"You like the army, don't you, Dake?"

"Yes, I do, better than anything I've ever done," he admitted. "I guess I'm just a natural-born rebel. Getting up and going to work every day, that's not for me."

"That's the way my father was," Jeanne said quietly. "I don't think he ever had a regular job in his life." She went on to tell how her father had spent his life wandering all over the mountains, hunting, fishing, trapping, and finally she fell silent when he gave her a curious look.

"I believe I would have liked him. I wish I could have known him. You miss him a great deal, don't you?"

"Yes, I do."

She was sitting close beside him, and something in the mournful tone of her voice touched Dake's sympathy. "Well," he said awkwardly, "I'm sorry, Jeanne. I wish I could do something to ease your sorrow."

"There's nothing anyone can do."

She was staring down at the creek and, to her horror, speaking of her father had brought back memories so sharp and so poignant that it caused a lump to rise in her throat. She tried to speak and found that she could not. All of the happy days she had known with her father suddenly came before her. She dropped her head and put her face against her knees, hugging them tightly, her shoulders beginning to shake. She had not wept like this since her father had died, and then only alone.

Dake was astonished at the girl. He had known that she must have missed her father, but she kept up such a good front that he had never guessed her grief ran this deep. He moved closer and put his arm around her and squeezed her, whispering, "I know it's tough. I'm sorry, Jeanne."

Her shoulders began to shake even more violently as she gave way to a paroxysm of tears that had been dammed up. Dake turned her around, and she fell against him. He held her tightly as she sobbed uncontrollably. Her face was buried against his chest, and he said nothing but held her and stroked her short-cropped hair. Finally, the sobs began to subside, and Jeanne pulled away.

"I didn't . . . mean to do that. I'm not usually such a baby," she whispered.

"No shame to it. It's not easy to lose someone you love so much."

Jeanne pulled out a handkerchief and mopped her face and then cleared her throat. "I don't do that very often."

"I guess it's all right to cry, Jeanne," Dake said quietly. He was a rough young fellow not given to emotional excesses, but something about the vulnerability of the young woman had touched him. He wanted to protect her from the sorrow and the grief. He actually wanted to put his arms around her again and hold her, but he felt that this might be misunderstood. "I wish I could go with you when you go to your aunt's," he said. "But I can't."

"I know, Dake, but it was good of you to get Colonel Knox to let me go. I'm very grateful for that."

The two got up and picked up the clean dishes and started to walk back toward the camp. By then the sun had dipped behind the hills, casting long shadows on the path. When they approached the campfire, Dake saw Clive there watching them carefully as they approached. Dake was aware that this tall cousin of his disliked him. He nodded toward Clive and then said good night to Jeanne before he headed for his tent to turn in.

As soon as Dake disappeared, Clive said to Jeanne, "It doesn't look good, your walking out with a soldier."

"Why, we just went down to wash the dishes!" Jeanne said, feeling a bit irritated.

"I know that, but it's a very tense situation, very unusual. I'd rather you didn't do it again."

Jeanne's eyes narrowed. There was, at times, a pompous streak in Clive that she disliked, and she saw it surface now. "I'll walk with anyone I please, Clive. You're not my father. I don't have to do what you say."

Instantly Clive realized he had blundered and said awkwardly, "I don't mean to be possessive. I . . . I just worry about you."

His quick apology softened Jeanne's anger. She took a deep breath and expelled it. Her brow suddenly furrowed. "Don't worry about me. I'll be all right." She turned and walked away, leaving Clive sitting by the fire unhappy and dissatisfied.

🔔　　　🔔　　　🔔

The next morning as they rode along, Dake said to Jeanne, "Clive doesn't like me very much. I don't think he trusts me where you're concerned."

Jeanne's face grew warm, for she knew that Dake was exactly right. "Clive is funny sometimes—but he's been very kind to me, and he can help my aunt."

Dake glanced over to where Clive was riding along, looking down at the ground. "Those English folks are funny, aren't they? I mean, so stuffy and everything has to be just right. Of course," he said, "I guess I could use a few fine manners myself."

"I suppose I could, too."

Dake grinned suddenly at Jeanne. "Maybe we could go to a charm school together." He made a joke out of it, and the two made the long ride easier by their talks. This, of course, left Clive out, and he grew more and more silent and morose as the journey went on.

The weather grew worse and accidents began to happen. Dake's horse fell as they were coming up out of a river. Dake's leg was twisted, and he could not walk. He tried to hobble around using a crutch he had whittled.

Dake's leg could not take the position necessary in riding a horse, so Colonel Knox commanded him to ride in a wagon. On the first day in the afternoon, Jeanne rode by and he sat up and called to her. "Jeanne, come and ride with me. I'm bored to tears."

"All right." Jeanne jumped out, tied the lines of her horse to the back of the wagon, then scrambled inside. They sat there on piles of supplies laughing as they were jolted over the almost impassable trails. Finally, Jeanne said, "This is awful, Dake. All this jostling around can't be good for your leg. Why don't you let Clive look at it? Maybe he could help."

"Just a twisted leg!" Dake's answer was short, and he absolutely refused to let Clive examine him.

However, Clive stopped by after supper with a bottle. "I've got some liniment here that might help that leg of yours. It's good for sprains and twisted muscles."

Dake looked up and nodded, "Well, that's thoughtful of you, Clive." He took the bottle and hobbled off to the wagon to try some of it on his wounded leg.

Jeanne had seen the gesture. She came up and shyly said, "That was nice of you, Clive. Dake hasn't been very nice to you.".

"I hope his leg gets better." He looked at her and paused, then said, "I'm anxious to get there, and I know you are too."

"Yes, I'm worried about Ma Tante. She's really the only one of my family left. Oh, I have an uncle—a half brother of my father's—but I haven't seen him in years. But Ma Tante, well, she's different. Even though we haven't seen each other in recent years, we've always been close."

"Tell me about her. Come on and sit by the fire." The two of them sat down, and for the better part of an hour Jeanne spoke about her aunt, who had taught her so many things. Once they had celebrated Christmas at her aunt's house, and she had given Jeanne some nice presents. It was a good evening for Clive—the best he'd had with Jeanne since they had left on the trip to Ticonderoga. Jeanne finally fell silent, and he said, "Jeanne, I want to tell you something."

"Yes, what is it?"

"I haven't been behaving well. I felt bad about Dake spending so much time with you. I guess . . . I am a little possessive of you. I mean, after all, your father did tell me to look out for you. I'm just trying to honor the promise I made him."

"I know, and I'm grateful, Clive." She looked at the young Englishman's face and sensed that despite his great height there was some uncertainty or immaturity in him. She knew he had never been forced to fend for himself and now wondered what he intended. "Are you going back to England, Clive, to be a doctor there?"

"I don't know." Clive picked up a stick, stuck it in the fire, and waited until it ignited. He held it up before his eyes, staring at the cone-shaped yellow blaze for a moment, then tossed it onto the bed of hot coals. There was an unhappiness on his face as he turned to her. "I know it's awful not knowing what to do. Here I've spent all my life studying diligently to be a doctor, and now I'm acting like a child, not knowing which way to turn."

"You'll find yourself. It's been hard times for you and your family. Tell me some more about England."

Willingly Clive began to talk about the home where he had grown up. They had moved a great deal during his father's career in the army, but they had been in one home for five years and, to him, that was always what he thought of when he thought of his childhood. He told Jeanne about the holidays there and the family traditions that made Christmas so memorable, and about the hunts he had been on with his father. When he stopped, he looked almost embarrassed. "Well, I'm talking like an old woman," he said.

"No, you're not. Tell me some more," Jeanne encouraged him.

"That's all there is!"

She smiled at him. "You didn't tell me about all the young ladies you charmed."

"Who's been giving me that reputation?"

"Your mother. She says girls always liked you."

"That's foolish. Mother ought to know better than to talk like that."

"She's a very wise woman." Jeanne thought of Lyna Gordon and said wistfully, "I never knew my own mother; she died when I was three."

"That must have been very hard growing up without a mother," Clive said softly. "I wish you had been in England. We could have been friends."

"No, you're older than I am. You wouldn't want a baby sister tagging along behind you."

"I see Grace has been talking to you," he accused her.

"Yes, she has. She said she idolized you when she was growing up and pestered you all the time, went everywhere with you. Isn't that funny, Rachel said the same thing about Dake. I guess sisters always idolize their brothers. I wish you'd been my brother. We could have had such fun together."

Clive laughed shortly. "Well, I'm not your brother—but I'm going to be your friend. You can always count on that."

Without thinking Jeanne reached over and put her hand on his. "I do think about that," she said quietly. When he looked at her, she smiled and said, "You'll never know what it's meant to me—to know you and your family. I was so lonely and scared when Papa died, but you've taken me in. Now I do feel like I have a brother."

Something about her words displeased him, but he smiled at her, knowing what she meant. "Well, it's been good for my mother. She always wanted to have a houseful of daughters. Now she gets to dote on you. I'm sure Grace appreciates you diverting some of that attention away from her!"

They grew quiet as they sat and watched the flames, and finally Dake came hobbling back on his crutch. "That stuff burns like fire!" he said. "What's in it?"

"I'm not sure, but it always works on horses," Clive drawled.

A laugh went up around the campfire, and Knox said, "That's just what we need, a horse doctor for a surgeon. All right, to bed everyone!"

☙　　☙　　☙

On December 1, 1775, Knox's force reached Albany on a cold gray day. The colonel was ushered into the office of General Philip Schuyler, commander of the Continental Army in the North.

Schuyler was surprised to see him. He stood up to shake his visitor's hand. When he heard of their errand he said, "Well, I'm happy to do what I can for General Washington. What might that be?"

Colonel Knox went right to the point. "General Washington sent us to Ticonderoga to bring back all the cannons there."

"And do what with them?"

"To take them back and break the siege in Boston."

Schuyler's eyebrows lifted. There was doubt in his voice as he asked, "You think you can move those cannons in December?"

"Certainly," Knox nodded vigorously. "The general's ordered the guns, and I intend to deliver them to him."

Schuyler shrugged his shoulders, still looking somewhat doubtful. "Well, I'm at your disposal, Mr. Knox. Now, what can I do?"

Knox had thought this all out. "We're going to need a great many oxen and horses. We're going to need sledges, perhaps even boats."

"Well," Schuyler shrugged, "horses are no problem. We've plenty of those. It may take a little doing to come up with sledges, and oxen are hard to come by in this country." He stared at the big form of Knox and inquired, "You intend to use these cannons to dislodge the British?"

"That's right. We'll drive those Redcoats out of the city in no time."

"About time!" General Schuyler arose and said to his officers, "Come, gentlemen. We'll see what we can do from this end to break the siege of Boston."

Schuyler did provide good mounts, but the cold intensified that very night. The temperature dropped below freezing as the men moved out the next morning. It was not until December 5, with a freezing wind blowing, that they reached Fort George, the small post at the southern end of Lake George.

When they finally were approaching Ticonderoga, Clive and Jeanne pulled away. "My aunt lives fifteen miles over there across that mountain," she said.

Dake was hobbling around now with the use of a stick. "It looks like a long way and you might get lost. Maybe I'd better ask the colonel if I can go."

"No, you can't do that. Your duty's with Colonel Knox," Jeanne said. "That's why he brought you."

"What will happen? How will you get back to Boston?"

"I'll see that she gets back, Dake," Clive said. "But it may be a long visit. If her aunt's very ill she may have to stay."

"That's right. But I'll write to you, Dake, if I do, and I'll come back to Boston as soon as I can."

"All right," Dake grumbled. Awkwardly he put his hand out and shook hands with her, saying, "Be sure you write. Time we get these cannons back it's liable to be spring, but I'll be worried about you."

"Don't do that," Jeanne smiled. He released her hand, and she turned and got on her horse. Clive mounted also, and the two turned the heads of the animals westward.

As they disappeared, Nathan Winslow came to stand beside Dake, who was staring discontentedly at the pair as they rode off. "I think you'd like to be going with them, wouldn't you?"

Dake turned and looked at the tall soldier. "I sure would, Nathan. How'd you know that?"

Winslow smiled, almost secretly. "It's not hard to tell that you're pretty attached to that young woman. Now, don't run off and desert just to be with her."

Dake grinned at him and said, "I would if this leg wasn't busted. I most certainly would!"

🛲   🛲   🛲

As soon as Knox and his company, shivering from the cold, reached Fort Ticonderoga after Clive and Jeanne had headed west, Knox was shown into the commander's quarters.

"Good to see you, Captain," Knox boomed. "I come from General Washington."

"Well," said Captain Bates, a lean man with a calm manner, "what are you doing up here this time of the year?" He listened carefully as Knox explained that he had come for the cannons that were stored there. Then Bates nodded, "Might as well take 'em. We can't use 'em here. You want to have a look around?"

"Certainly," Knox answered. He went at once with Captain Bates and examined the artillery pieces. Many of the cannons were old and worn out, but Knox pointed out a gun here and there until finally he had selected sixty artillery pieces that he felt could be used effectively. Most of them were cannons, ranging from four to twenty-four pounds. There were also half a dozen mortars, three howitzers, and enough cannonballs, flint, and powder to keep the big guns firing for a long time. Knox beamed and slapped his brother William on the back. "We'll have the Redcoats out of Boston before you know it!" he cried.

The entire garrison at Fort Ticonderoga was pressed into service. They set to work dismantling the artillery pieces, which were then placed on sturdy carts. The commander had managed to supply a heavy scow and two lighter flat-bottomed boats. The soldiers loaded the disassembled cannons, the barrels of powder, and the crates of cannonballs into the vessels. "I hope this thing doesn't sink," Dake said nervously.

Colonel Knox overheard him and said, "It won't do that, Private Bradford."

"I wish it'd warm up a bit," one of the men said.

"No! Warm weather would be the worst thing right now! We need frozen ground to use the sledges farther on down. Otherwise, we'd have to use wagons and the mud would slow us down. Nope! Pray for cold weather. That's what we need...!"

16

A Servant of the Most High God

MONTCERF WAS BARELY LARGE ENOUGH to be called a village. As Jeanne and Clive rode into the small settlement, he quickly took in the houses that were scattered about a rather barren landscape without the formality of streets. Some of the dwellings were simple log cabins, while others were constructed of milled lumber. Most of them had never known the taste of paint. The damp weather had coated all of them with a nondescript gray shade that seemed a little depressing to him. He did see what amounted to a general store flanked by a blacksmith shop with a corral in back where three scrubby spotted horses snorted and chuffed at them as they rode by.

"It's just a small village," Jeanne murmured, "but I suppose you can see that." She led him past several hogs that ambled up to inspect them curiously. A pack of dogs came up to yap rather lackadaisically, then returned to the barn where they found shelter from the weather. It was cold enough to numb the cheeks of the two riders, and as they made their way through the scrubby settlement, Clive wondered in what condition he would find his patient. Jeanne had told him nothing except that her aunt was very sick.

As they rounded a fence that made an unsuccessful attempt to keep in several goats, Jeanne motioned with her hand to a house set back under a small grove of spindly trees. "That's where Ma Tante lives," she said. She said no more but moved her horse forward quickly until they paused in front of the cabin. It was a simple structure, one and a half stories with two windows on each side and one that was framed by the "A" structure of the roof. The boards were aged and gray, and everything seemed to be in a state of disrepair.

As they stepped up on the porch, one of the boards gave beneath Clive's boot, and he hastily drew it back and found a safer footing. Jeanne knocked on the door, and there seemed to be a rather long wait until finally it cracked open. Then it opened wider and a short stubby woman greeted Jeanne with a string of rapid French, of which Clive understood not a word. Jeanne nodded and returned the greeting. Clive heard his own name mentioned.

"This is Ma Tante's sister-in-law, Marie St. Cloud," Jeanne said. "She and her husband have taken care of Ma Tante."

Clive nodded and said, "I'm happy to know you," but was aware that the woman understood practically no English.

Marie St. Cloud drew back and pulled Jeanne into the room, talking rapidly. As she spoke, Clive's eyes swept the room, noting that it was not as rustic as the outside. Some care had been spent, for there was a carpet on the floor. It was now old and worn and faded, but he could tell it had been expensive in its day. The furniture was surprisingly good for an outpost so far from any city. The room had several Windsor chairs and a lounge covered with horsehide, forming a small area to his right beside one of the windows. To his left was a large round table with a lamp set in the center of it on a crocheted mat made of what seemed to be blue wool. A door to the left of the table evidently led off to a kitchen, and another at the back of the room to a hall, which he thought must contain bedrooms. A steep staircase, little more than a ladder, led up to a balcony of sorts. He noticed that the top part of the structure had been converted into living space.

Jeanne turned to him, her eyes troubled, saying, "Ma Tante's not good, Marie says."

"Ask her what the symptoms are."

After Jeanne put the question in French and received an answer, she translated, "Ma Tante had a spell six months ago. She'd been ill before that. Marie says the last time she fell out in the garden and lost the use of her left arm and leg. She still can't use them very well. She says also the spell seems to have affected her mind."

"It sounds like a stroke."

"That is what Marie says. She's very good with sick people. But nothing, she says, seems to make Ma Tante any better. Will you come and see her now?"

"Of course."

Marie led them down the hall to a door, which she opened, then stepped aside. Jeanne went at once to the frail woman on the bed. Leaning over, Jeanne kissed her aunt while Clive stood back and watched. The woman Jeanne called Ma Tante was Lydia Revere. She was Pierre

Corbeau's only sister, and had married John Revere when she was a young woman. The couple had shared much happiness together, but had also suffered the tragic loss of all five of their children. Three were lost at birth, and the two who had lived had survived only until their early teens, when cholera took them. Many people would have become bitter in the face of such tragedy, but for John and Lydia, it drew them closer to each other and to God.

Clive's eyes narrowed as he studied the face of the woman. She had beautiful snow white hair. Though her face was lined by pain, there were still traces of an earlier beauty. Jeanne had told him that when her aunt was a younger woman, her hair had been as black as coal dust, blacker than could be imagined. Now, the only traces were the darkness of the eyebrows, which had not silvered as had her hair. She was lying propped up in the feather bed with several pillows behind her back, and when she reached up to receive Jeanne's embrace, it was only with her right hand. The woman was thin, but as she turned from Jeanne to meet Clive Gordon's eyes, there was a vibrant spark of life in her expression. Her dark eyes studied him calmly for a moment.

"This is my friend, Mr. Clive Gordon. He is a doctor, Ma Tante."

Clive was somewhat surprised when the sick woman spoke to him in English. "How do you do, Doctor?"

"I'm glad to know you, Mrs. Revere. Your niece has spoken of you quite often." He approached the side of the bed, pulled a chair up, and put his bag on the floor. "You're having considerable difficulty?" he remarked.

"I do not complain," the woman said. She had a sweet smile, and her eyes never left Gordon's face. There was no fear in her, and none of the bitterness one often found in chronic invalids. Instead, there was a placid expression and her lips were relaxed as she said, "It was good of you to make the trip—but I fear there is little you can do."

"Well, I must confess, I owed your niece a favor. Has she written you about what a great service she did for me?"

"No, tell me about it."

"Well," Clive began, "she saved my life. That's a thing a man doesn't forget." He went on to explain in detail what Jeanne had done for him, smiling at Jeanne across the bed as she flushed with embarrassment. "She doesn't like me to speak of it, Mrs. Revere," he said. "Quite literally, I would not be here if she had not come along and found me in the woods."

"Oh, do not speak of it!" Jeanne said. She turned to her aunt and stroked her hair with a gentle hand. "The doctor was good enough to offer to escort me here when I received your letter."

201

Lydia Revere listened to all this calmly, then a smile touched her lips. "You must have a small practice, Doctor, if you can leave Boston and come all the way to Montcerf to treat one sick woman."

Clive shook his head and returned her smile. "I'm afraid I have no practice at all, Mrs. Revere. I'm not long out of medical school and haven't yet begun one."

Jeanne sat quietly across from Clive, studying the face of her aunt. Her heart felt the pain of grief, for she had been shocked at how frail Ma Tante had become. She had not expected to find her so weak. She still had clear memories of her as a strong and healthy woman who laughed often—one who, out of a hard life filled with difficulties, had found a peace with God and with those about her. Now there was only a faint trace of the vibrant life that had once so filled Lydia Revere, and Jeanne knew that there would not be any healing for her beloved aunt.

Clive spoke gently and easily with the old woman, aware that she was watching him in a rather curious fashion. *Probably never seen many doctors, not English ones, I suppose,* was his thought. Aloud he said, "We'll see what we can do, Mrs. Revere. In the meantime, I'm sure you'll enjoy a visit with Jeanne."

Lydia Revere turned to face Jeanne and murmured something in French. When Jeanne answered, she turned back to Gordon, who was removing a bottle out of his bag. "I don't speak any French," he said, "or very little."

"I was just saying to Jeanne that God was good to send her to me. And you too, Clive Gordon."

Clive asked for a glass, and when Jeanne sprang up and came back with one, he poured some clear fluid into it and said, "Add some warm water to this, Jeanne. I think it will make you feel better, Mrs. Revere."

When the potion was prepared, Lydia drank it down, coughed, then handed the glass back to Jeanne. Lying back on the pillows, she turned to Jeanne and said, "Now, tell me everything. Tell me about Pierre."

Jeanne had written to her aunt about the details of her brother's death, but she saw that Ma Tante wanted to hear it from her directly. She leaned forward and spoke for a long time, giving all the details, not sparing her praise of Clive, who was somewhat embarrassed.

As Jeanne spoke, Lydia Revere listened intently. For a while, after Jeanne paused and broke off, her aunt lay there, then she turned her eyes on the doctor, giving him again that rather odd look, as if she were weighing him in the balances for some reason or other. She did not comment on her brother's last message but smiled faintly.

"It seems you are sent by God to take care of another one of our family. I'm grateful to the Lord Jesus for sending you to Pierre. It meant a great deal to him to have you there those last days, I know. You have taken your promise seriously."

"My promise?"

"To watch out for Jeanne. That is a noble thing and the good Lord will reward you for it." She was growing sleepy now from the medicine and said, "Let me rest awhile. Then you must come back. I want to know all about Boston and what you've been doing there."

Jeanne and Clive left the sick woman's room, and Marie St. Cloud met them and spoke to Jeanne in French. "Bring the doctor. I have fixed something for you to eat."

Jeanne translated this and the two sat down at the round table, which was placed in front of the fireplace. Marie quickly served them warmed-over stew, some cuts from a roast beef, and bread that had been baked recently. As Clive spread butter on the warm fresh bread he remarked, "This is a little better than what we've had lately." He saw that Jeanne was waiting and remembered himself. "Oh! The blessing—yes. Shall you do that?"

"No," Jeanne said simply, "it is a man's place."

Feeling somewhat flustered and caught off guard, Clive managed to struggle through a simple blessing, then the two began to eat hungrily. The food was served on pewter plates, and they drank tea liberally from the large mugs that Marie St. Cloud refilled several times. Marie sat down and drank her own tea, and Clive sipped his slowly while Jeanne and her aunt spoke in French. He supposed that Jeanne was filling the woman in on their journeys, and more than once he felt the woman's dark brown eyes come to rest on him, making him somewhat uncomfortable.

After a time, Marie got up and cleared the table then left. The two sat enjoying the warmth from the fire, which crackled cheerfully on the grate. The warmth soaked into them. They had been wet and cold almost since they'd left Boston, and Jeanne said, "It will be good to get dry clothes on." She rose and said, "Come, Marie told me which room you will be staying in."

They went to their horses first and unsaddled them, leaving them in a corral after having fed them some hay from the loft. "I'll have to pay for this, feeding the horses," Clive said.

"No, that would insult them," Jeanne said quickly. "Marie's glad to do it for you."

"Is she married?"

"Yes, her husband's name's Maurice. He cuts wood for a living—a timber man. He's off somewhere in the forest with his crew, though, and won't be back for a few days."

When they were back inside, she led him up the steep stairway, where, at the top, they turned into a short hallway. There was a door on each side. She opened the one on the right and led Clive inside. It was a cheerful enough room, though plainly decorated, with a single window that let in the rays of the sun. He put his gear down on the single bed, saying, "This will be fine—except for the bed."

She looked at it and saw that it was shorter than usual. Smiling, she said, "I suppose you always have trouble with beds being too short."

"Many times I've wished I could cut my legs off at the knees! But I'll make out."

Jeanne began at once removing the covers and the pillows and the feather mattress, despite his protest. "We'll fix you up a fine bed here," she said. "I'll have to get more covers. This won't be enough." She worked busily, then stood up and smiled. "Ma Tante liked you, I could tell," she said quietly. "It means a great deal to me, Clive, for you to have come all this way to help her."

Clive shifted his feet nervously and looked down at her. The light from the window fell on her face. It seemed to form an aureole around the black mass of curly hair. She had not let it grow, to his surprise, and he found himself liking it that way. He'd never seen a woman wear her hair like this and knew that it was a holdover from the days when long hair would be another difficulty. Several times he had felt the impulse to reach out and feel the silky softness of the curls, and he felt it now. But he said instead, "Your aunt is very sick. You see that, of course."

"Yes, I do. She can't live, can she?"

"Well, of course, no one can say. That's in the hands of God."

She looked at him with surprise. "You believe that? That God is in it?"

"Well, of course." He felt somewhat offended at her words. "You don't think I'm a heathen, do you?"

Jeanne smiled at his quick reaction. "No, but you don't talk about God. I'm glad that you do feel like that—that God is in it. She always loved God more than anyone I ever knew, even more than my father. I can remember sitting on her lap when I was just a little girl, and she would read to me from the Bible and make the stories so real. She taught me how to love the Bible." Reminiscence swept over her, and she was conscious then of the passage of time, even though it seemed in her mind that this had taken place only a short time ago. But those sweet times were all gone now, and the sadness and loss that grieved her reflected in her eyes and in the tightening of her lips.

"I wish I could give you better news, Jeanne, but obviously she's had a stroke, and from what I can tell and what she tells me, she's been growing weaker ever since."

"Yes, that is what Marie says too. She's weaker every day, it seems." She looked up to him and tried to smile. "But it meant a lot, your coming, even if she can't live. You can be a help during her last days, can't you, Clive?"

"Of course. I'll do what I can. She's a lovely woman."

"She was so beautiful when she was young and so full of life."

"Yes, I see some of that still in her. She must have been a beautiful woman, and despite her illness, she has not become angry or bitter. That happens often, you know."

Jeanne shook her head. "I can't imagine Ma Tante being bitter at anyone. It just seems that God is in her and love constantly flows out of her—and wisdom. She always knew just what to do when I'd come to her with something that was bothering me. It seemed God came down and talked to her personally." Her words embarrassed her somewhat and she said, "That sounds wrong somehow. But she lived very close to God all her life."

The two stood there for what seemed like a long time. Finally Jeanne said, "I'll be right across the hall. I'll bring you more blankets so you won't be cold."

Clive watched her as she left, then sat down on the feather bed. He sank down into it and grimaced as he looked at the shortness of it. "I wish I were short sometimes," he muttered. Some of the warmth from the lower part of the house was carried upstairs, but he knew the room would be colder when the fire was allowed to die. As soon as Jeanne brought more blankets, he followed her downstairs, where he spent what was left of the day. Both he and Jeanne were extremely tired from their hard journey and they both went to bed early that night. He went first, saying merely, "Good night, Jeanne. *Bonne nuit*, Madame St. Cloud." He tried his French, and she smiled at his efforts, wishing him a good night.

When he had gone upstairs, Marie questioned Jeanne more carefully. "He is not married?"

"No, not married."

"I'm surprised, but the English marry later than we do out here in this country." She questioned Jeanne more closely until finally an enigmatic look crossed her face. "Well, I trust he is a good man. It would not have been permitted once, a young girl like you, to travel all over the country with an unmarried man."

"It was something we had to do," Jeanne said quickly, "and besides, he would never hurt me."

"No, I do not think he would. He has the look of a good man." Then she said, "Go to bed now. You are tired."

Jeanne went upstairs and put on a heavy wool gown that Marie had insisted on loaning her. She snuggled down into the feather bed, pulling the blankets up high, and fell into a deep sleep almost at once.

🕮   🕮   🕮

Clive spent a great deal of time with Jeanne as the days passed. As he feared, Ma Tante, which he himself had now come to call her at her own request, grew weaker daily—weaker in the flesh but not in the spirit. Clive had seen a lot of people die, but this woman endured it with a grace and courage he had witnessed in but a few. Clive was fascinated by the faith of the dying woman. He had seen it in her brother and now again in Lydia Revere.

"Your aunt, Ma Tante, she's not afraid. She's like your father," he said once to Jeanne as they were sitting in the combination living area and dining room. Marie was gone on an errand, and the late afternoon sun was diffused through the light of the small windows.

"No, she's lived with God all of her life. He's been her best friend. She's told me that so often. She says now she's going to be with her friend, the Lord God."

"What a beautiful way to think of death!" Clive said softly.

"Yes, it is, isn't it? I hope when it comes time for me to die, I can face it as well as Ma Tante."

They talked for a while, then Jeanne picked up her book and began to read. Clive was restless and finally asked, "What are you reading, Jeanne? Most of these books are in French."

"This one is, too, but I can't make much sense out of it." She looked up at him and shrugged her shoulders, a smile in her eyes. "It's poetry. I never could understand poetry too well."

"Well, I understand poetry very well," Clive said. "Read it to me."

"But it's in French. You won't understand it."

"Translate it. What's the title of it? Who wrote it?"

Jeanne's eyes went back to the book, and she stumbled as she said, "It's something like, 'To the—' " She halted, then said, " 'To the Young Women They Should Have a Good Time.' "

Clive laughed aloud. "Is it by a man named Robert Herrick?"

"Why, yes it is." She looked up at him surprised. "You know it?"

"Oh yes, I know it very well. But you've got the title a little wrong. It's really, 'To the Virgins to Make Much of Time.' I memorized that one a long time ago."

She was amazed and said so. "Why would you memorize this? I don't understand, Clive."

"Why, it's easy," he said. "In English it goes like this:

Gather ye rosebuds, while ye may,
Old time is still a-flying;
And this same flower that smiles today,
Tomorrow will be dying.
The glorious lamp of heaven, the sun,
The higher he's a-getting,
The sooner will his race be run,
And nearer he's to setting.
That age is best when is the first,
When youth and blood are warmer;
But being spent, the worse and worst
Times still succeed the former.
Then be not coy, but use your time,
And while ye may, go marry,
For, having lost but once your prime,
You may forever tarry.

Jeanne had put the book down, listening to him carefully. She was curled up on the sofa, her feet tucked under her in a manner she had. "But what does it mean? Why doesn't he say whatever it is he means?"

"Some things can't be said directly, Jeanne."

"Why, of course they can. I can say, 'Hand me the porridge,' or, 'Shut the door.' "

Clive looked at her. He had had this argument before. "Yes, you can say things like that, but tell me how you feel about your aunt, about Ma Tante." He saw her face change and said quickly, "You see? Such things are hard to put into words—the deepest things in us. We can tell how many feet there are in a mile or how many ounces in a pound—but we have trouble trying to tell someone how we love them. Poetry allows us to say some of our deepest feelings."

"I didn't know that." Jeanne looked down at the words again and said, "Explain it to me."

"Well, 'Gather ye rosebuds while ye may, old time is still a-flying and this same flower that smiles today tomorrow will be dying.' It means what it says, Jeanne. If you want to gather a rose you have to do it while they're in bloom, because soon the bloom will be gone and the petals will fall off and the rose is gone. And the second stanza, it's almost the same, a different figure—'The sun rises, it goes up high and then he's gone.' The day passes, just like the rose."

"I see that," Jeanne said. She studied the rest of the poem and said,

"It says in this third verse that, 'Age is best when youth and blood are warmer.' I suppose that means that youth is better than old age."

"That's what the poem says, although some wouldn't agree. Some would say the last is better than the first." He was watching her, amused at her frown as she wrestled with the meaning of the words. "Do you understand the last verse?"

"No, not really."

"It simply says—I don't think you'll like it—it says you ought to yield yourself to love, for soon you'll be unable to love anymore, physically that is."

Jeanne looked up at him startled, "Is that what it means?"

"That's the way I understand it. Most poets, I guess, feel like that. Their poetry says so. But it's not a Christian way of looking at things."

Jeanne stared at him curiously. "What do you mean, Clive?"

"Well, this poet is saying that love is so important that we need to grab it when we can, never mind the results. I'm afraid most people try to do that, but I don't think Ma Tante would agree with it—nor your father. Nor my father and mother, for that matter."

Jeanne stared back at the poem as mixed thoughts ran through her head. She had not thought deeply about love, but now what he was saying began to take shape in her. Suddenly her eyes opened wide with understanding and she exclaimed, "This is a bad poem!"

"I'm afraid many devout Christians would say so."

"Don't you say so?"

"Well, I suppose I would have to, although love is very important to a man—and to a woman. It's a big part of our lives down here."

As they continued to talk about the poem, Clive was amazed at how quickly her mind grasped things.

Finally, she said, "I don't want to read any more poems by Mr. Herrick."

"Some of them are much worse," Clive said wryly. "I wish I had some English books here. I tell you what! You tell me what books you have there in French—and I'll tell you which ones you might like better."

T   T   T

Reading together during the long hours while Ma Tante slept became habitual with Jeanne and Clive. On the third day after they had arrived, Maurice St. Cloud came back briefly from logging. He was a short, squat man with enormous hands and a skin textured to leather by a life of hard work outdoors in the forest. He was glad enough to welcome Clive, but spoke so little English that the two had difficulty communicating. He stayed home only a day and then was gone again.

Every day Jeanne and Clive spent time with Ma Tante. Much of the time, Clive would simply sit there and listen as the two women would talk. Life was ebbing so fast from the old woman that her voice was now reduced to a whisper, and she would sometimes fall asleep suddenly, almost in the middle of a sentence. Early one morning when he had come to give her some medicine, she had waved it away, saying, "No need for that."

Clive stared at her. He knew she was right. He did it merely as a gesture, mostly for Jeanne's sake. But now, he obeyed, put the cap back on the bottle, replaced it on the table, and sat down. Jeanne was doing some washing. He could hear her singing in the other room, her voice floating faintly, but sweetly, into the sickroom.

Ma Tante opened her eyes and pulled herself up, as best she could, into a better position. Clive at once arose and helped her. "Is that better?" he asked gently, then sat back again.

"I want to talk to you about God," Ma Tante said abruptly.

"About God? Why, of course, Ma Tante," Clive answered, feeling somewhat awkward.

"You are a good man, but it is not enough to be a good man. You need God in your heart."

Her blunt words struck Clive like a blow. Such things as this he had not heard many times. Yet, he remembered now his mother had attempted to say things like this to him—and he had brushed them aside, giving it little serious thought. Now, however, in the confines of this small room, with the eyes of the dying woman fixed upon him, he could not do more than say, "Yes, of course, that's true of all of us."

"There's one important thing each of us is going to have to answer. When we die, we will not be asked," Ma Tante said in a weak but steady voice, "how much money we had or how much education. We will only be asked one question—" She hesitated and then said, "God will ask us, did you honor my Son that I sent to die for you? I want you to know this Jesus," she said, her voice growing somewhat stronger. "You must ask Him to come into your life."

"I've said prayers all my life, Ma Tante. Isn't that enough?"

"Nothing is enough but being part of God's family. You must become a son of God. This is why Jesus died. His blood will make you clean, Clive."

The use of his first name warmed him, and he sat there as she talked to him steadily for half an hour. He was aware that Jeanne had come into the room, moving quietly to sit on the other side of the bed in her usual place. He glanced up at her once, but she was silent, saying nothing.

Ma Tante talked on for a long time, always gently, but always persistently bringing his need of God before him. Finally, she grew tired and fell asleep.

"She's much weaker," Clive said quietly, looking up to meet Jeanne's eyes. "She can't last long, I'm afraid."

"I can remember when she talked to me about God as she's been talking to you. I was just a little girl, but she always insisted I had to know Jesus. Somehow, she made me believe it."

"I can understand that. She's a woman of faith." Clive felt uneasy, for he understood that the dying woman was asking something of him that he had never been prepared to give. Somehow, she seemed to be asking him to turn the reins loose of his own life. He had always prided himself on his self-reliance—and now she seemed to be saying that he did not have enough, certainly not enough to please God when he died.

The end came abruptly that very day. Clive was sitting in the front room, staring out the window, when he heard Jeanne call. He heard alarm in her voice and moved quickly. As soon as he entered the room, he saw that it was the end. He moved to the bed, sat down and listened while Ma Tante spoke, in French again, to Jeanne. Then she turned to him and, with almost the last strength that seemed to drain her of everything, began to bless him. "You have been a good friend to my Jeanne," she said, "and to my brother. Now you have been kind to me." Her eyelids fluttered and she seemed to draw some hidden strength. The pallor of death was on her already, but she opened her eyes and said in a surprisingly strong voice, "Clive Gordon—you will be a servant of the Most High God. . . !"

The words seemed to echo in the air, and Clive took the hand that she struggled to lift. She squeezed his hand once and then turned her eyes back to Jeanne, who was weeping. She said something once more, in French, took a deep breath, and then grew very still.

After a time, Clive whispered, "She's gone, Jeanne."

"Yes, gone to be with her Lord." Jeanne's eyes were filled with tears, but they were tears of joy. "Did you hear what she said to you? You will be a servant of the Most High God."

Clive did not know what the words meant. He was confused as he rarely was and said nothing. Jeanne reached out and arranged Ma Tante's hair and then straightened her arms in a final gesture. She said no more as the two turned to the things that must be done.

🕮   🕮   🕮

Two days later, the two arrived at Fort Ticonderoga. They found that Knox and his men had the cannons all packed. As soon as they rode in, Dake came forward. He was barely limping now and asked at once, "How's your aunt?"

"She is dead," Jeanne said calmly.

"Oh, I'm sorry to hear that," Dake said slowly, at a loss for words as usual at such times.

"She's gone to be with God." Jeanne once again spoke with a placid expression in her eyes. She looked around and said, "We arrived just in time."

"Yes," Dake said, "we're going back to Boston."

That was all the conversation they had time for, for everyone was busy preparing to leave for Boston with all the artillery pieces. Later that day, Knox rode out in front of the column and called out, "Forward! Back to Boston and give the lobsterbacks a bellyful of cannonballs!" The small column moved out and Knox, full of enthusiasm, encouraged them by calling out from time to time.

"It's gonna be a hard trip," Dake whispered to Jeanne. "I think he'd carry every cannon on his back if he had to. I never saw a man like Knox!"

Jeanne smiled at him and said, "I'm glad we got back when we did."

Dake nodded, "It was good you got to be with your aunt at the last." Then he had to move away to help with the teams.

After he left, Jeanne fell in at the end of the column—thinking of the last thing her aunt had said to Clive Gordon.

17

A Gift for His Excellency

A STRANGE MANIA SEEMED TO STRIKE the American leaders in charge of their new revolution. Somehow they strongly believed that Canada could be invaded and secured with little resistance. Even Washington was influenced with this zeal to conquer Canada, and he appointed General Philip Schuyler to direct the operation. When Benedict Arnold showed up at the Boston siege, he was given command of the military expedition. In September he headed toward Canada with a little over a thousand men. He marched his troops from Cambridge, then to the mouth of the Merrimac, where they boarded ships for Maine. For the next month and a half, the history of warfare held fewer more epic tales of abject misery than that suffered by General Arnold's expedition.

He and his men struggled through the swamps of Maine until they reached the outskirts of Quebec City in December. With the help of another commander named Richard Montgomery, the combined forces surrounded the city. Quebec was a difficult place to attack, and at the time they were in the middle of a blizzard. The morale of the troops was extremely low, for most of the men's enlistment time was to end the very next day.

It was a futile attack. Richard Montgomery was killed almost at once, which almost ended the attack right then. Arnold's men fared slightly better. About six hundred strong, they fought their way back. Arnold took a leg wound and collapsed. The route was cut behind them and the invasion of Canada was thwarted. It was a tribute to the two commanders that they mounted any attack at all.

With the loss of only five killed and thirteen wounded, General Guy Carlton, perhaps the most gifted of all the British generals in the New

World, inflicted nearly five hundred casualties on the American invaders and kept Canada for Britain.

But if Canada was being held by the Crown, the southern colonies were lost for it during this same period. In a series of small but significant actions, the rebels managed to secure control of Virginia and the Carolinas. These victories were a cheerful note to Washington, but he was a frustrated man. All winter he had sat in the hills around Boston and looked down on his adversary, Sir William Howe. Neither of them was able to do much. What Washington needed was a lever to shift the balance of the siege. Washington's hope, then, lay in the small force he had sent to Ticonderoga under Knox to bring back cannons—and day after day the eyes of George Washington turned and looked west, longing for the sight of the fat ex-bookstore owner turned artillery expert.

"Knox," Washington breathed once in the hearing of Nathaniel Greene, "where are you? Why don't you come back with those cannons!"

The tall Virginian knew he had made a terrible mistake. He had funneled Arnold to Canada in the middle of winter, throwing away rugged and valuable men. His first strategic move ended up in the senseless loss of half the force sent north to Quebec City. He hadn't relieved Boston from Tory control, nor had he brought Canada into the colonist side. He had simply sat outside Boston, unable to move because he had no powder and no guns. He had triggered a march to Canada that had ended in shambles. The Canadian fiasco was a sharp stabbing pain in his mind, but there was nowhere for him to turn. He simply had to wait until something happened.

⚜   ⚜   ⚜

Cut off by land and throttled by sea, General Howe and his fellow generals made do with what they had. London sent five thousand oxen, fourteen thousand sheep, ten thousand barrels of beer, one hundred and eighty thousand bushels of coal, plus oats and hay for the horses to supply the army in Boston. Most of it, however, arrived rotten, while other supply ships were driven by high winds to the West Indies.

Desperate for wood to keep warm and cook, the British soldiers tore down the Old North Church as well as the Liberty Tree, the arching elm under which Sam Adams and his Sons of Liberty had often met. Governor Winthrop's one-hundred-year-old home was razed to the ground for firewood. The Old South Church where Puritans had bowed their heads in solemn prayer was strewn with manure and hay and turned into a Cavalry School.

When the wind was right, the rebels would let leaflets flutter across their lines with messages comparing their lot with the besieged British. "Seven dollars a month, fresh provisions and in plenty, health, freedom, ease and affluence, and a good farm." Then they taunted with what the British troops were receiving: "Three pence a day, rotten salt pork, the scurvy, beggary, and want."

Howe proved himself an adequate general, but he was practically driven to his wit's end with the prolonged siege that held the city captive. He spoke one day with Leslie Gordon, saying, "Colonel, this is not war. It's a farce!"

Leslie agreed at once. "I've thought much about this business, General," he said quickly. "Can't they be made to understand in London that the more we pressure these people, the more they'll stiffen their backs?"

"I don't suppose anyone ever succeeded in getting anything through our sovereign's head. He's not a scholar. He's not a military man—and he's not a politician!"

Gordon was surprised at the vehemence of his superior officer against the Crown. "Those words could get you in considerable difficulty if they ever got back to King George, sir."

"Of course they could, but they'll never get there. You're not a man to pass such words along."

"No I'm not, sir, but I agree with you wholeheartedly. Is there any chance we could attack and break this deadlock?"

"And do what? Back in Europe, the military strategy would be to capture a city. Well, we've captured a city and now *we're* prisoners of it." Howe stared out toward the forest that surrounded Boston, somewhat in awe of the hundreds of miles of thick forest that seemed to stretch endlessly to the west. "Once we leave the city, what could we do? We could attack Washington's force. They would retreat into the forest. We would follow them and they would cut us to pieces. I see no hope for that." He shrugged his shoulders wearily and shook his head in despair. "It's a bitter business, this thing, Gordon. None of us are going to come out of it well. . . ."

🔔　　　🔔　　　🔔

While both the American and British generals stewed about the futility of their position, Jeanne Corbeau sat on a scow, her teeth chattering. Fort George was only thirty miles away from Ticonderoga, but the cold wind had cut through the party like a knife. Jeanne had never been on a ship of any kind and the trip down the lake was a harrowing experience for her. The temperatures continued to fall and ice formed at least a mile out from both sides.

"Are you as cold as I am?"

Jeanne looked up to see Dake, whose face was almost blue, his hands stuffed into his side pockets.

"Why is it so much colder over the water than it is anywhere else?" he said, plopping down beside her.

"I don't know," Jeanne said, her lips numb. "But there's no way to have a fire, not on a boat."

"No," Dake managed to grin. "That's the last thing we need, to have the boat catch on fire."

Even as he spoke he heard a shout, and Knox was yelling, "We're taking on water! Bring those boats over here before we lose these cannons!"

Instantly Dake rose and, along with other men, rowed hard until several flat-bottomed boats pulled alongside the stranded scow. They worked quickly to unload the guns into another boat, which made them sink even deeper into the water. "We're only halfway to Fort George, but the men," Knox said, "need a fire and some warm food."

William Knox, his brother, nodded and pointed toward shore. "We'll make camp over there." As soon as they reached the shore, the men hurried and set up camp. That night they sat around a roaring fire and ate some of the stew that Jeanne and the other cooks managed to throw together.

The next day they put out to the lake again. All day long the men worked hard rowing until they were dropping from exhaustion. Dake glanced over at Lawrence Hill, saying, "My arms are about to fall off my body. We've been rowing for ten hours now."

"Well, we can't quit now," Hill said. And shortly afterward, he straightened up. "Look! That must be Fort George."

A cheer went up from the tired men as they saw the buildings off in the distance along the shore. Although the trip down the lake had taken twice as long as they had expected, they were finally there, and the big guns were safe!

Dake worked hard along with the other men unloading the boats while Henry Knox's massive figure paced back and forth on the shore, overseeing everything. General Schuyler had made good his word. There were at least two dozen long heavy sledges waiting for them to transport the heavy artillery pieces back to Boston. The cannons could be loaded on their flat surfaces and lashed down for the next leg of their journey.

By now Dake's bad leg was beginning to trouble him. He had done too much. With the cold and the endless hours of rowing he had endured, he was completely exhausted. As he staggered slightly, carrying one of the crates of cannonballs, a voice said, "Here, let me have that. You're done in."

Dake looked up to see Clive Gordon. Glad for the rest, Dake made no protest as the tall Englishman picked up the crate and carried it to the stack.

"Go sit down. Go over there and get Jeanne to give you something to eat, and then go to sleep. You're going to kill yourself if you keep this up. Have you been treating that leg with that liniment I gave you?" Without waiting for an answer, he said, "Be sure you take care of yourself."

Dake hobbled over to where Jeanne was already busying herself about the fire. A sudden wave of weakness attacked him, hitting him like a blow, and when Jeanne looked up and saw his strained face she said, "Come sit down over here, Dake." She led him to a tree, then grabbed some blankets and put them down under him. As soon as he sat down, she said, "Wrap up in those. I'll have something hot for you shortly."

Dake was too tired to even speak. With the warmth of the fire and the blankets, he fell asleep almost instantly, sitting bolt upright. When she woke him with a bowl of hot stew and a mug of steaming coffee to wash it down, he ate hungrily. Looking up as he was finishing, he grinned faintly. "I feel like a baby," he said. "A man ought to be tougher than this!"

Jeanne shook her head. "You're not over that leg injury yet. You shouldn't be doing all you are." She came over and sat down beside him, a bowl in her hand. She ate almost daintily. The stew was so hot that it burned her lips, and she blew on it carefully. "Do you think we'll get there, Dake?"

"We'll get there, all right. Henry Knox is not a man to let a thing like a few mountains and rivers stop him. He promised General Washington that he'd bring these cannons back, and he'll keep his word even if it kills him." Dake ate more slowly now and stopped to ask her, "Are you still grieving over your aunt?"

"Not really," she said quietly. "Oh, I'll miss her, but she's gone to be with the Lord, and that's what she wanted most of all."

Dake looked at her face cautiously. It was pale from the cold, only two bright spots on her cheeks. The day had been hard on her as well as the others, and now she looked vulnerable somehow. "I'm sorry you lost her. It'll come to all of us, I suppose."

Jeanne nodded and said softly, "As it is appointed unto man once to die, but after this the judgment."

Dake stared at her. "Is that from the Bible?"

"Yes." She looked at him and smiled almost sadly. "It comes to everyone—death. I've often wondered if I'd be afraid to die. But Ma Tante wasn't—and my father wasn't. When their time came, they both seemed ready. I guess it's because they both knew the Lord so well."

Dake sat listening and did not make any comment. He himself had wondered about the same thing often. He had faced death when he had fought in battles, but during those times there was little time to think. The battle madness fell like a red curtain over your eyes—and you loaded your musket and fired and reloaded and fired again until you either killed the enemy or they killed you. But to die, to know death was coming and to wait for it, to think about it—that was not the same thing!

The two sat there for a while and finally Clive came over and fixed a bowl of stew, then picked up a piece of bread. He sat down beside them and said ruefully, "I'm not much of a worker, I'm afraid, Dake. I'm out of condition. How's the leg?"

"Oh, it's all right."

"Not the best way to recuperate," Clive shrugged. He ate hungrily, then said, "I'm going to bed. I think that maniac Knox will probably get us up at three o'clock in the morning to pull out!"

As the tall man went to his blankets and rolled up in them, Jeanne turned to Dake and said, "You do the same." She took his bowl and cup and then when he lay back, struck with fatigue, she reached out and took a branch and stuck it in the earth close to his head. "If it snows here," she smiled down at him, "we'll know where to find you in the morning. Here Lies Dake!" There was an elfin quality in her, almost playful. She suddenly touched his cheek. "Did you ever have a beard?" she asked curiously.

He grinned at her and said, "I did once."

"What was it like?"

"Almost red."

She stared down at him. "Couldn't be. Your hair is blond."

"It was, though." Her hand was lying on his cheek lightly, and he was very much aware of her soft touch. "Maybe I'll grow one again, a long one, down to my chest."

She looked at him almost seriously, then shook her head. "No, don't. I wouldn't like it. Good night," she said abruptly, then went to her own blankets and rolled up in them. Inside the cocoon of rough blankets she thought about the two men for a time, then dropped off to sleep.

T   T   T

Eighty oxen strained against the weight of more than a dozen sledges. The massive beasts cooperated as if they sensed the zeal of their human masters. The long caravan slid along over the snow-covered road. They kept moving all through the gray, snowy morning, all of them chilled by the raw wind that whipped around them. Henry Knox set a brisk pace as they headed back toward Albany.

The days of the overland trek had gone well, but soon the strength of the oxen diminished and the men grew weary. Snow fell steadily, so that the sledges moved slowly across it. It was a dry, powdery snow, fine little pellets that crunched underfoot and blew away. Some stretches of the road had been swept clean by the wind, which slowed the sledges down to a crawl.

A week passed after they left Fort George, and the temperatures stayed below freezing. Stream crossings were difficult, but they made them with no loss to equipment or men or animals. The bitter winds continued to howl and rage, finding every little opening in the tents the men had pitched. Jeanne snuggled in her blankets under the thin canvas and felt sorry for the shaggy-coated beasts that had to suffer through the night in the open. Sometimes it felt as if the cold was freezing her lungs, so she had to breathe very shallowly. "I don't know if we can endure much more of this," she said to Dake once. "The oxen haven't had enough to eat. What happens when they can't pull anymore?"

"I don't know." Dake's strength was stretched to the limits, and he could do no more than grunt. He was better off than some of the men who fell ill and had to ride on the sledges.

If Henry Knox had not passed around a bottle of brandy, no one would have known that 1775 was passing away and 1776 was beginning. It was just another cold, gloomy, muddy day, filled with hard work. They crossed the Hudson River at a place called Klaus's Ferry. One of the lashings broke and they lost one cannon there, but they finally reached Albany on January 7. Unfortunately, the weather began to warm, which made the roads impassable. Knox sent a letter to Washington with a rider explaining the delay. They had no choice but to wait for a new freeze. Knox chafed at the delay in the meantime, but Dake and Jeanne welcomed it. They spent some time together huddled close to a fire in front of the tents. Strangely enough, Clive Gordon did not join them often. Jeanne thought his absence strange and once asked him, "Why don't you come over and sit by us and get warm, Clive?"

"No, I think I'll walk."

The answer was moody, and when the tall man strolled away, kicking at the rocks under his feet almost viciously, Jeanne frowned, saying, "I wonder what's wrong with him?"

"I think he wants to be with you and he resents me."

"That's silly!" Jeanne scoffed.

"Not so silly," Dake said. "I feel the same way. After all, you're the only pretty girl here. Every man in the troop would enjoy being able to sit around a fire and talk with you."

Jeanne was wearing men's clothing, as she had since the trip had begun. Now bundled in a heavy wool coat with a red wool tam pulled down over her head, she said, "I'm just like the men."

Dake wanted to remark that imagination does strange things—that clothing did not always hide a woman's charm, but he said only, "Men are men, Jeanne. You might as well get used to it. You'll be living with us a long time."

She had found that she could joke with Dake, and now her eyes, with their strange blue-violet shade, lit up with humor. "I feel sorry for whoever you marry."

"I thought she'd be a lucky woman," Dake said in mock surprise.

"You *would* think that! You have an ego as big as that ox over there!"

"A man has to appreciate his good qualities. I don't think you've ever noticed mine, Jeanne."

She sniffed indignantly. "You can go find a girl somewhere who'll appreciate your 'good qualities.' "

Dake laughed and shook his head. "No girls out here. Nothing but ugly, smelly men and starving oxen. When we get back to Boston, maybe things'll be better."

"Why, you won't dare come into Boston, not with the British there."

"They won't be there always. Anyway, they're so dumb, they wouldn't know it if someone came and announced themselves as a patriot."

"That's not true. They've arrested quite a few men," Jeanne argued.

"They're just not as slick as I am." Suddenly he reached up and pulled her cap off her head. She made a wild grab at it, but he grinned and held it. "I never saw a woman with hair like that. Was it ever long?"

"Give me my cap back!" She made another grab at it, but he held it at arm's length, teasing her.

Stretching out his arm, he suddenly put his hand on her mass of black curls and caressed her head. "Sure is pretty. Just as curly as a dog's tail."

"Give me that cap!" Jeanne suddenly leaped on him and the two struggled for a moment.

"Hey! Watch what you're doing! You're gonna roll us into the fire!" Dake yelled. She was a strong girl, and he discovered they had come dangerously close to the glowing coals. He rolled her over and held her with his superior strength and grinned down into her face. "Now, will

219

you be good if I promise to let you go?"

Jeanne was looking up at him, half angry over his impetuousness, but there was a grin on his face, so that she could not hold her anger. "Please, let me up, Dake. You're hurting me."

At once Dake let her go. Reaching over, she grabbed a handful of snow. Before he could move, she smashed it right in his face. "There!" she said, grabbing her cap and leaping to her feet. He struggled to get up. Taking her foot, she shoved him backward so that he sprawled out. Then she laughed and ran away, calling back over her shoulder, "You're clumsy, Mr. Bradford!"

Across the way, General Knox and his brother, William, were watching the two. "I didn't think anybody had energy enough for horseplay," William Knox said wearily. His face was stretched taut, and he was thin from the effort of the long trek.

Henry smiled faintly. "I guess men'll always summon up strength where there's a pretty woman involved." He looked up at the gray, dismal sky and exclaimed, "Snow! Why don't you snow!" In exasperation he kicked a stump and hurt his toe. "Ow!" he said, rubbing it. "That helped a lot, didn't it? Why is it that it never snows when you want it to, and it always snows when you don't want it to?"

"I don't know, Henry."

"We've *got* to get these guns to His Excellency!" Henry said, giving Washington the title most of his men used. "If we don't, we will never break the Tories' hold over Boston!"

Finally, the temperature plunged and the ice began to form on the creeks once again. General Schuyler sent extra men to help them. Unbelievably, the worst part of the journey was yet to come. For the next few days, the caravan was plagued by broken equipment, muddy roads, and a storm that dumped inches of snow. Sometimes the snow melted, adding to the quagmire, so that the sledges could only be pulled inches at a time.

Ahead of them, the mountains lifted their heads as if challenging the expedition to try to cross them. A few times they had small skirmishes with renegade Indian tribes still trying to defend their hunting lands.

But somehow the mountains gave way. The oxen struggled through them, and finally only large hills were left to cross. The temperature stayed cold enough to freeze, so that they could move the sleds easily enough. The caravan toiled over the Taconics, then moved up and down the Berkshires, men shouting warnings as the heavy sleds gathered momentum like juggernauts. Sometimes the poor oxen perished in the traces, and replacements had to be found along the way.

As the column of men and artillery drew closer to Cambridge, however, they found refreshments and festive welcomes for the success of their journey. They enjoyed warm dinners in the roadside inns and taverns along the way. When they reached Westfield, Massachusetts, the entire town turned out to greet the column with cheers and mugs of cider. All the townspeople gathered around to gape at the guns and touched them as though they were live creatures. Henry Knox, never a man to forego a frolic, would shoot off one of the monstrous guns from time to time for the entertainment of the cheering crowds.

And so it was that eventually the happy column lurched into Cambridge in mid-January of 1776. The movement of the guns had not taken two weeks, as Knox had anticipated, but six long ones.

🨤   🨤   🨤

"Just one minute more, Miss Howland—"

Matthew Bradford carefully moved and added a touch of paint to the canvas propped in front of him, his concentration utter and absolute. He was always this way when he painted. Everything else seemed to fade away as he threw his whole being into capturing on a canvas what his eyes beheld in front of him.

"Now," he said, turning with his brush and palette in hand, "you can relax."

Abigail Howland pulled her shoulders back, throwing her figure into firm relief against the rose-colored gown that she had worn for the sitting. Her brown hair seemed to shine in the golden sunlight that filtered through the window. She had chosen this particular dress to be painted in because it flattered her figure so well. "I didn't know it was such hard work just to get your portrait painted," she said. She smiled demurely and asked, "May I see it?"

"If you like. It isn't quite finished," said Matthew as he added another stroke. Abigail came over and stood so close to Matthew that he could feel the touch of her arm against his.

"Why, do I really look like that? I'm quite beautiful, aren't I?" she said saucily.

Matthew could not help but laugh. He had come back from Virginia confused and upset over his relationship with Leo Rochester. With time on his hands, he had taken Abigail Howland's words at face value, informing her that he was available to do her portrait. She had been delighted and insisted that they get started immediately. For a week now, Matthew had been coming to the Howland residence to work on the portrait. Now as he looked at it, he said, "That isn't bad, but of course, having a beautiful subject doesn't hurt any artist."

"Why, thank you, Matthew," Abigail said. She was a beautiful young woman with a lively expression and a way that was pleasing to most men.

There was a knock at the door, and when Abigail turned with surprise and said, "Come in," Paul Winslow entered. He walked straight over to the canvas and stared at it almost moodily.

"Very well done," he said. Then he smiled at the painter. "I don't see how you fellows accomplish that. That kind of talent must be born in you."

"I don't know either. I feel the same way about musicians," Matthew shrugged. "I've got no musical talent at all. To see someone sit down at a harpsichord and use all ten fingers doing different things—well, I just don't understand it."

They talked about art for a time, with Abigail making some comments about her portrait, and then finally Paul said, "Are we having dinner, Abigail?"

"Of course." Abigail hesitated, then said, "Won't you please join us, Mr. Bradford?"

"Oh no. I'd just be in the way," said Matthew as he cleaned his brushes.

"Not at all," Paul Winslow said. "My family would like to meet you. You might even get some more commissions," he grinned. "Come along," he said cheerfully.

Matthew was not inclined to go home again. Ever since he had returned from Fairhope, there seemed to be a tension in his house. It was not of his father's making—but that which was in Matthew's own makeup. All that he had learned in Virginia about the man who now wanted to claim him as son had left him troubled and confused.

"Why, thank you. I think I will join you." Quickly Matthew cleaned his hands with turpentine, put a damp cloth over the wet paint to keep the dust off, then accompanied the couple to the home of Paul Winslow's parents.

When they went inside, he was introduced to Charles and Dorcas Winslow. Charles Winslow was obviously in bad health and made reference to it at the dinner table. Watching the others eat heartily, he said, "I can remember when I could eat almost anything. Why, when I was a boy," he remarked, "there was nothing I liked better than getting a raw onion and eating it like an apple."

Paul grinned at his father. "I can't believe you used to do that!" he remarked. "You must have smelled terrible."

But Charles Winslow said thoughtfully, "When you get older, the pleasures aren't there anymore."

Dorcas Winslow turned to Matthew and remarked, "Boston in the grip of a siege is a strange place for an artist to be, Mr. Bradford."

"Well, I've been in England studying art for the past few years, Mrs. Winslow. I just came home recently."

Abigail said at once, "Oh, it must be heavenly to be in England! I'd love to be there now."

Paul spoke up at once, "You may be there quicker than you think."

Abigail stared at him in astonishment. "What does that mean?"

"It means that if the rebels succeed in taking over Boston, we'll all have to run somewhere. Our officers and men have been pretty hard on the patriots. I think they'll be wanting a little of their own back if they ever get inside this town again."

"Why, they can never do that. Not with General Howe and his fine army here!"

"I wouldn't be too sure about that," Paul said. "General Howe's got a lifeline three thousand miles long. If it were snapped, we'd starve to death here. What about your family?" he asked Matthew abruptly. "Are they Tory or patriot?"

"Patriot, Mr. Winslow," Matthew said.

"But you, yourself?" Paul insisted. "I thought artists were more or less neutral when it comes to politics."

Matthew shrugged. "So we are, I suppose. I feel strongly that a grave mistake is being made in this whole thing."

Talk went around the table for some time and finally, when they had coffee in the parlor, Abigail spoke to Matthew about his prospects. He hesitated for a moment, then said, "At the moment, they're very firm."

"Do artists make a great deal of money?" she asked curiously.

Matthew grinned at her blunt question. "Some of the more famous ones do. Most of them don't—unless they have a wealthy sponsor."

"And do you have one?"

Matthew hesitated, then said, "Sir Leo Rochester has been kind enough to offer me his help."

At once Abigail's attention was caught. She glanced at Paul, who was sitting with his head back on the chair, half listening. "Sir Leo Rochester?"

"Well, he has the title in England. I don't think he uses it here much," Matthew said.

Without looking up, Paul said, "I know him very well—a very wealthy Virginian." He straightened up and winked at Abigail. "If you decide you won't have Nathan or me, perhaps you'll have Mr. Bradford here. You could be the wife of a famous painter."

"Oh, don't be foolish," Abigail said, but there was a coy smile on her face.

Matthew regretted he had even mentioned Leo's name, for Abigail seemed to have a thousand more questions about Leo Rochester's offer to sponsor him. Her curiosity made him uneasy. Finally, he stood and thanked them for the meal and excused himself.

When he left the two to make his way home, Paul said to Abigail, "There's another possibility for you, Abby."

"Oh, don't be foolish, Paul." She came over and kissed him, leaning her body against him. "You're the one I really love."

Paul Winslow took what was offered. He held her tightly, enjoying the pressure of her soft body against his, then grinned sardonically. "You're handsome baggage, Abigail Howland, but I never know what you're thinking."

☙   ☙   ☙

When Knox led the procession to meet the commander in chief, he pulled off his hat and gestured dramatically. "Your Excellency, the cause of liberty is safe!" he exclaimed.

Washington strode forward laughing. He had a great affection for this huge man, so strange looking in appearance yet so effective in the cause of the patriots. "Henry," he said, "I congratulate you. You have done a magnificent service for your country."

"Now, Your Excellency, we can get down to the business at hand," Knox said, shaking Washington's hand.

Washington sobered and said, "It's going to be a matter of powder," he said. "We'll have to have enough to blast the British out of town."

Henry Knox waved his hand confidently. "All shall be done, Your Excellency. Now that I have my guns, we shall see what General Howe will say when he receives what we have to offer."

Clive and Jeanne had been standing close enough to observe the encounter of the two officers. Clive turned to her, saying, "I'd like to take you home. You must be exhausted; I know I am."

"I *am* tired." Jeanne turned to go with him but saw Dake standing over by one of the cannons. She went to him at once, saying, "I won't be seeing you very soon, I suppose."

Dake grinned raffishly. He had recovered his strength now and looked ready for anything. "Don't bet on that, Jeanne," he said. "If you hear a stone rattling your window some night, don't toss a bucket of water outside. It'll probably be me."

"Don't be foolish," she responded quickly, a strain of worry causing a crease between her eyes. "You could get into serious difficulty if you come into town. If you get caught, you could be arrested and even hanged."

But Dake merely shook his head and grinned. Turning away, Jeanne rejoined Clive and remained quiet as they made their way home. When they reached the house, Lyna, Grace, and David all converged upon the pair, wanting to know all that had happened in the last several weeks. Lyna and Grace hurried about making a meal, and when Colonel Gordon came in, he shook hands with the pair of them, saying, "I'm glad to see that you made it back safe. I was worried when I found out you and Clive had left with all the hostilities going on around us."

"She's gone to be with the Lord," Jeanne said simply. She saw the sympathy in Gordon's fine blue eyes and smiled.

Lyna said, "It's hard to lose someone, isn't it?"

Jeanne turned to her, her eyes getting wider. "Oh, but I haven't lost her. I know where she is. If you know where something is, you haven't lost it, have you?"

"By George!" Leslie Gordon exclaimed. "I never thought of that. I've never heard it said like that. That's very fine, Jeanne, very fine indeed!"

The warm welcome Jeanne received from the Gordons made her feel as though she belonged. She, who had no home, felt that this family had accepted her, and she felt secure in their love and care. She and Clive spun out their adventures long after supper, until finally she went to bed and lay there for a long time thinking of Dake's last words. *He'd better not come here*, she thought. At the same time, she half wished he would. There was a simplicity about Dake Bradford that she liked very much. She saw some of her father's adventurous spirit in him, in his easygoing ways, his love of the wild, and his independence and reluctance to accept authority. At the same time, she thought of Clive, who had put himself to such trouble and who had been so kind to both her father and her aunt. She wavered between thoughts of the two of them and finally, firmly, said, "You must go to sleep. Don't be a silly girl!"

18

A Surprise for Jeanne

AS MARIAN ROCHESTER ENTERED THE FOUNDRY, she was acutely aware that business had fallen off sharply. Before the city had been seized by the British army, the Boston Foundry, her father's and Daniel Bradford's business, had hummed like a beehive. Now, as she walked down the long building that housed one unit, she noted how few men were working. It seemed almost silent after the din that she was accustomed to in the place. A sadness came to her as she thought about how the war had ruined so many things for so many people.

"Hello, Mrs. Rochester."

Marian turned to see Sam and Micah Bradford working on a forge. They both had on leather aprons, and Sam was pumping the bellows while Micah was pounding a piece of white-hot steel bar with a large hammer.

"Hello, Sam," Marian said.

She moved closer toward the forge to speak to them. As Micah put down the hammer and smiled at her, she thought, *What handsome sons Daniel has!* Micah, of course, was the mirror image of Dake. His wheat-colored hair was ruffled, and the thin shirt he wore stuck to his deep chest and the brawny muscles of his arms. He reminded her of Daniel when she saw him working the forge years ago in Fairhope.

"Good morning, Mrs. Rochester," Micah nodded. "How's your father?"

"Not as well as I'd like, Micah." She didn't want to talk about her father's health and inquired, "What are you two working on?"

"Oh, just an invention of mine," Sam said nonchalantly. At the age of fifteen he was a strongly built young man with auburn hair and blue eyes that usually were bright.

"Shows what we've come to," Micah grinned. "Not enough work to do, so we have to pass the time making one of his fool inventions."

"I notice you don't mind using my water heater at home," Sam snapped, casting a hard glance at his brother. "You stay in that bathroom almost as long as Rachel."

"What's this about a water heater?" Marian asked.

"Why, it's my new invention," Sam said quickly. "There's nothing like it, I don't think, in all of Boston."

"What does it do, Sam?" asked Marian.

"Well, it heats water up outside the house in a special iron tank, you see. Then the tank is hooked up to a pipe that lets the hot water run right through the wall and into a copper bathtub. So, when you want to take a bath, you just turn the faucet on. Hot water comes out—and there it is!" he said, smiling proudly.

"Why, that sounds wonderful!" Marian exclaimed. "I've never heard of such a thing." She sighed and shook her head. "My servants seem to spend half their time carrying water back and forth from the fire."

"Well, that's the way it was at our house and I got tired of it," Sam nodded wisely. "Everybody said it wouldn't work, but it works fine. Rachel, she just loves it. And, Micah here, too. 'Course, I ain't much on bathing myself, but at least it gets me out of toting the water anymore."

Marian thought for a moment, then said, "Well, since you're not doing anything, and since business is so slow these days, do you think you could make one of those water heaters for my father's house? It would be nice for him and for me, too."

"Why, sure we could, Mrs. Rochester," Sam said energetically.

Micah said thoughtfully, "Haven't figured out a way to get water up to the second floor. Does your house have bathrooms on the second floor?"

"Yes, it does."

"Oh, that won't be any problem," Sam said loftily. "I'll figure out some way to get it up there." He added quickly, "But, you'll have to talk to Pa about it. It'll be okay, of course, since your father and him are business partners."

"Well, I'll certainly do that," Marian smiled. "I think it's a *wonderful* idea, Sam."

Sam grew eloquent. "Why, there's nothing like it, Mrs. Rochester. You just get in there and take all your clothes off and sit right down—"

"Sam!" Micah protested. "That's no way to talk to a lady!"

Sam flared at Micah. "What'd I say? Oh! Well, you can't take a bath with your clothes on, can you?"

Marian was amused by Sam's indignation. "That's all right, Sam. I can put up with almost anything to have some of that heavenly hot water for a bath. I'll talk to your father about it right away." She hesitated, then started to ask about Dake, but decided that it would not be wise to bring up the subject.

Nodding at the young men, she turned and made her way to the office, where she found Daniel not working for once. He was sitting in a chair, staring out the window, lost in thought. When she closed the door, he turned his head at the noise.

Seeing her, he stood up at once. "Why, Marian," he said and came to her. "What brings you here?"

"Father sent these back," she said, handing him a small leather bag. "It's the drawings you sent him on the project for the cannons."

Daniel took the bag and then shot a keen glance at her. "I hope you didn't let anybody else see these."

"Why, no, of course not." Marian looked at him with surprise. "What's the matter?"

"Well, I wouldn't exactly welcome the British army knowing we're planning to cast cannons that will probably be used against them."

"Oh, I see. Yes, of course you're right," Marian said. "But I didn't talk to anybody."

"I was just going to make a pot of tea. Sit down and tell me about John. How's he feeling today?"

Marian sat down, and as he busied himself making tea, she told Daniel about her father. "He doesn't get any better, Daniel. In fact, he seems weaker by the day. I'm afraid for him. I've been trying to convince him to go to a warmer climate, but he won't hear of it. You know how set in his ways he can be at times."

Daniel smiled and listened as she spoke of her father, thinking of how fortunate he had been to be taken as a partner by John Frazier. He could have worked for a lifetime and never accumulated enough money to do this sort of thing for himself. Finally, the tea was ready, and the two of them sat down and sipped it, speaking quietly. It was one of the things he liked about Marian. She could endure quietness—even enjoy it—in a way some people could not. He mentioned that now. "You know, most women have to be talking all the time."

Marian laughed at him. "Some men are that way, too."

"Oh, I suppose so, but I feel so—well, comfortable with you. When you're not comfortable with people," he observed, "you can't just be quiet and enjoy their company. You have to be constantly talking about something."

"We've always been that way, haven't we? Remember when I first met you when I came to Fairhope for a visit? I talked your ear off, though," she said. "I questioned you about horses day and night, didn't I?"

"Yes, you did." He grinned at the fond memory. "I never saw such a talkative female in all my life! But, I liked it, though."

"That seems like a lifetime ago, doesn't it, Daniel?"

He hesitated then and, without speaking, nodded. It was difficult for him even to be in the same room with Marian Rochester. While his wife had lived, of course, he had not thought of Marian except as a young woman he had kissed once and been infatuated with. After Holly had died, Marian had been married and that had ended any hope of a relationship. When he had moved his family to Boston to become a partner with John Frazier, it had been against his better judgment. He knew by that time that he had cherished a feeling for Marian that had not lost its force over the years. Now, as he looked across at her, he admired the placid look on her face, the green eyes that he'd always found extraordinarily attractive. She was still slender, with the figure almost of a young girl. He pulled his thoughts back, away from such things, and said, "What have you been doing?"

Marian knew him better than most. She knew that look and realized that he was still attracted to her. She could not be sorry for this, although she knew there was tragedy inherent in their relationship. He could not hide his feelings from her, nor she from him. It was an uncomfortable situation at times, and now she said quickly to cover the moment, "I was just talking to Sam. He was telling me about his new invention—the water heater."

"Oh yes," Daniel grinned. "One of his more successful attempts. I swear that boy's going to blow himself up one day! The water heater works, though, I'll have to admit."

"He said that Rachel likes it very much."

"Well, she does, and I don't mind it myself." He looked at her and asked, "I take it you'd be interested in having one of the outfits in your home?"

"Yes, I would. It would be so nice, especially on these cold days. Sam tried to explain it to me, but I don't think I understood it all. How does it work?"

"Oh, it's just a boiler on top of a firebox with a pipe running out of it. You heat the water outside; then it runs through a pipe through the wall into the tub. You've got a valve over the bathtub. You turn it on when you want hot water. That's all there is to it."

"I was thinking once, not long ago, about how nice it would be to have water flowing down over you. You know, like standing under a waterfall."

"Well, I suppose Sam could build something that could do that. Just tell him. Or I will."

"Thank you, Daniel. It'll be something to look forward to." She hesitated, then said, "Have you talked to Dake recently?"

"Yes. I made a trip to the hills the other night to meet with some of the officers. Dake's doing fine. I think he's interested in that young woman that Clive Gordon brought back out of the hills."

"Yes, I heard about her."

"She's a lovely young woman."

"And you really think Dake's fond of her?"

"Dake's been fond of lots of young girls. I don't suppose anything'll come of it."

She hesitated, then asked, "What about . . . Matthew?" At once his face changed, and she knew she had touched the sore spot of his life. "Has he said anything to you since he came back from Virginia?"

"We've talked some about it." Daniel's reply was brief and he bit his lip nervously. He turned to her and said, "Matthew's in a bad spot, Marian. I've never heard of a man having to make this kind of choice. I've left it up to him, of course."

"I don't think it would be good for Matthew to be under Leo's guidance." She hesitated, then said, "You know . . . what kind of man he is."

Daniel was astonished. It was not like Marian to speak this way. He knew she believed strongly in honoring her marriage vows, which, to her, meant that as long as she and Leo lived they would be husband and wife. He had felt the wisdom of her attitude and deeply respected her for it. She never complained, although he was sure that Leo abused and mistreated her. Now, he stared at her and nodded slowly, "I think you're right, but it'll have to be Matthew's choice."

The two talked for a while about Sam's inventions and her father's health, then she stood up and moved toward the door. "Come and see Father, if you can. He thinks so much of you, Daniel."

"I will. I'll bring Sam with me tonight, if you wish, and we can talk about the possibilities of a water heater. I can talk to your father while Sam's puttering around and taking some measurements."

Marian realized his wisdom in bringing along his son to ward off unnecessary gossip, and she appreciated his thoughtfulness. "Bring Rachel," she said, "and Micah. We'll make a family dinner of it." She smiled then and was gone.

🔔   🔔   🔔

"Wonder who that could be? Sounds like they're trying to break the door down." David Gordon had been talking with his sister, Grace. He got up and went to the door. When he opened it, he was rather surprised. "Well, Sam!" he said.

"Hello, David," Sam said. "I bet you're surprised to see me."

"Oh, not at all," David said smoothly. "Come on inside."

David led the way down the hall and said to Grace, "Look who's here."

Grace smiled from where she sat. "Hello, Sam. Did you come alone?"

"Yes, I did." He looked around and said, "I've really come to see Jeanne. Is she here?"

"Oh yes. She's upstairs in her room. I'll get her."

As soon as Grace left, the two cousins studied each other. They were the same age, these cousins, and had been molded by different ways of life. David was English to the core, having grown up in England and being totally sympathetic to the House of Hanover. He was proud of his father's service and was, at the same time, not quite sure how he should act toward the son of a man suspected to be a rebel.

Sam was aware that David was staring at him strangely and he felt awkward, an unusual circumstance for Sam Bradford. "Well, what are you doing these days, David?" he asked to break the silence.

"Studying Latin mostly, and some mathematics."

"I hate Latin. Don't see any sense in it." Sam scowled. "There aren't any Latins around, are there? When they told me it was a dead language, I lost all interest."

David found this amusing. "It's an exercise for your mind—stretches it."

"My mind's big enough as it is. I've got important things to think about."

"Come on and sit down. You can tell me about them. How about a glass of cider?"

"Sounds good."

The two young men went into the kitchen and found Lyna mixing dough for bread. She loved to cook and now, when she saw Sam, she said, "Oh, how's my favorite nephew?"

"All right, Aunt Lyna. I came over to see Jeanne."

He'd no sooner spoken than Jeanne came in and Sam turned and said, "Hello, Jeanne."

"Why, Sam!" Jeanne said, a ready smile on her face. "It's good to see you. Is everything all right at your home?"

"Well," Sam said, "not exactly." He hesitated and frowned. "Rachel's not feeling too well. She asked me to come over and see if you could come and help her with the housework, you know. Takes a lot of cooking to feed me and Pa and Micah and Matthew. Mrs. White's been ailing. That's our housekeeper, you know."

"I'd be glad to go—if it'll be all right, Mrs. Gordon?"

"Why, of course," Lyna said. "How long do you think you'll want to stay?"

"Well, until Rachel's better, I think. I'll go get my things, Sam."

After she left the room, Lyna asked, "How's your father? We haven't seen much of you in the last week or so."

"Oh, Pa's fine and so is Micah." He wanted to say something about Dake but felt that might be a little bit dangerous.

"I'm building a water heater for Mrs. Rochester," he said. "Just like the one we've got at home."

"What does it do?" Grace inquired.

They all listened while Sam explained his invention, and Grace said at once, "Every house ought to have one of those."

"I don't know," David said with a frown. "Seems like a lot of trouble to me."

Sam defended his invention until Jeanne came back carrying a small bag. "Tell Clive goodbye for me—and Colonel Gordon. But I won't be gone long," she said.

The two left the house, and as they made their way back through the winding streets of Boston to the Bradford household, Jeanne listened to Sam boast of his exploits. "I've been up to the hills more than once to see the soldiers," he said. "I've seen General Washington, too. Boy, he is something now! Big as a house, he is."

When they got within sight of the house, Sam stopped and said, "Wait a minute. I've got to tell you something."

Jeanne turned to look at him. "What is it, Sam?" she asked curiously. He was such a straightforward young man, she could not imagine his having a secret. Nevertheless, he had an odd look on his face.

"Well, you see, I didn't exactly tell the truth to Aunt Lyna and the others."

"The truth about what?" asked Jeanne, puzzled at Sam's words.

"Why I came to get you."

"Well, what is the truth?"

"The truth is that Rachel's not sick at all." He saw surprise wash over Jeanne's face, and he burst out hurriedly, "Dake's here. Oh, he's hiding out, of course, but he wanted to see you. He was gonna go over to the Gordons' tonight, but I told him that'd be too dangerous, so I came up with this scheme. I said, 'I'll go bring her to the house.' He said I couldn't do it of course, but"—Sam grinned broadly—"here you are."

"You shouldn't have done it, Sam," Jeanne protested. "It's not right to lie like that, especially to your aunt, or to anybody for that matter."

"Well, I had to do something. I didn't want Dake to get captured or

232

maybe shot for a spy. You wouldn't want that, would you?" Sam was rather anxious now. He had not felt comfortable with that part of his scheme, but now he pleaded, "Oh, come on, Jeanne, Aunt Lyna wouldn't have wanted me to put her nephew in danger. We have to think about her, don't we?"

His twisted logic suddenly amused Jeanne. "Oh, so now we're doing all this for Lyna's sake? It's all right to lie as long as it helps somebody. Is that the way you think?" Then she laughed and squeezed his arm. "It's wrong to lie, Sam. And I forgive you. But next time, tell me about your plan without lying, all right?"

"Sure, all right, Jeanne. Boy, Dake really wants to see you! Come on."

Jeanne entered the house and at once found Rachel and Dake in the kitchen. Dake looked pleased with himself. He got up and came over and squeezed Sam's shoulder. "Well, you did it! I owe you for this one, Sam." He turned then to Jeanne and said, "It's not much of a way for a young man to come calling on a girl—to make her come to him. But I didn't intend to let any grass grow under my feet."

"You must be crazy, Dake," Rachel sniffed. Her red hair gleamed in the sunlight that came through the window and she spoke fondly, although with some severity. "Pa'll probably take a stick to you when he finds out you sneaked away from camp."

Dake looked injured. "I didn't sneak away. I came on a mission. I told you that. I've got some letters for Pa, and General Greene wants to know some things about what's going on that Pa's supposed to tell him about."

Jeanne was amused, and as the four young people gathered around the table, eating a cake that Rachel had made, she felt very comfortable. It struck her a little strange and she thought, *Here I didn't have any home at all, and now I feel like the Gordons and the Bradfords both love me.* That gave her a warm feeling, indeed. She sat there enjoying the company of those she had grown very fond of.

When Daniel came home and found Dake there, he frowned. But when he found out Dake's mission, he shrugged, saying, "It's a little dangerous, Dake, but I know you'll be careful." Then he looked over and said, "We're all supposed to go to the Fraziers' tonight. Marian's cooking supper for us there. Sam, you're supposed to take the measurements for that water heater you promised her."

"All right!" Sam said. "I can do it."

"You two'll have to shift as best you can," Daniel said. "I suppose you can keep our guest entertained, Dake?" His face was straight, but Dake flushed, knowing he was being teased.

The family left early for dinner, and Dake had Jeanne all to himself. He said, "Let's make donkers."

"What's that?"

"You don't know what donkers are? Well, I'll show you." It was quite a production, and they laughed a great deal as Dake showed her how to make the delicacy. He took all the week's leftover meat and chopped it together with bread and apples and all kinds of savory spices. Then they fried it and served it with boiled pudding. As they were eating the donkers and washing them down with cider, Dake said, "You see. You said one time you pitied the woman that had to live with me. Not many women have a husband that can make donkers like this."

"What else can you make?" Jeanne smiled at him.

"Nothing."

"It would get awfully boring eating donkers all the time, Dake."

"Well, I figure my wife can cook everything else and I'll make the donkers."

The two ate with healthy appetites, then cleaned up the kitchen. By then darkness had fallen, so they went out in the back where Dake was not likely to be seen. "Look at those stars," he said. "There must be millions of them."

"They all have names, but I don't know many of them."

"I had a friend once who had a telescope. He knew all of their names. We used to set up that telescope on a tripod and gaze up at the stars all night. Look at that bright one up there, twinkling. Looks like it's on fire, doesn't it?"

They stood there in the darkness, ignoring the cold and looking up at the stars as they spangled all across the night sky.

They talked for a time and then went back inside the house, where Jeanne made tea and they ate the teacakes that Rachel had made that afternoon. Later, they moved into the parlor, where Dake showed Jeanne the books that he had read as a boy. "I used to like to draw," he said. "Pa liked it. He said I had a gift. Fathers always think that."

"Do you have any of them left?"

"Oh yes. They're all here somewhere." He rummaged through a chest over beside a window and came out with a large brown leather portfolio. Untying it, he pulled them out, and the two sat down on the sofa to go through them.

"Why, these are fine, Dake! I didn't know you could draw like this!"

"Oh well, of course, Matthew's the real artist in the family. I gave up drawing a long time ago since he was so much better than I was."

"Well, that's not right. I've seen people that could shoot better than I could, but I didn't give up hunting because of it."

"Well, I don't have the heart for it like Matthew does. That's all he ever thought about when we were growing up. Always had a pencil or piece of charcoal in his hand. He's real good at it, too."

Jeanne was looking at a picture of a woman who was sitting in a chair. It was a simple drawing, but somehow it captured the strength and sweetness of the woman's face. "Is this your mother?" she asked.

"Yes," Dake said quietly, "Matthew drew it."

"I wish I could have known her. She looks so sweet."

"I never heard a harsh word from her—none of us did. I still miss her, even to this day. I think about her sometimes and wish she could have lived to see us all grow up."

"She would have been proud of you, I think."

"You don't remember your mother?"

"I was only two when she died. But I can remember sitting in her lap and her reading to me, and singing to me. She loved to sing."

The two sat on the sofa and went through the drawings slowly. Jeanne was very interested and commented on each one. She had so little family history herself, and she found it wonderful that this family still had mementos—childhood drawings, going all the way back to the beginnings of the family. Finally, she said wistfully, "It must be nice to have a family."

"Why, yes it is. I guess I've taken it for granted all these years," Dake said. He looked at her quickly and said, "It was just you and your pa, is that the way it was?"

"Yes, mostly," Jeanne said quietly.

She did not speak for a while and Dake said, "I wish you could think of *us* as a family."

She turned to him quickly and tears suddenly brimmed in her eyes. "That's the nicest thing you could have said to me, Dake. I do feel a love for your family."

Dake was swayed by her obvious longing for a place and for love. He reached over and said huskily, "You're a sweet girl, Jeanne." Before she could protest, he drew her to him and kissed her.

For Jeanne it was a shock. She had not expected Dake to do this, although she had not been unaware that he liked her. Having no experience with men, she was unsure of her own emotions. He held her for a moment, and then she drew back. "Dake, we shouldn't be doing this."

"Why, it's just a little kiss," Dake said in surprise.

"I . . . I just don't know about those things." Jeanne turned her head away, unable to face him for a moment. "Pa raised me as a boy. I missed out on courting and boys and all that."

"Well, you're only seventeen," he said. "You've got plenty of time to learn." When he saw that she was disturbed, he said awkwardly, "I didn't mean to bother you. But I meant what I said. You are a sweet girl."

She turned to him then and said quietly, "Thank you, Dake. It's nice of you to say that." Then, feeling the tension that had built up in her, she said, "Come on. You said you were going to teach me how to mold bullets with that new bullet mold."

"All right. Come along." The two left and went to the small workshop in the back of the house. By the light of the candle, Dake proceeded to show her the new bullets he was making.

As he got busy removing bullets from the mold, his head bent over his work, Jeanne studied him, thinking, *He's so different from Clive.* Thoughts of Clive came to her and she was suddenly filled with remorse. *I've let both of them kiss me. What kind of a girl am I, anyway?* She still remembered how Clive had shown up at a very difficult time when she needed him, and now, looking at Dake's strong hands as he handled the bullet mold, she thought of how much fun Dake was to be with, how he loved the outdoors as much as she did. There was a sudden feeling that came to her that she had not felt before, and yet she sensed that it was part of the things a woman had to feel. She knew that sooner or later she would have to make a choice, and the thought troubled her deeply. She felt worried that she would not know what to do when that time came.

🔔 🔔 🔔

Leo had not approached Matthew since coming back from Virginia, not wanting to frighten him off. He knew the lad had much on his mind to sort out. And to press Matthew would thwart all his attempts to win the young man over. Yet Leo was a man who once having set his sights on something did not give up easily. He was determined to have someone to carry on the family name. Finally, however, Leo encountered him on purpose late one afternoon at the dock. He knew that Matthew came here often to paint. He came up, greeted him, and saw that Matthew was disturbed at his presence.

"Let me have just a word, Matthew," he said quickly. He began by admitting again he had not been innocent in the least concerning his dealing with Matthew's family. "All I can say is, I regret it and it's over as far as I'm concerned."

Matthew stared at Leo and tried to think. "My head's in a whirl, sir," he said. "I can't seem to concentrate. Every time I think about what you say to me, I just get more confused."

Leo decided to use more force. "Come with me to England—just for a visit. Things are getting sticky around here, anyway. You're not involved with this war. You're not even in favor of it, are you, Matthew?"

"No, sir, you know I'm not. I think it's foolish, and I think the Colonies will suffer for it. Green troops can never beat the king's forces." He had seen the king's army parade and drill in England, and he could not imagine men like Dake or his father standing up to British practiced military discipline.

"That's a wise thought. We'll hope they'll come to their senses and realize it before it's too late. But it's going to be a difficult thing. Look!" Leo said evenly. "What can you lose? At the most, a little time. But I think it might open your eyes. Come along, my boy. All I want to do is introduce you to some of the most talented men that make painting what it is today. It's the opportunity of a lifetime."

Matthew was tempted, and before he thought, he said, "I couldn't agree unless I had my father's permission."

Leo's eyes glinted at the words "my father," but he said, "Well, ask it, by all means. I can't think Daniel would stand in your way."

Matthew was tired of being confused and in a constant state of turmoil. "All right," he said briefly. "I will." He began to pack his paints and then picked up his canvas and the easel and said, "I can't offer you any hope, sir. I know he doesn't care for you at all."

"That's neither here nor there," Leo said. "The thing is—what's best for you? Send word to me after you've talked with him."

❉   ❉   ❉

The next day Daniel had an angry visitor. "Come in, Leo," he said wearily. Rochester had come to the foundry and opened the door to Daniel's office without knocking. "I suppose you've come about Matthew."

"Yes, Bradford, you know that I have."

"Leo, I'll be candid with you. I think it would be a grave mistake for Matthew to put himself in your hands."

"You pious hypocrite! You took advantage of my wife behind my back while I was in England on business and you talk to me about what's *best* for your son?"

"I've already explained that to you. You have a fine woman for a wife. She wouldn't do anything wrong. What you saw was not what you chose to think."

Leo argued vehemently. His voice rose. But when Daniel insisted that he would never give his permission for Matthew to accompany him to London, Leo's face grew pale. He whispered, "You'll be sorry for this,

Bradford! I guarantee, you'll be sorry for it!" He whirled and stormed out of the room, slamming the door.

Later, when Daniel talked with Lyna about Leo's offer to Matthew, telling her all that had happened, she was apprehensive. "You know what he's like, Daniel. He did us enough harm. He's cruel and capricious. There's nothing he won't do to get what he wants. You must be very careful, Daniel. Don't give him any opportunity to hurt you or your family."

Daniel agreed with his sister, for though many years had passed, he still remembered the cruel things he and Lyna had suffered at the hand of Leo Rochester. His love for Matthew had grown over the years. He felt that the boy *was* his son, in everything but blood, and what he feared most of all was that Leo would corrupt Matthew as he had corrupted everything else he had ever touched. He nodded finally, saying wearily, "I'll do all I can, but it's in God's hands, Lyna."

As he walked through the nearly abandoned streets toward home, his shoulders drooped from the weight of the situation. The strain of the war had worn him down. He longed to be with the troops, but General Washington had asked that he remain in Boston at the foundry. Even though he was working on plans for casting cannons, he felt himself to be little more than a spy and he despised that thought.

He thought of Marian—her face as it had been when he had last seen it—but immediately pulled his thoughts violently away from that.

"Matthew!" he said. "I've got to do all I can to save Matthew from what Leo would make of him. . . ."

PART FOUR

GUNS OVER BOSTON

Winter 1776

19

"I Already Have a Son"

OCCASIONALLY, EVEN THE BEST OF CHESS PLAYERS find themselves unable to make a move. Even more occasionally, both players seem to be pinched into a corner so that each sits there staring at the board for long periods, looking up from time to time trying to gauge the will and the intention of his opponent. So it was with Generals George Washington and William Howe throughout the fall and winter of 1775 and into the early months of the new year.

Washington had under his command a superior force numerically, but Howe and his troops had the better defensive position. Washington knew he had made a great mistake sending Arnold to Quebec and losing valuable men. Now he had sent General Lee to New York, laying plans to defend that city. With the men that stayed behind, Washington perched on the hills staring hungrily down at Boston. He simply sat there, unable to move, for he did not have enough powder for the guns that Colonel Knox had brought back from Ticonderoga for a sustained attack. His mind sometimes swirled with obscure and frantic thoughts—although those who surrounded him never saw this side of the commander. They looked to him already as a father as much as a commander in chief. Watching the tall form of Washington stalking back and forth staring down at Boston below, Greene once said to Putnam, "Look at him. Just look at him."

"Quiet, isn't he?" Putnam replied.

"Yes, he's quiet. He'd be that way if the skies fell on him."

"In a way, I guess they have," Greene said, "unless a miracle happens to break this gridlock."

Finally, the officers were called into counsel. They sat there staring

241

at Washington: Greene, Gates, Sullivan, Putnam, Lincoln, and Thomas. Though General Washington was a man of few words, he was very perceptive and saw a resurgence of hope in the faces of the men. Though doubt rose in him almost like a cloud, he knew he could wait no longer and had to force the issue.

"Gentlemen," he said slowly and deliberately, "we must make a move. We have Colonel Knox's cannons, fifty-two of them, nine big mortars, and five cohorns."

"But the powder! What about the powder, Your Excellency?" Greene spoke up.

"We have enough powder to serve them for one attack."

They had sat out a good part of the winter waiting, anxious for battle. Now that the possibility for action lay before them, there was a stir in the room as hope began to show more upon the faces of the officers. "Bunker Hill has been taken from us. It's too strong to be recaptured. But the ice is frozen solid across the channel all the way to Boston. We could assault Boston across the ice."

"Sir," Greene spoke up, his eyes narrowed, "what are our forces?"

"About seven thousand militia, eight thousand Continentals."

"Are you proposing," General Thomas asked slowly, "to advance on Boston, across ice with nothing more than musketry?"

Quickly Washington said, "Howe can count on no more than five thousand on foot. We're three to their one."

"But they're in a defensive position," Greene interrupted. "It would be a hard matter, sir. And two thousand of our men have no muskets at all. Most of those who do have only nine or ten rounds of ammunition."

For the next hour, the arguments went around the room and Washington sat back, allowing all the men to have their say. Eventually, he knew he would have to make the decision. That was the penalty of being commander in chief. Whatever his decision, he knew he would have to bear the responsibility.

Finally, General Sullivan asked, "I wonder why Howe hasn't marched out against us?"

"He hasn't enough transport for a campaign," Putnam said. "And you can't strike England without rousing the militia."

Washington had given the situation considerable thought and had been waiting for this last argument. "Howe may be reinforced before he strikes, and in that case, he could launch out. He could devastate us. I'd like to attack him now before he has that opportunity. Would you give me your votes?"

One by one the generals spoke—and all were against Washington's plan.

All the rest of the day, Washington kept to himself, pondering what he had to decide. Finally, late that night he sent for Knox. When the massive figure of Knox stood across from him, he looked up and said, "Dorchester Heights, Knox—if your guns were set up there, would they control the city?"

In a sense it was strange that Washington, who had known military service, was asking advice from a bookstore owner who had never seen a major battle in his life. But Knox had studied the science of artillery so that his head was full of it, and Washington trusted the man's judgment.

"They would, sir!" His voice was confident and his face began to beam at the thought. "We could drop shells right on top of General Howe's head, Your Excellency."

"I haven't fortified Dorchester up until now," Washington said slowly, "because we didn't have enough forces and gun power to defend them. But I think now we must make our move. We must strike now, and be decisive about it. Can you do it?"

Knox was still exhausted from slogging through winter mud and ice, dragging metal monsters along impassable trails from Ticonderoga, but he straightened up and a determined look wreathed his face. "Yes, sir, I can do it!"

"Very well," Washington said firmly. As he spoke, he had the sense of passing through a door that led to a dark passageway—or perhaps of coming to a fork in a road, not knowing what lay down each trail. But he let none of the burden of responsibility he carried show to Knox. "Very well, Colonel, put your mind to it—and your men. All that you have—we must strike at once!"

🔔   🔔   🔔

Dake found himself thrown into a furor of activity, spurred on by Knox, who was even more determined than he had been with his cannons. Every available man was set to making what Knox called "fascines." These were prefabricated wooden structures for fortifications that could be made into bulwarks.

"These barrels ought to get a few lobsterbacks," Dake grinned. Sweat was pouring from his face as he muscled one of them in place. "We can roll barrels down on them if they try to attack."

Everything had to be done secretly and by cover of night. As Knox explained, if Howe perceived that Dorchester Heights was being fortified, he might come marching out with his troops. That would spoil the game, Knox knew. So, large parties of men, up to two thousand of them, began hauling fascines, pressed hay, dirt, and carts that remained hidden from the enemy. All was kept out of sight from the unsuspecting British troops that waited in the city below.

Dake, along with his fellow soldiers, was excited about the new development. After all the months of waiting, he was ready to see some action. He was called aside by Knox, who pulled him into the privacy of his tent.

"I've got a rather dangerous assignment for you, Bradford," the burly colonel said slowly. "One that might not be to your liking—but it will be a great service to our forces."

"What is it, Colonel?" Dake inquired curiously.

"We need as much information as possible about the British down there." He indicated the general direction of Boston. "We have our agents, of course, but their information's not always very reliable. We need a man with a cool head."

Knox stared down at the smaller man and said, "Your father has sent the most accurate information. Do you feel you might make your way to your home without being caught?"

"Why, of course I could," Dake said confidently.

"Careful now! If you're caught, it means a rope."

Both men sobered when they thought of some brave Americans captured by the British and executed as spies. Dake grew quiet at the thought of facing a similar fate. "I don't see how the British could tell I was a patriot. Of course, they know my family is, but my brother's working at the foundry. I don't think they'll notice one extra man."

"Good! You'll leave at once. We'll be on the move soon. Collect what information you can and get it back to us as soon as you can." Knox's broad face broke then in a smile. "Now we'll show Howe what it costs to disturb Americans!"

⚜   ⚜   ⚜

Marian opened the door and, upon seeing Daniel, said quickly, "Come in, Daniel." She stepped back, and as he removed his heavy coat and hung it on the hall tree, she said, "I'm sorry to bother you, but Father wanted to see you."

Hanging his wool tricornered hat on another peg of the hall tree, Daniel turned to her. He studied the intense expression on her face and asked quietly, "Is he worse?"

"Yes. I had the doctor in."

"What did he say?" Daniel asked, noting the strain on her face.

"Nothing! The same thing he always says." Marian was a strong woman, but the pressure of her father's illness had worn her down. Her shoulders, usually straight as a soldier's, were slumped, and fine lines around her mouth told of a weariness that weighed her down inside. "He keeps asking for you," she said.

"I'm glad you sent word. I always want you to feel free to do that." He hesitated, then said, "Your father's such a fine man. I've always loved him."

Marian looked at him quickly. "And he's always loved you—and trusted you. Ever since the first time you came to the house, I think. I remember so well the day you arrived with those horses."

"Seems like a long time ago."

"I know, but I remember it." A smile lifted the corners of her tired mouth. "I think he was expecting a rough blacksmith, from what I'd told him about you before you came."

"Well, that's what he got. That's what I am."

"That's not true." She turned then and walked down the hall.

Daniel followed her silently, and when they entered the sick man's room, he noted quickly that John Frazier was much weaker than he had been three days earlier when he'd made his last visit. He covered his thought, however, smiling and walking over to the bed, saying, "Well, here I've come to bore you to death again, John." He seated himself beside the bed, reached over and took the thin hand that Frazier offered. He began to speak of work that went on at the foundry, and for thirty minutes the two men talked quietly, speaking of the plans to build cannons. Marian brought tea, then left them to themselves. Finally, Frazier had a severe coughing fit that disturbed Bradford. *What a helpless feeling it is*, he thought, *to see someone hurting and not be able to do anything about it!* Then aloud, he said, "That's a bad cough. There's a lot of illness going around. This has been a bad winter."

Frazier gained control of himself after a few minutes, dabbed at his lips with a white handkerchief, then cleared his throat. "Tell me about your family, Daniel. Are they all well?"

"Yes, they are." He hesitated, unable to mention Matthew. He was not sure how much of Leo's real nature Frazier was aware of, but he was relatively sure that this man was not totally blind as to the sort of man his son-in-law was. John Frazier was a wise man, able to read others, and Leo could not have concealed his true character all these years, given the rumors that ran about the town. He did not mention Matthew, however, but said, "I'm worried about Dake."

"Is he still with Washington up in the hills?"

Daniel hesitated, then shook his head. "No, he's at my house."

Frazier's eyes opened wide with shock. "At your house! Isn't that dangerous, Daniel?"

"Yes, it is. But it's what Colonel Knox assigned him to do. I'm supposed to move around and determine the strength of the British—just exactly what's going on inside Boston—then pass the word along to Dake. Then he's to take it back to Knox." Daniel shifted his big frame in the chair and rubbed his chin, almost nervously. He had a cleft chin that embarrassed him, and he'd thought of growing a beard to cover it. Dake and Micah had the same trait. A scar on the bridge of the nose— a reminder of a fight he had had when he was a younger man—gleamed whitely as Daniel sat there reminiscing. Finally he grasped his hands and squeezed them together. "You know Dake—he loves it! Anything dangerous, he's for it."

"He's so different from Micah," Frazier observed. "They look so much alike—yet are so different in their ways."

"Yes, I guess so. I think Dake gets all of his ornery qualities from me." He grinned suddenly, adding, "And Micah got the good things from his mother. Sam, of course, if anything, is more rambunctious than Dake." He shook his head. "I don't know how much longer I'll be able to keep him out of this war. He's pestering the life out of me to join up."

"You have a good family. Rachel is such a beautiful young woman! She came to see me yesterday. Did you know that?"

"No, she didn't tell me," Daniel said, surprised.

"Yes, she brought some soup and a cake that she'd baked. How she found out it was my birthday, I'll never know."

"Your birthday? I didn't know that."

"I don't brag on it. When you get to be my age," Frazier said, "it's not a thing to celebrate." He was not a man who complained, this John Frazier, and did not do so now. He merely shrugged, saying, "Now, every day I celebrate making it through."

"You've been patient in your sickness, John." Daniel shook his head and spoke his private thoughts. "I don't know how to pray anymore, it seems. I pray over and over again, day after day, month after month, sometimes year after year and nothing seems to happen. Yet, the Scripture says we're to keep on praying."

Frazier studied the broad-shouldered man who sat beside him. "You really believe that prayer changes things?"

"Of course. Don't you?"

"I don't know. I did once—but now, I'm not sure," Frazier admitted. Disappointment showed in his eyes. "I have no grandsons. That's been a grief and a sorrow to me. Not that I blame Marian," he said quickly. It was as close as he'd ever come to speaking of the failure of his daughter and Leo Rochester to have any children. Quickly he covered the slip by saying, "You tell Dake to keep his head down. I always liked that boy. He's wild as a hare, but always fun and ready for anything."

Finally, Daniel saw that Frazier was growing tired. He got up, wished him goodbye, and left.

As Marian met him outside in the hall, she asked him at once about Matthew. "Leo's furious that you won't help him. I've never seen him so angry and bitter."

"I can't help that." He looked at her and tried to smile. "You've got enough worries without taking me and my family on."

Marian shook her head, her full lips pursed suddenly in a strange expression. "I suppose you and I will always worry about each other, won't we, Daniel?"

He looked at her with surprise and then nodded. "I suppose so. Well," he said abruptly, "I'll be praying for your father." With that, Daniel turned and left the house.

As soon as Daniel was gone, Marian went back up the stairs to check on her father. He was almost asleep, but as she tucked a blanket around him against the cold, he looked up at her.

"Fine man, Bradford," he said, smiling at Marian.

"Yes," she said softly. Her eyes were thoughtful, and she wanted to say more but was afraid to trust herself. "Go to sleep, now," she whispered. "You'll feel better tomorrow."

🜚   🜚   🜚

Dake sat back in the Windsor chair propped against the wall and balanced the dish in one hand. He smiled and looked across the table at Jeanne. She was wearing a light blue dress that made her very attractive. It had actually belonged to Rachel, and Dake remembered it. He had seen it on his sister often enough. Taking a huge bite of the chocolate cake, he swallowed it with evident pleasure, then said, "This is fine cake, Jeanne. I didn't know you could cook so well."

"Mrs. Gordon has taught me how to make a cake. This kind anyway."

"It's so good I think I better have another piece," said Dake as he reached for the cake.

"Don't eat so much," she scolded. "You'll founder."

"A nice way to go," Dake grinned. "There's worse ways to die than overeating chocolate cake."

Jeanne had been taken by surprise when she had come to visit Rachel and found Dake there. Rachel had warned her, "Don't mention a word about him being here. If the British found out, he'd be arrested and hanged." Rachel had explained how he was here as a spy, more or less, for Washington's forces, and Jeanne had been quick to assure her that she would say nothing.

The two had spent the morning together, and since Dake was not free to go out of the house, they sat in the kitchen as she worked on the noon meal. They were alone, for Micah and Sam were at the foundry along with their father, while Rachel was at the church working with the ladies on some project for the poor.

After Dake had devoured all of the cake Jeanne would allow him, they sat there drinking tea. Dake probed into her past, curious to know what it was like for a girl to grow up in the wilderness. He was surprised when she spoke of the times she had gone out by herself to check the traplines.

When she had finished talking about her life, she looked at Dake and wanted to know all about his childhood. "It must have been wonderful, having brothers and a sister. I bet you didn't always get along, though, did you?"

"Nobody can get along with those people," he said, looking pious. "The good Lord knows I've tried to make this house a home—but, you know how difficult they are, impossible to get along with!"

Jeanne could not help laughing at his solemn expression. "You are *awful*, Dake Bradford, just awful! If anyone's hard to get along with, it's *you*!"

"I don't know why you say that!" he said in mock surprise. "Why, all I want in this world is just to have my own way."

"I'll just bet you do—and you're not going to get it!"

Dake was sitting on a tall stool, looking down at her as she sat in a lower chair. Her oval face glowed with health, and he admired her openly. "You are a good-looking woman," he remarked critically. "I'm an expert in things like that, you understand?"

Jeanne flushed and dropped her eyes. She had not yet learned to handle Dake's outlandish statements. "That's enough of that!" she retorted sharply.

"You know, I've always said that us folks that have dimples in our chins are smarter than anybody else." He studied the tiny cleft in Jeanne's chin, then touched the one in his own. "I think it's a mark of superior intelligence, charm, and wit, don't you? Oh, all the great men and women of history have had them. Just check the records."

"I don't recall all that many great people having chins like this." She did not like the slight dimple in her own chin.

After she'd cleaned up the kitchen, he said, "Come on to the parlor and I'll let you read to me for a while." They moved to the parlor but did not read, for Dake was still not finished with talking.

Finally she said, "Dake, what will you do after the war?"

He looked at her thoughtfully. "I've thought about that a lot," he said. "I'd like to get away from here, see what lies over the mountain."

"What mountain?"

"Any mountain. I'm always anxious to see what's on the other side. I've been stuck here helping Pa in the foundry and going to school. Now, first chance I get, I'm going to head west and do some exploring."

"I like that," she said quickly. "Maybe I could show you how to trap a beaver."

He laughed, saying, "I'll bet you could. We don't have many of those around Boston here. Have you actually trapped beavers?"

"My father and I trapped just about everything." She began to tell him more about her life—the freedom and the joy she'd experienced in living outdoors.

Dake listened intently, then finally he asked, "That's the kind of woman you are, isn't it? Not much for society things?"

Jeanne shook her head. "It's been different being here. Mrs. Gordon and Grace have been so kind trying to teach me how to behave properly, but I don't fit here exactly. I really miss the way I grew up."

"Well," Dake said with an odd look sweeping briefly across his face, "we'll see about that beaver when there's time to think about it. First we have to settle this matter with the lobsterbacks, though."

She looked up quickly, saying, "Be careful, Dake. It's very dangerous, you being here. I . . . I wouldn't want anything to happen to you."

"Aw, I just have to go back and make my report—I'll be all right!" He was sitting on the sofa beside her. Reaching over, he took her hand—then did something he'd never done in his life. He kissed her hand, and seeing the shock in her eyes, he said, "I've never done that before—but I kinda like it. Do you?"

Jeanne tried to pull her hand back, but he held it fast. "Never mind that. Let me go, Dake."

He released her at once. A strange light brightened his eyes, playful, but at the same time serious. Seeing that she was embarrassed, he shrugged, "Well, come now, you can read to me." He made light of the moment, saying loftily, "You can read me something heavy and difficult. Something to challenge my mind." He was glad to see that she was able to shake the embarrassment that his kiss had caused. She picked out a book from the shelf and sat down and began to read. The two sat there letting the time flow by without noticing it.

Leo came into the house, his face stormy and his lips pulled down in a scowl. He went at once to the parlor, where he found Marian reading. "Have you talked to Bradford?" he demanded.

Marian put down the book and stood up. "Leo, there's no point in discussing this further. I don't have any influence over Daniel's decision."

"Oh, you have *influence*, all right! The fellow's so in love with you, he'd stick his head in a furnace if you told him to!" Throwing himself into a chair, he sat there staring at her, his eyes half shut. He had not known her as a husband knows a wife for years—yet often was struck by the beauty she had retained over the years. *If she had borne me a son,* he thought abruptly, *we might have had a good marriage.* But knowing himself well, he realized he had never really been in love with her—nor she with him. Now he said aloud, "The servants said he was here today."

"Yes, he came to see Father."

Leo grinned sourly. "Handy to have a lover who's a partner of your father's, isn't it? He can come and go in the house any time—no questions asked. Did you talk to him?"

"He didn't say anything about Matthew."

"Blast him! I wish I'd never heard the name of Bradford! He and that sister of his have been nothing but a plague to me ever since the first time I laid eyes on them!" He got up and began to pace the floor nervously. Finally, he swore and started to leave the room, but wheeled when she called his name. "What is it?" he snapped.

Marian rose and came to stand before him. "Leo," she said quietly, "I've been thinking of something for a long time, something that might be the answer for us."

"For us?" He stared at her. "You're not trying to make a loving couple out of us, are you, Marian?" he said sarcastically. "I'd think that's all been shaken out of you over the past few years."

"You're my husband, Leo," Marian said, her voice quiet. She had thought for a long time and prayed about a way to find peace with this man. He had abused her verbally and physically for years. He had taken more mistresses than she cared to know about, then boasted of them to her face, shaming her terribly. But Marian Rochester had a strong conviction about the view of marriage in Scripture. She would honor her God and her vows to this man no matter what she had to suffer. He was her husband as long as he lived. Only death could break the marriage vow. She had spent sleepless nights thinking over the long years that lay ahead of her like an endless road, had shed her tears in private—and hidden all of this from her father and the servants.

"Leo, why don't we adopt a child? A boy. Then you'd have the son you long for."

"*Adopt* a child?" he said, surprised at her words.

Leo stared at her, for once taken off guard. Suspicion rose into his eyes and he half shut them. "When did all this come to you?"

"I . . . I've thought of it before, but I kept hoping that we'd have our own children. That hasn't happened," she said, "and I'm truly sorry for it. But it's not too late. There are plenty of children without fathers. I understand the orphanages are full of them." Marian stood there looking at Leo, hoping that this offer might bring an answer to their troubled marriage.

Leo Rochester stared at his wife. For a moment the idea seemed to appeal to him, then he shook his head almost angrily. "No, I won't have it! I already have a son—my own blood. That's what I want to see— Rochester blood, the Rochester name." For once he was not striking out at her but speaking his deepest feelings. "I know I haven't been much— but I could be better if I had a son to pour myself into, someone to bring up—a young man who could carry on the Rochester line."

"An adopted son could do that," Marian said.

"It wouldn't be the same!" he exclaimed. "Don't you see that, Marian? It's in the blood. You didn't know my father. He was a good man—not like me. Somehow, I . . . I was the bad seed. But I see some of my father in Matthew. He resembles him in his manner a great deal. No, I'll have him!"

"Leo—"

"Don't speak of this again," he said harshly, then turned and left the room.

Marian stared after him, futility rising up, almost choking her. Despite her honest attempts to be civil with him, her life had been nothing but a series of hopeless encounters with Leo. She knew she could never please him, but she had thought that a child might somehow modify his behavior and make him into a different sort of man. Deep down she had little hope of it, but she was desperate enough to try anything. Now, as the door slammed, she sighed, knowing that her suggestion had been scorned and rejected.

T   T   T

"I need a man," Leo said, leaning over the bar staring at the barkeep intently.

"Wot kind of a man would you be needin', Mr. Rochester?" The bartender, a slender man named Mooney with sepulchral features, was accustomed to finding women for his customers. He was somewhat surprised when Leo Rochester showed up, though. He knew Rochester for a gamester with a terrible reputation with women, and he thought at first that the tall man had come looking for a harlot. That would have been simple enough. When Rochester had said, "I'm looking for a man," however, Mooney put up his guard. "Wot do you 'ave on your mind, sir?"

Ever since Rochester had stormed out of the house, sinister schemes were swirling in his mind, indeed. He leaned forward, lowered his voice, and spoke for some time to Mooney, saying, "Do you know of a tough, shrewd man that can keep his mouth shut?"

"I might know a fellow like that. 'E comes high, though."

"What's his name?"

Mooney leaned forward and said quietly, "Theo Wagner. 'E's no man for rough work, you understand."

"I don't need that. Where do I find him?" Leo listened as Mooney gave him instructions on where Wagner could be found. When the barkeep was finished, Leo took his wallet out and laid some bills before him. Leaving the inn, he went at once in search of Wagner. He found him with little trouble at a rather good inn.

"Your name is Theo Wagner?" he asked when the door opened.

The man who looked at him was small, no more than five seven. He had sharp black eyes, black hair, and a face somewhat like a ferret. "That's my name. Will you come in?"

Leo stepped inside the room and stood staring down at the smaller man. He was not an impressive-looking figure, but that might be all to the best for the type of scheme Leo had planned. "I need something done. I want to see if you're the man to do it."

Wagner at once smelled money. He took in the expensive cut of Leo's clothes, the arrogant face that spelled aristocracy, and said smoothly, "Why certainly, sir. Have a seat. Will you have ale or will whiskey do you better?"

Within fifteen minutes, Wagner had listened to Leo's proposition. "You want me to put the squeeze on this man, Daniel Bradford, as I take it?"

"The man's tied in with these rebels. I'm convinced he's a spy for them. You bring me proof of that and you'll be well paid."

Wagner was used to such things as this. He was a spy himself, or had been, and knew how such things worked. Sipping the whiskey from the cut-glass goblet, he nodded. "I think something might be done, Mr. Rochester."

"I want him hanged!" Leo said sharply. "Or at least I want enough evidence to hang him. But don't take it to the authorities. Bring whatever you discover to me. You understand that?"

"Oh yes, sir, of course. Now, I'll get on this at once. Things are happening. You know sooner or later Washington's force is going to try to take Boston."

"Do you think they can do it?"

"The British are not as strong as most people think. I wouldn't be surprised. If Washington gets the arms, he can do it. He's got plenty of men to do it right now."

"Bradford's part of that. I *know* he's in contact with Washington. He's got a son who's up there with him, too. Somehow I've got to get enough evidence to put pressure on the man!"

Leo rose to his feet, finished off his drink, and gave the man money. "There'll be plenty of this if you can get the evidence, Wagner."

"Yes, sir. I'll see to it. Money's a good thing, and I like to have lots of it."

"Don't we all!" Leo snorted, then left the room.

After Rochester was gone, Theo Wagner held the bills up before his eyes and caressed them lovingly. Then, as he put them into his pocket, he smiled and leaned back to lay his plans for Daniel Bradford's demise. It wasn't necessary for the man to actually *be* a spy. There were ways to make it appear so, to juggle the evidence, so to speak. He knew well that Leo Rochester would never inquire whether the man was actually guilty, for the deep hatred for Bradford had shown in his eyes. This was all to the good—for Theo was, even as he sat before the fire, thinking of ways to create evidence if none existed.

20

SAM MEETS THE ENEMY

GROANING LOUDLY, SAM BRADFORD snuggled down under the covers, burrowing deeper into his feather bed. But Rachel's call came sharper: "Sam, you come out right now or I'll come in with a bucket of cold water!"

"I'm coming! Can't you give a fellow a minute!" Sam threw the covers back, jumped onto the bare floor, and almost cried aloud. Stumbling quickly to the washbasin, he found the water frozen in the pitcher and mumbled angrily, "Blasted water basin! How's a fellow supposed to wash in ice?" Wearing only a pair of knee-length drawers and a vest, both made out of cotton, he hurriedly began pulling on his clothing. He grabbed his shoes and a pair of wool socks, then dashed out of the room, stomped down the stairs, and burst into the kitchen, going at once to stand in front of the fireplace.

As he stood there rubbing his hands in front of the fire, Rachel gave him a caustic warning. "You're not getting any breakfast until you put your clothes on."

"All right—all right!" Sam pulled on his socks, then pulled a pair of britches over them and struggled into his shirt. "This thing itches!" he complained. "Why does everything have to be made out of linsey-woolsey? I hate that stuff!"

Rachel said, "Hush and put your shoes on." If anyone hated linsey-woolsey, she did. Most of their clothes were made of a fabric woven of threads of linen and wool. The flax plant had to be grown and harvested, then made into threads. The wool had to be shorn from the sheep, then both wool and flax had to be broken down and combed and spun into thread. After that, the two fibers had to be woven into cloth. Finally, when all that was done, the garment could be cut out and sewn. Rachel took more care than most, for she dyed her linsey-woolsey red from the juice of pokeberry, brown or yellow from sassafras or butternut

254

bark. Since many of her dresses were made of the same material, she agreed with Sam that it itched, but would not say so.

"It's warm and that's what counts. Now put your shoes on."

Sam picked up one shoe and stared at it. It was one of a pair of new shoes, and the cold had frozen it almost as hard as iron. Staring at them, he looked at his own foot. "Rachel," he said thoughtfully, his inventor's mind working, "did you ever stop to think that your left foot and your right foot are different?"

Looking at him disgustedly, Rachel snapped, "Of course, I know my feet are different! What about it?"

"Well, if feet are different, why don't we make shoes different? One for the left foot and one for the right foot?"

"That's nonsense, Sam! It'd be a waste of time. Now, put those shoes on and come and get your breakfast."

Sam pulled on his shoes, muttering, "Someday, they'll do it. Why is it I have all these *great* ideas—and a few years later somebody comes by and thinks of the same thing and makes a lot of money out of it?"

Rachel laughed aloud at him. "You'll be wealthy someday, Sam, no doubt. Why don't you invent a carriage that would go without a horse. That'd make you rich!" Picking up his plate she filled it with cornmeal mush, which he immediately drowned with molasses. She brought a fresh loaf of bread over, sawed a piece off with a sharp knife, and put it down along with a pat of butter. "That's the last of the butter," she said, "so you'd better enjoy it." She sat down beside him and they bowed their heads while Rachel asked the blessing. As the two began eating, washing down their breakfast with cider, she asked, "What are you going to do today?"

"Mrs. Rochester has commissioned me to make her a hot water heater like the one we've got here," Sam said importantly. "She already gave me the money to buy the parts and hire whoever I needed to help me put it up. But Micah's working on something else, so I'll just have to hire another man, I guess."

Rachel took a drink of the cider and dabbed at her lips with a napkin. "I talked to her about it. She's so excited. Poor woman. She needs all the comfort she can get!"

"Poor?" Sam stared at her. "She's not poor. She's got lots of money."

"There's not enough money in the world to make living with a man like Leo Rochester tolerable," Rachel answered grimly.

After the two finished their meal, Sam pulled on his coat and cap and left the house. He went at once to the foundry, his breath frosting in the air. As he moved along, he kept a close watch on the Redcoats in the street, glaring at them but saying nothing. From time to time he glanced up to where he knew Washington's army was encamped along the line of hills and muttered, "I wish you'd hurry up and get down here and knock these Redcoats winding!" When he arrived at the foundry, he reported to his father, saying, "Micah's promised to help me, but you've got him doing something else."

"I know it, Sam. I've got Micah on a job that pays money. We're not charging Mrs. Rochester for doing this. After all, her father owns half the place."

Sam did not think it prudent to acquaint his father with the fact that Marian Rochester had already given him enough cash to pay for his time and for a helper. When he left the office, he muttered, "If Micah doesn't want the money, I'll find somebody else. . . ."

Going hurriedly to the project, he spent most of the day pulling the units together. Actually Micah had done a great deal of the more skilled work, but by midafternoon, Sam stepped back and nodded with satisfaction at his completed work. "Well, that ought to do 'er. All ready to be hooked up."

He procured a wagon used to haul iron and the materials and the finished products of the foundry. But after he had hitched the team up, he discovered that there was no one free to help him. Most of the men had been let go anyhow, and the few that remained were only working part of the time. "I'll have to go get Jed Bailey to help me. He doesn't have much sense, but he's got a strong back."

Moving toward the door of the foundry, Sam put on his hat and coat, then stepped outside. The air was very cold and seemed to suck his breath out of his lungs for a minute. He turned to go to the residential section where the Baileys lived when a voice from behind him spoke up suddenly. "Know where a man could get a bit of work?"

Sam turned and was surprised to see that a British soldier had come from the opposite direction and now stood dejectedly, his face blue with the cold.

Sam knew that the British soldiers had been hired by many of the citizens of Boston, but he himself despised the practice. "No!" he grunted roughly. "There's nothing for you to do around here."

The soldier was a small man in his late thirties or early forties, as well as Sam could judge. He had a thin, pinched face and was at least three inches below Sam's five feet seven. He licked his lips and hunched his shoulders and seemed about to turn and walk away. Then he said, "Just any kind of work. I'll do anything. Just for something to eat."

Sam was curious. He had a strong hatred for the British army—but it was a hatred that fixed itself on a regiment or a larger unit of the army coming to destroy his freedom. It was the army that had killed Americans at the Boston Massacre. But somehow, this undersized, worn-looking man did not seem to be threatening. Hesitating a moment, Sam asked curiously, "Don't they feed you? You're a soldier. I know that there's such a thing as soldiers' mess."

"Yes sir, there is, and mighty poor pickings, it is! Not enough to keep body and soul together. All I had today was half a bowl of mush and some old bacon that liked to turn my stomach. Not enough to do a man," he added, shrugging his thin shoulders.

Something about the small figure engaged Sam's sympathy. "What's your name?" he asked.

"Oliver Simpson. Ollie, they call me."

"My name's Sam Bradford."

The giving of the name seemed to encourage the soldier. He straightened up a bit and said, "I ain't very big, I know, but I ain't known nothing but hard work all me life. Mr. Bradford, just anything will be duly appreciated."

There was something pathetic to Sam about this man, already in his thirties, calling a boy of only fifteen "sir." This was certainly not the conquering hero that British soldiers were sometimes made out to be! An impulse struck him and he heard himself say, "Well—come on inside, Simpson. I don't have any work, but there's some grub left over here. You're welcome to it." He turned and walked inside, followed by the soldier. Moving to the middle of the foundry where one of the forges was still glowing with coals, Sam pulled a box off a shelf and said, "My sister packed too much for me to eat today. If you don't mind taking seconds, you're welcome to it."

He handed it to the soldier, who bit his lip and then nodded. "Thank you, sir. It's good of you."

He sat down and began to eat with such ferocity that Sam was embarrassed by it. "I think there's some tea. Hang on, I'll see if I can get you a pot of it." Soon he was back and discovered that the man had eaten almost all that was in the box. He stopped and drank the tea thirstily. Sam sat down and tried not to watch while he finished.

Simpson said, "That was fine, sir, the best I've had! Now, I insist, let me sweep the floor, clean up after the horses—anything! I don't like charity."

Sam said slowly, "Here, have some more tea. There's plenty." He poured some more into the mug, and then as Simpson sat back and sipped it carefully, obviously enjoying it, Sam gave him a curious glance. "I don't understand why you're here."

Simpson looked up. "You don't? I don't understand it myself." He twisted the mug around in his hands and stared down at it as if to find some answer there. After a while, he lifted his eyes, which were a rather watery blue, and his mouth twisted as he said, "I didn't come to get rich, that's for sure! I don't really know. I got drunk one night. I was in a pub, and when I woke up they told me I'd taken the king's shilling."

"What does that mean?" Sam asked.

"Oh, that's the way they get young men to join the army. Parade into town with their scarlet coats and the drums beating and the bugles blowing—and a young silly idiot of a lad signs up and gets a shilling. Once he takes it he belongs to the king, body and soul."

"What's it like?"

"What's what like?" Simpson asked.

"Being a soldier in the British army."

"Well, it's no life for a man, I can tell you that," Simpson said. "I've got a wife, two children, and you know what the army pays? Eight pence a day!"

"Eight pence? Is that all?"

"Eight pence. But we never see it. Sixpence every week they withhold to pay for our uniforms. We have to pay for shoes, gaiters, mittens, even our knapsacks. By the time the money gets to us, the quartermaster's taken his cut. 'Course, there's always charges. This uniform," he looked down, "ain't it splendid?" There was irony in his thin voice as he waved at the scarlet coat, the white belt, white britches, knee-high gaiters, and a cocked hat. "Has to be brushed and whitened every day. If we don't do it, we'll get the lash."

"They actually use a lash on you?"

"On my word! A man can be sentenced to five hundred lashes across the bare back with a cat-o'-nine-tails. A thousand if he strikes an officer—or either the gallows. That's why they call us lobsterbacks."

A hammer from down at the other end of the foundry was striking on an anvil, making a musical cadence of a sound. Simpson stopped and took a sip of his tea. "Don't ever think it's a glorious thing, sir. We have to carry up to a hundred and twenty-five pounds. And our muskets—them they call Brown Bess—weigh fourteen pounds. A ball from it falls to the ground from a hundred and twenty-five feet. For a small chap like me, carrying that weight under the hot sun . . . well, you can imagine."

"Were you at Bunker Hill?"

"Yes, I was—and I wish I hadn't been." Simpson passed a hand nervously across his eyes. "My best friend got shot in the stomach. Took him three hours to die, it did—out there under the sun. We couldn't get back to pull 'im off the field."

"Well, some of our people got shot, too," Sam said defensively, but somehow he no longer felt the belligerence he had been carrying for weeks. "Some of my best friends got killed that day."

Ollie Simpson looked up. "I'm sorry for it, sir, but you won't find a man wearing the red coat who wants to stay here and fight. Our people in England hate this war!"

It was a thought that had not occurred to Sam, and for some time he listened as Simpson told about how in England the revolution was an unpopular war. "We'd pull up and sail back to England in a minute, but them what's over us ain't got the sense to know that it's a bad thing." Simpson stood to his feet and said, "I'd like mighty well to help you. To pay for the meal."

"The meal's free. You're welcome to it," Sam said. He hesitated and then said, "I have got some work. I've got to put up a hot water tank. It takes a strong back—but I'll pay you if you want the job."

"Thank you, sir," Simpson said instantly. "I'll be grateful for any help you can give me."

🔔   🔔   🔔

That night at the supper table, Sam was strangely quiet. Everyone noticed it and finally Rachel said, "What's the matter with you, Sam? I never knew you to be so quiet."

Sam was chewing slowly on a piece of tough beef. He swallowed it and then said, "I hired a British soldier to help me put up the water tank over at Mr. Frazier's house today."

"You did what!" Micah exclaimed, almost choking on his food. He stared at Sam as if he'd announced he had decided to go to the moon. "Why did you do that?"

"I don't rightly know," Sam mumbled and wished he had not mentioned it.

"Tell me about it. I'd like to know," Daniel Bradford said. He leaned back in his chair, keeping his eyes on his son's face. He was thinking how quickly this youngest son of his had grown up. Fifteen years ago his mother had died bringing him into the world. Since Daniel had been both father and mother to the infant, he had grown especially fond of him—though he never showed preference. "Why did you do it, Sam? I know how you feel about the British soldiers."

"Well, he was such a . . . a *little* fellow. Not near as tall as me . . . and skinny, too . . ." Sam stumbled through the story, and when he had finished, he looked around, noting how they were all looking at him in a peculiar fashion. "Well, I didn't know how bad it was for him until he started talking. He was hungry and he's got a family—and it's a miserable thing to be a British soldier. I didn't know they treated their men like that."

Rachel suddenly rose, moved to get another piece of cake, and put it down before Sam. She put her arms around him and kissed him on the cheek, her eyes bright. "I'm proud of you, Sam! Next time, bring him here and we'll give him a *real* meal!"

Sam stared at her with astonishment. He looked around and saw approval in the eyes of all. It was Matthew who said quietly, "I think that was noble of you, Sam."

"So do I," Daniel Bradford said. "I'm glad you had that experience." His eyes grew moody, and he clasped his hands together in front of him, a habit of his. He stared at them, then looked up, saying, "This is going to be a bad war. It would be easy for us to let hate fill us, but I'm glad you saw that soldier. He's got a wife and children who love him, I suppose."

"They're caught up in the wheels of a big machine, just as we are," Micah said. He was a deep thinker, and spoke for a while about how the individual often was victimized by forces too large for him. "We're going to see some terrible things," he said. But then he smiled. "I'm glad you gave the man work. Don't ever let hate take you down, Sam. It'll poison you quick as arsenic. . . !"

⚓ ⚓ ⚓

Lyna Gordon was patching one of Leslie's uniforms and looked up to study Clive, who was sitting across from her. He had been reading a book as she sewed, but now she saw that he had closed it. He was wearing his oldest clothes, for he had been working around the house gathering wood for the fire. Now, he looked somehow unhappy.

"What's wrong, Clive?" Lyna asked quietly. She bit off a piece of thread, started a new stitch, and asked, "Don't you feel well?"

"Oh, I feel all right." Clive weighed the book in his hand, as if considering her question, then shook his head. "I'm just bored, I suppose."

"You do need more to do. Have you thought more about going back to England and starting your own practice?"

"Yes, I've thought quite a bit about it."

"Well, what have you decided?"

"Oh, I don't know, Mother!"

She heard the frustration and impatience in his tone, but it was, she saw, directed at himself.

He rose and moved to put a piece of wood on the fire, poked it with an iron poker, then watched the sparks fly up the chimney. "We're going to run low on wood," he murmured. "I'd better go out and find some more pretty soon."

He stood staring down in the fire, the flickering yellow flames throwing his face into relief. *He's a fine-looking young man*, Lyna thought. *I'm surprised that he's never been serious about marriage.* This train of thought prompted her to ask abruptly, "Where is Jeanne?"

"Gone to the butcher's with David." He smiled briefly. "I hope they don't come back with a haunch of bear or some terrible thing that these Americans seem to like to eat!"

"You think a lot of Jeanne, don't you, Clive?"

It was a calculated statement. Lyna and Leslie had not been unaware of their son's interest in the young woman. It had been Leslie who had said, "I wouldn't be too surprised if he took an even more *personal* interest in her. She's a fine-looking young woman, and they've had some unusual adventures together—very romantic."

Clive looked up quickly. He knew his mother was an intuitive person, and seeing her gray-green eyes fixed steadily on him, he slumped down in the chair, shrugging expressively. "I never could hide anything from you, could I? There ought to be a law against mothers knowing too much about their sons!"

"Then you are interested in her?"

Clive hesitated. "I've never known anyone like her, Mother."

"Well, she's had a strange rearing," Lyna said calmly. "Not many young women were brought up in the middle of a dense wilderness, learning to shoot and skin animals and trap wolves. That's bound to have made her different."

"She gets so . . . so *upset* because she doesn't know things other women know. You and Grace have done so much for her—and Rachel Bradford, too, but when we went to that party the other night, I noticed the other young ladies hung back—wouldn't admit her into their precious little circle! It angered me! They're snobs, that's what they are!"

"What did Jeanne say?"

"She didn't say anything—but I could tell she was hurt by it. She's as sensitive as any young woman I ever saw."

The two talked for some time. Lyna had always been a good listener to her children, as had Leslie. She knew that if she sat there long enough and simply listened, sooner or later Clive would come out with what had been troubling him for the past few weeks.

"Mother," he said tentatively, "I think I love her. Does that shock you?"

"Shock me? Why, no indeed! It surprises me, though." Lyna put her sewing down and came over to sit beside him. She picked up his hand

and studied it, admiring the long fingers and their strength. "You have good hands for a surgeon," she murmured. "You'll be a fine doctor." Then she looked up at him and answered his question. "You've got to be careful, of course. Everyone should when they think they're in love."

"How does one 'be careful' in a matter like love?" Clive asked in a rather confused manner. "You can be careful when you're choosing a business partner or deciding on a profession. But love's not like that, is it? When you fell in love with Father, were you *careful*?"

"Your father and I had a rather unusual courtship," Lyna spoke thoughtfully. "He didn't even know I was a woman at first." She referred to the fact that she had met Leslie while she was a runaway. In order to protect herself from unwanted male attention, she had cut her hair and dressed up as a man. Leslie, on his way to the army for the first time, had hired her as his personal servant. Clive knew all of this, of course. It was part of the family folklore. "The first time he saw me in a dress," she said, "I think your father nearly fainted." She smiled fondly at the memory and said, "He married me to save me from—well, Leo Rochester. You know the story. I was a bound servant to him—both Daniel and I were for a time. I had run away because of his attentions."

Clive listened carefully and then said, "Well, when did you know you were in love with Father?"

"A long time before he knew he was in love with me! Of course, I was with him in India and nursed him after he was wounded. He was so weak and helpless—like a child." She studied her son's hand again, stroked it, and shook her head. "He was always so . . . so *kind*! I couldn't help it, Clive—I just loved him."

"Well, I guess that answers my question. Poets are always talking about the power of love. Novelists write reams of books about it—but I never thought it would be anything like this."

"What is it like, son?"

"Well, I stay confused most of the time," he admitted ruefully. He ran his hands through his reddish hair, mussing it up, then shook his head woefully. "I don't know where I stand with her. Oh, I've chased a few ladies, you know about that. None of them seriously. But somehow, I feel something—different for Jeanne." He stopped abruptly and his jawline grew tense. "I've been trying to make up my mind if I should say anything to her."

"Well, what have you decided?"

Clive nodded. "I'm going to tell her tonight. . . !"

🔔　　　🔔　　　🔔

It was half an hour after the evening meal that Clive rose from the table, saying, "Jeanne, let's go outside. I need to walk this supper down."

After the two left, Lyna informed Leslie of what Clive had told her earlier.

Leslie stared at the door. "What do you think? Does he love her?"

"I think so, but who's to know?"

"What about her? You ought to have seen something in her."

Lyna was perplexed and shook her head slowly. "I just don't know, Leslie. She's so different from any other young woman that I've ever met. It's hard to say. She's very vulnerable, I know that. She'd be a good wife in most ways."

He glanced at her curiously. "Most ways? You mean in some ways she wouldn't?"

"Clive will be a physician. He'll be moving in high society. Jeanne missed out on a great deal of that sort of thing. She'd have to learn a lot."

"She's a bright girl; she could learn," Leslie said.

"Yes, I know, but she'll have to make that decision. It might be too hard for her. And I'm not so sure that is the kind of life she would choose."

As the two were talking, Clive and Jeanne were strolling along the streets of Boston. It was dark and the streetlights were not lit. Overhead the moon was casting its pale beams down on the streets. As they moved along, Clive noticed Jeanne was unusually quiet. "What have you been doing?" he asked.

"Oh, nothing much. Your mother's teaching me how to cook—I mean things like cakes and pies and tarts. She's teaching me how to sew, too."

"You never learned how to sew?"

"Just animal skins. Remember my buckskins? I made those."

They walked along slowly, and Clive sought for some way to speak his feelings to her. Finally, when they'd gotten to the end of the street, he said, "Let's go back." Turning around they walked home, and when they stood in front of the house again, he said, "Jeanne, there's something I want to say to you."

Jeanne turned to him, surprised. "What is it?" she asked. By the moonlight she saw that he was troubled and tense. "Is something wrong?"

"No, well . . . well, yes, there is," Clive stammered.

"What is it, Clive?"

Clive reached out and put his hands on her arms, which surprised her. He held her for a moment, then looked down at her and said simply,

"Jeanne, ever since I met you, I thought you were one of the most un-usual women I've ever known. It's not just that you saved my life—though I'll never forget that! But there's a sweetness in you and a sim-plicity that I've never seen in another woman."

Jeanne was acutely conscious of his hands holding her arms. "Why, that's sweet of you, Clive, to say that."

"That's not all I want to say." Clive hesitated. He felt like a man on the edge of a cliff, about to jump off—but that was the wrong figure, he thought suddenly. *A man in love doesn't think of jumping off cliffs!* He looked at her steadily and saw that she was watching him, her eyes wide with curiosity. "I love you, Jeanne. That's what I'm trying to say." He leaned forward then, drew her into his arms and kissed her. It was a gentle kiss and did not last long. Her lips were soft and sweet under his, but he stepped back and released her at once and saw that she was shocked at his words. "I mean what I say—I want to marry you."

"Marry me?" Jeanne said, shocked at what she had just heard.

"Why, of course. Why does that come as a surprise? That's what peo-ple do when they fall in love."

"But, Clive—we haven't known each other very long."

He shrugged impatiently. "I've known people to court for five years—and not know each other as well as we do. I don't think it's time that matters. It's somehow—well, it's the *intensity* of things. And I can't explain love, but I feel for you what I've never felt for another woman."

Jeanne was not shocked to discover that he had an affection for her. She had known that for some time now, but this sudden declaration had taken her by surprise! She had not expected a proposal, and now she grew confused. "I . . . I can't answer you, Clive."

"I know. I don't expect one right away—but I wanted you to know how I feel." He paused abruptly and a thought came to him, "How do you feel about me? Do you care for me at all?"

"Of course I do," Jeanne answered quickly. "How could I not, after what you did for my father and for Ma Tante?"

"I don't want gratitude," Clive said, shaking his head slightly. "Do you think you could ever come to love me?" He discovered he was tense as he waited for her reply—which did not come immediately. She was poised, it seemed, to leave him and go into the house. He could see his proposal had confused her, but he had to know. "Am I a man you might think of marrying?"

Jeanne had no experience with things like this. She was shaken ter-ribly by the suddenness of it all and even seemed to be physically weak-ened. "I just don't know, Clive," she whispered. "You'll have to give me time." She hesitated, then said, "I'm not the kind of woman you should marry."

"What does that mean?" he said, taking a step toward her.

"It means, you need someone who knows how to live with important people. You'll be going back to England. You'll be a famous doctor someday. I don't know how to behave in that world."

"Why, you can learn, Jeanne. Mother will teach you, and Grace."

But Jeanne was too moved by the emotion that had struck her almost like the blow of a fist. Somehow she had never anticipated this—although now she saw, if she had been a girl more used to this situation, she might have known it could happen. She liked him very much—and yet there had to be more than that! "You'll have to give me time," she whispered, then turned and walked into the house.

Clive followed her, somehow feeling that the battle for this young woman lay ahead of him.

🜊   🜊   🜊

Even while these two were speaking, a conference was going on in the hills surrounding Boston. On March 2, Washington had ordered a heavy bombardment on the city. Now, on March 4, the day before the anniversary of the Boston Massacre, the commander in chief was ready. Calling his officers in, Washington stared at them and gave the order in firm tones: "Gentlemen, we will begin the assault and victory will be ours!"

21

General Howe Has a Rude Awakening

THE GROUND WAS STILL FROZEN too hard to dig entrenchments, so Washington's soldiers built defensive walls, strengthened by the fascines which they had brought with them in three hundred heavily loaded carts. The covering party, consisting of eight hundred men, led the way. Then came the carts and the main working body under General Thomas, consisting of about twelve hundred men.

The carts were loaded heavily with the fascines, and the pressed hay in bundles of seven or eight hundred. Everyone knew his place and business. The covering party went before, and throughout all that night of March 4, strict silence was commanded. What noise could not be avoided by driving stakes was carried by the wind into the harbor, so that the troops of Howe never heard it.

The soldiers of Washington's fledgling army might not be much on parade ground drill, but that night, under the cover of darkness, they accomplished something that would turn the tide of the battle. Two hours before midnight they had erected two forts capable of protecting them from grapeshot or small arms fire. Then, fresh working parties relieved them at three in the morning and the work continued at a feverish pace. Although the night was mild and a bright moon was visible, a low-hanging mist on the harbor shielded them from British eyes.

    🐿   🐿   🐿

"General—General! You must wake up, sir!"

General Howe was awakened roughly by an aide shaking his arm. The general had spent part of the night gambling, the rest with Mrs. Loring. His head ached, and he held it as he sat up abruptly. Striking off the aide's hands, he groaned, "Get your hands off me."

"Pardon me, sir, but you must come!" the man insisted.

"What the devil is it?" Howe demanded.

"Sir, it's the rebels."

"Well, what've they done? Is it an attack?"

"No, sir—"

"Let me get my pants on." Howe dressed rapidly, then stalked out of the bedroom into the living area, where three of his staff officers stood with ashen faces. He took one look at them and then demanded, "What's the matter?"

"Sir, Dorchester Heights—"

"Well, what about it?" Howe snapped.

"Sir, there are forts on the Heights."

"Impossible!" Howe walked to the door, stared up at the Heights, then gasped. Looking up, he saw a fort on a hill where there had been absolutely nothing the night before.

"General Howe—" General Robertson, who came to stand beside him, was agitated. "To accomplish that in one night, the rebels must have a force of twenty thousand men!"

Howe could not speak for a moment. He stared upward, knowing that this marked a terrible defeat for him. However, he stiffened his back and turned, saying, "We must prepare for action! Gentlemen, the honor of the British army demands an immediate attack on that position!"

After having wasted all winter in Boston when he might have marched forth at any time, now Howe's hand was forced. All day he moved among the troops, practically driving his officers, as he shouted, "We will attack tomorrow! We will strike those fortifications, and we will drive them off the hill!"

Up on that hill, Washington was fully expecting an attack from the British. He looked over his officers and said soberly, "Remember, it is the fifth of March, the anniversary of the Boston Massacre. We must avenge our brethren who gave their lives for the cause of freedom!"

Howe's plan to mount an offensive attack was completely and wildly unrealistic. He set up a nocturnal amphibious invasion—an operation more fraught with danger and difficulty than he could imagine. His soldiers, even down to the ranks, sensed a fresh embarrassment coming. Knowing the penalty for desertion, Howe's troops climbed into their boats, but they were pale and dejected and utterly spiritless.

Fortunately for them, a violent storm broke that night, and Howe quickly called off the operation. As Howe canceled the mission, he admitted to his generals that the foolishness of the attack had been his own sentiments from the first, adding, "But I thought the honor of the troops was of concern."

General Howe should not have been surprised when the troops did not demand to throw themselves into a suicidal mission much as they had endured at Bunker Hill. Howe's army now was trapped. There was obviously no way for them to turn. The Boston Tories were amazed and terrified when they got the news, for they were instantly aware that the next order from the general would be to evacuate Boston. Washington later said, "No electric shock, no sudden clap of thunder—in a word, the last trump could not have struck them with greater consternation."

Dake rejoiced with the rest of the army in what had been accomplished. There were cheers that night all around the camp, and considerable drunkenness among the members of the Continental Army encamped in the hills around Boston. But Dake had no time to join the party, for he was summoned immediately by Knox.

"Get down at once to the town. Tell your father that the time has come. The British will be leaving, but we want him to be ready to protect the city along with other patriots who are there. The British might try to burn it. We want to know what their plans are, so that His Excellency can answer it."

Dake nodded and was off like a shot. As he disappeared into the night, running his horse hard, Knox smiled and said aloud, "We'll all be coming for a visit to Boston now that we've blasted the rabbits out of their holes!"

☙   ☙   ☙

Leo opened the door, a frown on his face. He had not been expecting visitors. For one moment he blinked, for the man stood outside in the shadowy darkness, the large floppy brim of his hat pulled down low over his eyes.

"Well, what is it? What do you want?" he growled.

Slowly the man lifted his head, took half a step closer, and Leo recognized the features of Theo Wagner.

A slight grin twisted the lips of Wagner, and he whispered in his husky voice, "You're not happy to see me, Sir Leo. I'm hurt."

With a scowl, Leo stepped back. "Stop being a fool and come in. Quick! I don't want anyone to see you."

He waited until the small man moved inside, noting that Wagner walked with a sidewise gait, as if one leg, perhaps, were damaged. He was wearing a long black cloak and boots that were muddied by the streets outside. Pulling off his hat, Wagner's lank, flaxen hair lay flat against his skull, and he bared his teeth, which were yellow and crooked. "I don't suppose a man could get a drink to warm him up?"

"What've you got?" Leo demanded.

"Thirsty work it is. My throat's about dry, but I think some good Irish whiskey might give me a bit of a voice."

Rochester stared at him, tempted to grab him by the scruff and throw him out—but there was a light of triumph in the man's face. Something in Wagner's crooked smile warned Leo to take a less radical view. Moving to the mahogany cabinet against the wall, he picked up a square brown bottle, then two glasses off a shelf. "Sit down, Wagner," he said brusquely. When the man was sitting, Leo put the two glasses down on an oak table, then poured them full and sat down himself. Carefully he studied Wagner, knowing that he was about to be asked for more money. It was part of the knowledge that had come to Rochester in his dealings with men. His philosophy was that one could get anything if he paid enough for it! Now he settled on a figure in his mind and waited until Wagner had drunk his drink. Without asking, Leo poured again. Then he sat back, sipped his drink, and said, "What've you got?"

Wagner's thin neck had a large Adam's apple. As he swallowed the whiskey, it bobbed up and down, as if he were swallowing a small animal that refused to go completely down but kept struggling up. He put the glass down, coughed loudly, and wiped his eyes as they filled over with moisture. "That's good whiskey, Sir Leo," he gasped. "Does a man good on a cold night like this." He saw that Leo was waiting and intended to say no more. "Wot've I got? I've got your man, that's what I've got!"

Leo at once leaned forward, his eyes bright with anticipation and pleasure. He even smiled, so that the one false tooth that did not match his others was exposed. "What do you mean? What's Bradford done? I knew it! He's nothing but a dirty traitor! What's he done?" asked Leo.

"If you mean Mr. Daniel Bradford," Wagner shrugged his bony shoulders, "why, nothing that I can see."

"You're no good to me! What do you think I'm paying you for?"

"You're paying me to find out something rotten in Bradford's house, and I've got that."

"What do you mean? Stop beating about the bush, Wagner. If you've got anything, let's have it!"

Wagner was drawing his pleasure out. He was very good at this sort of thing, having been hired for many sinister deeds. He stopped short of violence—but aside from that, there was little that he would not do for a price. "Here is what I've done," he said. "From what you told me, I was sure the Bradfords were caught up with the rebels in the hills. I asked around, and some of the neighbors told me as much—the Tory ones, of course. Bradford's a rebel to the bone, they said—ought to be hanged! Well, Sir Leo, that's well enough, but there's a thing called evidence a man has to have. So, I set about getting it!"

Wagner coughed and nodded his head toward the whiskey, his eye glittering like a bird's. "A bit more if you don't mind." He waited until Leo nodded reluctantly, then filled his glass to the brim. Once again, the Adam's apple bobbed up and down, the eyes watered, and after he had gasped and cleared his throat, he said with satisfaction, "They had me fooled at first. I took a room where I could get a good view of the Bradford place. Right next door to it, it was, an upstairs room where I could look down. The fools don't draw their drapes half the time! I could see everything going on. Of course, I could see anybody coming in, and anything out in the back where the stable is. Well, I watched and I watched—did without sleep, I did. They nearly had me fooled." He cackled then, a high-pitched sound that ended in a wheeze.

"What did you find? Tell me, man!"

"What I found is what you might have told me at first. There's *two* young men in that house. One's named Micah and the other's named Dake."

"Of course there are! What does that have to do with it?"

"Why, they're identical twins! That's what you didn't tell me, Sir Leo. Might have saved some time and money if you had. I'll have to charge you, you understand, for the extra time I've spent. If I'd known they were as alike as two peas in a pod, it might have been a lot easier."

Leo shifted, gnawing his lip. He had not informed Wagner of this and frowned. "So, what have you found out?"

"Well, I kept seeing a young man go out. He had light-colored hair and hazel eyes, a tall, strong young fellow he was. He went out a lot, it seemed to me. The only trouble was, it wasn't always the same one I saw."

"What do you mean? One of Bradford's sons is up in the hills with Washington."

"No he ain't. He's in that house. Didn't know that, did you?" smiled Wagner.

Suddenly it all became clear to Rochester. "He's come back, then. He's acting as a spy."

"That's the way it was—but you'd never known it. I wouldn't have found out myself, but they made one little mistake." Theo Wagner grinned and gave the gem of his little campaign with a note of triumph. "They made the mistake of going out in the backyard at the same time, together, don't you see? Then I realized that the one that's from Washington's crew would go out and tour the city while the other one stayed home; then the other one would take his turn. But he's there all right! At least, he was when I left to come and see you—and, of course, settle our account."

Leo's mind was working. He thought to himself, *That's what I need! If I can prove Bradford's son is a traitor, that'll put the screws on Daniel—he'll do anything to save him!* Without showing the pleasure that he felt, he shrugged. "It may be of some good to me. But you've got to go back. I've got to know what's going on. There's one more act in this little drama."

"You aiming to do him in, ain't you? The son from Washington's army? Well"—he spread his hands expansively—"it's none of my affair, but I've got to have some money."

A skirmish took place in which Wagner demanded more and Leo gave less. Finally Leo managed to satisfy the man's greed—at least temporarily. "Get back at once. I've got to be sure that he's in the house. We can't make a mistake, Wagner. When I have him arrested, it can't be Micah. It's got to be Dake Bradford. Find a way to do that, and I'll see that you're not sorry for it."

"Right, Sir Leo. I'll see as it's done."

T   T   T

Leo slept little that night. He got up long before dawn and stirred the fire. As he sat there staring into the dancing flames, his mind was filled with schemes and devices. He was a man of intense selfishness, clever beyond the usual range of such things. He finally decided to try to gain control of Matthew Bradford one more time without a scheme to implicate Dake Bradford. Dressing hurriedly, he left his quarters and went at once to the Frazier house. He was met at the door by Cato, who said evenly, "Good morning, Mr. Rochester. Come in, sir."

"Where's my wife?"

"She's up with her father. Shall I ask her to come down?"

"Yes, tell her to come to the library at once." Leo moved to the library and paced the floor nervously as he waited.

When Marian came in, she was wearing a blue woolen gown gathered at the neck, and she said at once, "What is it?" Her eyes were cautious. "Is something wrong?"

Leo Rochester turned to her. He had made up his mind what to say. "Marian, most of life is a rather crooked, twisted thing. I have no confidence or hope in most of mankind—or womankind, as you well know. You, however, are not like many women." A streak of honesty suddenly surfaced in Rochester's thoughts, and he turned his head to one side and said almost gently, "No, you're not like that, and though you haven't given me what I want most in the world, I've admired you. You're like my father. He had that streak of honesty in him. It was left out of me, though," he said almost regretfully. "Don't know why some people are honest and others can't seem to be."

"Leo, you can't really believe that. It's in our hands, what we do with our lives," Marian said gently, not wanting to anger him.

"No, that isn't true. We're like chess pieces on a board." He looked up, almost as if he expected to see a gigantic figure, and his fancy took him for a moment. "We're on a board and we're in a game—but we don't decide which square to move to. Some power does that for us. We may think we're in charge, but we're not. We're marionettes. I don't even know what that power is, but I know one thing"—he shrugged his shoulders and his lips grew tight—"whoever that great chess master is, he's a pretty cruel chap!"

"I can't believe that, Leo."

"All you have to do is look around and see the pain and agony and misery in the world. If he were any good—that chess player up there—he wouldn't let all that suffering happen. But I didn't come to talk about that."

Marian had seen Leo in these fits of fantasy before. Outside he was hard and there was a streak of cruelty in him—but deep down, on occasion, she had sensed what seemed to her a longing in her husband for something else. It was as if he wanted to see the good in the world, to participate in it, but would not allow himself to do so. Sadly she shook her head. "You have all the gifts, Leo. You could have been such a good man. You still could be."

"All right, maybe I will be," he said. For a moment he stood there silently, staring at her. His eyes half closed as he said, "When I get the one thing I want, I think I might be a better man."

"You're back to that again?" Marian said, shaking her head sadly. "You'll never do it, Leo."

"Oh, I think it might be arranged. As a matter of fact, I think I've about made the necessary arrangements. But to tell the truth, I'm wishing there might be another way." He hesitated, and his eyes seemed to bore into her as he said, "It's going to be a very painful ordeal for Bradford if it goes on as I've planned it."

"What are you going to do?" Fear leaped into Marian's voice. She could not control it, for she knew what a ruthless and merciless man Leo Rochester could be. She had not been married to him a month before that side of his debauched character had become obvious to her, though she had only suspected it before. And now, she stood there helpless and vulnerable, knowing that Daniel Bradford would never be safe as long as Leo held this mad plan—whatever it was—to ruin him.

"I see you know what I'm capable of, my dear," he said. "Well, that's good. I don't think I'll let you in on my little secret." Leo stood there and suddenly put his hands behind his back and locked them together. He moved back and forth, heel to toe, rocking slightly, saying finally, "I don't want to hurt Daniel if I can help it. I've hurt him in the past, I know that. This time it doesn't have to be that way. If he'd just give me this *one* thing. If he'd just listen to reason!" Then he unlocked his hands, slapped them together, and shook his head. "Tell him, Marian, that he's standing on the brink of a cliff. All I have to do is give him one touch— and he's over the edge. He'll be ruined if he doesn't give me what I want. All he has to do is give Matthew the word to come with me to England where he can make his own choice about his life. I'll even agree to this," he said slowly. "I'll put the matter to Matthew as we're traveling. If he wants to be my son legally, that's fine. If he doesn't, of course that's his choice."

"I can imagine the way you'd put that. It wouldn't be much of a choice at all," Marian said, feeling a panic starting to rise at the threat Leo had just spoken against Daniel. She knew Leo was unscrupulous and would go to any lengths to gain what he wanted.

"Perhaps not, but it's the best offer I can make. I'm serious about this, Marian. I'm holding a gun, and it's pointed at Daniel Bradford's head. I'm giving him one chance to escape. All he has to do is bend that precious little moral judgment of his one time. And we all have to do that, don't we? He's not a saint! Just *one* time I'd like to see him give in. If he doesn't," he whispered in a voice that was as cold as polar ice, "I'll ruin him, Marian!"

Without another word, he wheeled and left the room. At once Marian dressed and went to the foundry, where she found Daniel at work. Without preamble, she entered his office and, seeing that he was alone, said, "Leo just came to me." She paused before him, and he arose to stand before her. "I don't know what he has, but he says if you don't advise Matthew to go with him to England, he'll ruin you."

"He's already threatened to do that."

"No, this is different. It's not just an idle threat. I know him, Daniel. He's got something in his mind—some sort of leverage to use on you. I have no idea what it is, but he's clever about things like this. You know he is! He's done enough to you in the past. Look what he did to you and Lyna—deceived you both most of your lives. Daniel," she said, and her voice broke, "I think you must give in this time."

"Marian—"

"No, I don't want to hear what you have to say. I know your principles are as firm as any man's—but look at it this way—you're not really giving Matthew to him. Matthew's been with you for years. He knows you. He knows what's good. He'll see through Leo. Trust him, Daniel!"

"He might not. Then I'd lose him," Daniel objected.

Marian came closer and reached out, almost involuntarily, and put her hand on his chest. It remained there with an insistent pressure, as if she would force him to see things her way. "*Trust* Matthew. He's got good blood. I know he's Leo's son, but you've had him for nineteen years. He's taken that in, and Holly was a good woman. His mother's blood is in him, too. You told me what a gentle woman she was." Her voice grew more insistent, and she stood there for a while urging him, pleading with him.

Slowly Daniel reached up, took her hand, holding it gently for a moment. It was very small, and he held it as if it were a tiny captive bird, so fragile he might hurt it. He looked up and said, "I'd do almost anything for you, Marian. But I can't send Matthew off with Leo. If I did, and he were corrupted, I'd never forgive myself."

Marian knew she had lost. She had little hope of persuading him to give in to a man like Leo, and now she said quietly, "Then we'll have to pray that whatever scheme he has for you will fail."

The two stood there, frozen for a moment in time, very conscious of the touch of their hands together. Then she removed her hand, turned, and walked slowly from the office.

𝕋 　　　𝕋 　　　𝕋

"Well, this hasn't been a happy assignment for us," Leslie Gordon said slowly, "but we knew a change would come." He had come to stand beside Lyna, who was looking out the window. Clive, Grace, and David were there also. Leslie had called them into the room to inform them that there would be a change in their lives. He saw that they were waiting for him to say more, and he shrugged his shoulders. "General Howe knows we have to leave. With those guns up on Dorchester Heights, we don't have any other choice."

David piped up at once, "When will we be leaving, Father?"

"I can't say that, but right away. That's why I've called you here. Get your things ready, because when the marching order comes, it may come very fast."

"How will we leave?" Grace asked.

"It will have to be by ship, of course. We still control the seas. If it weren't for that," Leslie Gordon said grimly, "we'd wind up in a prison, I suppose."

Clive shifted uneasily in his chair. "What about Jeanne? She'll have to go with us."

Lyna refrained from meeting Leslie's eyes as he glanced at her. They'd already spoken of this. Now she said gently, "I'm not sure that she'll choose to go."

"Why, she'll have to go," Clive rapped out sharply. "She can't stay here! What would she do?"

Grace put her hand on her brother's arm. She, too, had thought of Jeanne's situation and had talked to her more than anyone else. "She feels out of place with us, I think, Clive. I wouldn't be surprised if she tried to go back to her old homeplace."

"She can't go there!" Clive protested. "That's no life for a woman! It's not safe."

"Probably not," Grace shrugged, "but she's been very unhappy here in Boston."

"It looks to me," David said, "like she's spent more time with the Bradfords than she has with us. I'll bet she goes to live with them." He nodded and his lips were tight together. "The rebels will rule the roost now that we're being forced to leave."

Clive cut his eyes around and glared at David, although his brother had said nothing that he had not thought himself. "Well, I'm not going to let her do it!" Clive stood up and turned to leave the room.

"You can't force her to go with us, Clive," Lyna called out. But he ignored her, and they heard the door slam. Turning to Leslie, Lyna shook her head. "He's headstrong."

"I can't imagine where he gets that from," Leslie said, trying to make light of the moment. But then he, too, sobered and said, "He'll just have to learn to live with it. Of course, he could stay here, but it would be unpleasant for him. The patriots are going to make it pretty hard on anyone connected with the British army. I expect there'll be a wholesale exodus of Tories that'll be on the ship with us. In any case," he said, "we'll be leaving shortly, and Clive will have to make his own decision."

Clive took the buggy without asking permission and made his way toward the Bradfords' house, aware that there was a tension in the streets. The soldiers, who had been loud and raucous and hard on the citizens, were saying little now. They gathered together in small groups with a furtive look about them. They had the appearance of beaten men.

The horse's hooves sent the mud flying, for the weather had warmed, turning the streets into quagmire. Even now there was a hint that it might rain, for the air was thick and muggy and humid. Although it was still afternoon, three hours before sunset, the dark roiling clouds lay over the city like a thick blanket blotting out the sun so that there was a strange murky sensation, almost like being under water.

When Clive reached the Bradford house, he jumped out, ignoring the mud, tied the horse to an iron hitching post, and then walked up to the front door. When he sounded the brass knocker, he waited impatiently. The door opened and Mrs. Lettie White stood there.

"Hello, Mrs. White. I need to see Jeanne at once."

"Why, she's in the parlor—"

"Thank you. I can find the way." Ignoring Mrs. White's look of astonishment and resentment, Clive strolled right by her. For some reason he had conceived the idea that the regiment might pull out that very day, and he did not want to leave Jeanne behind.

He turned into the parlor and stopped abruptly, for Jeanne and Dake were sitting on the horsehide settee looking down at a book. They were sitting very close together, and Dake's arm was around the back of the settee, his hand on her shoulder. When Jeanne looked up and saw him, Clive could not identify the expression that came into her eye, but certainly it was partially embarrassment.

Leaping to her feet she said, "Why, Clive—I didn't expect you."

Clive said tersely, "Obviously not." He looked at Dake and said, "I'd like to speak to Jeanne alone, if you don't mind."

Dake shrugged his shoulders. "That's up to her." There was a challenge in his voice. His hazel eyes were half hooded, as if he would welcome trouble.

Jeanne saw that the two were facing each other almost like strange dogs that she had seen in the street, circling and looking for an opening. "What is it, Clive?" she asked quickly.

"I've come to take you home," Clive said, biting the words off. He would not have been so rough if he had not seen the pair together. It was not that he distrusted Jeanne, but he felt that Dake was misusing her. Clive faced Dake squarely, saying, "That's all she needs, to get caught here with a spy! I thought you were up in the hills."

"I came for a visit," Dake said easily. "What's this about taking Jeanne home? Are you running for cover with the rest of the lobster-backs?"

The truth of Dake's words hit home, and the grin on his face infuriated Clive Gordon. He was filled with a sense of humiliation that the British army could be beaten by a rabble in arms. Even now, he could not accept it. He felt shame for his father and the profession that he loved—still there was no answer for it. He gritted his teeth and said,

"Yes, I suppose you figured that out. We'll be leaving—" He turned to Jeanne and said, "And you'll have to come with us, Jeanne. You can't stay here."

"She can stay anywhere she wants to. This is her home as long as she wants it," Dake said.

"Bradford, I'd appreciate it if you'd either leave the room or keep your mouth shut!"

Instantly, Dake's jaw hardened and the smile left his face. "I don't care for your manners, Gordon."

"Oh, you don't?"

"No, and furthermore, I'll have to ask you to leave the house. Jeanne is a grown woman; she can make up her own mind."

Jeanne was caught as between two strong gusts of wind that pushed and pulled at her. She could see Dake's muscles tensing as he rose, and he seemed dangerous as he stood there. "Clive," she said quickly, "I'll come to your home later and we'll talk about it."

"No, I'm taking you now," he said, and made the mistake of reaching forward and taking her arm. This rash action was an indication of how flustered and frustrated he was. It was an act he would never have committed under ordinary circumstances. But the pressure of time was on him, and he could not bear the thought of leaving Jeanne here in this city while he sailed away.

Dake reached out and slapped Gordon's arm away. "Keep your hands off her! She's not a child to be hauled around—!"

Gordon was not a fighting man. He'd had his schoolboy fights, but that had been years ago when they had been merely scuffles, but anger now coursed through him and suddenly exploded. He struck Dake in the face, his fist catching on the cheekbone.

Dake had been a fighter all his life, and his skills had been sharpened on hard, tough young men. There was an instinct in him that he could not explain—or control. It was like a match being touched to powder when someone challenged him. Now, the sting of Gordon's blow did not hurt him, since he had been struck harder many times. But somehow it touched off this innate fury that lay somewhere deep inside him. Without thought he planted his feet. His right arm shot out in a powerful blow, his fist exploding against the chin of Clive Gordon. The blow drove Gordon back and he struck the floor limply, not trying to save himself, almost unconscious.

"Clive—!" Jeanne had seen fights in her own time, and she fell down on her knees and touched Clive's head. She turned back and said, "You shouldn't have done that, Dake!"

Dake knew she was right, which made matters worse. "He doesn't have any business coming in here telling you what to do and man-handling you!"

"He wasn't manhandling me." Jeanne had been angry at Clive at first, but now seeing him lie helplessly on the floor with a line of blood trickling down his cheek, she transferred that anger to Dake. "Get out of here, Dake!" she snapped.

Dake stared at her and an apology leaped to his lips, but he had never been one to apologize. Without a word, his lips drew tight and a flush touched his cheeks. He stalked out of the room, slamming the front door behind him.

Jeanne leaped up, got some cool water on a cloth, and bathed Clive's face. His eyes fluttered open finally, and he looked up into Jeanne's eyes and said, "What—?"

"Are you all right?" Jeanne asked.

Clive started to get up and, feeling rather foolish, said, "Where is he?"

"He's gone. Don't think about it. I'm sorry it all happened," Jeanne said. "You two shouldn't fight. I mean, after all, you're cousins."

Clive was not thinking about claiming familial relationships at the moment. He felt like a small boy who had been slapped. The ease with which Dake Bradford had conquered him was bitter in his spirit. "I suppose I shouldn't have come barging in here. I apologize." He thought then of how the two had been sitting so close and could not keep the jealousy out of his voice. "If you'd rather stay here with Dake, I suppose that's your decision."

"Don't be foolish, Clive," Jeanne said quickly. "Things are happening so fast, and I realize you're disturbed. Wait a minute and I'll get my coat. I'll go home with you and we'll talk." She got her coat and the two left.

Dake, who had not gone far, saw her get in the carriage, followed by Gordon. As it drove off, he stared through the murky gloom, which was somehow very much like his own mood. He turned and began to walk blindly. The anger that had fluttered in him was gone now, and he realized he had made a fool of himself.

"There wasn't any need of putting Clive down," he said aloud. "Men ought to be able to talk without using their fists!" But, as always when such things are done, they leave a bitter taste, and for hours Dake stayed outside near the house, thinking how he would have to find Gordon and apologize. "I'd rather take a beating," he said, "but it's got to be done."

In the end, Dake could not bring himself to hunt Gordon up and apologize. "I'll just go up to the hills and report to the colonel," he told

Rachel when he came back in later. "I'll be back soon."

"You can't go out! The patrols are out, it's not safe!" Rachel argued.

Dake said rashly, "They'd better not catch me, then." He was carrying in his breast pocket the notes that he had made for Knox, although they seemed rather futile now. The city was going to be captured without them. "All my work for nothing," he said grimly, but he stuck the notes in his pocket and left the house, saddled his horse, and left the stable. It was a dark night and gloomy with no stars. He had not gone more than fifty feet when suddenly dim forms moved ahead of him.

"Hold it right there!"

Dake knew it was the patrol. He also was suddenly aware of the incriminating papers in his pocket. Quickly he turned his horse and gave him the spurs. But, almost instantly, a shot rang out and he felt the animal falter, then go down. He cartwheeled, falling full length, the breath knocked out of him. He struggled to his feet, but instantly iron hands clamped on him and a tall form loomed over him. "Hold on to him! Put the irons on him, Corporal."

Dake felt cold irons clamp on his hands, and then rough hands searched him. A lantern was produced and the sergeant, a tall man with a brutal face, scanned the papers. He looked at Dake, a smile breaking forth on his thick lips. "You're a spy," he said with pleasure. He winked at the other members of the squad who stood surrounding Dake, holding their muskets. "Well, we'll have a nice hanging for this one! Take him now and don't let him get away. Ain't nothing we need more than to see one of these rebels turning purple in the face and doing his dance at the end of a rope."

Dake struggled and tried to break away. The sergeant simply lifted his musket and rapped him alongside the head. The world seemed to turn into a brilliant display of stars, and pain ran along his head. He felt himself fall and rudely was plucked up.

"Ain't nothing like a good hangin' to put heart in a soldier, I always say. With a slimy rat like this 'un, it'll be twice as much fun," the sergeant proclaimed. "Off now, we'll take him to the general. . . !"

22

DANIEL'S CHOICE

GENERAL HOWE, LEFT WITH LITTLE CHOICE, began at once to prepare for the evacuation of the city. The Boston Tories, those who had lived well during the occupation of the British, were now aware that the deluge awaited them. When the patriots came swarming back to reclaim their city, they knew that not even their lives would be safe—certainly not their property!

Howe's headquarters was flooded with the most illustrious names of Massachusetts—Olivers, Saltonstalls, Mathers, Hutchinsons. They had already begun gathering what few valuables they could carry to leave their homes—many convinced they would never see them again. Among them, strangely enough, were Henry Knox's in-laws, the Fluckers.

None among these was more frightened than Abigail Howland. Her parents had been staunch Tories, and though her father was very ill and too sick to leave, she knew what to expect. In truth Abigail had only recently gotten engaged to Nathan Winslow so he could protect her during this time, as he was a patriot. She had accompanied Paul Winslow on a walk through the city, and the scurrying Tories disturbed her greatly. They entered an inn and saw Sir Leo Rochester and Matthew sitting at a table. Rochester saw them and motioned them over. "Have a seat, Winslow," he said, and when they were seated, he grinned sardonically. "It looks as though our sort have come up a little short."

"Oh yes," Winslow said coolly. "I expect to be tarred and feathered properly." He winked at Matthew Bradford, saying, "Will you put in a word for us with your governor, Bradford, just before the ax falls?"

Matthew flushed. He was not at all comfortable with the situation. "I'm sure that it won't be too bad," he said.

"Are you? I don't know why you'd think that," Paul said. He waited until the waiter had brought more wine for them and then drank down a glass, almost without stopping. His face was flushed, for he had already been drinking heavily. "We've put the poor devils in jail, broken their homes up, made life as miserable as we can.

"It can't be that bad," Abigail said. She had always been able to smile her way out of any situation, and where men were concerned, she could usually get what she wanted. Now, however, she felt helpless and suddenly fixed her eyes on Matthew Bradford. "Your family are patriots, Mr. Bradford? You won't be in any trouble?"

"Of course not."

Leo said abruptly, "Well, he might be in some. After all, he's been consorting with Tories like myself and you two. That'll be enough, perhaps, to get him tarred and feathered, as Paul suggests."

"Oh, I hardly think so," Matthew protested.

"You don't know mobs, Matthew," Leo shrugged. "When they get out of control, they're mindless. Anything that gets in their way, they strike at it." He glanced at the two and said, "I've been trying to get this young man to come with me to England. I want to make a wealthy young painter out of him, known all over the world. Perhaps even give him the Rochester name. I have no sons, you know. But, if I ever saw one I'd like to own, it's this young man, here."

Matthew glanced quickly at Leo. It was the closest to a public announcement he had ever made. He swallowed hard as Leo continued in a practical voice.

"How does Sir Matthew *Rochester* sound, Winslow?"

Winslow grinned sardonically. "Are you sure you wouldn't like to make that Sir *Paul* Rochester? I'd be glad enough to find a rich benefactor who wants to give me everything I want." He looked suddenly at Abigail and saw that she was staring at Matthew. "Well, there you are, Abigail! If all else fails with Nathan, you can always charm Sir Matthew Rochester. Then you'd be Lady Rochester, and none of these riffraff could touch you."

"Oh, don't be foolish, Paul," Abigail protested, but she eyed Matthew with a covert interest.

They had their meal together, talking about the problems that were about to fall on Boston. Leo was not displeased at the crisis. After Winslow and Abigail Howland left the table, he grinned. "That's a toothsome wench. Did you get to know her while you were painting her portrait?"

"Oh, it was just a job."

Leo grinned, saying, "Well, you'll have beautiful women like that swarming to you when you take your rightful station in life. You can take your pick then."

※　　　※　　　※

As soon as Lyna looked up and saw Leslie's face, she knew something dreadful had happened. His lips were drawn tight together and he seemed to be gritting his teeth. "What is it?" she asked at once.

"It's Dake! He's been captured." Shaking his head, he added grimly, "The charge is that he's a spy. You know what happens to spies."

"No! That can't happen," Lyna whispered. "Does Daniel know?"

"I don't think so. I was at headquarters when he was brought in. The sergeant said they arrested him as he was coming out of Daniel's house. He had incriminating papers on him." Leslie slammed his fist into his hand. "Blast! Why did this have to happen now? Why didn't the young lad stay up in the hills? It's all over now. There was nothing to gain by carrying such messages."

"We've got to do something!" Lyna cried.

"I'll talk to General Howe—but he's not in a good mood. I've already tried once, but I'll try again." He looked at her and saw that her face was white. "You've got to go to Daniel. Tell him about Dake—or would you rather I go?"

"No, I'll do it myself." She looked so fragile for a moment that he came to her and put his arms around her. He held her and they clung to each other. "The world's falling down. Most of all for Daniel. I must go."

Leslie drove her to the Bradford house and said, "You want me to come in?"

"No, Daniel may want me to stay for a while."

"I'm going back to headquarters," he said. "Where will you be? Here, or will you come back home?"

"I don't know, dear," she said. "You go on and *try* to talk to the general again. I mean, after all, the battle's over."

"Not to him, it's not! It'll be in every newspaper in England—how he lost the Battle of Boston. He'll be looking for a sacrifice."

Lyna kissed him, got down from the carriage, and went immediately to the house. It was Daniel himself who opened the door to her knock.

"Why, Lyna, I didn't expect you. Come in."

Lyna knew from his greeting that he had not heard the terrible news. "Daniel," she said, "you haven't heard about Dake?"

At once a cold chill ran through Daniel. He knew at once without being told. "He's been captured?"

"Yes, and held by the authorities. They say he was carrying incriminating papers."

Daniel groaned and clenched his teeth together. He closed his eyes and seemed to sway. Then he pulled himself together. "I'll have to go and see what I can do."

"Leslie says General Howe's furious at losing Boston, that he's looking for a sacrifice. He says he'll not listen to reason."

"We'll have to tell the family. I want you with me."

Lyna waited until Daniel had called all the family together, then he stood looking around them, saying grimly, "Dake's been arrested."

"Arrested? For spying?" Micah said, a grim look on his face.

"Yes."

Samuel swallowed hard. "What'll they do to him, Pa?"

"You know what they do to spies, Sam."

"No! They can't do that! Not to Dake! We'll have to get him out!"

"He'll be well guarded," Daniel said slowly. He had been shocked, almost as if he had been thrown into icy waters. His mind seemed to have stopped working, but now he had begun thinking. *This is what Marian was trying to warn me about*, he thought grimly. *Somehow Leo is at the bottom of this.* Aloud, he said, "I want you to stay here. I'll go see what can be done." He ignored their protests and shook them off. "There's nothing you can do." He turned to Lyna and said, "Stay with them, Lyna, please. I'll try not to be gone too long."

He left, and just as the door slammed, Jeanne came down the stairs. She had heard the talk but had not been able to distinguish the words. At once, she felt the tension in the room. "What's wrong?" she asked.

"It's . . . Dake," Rachel said with difficulty. Her face was pale, and she had to swallow before she could speak. "He . . . he's been arrested for spying."

"And they're gonna hang him if we don't do something!" Sam broke out.

Instantly, two thoughts came to Jeanne. The first was, *I can't bear it if they hang Dake!* And the second was, *It must have been Clive who told them! He was the only one of the British who knew he was here. . . .*

She stood there struggling, and the confusion was plain on her face. Rachel went over and said, "We'll all have to pray now, Jeanne. That's all we can do."

Jeanne said, "How much . . . how much time is there?"

"Daniel's gone to find out what can be done. It may not be as bad as we think," Lyna said. "Leslie's trying to talk to the general. Howe's always liked Leslie. We'll just pray that he'll listen this time."

They all looked at one another helplessly, and finally Rachel said, "I'll make us some tea." It was a gesture of something to do. None of them were hungry or thirsty, and as the time dragged on, it seemed that more and more the situation was totally hopeless.

✠   ✠   ✠

Still filled with anger about Dake and Jeanne being together, Clive found himself unable to do more than roam the streets. He went to a tavern and sat for hours drinking ale, but it did not seem to affect him. Finally, he went by the hospital to visit a patient—one of the British soldiers who had struggled with a bad wound taken at Bunker Hill. He did not seem better, and Clive comforted him by saying, "We'll be out of Boston soon. Wherever we go, they'll have better facilities than here."

"Where will that be, Doctor?"

"I don't know. New York or perhaps even Halifax, but it'll be better than here."

"I wish they'd take me back to England," the soldier said, a pitiful look on his face. "If I've got to die, I'd rather do it there. Not here!"

Clive stayed with the man for a considerable time and finally, instead of going home, stretched out on one of the empty cots. He awakened with a splitting headache. Checking with the patient, Clive saw that he was asleep. He straightened up and stretched, then made his way out of the hospital. The streets, he saw, were crowded with soldiers, some of them going around with their rifles, breaking in the windows of businesses and doing what damage they could before they fled the city.

He went to his home and was met at the door, surprisingly enough, by Jeanne. "Why, Jeanne—" he said.

"I have to talk to you." Her lips were white and her eyes glinted angrily. She walked outside, shut the door, and said, "Come this way. I don't want anyone to know what you've done."

As he followed her, his mind went at once to the scene that had taken place at the Bradfords' house the night before. "Well, I know I was wrong," he said. "I shouldn't have come and treated you as I did. But I—"

"I'm not talking about that!" She turned to face him and there was defiance in her look. She kept her body still and straight, and an underlying strain of fury edged her voice as she cried, "Why did you do it, Clive?"

"Why did I do what?" asked Clive, looking at her puzzled.

Jeanne stared at him, and for a moment doubt took her. "Don't pretend. You're the only one that knew Dake was at home."

Clive shook his head to clear it. "Dake? What about Dake being home? What's happened?"

"He's been arrested and they're going to hang him." Her voice broke on the last syllable, and to her dismay, Jeanne felt her eyes begin to moisten. She batted them furiously and then said, "You were the only one who knew he was there—and you were angry with him. You told the authorities, didn't you, Clive?"

Clive stared at her in astonishment. He could not believe what he was hearing. "Why, Jeanne, I can't see how you could even think that!" He shook his head. "I didn't tell anybody. I've been walking the streets, then I went to the hospital and sat up with a wounded soldier till early this morning. I've just come from there. I didn't even know until you told me."

Jeanne said, "Are you telling the truth?" There was hopefulness in her voice, for she did not want to believe that this man who had been so kind and with whom she had shared so many experiences would be guilty of such a vile betrayal. She studied his face, which was drawn and almost frozen now with intensity. He was rather a pompous man at times with strict ideas of the way things should be that she did not agree with, but she had always thought him one of the best men she had ever met. Now, with this hanging over her, she wanted desperately to believe in his innocence.

Clive saw some of this in Jeanne's blue-violet eyes as they looked up at him. He put his hands up awkwardly and grasped her shoulders. "I swear to you, Jeanne, I was angry with Dake, but that's all. I thought you would be hurt if you stayed here. I just wanted what was best for you. But I swear, on the Bible if you wish, I didn't know a thing about this—" He swallowed and said, "I'm sorry for it. Dake's a good man."

Jeanne felt relief rush through her. She had been so tense and frightened over Dake's predicament, and now her anger with Clive had almost brought her down emotionally. Now she whispered, "I believe you, Clive, and I'm glad!"

"Come, let's go in the house," he said. "Tell me about it." They went into the house and he listened carefully. When she was done, he said, "My father—he'll do something."

"No, he's already tried. General Howe says he's going to hang Dake."

"They can't do it!" he answered. But he remembered the mood that the whole army was in—he had seen them smashing in doors and windows and tearing off siding from houses, even on his way here. He knew that all they needed was an excuse—and now they had it.

The two sat in the room for a long time, and finally Jeanne said timidly, "I'm sorry about what happened. With Dake, I mean. There was nothing, really. We were just looking at a book."

"I know," Clive said. He wanted to hold her but felt that would be taking advantage. "I was going to tell Dake I was sorry. I will anyhow."

"They can't hang him! They can't!" Jeanne said, holding her face stiff.

Clive did not answer. He *had* no answer, for he knew very well that they *could* hang Dake Bradford.

🔔   🔔   🔔

"I don't know why you came to me, Bradford," Leo Rochester said.

Daniel had come to his room downtown, and as soon as he'd stepped in had said, "I know what you've done, Leo, about Dake."

"I'm not the one who's arrested him."

"Don't lie to me, Leo," Daniel said. "This is what you've been threatening me with. I knew you were low, but I never thought you'd be low enough to kill an innocent man to get what you want."

Leo could not meet Bradford's eyes. He realized suddenly he never had been able to meet Daniel's eyes. There was an honesty in the big man that somehow caused him to feel strangely inferior—something he had never felt with another man. He had intended to gloat over the situation, but now he said, "Look, Daniel, it's a bad situation, but something can be done, I'm sure."

Daniel stared at him and said in a flat voice, "They're going to hang him for spying. That's what you've done, Leo."

"Wait a minute!" Leo protested. "These things are hard, but as I said, it's not impossible that something might be done. I'm on very good terms with some of the officers, even with General Howe. I'm not even certain he knows that Dake has been captured. He's a busy man these days."

"He knows—and he's already said Dake will be tried and found guilty and hanged."

"Well, that's what he has to say publicly, but of course, there are—well, things that can be done privately."

"You mean, you'd bribe General Howe?"

Daniel's words were hard and hit Leo Rochester like a shock. Once again he felt that same sense of frustration and even inferiority that he'd always felt in dealing with this man. "Well, would you rather your son die, or are you willing to give up that fool stubbornness of yours? I tell you, I can get Dake off with a prison sentence. It may be rough, but he won't be dead."

Daniel could not contain himself. Without willing it, his hand moved forward and he slapped Leo in the face. He had done so once before, and Leo had never forgiven him. Now, as Leo staggered back, Bradford's eyes were cold. "You're worse than any man I've ever known."

Touching the imprint of Daniel's hand on his cheek, Leo whispered, "I told you once, if you ever laid a hand on me, I'd kill you. You don't learn very quickly, do you?"

Daniel turned to go but Leo said, "Wait a minute." He moved forward and placed himself between Daniel and the door. "Don't be a fool, Bradford. Think what it is you're throwing away."

"I have thought. You'd corrupt my son."

"You can't know that."

"I know you. You corrupt everything you touch."

"I won't argue with you—but listen, Daniel. Let's try to stop and think for a moment." Leo deliberately forced himself to speak rationally. "All I want—all I've ever wanted—was the chance to let Matthew make his own choice. I have to have some time with him to show him my side of it. You've had him for all his life. All I want is just a little time. By then I may find he's not what I want—or he may find he doesn't want me. He knows what kind of a man I am."

"I don't think he knows that you've put Dake's head in a hangman's noose."

Leo refused to be sidetracked. "You've got to listen! I know you love your sons. I have only one chance. Believe it or not, I want to do better. I want Matthew to be a better man than I am. You remember my father?"

"A little."

"He was a better man than I am, a good man, in fact. A little harsh sometimes, but basically a good man. You remember how he tried to stand between me and your sister?"

"Yes, I do remember that."

The words were so cold that Leo regretted mentioning it. "All right!" He threw up his hands. "I was wrong. I can't spend the rest of my life repenting and apologizing every time I see you! The question is, do you want Dake to live? If it comes to it, would you rather give up that stubborn foolish pride of yours and keep your son, or do you want to see Dake hanging? It's that simple."

Bradford could not face Leo anymore. He turned and walked out, leaving the door open.

"He'll be back . . . he'll be back!" Leo whispered, gritting his teeth. "No man could stand seeing his son die when he has it in his power to get him free!"

☕   ☕   ☕

Dake stood up as his father entered the room. "Hello, Pa," he said evenly, and as his father's big arms clamped around him, Dake felt his resolution shaken. The two stood together, and Dake put his arms around his father and held him tightly. They seemed to find some sort of strength in each other. Then Dake stepped back, saying huskily, "Well, I always manage to find some kind of a way to make a fool of myself. Sit down, Pa. Make yourself comfortable."

There was little comfort indeed in the cell where Dake had been put inside the prison. There were no windows, a single cot, a bucket of water on a rough table, and a bucket for sanitation. A single candle burned, set in a sconce in the brick wall.

"Tell me about it, Dake."

"Not anything to tell. I was a fool, that's all. If I hadn't had those papers they might have roughed me up, but I wouldn't be facing a hanging."

"That won't happen," Daniel said quickly.

Dake had been thinking hard. He had been alone in the semidarkness, and now he said simply, "Yes, they can. You know they can, Pa. Who's to stop them?"

Daniel sat down and Dake sat beside him on the cot. Far off in another part of the prison they heard someone yelling and banging against a set of bars. The sound stopped suddenly, as if the perpetrator had been struck down by an angry guard. There was the smell of old, rotten straw in the air, and the candle needed snuffing, so Dake reached up and pinched off the wick with his fingers. "They have me this time, sir," he said. His voice was even, and when he looked at his father, he said quietly, "I have to tell you this, Pa—I'm pretty scared."

"Every man's afraid when he faces a time like this. I was pretty scared at Lexington on the way back from Concord. I was pretty scared at Bunker Hill, too, with men dying all around me."

"That's different, Pa! When the bullets are flying and you're loading, you don't have time to think. Now, I've been sitting here in this cell, and I know there's nothing I can do. I know they're going to come and get me tomorrow or right away and take me out and hang me as they've hanged others." He bit his lip nervously, then nodded, "I'll try to do as good as they did, Pa. I wouldn't want you to be ashamed of me."

Daniel Bradford had been in some dangerous positions in his life. He had faced battle more than once, convinced that he could not live through it. This, however, was much worse! Even as Dake had said, in battle a man can forget things—but when you're locked in a quiet cell with no one to talk to, every silence reverberates with some sort of fear that soaks into a man. His heart went out to Dake, and he said quietly, "I'd never be ashamed of you, Dake. You've been the best son a man could have."

"No, that's not so, Pa."

"To me you are."

"No, I've been a burden to you. Always been a streak in me that gave you a lot of grief."

"Let's don't talk about that."

"Yes, I've got to!" Dake did not say that there would be no more time for such talks, but it edged in at his mind and nibbled at him. The gnawing fear—he kept back only by tremendous strength of will. He knew that if he gave up, he would wind up crying and screaming and battering on the door. Now he forced himself to be calm. "I've always wondered what it would be like to come to the end of everything. Now I guess I know."

"We serve a big God. With Him all things are possible."

Dake looked at his father silently. He let the quiet run on for a time and said in a subdued voice, "I haven't ever let God do anything in my life, Pa. I know that's been a big grief to you."

"It has, son, but it's not too late."

"Why, Pa, I can't come groveling to God now! It wouldn't be the right thing to do."

"Why wouldn't it be?" Daniel said calmly.

"Why, it just wouldn't! Here I've lived my whole life to please myself. Now that I'm about to lose it, what kind of a man would I be to go whining and begging God to forgive me?"

"I think you'd be a wise man to do that, son. We all go 'whining and begging' to God. It's the only way we can go. I went that way myself."

"Oh, Pa, it was different."

"No it wasn't. Dake, I think every man has a time. There's a verse I've always liked. It's found in Titus, second chapter—I forget which verse but it says, 'For the grace of God which bringeth salvation hath appeared to all men.' I always liked that verse, Dake. You know, I always used to worry about what happened to people who lived in dark lands where there was no gospel, but this verse says that somehow the grace of God has appeared to them. I don't understand that. I used to think a man had to have the whole Bible and a preacher or evangelist—but somehow God's grace appears to all men. And I think it comes at the best time for them."

"What do you mean, the best time?"

"I mean, sometimes we're ready to listen, and sometimes we're not. It's always that way. It was with me. If God had come to me at an earlier point, I might have turned Him down and been lost. I heard the gospel many times before I was saved, but God didn't really speak to me until I was ready to hear."

289

"What do you mean, ready to hear?"

"Dake, I don't know exactly how to explain it." Daniel was praying silently for just exactly the right words. He had tried to talk like this before to his son, but Dake had merely put him off, saying he would think of it later. "I mean that there's a *readiness* in men. I've seen it, for example, in children. You try your best to teach one to read. He works and you make him work and study, but it just doesn't take. He's just not ready. Then, one day, he *is* ready, and everything you had to beat into him, it's suddenly easy for him."

"That's Micah and me. He learned way before I did."

"That's right, you just weren't ready, but when you were ready, it came easy for you. That's the way it is, I think, with a great many things. We're just not always ready for God's wisdom. He has to wait until we are. I think sometimes the most important part of being a Christian is learning to listen to the voice of the Lord. Not doing what we please, but just waiting, just listening, being ready. I had a friend that used to always say to be a Christian you had to be always available and instantly obedient. Always ready to hear God—then always ready to do what He says when He speaks."

"Pa, I've heard a thousand sermons. Why, I've even called on God more than you know. When I was in trouble, most of the time."

"I think all of us do that, but let me tell you what it means, I think, to really come to know God." Daniel began to quote Scripture. He did not have his Bible with him, but all through the Bible he moved. He spoke of the fourteenth verse of the second chapter of Titus. "It says, 'Jesus Christ who gave himself for us that he might redeem us from all iniquity and purify unto himself a peculiar people, zealous of good works.' That's what Jesus does. He came and gave himself, and *He* has to do the work."

"You've always been strong on teachings about the shedding of blood for the forgiveness of sins, Pa. I never understood that much. Somehow, even now, it gives me a kind of a thrill to hear it, the blood of Jesus. You always said it so well, so strongly. But, I've never understood how that blood shed way back in those days could help a man living today."

"That's because we're living in time. We were born at a certain time; we live a few years and then we die. But God isn't like that. He was never born. He'll never die. Today to Him has always been there. It's hard, Dake, but you see, when Jesus died, for us it was a particular time in history. But for God, it just *was*. He's the great I AM. That's His name. So, the Scripture says that Jesus—in God's sight—died before the foundation of the world. God now has seen the blood. Do you remember in the book of Genesis about the Exodus?"

"Sure, I remember that, Pa. I've heard you read about it enough."

"You remember they took a lamb and they killed it and they splashed the blood on the doors of their houses. That night, you remember what happened?"

"Sure, the angel of death came."

"That's right. And it says, 'When he saw the blood, he passed over the house.' So, one day, Dake, you're going to die, maybe tomorrow, maybe fifty years from now. So am I. But, whether it's today or then, when we get before God, He'll be looking for one thing—the blood of Jesus."

On and on the two talked. The guards did not interrupt, except that one came after an hour and stuck his head in, studied the two silently, then shrugged and closed the door.

Finally, Daniel fell silent. He sat there thinking about this son, so precious in his sight, and said, "The Bible says whosoever will may come. That's the only question, Dake. Will you do it? Whosoever will. God's not going to force you. I hope I've shown you that it's not your good works that are going to save you. Maybe God put you in this tight spot just to get you ready. Are you ready, Dake? Will you let God come into your life?"

As all men and women do, there was a moment when Dake Bradford seemed to teeter—like a man caught in a high wind, blown first one way, then the other. Something in him was tremendously drawn. He had felt his heart grow frightened as he thought of an endless hell where he might spend eternity. But, as his father had read about heaven, about Jesus, about this same Jesus coming back again, somehow coupled to that fear was a longing. He'd felt it before, he remembered now, more than once when he'd heard the gospel preached, but he had always quickly snuffed it as a man would snuff a candle.

Now, however, in the darkness of the dank cell he felt this desire for something more grow within him. Something was telling him it was all foolishness, that he could not change. But his father kept quoting Scripture, saying, "It's Jesus who's made the way. Let Him come into your life."

Finally, Dake Bradford bowed his head and nodded, "I reckon you may be right, Pa. I never was willing to listen before. Now, if you'll tell me what to do, I want to get right with God—whether I die tomorrow or not."

Tears swam in Daniel Bradford's eyes. He put his arm around his son's broad shoulders and whispered huskily, "It's not hard to get home to God. You remember the Prodigal Son?"

"Yes, I remember."

"You remember, he was ashamed of the way he'd behaved just like you are—just like I was—he said, 'I'll just be a servant in my father's house.' But when he got close to the house, you remember what happened?"

Dake's voice was choked and he said, "The father—he came to meet him."

"He did and he put his arm around him and kissed him and said, 'Kill the fatted calf for this is my son that was lost,' and there was rejoicing in all his house. You're coming home, Dake, and God's coming to meet you!"

Dake Bradford bowed his head and the two began to pray. The candle flickered, casting its amber shades over the two men. The walls had never heard words such as were spoken, nor had they heard the cries of joy that came from Daniel Bradford when he said, "This, my son, is home at last!"

23

A Piece of Paper

THE SENSE OF FEAR THAT HAD COME to cover Boston like a miasma was almost palpable. Clive Gordon had felt it as he had walked the streets and tried to think of some way to help Dake Bradford. Somehow, in a totally illogical manner, he had come to feel that he was responsible for Dake's plight. It made no sense, yet still he could not put away the thought that he was implicated in the young man's capture.

He had been told by his father that General Howe would not relent, that Dake would be hanged without a trial. It was the usual fate of spies when the evidence was clear. But the very thought of seeing his cousin hanged nauseated Clive.

As he walked down a half-deserted street late on Thursday afternoon, he began to do something that almost shocked him. He was not a praying man, Clive Gordon. His religion had been more perfunctory than he cared to admit, and more than his parents would have liked. The times he had spent with Jeanne and Pierre and later with Ma Tante, those had been the times of reality for him, at least in his spirit. They had brought before him the concept of a God who was not far away, but close—so near, in fact, that he had clearly seen God in the faces of the two older people as they faced death, and he had sensed it in Jeanne. A vague longing had been with him ever since these encounters. Now, as he strolled along, he was struck with a desire to know God in that same way. He began trying to pray—and found that it was almost hopeless. His thoughts wandered. No matter how much he tried to pray for himself, he could only think of that moment that would soon come when Dake Bradford would be strangled terribly, grotesquely, at the end of a piece of rope.

"God, I've got to do something—help me to get Dake out of that prison. . . !"

The prayer sprang to his lips spontaneously—not something that he

293

had planned. He had always held those who asked for specific things in a slight contempt. His sister, Grace, had told him once, "Prayer is like taking a wagon to the door of the warehouse and telling someone to fill it up." Her gray-green eyes had almost laughed at him when she had seen his expression. "We need things from God, Clive. How else are we going to get them if we don't ask for them?"

Grace's voice seemed to echo in Clive's ear as he moved slowly along the streets, already beginning to darken in the late afternoon. Clive, however, was thinking about the prayer. *Why did I pray like that*, he thought. *If people could get anything they want from God, why, it would be a strange world indeed!* Still, the prayer had been his. It had sprung to his lips and been uttered audibly. Yet, he knew somehow that it had not come from him. Something inside had urged him to pray that particular prayer. As he halted and looked up at the sky as if expecting an answer, he was aware that something in him was moving. There was an odd stirring in him such as he had not known before. There was a longing, but yet the longing was for something he could not even identify.

"Well, that's definitely enough, getting Dake out." Clive muttered these words aloud and then proceeded down the wooden sidewalk. *All right*, he thought, *if you want me to believe in you, God, I'd like to have some evidence. I don't have a clue as to how to help Dake Bradford. Not an idea in my head. I don't think there is any way.* "But I promise you this," he said almost logically, as if he were dealing with a merchant, "if you'll put something in my head that will get Bradford out of prison, I'll do it—and if it works, and he gets free, I'll know that you're really the God that I've seen in Jeanne and her people!"

🕇   🕇   🕇

Jeanne was taken aback when Clive walked into the room. There was a set quality to his face, a sternness that she could not explain. At the same time, there was a light in his blue eyes that seemed to flash. This combination made her ask, "What is it, Clive?"

Sam had come to answer the knock at the door almost at the same time as Jeanne. He had heard Jeanne explaining that only Clive Gordon had known about Dake's presence in the house, and had jumped to the conclusion that Jeanne herself had reached. "We don't need you here, Gordon," Sam said. "Get out!"

"Hush, Sam!" Jeanne said, putting her hand on his arm and holding him back. She turned to Clive and repeated, "What is it?" Her expression was set, for the fear of what lay ahead of Dake had stiffened her and made her afraid.

Clive looked at Sam, noting that the young man's squarish face was stretched taut. There was a bitterness in the electric blue eyes, the young man's most fetching feature. His reddish hair was mussed and his fists were clenched, as if he longed to throw himself on the visitor.

"Come along, Sam and Jeanne. I've got to talk to you."

"I don't want to talk to you!" Sam said bitterly. "You're the one that turned Dake in."

"No, I didn't."

Sam stared at Clive, anxious to find something in the tall man's face to belie his words. However, he saw only a calm steadiness.

"I have something to propose," Clive said. "It will be a little dangerous. If you don't want to be in on it, Sam, I'll talk to Jeanne alone."

Clive could not have said anything more calculated to bring Sam into the scheme that he had come to share. He had continued to walk for an hour after his prayer, and slowly a scenario had formed in his mind. He had waited until it was complete and then had turned at once to the task at hand.

"I'm not afraid. What is it?" Sam demanded.

"Let's go into the sitting room and I'll tell you about it." He looked at Jeanne and asked, "Do you believe God tells people things?"

"Yes, I know He does."

"Well, I'm a strange one for God to be speaking to, but I think you'll be interested in what I believe He's given me."

Jeanne and Sam stared at the tall form of Clive Gordon, then Jeanne said quietly, "Come along. I always want to hear what God has to say."

T   T   T

"What's this you say?" asked the guard in charge of the prison. He held the rank of sergeant, and was almost as tall as the colonel who had entered the room. "I don't believe I've met you, Colonel."

"No, I've just been assigned to the regiment. My name is Colonel Jones, Horatio Jones."

"What can I do for you, Colonel Jones?"

The tall man spoke lazily, almost as if he were bored. "Oh, General Howe has a bee in his bonnet. You know how generals are."

The guard, flattered that he would be included in such august company, could do no less than grin. "They are strange, sir, although it's not for me to say so. What's on the general's mind?"

"Oh, he wants to talk to one of the prisoners. As a matter of fact, he wants him transferred to one of the ships down in the harbor, the *Cerebus*."

"And which prisoner is that?"

The colonel frowned, seemingly bored. "Dear me—what *was* the fellow's name?" He removed a sheet of paper from an envelope, unfolded it, then seemed to peer at it in a nearsighted fashion. "I have to get my spectacles. Left them back in the quarters. I can't see. Here it is."

The guard took the paper, which he saw bore the insignia of the Royal British Army. He glanced at it for a moment, then said, "Why, this is for the spy Bradford."

"Yes, I do believe that's his name. Bradford, yes." The colonel nodded and yawned languidly, then murmured, "Bring the fellow out, will you? I have a young lady waiting for me." He winked lewdly at the sergeant. "You know how it is with young ladies, eh?"

Once again the sergeant was flattered. "Well, sir, being men of the world, we both know how young ladies are."

"Right-oh! Now, just trot the fellow out, and I'll sign whatever paper's necessary for release."

The sergeant, however, said, "Why, sir, I couldn't release a prisoner. The lieutenant would have to do that."

"The lieutenant?"

"Why, yes, sir. That's regulations. Lieutenant Simington."

"And where is Lieutenant Simington?"

"Why, sir, he's gone for the day. You can probably find him in his quarters."

"I'm not about to waste my time looking for a lieutenant when I have papers signed by the general himself!" snapped the colonel. Then he shrugged, saying, "I'll be responsible. Get Bradford now and get the papers ready, like a good chap."

"Oh no, sir. On no account!"

The manner of the tall colonel suddenly seemed to change. "Sergeant, do you enjoy your rank?"

"Why—yes, sir!"

"How would you like to be a private again?"

The question was blunt enough, and the blue eyes of the tall colonel seemed suddenly to come alive. "I think it could be arranged. As a matter of fact, if you disobey a direct written order from General Howe, Commander in Chief of His Majesty's forces in the Colonies *and* from a colonel such as myself, all for the sake of one pitiful Lieutenant Simington—well, there you have it."

The sergeant swallowed hard. He had a sudden grim vision of losing his rank and being thrust in with the privates he had abused quite rigidly. It was a future he did not care to contemplate, and after all, he had the order and the colonel could sign a release.

"I'll be right back, Colonel. Just wanted to be doubly careful, you know."

"Very commendable, Sergeant. Now, let's get on with it. The young lady, you know!"

The sergeant turned and bustled out of the room used for records, snatching a key from a nail. As he passed a guard down the way who questioned him, he said, "There's a colonel come to take Bradford."

"Take Bradford? Take him where?"

"That's not your affair. General Howe himself has signed the order. That's enough for the likes of you."

It gave the sergeant some satisfaction to berate the lowly private. He reached the cell where Bradford was kept, unlocked the padlock, then swung the door open. "All right, Bradford, get your coat. On your feet!"

Dake Bradford was sitting on the cot and looked up calmly. "Is it time?"

"Oh no," the sergeant said hurriedly. "Not for—well, you're just being transferred out to one of the ships, the *Cerebus*. General Howe wants to talk to you."

"That's better than the alternative, eh, Sergeant?"

"Oh, indeed it is, Bradford! Well, come along with you now. The colonel's impatient."

Dake Bradford picked up his coat and the Bible that his father had succeeded in getting to him, then settled his tricorn hat firmly on his head. "All ready, Sergeant."

Dake preceded the sergeant, who followed him closely. When they got to the outer part of the prison, the sergeant said, "In there, Bradford."

Dake stepped inside a door, and when he hesitated slightly, the sergeant said, "Move on there." As soon as the two were inside, he said, "Here he is, Colonel. Now, if you'll just wait, I'll get the release papers for you to sign."

"Very well, Sergeant."

Dake found himself standing in front of a tall British colonel dressed in the colorful uniform of the Royal Fusiliers. He took in the crimson coat, the white shirt, the epaulets, and then stared into the eyes that did not blink. The two men remained quiet, and finally the sergeant said, "Here, if you'll just sign here, Colonel."

"Oh, of course." The colonel bent over, signed, and said, "Thank you, Sergeant. I'll commend you to the general for your prompt cooperation."

"I would appreciate that, Colonel. Now, I'll have the two guards accompany you."

"I hardly think—"

"Oh, I'm sorry, Colonel. That is a firm regulation. They'll accompany you down to the dock." The sergeant quickly stepped to the door and called out, "Jennings—Waite, on the double!"

Two guards, privates armed with muskets, appeared, and the sergeant snapped, "You'll accompany the colonel to the docks. See that the prisoner's turned over to our people there." He did not wait for an answer but said, "I'd be appreciative if you'd put in a good word for me to the general."

"Of course, and to your good lieutenant, too. Well, come along, fellow." He reached out and prodded Dake, who did not say a word but turned and stepped outside. He was followed by the tall colonel and the two soldiers.

As they moved down the street and headed for the dock, the colonel said, "Sorry to trouble you men. I could have handled it, but regulations, you know."

"That's all right, Colonel," a short, stocky man grinned. "Maybe he'll try to break and we'll have to shoot him."

"No," the other one said, "he'll be good for 'anging." He grinned at Dake, who looked back at him steadily.

The colonel kept up a lively conversation with the two soldiers, speaking mostly of the duty that they would have when they got out of Boston.

Finally, they got to the dock, which was fairly busy. "Oh, there they are," he said. The two soldiers looked up and so did Dake. There, ahead of them, two privates holding muskets were waiting for the arrival of the prisoner.

"Here you are!" The colonel took money from his inner pocket, handed it to the two guards from the prison, and said, "On your way now. Have a good time on me."

"Why, thank ye, sir." The men took their money, touched their forelocks, then turned and moved away.

Dake did not say a word. He was staring at the faces of the two soldiers. When the soldiers were out of hearing distance, he said, "Jeanne, Sam, what—"

"There's no time for talk." Clive Gordon acted swiftly. He untied the rope that bound Dake's hands behind him and said at once, "You've got to get out of town. Don't go home. They'll look for you there first."

Clive turned and walked away slowly. The others followed and he said, "Don't move so fast; we have to look natural." He walked until they reached the stable door. When they stepped inside, Dake saw his horse, Captain, saddled and bridled.

Turning to Clive, he said, "What does this all mean, Gordon?"

Clive Gordon shook his head. There was a grim expression on his face. "Get out of town as quickly as you can. They might have already found out that that note's a forgery. I've got to go." He turned and would have left, but Dake reached out and held his arm.

"I don't understand this," Dake said, "but I'll never forget it, Clive." He saw that the other man's face was tense and said, "I've had bad thoughts and I haven't acted right, but God knows I mean to do the right thing. I just want the best for you—and for Jeanne."

Jeanne said quickly, "He did it all, Dake. He took the uniforms and thought up the whole scheme. And he says, Dake, he felt strongly that the Lord gave him the idea."

Dake stared at the tall form of Clive Gordon. "Well," he said softly, "I guess we're both learning something about the ways of God." He put his hand out. It almost swallowed the other man's smaller one. "God bless you, Clive. I'm proud to have a cousin like you."

Clive Gordon felt the power in the hand of Dake Bradford. Their eyes met for a moment, then he glanced at Jeanne and almost spoke. Instead he wrenched himself away, saying, "You get in there and change clothes again. I've got to get these uniforms back before anyone finds out."

Jeanne and Sam darted into the inner recess and soon came out wearing their own clothing. Clive had stripped off his own officer's uniform and packed it carefully. When all the uniforms were stowed in a bag, he said, "I've got to get these back. Get out of here, Dake. If they catch you again, they'll hang you for sure."

Clive was gone then, and Dake stared after him in the gathering darkness. He turned to Jeanne and Sam, and it was Sam who said, "He risked his life for you, Dake. But you know what bothered him the most?"

"No, what was that?"

"He was afraid his father would be tied somehow to this jailbreak." He stared out in the direction Clive had disappeared. "He's quite a fellow, isn't he?"

Jeanne had her eyes turned in the same direction. "Yes, he is quite a fellow." Then she said, "You've got to leave, Dake."

Dake nodded. He swung into the saddle and looked down at the two. "Well, I'll be seeing you soon. I have the feeling that the British won't be here too long."

He looked at Jeanne and a thought struck him. "Are you going with the Gordons?" he asked abruptly.

Jeanne shook her head. "Go on, Dake, quickly!"

Dake accepted her look, which told him nothing, then turned Captain's head and moved out of the stable.

† † †

Daniel Bradford approached the Frazier house, a dragging reluctance in his steps. He had thought this over in his mind and knew that he really had no other choice. He had realized that there was no hope for Dake—unless Leo could somehow manipulate the authorities. He had done all he could, prayed until his mind almost seemed a blur. Finally he had groaned, from the depths of his own spirit, "I've got to do it! I've got to give Matthew into the hands of Leo." He approached the door, knocked, and Cato answered it.

"Why, good evening, Mr. Bradford."

"Hello, Cato. Is . . . Mr. Rochester here?"

"Yes, sir, he is. He's in the library with Mrs. Marian. You want me to announce you?"

"No, that won't be necessary. Thank you, Cato." He gave the servant his hat and coat and moved on down the hallway. When he entered the library, Marian, who was sitting on the settee, rose at once. Leo had been standing, looking down into the fireplace. He turned, and at the sight of Daniel Bradford, instantly grew alert.

Daniel stopped abruptly and then turned to face Leo squarely. His distaste for Rochester went deep. He had to struggle constantly to keep hatred from forming. He knew what hatred could do in a human heart. Time and time again, when this fierce hatred for Leo Rochester would rise up in him, he would have to seek strength from God. So far he had succeeded, but now, looking at the cruelty in Rochester's eyes, he could hardly speak.

"Well, Bradford," Leo demanded, "have you come to your senses?"

Marian watched the drama between the two. She knew the depth of love Daniel Bradford had for his sons and knew what it cost him to come. There was a surrender in his shoulders. They slumped, which was unnatural, and her heart felt a pang as she saw that his eyes were gloomy with grief.

"All right, Leo. You win," Daniel said wearily.

"You'll do what I say?"

"I've said you won!"

"Well, *now* you're showing a little sense!" Leo exclaimed, and his eyes gleamed as he slapped his hands together, rubbing them. He glanced at the two, saying, "Now, don't be so confounded gloomy! I'm not going to eat the boy. I'm going to do something for him that you couldn't do!"

"I don't want to talk about it," Daniel said. "I'll agree to counsel him to go with you. That's what you wanted, and that's what you'll get."

Leo was already making plans, but Bradford interrupted, "Now, what about Dake?"

"Oh yes, well, I'll go at once to Colonel Matteringly."

"Colonel Matteringly? Who's he?"

"A very greedy member of General Howe's staff. The fellow has an insatiable love for money. It'll be the undoing of him someday."

"What does he have to do with Dake?"

"He's in charge of prisoners, for one thing—executions, all of that."

"You're going to bribe him to turn Dake loose?"

"Oh no, that wouldn't do. He'd never be able to handle it—but he has great influence with Howe. Howe himself isn't adverse to the better things of life. I'll have to pay the both of them before it's over, but I think I can guarantee that he'll be committed to prison. At least, it won't be the rope."

"That's almost as bad from what I hear. If they put him on a hook somewhere, he'll die of sickness or disease."

Leo shrugged. "I can't guarantee that. I can practically guarantee that he won't hang. That was our bargain. Are you willing?"

Daniel had no choice. As long as Dake was alive there was a chance. He nodded slowly, "I agree."

Triumph washed across Leo's face and he grinned unabashedly. He had won—and suddenly it seemed that all of his life he had been frustrated by this man, Daniel Bradford. But now, he had finally conquered the man. Already, he was thinking of how he and Matthew would begin their new lives together. "All right," he said, "I'll go at once—"

He was interrupted by a voice down the hall and then turned as the door to the library opened. "Why, Matthew," he said, "come in. I think we have something to say to you. Quite a surprise, eh, Daniel?"

But Matthew was not listening. "Pa," he said, bursting out. "You haven't heard?"

"Heard what?" Daniel asked in bewilderment.

"Why, Dake. He's escaped!"

"Impossible!" Leo cried out, a wild expression sweeping across his face. "No one's ever escaped from the prison!"

But Matthew had gone up to face his father. "It's true. It's all over town. He got away."

"How did it happen? When did it happen?" Daniel asked, his mind reeling at the news.

"I haven't heard all of it yet. I don't know how. I went by the prison—and sure enough, they're going crazy over there." He laughed and slapped his hands together exultantly. "Some heads will roll for this, but he's gone all right. He's back up in the hills with Washington by this time."

Instinctively, Daniel turned to face Marian. He saw tears in her eyes and a smile on her lips. He knew that Leo was aware of this. He turned toward Leo and waited for Rochester to speak.

Matthew sensed that something was going on. "What is it? What's the surprise, sir?" he said to Rochester.

Leo knew that he was defeated. He ground his teeth together and glared at Daniel Bradford. There was no point in his asking, although for once he wanted to beg. "I see I have nothing to bargain with," he said. He looked at Matthew and forced himself to be calm. "I'll be leaving with the British," he said. "Will you come with me?"

"I've already told you, I could only do that if my father advises me to do it." Matthew turned to look at Daniel and said, "What shall I do?"

Daniel hesitated and once again he caught Marian's eye. It was as if they were in a conspiracy of some sort.

Leo Rochester saw the unspoken communication. *It's almost like they're married*, he thought bitterly.

Daniel said slowly, "Matthew, I only want the best for you. I know Leo could give you many things—but I can't agree for you to go with him. I think it would be dangerous."

"You don't trust me, Pa?"

"I don't trust myself," Daniel said evenly. "You're a young man and you're old enough to make your own decisions. You've been on your own for a time. I can only say, if you go, it won't be with my permission."

Somehow, Matthew seemed curiously relieved. He turned at once to Rochester, saying, "I'm sorry, but I can't go."

Leo Rochester glared at Daniel. He dared not lose his temper in front of Matthew, for he had not given up—he would never give up! Then he forced himself to say calmly, "Very well, I'll be leaving, but I'll expect to be hearing from you, Matthew. Perhaps we can still meet and talk about painting." Leo turned at once and left the house.

When the door slammed, it was as if a weight had fallen off of Daniel. He moved over and grasped Matthew and said huskily, "I'm proud of you, Matthew. Never prouder than right now. I know what this means to you, but I'll do all I can to help."

"I guess you'll be fighting in a war, Pa, but you know my feelings. I won't go with Leo Rochester until you tell me—at least not until I've thought it out." He said, "I've got to go now. There's a celebration at home."

"Wait, I'll go with you."

Daniel turned to Marian, and because Matthew stood there, he could only say, "Will you be leaving with Leo?"

"No," she said quickly, "Father's too ill for that."

"You'll be all right here—but it might be dangerous for him." It was not what he wanted to say. She was looking at him in a way he had learned to recognize that went beyond politeness. Now he said, "Goodbye, I'll see you later."

The two men left the house and Marian went up to tell her father the news. As she went, she knew somehow that Leo Rochester had not given up, that he would try again to get his son by any means that he could.

24

A World to Live In

"AND SO IT'S COME TO THIS AT LAST."

Leslie Gordon stood slightly to one side as General Howe gazed out the window. The two officers had been discussing the final plans for evacuating Boston. It had been a distressing chore, one which neither of them had enjoyed. Finally, Howe had moved to stare out of the window. Now he repeated, "And so it's come to this. Eleven months after the opening of hostilities, the Battle of Boston is over."

"Yes, sir."

"We've been defeated at every step. We were defeated on the road back from Concord to Boston. We were defeated at Bunker Hill—and now, they've driven us out of this city. The rebels have New York, Ticonderoga, and Crowne Point; Virginia and the Carolinas have defected to the rebels too."

Leslie Gordon tried to think of some comment that might ease the pain that the general felt. Actually he had none and felt none—for all along he had been one of many officers who believed that the whole war was useless and futile. Now he said, "Perhaps the government will see things differently."

"No, they won't." Howe's words were clipped and dogmatic. He turned to face Gordon, his lips drawn down in a scowl. "These Americans—they've been a surprise to all of us." He lifted his fingers and began to enumerate the accomplishments of the Colonies. "They've created state governments. They've put together a political union. They've organized and maintained an army. Why, they've even inspired an American party in Parliament and excited the sympathy of the French!"

"I fear that is all true, General Howe," Gordon said quietly. He hesitated, then asked, "What are your orders?"

"I have no choice, Gordon. What is this? The sixteenth?"

"Yes, sir."

"March 16, 1776." Howe's face darkened and he shook his heavy head. "I won't forget this day."

"But the orders, sir?"

"We'll weigh anchor tomorrow. Have everyone on board ship as early as possible."

Gordon asked quietly, "And all of the Loyalists in the town that want to go?"

"Take them all—all that will fit on the ships. We won't be going far."

"Will we go to New York, General?"

"No, we'll go to Halifax in Nova Scotia. There may be action in New York. I want to get the men rested and ready for the new invasion." He turned and nodded sternly, "That will be when we go to New York, Colonel Gordon." He looked at the tall form of Gordon and said, "A bit hard on you with some of your wife's relatives siding with the rebels."

"Yes, sir, it's not unusual, I believe."

"Well, I'm sorry for it, but we'll have to come back. They can't win, of course, but they can create the devil's own time of it for us for a while."

Gordon stayed long enough to finish writing out the orders for the general, then left. After checking with his own officers and other commanders, he went home, where he found things in an uproar. Trunks were being stuffed, bags packed, and amidst all of it, Lyna was directing the operation.

"We'll leave in the morning," he called out, overriding the voice of David, who was yelling at Grace about something. "Will you be packed?"

"We'll take what we can," Lyna said. "We've done it before."

"Yes, we have." He went to her and held her for a moment. Then he kissed her and said, "I'll help with the packing."

They threw themselves into the work and were interrupted when a knock sounded at the front door.

"I'll get it!" Clive said, stopping with the crate he was packing. He went and opened the door, and then said, "Oh! Why, Uncle Daniel! And all of you! Come in!"

As Daniel led his family inside, including Jeanne, whose arm he held, Clive called out, "Sir—Mother, it's our relatives, come to call."

Daniel smiled at Clive, then came over and stood beside him, clapping his hands across the tall young man's shoulders. "I haven't thanked you properly yet," he whispered, "but you know how I feel." They had thought it best not to say anything about Clive's part in getting Dake free. It would be too easy for the officers of the Crown to put together the ability to get uniforms with the son of a colonel. They did

305

not want to bring Leslie Gordon into it.

Leslie and Lyna Gordon came to the front hall and greeted them all by name. For a moment, they all stood there looking a little embarrassed.

"Well," Daniel said, "I knew you'd be leaving, so I couldn't let that happen without saying a proper goodbye."

Lyna came over and took his hand. "After years of thinking you were dead, we found each other. Now, we're losing each other again."

"No, it's different this time," Daniel said. "This'll be over one day. In the meanwhile, our two broods have gotten to know each other."

Rachel went over and hugged Grace. The two had become great friends, and Rachel said, "I'll miss you so much."

Grace turned her gray-green eyes on her cousin and whispered, "I'll miss you, too, Rachel." She looked around and said, "And all of you. It's like losing a family again."

"Well, come," Lyna said. "We've got cakes made and tea. Come along, now."

They all crowded into the kitchen, where the women served the cakes and tea. Samuel and David sat together, arm-wrestling down as many of the delicious small cakes as they could. They felt a little ill at ease, but finally Sam said, "I want you to know, David, even if you are with the lobsterbacks, you're still my family."

David grinned broadly. "And even if you are a ragtag rebel," he said, "you're still my family."

Micah and Matthew were cornered at one point by Leslie, who said, "What are you two chaps going to do? Not join the army, I take it."

"No," Micah said. "I'm not one with my family on this war. I think it's a mistake."

"What about you, Matthew?"

"Oh no, I'm with Micah. I've never agreed with it. I thought about going back to England. Takes money, though. I'm just not sure, Uncle Leslie, what I'll do."

While the talk was running around the kitchen, Clive suddenly took Jeanne's arm and simply walked her out. Almost everyone watched them go. When they were outside in the hall, he said, "Come, I have to talk to you."

"All right, Clive," Jeanne said. She followed him as they went to the small sitting room.

He turned at once and said, "I've already told you how I feel about you. Come with me, Jeanne. Marry me. We don't have to go to England. We can go to New York. I can start a practice there."

Jeanne had already known that he would ask her to go with him.

She bit her lip and looked up at him. "I think all the time about how you came to us out in the mountains. I'll never forget that. I'd never met a man as kind as you, Clive." She went on speaking of all that he had done for her father and aunt.

All the time his face was growing stiffer. He finally interrupted, saying, "All this is to say no, isn't it, Jeanne?"

"I wouldn't hurt you for anything," she said, "but you know how I feel. I'm not in love with you—though I thought I was for a time. I've never known much about love, but I know one thing, Clive—I wouldn't make you a good wife."

"Of course you would!"

"No, you need a woman who knows your kind of life. One who knows how to dress and which fork to eat with and who is able to make the kind of talk a fine doctor's wife could make. I could never do that."

"You could learn."

"But it wouldn't be me, Clive. It's not what I am." Suddenly she reached up, pulled his head down, and kissed his cheek. "I'm sorry, Clive," she said, "but we wouldn't be happy."

He knew that her answer was final and he summoned up a grin. "Well," he said, "I don't suppose I can grab you by the hair and *drag* you off to New York or England. Wouldn't do much good, would it?"

"No, it wouldn't."

"So, God bless you, Jeanne. I'll never quite get over this, I think."

"Yes you will. You don't really love me, Clive. I'm just different."

"You're different, all right," he said. "Come along, they'll be talking about us. What will you do?" he asked.

"I don't know. I just don't know."

They went back into the kitchen, and the Bradfords stayed for another half hour. Finally, they stood to leave. Daniel went over and held Lyna in his arms, whispering, "Well, sister, this is goodbye for a while. But you know, Christians never say goodbye."

Lyna smiled at him with misty eyes. "Daniel, be very careful. Don't let anything happen to you. It's going to be a terrible time, but I'll be praying every day for you and your family."

☙ ☙ ☙

In their final days in Boston, the British soldiers, frustrated at every turn in their six-year occupation of the Colonies, turned on the old town with a vengeance. They destroyed many houses. Military supplies that could not be taken aboard the fleet were smashed and thrown into the river. And finally, with General George Washington watching through a spyglass, the last of eight thousand, nine hundred soldiers and one thousand, one hundred Tory refugees crammed on seventy-eight vessels and sailed out of the harbor north for Halifax.

General Sullivan rode down toward Bunker Hill, where he saw some of the Redcoats shouldering arms as if on sentry duty. He noticed they were not moving. He soon discovered they were dummies. Sullivan, then, bravely took the fortress defended by lifeless sentries, one of whom bore a sign. It read, "Yankees, Goodbye!" Thus on March 17, the British army set sail and Boston was free again.

Dake was not allowed to come into Boston with the first troops. For over a week he was kept in the hills, for the rumor was that smallpox was raging, and only men that had already endured that disease were allowed to go. Finally, however, he and the others were led out of the hills and they went at once into the city. Dake ran the last hundred yards to his house and burst through the door, calling out, "Pa! Sam! Where is everybody?"

Instantly he was swarmed by Rachel, Sam, and Micah as they came running into the foyer. They greeted each other happily and then Dake looked around. "Where's Jeanne?" he asked.

Micah glanced at the other two, then said, "Why, Dake. She's gone back home."

"You mean with the Gordons?"

"No. I mean she's gone back to where she came from. She said she couldn't take this town living anymore."

"I think she was really sick of it, Dake," Rachel said quietly. "She left a note for you. I'll get it."

Sam saw that Dake's happiness had evaporated, and he tried to cheer him up. "It's gonna be great, Dake! General Washington's gonna double up on the army, and I'm gonna ask Pa to let me go with you."

"He won't do it," Micah said shortly. He turned to Dake, saying, "Pa's gone to see Mr. Frazier. He's real bad."

"I'm sorry to hear that," Dake murmured. He waited until Rachel returned, then ripped open the note. The others watched him as he read it, trying to discern something from his face. They saw his brow begin to crease as it did when he was worried or angry. They could not tell which it was.

Finally, Dake looked up and saw them watching him. He shoved the note in his pocket and said, as though nothing had happened, "Well, can a man get something to eat in this house?"

At the same time Dake was entering his house, Daniel Bradford was standing beside his partner, John Frazier. "It's all over here in Boston, John."

"But not over completely." Frazier was pale. He'd had a bad night and he spoke faintly. Marian stood beside him and he looked up and said, "Where's Leo?"

Without meeting Daniel's eyes, she said, "He's gone back to Virginia. I have a letter from him."

"I suppose he wants you to come home?"

That was indeed Leo's demand, but not wanting to add to her father's burden, Marian said, "Oh, he'll get along very well. I have some new recipes to try out on you, Father."

Frazier relaxed. He had been dreading the loss of Marian, but now he seemed content, knowing that she was staying behind to care for him.

After Daniel had talked with his partner for a while, he left the room. He and Marian walked down the hall silently. When they were in the foyer and he was about to get his hat, she said, "Daniel—"

"Yes?" He turned to meet her and saw that her face was drawn and serious. "Leo wants me to come home—but I can't leave Father like this."

"I don't think you should. Leo will just have to understand."

"He never understands anything. You know he doesn't. All he cares about is himself." She drew her lips tightly together and shook her head. She touched her hair then in a futile gesture. "I'm sorry, I didn't mean to say that. What about Matthew?"

"I think he'll go to England, but not with Leo."

"Leo will follow him there."

"I suppose he will. Nothing I can do about that." Daniel stood looking at this woman he loved above all things on this earth, except for his own family. Everything in him cried for him to reach out and take her in his arms. They had stood like this before, on the brink of moving into a relationship that could only destroy both of them. *I love her too much to let that happen*, he thought. Then he summoned up a smile, "I'll be going into the army now. General Washington has asked me to come in as an officer."

"Dake will be going, too, I suppose?"

"Yes, but not Micah—and not Sam, as long as I can keep him out. That's what I want to ask you. I may be called to leave at any moment. Would you keep an eye out for Sam? I don't have anyone else to ask."

She looked at him and saw that he wanted her. Though his face remained set, trying to hide his true feelings, his eyes could not lie. A woman knows that, no matter how much a man tries to hide it, and she found herself happy that he did. She had lived with sadness and remorse for her marriage for years. Now, she saw this man, so full of goodness and honor standing before her. Knowing that she had missed all of it—and could never have it—saddened her. She knew also that all she had to do was make one move and she could melt that resolve she saw summoned up in his eyes.

But she did not move. Instead, she merely put her hand out and said, "We'll see each other before you leave?"

"Yes." Her hand was soft but strong in his. He bent over it, kissed it, then straightened and released it. Without another word, he left the house. If he had turned around, he would have seen tears in her eyes—but he did not turn around. He moved away toward what he knew would be a long and hard and bloody war.

🔔   🔔   🔔

Thin lines of clouds moved across the gray sky over Jeanne's head. A sharp breeze touched her face and seemed to suck her breath, but she ignored it and kicked her horse into motion again. There was snow in the air somewhere, she knew, and she wanted to get home before it began. "Come on, girl," she said. "Get me home again. We don't want to be caught out like this."

The roan mare lifted her head and whickered eagerly, then broke into a lope. There was a pleasure to Jeanne just feeling the horse beneath her. She savored the smell of pine and loamy earth as she rode the crooked trail that wound in a serpentine fashion through the dense woods. For two weeks, since returning to her cabin, she had gone every day on long rides. She had not set the traps, but it was not hard to fill the pot with game. She had seen no one except a pair of hunters that had stopped by a week earlier. They had known Pierre, but had not heard that he had died. One of them, a tall rangy man in his late thirties, had come to her before he left and said awkwardly, "Miss Jeanne, I lost my wife. I got those three kids to care for. I know it ain't proper to speak so soon, but I'd like it mighty well if you and me was to marry—be a home for you and you'd never know meanness from me."

Jeanne had smiled at him, touched by his kindness. "Thanks, Thomas," she had said. "That's a fine offer and a compliment."

She had put him off gently and he had left, saying, "If you change your mind, I'll come a runnin'."

Now, as she cleared the forest and moved down toward the opening where the cabin sat, it gave her a sudden thrill to see it. She had not known how much she had missed all of this, and now just the sight of that plain cabin, aged to a fine gray color by the passage of time and weather, made her content. She had not been for the first few days. Somehow, as she settled in, she had wandered over the cabin, touching things, remembering the times she and her father had read this book together. How they had made these skinning racks. He seemed very real to her, and often she had gone to stand beside his grave, not finding consolation in the mound of raw earth. She had come to realize that this was not the part of him she missed, but his strong and noble spirit.

Now she rode into the open space but suddenly drew the mare up. Someone was in the cabin!

Quickly she reined the horse around, tied her to a sapling, then slipped the musket out of the leather case. She checked the loads and the powder, then moved forward stealthily. She had seen smoke rising from the cabin, and knew that the fire that she had left would have burned down long before.

It's probably only a hunter—one of Pa's friends, she thought. Nevertheless, there were men around she would not trust, and she moved quietly toward the door. Stepping up on the porch, her foot made no noise. The door was shut and she laid her ear against it. She could hear nothing. Taking a deep breath and putting her finger on the trigger, she tried the latch and saw that the door was open. Instantly, she shoved it with her shoulder, and as it burst open on its leather hinges, she leaped inside and aimed the rifle on a man who was bending over the fireplace.

"Don't move a muscle or I'll blow your backbone out!"

The man froze. He had a strong-looking back and had taken off a heavy coat, which lay on the floor. A cap lay beside it and she said, "Turn around!"

The man turned slowly, and when he was fully turned, she saw who it was! "Dake Bradford, I ought to shoot you!" she cried. She lowered the rifle and shook her head. "People just don't come in and make themselves at home out here!" She saw that he looked tired. There were circles under his eyes and he had lost weight.

"I thought I'd find you here," Dake said, coming to stand before her. "It's too cold to stay outside. I didn't know how to track you down."

"What are you doing here?" she said. She went over to the fireplace and put the musket on its pegs and then turned to him as she pulled off her coat and tossed the wool cap on the table. She was breathing a little harder, for the shock of finding him here had hit her more than she thought it might.

"I came to see you," he said. "You left without saying goodbye." He grinned crookedly and said, "Never could understand why a woman would leave a good-looking fellow like me without saying goodbye. I must be losing my touch."

"You're losing your mind!" Jeanne snapped. She stood there, trying to ignore how glad she was to see him—how *very* glad. The loneliness had gotten to her more than she had thought and now she said hurriedly, "Well, I'll let you skin those squirrels I've got out there. I'll make some corn pone."

"Bless your heart," Dake said. "I do believe I'll take you up on that." He slipped into his coat and clapped his wool cap on his head and disappeared outside.

Jeanne drew a quick breath and turned at once to throwing together the elements for a meal. He was back sooner than she had anticipated and she said, "You want these squirrels in a stew, or roasted?"

"Let's make a stew. Sounds good to me." He drew up a chair and watched her as she busied herself cooking the meal.

Soon the cabin was filled with the delicious smell of bubbling stew and corn bread. Dake kept her entertained by telling her news of the family.

After he had finished telling her what his family had been doing, he said, "The Gordons are in New York. Clive, too. I thought he might stay in Boston, set up practice."

"No, I didn't ever think he'd do that. New York's the place for him— or London."

He listened carefully to her words, seeming to try them. Her face was smooth and undisturbed as she moved to the fireplace, stirring the stew. Her black curly hair framed her face, and he thought again of how much he loved curly black hair on a woman, although he'd never seen it cut that way except on Jeanne Corbeau.

"I . . ." He hesitated, then picked his knife out of its sheath and began toying with it. "I . . . was a little surprised."

"Surprised about what?" asked Jeanne as she set the table.

"About you. I couldn't get back out of the hills for a week. All the time I was thinking that when I got back, you and Clive would be married."

Jeanne looked at him, raising her head up abruptly. Their eyes met and she flushed. "No, there was nothing like that."

"He asked you to marry him, didn't he?"

Jeanne turned back to the stew. "Don't be so nosy! You're the nosiest man I've ever seen! Curious as a coon."

He studied her carefully, put the knife back into his belt, then sat down, saying, "Tell me about what you've been doing."

He listened as she related her travels back from Boston, how she had come back to the cabin, opened it up, and had spent the days simply wandering through the woods, hunting, and reading by the fire. "I suppose that sounds boring to you."

"No, it doesn't." Dake shook his head definitely. "Sounds like a mighty good way to live."

The meal was ready soon and they sat down. Dake said, "How 'bout I ask the blessing?" When she nodded, he said, "Lord, I'm thankful for this food. I thank you for my family and for the Gordons, and I thank you for this young woman and ask your protection on her. In Jesus' name. Amen."

"I didn't know you were a praying man, Dake," Jeanne said, surprised at the tenor of Dake's prayer.

"Not much of one, I guess. But I'm learning." He sat silently, and when he looked up, there was an odd look on his face. "I want to tell you what happened to me after we get through eating."

"All right," Jeanne said as she filled their bowls with stew.

They enjoyed their meal. Afterward Jeanne fixed strong cups of tea, and they sat back and drank them. She waited, for she sensed the seriousness of the moment.

Soon Dake began to speak of the night that his father came to him in the jail. He related how he'd been running from God all his life, and then how that night, things became different. "It was a low limb for me, Jeanne," Dake said quietly.

His face was serious. His wheat-colored hair caught the light of the fire. The scar on his left eyebrow showed clearly. There was a pensive quality about him that was unusual and strange. He was, Jeanne knew, the most outspoken and fiery-tempered young man she had ever known. Now, however, there seemed to be a placid center to his being as he sat there, his big hands idly clasped over his knee.

"I can't ever explain, although I guess you'd know," he said finally. "Pa came to see me and some of the things he had tried to tell me about God finally made sense that night as we talked. I just called on God and can't even remember how I did it, but Jesus Christ came to me that night. Been different ever since."

Jeanne's eyes were misty and she whispered, "I'm so glad for you, Dake!"

They talked long into the night, then finally he said, "I guess I can sleep out in the barn?"

"Why, no. I don't have any nosy neighbors. You can have my father's old room over there." They said good night and Jeanne went to bed in her small room.

Early the next morning she fixed breakfast and was surprised to find how much better it was to cook for two than for one. After breakfast, they went on a long ride. She showed him her country, and his face glowed with health and excitement, his eyes taking in all that she showed him. They stayed all day long, coming back late, frying up deer steaks from a buck that he had shot. Once again they sat drinking tea, talking, and then went to bed again.

She said nothing to him about his leaving, for she suddenly realized her life had become filled with his voice, his laughter, idle talk that went on late in the night. She knew he was in the army and would have to go back, but she dreaded to think of it.

On the afternoon of the fourth day, they had gone for a walk alongside the creek. The ground had frozen and the ice-covered weeds snapped beneath their feet. "You couldn't sneak up on anything in this," he said.

"I bet I could."

He looked at her and grinned. "You always think you're the best hunter in the woods."

"Well, until I see a better one—" She smiled. There was a quietness between them, and finally they turned and started back. When they were in sight of the cabin, he took her arm. "I've got to go back, Jeanne."

His words brought regret and it showed in her face. "I wish you didn't," she said quietly. "It's been wonderful having you here, Dake. I'm so glad you came."

He was looking into her face, admiring the smoothness of her cheeks, the clean lines of her lips, and her blue-violet eyes. The tiny beauty mark on her left cheek, near her lips, caught his attention. He studied it. Suddenly, he reached up and with his hand stroked her high cheekbone, put his finger on her chin, and smiled. "I always liked that cleft in your chin."

"I hated it—always have." Jeanne was feeling most peculiar. His hand on her face had stirred her somehow. She felt strange, and when he dropped his hands and stood looking at her, she felt somehow alone. She realized that the next day, after he left, she would be lonely beyond anything she had ever known.

And then she saw something come to his face. Although she was not experienced with men, she recognized the desire that was in his eyes. She did not move for a moment as he put his arms around her. But then, as he drew her close, she stiffened for a moment.

He released his grip at once, saying, "I'm sorry."

Without thought, she cried, "Oh, Dake!" and threw herself against him.

Dake was shocked at Jeanne's movement. Even through the heavy coats, her femininity was unmistakable. He put his arms around her

314

and they stood there, holding to each other, her face buried against his chest. It was a hard matter for Dake Bradford. A sense of honor kept him from this girl, yet when she finally lifted her head, he saw a loneliness in her that grieved him. "You shouldn't be lonely, Jeanne." He lowered his head and put his lips on hers. They were cold but soft, and he felt her arms go up around his neck. She added her own pressure to the kiss and they clung to each other almost violently for a moment. She moved her head and he lifted his lips.

"I guess I might as well tell you, though it'll do me no good," Dake said. "I love you, Jeanne." He waited for her to speak. Her lips opened for a moment and then she turned from him, her head down, and began walking slowly along. *Well, that tears it, I guess*, Dake thought. He moved along beside her saying nothing.

They had gone fifty yards and she had not said a word. Then she said abruptly, "I've been so lonesome—but I hated Boston. I don't think I could ever be a town woman."

Dake took her arm and turned her around. "That's what I came to tell you, Jeanne. I thought you were in love with Clive."

"No. He's a fine man," she smiled, "but he's too fancy for me."

Her words caught at Dake. Once again, he took her arms and forced her to look up. "Well, I don't think *I'm* too fancy for *anybody*."

He shook his head and said earnestly, "Jeanne, there's a war that I've got to get into. But, after it's over, I'm never going back to live in Boston. It's all right for Micah and maybe for Sam. But this is what I love." He swept his hand toward the vast expanse of trees that shelved way back into the mountains for hundreds of miles. "That's the kind of country a man can get a breath in. After it's over, I'm going as far back in those mountains as I can go. So far back that even the hoot owls never see a man."

"Are you, Dake?" Jeanne's eyes had brightened and excitement stirred her eyes. "I've always wanted to do that. I love it here, but I've always wanted to go farther. The hunters come back and tell me what they've seen. Pa and I were going to do it, but we never did."

Then suddenly Dake said, "Do you love me, Jeanne? Like I love you?"

Jeanne thought hard for a moment. "I don't know much about love," she said, "but I know I'd like to spend the rest of my life with you, Dake."

He kissed her again and once again time ran slowly. Finally, they turned and began walking down the path. But there was a lift to their steps as he said, "Come and stay with my family until the war is over. That way I'll be able to see you when I get leave. When it's over, you and I will get married and we'll find out what's on the other side of those mountains."

They reached the doorstep and turned. His arm was around her and hers around him. She looked over where the sun was cresting the mountains. Far away a purple haze lay on them and she murmured, "It's a whole world to live in, isn't it, Dake Bradford?"